VAMPIRES IN WONDERLAND

VAMPIRES IN WONDERLAND

CANDACE ROBINSON

AMBER R. DUELL

For anyone who ever wanted to visit Wonderland

PREQUEL

RAV

CHAPTER ONE

RAV

The mortal world was a vampire's amusement park. There were rides to suit everyone's tastes—bars, seaside towns, sporting events. Rav preferred the adrenaline rush of night clubs. The bigger, the better. All those pitiful humans with racing heartbeats and building sexual desire as they ground against each other on the dance floor. The scent never failed to make his cock as hard as a rock. Just thinking about it made him crave the satisfaction of sinking into a warm body … in more ways than one.

Tonight, Rav had very particular plans, however. He made his way through the underground tunnel that led from Wonderland to the mortal realm. The white flames burning on wall torches reflected against the black slate walls and, before him, the portal gleamed. A shimmery red and black vortex that would spit him out into a wretched dirt hole in the ground of the mortal world. Once, centuries ago when he was first turned, Rav mused to the queen when he met her how the *rabbit hole* worked in Ivory compared to Scarlet, and she'd called him *Rabbit* ever since. His pet name from her, and he allowed it. She was too good a fuck not to.

With the task of bringing back a human—to turn immortal—hanging over his head, Rav pictured the outskirts of London in his mind and stepped through the portal. The trip was slightly less fun with a job to do, but only *slightly*. He and the Queen of Hearts were running low on servants—not surprising as they killed them nearly as quickly as they became vampires—and they needed to replenish their stock. At least he got to play for the night before returning, and he knew just where to do it. The man-turned-vampire who he brought back last week had piqued his curiosity with tales of a vampire club in London.

It took some convincing to get Rav to believe the place existed—apparently many did all around the mortal world—but it was such a far cry from the mobs with pitchforks from centuries ago. Back then, leave one villager drained of blood and the whole town was up in arms. He simply *had* to see this club with his own eyes.

Dressed in a sheer black shirt with metal rings running down the sleeves, his abs were clearly visible. His black jeans were slung low and the boots he wore were heavier than he was used to, but he wanted to blend in. The now-vampire who had told Rav of the club assured him this clothing would do the trick.

Rav brushed his white hair over his shoulder, the blood-red tips dancing in the cool London breeze, and approached a brick building with *Bloody Hell* in neon lights. He chuckled to himself at the name. Many new vampires compared Wonderland to Hell when they first arrived, and it certainly *was* bloody. But he doubted the club would live up to the name.

The bouncer—a broad, tattooed man with a safety pin shoved through his brow—opened the door without a second glance, allowing him entrance. Hard rock music raged with a furious strum of the guitar and chaotic drumbeats, while a fog machine coated the floor in a low cloud. Red brocade wallpaper clung to the walls. Velvet chairs and matching couches were arranged on one side of the club, a dance floor with red lights and flashing strobes on the other, and the bar in between.

The energy nipped along Rav's skin. He smiled, his fangs on full display, and sauntered to the bar. With a quick glance at the list of drinks hanging on the wall, he flagged down the bartender. Her tight red corset lifted her breasts in a way that made his mouth water. Blue veins snaked beneath her skin just *asking* for someone to take a bite, but he was better off with someone else. She would have to wait until she was finished with her shift to follow him, and he didn't want the hassle.

"Type AB," he ordered. There was no way they served real blood, was there? He couldn't smell any of the metallic delicacy, but he was going to find out.

Someone with the rich, intoxicating scent of lavender brushed up against him. Rav glanced down to find a girl no more than twenty leaning over the bar. Wavy black hair reached her waist, but he noticed it wasn't her natural color as blonde roots were beginning to show. Dark makeup swept upward from the corners of her eyes and her lips were stained black. A silver bar pierced through the bridge of her nose and two more piercings dotted her cheeks like dimples.

"Like what you see?" she asked, looking up at Rav.

He lifted a brow. "Pardon?"

"You're staring." She turned to face him and propped an elbow on the bar.

Fingerless black lace gloves ran up to her elbows, but that was where she stopped fitting in with the sea of black and red. The dress she wore was pure white with straps and buckles around the waist. Tulle peeked out from the skirt, hitting just above her knees. She looked positively *delicious*.

"Can you blame me?" he asked with a smirk.

Her eyes flicked down to his mouth. "Nice fangs. Where did you get them done?"

He swiped his tongue over a pointed tip. Why had no one told him about these clubs before? This was almost too fucking easy. "Wonderland," he told her.

The bartender returned with a thick red drink and Rav sniffed it. *Definitely not blood.* He frowned into the glass and stirred the little stick, making the ice clink. *Should've known.* It was better straight from the source anyway.

"Is that here in London?" she asked.

"Hmm?"

"Wonderland," she clarified. "Is it in London? I've been looking for a place to get my fangs done, but no dentist wants to file them for me."

Rav pushed the glass away and scanned the room once more. He could stay and play, grab a bite to eat, and take his chances luring another vampire wannabe to Wonderland. It didn't seem like it would be difficult. But would they be bearable? Rav lived in the Queen of Heart's castle and relied on the servants as much as anyone there.

And this girl had a bit of flare. A spark.

"I can take you there. It's not far," he said. "Get you an appointment."

Her smile faded, replaced with uncertainty. Rav caught the slight uptick in her pulse. "Oh… I don't think that—"

"They only accept new patients by referral," he interrupted. "And they close soon, so if you want in, we should go now."

The girl chewed her bottom lip. "I don't even know your name."

"I'm Rav."

She hesitated before holding her hand out to shake. "Alice."

"Alice," he purred, gripping her hand. "You would look divine with a set of fangs."

She smiled again and glanced around the club, hesitating. Then she rolled her eyes. "Okay, fine. I've been desperate to do it. Hell, I'll be a rebel for the night. Let's go."

Rav beamed down at her before motioning toward the door. "After you."

CHAPTER TWO

IMOGEN

Under a vampire's touch, anyone's heart could be crushed.

Imogen adjusted herself in the red, velvet high-backed chair and crossed her legs, allowing the long slit of her gown to show off her pale flesh to Ferris, her Knave.

She'd brought the tall and muscular male through the portal to her palace several years ago to be her servant. The newly-turned servants came and went when she grew enraged, or the Rabbit—Rav—became bored. Ferris had been too willing to fuck when she'd met him at a club, desperate even. Before making him her servant, she gave in to the desire. With his lean muscles, dark hair and eyes, it was a worthy distraction. The temporary rush of euphoria along with the taste of crimson ecstasy was the itch that she'd needed scratched. But once a human became an immortal servant, that was all they were.

For the past two years, she could tell by the way Ferris watched her that he was aching for another fuck, but she was finished with him. Just as she'd been with her first husband, that

5

pathetic male who had believed himself to be an actual king, who she and Rav had murdered together. Imogen had ripped his heart out—a signature death that made her known as the Queen of Hearts—and Rav became her permanent lover. Even though they relished in other's pleasures, no one could satisfy them completely except for each other.

Imogen felt eyes on her once more. "You're looking again," she cooed at Ferris.

"I'm only doing as you asked," he said softly. "Straightening your paintings."

Imogen stood from the chair, swaying her hips as she sauntered toward him. Her red gown dragged across the onyx floor as she stopped in front of him, her feathered collar swaying. The sitting room was scarlet and white with ivory anatomical hearts painted along each bricked wall. Several portraits of game cards hung around the area.

Ferris's hands nervously twitched as she reached inside her dress, feeling for the solid textures of her prized possession.

"Ah, don't be frightened, precious Knave." She fished out the deck of cards that she always carried with her. "I know you like games." With a smile, she patted the end of his nose.

His eyes widened as she shuffled the cards, her long, pointed scarlet and black nails tapping the top of the deck. Slowly, she spread them out before him, fanning herself. "Pick a card," she whispered. "Only one."

Ferris pursed his lips but knew not to deny her. If so, she would cut out his heart. He blinked rapidly as he tugged out a card. Flipping it over, he released a relieved breath. She fought back a smirk for causing him stress.

"Diamond," he murmured, his dark eyes catching hers.

"Looks like you won't have to watch me and Rav fuck tonight then, will you?" She ran a finger down his lips, catching on the bottom one. "I know you desperately want to get between my legs again, but you're weak, and your cock is nothing like his." Turning away from him, she laughed as she headed toward the door. She glanced back one more time before leaving and purred,

"Oh, and don't forget to finish dusting the whole room … with your tongue."

Rine, one of her female servants, walked up to Imogen as she exited the room. "You have a guest waiting downstairs."

Imogen wasn't a bitch to all her surviving servants, more so to Ferris because it was fun toying with him. "Who is it?"

"The hat maker." Rine rolled her eyes.

"Ah, that crazy fool finally showed up. Can you make sure the Knave is cleaning up the dust with his tongue?"

"Only if I can play with him too?" Rine smiled wickedly.

"Do as you wish." Imogen brushed past her and descended the checkered steps to where she found the hat maker—Maddie—sitting in the middle of the black settee, tapping her feet in a mad rush. She wore bright purple arm sleeves, and her hair fell to her chin in spiraled curls that matched in color. Lace crisscrossed up the front of her tight black dress. Her skirt flared out to mid-thigh, and violet hues peeked through the black.

She wasn't beautiful in the slightest. But if Maddie wasn't so fucking crazy, Imogen would still have invited the hat maker to her bed, but she didn't do *mad*.

Maddie was always so antsy that Imogen only wanted to collect her commissioned hats, then quickly send the nuisance on her way. Imogen could just find another hat maker, but there wasn't anyone in Wonderland who made them the way Maddie did.

"Where is it?" Imogen snapped as she stood in front of her guest.

"Payment first," Maddie sang.

Imogen clenched her teeth. "You know very well that your payment is me not killing you after you allowed the White Queen to disappear. So quit fucking with me."

"I've told you I don't know where she is."

Imogen was certain Maddie *did* know—the Hatter was such good friends with the traitor, after all—which was precisely why she was still alive. One day, Maddie would lead Imogen to her enemy, whether by slipping up or giving in. The White Queen—

Ever—wanted to put an end to snatching unwilling humans from the mortal world. That wouldn't happen. Even Rav wanted Ever dead and she was his sister.

"You will give me one more hat in a month's time and then we'll come up with a new arrangement." Imogen lifted Maddie's chin harshly. "Understand?"

"Yes, Your Majesty." Maddie moved out from the queen's touch and stood from the settee. "Can I see Mouse before I leave?"

"No." Maddie's sister was still serving in the palace and, until Ever was found, would continue doing so.

Imogen didn't miss the flex of the hat maker's fingers before her shoulders sagged and she scampered out the door.

The Queen of Hearts smirked. Even if Maddie grew a backbone, what could she do? Try and stab Imogen through the heart with a hatpin? If the female attempted anything, she would be dead on her back before laying a finger on Imogen.

Forgetting about the Mad Hatter, Imogen lifted the purple box to inspect it as she headed into the throne room. She removed the lid and drew out the hat. It was perfect, delicate and oval with a fishnet veil. She placed it on top of her red waves and clipped the hat into her locks.

"I have a gift for you," a deep voice said from behind her.

Imogen whirled around, catching a lilac scent before seeing the human's face. Beside the new guest stood Rav, his white, scarlet-tipped hair pushed back over the shoulders of his sheer black shirt that displayed his taut chest and abs. She could lick him right here. But the human's scent made her pulse race.

Without blood, a vampire's heart would quit beating, and she would make sure hers never stopped.

"This is where you went to get your fangs done?" The girl's bright blue eyes were as wide as saucers as she glanced at Rav. Thick black hair with blonde roots fell to her waist, and the belted dress she wore was hideous. She appeared to be somewhere in her early twenties—a good age for the change.

"Yes, right here in Wonderland." Rav stroked the tip of one

fang with his tongue as he smirked, his brown eyes blazing. "Hundreds of years ago."

"I don't know what's happening." The girl's chest heaved, her body trembling. "But I want to go back home."

"That's funny." Imogen crept close to the girl, backing her up into the wall so she had nowhere to escape to. Leaning forward, she brushed her nose against the fluttering vein at the girl's throat. "Because you *are* home."

CHAPTER THREE

RAV

One brush of power and Rav had Alice following silently at his heels. He didn't always bother compelling the mortals before leading them through the portal to Wonderland, but it really depended on the person. Some ignored their fight-or-flight response right up until he told them to hop into a hole in the ground. A good chase could be entertaining, but he wasn't in the mood for running tonight. Alice had followed him from the club willingly enough. Leading her into a wooded park at night seemed like a stretch though—she was too self-aware. So a compelled human it was. That way, he could do whatever the fuck he wanted. Even if he were to drain every ounce of a human's blood, the mortal wouldn't bat an eyelash.

"After you," Rav said with a flourish.

He took Alice's warm hand and helped her leap into the hole at the base of a giant, ancient tree. Moss concealed the entrance while Wonderland magic deterred everyone who ventured close enough. Well—not *everyone*. Some people still hopped into the perfectly circular dirt hole and bravely went through the portal, finding themselves lost in a world of vampires. Just like Rav and his sister had all those centuries ago through the one in Ivory.

Rav jumped into the hole after Alice. Six feet from the bottom of the hole was the gleaming portal that led straight into the lower levels of his castle.

Because of his compulsion, Alice had landed on her feet without stumbling. He slipped down beside her. Alice's body shook with nerves as he pressed a hand to her lower back and escorted them both into Wonderland. It was a testament to how strong-willed she was—that she could still retain enough consciousness to feel fear. Rav smirked. Her blood would be all the more delicious for it. He loved the extra tang that terror added to the flavor.

"You're going to meet with the Queen of Hearts," he said conversationally. Her footsteps echoed throughout the gleaming slate tunnel while Rav's were completely silent. "And live in her Ruby Heart Palace."

A whimper escaped Alice's throat, sending a jolt straight to Rav's cock. *Fuck*. He pressed a hand to her lower back again and forced her to walk faster. The queen was waiting for him in the throne room and the sooner she turned the girl into an immortal servant, the sooner he could sink into Imogen's wet heat.

The palace blurred out of focus as his attention zeroed in on the fastest path to their destination. White marble hallways decorated with blood-red tapestries and paintings, low-hung chandeliers with glowing candles, and a crimson carpet stitched with anatomical hearts running down the center of the corridors. The glamour had faded for Rav centuries ago, but the pleasure he was about to partake in was another story.

Bursting through the tall doors, Rav led Alice straight toward his immortal queen. Imogen stood in front of the arched windows behind the throne. The city of Scarlet stretched out below the castle with a million lights burning through the constant dark of Wonderland. That, too, had lost its wonder for Rav, but Imogen still reveled in the power they held over so many. But Rav wanted more. He'd held authority in the palm of his hand since the day he became immortal. If he knew then what he knew now about his twin sister, the White Queen, he would've driven a stake through her heart and taken the Ivory kingdom the moment the late rulers made her their heir.

Then there'd been Imogen. He'd wanted her. And he *had* her.

Seeing Imogen in his favorite red gown, the train skimming over the black floor, the feathered collar caressing her neck, had him ready to take her before dealing with the mortal. But the queen didn't appreciate rash behavior. It's what kept the kingdom of Scarlet and their subjects in line.

"Imogen," he purred. "I have a gift for you."

She pivoted around slowly, her red lips curling into a smile.

Alice turned to face Rav with wide blue eyes. "This is where you went to get your fangs done?"

Rav cursed himself for letting his control of her slip. He couldn't help it though—Imogen made him irrational in every way. "Yes," he told her, flashing his fangs. "Right here in Wonderland. Hundreds of years ago."

Alice looked back and forth between him and the queen, and her body began to shake. "I don't know what's happening, but I want to go back home."

Rav tightened his compulsion over her to avoid the stage where she begged for her life. She would still have a life when they were finished—she just wouldn't be mortal.

"That's funny." Imogen backed her up into the wall so Alice had nowhere to move. Leaning forward, she brushed her nose against the girl's neck. "Because you are home."

Rav stepped closer to them and trailed a hand down the girl's throat. "I found her at one of those *vampire clubs*." His voice was coated with amusement. It was rare that something surprised him, but the existence of such places was a splendid novelty. "She was admiring my fangs."

Imogen's yellow eyes sparkled with cold humor. "You do have impressive fangs, Rabbit."

He grinned, exposing the sharp canines. As soon as she fed

from the girl, he would sink them into the queen's wrist. Taste her blood. Then he would taste between her legs.

"Would you like a pair of your own?" Imogen asked Alice. When she didn't answer, her eyes glazed, the queen spared Rav a disappointed look. "You compelled her?"

"I was eager to get back."

Her gaze trailed down his body, pausing at the large bulge in his trousers. She rubbed a hand over her chest and grinned. "You always come back to me *eager*."

Rav's lust built at the sight of his queen's chest rising and falling faster than before. Paired with the quickening of Alice's pulse, he wasn't sure he could wait long enough for the business with the mortal to be finished.

"Hurry with this one and I'll *show* you eager," he vowed.

Imogen leaned down to lick Alice's neck and glanced up at Rav from beneath her lashes. "Let her scream. You know how much I like it."

Rav suppressed a moan and lifted the compulsion just enough for Alice to have her voice. The ear-piercing scream that followed was enough to rattle the crystal goblets sitting beside the throne.

Imogen gripped Alice's shoulders, her nails biting into the skin and staining the white dress with tiny drops of blood. The scent instantly filled the room and the queen inhaled deeply. Rav unbuckled his belt in anticipation of fucking Imogen when she was finished.

Then Imogen opened her mouth and bit into the girl's creamy flesh.

Drinking.

Drinking.

Drinking.

Fuck, Rav thought as he struggled to control himself. Blood-lust raged alongside his carnal desire, and his cock swelled eagerly.

Finally, Imogen lifted her head from Alice's neck. Twin puncture wounds marked the mortal who now slumped in the queen's hold. Imogen licked her lips and held out one hand to Rav. "Hurry," she rasped.

Rav wasted no time. He lifted Imogen's wrist and bit the tender flesh below her palm. Warm blood oozed into his mouth, but it wasn't meant for him so he pulled back. Imogen pressed her bleeding wrist to Alice's lips and held it there. Thick ruby liquid smeared the girl's mouth, a small line racing down her chin.

Seconds ticked by as Rav undressed the queen with his eyes. *For fuck's sake!* He was going to come in his trousers if she didn't speed the process along. The rich, spicy scent of Alice's blood clung to the air and soon he would get to taste it straight from his lover's lips.

"Ferris!" Imogen shouted, calling for the Knave. A series of heavy footsteps pounded against nearby stairs. When the side door swung open, the queen let Alice slide down the wall and collapse on the floor. "Lock her in the dungeons while she turns."

Ferris eyed Rav with fire in his gaze. The Knave wanted his queen … but she didn't give two shits about him. Rav rubbed himself over his trousers with a smug smirk as Ferris lifted Alice into his arms.

"Enough teasing him," Imogen whispered in Rav's ear. "I want you to tease *me* now."

"No." Rav prowled around Imogen. "You don't want to be teased. You want to be fucked."

CHAPTER FOUR

IMOGEN

Alice's blood was one of the sweetest Imogen had ever tasted. So lush, so perfect. The girl may not have appeared innocent by her various piercings, the clothing she wore, but Imogen had seen everything in the girl's blood. How Alice's family had wanted her to be more outgoing like her brother, not so reclusive. She'd never had many friends, never even had a boyfriend—she'd always been too focused on school, her grades. So Alice had decided to change, but not in the way her family had wanted. She'd started taking a liking to the vampire culture after researching mythology online, then attempted to alter herself, but there was no masking the innocence still hiding there.

"You have a little something on your lips," Rav whispered, his voice low, so delicious that she could almost taste his desire.

Before Imogen could lick the lingering drops of blood clean, Rav's tongue trailed slowly along the edge of her lips. A rush of heat went straight to her core, lighting her on fire.

"There," he murmured in her ear. "Got it."

Imogen pulled closer to him, draping her arms over his strong shoulders before wrapping her legs around his narrow hips. "Take me upstairs. To Ferris's bed."

He growled in approval and held her tight, his nose nuzzled into her hair.

Rav led them out of the throne room and walked them up each step, not once stumbling as his lips found hers again, their tongues entwining. Their kisses became frantic when he reached the top of the stairs. He threw open the first door at the start of the hallway—Ferris's room—and took her inside. Ferris shouldn't have given Rav that fiery look earlier, which was why the Knave needed to be disciplined. Rav was his king, and Ferris needed to treat him as such. The scent of their fucking would remain in his bed long after they finished, and the thought pleased her.

"Unbutton me," Imogen demanded as she stepped to the floor, gliding her breasts down his muscular chest.

Rav spun her around, his fangs grazing her neck as he slowly unbuttoned the back of her dress, inch by agonizing inch. He pushed the fabric from her shoulders and the gown pooled to the floor, her body now bare before him.

Kicking the dress away, Imogen licked her lips and turned to face him. With anxious fingers, she stroked his cock through his fabric. His buckle was already undone and she unbuttoned his trousers while he hungrily watched. Rav removed his boots, shoved his trousers the rest of the way down, and tossed them to the other side of the room. In one swift swoop, his shirt was lost somewhere too.

Imogen drew him toward the bed by his wrist. "You brought an extra delectable treat to serve us, so I want to return the favor."

Rav smirked as Imogen lowered herself to the bed and scooted backward until she felt the hardness of the headboard against her flesh. With her index finger, she motioned him to come to her. His fists hit the mattress and he crawled his way to her, straddling her body, and she grabbed him by the hips. He knew exactly what to do, what she craved, as he got on his knees, his cock gloriously before her.

The veins throbbed on his hardened length, desperate as much as she was. Imogen brought her head forward, swiping her tongue across the tip. She clenched her hands harder on his hips, her fingernails digging in as she urged him closer. Rav slowly rocked back and forth inside her mouth—low groans escaped his throat as she worked her way up his cock in the way he liked. He tasted salty to perfection as she relished in his flavors, and his skin was like velvet on her tongue.

Rav removed the hat from her hair, then interlaced his fingers through her red locks. With a growl, he gently tugged himself from her mouth. "I'm about to come. Turn over."

A wicked grin spread across her face and she pushed him back by his chest, then did as she was told. Imogen placed both hands on the headboard, gripping it tightly, her body tingling with anticipation, demanding him to fill her.

"Fuck me!" she shouted, knowing the entire palace could hear her. And pleased they had.

Rav's body pressed against hers, his fingers stroking between her wet folds. "We will be doing this all night, my queen." And with one swift thrust, he was inside her, the headboard slamming the wall as she lurched forward.

She moaned, arching her spine into him, the pads of his fingers running down each vertebra.

Again and again, Rav thrust, his hands on her breasts, toying with her nipples in a way that made her body hotter than lava. Then his teeth were at her throat, making her moan even louder. Imogen reclined her head back as her second favorite part of him sank into her. The ecstasy rolled through her veins as her blood filled his mouth. Each roll of his hips, each suction at her throat, had the desire building until a rush of crimson colors rocketed within her, the pleasure seeming as if it wouldn't end.

Then he ripped his fangs free of her flesh and with her name on his lips—the sound filling the room in a violent, exquisite way—he erupted too. His chest heaved against her body, hers inflating and deflating just as savagely.

When Imogen finally caught her breath, she glanced over her shoulder, giving him a devilish smile. "We're not done yet, Rabbit. Lay on your back."

Rav chuckled, uncaging her, as he flipped to his back, his head resting on Ferris's pillow. Imogen's fangs lowered while she cradled his hips with her thighs and leaned forward, inhaling his musky scent. Her tongue swiped the vein of his throat, his pulse beating rapidly.

Imogen sank her teeth into his soft, delicious flesh. She drank and drank until he was hard once more, desperately growling her name.

And now, she would ride her king.

CHAPTER FIVE

RAV

The sun never shone in Wonderland. If it did, vampires would be trapped inside nearly half their lives to avoid turning to ash. So, instead, time was told by how dark the sky was: pitch black at night, ash gray at midday, and varying shades between. Judging by the deep charcoal, Rav had spent the entire night with Imogen in the Knave's bed. Ferris had undoubtedly attempted to sleep at some point, and Rav hoped the fool had heard the queen screaming *his* name.

Fucking shitbag. He'd never understand why, out of all the servant's Imogen killed, it had never been *that* one.

Alice, on the other hand, would be interesting. A mortal who wanted to be a vampire and thought them to be romantic instead of ruthless... What would she do now that her wish had been granted? Over the centuries, only a handful of humans had wanted to be turned, but this was different. Humans no longer truly believed in the existence of Rav's kind. He couldn't help being curious about how she would react. Would parts of this world live up to her expectations, or would she mope about because it was so vastly different? And the first feeding—would that intrigue or repulse her? There were so many questions that he wanted answers to.

"What are you thinking about, Rabbit?" Imogen asked as she stepped into her gown.

Rav slipped his shirt over his head. "Hmm?"

"You look as if you're ready to cause trouble."

Rav ran a hand through his tumbled hair. "No trouble. I'm just thinking of the girl."

Imogen's gaze took on a hard edge. She raised an eyebrow, silently letting Rav know he needed to elaborate.

He stepped forward, buttoning the back of her dress without her having to ask. "I'm curious how similar we are to what this new … vampire culture thinks. Do you suspect that it will affect her change at all?"

"I don't see how similarities between her expectations and reality would have any impact." Imogen bent and grabbed one of her shoes from under the bed. "It's not their mental strength that's tested."

Rav nodded, though he already knew that. The change could be brutal. A vampire—one stronger than Ferris or any of the dungeon guards—sometimes had to coax them through it. Even then, there was no guarantee they would survive. Some bodies were simply not equipped. Humans called it survival of the fittest.

"You want to study her," Imogen said with a roll of her eyes.

Studying things was a habit of his, not that he always knew what he was searching for. Just … *something*. And it gave his life a touch of focus. After centuries, living could become dull without a purpose. Even a meaningless one. Rav shrugged. "Let me have my fun."

"Fine." Imogen swiped her second shoe from the floor and crossed the room, running a finger down his cheek. "Conduct your little experiment, quench your thirst for useless knowledge, then come back to me. I'm going to bathe."

"I'll join you after," he promised.

The queen sauntered past him, swatting his naked ass. Rav chuckled and quickly pulled on his trousers. If things had gone well, Alice would have already finished transitioning into a vampire. It took less than thirty minutes, ideally, and he'd spent six times as long fucking Imogen.

Rav left the bedroom, skipping down the stairs, and smiled to himself. When he saw Ferris sitting on the bottom step, his smile widened. The Knave stared straight ahead at the wall, his lips pursed, with his hands in fists.

"What's wrong, Knave?" he asked, smug.

Ferris shot him a look hot enough to burn. "Nothing."

"Nothing?" Rav laughed at the obvious lie. "Enjoy the new scent all over your sheets."

One second, Ferris was sitting, then the next he was standing, his face an inch from Rav's. "Remember, *my king*. Those with the most, have the most to lose."

Rav pushed Ferris away with a single finger to his chest. "Is that a threat?"

"Who am I to threaten you?" he asked, feigning ignorance.

Rav groaned. He didn't want to deal with Ferris, not even to taunt him. He wanted to see how Alice was progressing. "One day, Knave, your disrespect will get you killed."

At that, Ferris smirked.

Rav smirked back, though rage boiled within him. He couldn't let the pathetic bastard see how he was getting under his skin. The Knave knew what he was doing, the fucker, but Imogen clearly wanted him alive. It was hard to find loyal servants and, to her, that was exactly what Ferris was. Rav had to respect that, just as she respected his interest in Alice. So, he hurried to his own room to change into a clean outfit more befitting him.

Once in a comfortable pair of black linen trousers and a plain red shirt with a black jacket, Rav made his way past the throne room, and down a winding stone staircase to the dungeons.

A muscular male vampire stood watch at the front of the

room wearing the queen's crest on a crimson tunic. The tang of old blood hung in the air, mixing with the damp, musty scent from the straw sprinkled across the floor. Six-by-eight cells stretched down the long, dark passageway, separated with metal bars. Shackles hung from the walls to help keep the prisoners from breaking free. At the other end of the room was a door that led to the *interview* room. All the fun toys were kept in there.

The only guest today was Alice and, judging by the silence, the change had gone well. Or killed her already. Rav peered through the rows of metal bars, not catching a glimpse of Alice's white dress.

Brows lowered in confusion, he turned to the guard. "Where is the girl?"

"Girl, Your Majesty?" he asked.

"Yes. The girl the Knave brought down hours ago to complete the change." He flicked a hand at the cells. "Where is she?"

The guard's throat bobbed. "The Knave didn't bring anyone here today."

Rav blinked, sure he'd misheard. "White dress, dark makeup, about this tall," he said carefully, holding his hand up at roughly Alice's height. "The queen's bite mark on her neck…"

The guard shook his head, his expression wary.

Rav's rage stirred, foaming at the brink, threatening to spill over. "That motherfucking piece of shit!"

The guard blanched as Rav spun on his heel and stormed out of the dungeons. He would kill Ferris. Chop him into tiny little pieces and scatter him from the balcony. Except his head. His head, he would stick on a pike outside the palace as a warning.

"Imogen," he shouted once he hit the main floor. He would deal with the Knave after they found Alice. "We have a problem!"

CHAPTER SIX

IMOGEN

The water was warm against Imogen's skin as it lapped at the edges of the bathtub. She spread the soap up and down her pale breasts, then sank her head below the water.

A shout came from somewhere within the palace and Imogen jerked forward, creating waves along the bathtub walls. Her eyes narrowed as she cocked her head, listening for the sound to come again, wondering if she'd imagined it. Then it reverberated through the palace walls. Rav calling her name. If it had been anyone else, the interruption would have irritated her. But for him to yell for her meant something was important.

Imogen didn't bother wiping the liquid droplets from her skin as she stepped out from the cast iron bathtub. She flicked her wet hair over her shoulders and grabbed a raven-colored robe from the hook on the wall beside the sink. She shoved the silk on as she opened the door, her nipples pebbling from the cool air. With the robe still open, she stepped into the hall.

Furrowing her brow, she looked both ways into the empty

area. "Rabbit?"

Footsteps thumped against the stairs and Rav raced toward her, his face red with fury.

"What is it?" she asked, staring at his disheveled hair. The last time she'd seen her king this furious was when one of their servants had attempted to stab Imogen through the heart with a dinner knife. That servant lost his head and heart before the blade could even touch her flesh.

Rav struck his fist against the wall. "I told you the bastard wasn't trustworthy."

"Who?" Imogen wrinkled her nose.

"That fucking Knave of yours."

Ferris. Her eyes turned to slits as she thought about him, replaying every single interaction between them. He never once disobeyed her, and if he truly did deceive her, she would rip his heart out and crush it. She and Rav could always detect the untrustworthy ones right away, and she didn't see how she could have missed it.

"What did he do?" Imogen asked, while tying her robe. She then straightened her shoulders and released her fangs.

"The girl is gone," Rav spat. "I went to the dungeons, and the guard said the Knave never brought in anyone. I saw the smug bastard before I went down there, sitting on the steps outside his room."

Imogen felt her temper rising as her heart quickened. Nothing ever slid past her. Ever. But something wasn't right about this. "Where did he take her then?"

"I don't know, but we need to find them." Rav struck the wall again.

If Rav had just seen Ferris, then he still had to be in the palace. Somewhere.

"Knave!" she screeched, brushing past Rav.

Imogen rushed straight to his room and threw open the door. His drawers were wide open, clothing dumped all over the floor, as if he'd taken things he'd hidden. *That bastard.*

Gritting her teeth, she drew Rav out of the room as soon as

he entered. They then went up and down the palace, gathering all the servants to help them search for the traitor. There wasn't a sign of him anywhere. Not a single cabinet, wardrobe, or curtain had been left unsearched. No one had seen him with Alice. No one had even seen him since Rav.

A sinking feeling nagged at her. "Did anyone check your portal?"

"No," Rav growled, already taking off in the direction of it. They turned down several of the red and black checkered hallways, then flew down the glistening steps leading to the lower levels of the castle. A sulfuric scent filled the air, as if a match had just been struck. Someone had used the portal.

Imogen picked up her pace, remaining right on Rav's heels. Just as they were about to reach the last hallway to the portal, a shadow slinked around the corner before she caught sight of the figure.

It wasn't Ferris but her *son*. Chess. He looked nothing like his father besides his chestnut hair. It fell to mid-neck, shorter locks framing his face, his yellow irises matching hers. He wore his usual dark vest, nothing underneath, paired with leather trousers and boots.

"Did you use Rav's portal again?" Imogen hissed, already knowing his answer.

"I did." He smirked, stroking a finger along the wall. His gaze flicked between her and Rav. "I suppose you were too busy fucking each other to notice what's been going on."

"How long have you been lurking around down here?" Rav asked.

"Long enough," Chess said coyly. "My pleasant feast was interrupted when the Knave rushed a girl through the portal."

"And you didn't stop him?" Imogen grabbed her foolish son by his vest.

Chess didn't bat an eyelash. He had so much of her in him that she didn't know whether to be proud or furious.

"Why should I care about a human girl he wanted to feed off and send back?" He shrugged.

"She was turned, Chess." As precious moments ticked by, it didn't matter that he was her son—she wanted to kill him.

"Funny thing." Chess grinned, removing Imogen's hand from him. "Ferris went out the secret door, alone, only minutes ago."

"Chess!" No one should have known about the hidden door besides the three of them.

"I don't think Ferris realized he sent the girl up the portal just as the sun was rising." He bit his blood-stained lip. "Oops."

Imogen wrapped her hand around Chess's throat. "Find the Knave and bring him back here. You know better than anyone how to get around Wonderland without being seen. If you screw this up, you'll meet the same fate as your father."

"You don't have to be so dramatic, Mother. I'll bring your little toy back so we can be one big happy family again."

He'd better.

Imogen removed her hand from Chess's throat and watched him saunter toward the hidden panel in the wall. For now, they would have to seal it up to make sure Ferris couldn't slip back inside on his own.

"I think there's more to this than you refusing to bed Ferris again," Rav finally said when the door shut behind Chess.

Imogen thought about the way Ferris had always been watching her. His lust-filled gazes now seemed as though they could have been false, as if he'd been using the tactic to spy on her instead. For something… Or for *someone*.

"Chess will bring him back"—her gaze connected with Rav's—"then you'll pry the Knave's fangs from his severed head. As for the girl, if the sun doesn't kill her, we have to find her. A newly-turned vampire can't be allowed to run around the mortal world. And, if she *is* dead, then we need to collect another human to take her place."

BOOK ONE

MADDIE

CHAPTER ONE

MADDIE

Creating a hat was like creating a heart.

For Maddie, it had always been that way. The threads were the hat's veins and arteries. The fabric, its muscle. The pulse seemed to come to life as soon as the hat was placed atop one's head.

Or, at least, her head.

Maddie's fists tightened as she fought to keep her wandering thoughts on hats—wide brims, curving crowns, silk lining, velvet bands, feathered decorations—but all she could focus on was her latest creation, the headpiece she'd just handed over to the Queen of Hearts. *Imogen*.

That *bitch*.

Gritting her teeth, Maddie shook out her hands and exhaled a harsh breath as she stomped away from the Ruby Heart Palace. Her fingers twitched for the collection of hatpins back at her cottage. Plunging a particularly sharp hat pin straight through Imogen's heart and then using it to stitch together a hat made of her flesh sounded enticing. She would love to parade it through Wonderland, giving the queen exactly what she deserved for taking Maddie's sister and holding her as a prisoner in her palace.

Mouse.

Mouse.

Mouse.

Maddie had given Margo the nickname as soon as her baby sister had been born. Margo had been so quiet—always quiet. The mad one and the quiet one. If only Maddie hadn't come back to London after becoming immortal—if only she'd let Mouse believe she had vanished. Mouse had been a child of only ten when Maddie left. She'd returned ten years later to catch a glimpse of her sister each night in her sitting room window after the sun sunk deep into hibernation. Even her hats had ceased to fill the void in Maddie's heart from missing Mouse.

Maddie crouched in front of her old home and gazed through the glass, finding Mouse alone and quilting in front of the fireplace. Several lit candles lined the grime-covered windowsill.

No longer was Mouse a child, but a grown woman. Still small, still frail, her unique pixie-like face seemed straight from a faerie world. Chestnut curls spiraled from her head, the exact color Maddie's had been before they'd shifted to violet once immortality flowed through her veins. Sometimes it was one's eye color that would change, for others it was hair color. Sometimes both, and sometimes nothing at all.

After several long moments, Maddie pushed away from the glass window and the flickering candlelight, then headed back toward the portal to Wonderland. She hadn't made it far from her old home when a hand snatched her arm, making her gasp.

"Please don't go, Madelyn!" Mouse shouted, studying her face.

With Mouse's quiet, stealthy movements, Maddie should have known she would be caught. A mixture of relief and fear flooded her as she faced her sister, who held a lantern, casting yellow light around them. Her white nightgown dwarfed her tiny frame.

"You look different," Mouse continued. "But you're my sister. Don't deny it. You've been coming by the house every night." Not a single sign of terror darkened her sister's eyes.

Maddie's fingers fluttered by her sides, her voice trapped in her throat. The scent of blood wafted through the air, hidden within her sister's veins. Even though she yearned to taste it, she controlled her fangs from lowering. "I'm not the same person anymore."

"It doesn't matter." A tear slid down Mouse's cheek, and she brushed it away. But that didn't stop more from following. "Anything is better than here."

"What happened?" Maddie whispered, her chest tightening. Their home had always been a happy one when she was a mortal.

"While you were away, Mr. Taylor… He took everything from me. Without my consent," she said, her eyes peering down at her feet, her lower lip trembling. "If I stay here another day, I won't survive. I'd rather die."

Fury ignited within Maddie. Their bastard neighbor dared touch her sister? "I won't leave you again," she promised. Maddie wrapped her arms around Mouse, holding her tight as her sister sobbed, and vowed to make Mr. Taylor pay.

And pay he had.

Maddie ensured he'd received no pleasure from her bite, murdering him slowly with her hatpins and knives. Piece by piece.

Mr. Taylor was the only human she'd ever killed. Vampires were another story.

A cloud of bats zoomed over Maddie's head, interrupting her thoughts. Through the trees, howls echoed in the distance, the gray of Wonderland darkening to black. Buildings of obsidian and crimson quickly blocked out the horizon while she ventured farther into the city. She shivered as she passed a dressmaker's shop and cast a glance over her shoulder.

"Bloody hell," Maddie squeaked. "Tonight just isn't my night." She quickened her pace as the howls increased, drawing nearer. The rogue werewolves didn't frequent this side of Wonderland often—unless they were hungry. Most of the queen's guards kept them out, but they sometimes managed to slip into the kingdom of Scarlet. While throats could easily be torn apart with her teeth, she would need much more than that to kill a werewolf. She would need a silver bullet, but she hadn't brought any of her guns to the palace since Imogen didn't allow guests to have weapons.

Maddie's boots pounded the cobblestone path, the ruby lanterns guiding her way. "Hats, Maddie. Focus on hats. Sewing and stitching," she sang to herself, while barreling through the night, passing row after row of red and black homes until she entered the fringes of Scarlet.

Trees replaced buildings and the glow from the ruby lanterns ceased. She darted over wilted plants and hurdled fallen logs until her lone cottage slipped into view—the crooked roof, the black and purple painted exterior, the circular door, the garden filled with red roses. Imogen only allowed red roses in her kingdom.

Tearing open the door, Maddie sprinted inside and slammed it shut, her breathing ragged. Her gaze flicked to the walls lined with hats of all shapes and sizes. Bright pinks, deep crimsons, blacks, grays, velvet, wool, cashmere, lace. There wasn't a single empty spot. Without them—her *safety*—she would slip into madness.

Maddie's thoughts again turned to Mouse as she peered at her sister's favorite blue hat resting on the desk. Imogen and her king, Rav, imprisoned her sister because they believed Maddie knew where the White Queen, Ever, resided. She didn't know, but even if she did, Ever was her friend. Imogen and Rav would murder the White Queen for wanting to put an end to their taking of unwilling humans. It didn't matter that Ever was Rav's sister.

Regardless of the White Queen's location, Maddie remained loyal to Ever and her mission. Feeding or ending a life was one thing, but forcing someone to become immortal was *wrong*. And Rav—

Maddie screeched as she thought about that snake and how her sister was locked up in the palace where *he* resided. She ripped a partially-finished hat off the desk and plopped down on her chair. She shoved the needle into the material as images of Rav spun through her mind. If only it were his eyes she was sewing shut.

Back in London, a couple of centuries ago, Maddie had worked at her mother's millinery shop, dreaming of one day making hats for the queen. While other women yearned for a husband, that had never been her wish. She'd never considered herself pretty enough to receive a second glance from a gentleman. Her sister, yes—but not her. She had neither the looks, the grace, nor the wealth to be considered suitable for marriage. In adolescence, the boys had always found her odd, and it wasn't until she was twenty-two years old that someone gave her any attention, sweeping her off her feet when he'd encountered her mother's shop.

"The queen needs a hat maker, and I hear you're quite good at it," the stranger said. His hair was tucked under a curled white wig, and his brown eyes sparkled as they caught hers. "I'm Rav. And dare I say, you're beautiful."

Maddie quickened her movements, stabbing and yanking the thread through the hat. She hadn't known then, when she'd agreed to accompany him, that it would be for a queen in another world—a world known as Wonderland which had existed just as long as the mortal realm. How could she have known he was the queen's lover? A liar, he was. Deceitful, he was.

Angry. Destroyed. Weak.

Within a few hours of knowing him, he'd made her feel all those things. She'd been green then. Naïve.

The entire town would've called her a fool for being so infatuated with someone after such a short time. All because he'd been the only man to ever pay her any attention. She'd given all of herself to him in the forest that day. There, he not only took her innocence but her mortality, too.

"I hate this hat!" Maddie chucked it at the wall, wishing it would've hit with a loud bang instead of a teeny thud. A melancholy feeling washed over her at the dent she'd just put into the fabric. She didn't really hate the hat. Scooping it from the floor, she dusted it off and brought it up to her face. "I'm sorry. I didn't mean it." She set it down and snatched up a new hat to work on.

Maddie couldn't let Rav and Imogen get to her. She wouldn't allow herself to once again spiral into that dark, mad place. The one where she would either fuck or find a victim to drink the night away. Until her sister helped her to get past those gloomy memories.

The earlier visit to the palace, where she hoped to get a glimpse of Mouse, didn't go as planned. No, not at all.

"You will give me one more hat in a month's time and then we'll come up with a new arrangement." Imogen lifted Maddie's chin, and she studied the queen's yellow irises. "Understand?"

"Yes, Your Majesty." Maddie moved out from the queen's touch and rose from the settee. "Can I see Mouse before I leave?"

"No."

In that moment, Maddie was pleased with herself for rubbing saliva all over the queen's hat before delivering it.

Maddie adjusted her bright purple arm sleeves, the fabric covering her flesh from elbow to a few inches of her palms, her thumbs peeking out through holes made specifically for them. She plucked up a spool of tulle, twisting the material around the center of a silver hat, creating a golden fishnet veil. Her stomach ached with hunger—she would need to find a human to feed on soon. But even blood cravings failed to pull her focus from her sister and how she continued to let Mouse down.

Maddie's sewing picked up, faster, faster, as she concentrated on her work. For hours and hours, unable to sleep, she added more ribbon and stitching to the same hat, then took it apart before doing the repetitive movements again and again until it was perfect. For all her clients in Wonderland, she wouldn't allow anything less.

A loud rapping at the door startled Maddie, and she lurched forward, the hat falling to the floor. She jumped from her seat, her stiff muscles aching from sitting in the same position for so long, and hurried to the door. Standing on her tiptoes, she opened the small square peephole and peered out. Her breath caught, her lungs halting as her gaze settled on a familiar figure standing outside, shrouded by the gray fog.

What is he doing here? A wave of excitement crashed over her. *He did it!*

Throwing open the door, she grabbed Ferris's arm and yanked him inside, studying his short black hair, dark irises, and flushed cheeks. He'd been working as the Queen of Hearts' Knave. Maddie and Mouse had met Ferris at a club four years earlier. He'd agreed to let them feed on him when their hunger rose, mostly for his own reasons—past demons. Their feeding was his own escape, his high.

"Where is she? You have her, right?" Maddie asked, gazing out the door, hoping to catch a glimpse of her sister. Her heart pounded, trying to free itself from her rib cage when she couldn't spot her.

"I couldn't get her out." His lips tugged down into a frown. "We need to find another way to save Mouse."

"Why so suddenly? You've been there for *two years.*" It wasn't his fault, though. His dangerous tenure there hadn't gotten them any closer to saving Mouse.

"I'll get to that in a moment. I just need to catch my breath."

Maddie sighed and gripped his shoulders, though he was much taller than her. "You didn't have to stay so long. Risk yourself. But thank you for doing this, not only for me, but for her. How is she?"

"Quiet." He ran a hand through his hair. "But strong enough not to be broken."

Two years earlier, Maddie hatched a plan—one Ferris agreed to—for him to show up at a club where Imogen frequented to retrieve her male servants. The queen would pluck them from there, fuck them, then make the males immortal. But no one would ever replace her Rabbit, no matter how many lovers she or he took on the side.

After Rav stole Mouse, Maddie needed someone to infiltrate the palace, find out things, and attempt to retrieve her sister. Ferris consented, even though his mortality would be stripped away.

"Now, to answer your question about giving up so

suddenly… There's something else you should know." He bit his lip and gripped the back of his neck. "I have a new problem. A big one."

Maddie released his shoulders and stepped back. "What is it?"

"Rav brought a human girl to become a new servant. I was supposed to bring her to the dungeon so she could go through her transition, but I stopped to see Mouse on the way. She asked me to save the girl—Alice."

"You didn't!" Maddie's eyes widened. Why had he listened to her? "Bloody hell. What did you do?"

"Imogen had me dusting rooms with my fucking tongue, and this girl would've suffered the same atrocities. I couldn't deny Mouse's request. I could only stay long enough after rescuing Alice to grab Ever's keys that you gave me from my room or they would've found them." Ferris clenched his jaw. "Alice is back in London."

"As a vampire?"

"A new one…"

"No…" Maddie clasped her hands over her mouth. Not all new vampires made a mess of things, but this was a fifty-fifty stab in the dark.

"She seemed stable enough." He shrugged. "Not wild like some of the others I've seen transition. I promised to help her and will bring her back before anyone gets hurt."

"Not you." Maddie shook her head, her hat sliding against her hair. "We."

Ferris's nostrils flared.

"You know Imogen and Rav will still go after her." If they found her then tortured her, they could discover that Mouse was part of the reason why Ferris helped the girl escape. What would they do to Mouse then? *Horrid things.* "Where are you supposed to meet her? I'll help you."

"Her brother's place. She wanted to tell him goodbye."

CHAPTER TWO

NOAH

The scent of freshly brewed coffee clung to Noah's clothes. He hung his apron near the back door of Bean & Brew and stretched his arms with a satisfied groan. He'd worked a double shift making overpriced cappuccinos and lattes to keep his mind busy. Better to work himself into the ground than to have a weak moment and text his fucking ex.

"Heading out, Noah?" Ava, his co-worker, asked.

He wanted to, but it was getting late. Though London was generally safe at night, one never knew who was lurking about. Ava was a petite girl with a doll-like face and long blonde hair, so he felt better if she didn't lock up alone. "I'll wait and walk you to the Tube."

"Okay." Ava blushed. "Let me grab my purse."

She returned a second later, bag slung over her shoulder, and flicked off the lights. Noah opened the back door and let her step out first. The minute he was out of the shop, he dragged in as much fresh air as he could. Coffee was great, but too much of a good thing … or whatever.

Ava locked the door and turned to him. "Ready?"

"Hell yes." He couldn't wait to take a long shower and crawl into bed until noon. It had been entirely too long since he'd gotten more than the bare minimum of sleep.

"What are your plans this weekend?" she inquired as they walked side-by-side toward the Tube entrance.

"I'm not sure yet. I haven't had one free in a while, so I'll probably hit up some friends." One of them would undoubtedly be throwing a party and he wasn't about to pass up a chance to drown his break-up woes. Even though Noah had been the one to end things, walking in on her fucking someone else in *his* bed was a bit of a blow to his ego. "What about you?"

"I'm going dancing with some friends." She paused and bit her bottom lip. "Do you maybe want to come along?"

Noah hadn't missed how Ava blushed whenever they spoke or how her gaze landed on him more often than necessary. It had always made him feel good, but he never expected her to shoot her shot, even now that he was single.

"Noah!" Harper's voice carried down the street with a shrill edge. He winced and kept walking as if he hadn't heard his ex call out. "I know you heard me!"

Fuck. "Hang on, Ava. Sorry."

"It's okay," she said, backing away. Ava had been a witness to Harper's meltdown at the company New Year's party last year when Noah had tipped the barista more than Harper thought was acceptable. Months later, he still didn't know if it had been jealousy or because she wanted the money herself. He couldn't blame Ava for wanting to escape. "I'll be fine from here—I can see the Tube. Let me know about this weekend?"

"I will," he assured her. "G'night."

With a fortifying breath, Noah turned to face Harper. She'd already closed the distance between them, so he held his hands out to keep her at an arm's length. Mascara trailed down her freckled cheeks and her dark hair was in a messy knot atop her head.

"You're dating *her* now? I should've known! She was always staring at you," Harper spat.

"I'm not dating anyone," Noah said in a calm voice. Rising to meet her anger only made things worse and they were in the middle of a public street. "After dealing with your shit, I doubt I ever will again."

Her eyes narrowed. "I said I was sorry. You make me lose my mind, is all."

Noah still hadn't told his parents that, after the breakup, she had splashed paint all over their hand-crafted wall mosaic or purposely snapped the wings off the cherubs sculpted on the living room fireplace. The walls were fixable—a little elbow grease, the right chemicals, and a lot of time would take the paint right off. But the wings were another story.

"Don't make this my fault, Harper. Your issues are your issues and I have too much going on to put up with them, okay? We had a good run." *Good sex, at least.* The rest of the relationship was rather brutal on his psyche, if he were being honest. All two years of it. "But it's over now."

She grabbed his arm as he turned to leave. "Please, just give me another chance."

"You cheated on *me*." With his best friend, no less. "Go leech off someone else, yeah? I'm done with you."

"Noah, *please*," she begged.

But he wasn't having it and hailed a taxi, price be damned. It was worth it to get away from Harper. She'd gotten more chances than anyone should have, and now he was going to relax and enjoy his last year of university. No more drama, no more gold-diggers. Just studying during the week and letting loose on the weekends. When he didn't have to work, that was. His parents were letting him stay in their London flat rent free with two conditions: keep a job and make sure his sister, Alice, stayed out of trouble.

One of those was easier than the other. His little sister had taken full advantage of the freedom university bought her. She'd always been well-behaved and had gotten straight-As, but there hadn't been any other option. Their parents would've skinned them alive for any less. But now that Alice was out from under their thumb, she'd made some … interesting choices. Not that it mattered to Noah. He was actually proud of his sister for trying to find herself.

"Girl trouble?" the driver asked.

"You have no idea." Noah rested his head on the back of the seat and gave his address. Harper wasn't worth all this trouble.

By the time they reached the front of Noah's house, his eyes had drooped, his head bobbing with sleep. He shook himself out of it and swiped his credit card. "Thanks, man."

"You bet," the older driver said and pulled carefully back into traffic.

Noah walked around the corner to the back entrance in case Alice was napping. Her room was adjacent to the front door, and she was a notoriously light sleeper. If she had any plans to go out again tonight, she would need the rest. She and her friends partied harder than he ever had—he wasn't even sure if she came home last night. *More power to you, sis.*

The gate clicked shut behind him as he entered the small garden. Tall bushes lined both sides of the stone pathway and every inch of dirt between them bloomed in bright flowers. Above them, creeping vines snaked over the brick exterior of the house.

Noah's phone buzzed in his pocket, and he pulled it out to see a text from Harper. He rolled his eyes and unlocked the screen to block her number without reading it. Before he could manage it, he tripped over something large in the middle of the pathway and landed on the ground with an *oomph* next to his sister's prone body. He recognized her black hair and blonde roots immediately as well as the new piercings through the bridge of her nose and in her cheeks.

"Alice?" He pushed himself up with a grunt. "What the hell are you doing out here?"

When she rolled away from him and curled into a fetal position instead of answering, he got to his feet. "You're pissed again, aren't you? I told you not to drink so much."

"Help me, Noah," she moaned.

Such a lightweight. He grabbed her arm and tugged her into a sitting position. "Come on. You're just knackered. Let's get you to bed."

Alice shook her head. "I have to leave."

With another tug, she was on her feet, clinging to his upper arms. Her hair was a snarled mess, the straps and buckles of her white dress were covered in dirt and grass stains, the tulle skirt ripped in places, and her skin appeared paler than usual. His brows rose at the sight. "What happened to you?"

"Vampires," she breathed, her expression wild. Alice's irises were a light blue which was a change from the red contacts she'd been wearing most of the time lately.

Noah rolled his eyes. He knew about her obsession with the mythical beings, knew about the clubs she went to with her new, like-minded friends. She must've meant one of them. Each one he'd met dressed in all black, bodies laden with tattoos and piercings, and a few even sported fake fangs. Still, they'd all seemed decent, harmless. Either he wasn't as good at reading people as he thought, or he hadn't met the person responsible for her condition.

"Who hurt you?" he asked softly.

"There was a man with white, red-tipped hair and fangs..." She released Noah to prod at her own teeth.

"Yes, a vampire. They have fangs." He spoke carefully, running through his memory of her friends for one who fit that description. Demanding their name when Alice was in this state wouldn't do any good. Demanding *anything* from her in any state never ended well, actually. It was just who she was. He had to go easy to keep from spooking her into utter silence. "What did he do?"

"He took me to a hole in the park."

Noah drew a steadying breath. *Sure, he did...* "Come inside, and I'll put on some tea."

"You're not listening!" she shouted, ripping herself from his grip. "I don't have time to make you believe me. I only came back to tell you that I love you. And … and goodbye."

His mouth fell open and he blinked, not understanding. "What are you talking about?"

"A … friend will be coming soon to help me." She paced back and forth, her vinyl Mary Janes clicking on the pavement as she mumbled incoherently to herself.

Noah searched the garden path for Alice's purse. If he could get his hands on her phone, he could call one of the friends she went out with tonight. Ask if they'd seen anything. Maybe someone slipped something into her drink, but he didn't want to get the police involved without knowing more. When she'd started acting out in little ways to find herself, Noah was proud of her, but he was also worried how far she would take her new freedoms. The piercings and vampire clubs were one thing, but he'd made her swear to never touch drugs. If she broke that promise tonight, they would fucking talk about it in the morning.

"Let's wait for your friend *inside*," he urged. A murmured voice sounded behind the gate and Noah spun to face it, putting himself between his sister and whatever *friend* was coming.

"This should be it," a man whispered.

"We need to hurry," a woman urged. "Maybe we should knock on the door, or I can shimmy through a window?"

"She said she would wait in the back garden, so no one saw us."

Noah glanced at his sister over his shoulder. "Are these your friends?"

"I don't know." She sucked her bottom lip between her teeth. "It was just supposed to be the Knave."

"The *what*?" *Knave*? Noah shook his head at the ridiculous nickname. "Never mind. I'll get rid of them. Go inside."

"Wait!" Alice called after him as he approached the gate and swung it open.

A man wearing black trousers and a matching long-sleeve shirt with rope-like rips stood on the other side. A young woman, a head shorter than him, flanked his side. The street lamp behind the duo cast the woman's face in shadow, but she wore an odd hat pinned to the side of her purple hair.

She stepped forward, her hands toying with the skirt of her dress. "Is Alice here?" Her honey-colored gaze shifted past him, her fingers tapping anxiously at her thighs.

Something about the pair made the hair on Noah's arms rise. He couldn't put his finger on *why*, but he knew instinctually they were up to no good. "Sorry, she's not seeing anyone tonight."

"Unfortunately, that's not an option," the man said, and promptly pushed Noah aside before entering the garden.

CHAPTER THREE

MADDIE

This wouldn't go well. A simple task was what Maddie needed. Simple would not be today.

"Noah!" Alice screamed, her dark hair and blonde roots bouncing. Maddie prayed that every door in the building would remain shut. Influencing all the neighbors to go away would waste precious moments.

She assumed the ridiculous blond man, who Ferris shoved out of the way, was Alice's brother. Ferris wasn't one to get aggressive, but they didn't have time to deal with this mortal slowing things to a snail's pace.

Noah pushed off the wall and Maddie adjusted her hat, knowing what he was going to do next as he zeroed in on Ferris. She supposed she should intervene before Ferris, who was too focused on Alice, received a hit to his pretty face.

Leaping forward with the grace of a predator, she clutched Noah's shirt and hauled him back, just as he was about to slam his fist into Ferris.

"What the hell?" Noah growled, attempting to whirl around to face Maddie.

Alice watched with wide eyes as Ferris spoke quickly to her, calming her while Maddie finished dealing with her brother.

Despite her thinner frame, she used her immortal strength to yank him down so he was eye level with her, his back in an awkward position. Her nose skimmed his throat as she drifted closer to his ear, but she couldn't stop herself from inhaling his cedarwood scent and the crimson buried below his skin, all with the bitter scent of coffee mixed in. She'd had a snack in her teacup back in Wonderland before she left with Ferris, but it had been cold. The warm blood flowing through Noah's throbbing vein tempted her. To keep her heart beating, she, and every other vampire, needed blood. It had always been that way in Wonderland. At least, since she'd been there. She yearned for a taste of his blood. *No time.*

"Listen to me," Maddie sang while he cursed and jerked in her grasp, "and listen well. We are not the threat to your sister. She's in danger, and you need to stop fighting us. If I release you, will you do as I say?"

He nodded. Yet by the way his full lips pursed, she knew this wouldn't be the end of it. But she would let him lose his first chance.

Maddie let go of him, and he spun to face her just as she foresaw. *Dear humans, always making bold, yet terrible mistakes.*

With what he most likely believed were quick motions, Noah had her backed into the wall. His hands gripped her arms, his chest pressed against hers. She glanced at Ferris who watched her, his gaze rolling to the sky. He had to know Maddie was having a little fun with the mortal by allowing him some sense of control.

"Just leave him alone," Alice pleaded while Ferris held onto her. "He doesn't understand."

"Listen," Noah said, his voice low. "I don't know what drugs you're on, but you need to get the fuck out of here before I call the police."

Maddie chuckled then, and he looked at her as if she were mad. But that was nothing new. She quirked a brow and slowly raked her gaze down his lean and muscular form. Now that she was looking, his body wasn't a bad one at all, but it wouldn't tempt her today … or tomorrow. "You wouldn't have time to pull it out of your pocket and make a call." Noah was a fool for even threatening a vampire. If Rav and Imogen had shown up first, he would've already been dead.

"Now you—"

"Tut, tut." Maddie interrupted his pathetic threats and stared into his green eyes, luring him in with her influence. "Now, step back."

When he obeyed with glazed eyes, Alice gasped, her hands balled into fists against her tulle skirt. "You did to him what Rav did to me."

"It's fine. It had to be done." She turned to Ferris and, with a flick of a hand, said, "Time to go."

"He's going to have to come with us." Ferris sighed as he glanced at Noah. "Rav has her purse, so he'll know where they live. He'll kill him."

Maddie peered up at the mortal, who blinked at her, waiting for her next command. "No. He stays here, Ferris."

"Please," Alice begged, tears sliding down her cheeks, over her silver piercings. "This is all my fault. I—I can't leave him."

Maddie narrowed her eyes. She couldn't let this man or Alice ruin her plans to save her sister, but damn it all, Ferris was right. "I suppose. We'll bring him back for a few days, then he can return home. However, the influence remains on for now. No argument."

Alice nodded, yet her body trembled, still fearing Maddie. But Maddie was nothing like Rav—he used his influence to torment humans in a variety of ways before killing or turning them. Sometimes even experimenting on the ones he turned.

Footsteps sounded and a couple rounded the corner. Maddie stilled as her gaze latched onto long red hair falling down a woman's back. The breath in her lungs pumped again when the woman's face looked nothing like Imogen's, and the darker-haired female she held hands with wasn't Rav.

The couple didn't spare them a second glance.

"*Maddie*," Ferris warned, his voice serious, "we need to leave now."

Maddie focused once more on Noah's green gaze. "Continue to stay quiet and stick close to me."

Ferris moved down the path first, checking both ways before motioning them on. She wasn't certain Imogen and Rav would appear tonight, but something in her bones told her they would.

Maddie glanced at Alice's still-trembling form. Rav had been the one to take her, and she knew the tricks he liked to pull with his victims.

"Did Rav fuck you before the change?" Maddie asked, her nostrils flaring.

"No," Alice gasped, a look of horror crossing her face. "Nothing like that."

Lucky duck, then.

Alice groaned, clutching her stomach and hunching over.

Perhaps she hadn't turned as easily as Ferris had thought.

"Have you fed?" Ferris asked and pointed at his throat.

"No." A look of disgust crossed Alice's face. "I was hiding in a bin all day until the sun set."

Alice hadn't fed, and if she didn't soon, she might not complete the change and die, or she would grow mad and try to drink from the entire city of London.

"You need to feed," Maddie said as she walked beside Alice. "When we get to the safe house, you can drink from the pouches stored there."

"No!"

"That's your only option for a bit." They didn't have time to scavenge a human in Wonderland to please Alice, and Maddie was certain she wouldn't want to feed from her brother.

"I'll help you through it," Ferris said. "Compared to Maddie, I haven't been a vampire for long."

"I love the lore, the style, but I never wanted to be *this*." A few tears streamed down Alice's cheeks.

Maddie hadn't either, but she'd grown used to it.

"We need to pick up our pace," Maddie whispered. She then turned to Noah, his eyes still glazed. "Follow us and keep up."

No one said another word as they hurried to the park portal near Noah's home. A few stars shone brightly in the night sky, and every now and again the group passed a civilian or a car roared down the street. There were a number of portals throughout London, but the one Rav frequented was in a different city park near the nightclubs. That particular portal led straight to the Ruby Heart Palace. Somehow, Ferris had snuck Alice out through it.

Adjusting her arm sleeves, she looked again at Alice who continued to quiver. Maddie would attempt to lighten the mood while they kept their pace. "By the way, I'm Maddie."

"I'm Alice." She turned to her brother, tears glinting in her eyes, her shoulders sagging. "I only wanted to tell Noah goodbye."

"That's what we all think, but it's never that easy." Maddie peered at Noah in his calmer state, wondering what he was like when not encountering vampires. No human would be able to tell he was under an influence, but any vampire could. If Noah was as close to Alice as Maddie was to Mouse, then Alice would never have just been able to say goodbye. She would've continued to come back, the same way Maddie had returned to see Mouse.

"Which hideout should we take them to?" Ferris asked.

Ever had given Maddie half her set of keys so they would both have protection in case they needed to escape Imogen and Rav. The keys unlocked secret places across Wonderland. Maddie had later split them with Ferris so he could use them once he'd gotten Mouse, which he hadn't. But he'd been able to use one to escape through the palace's hidden back door.

"Rock, paper, scissors to decide?" she finally said.

Ferris rolled his eyes. "Let's just go to the one at the edge of Scarlet."

Ah, Maddie had missed Ferris's eye rolls. "Perfect, my dear." She'd first found him at a club where he'd played drums with his band, or in truth, Mouse had discovered him. He'd been passed out in the hall outside the club's back room, drunk and high. Maddie had said to leave him be, but Mouse chose to save him from overdosing. He'd thought Mouse was an angel when she first drank from him, taking the poison from his blood. After that, he'd wanted that high instead, and it worked out for Maddie and Mouse when they needed their appetites satiated.

The group approached a nearly-empty street and headed across it into the secluded park. Not many humans ventured there. Graffiti covered the playground, and a long crack ran up the yellow plastic slide. A lone swing creaked from the wind, the rest missing from their rusted chains, and a large rat scampered into a tunnel across from a leaning merry-go-round. The picnic tables, long disappeared, had never been replaced.

"I'll let things settle for about a week, then find a way to get Mouse out," Ferris whispered.

The best plan would be for Rav and Imogen to die by the sun's hand. Maddie was about to say just that when the strong scent of sulfur hit her nose. *The portal.* Someone was using it.

Maddie's heart pounded, her gaze settling on the spot beneath a cluster of bushes beside a row of hazel trees. Vampires from all sides of Wonderland frequented any of the portals they wished, besides Rav's, but she hoped no one was on the other side of this one who could identify Alice or Ferris. Imogen wouldn't give up her search until they found them, alive or dead.

"Hide," Maddie whisper-shouted, shoving Ferris and Alice toward a covered footpath, leading to the playground tunnel that could easily fit two.

She was about to haul Noah with her to take shelter behind— she pivoted her head, searching their surroundings—apparently nowhere. The tree trunks close to them were too narrow, and climbing them wouldn't do with their thin and wiry limbs.

Next option. Act natural. Maddie would look like anyone else coming or going from the portal with an influenced mortal, and no one would recognize Noah.

"You'll thank me later for this." Maddie looped her arm around Noah's waist. She pulled him close to her, like a lover, and walked toward the portal as though they were waiting their turn to enter. "Act like we're *together*."

Out from the bushes, a masculine, yet elegant, hand appeared, then a body. *Bloody hell.* Not what she wanted. Not *who* she wanted.

Scarlet's prince. Chess.

That bastard. Right before Ever went into hiding, she'd told Maddie that Chess had tried to murder her. It had been on his mother's—Imogen's—orders. The White Queen had stabbed him in the chest before fleeing her masquerade ball once she discovered her guards had also betrayed her. But like a cat with nine lives, he lived. Ever should've aimed straight for his heart then twisted the blade like he was a wind-up toy.

It took everything in Maddie not to clench her teeth, but her fingers still dug into Noah's waist, his arm draped over her shoulder. She hadn't asked him to do that, but she didn't shove it off.

Chess wore a tight, dark vest, his full chest on display, his lean muscles flexing as he lazily pushed himself up to stand. He scented the air and his yellow gaze latched straight on them. Layers of brown hair fell to his chin and neck and he tucked them behind his ear.

Damn it.

"What are you doing out here?" Maddie cooed, pretending as if it were any normal night. "Don't you have your own hole to crawl out from?"

"Maddie, Maddie, Maddie, you still haven't learned how to speak to royalty?" Chess purred, licking his lower lip, his gaze flicking to Noah as he stepped closer to them. "Seems you found yourself quite a treat."

"He's mine. Go find your own."

"I'm still full from my earlier dessert." The prince grinned, inching closer to her. "Perhaps when you come to the palace with your next hat, you can stop by my room before you leave." Leaning forward, he whispered, "We can put some of that madness to good use."

Maddie tried not to hurl up her earlier snack. "Tempting, but no."

Chess only leaned in closer, his grin growing wider. "I'm going to find your White Queen soon. Perhaps I'll have a different, *bloodier*, sort of fun with her."

Maddie's heart lodged in her throat, and she held back taking a deep swallow. "Why should I care what you do with her?"

"You may not." He shrugged, then straightened as if he were becoming bored. "But I do know you care about your sister."

"If you touch her—"

"Relax." Chess chuckled. "She isn't my type. She's too quiet. Probably wouldn't even squeak when I fucked an orgasm out of her." He glanced between her and Noah. "Well, I'm afraid I have more important matters to see to…"

With that, he sauntered away. She clenched her teeth then, so hard she thought she felt one crack.

"I hate that fucking pretentious ass," Ferris said under his breath. Maddie hadn't heard him approach, hadn't known how long she'd been standing there thinking about stabbing several hatpins straight through Chess's villainous heart.

"I feel … I feel," Alice murmured, collapsing onto Ferris. He scooped her up just as her body convulsed, her mouth foaming.

"We have to get her into hiding *now*," Maddie rushed out. "I don't know if feeding will even help her. Something's wrong."

Ferris nodded and lowered Alice to the portal, hurrying them both through.

Maddie turned to Noah and grabbed his hand, tugging him toward the hole next. "Crawl through. Quickly."

After his form slid past the bushes, Maddie pushed the branches back and went in behind him on all fours. A warming sensation tickled her skin as she slipped into the entrance to her home. Deep brown dirt surrounded her while she crawled forward, and a slew of bright scarlet beetles and black and blue caterpillars accompanied her.

Maddie finished venturing the short distance and brought herself to stand back in Wonderland, darkness sweeping around her.

Ferris held Alice, who was now unconscious in his arms, no longer convulsing. To his side, Noah patiently waited, eyes still glazed.

With a grin, Maddie grasped Noah's face between her hands, tilting it down so their gazes met, and she released him from her influence.

He blinked, his breathing hitched, yet his eyes stayed trained on hers as she held him in place.

She parted her lips and her fangs lowered. "I'm giving you this one opportunity to help us with your sister. She's no longer human. As you can see, I'm not either."

CHAPTER FOUR

NOAH

*N*ot *human.*

Noah heard what the young woman—Maddie—had said. He saw her teeth. *Fangs.* But somehow, it wasn't processing. There was no such thing as vampires. If it wasn't for the fact that Maddie had somehow controlled his mind to get him to—where the bloody hell were they?—then he would've thought the fangs were prosthetic.

But the conversations he'd overheard, a man crawling out of the *ground*, his sister seizing… It was all real, right? And then Maddie had crawled through the very same *hole* in the ground, pulling him along with her, and entered another place entirely. *What in the ever-loving fuck?*

"We have to *move*," Ferris whispered through gritted teeth.

Noah scanned the city behind Maddie. Buildings stood two and three stories high, made from glossy red and black stone and aged wood. Red lights hung in lanterns, casting the entire street in an ominous glow. He stopped breathing when his gaze landed on a man—*vampire*—through one of the open windows facing them. A vampire and a woman. Moving her hair aside, he struck hard and fast, biting her neck. And she arched into him as if she *enjoyed* it. Noah backpedaled from Maddie and Ferris as he looked desperately for somewhere safe to get away from this crazy shit.

No. He couldn't leave without Alice. But she was still in the arms of a damn monster. His gaze snapped to where Ferris held Alice, and his breath left him in a whoosh. The stranger scanned the area like a predator, shifting nervously as he waited for prey. She was one of *them* now. A vampire. *An actual vampire.* Did that mean she was dead? Did she need blood to live? How would he keep her safe when they returned home? Why, *precisely,* couldn't they return home? And how was he going to keep her … "condition" a secret from their parents? From the world? *For fuck's sake.*

"I need answers to a *lot* of questions before I agree to anything." Noah crossed his arms and dug his heels into the ground. "I won't go anywhere until I have them."

A snarl sounded and Noah whipped his head to the side. Two males seemingly appeared out of nowhere—though likely from behind one of the nearby buildings—and rolled on the ground together a few meters away, their movements a blur. Paired with how dark it was, Noah had trouble making out what was happening. He could hear just fine though—every tear of fabric, each growl. *What the…?* He squinted at the fighting duo and a spray of blood sailed through the air.

"Ignore them," Maddie said, grabbing Noah's arm just as he was about to make a run for it. "We don't have time for questions, but you may ask *one.*"

One. How was he supposed to choose? They all seemed important. What were they running from? Where were they running to? Vampires? Mind control? What were they planning to do with him and Alice? Kill them? Why the fuck were they ignoring the fact that two vampires were tearing each other apart? "What's with the underground tunnel?" he asked before he could stop himself.

"This is where the portal to Wonderland is, and you're in the city of Scarlet. All of the portals are underground. Now"—she put her hands on her hips and looked up at him—"are you coming?"

Noah stared at her as if she'd spoken gibberish. It was a little late to ask him that now, considering she'd already dragged him into this hellscape. What else was he going to do but follow her? Run? With his luck, he'd only get himself drained dry within the hour. Besides, they had his sister. He grunted in anger which Maddie must've taken as a *yes*.

"Welcome to Wonderland," she sang. "I really don't prefer to influence humans but most of the time it's necessary." With a flick of the wrist, she whirled away from him, then glanced back over her shoulder. "Shall we go?"

"Give her to me." Noah stepped up to Ferris and slid his arms under Alice, pulling her away from the vampire. It didn't matter how far they had to travel—he'd be damned if he let anyone else touch her, no matter their motives.

"You sure you can carry her all the way to the safe house?" the vampire asked, relinquishing Alice.

"Don't worry about me." Noah hoisted Alice higher, adjusting his grip. "What's going to happen to her? Will she be okay?"

Maddie ushered him forward and gave a surprised gasp. "I almost forgot! Drink this."

"Drink wha—"

She pressed a smooth glass bottle to his lips. Cool, tasteless liquid flowed over his tongue and down his throat. He sputtered, half of it spraying Maddie in her face.

She wrinkled her nose in distaste and wiped it off with her arm sleeve. "It will allow you to see better since Wonderland has no sun. The muted grays in the morning will be fine for you, but tonight we're going into a lowly-lit part of the city." Maddie poked at his back to make him walk faster. "Now, chop-chop. We don't want to get separated from Ferris."

Get separated? Ferris was right—*gone*. Noah searched the lit street and watched him turn left at a crossroad. How had he moved so fast? It wasn't— Noah winced. *It wasn't natural*, he thought. But it was … *for them*.

"Go on then, slowcoach," Maddie insisted. "Ferris has the keys to the safe house."

A sharp scream sounded in the distance, quickly turning to a moan. Noah's heart pounded and his breath came quicker. How did a nightmarish place like this exist and no one know about it? If anyone found out, he was sure the world leaders would find a way to bury these portals. They could block the tunnels with cement or throw a bomb down the holes.

"Bloody hell," he whispered to himself. "Where are we?"

"Have you been listening to anything I said, mortal? Your sister has enemies searching for her." Maddie placed her hands on his back and pushed him, holding Alice, farther into the city. "There are many vampires who travel here for the portal. We have to get to the safe house before we draw too much attention."

Noah heard the truth in her tone and hurried his steps to where he'd seen Ferris disappear. It must've been the right direction since Maddie finally stopped shoving him and moved to walk at his side.

Noah kept her in his sights while canvassing their surroundings. No shops stood nearby, but some of the homes featured balconies. Instead of the planters and patio furniture people decorated them with in his world, these were empty. At least for the most part. Two or three contained strange, abstract sculptures that filled the entire space. Spirals and jagged edges, pieces that appeared unfinished. The red lanterns only made them more ominous.

"What are you thinking?" Maddie peered up at him.

Noah swallowed hard, fighting the urge to put some distance between himself and this vampire. He needed her though. Someone had to help him save Alice, and it wasn't like he knew anyone else willing, or even capable, of it.

"Not sure what to think," he mumbled. It wasn't a lie.

"Your sister will be... Well, she'll be fine for now." Maddie gave him a look of sympathy. "Let's have hope that a little blood will fix her right up and one day she'll be able to control her bloodlust."

Bile rose in the back of Noah's throat. His sister, drinking blood... What the fuck was actually going on here? If only he could wake up from this damn nightmare.

"Here we are." She stepped through an already-opened door into a pitch-black room.

Not quite pitch black. Noah blinked a few times until vague shapes formed. Inside the black stone building, Maddie, Ferris, and a few blurred pieces of furniture stood, waiting. He blinked again and an ornate grandfather clock came into focus.

"Get in here, dumbass," Ferris snapped, suddenly in the doorway. He grabbed Noah's arm and yanked him inside before shutting the door.

Noah stumbled over the threshold and nearly dropped Alice. Maddie clasped Noah's shoulders, steadying him, as his gaze fastened on her honey-colored eyes. "Thanks" he said, shuffling away from her touch.

"Set your sister on the settee," she told him, then scurried into an adjoining room with rows of cupboards. She opened one at a time, rifling through whatever was stored there. "Ferris, can you bring me some water?"

Noah's arms ached with the weight of carrying his sister, even though it had only been a few streets, so he took Maddie's advice. After laying Alice on the black velvet settee, he grabbed one of the round decorative pillows and lifted her head. She groaned as he adjusted it beneath her.

"It's okay, sis," he lied, and felt her forehead as if seeking a temperature. Ridiculous, maybe, but what did he know about becoming a vampire? She looked like herself, as she always had, and it was hard to reconcile that she was something different now. "We'll get you sorted."

Alice's eyes snapped open, glowing a bright blue. There was something wild in her expression, a desperation he'd never seen, like the gleam of an animal on the verge of starvation. A growl rose from her throat, low at first, then louder, monstrous. Her fingertips scraped across the velvet cushions. Noah tensed. She dug them in harder, ripping lines through the fabric.

And then she lunged at him. Noah reared back, tripping over his own feet, and landed hard on the wooden floor. Alice was on top of him before he could make sense of what had happened. Something sharp grazed his throat.

Alice disappeared almost as quickly as she'd attacked. Ferris held her to him, her back against his chest, as she snarled at Noah. Blood—*his* blood—dripped off two elongated fangs.

The world slowed as Noah raised his hand to cover the scratch she'd given him. His sister almost *bit* him. What the fuck?

She tried to bite me.

Bite. Me.

"Up you go," Maddie said and lifted him to his feet with far too much ease. "No use crying over a little spilled blood, right?"

He whipped his head to Maddie and stared, mouth open, at her. Was she serious?

"I have to leave now." Maddie shouldered a small bag. "It seems you're coming along with me instead of staying here. Unless you're interested in feeding your sister?"

Noah felt the blood drain from his face. "I'm not feeding *anyone.*"

Maddie shrugged and gave a lighthearted *hmm.* "There's powdered blood in the cabinets for you to mix with the water," she told Ferris. "Use however much it takes."

"It tastes like shit," he grumbled.

"Yes, but it will do." Maddie laughed. "Besides, we can't risk bringing a human here for her."

Ferris fished out a large ring of keys and plucked one off, handing the others to Maddie. "Fine, but don't take too long."

"Wait," Noah rasped. "Where are we going now?"

"You used your one question already." Maddie bopped him on the nose with the tip of her finger. "Let's go, mortal."

CHAPTER FIVE

MADDIE

"Seriously, where are we going?" Noah asked, jogging up beside Maddie in the city street.

The night grew darker, making the red lanterns in Scarlet seem to glow brighter. Maddie hadn't wanted to take the little mortal—or rather, big mortal—with her, but anyway, his height was beside the point. His sister had tried to make a meal out of him, and if Maddie and Ferris hadn't been there, he would've been a dead human.

Noah's warm hand wrapped around her arm and tugged her to a stop. If she wanted, she could easily pull from his grip and toss him to the ground, but she would give the mortal his moment.

"You're a bold one, aren't you?" Maddie grinned. "Any other vampire would've bitten your arm off."

Noah's eyes widened as he dropped her arm.

"I'm only teasing." She paused, laughing silently to herself. "Or am I?"

"Listen, Maddie. At least tell me where we're going."

Maddie had told him she would give him one question, but to be fair, perhaps she could do another. After all, he did look a bit tense out here. She knew a good way to loosen those tense muscles of his, but with him as frightened as a kitten, a roll in bed would probably not go over so well.

"To my home." She waved a hand in the air and continued her brisk pace.

"Your home?" Noah's voice went up an octave. "For *what?*"

"Quite the little questioner, aren't you?" Maddie cut between two tall buildings lined with diamond-shaped windows. Boisterous growling and screams came from one of the structures. At the other, several of the vampires were feasting and fucking at the windows while some had their curtains drawn tight. Maddie preferred to take a lover behind closed doors, but there was always time to be venturous.

"Well?" Noah asked, arching his impeccable brow at her.

Maddie had only spent a little while with Alice, but already she wished the female's role were reversed with Noah's. Alice wouldn't have been as much of a nuisance.

"We're going to my house to make a hat." She pulled her index finger and thumb across her lips. "Now put a sock in it."

"What the fuck? *Why?* Actually, no. Spare me the illogic," Noah said, rubbing his temples. "We're going to make a hat, then what? Have a tea party?"

Maddie stopped and turned to him with a big smile on her face. "Precisely, my friend. Less talkie and more walkie."

Noah glared but followed beside her, this time keeping his lips sealed. It was a good thing, too, because she didn't want to have to threaten him with needle and thread. He wouldn't find her teasing funny, but a part of her wanted to see the mortal's reaction.

The red lanterns leading to her home grew distant, giving way to the darkness. If she hadn't given Noah one of her elixirs, the trek home would've been unbearable. No beastly things stirred in the city this night—the werewolves must've gotten their fill, their appetites satiated. However, she did have her gun loaded and ready in the side of her boot.

Maddie and Noah slowed to a stop in front of her door. "How do you like my home?" Maddie sang. It had been a bit since she'd brought a human guest there. She'd been going to the mortal world or the donor compounds in Wonderland for her feasts. Since Ever had been gone, and while Maddie had been plotting to get Mouse out from the Ruby Heart Palace, she hadn't wanted anyone to get too close in case Imogen and Rav tortured them to try and obtain any information about the White Queen.

"It's lovely," he answered sarcastically.

"Such a party pooper, you are." Grinning, she unlocked the door, pushed it open, and waved him in as if he were attending a circus.

"Cut the theatrics." He rolled his eyes, but she could've sworn his lips twitched. As his gaze roamed around the sitting room, a confused expression crossed his face. "What. The fuck. Is this?" He whirled to face her. "You have hats *everywhere.*"

"Are you going to be surprised by *everything?*" She stepped over a clump of fabric on the floor and picked up a bonnet from her chair to take a seat. "Yes, dear mortal. They are *mine.* You should try one. It would suit that inquisitive head of yours."

The lack of torture devices was likely a *surprise* to him too, but she kept a respectable distance, making sure he didn't feel threatened. Noah furrowed his brow, his pulse slowing as he examined her home. She'd done her duty—he wasn't frightened anymore. For now.

"So, this is your job? You make weird hats?" he asked.

"Hey now," she whispered and pressed a finger to her lips. "They can hear you. You don't want to hurt their feelings."

"Whatever." He shook his head and settled on the settee near the wall. "Is Alice going to be all right?"

Maddie truly didn't know. She could be dead when they returned if her heart didn't take well to the blood. The change from mortal to immortal wasn't as easy as one might think. The human body was a very fickle, fickle thing.

"Let's hope. Ferris will make sure she feeds regularly, which will help." Maddie opened her cooler, the contents always cold courtesy of the special ice chests made in Wonderland. She fished out a blood bag and her teacup, then poured the red liquid in. Cold wasn't the best, but it would do to avert her from the lovely smell flowing from Noah's veins. This mortal's unpleasant attitude clashed with his pleasant scent. His cedarwood smell enveloped her once more, sweet as a summer night.

"You weren't kidding about a tea party, were you?" Noah's nose wrinkled in disgust, but his eyes danced with curiosity.

"Nope." She gestured behind her at a pail on the wooden table. "There's water if you're thirsty. I haven't had a human guest here in a while, but I usually refill it just in case. Wouldn't want you to dehydrate and create another problem for us."

Not bouncing back with one of his ridiculous questions, he went and poured water into a teacup.

She lifted her own snack and drank the cold liquid down. A low moan escaped her mouth—it had lost some of its richness due to the chill, but the metallic notes hit her tastebuds just right. When she glanced up, Noah was studying her with an unreadable expression.

She took out a roll of tulle along with a spool of thread.

"You can sleep on the settee if you wish," Maddie said. "I need to finish this fascinator for one of my clients before the morning." She should've had it completed before leaving to retrieve Alice, but her thoughts had been a horse race circling her brain. Or more like a slow drawn-out song that would never end while waiting for night to fall.

Noah relaxed on the settee and took a sip of his water. "Not sure I'll ever be able to sleep, to be honest."

Maddie shrugged and picked up a pair of scissors and a sheet of polka dot felt. She then cut out a large circle and concentrated as she folded, stitched, tore, and looped.

After a while of getting lost in her creation, she glanced up to find Noah asleep, light snores drifting out from between his plump parted lips. Smiling to herself, she grabbed a bowler hat off the wall and placed it onto his head. *There. Now he looks like a gentleman, even if he doesn't act like a proper one.* She then took the folded blanket beside him and draped it across his body, her eyes unintentionally sliding down his muscular form.

He was an unpleasant guest, but it didn't mean she wouldn't have manners. Maddie picked up her project once more and worked and worked until her fingers were tired and her lids shut.

A knock pounded at the door and Maddie jerked out of her seat, snatching a hatpin. Noah studied her hand where it gripped the metal, but he didn't say a word.

"Stay quiet and act natural," she whispered.

He bit his lower lip and nodded, his hands clenched into fists. Those human fists would do nothing to save him here.

The bowler she'd placed on his head was now tossed to the side on the floor. *Poor hat.*

She peered out the speakeasy, expecting to see one of her clients there. Her entire body stiffened. This was bad. Bad. Bad. Bad. What were *they* doing here?

Imogen and Rav.

Not waiting a moment longer, since that would only make them suspicious, Maddie tossed the hatpin aside and flung open the door with a grin. "How may I serve you, Your Majesties?" She bowed, keeping her gaze trained on Imogen because Rav was more of a piece of shit than the Queen of Hearts.

Without an invitation, Rav bounded into her home, Imogen at his heels. His white, red-tipped hair was pristine as ever, and his brown eyes settled on Noah. Imogen's scarlet curls fell down her back and instead of her usual gown, she wore crimson breeches and a red and black coat with tails.

"It appears we're meeting again, sooner than I expected," Imogen purred, her yellow irises, matching Chess's, met hers. She then sniffed the air. "The treat you brought home smells rather tasty."

Noah's fists tightened even more, and Maddie fought a grin.

"I can share if you want," she sang. "I was just about to have two kinds of breakfasts with him."

"I'll find my own, Hatter." Imogen's lip curled as she retrieved her blasted deck of cards out from the pocket of her trousers. "Now, have you seen my Knave?"

Maddie's heart thumped an extra beat. If Ferris had still been there… But he wasn't. He was safe with Alice at the moment.

She furrowed her brow, putting on false confusion. "The tall one?"

"You know who I'm talking about," Imogen snapped.

"Can't say that I have, but if I do, I will cut out his heart and bring it to you." Maddie knew that answer should please Imogen enough since the queen relished removing the bloody organ of her enemies.

"Hmm," Rav said, pressing close to Maddie and fishing out a photograph from his pocket. "Hopefully you please this human more than you did me." He lifted her chin, his finger caressing her jawline, and she couldn't stop herself from shuddering. "Now, listen close, have you seen this girl?"

Maddie studied the photograph that he held up a few centimeters from her eyes. She focused on keeping her breaths steady because it wasn't just a young Alice in the photograph— a boy, who was maybe sixteen at the time, stood beside her. Even though Alice looked the same except for her locks being completely blonde in the picture, Noah appeared nothing like himself. In the image, he was heavier, sporting a choppy haircut, and he wore glasses and braces. If she hadn't known he was Alice's brother, she would never have guessed this was the same mortal.

"I'm afraid I haven't." Maddie shrugged.

"If you do find the girl or Knave," Rav said, "bring them straight to the Ruby Heart Palace and we will reward you."

Fuck their rewards.

"Come on, Rabbit," Imogen said, shuffling her deck of cards.

"I knew coming here would give us no results." She then turned to Maddie. "For wasting my time, bring me a new fascinator in two weeks instead of a month. It had better please me, or Mouse will answer to me again."

Maddie took a deep swallow. "I will." If one thing could make her nervous about anything, it was her sister.

Without another word, Imogen and Rav left her cottage, but not before the bastard gave her a wink while running his hand over his cock. She closed the door behind her and took breath after breath.

"Who's Mouse?" Noah asked, his voice softer than she'd heard thus far.

"My sister. She was the one who told Ferris to save Alice from the palace." Maddie sank down on the settee beside him, his lovely scent surrounding her. "That was the Queen of Hearts and her king, Rav. They are the ones who changed your sister."

"*Them?*" Noah whisper-shouted. "They were in my home, took my picture? And they also have your sister?"

"It's a long story." Too long to discuss with him now—she didn't have the energy to tell him everything in its entirety at the moment. Not after Rav had put his fingers on her flesh again, caressing, taunting.

"Why is she called the Queen of Hearts?"

"Because she's obsessed with the organ and will easily rip out anyone's heart who she sees as her enemy, then decorate the palace grounds with them. I'm lucky she still hasn't taken Mouse's. My sister has been in her palace for two years, and I just want her home."

"I'm sorry." He blew out a breath. "Once a vampire is changed, can they ever become human again?"

It had been a long time since she had asked herself the same question. There was a time when she'd wanted to return to humanity, but she preferred the cards here. Mouse did as well.

"It would take moving heaven and hell to change back." She paused and then added, "No more questions. Come on, we need to get this hat to my client. It's a good friend of Imogen's which is why it can't be late."

CHAPTER SIX

NOAH

The vampires who'd turned Alice were worse than Noah imagined. Imogen and Rav carried an air of superiority like he'd never experienced. As if they ruled the world and would damn anyone who stood in their way, which, he supposed was true. Except *he* was blocking them from Alice. So were Maddie and Ferris. He would never give his sister up to those two arseholes, yet what motive did Maddie and Ferris have to protect her? Like Alice, Ferris was wanted by the royals, but what about Maddie? He narrowed a suspicious gaze at the purple-haired vampire walking briskly beside him, looking her up and down. His gaze lingered on her legs for a moment—they were rather shapely … not that he should've noticed…

If Maddie's customer was anything like Imogen, he didn't want to meet the slag. It was likely though, given that the two females were friends. Still, he carried the bright yellow hat box with its oversized, ridiculous blue ribbon through Scarlet while avoiding stepping in the tacky-looking blood stains on the streets. "Are you certain I can't wait at your house while you deliver this?"

Maddie gave an exaggerated sigh. "I've told you already. No, mortal."

"Right." He scowled at the back of her head, a black tulle hat perched on her purple hair. "But *why*?"

"Curiouser and curiouser, aren't you?" She hooked a sharp right down another street.

This one contained only homes made of deep red glass. The walls were too thick to see clearly inside, but he could make out general shapes. Tall furniture, moving bodies. Maddie took another turn and he almost missed it—his gaze riveted to the craftsmanship around him.

"When can we check on my sister?" he asked, almost plowing into Maddie's back as she slowed to match his pace.

"When it's safe."

It would never be safe here, and Alice could be dead for all Noah knew. *No.* He refused to entertain the idea. Ferris was looking after her, and although a vampire and a stranger, he didn't seem to want to harm her. He believed she would be fine until he found a way to reverse what happened.

It would take moving heaven and hell to change back. Maddie's words played over and over in his head. That meant there was a cure, even if she'd refused to elaborate. But whatever the hell it was, getting it was instrumental. "Don't fret about your sister—we'll go soon enough. I cannot drag a mortal around Wonderland with me and hope to succeed," she continued.

"Succeed in saving your sister?" he asked.

Maddie whirled around and placed a finger on his lips. "You talk too much about things that shouldn't be spoken of."

Noah arched a brow and inched his head back, away from her warm touch. While it was clean now, he could only imagine how many throats she'd ripped out with the same digit. "But you *are* dragging me around Wonderland."

Maddie rolled her eyes and continued down the street, this time at his side, her arm brushing his. "I won't be going directly home after making this delivery, and I can't very well leave you alone. What if Imogen and Rav return, hmm? So I need to take you somewhere else—somewhere safe—to wait."

He certainly didn't want to run into those two, but more importantly… "What am I waiting for?"

Maddie patted his shoulder as if comforting a simpleton. "To go home, of course."

"I can't go home." Noah clutched the box tightly. "I need you to tell me more about the cure for Alice so I can find it."

Maddie released a high-pitch laugh. "Impossible."

"You said one exists," he insisted.

"And it does. Deep in the swamp, in the heart of werewolf territory. The beasts would eat you long before you came close to the cure. A simple mortal man against an entire pack of wolves? No, no. It's best to accept your sister's new life and move on."

A sudden burst of rage seared Noah's veins. Accept that Alice would be reduced to a blood-thirsty creature? That she would live in this alternate world under the rule of arseholes as fearsome as Imogen and Rav? Fuck no. What would he tell their parents? Not the truth, obviously, but to let them think she ran away would be torture.

"Then I suppose *you* should accept *your* sister's imprisonment," he snapped.

Maddie inhaled sharply, immediately stopped walking, and dug her fingers into his upper arm. "Watch what you say, mortal."

"Don't threaten me," he said, pulling from her grip. It was stupid to taunt the one vampire who was helping him. She could easily turn on him, kill him, and lie to Alice about it. If Alice was told he returned home, she would believe it—she was too trusting. There would be no reason for her to question it when Wonderland was a deathtrap for humans. But if she ever returned to visit, only to find their flat empty, what would she think? That he was murdered or he'd moved on with his life? Still, he had to do whatever he could to help his sister now, while he could. "Tell me where this swamp is and how to get there, and I'll be out of your hair."

Maddie reached up and twirled one of her curls. "I don't have time for this now. We'll be late."

"Tell me where it is." Noah lifted the hatbox into the air, high above his head. "Or you won't have anything to deliver."

Maddie blinked at him in surprise, then brought the outer edge of her hand down in the crook of his elbow. His arm bent under the hard blow, and she easily snatched the box away from him, cradling it to her chest. "If you behave yourself, we'll discuss her situation *after* I complete my sale."

Noah rubbed his arm and grinned. Damn, she was strong as fuck. He could wait the few minutes it would take to drop off the hat. "Deal."

With a nod, Maddie strode down the empty streets, her skirt riding up her toned legs. The faint hint of death lingered in the air, pulling him back to the present. Noah had attended an autopsy for one of his university classes and he would never mistake the distinct scent of human decay. He pushed the knowledge away before it was able to take root. Losing his mind wouldn't help Alice get out of this shithole. He held his breath, hoping by the time he needed another, they would be far enough away from whatever corpse was nearby. A bat swooped down from a hidden perch, streaking straight at his head. He cursed, ducking, and tasted the scent on his tongue. A cough shook his chest as he fought not to vomit, especially when his gaze connected with half a skeleton resting beside a rose bush.

"There, there," Maddie said without a hint of sympathy. "Pull yourself together."

Noah slapped a hand over his mouth and tried to drag in a breath without smelling anything.

"We're here," she added.

Noah took in the large stone house she stared at. *Of course, their destination was likely a murder scene.* The building was three stories high with a slate roof, a small stone gargoyle fixed to each corner, and massive, arching windows draped in red curtains.

Maddie didn't wait to see if Noah followed as she climbed the six steps to the door and lifted the knocker. A snarling wolf's face peered back at him with a chain wrapped around its snout and something about its carved expression made Noah uncomfortable.

A few moments later, the front door swung inward to reveal a woman with sunken eyes. She wore a long black dress, a large white bow tied neatly in the front, and her dark blonde hair was pulled into a tight bun at the base of her neck. Noah couldn't tell if she was human or vampire, which, he supposed was going to be an ongoing problem now that he knew the sun-fearing creatures were no fucking myth.

"May I help you?" the woman asked.

"Hello, Robin. I've come with Osanna's new hat." Maddie held the box up in the woman's face as if she would've missed it otherwise. "She's expecting me."

Robin wordlessly stepped aside, and Maddie waltzed in. "Come along, mortal," she sang when Noah didn't immediately follow.

He cleared his throat and slipped in after her. Robin clanged the door shut behind them and Noah swallowed hard. This was nothing like Maddie's home, but empty, a shell of a house, devoid of all life. The stone walls were bare, the marble floor gleaming. No furniture decorated the entrance hall, but a large crystal chandelier hung from the ceiling. Two sets of stairs curved up either side of the room.

"In here," Maddie said, and entered through a door to the left without waiting for an answer. When Noah caught up, she leaned in. "I *always* meet her in here."

Noah studied the room with the red curtains he'd seen from outside. Pleated silver fabric covered the walls, and a large black settee faced the door. Two iron lamps hung from the ceiling, candles burning behind the metal bars. On the matching black ottoman, sat a tray with two glass goblets full of thick red liquid.

Blood, Noah realized. His skin crawled, not only because of what it was. *Where—or who—had it come from?*

"We always have a drink," Maddie said, following his gaze. "Sit there."

Noah slipped around the ottoman to take the corner of the settee. The metallic tang of blood floated in the air, and he pulled in a shallow breath. A drink with an enemy in exchange for a hat? He rubbed his forehead against the first hint of a headache.

"Hatter," a female cooed, bursting into the open doorway a moment later. "I'm dying to see what you've brought me this time."

Noah's lips parted as he took in the vampire. A gold silk robe hugged her body, the color bringing out the bronze tones in her flawless skin. She looked as if she had just stepped out of a magazine spread with her high cheekbones and winged eyeliner.

"Hello, Osanna. It's just what you ordered," Maddie told her as she handed over the box.

The vampire lifted the lid and pulled out a cobalt hat with stiff, curled ribbons and a giant sapphire. She placed the hat on her sleek emerald hair and turned her head this way and that to see if it fit. Then, her gaze finally landed on Noah.

"Who's this?" she asked, swiping her tongue along her lower lip.

"My mortal," Maddie answered, her voice sounding protective. "He's staying with me for a little while."

Osanna removed the hat and returned it to the box with a curious expression. "I thought for a moment, perhaps, you brought refreshments this time."

Maddie laughed, the pitch higher than what he'd heard prior to this moment. "Unfortunately not. He's already given what he could for today."

Noah's eyes drifted between the two vampires, his pulse quickening. Osanna didn't mean she wanted to feed from him, did she? *She did.* He was no vampire expert, but the drop of her fangs seemed like a damn good indicator. At least Maddie was lying to try and keep his blood where it damn well belonged.

"He does seem tired," Osanna admitted. "Perhaps you would allow me to entertain him briefly? Just to see if he would be interested in extending his stay once you've finished with him. He's *very* attractive."

Maddie hesitated. Her gaze met his and she gave him a look that told him to play along. Why did this feel like part of her plan *before* they'd struck their deal in the street? Noah narrowed his eyes at her, letting her sense his suspicion. He had promised to behave, but that didn't mean Maddie was allowed to throw him to the wolves.

"That would be fine," Maddie agreed, wringing her hands in front of her.

"Splendid." Osanna licked the corner of her lips. "Go see Robin about payment."

Maddie cast him one final, almost guilty, look, before slipping from the room faster than it took Noah to realize what the hell was happening. Then Osanna sat beside him, and he caught a whiff of her perfume—a horrible cross between baby powder and coffee beans. He hadn't even seen her move. "Hi," he murmured. Every alarm bell in his head alerted him to her proximity.

"Hello." Osanna trailed one of her gold-painted nails gently down the side of his neck. "You have no marks here. I didn't expect the Hatter to prefer more private feeding locations."

"Wh—"

Osanna's hand landed on his knee and slid up his inner thigh. Noah attempted to shift away but she tugged him closer. "Don't be coy, human," she whispered in his ear. Her hand skimmed down the opposite thigh and back up. "You seem not to have any sensitive bite marks hiding here. Did she bring you here to feed a different sort of appetite?"

Noah opened his mouth to tell her he had no idea what she meant when Osanna cupped his balls over his trousers. He attempted to wiggle out of her touch, but she simply began stroking him, effectively holding him in place. "Excuse me," he shouted.

"Unlike her, I like to mix business with pleasure." This time the words took on an edge of anger—anger directed at Maddie.

"If the Hatter wants to hide Ever from my queen, I will see no reason not to break her toy."

"I'm not a toy." His heart pounded in his chest, his muscles begging him to *run!* But he was trapped. Paralyzed by fear and cornered by a predator.

"Silly boy." Osanna laughed. "Of course you are."

Osana lunged forward, her teeth slicing through the flesh of his throat. Blinding pain radiated from Noah's neck. He sucked in a breath to shout when she covered his mouth. Pressure built beneath her bite, the agony coming in waves as she sucked and released with each mouthful of his blood. He kicked out, sending the goblets of blood on the table shattering to the ground. Then the pain dissolved into a wave of pure ecstasy. Noah moaned, feeling the suction at his neck all the way down to his swelling cock. Osanna's hand stroked him over his trousers as she continued to drink from him. His eyes fluttered and his back arched into her touch.

Noah's limbs fell limp at his sides, useless and weak. But he didn't care. Not when he was experiencing the most intense pleasure of his life.

Osanna ripped herself free from his throat. Noah slumped backward and slid down, his head bent at an unnatural angle into the crease of the cushions. He didn't mind the discomfort as euphoria washed over him.

"Delicious," she rasped. "You would've been wonderful to bottle. Too late now."

Noah moaned as the room faded in and out of focus. "Maddie," he called as pain began to leak through the bliss. Or … he tried to call for her. His voice didn't seem to be working anymore. *No,* he cried out, the word never making it to his mouth. *I can't die here. Not like this! I still have to save Alice.*

Osanna stood, wiped at the corners of her mouth, and lifted her new headpiece again. "I shall let the Hatter know I'm finished," she purred as Noah continued to bleed out.

CHAPTER SEVEN

MADDIE

Maddie wandered the bare halls to the library to meet Osanna's housekeeper, Robin, for her payment. Osanna was a flashy female, golden and silver gowns, sapphire and emerald headpieces. But she wasn't much for decoration around her home. Maddie could easily spiff up the place if Osanna asked her to. Walls lined with ruby cloches and bronze bowlers would be positively delightful.

And then she remembered Noah... She hadn't wanted to leave the mortal with Osanna, yet it wasn't as if she hadn't left humans with her unattended before. If anything, she may take a small bite from him, have a quick drink, but no permanent damage would be done.

Maddie rounded the corner to find the library door wide open. Inside were two high-back green velvet chairs, an elegant ivory table, a fireplace accompanied by walls and walls of books, mostly erotic. She didn't think Osanna even knew how to read— it would be too much work for her. The tomes were just there to look pretty or to supply her with pictures for browsing in her boredom.

Where was that blasted Robin? She was usually in here. While waiting for the housekeeper to show up, Maddie pored over each pristine book, not a single crack or bend in their spines. "Oh," she said, coming to a stop on a bright white one with golden letters. She drew out the *Kama Sutra* book and flipped through its crisp pages.

She arched a brow as she took in each position—delicate, rough, unusual. "I've done that one. Definitely that one. Wouldn't do that one. Ah, that one I certainly like. Bloody hell, how do you even get in that position?"

Footsteps echoed in the hallway, pulling Maddie out of her rehashing of past partners. She pushed the book back into its place and peered up as Robin's blonde head entered the room. "There you are," Maddie sang, gliding toward the housekeeper across the floor and holding out her hand. "Payment?"

Robin bowed with a strange smirk and took out a silver key from her pocket. The housekeeper had been here for years, unlike the Queen of Hearts who constantly replaced the majority of her servants after she grew bored. Osanna kept hers, or the one. As long as Robin didn't speak too much, anyway. But Robin would help Osanna with her vicious deeds when necessary. A follower, like Igor was to Dr. Frankenstein.

Robin went to the wall beside one of the bookshelves, wiped away a few specks of dust, and placed a key into the small rectangular jeweled door. It squeaked open and she withdrew a velvet sack that clinked with coins.

Maddie wiggled her fingers as Robin dropped three scarlet coins in her hand, which the Hatter quickly tucked into the skirt of her dress.

"Good day, Robin." Maddie waved a hand in the air and spun on her heel. Now that she was finished with Osanna for a few months and wouldn't have to see Imogen for another two weeks, Maddie had the freedom she needed to focus on saving Mouse.

It was time for her to take the mortal and head back to Ferris to figure out what their next step would be. When Maddie delivered Imogen's hat to the Ruby Heart Palace, she would have to try and make a move—Mouse had been there too long. And she also needed to figure out what the bloody hell to do with Alice, who couldn't stay in hiding for the rest of her life. But wasn't that what Ever was doing? When, if ever, would the White Queen finally make her appearance? Maddie had thought she would've already returned by now. Unless something was wrong...

As Maddie turned the corner of the hallway, Osanna's green hair flowed around her when she stepped out from the sitting room, her golden robe dragging on the floor. The sapphire hat Maddie had made was atop Osanna's head, and the immortal brought a hand to her own face. To wipe away a streak of blood from her chin... Maddie halted. She must've decided to have a small snack from Noah. Maddie would apologize to him, then they would be on their merry way.

"Your human tasted lovely, Hatter." Osanna grinned, bringing a hand to her fascinator. "But I may have *purposely* gotten carried away. Now, clean his body up and leave. Robin will walk you out and I'll see you in two months." She paused, her grin growing wider. "You know better than to cross my queen—she'll find Ever soon enough."

Maddie couldn't show her concern. Not for the mortal and not for Ever. Even though her heart thrummed faster in her chest. "As I told our queen, if I stumbled upon Ever, I would escort her myself to the Ruby Heart Palace with a brand-new white hat atop her head. I have the perfect one ready with lace and—"

"Next time, bring each of us a dessert, along with the hat that *I'll* use on Ever." With that, Osanna turned on her heel, swaying her hips as she headed down the hallway.

Gritting her teeth, Maddie rushed into the room. The metallic scent of Noah's blood permeated the air, strong, so strong. She yearned for just one taste, for her tongue to gather his flavor. But she shook the allure away and found Noah slumped on the settee, deep crimson blooming at the spots where Osanna drank from him. "Oh dear." What did the curious mortal do? Ask too many questions?

Maddie grabbed Noah by the shoulders. "Mortal!" she hissed. "Wake up."

He groaned, his breath ragged. At least he wasn't dead … yet. His tan skin grew paler by the second. She had to get him home because he was running out of time. Once she got him there, she could … what? She wasn't a human doctor. She didn't have a way to give him a blood transfusion, and he sure wouldn't last long enough for her to get him out of Wonderland and to a hospital.

There was one way to save him, though…

The cool steel of a knife was at her throat, interrupting her thoughts. "Osanna said to clean his body up," Robin growled in a low voice. "Not turn him."

"Deepest apologies," Maddie said. "I shall carry him out the door then."

As soon as the blade was lifted, Maddie whirled around and ripped the knife from Robin's hand. "After I kill you, that is," Maddie sang. Then she shoved the blade into the female's heart. The housekeeper's body collapsed to the floor, her eyes closed. She knew she should leave things how they were, but the need for revenge pulsed through her. Maddie searched around for something to decapitate Robin with, but the walls were bare of anything useful and the knife, too small. So she would just get messy. She gripped Robin's head between her hands and twisted it hard to the right, tearing it from her body. Thick blood spilled from Robin's neck, and Maddie tossed the head on the floor beside the vampire's still body with a sickening *thump*.

Shrugging, she spun to face Noah. Enough time had been wasted. Maddie didn't think—she brought her wrist to her mouth and sank her fangs into her flesh. A slight sting came as she bit down, hot crimson blossoming to the surface. She shoved her wrist to Noah's mouth, and it took a moment for his lips to move. But she knew as soon as a drop touched his tongue, he would crave it. She knew because she remembered that first taste when Rav had held his wrist to her mouth, when ecstasy rolled over her in waves, how she wanted more and more of his blood, him inside her. The *bastard…*

And then Noah's lips brushed her flesh in an almost caress, drawing her away from thinking about Rav. Noah flicked the tip of his tongue across her skin, his lids closed, as he began to suck. His eyes fluttered while he groaned. It felt just as good to her as she knew it did for him, maybe even better than making a hat.

But a mortal who hadn't changed yet didn't have the control to stop on their own, so she forced herself to rip her arm away when she'd given him enough. "You don't want to bleed me dry because then how would we help you-know-who?" Maddie whispered.

Noah's eyes cracked open, dazed, but his skin wasn't as pale as before.

"Now, off we go."

He mumbled something when she pulled him to stand. His body sagged as he leaned his weight on her. Maddie helped him wrap an arm across her shoulder and she looped hers around his waist.

Osanna was a bitch and Imogen's friend, but Maddie truly didn't think she would've drunk him almost dry. And why should Maddie care anyway? Noah was just a mortal who was getting in the way of her trying to help her sister. Besides, Mouse had asked Ferris to save Alice, not Noah.

And then… Maddie had done the one thing Ever was fighting against: turning mortals into vampires without their consent. But if she hadn't, he would've died, which was a practice generally accepted by both her and Ever. Dying was a natural part of life, but being turned wasn't, so it should always be the human's choice. However, she didn't *want* him to die, even when he made her life harder than it already was. He might still die though, if his body wasn't made for the transition…

As Maddie and Noah left Osanna's and hobbled down street after street, the sky became a lighter shade of gray. A storm of bats beat their wings as they flew above, their squeaks echoing across the city. When Maddie had first brought her sister to Wonderland, Mouse had wanted to keep one for a pet. Maddie would've gotten her one too, but those bastards were impossible to catch.

Noah groaned, his pace slow, his weight becoming heavier.

"Keep going," she said, lifting and tugging him along. "You're lucky I returned when I did." If she'd left him at her cottage, he wouldn't be in this position. But all things happened for a reason, good or bad. If he'd had enough strength to hold onto her, she would've attempted to carry him on her back.

It didn't take much longer for her cottage to slip into view. A light fog covered the rose garden surrounding her home. They walked through the light mist with baby steps until she finally thrust open the door.

She stumbled into her home with Noah in tow. As his body started to slump, she thought about just dropping him there on the floor for now. She used more of her strength instead and picked him up, cradling him in her arms. She should've probably just done this earlier—it would've been easier. Vampire strength and speed were highly advanced, but a pity it only lasted short increments before a rest was necessary. She could've handled the distance to her cottage, however.

With a sharp turn, she sat him on the settee, his body collapsing into the cushion. She wiped a hand across her cheek with a sigh. "How about we *not* play that game again, all right?"

Beads of perspiration dotted Noah's upper lip and forehead. Bloody hell, what a nuisance he was. She still needed to meet with Ferris, but now she must tend to this mortal to make sure his arse didn't die. It was all for Mouse because this was what her sister would've wanted her to do.

She stared at his features—the light stubble on his face, his square jaw, his plump lips. Then her gaze dipped to his tight black shirt, his broad chest, his muscular arms—she couldn't help noticing how attractive he was. So different than that picture Imogen and Rav had showed her of when he was younger. What had happened to him? Damn. Now she had questions for him about his magical transformation.

Maddie stepped over rolls of tulle and a pile of cut squares of different furs and leathers. She picked up a piece of cloth and poured cool water from the pitcher onto it. She then walked back to Noah and placed it on his forehead. There would be blood bags in her ice chest for when he woke, and she still had boxes of bottled powdered blood for emergencies if he needed them. Once he was well enough, she would need to find a live donor and teach him how to feed properly. Alice would eventually need that too.

She propped her fists on her hips and stared down at him. "There, all better." She was about to call it good and begin working on a new fascinator until he needed her, when his hand gripped her wrist.

Already?

Noah released another groan and drew her toward him. His groans were starting to sound like those zombie films mortals tended to watch.

With a strong tug, he pulled her into his lap, and she squeaked when her legs straddled his thighs. She arched a brow as his strong hands gripped her waist, his fingers digging into her hips. His eyes were still shut.

And then she felt his cock against her, hard and ready. Maddie's breath hitched when he rolled her hips forward. Her heart pounded, all her heat rushing straight to her core. And she wasn't even sure if she liked this man. But she knew how mortals were during their transition, some more lustful than others.

"Tut, tut, mortal." She grinned, lifting both his lids so he could see her. "I don't think this is what you want after such a dreadful day of suffering."

Maddie released his lids and he blinked. His bright green eyes focused on her and widened, his hands stilling on her hips, his fingers digging in harder.

"No, not mortal anymore, is it?" She shrugged and gave him a sympathetic look. "Immortal."

CHAPTER EIGHT

NOAH

Noah used every ounce of strength he had to lift Maddie from his lap. *Damn.* He'd been dry humping her like a fucking teenager … and he'd *liked* it. *And* she'd *let* him. Maddie cocked her head and stared at him, then shrugged.

"Sorry," he muttered, leaning back into the settee.

"Don't be." She padded through the living room, carefully moving hat materials from her path. Noah found himself staring at her long legs as she bent over to chase a rolling bobbin. Her skirt was just long enough to prevent him from seeing more. The view of her legs was tantalizing enough but he still cursed the extra inch of tulle.

Get it together, man.

Maddie finally made her way to the cupboards and grabbed a teacup, quickly filling it with bagged blood. "You need to drink."

His veins were parched, his mouth a desert. There was no pain in his neck like he expected and, when he lifted his hand to Osanna's bite, it was already healed. But the ache in his chest intensified with every slowed beat of his heart. *My heart is still beating.* Vampires were dead, weren't they? He was still very much alive, though he was quickly coming to regret that fact as pain rattled through his bones. His body spasmed, joints locking, jaw clenched, as he fell over onto the cushion. Maddie rushed to the settee and rolled him to his side. The fit lasted only a handful of seconds but left him sweating through his shirt.

"Here," Maddie said softly, holding the teacup right under his nose. "It will make the pain go away."

Drink blood? Never.

But his body disagreed. It begged for the thick red liquid. *Craved* it. His eyes had tracked Maddie's movements as she poured it, but the idea sent chills through him.

Soon though, he would need to. He knew it, even if he didn't want to admit it. There would be a point where he couldn't deny the mounting hunger. His gums tingled at the mere thought of a sip, and he squeezed his eyes shut to erase the image of Maddie's fangs dropping down.

"I have to check on Alice," he croaked. If she'd experienced even a sliver of this agony, he needed to see her.

Everything made sense now: why she'd been sprawled on the ground behind their flat, the reason Ferris had carried her, why she'd attacked him at the safe house.

"Drink and live. Don't and die. It's all the same to me," Maddie said with a flippant wave of her hand. "But you can't see your sister if you don't survive the transition."

He scowled. "You turned me. You *should* care if I survive it."

Maddie cast her gaze to the floor and chewed her bottom lip. "If you don't pull through, it will be the same as if I didn't turn you. This was the only way to give you a chance."

"Vampires are dead either way," he said, focusing on the painful *thump thump* in his chest.

"No." Her laugh came out high-pitched as she sat beside him. "Mortals all think that, but it isn't true. We are alive and we will remain that way forever."

Alive? He'd think more on what that meant later, but it gave him hope. It would be much harder to cure death, yet, if what she said was true, this seemed like more of a disease. The cure existed—Maddie had confirmed it. All he needed to do was find the location of this werewolf swamp. *Because werewolves were a fucking thing now too…* "Unless someone drives a stake through your heart," he said.

"More nonsense. We die by sunlight, fire, or if someone cuts off our heads." Maddie shrugged. "Imogen removes hearts, which is also effective."

At the mention of the queen who'd turned his sister, Noah pushed up into a sitting position. "We have to go—"

"Hush." Maddie slipped from the edge of the settee where she'd perched and spun to face him. "You need to drink and finish the transition before we do anything. I'd prefer you do it quickly as I have my own sister to save."

Noah swallowed hard. He'd forgotten Maddie's sister was imprisoned, and that she was the reason Ferris saved Alice. "Fine," he said through clenched teeth. "Hand me the cup."

Maddie scooped it off the end table and placed the cup into his hands. "I promise you'll like it," she said as if that made drinking blood any better.

She's completely mad. Noah raised his brows and gave her a final look before bringing the cold liquid to his lips. The metallic scent filled his nose and a groan slipped from him, unbidden. *Bottoms up*, he told himself and took his first sip.

A bright memory exploded behind his eyes. One of a sunny day at the beach with his parents and Alice—years before impossible rules controlled every moment. He was three, Alice two. His father spun Noah and threw him up into the air, only to catch him a moment later. That was what drinking blood felt like. A rush of soaring, the fear of falling, and the relief of being caught all at once.

And Maddie was right—he *did* like it.

Noah tilted his head back, downing the cup's entire contents in two gulps. Then he licked the inside of the porcelain clean, followed by his lips. Whatever reservations he'd had about his new diet were officially gone and he couldn't bring himself to feel ashamed. He glanced into the cup to find it spotless, and he frowned at Maddie. "More."

"No." She plucked the cup away. "You'll become ill if you drink too much at once. Rest and let this settle, then you may have more."

"But—" A mild cramp twisted his stomach and he clutched at his abdomen. Perhaps she was right.

Maddie tutted. "Told you so. Now, lay back and sleep."

Noah had no choice but to listen as a stronger cramp took hold. Another round of cold sweats broke out along his forehead. Maddie tucked a blanket around him as he drifted away from the pain. While he slipped toward peaceful sleep, he clung to the memory of that day at the beach—the laughter and the warmth of the sun—and he smiled.

Hours blended together as Noah slept. At one point, Maddie had dragged him into her bedroom in case Imogen and Rav made another visit, but he slept better on the bed anyway, so it was worth the struggle to get there. He had woken for another cup of blood before his eyes slipped closed again. Each time was easier. The cramps stopped, the pain in his chest subsided, and the dryness in his mouth quenched.

He owed Maddie for taking care of him so diligently—though, he supposed, she owed him. After all, she *had* turned him. It was only fair that she wiped the sweat from his forehead and set cool cloths on the back of his neck. Regardless, he was grateful for her attention. For a vampire, she wasn't half-bad.

When Noah roused again, his body hummed with energy. He kept his eyes closed, scanning himself, concentrating on each part to ensure nothing was wrong. Arms, shoulders, neck, hips, legs, ankles. Everything seemed to be in working order, and he felt … almost normal. Except he could smell *everything*. Scents of wood furniture, to soft linen blankets, to old metal spicing the air in Maddie's room. *Blood*, he instinctually knew, noting the difference between that metallic aroma and the metal tools Maddie kept for hat making. It carried a tangy undercurrent that made his fangs threaten to drop.

"I know you're awake," Maddie sang from another room.

Noah opened his eyes and sat up slowly, waiting for his body to revolt. When it didn't, he released a breath and slipped from Maddie's bed, walking toward the living room. There, he found Maddie pleating pieces of felt. She sat cross-legged on a large, padded chair, the skirt once again teasing him with what was beneath. He pursed his lips. Why were his thoughts so focused on seeing Maddie hike up her skirt? There was no denying she was attractive, and anyone would be drawn to the perfect swells of her breasts, but there wasn't time for fantasizing. Both he and Alice were fucked if he didn't learn how to reverse their conditions.

"I'm surprised you let me sleep in your bed," he said with a small smile.

Maddie shrugged. "You looked uncomfortable."

Undoubtedly, she was correct seeing as he was at least a head taller than the settee. He plopped down on it and watched her work on her hat. "How long was I sleeping?"

"This time, about two hours." She stuck the dull end of a needle between her lips and brought the felt closer to her face. After a moment of inspection, she lowered it and plucked the needle from her mouth. "If you're asking how long since you started the transition, it's been five days."

"Five *days?*" he blurted. That was impossible. It couldn't have been more than one day and one night at most. Every time he looked outside Maddie's window, it had been dark. But *how* dark? The gray mornings in Wonderland were comparable to London's evenings. He was certain he'd been fired from his job, but who gave a fuck about making coffee at this point? It was all a blur now, but he knew one thing for certain: they needed to get back to the safe house. "We have to go."

"If your sister died, Ferris would've returned by now," she mumbled, narrowing her gaze at her work.

"How do you know?" he demanded. "Maybe he ran off alone."

She smirked. "I have all the other keys."

"Fuck the keys," Noah growled. The last time he'd seen Alice, he'd left thinking she was a monster, but now he understood. What a shit brother he'd been. He had to go back to help her, to *cure* her. And himself. "I need to see my sister."

"Noah." Maddie sighed and set the pleating down on her lap to look him in the eye. "Ferris would never abandon me, and he would never give up on saving Mouse. We're days late in returning, so he would've come searching by now. Since he hasn't, it's because he's stuck watching Alice."

"Or because Imogen found them." The thought stole his breath.

Maddie sucked her bottom lip between her teeth and Noah's cock stiffened slightly. What would it be like if she sucked *him* into her mouth instead? Ran her tongue slowly up the length of him from tip to base? He raked a hand through his hair and looked away.

"Unlikely," she said after a moment.

"Not impossible though," he insisted.

Noah tensed when a soft knock sounded at the door, but Maddie simply stood and placed her supplies in a basket. "That will be your meal."

Meal? Had she ordered more blood bags to be delivered? How was it she even got the blood bags? Stole them or bottled them herself? Never mind, he didn't want to know.

Maddie opened the door and motioned in a man in his mid-thirties. He was dressed in a nice pair of trousers and a neatly pressed dress shirt as if he'd just come from a day at the office. Following him was a rich, warm scent that immediately made Noah's fangs drop.

"Hello," he greeted. "My boss sent me."

"Yes, I've been expecting you." Maddie quietly shut the door behind him and turned to look at Noah. "While you were asleep, I left for a moment to secure a mortal for you."

"You left to *secure a mortal?*" Noah repeated in disbelief. Humans weren't *things* to be acquired.

"There's a company in Scarlet that contracts us," the man said with a big smile. "We get paid handsomely and enjoy the work."

"This is his first feeding," Maddie whispered to the stranger.

"I figured as much." The man's smile was kind as he rolled up his sleeve and approached the settee. "My name's Elijah."

"Noah," he replied through clenched teeth. He did *not* want to bite someone. Let alone some stranger they pulled off the street like some sort of prostitute. People couldn't just go around drinking random blood. *Or any blood*, he reminded himself. But he was a vampire now—that was exactly what he needed to do to survive.

"Nice to meet you." He held his arm out to Noah. A few light-colored scars dotted his skin from prior bites. "Don't worry. As a vampire, you can't catch anything from blood—not that I have anything to catch."

"Are you a mind reader or something?" Noah grumbled.

Elijah laughed. "No, I just recognize that look. I've been doing this for a while."

Maddie hovered beside them, glancing from Noah to Elijah and back as if she was worried that Noah would refuse. He damn well *wanted* to refuse, but the sound of the steady heartbeat mixed with the warm, heady scent wafting off Elijah had his mouth watering.

He sighed in defeat and took Elijah's proffered arm. "Let's get this over with."

"You'll like this even better than the bags." Maddie smiled encouragingly as Noah swiped the tip of his tongue across a fang. "And I'm right here to stop you."

Noah closed his eyes for a moment, mentally preparing himself, and lifted the wrist to his mouth. Saliva flooded his tongue as an intoxicating scent reached his nose. *Ah, fuck it.*

Instinct took over and he sank his fangs into Elijah's soft flesh.

Hot blood exploded into his mouth and he moaned as the different flavors mingled together on his readied tongue. Iron and … and he couldn't identify everything he tasted. Whatever it was, it was euphoric. A crackling fire on a cold day, bringing him back from the edge of death. This was so much different than the bagged blood. Those bags quenched his thirst, but this was like drinking life itself.

Noah pulled in a deep mouthful and swallowed, again and again. Energy sparked through his body, blazing through his veins. And still he drank. Until it felt as if he would explode with power. And then he drank some more.

"Noah," Maddie called through his haze.

He ripped his mouth away from Elijah's arm and gasped for breath. His body practically hummed, and his cock was hard as steel. *Shit.* He'd just gotten a hard-on from drinking blood? Was that supposed to happen?

Elijah said something, but Noah was too preoccupied with the new sensations flowing through his body to comprehend. Maddie leaned down to look Noah in the eyes. "He's fine," she chirped to the human. "I'll see you out."

Noah's gaze landed on Maddie's arse as she led Elijah to the front door and placed a coin in his palm, exchanging a few quiet words. How he wanted to see that arse bent over for him, him unbuttoning his trousers, freeing his cock, then sliding into her with one swift thrust and… *Stop.* He rubbed a hand over his face and his fangs retracted on their own.

"Feeling better?" Maddie asked, returning to him.

Noah let out a long breath and peered down at himself. Other than the raging boner straining against his trousers, there was blood dried into his clothes from where he'd bled out on Osanna's settee. He sniffed himself and blanched. Sweat and blood—not a good combination. If everyone in Wonderland could smell as well as he could, it would definitely draw attention. "Do you have anything else I can wear?" he asked.

"I stashed some clothing for Ferris here, but they might be

large on you." Maddie quickly disappeared into her bedroom and Noah winced at how loud the squeak of the dresser drawer was.

"Are sounds always this … grating to the ears?" he called.

Maddie laughed as the sound of her rummaging through fabric filled the air. "It's only because there's nothing but us here to make noise so your ears pick up on more. Outside, for example, there's the sound of animals and bugs and the wind to contend with."

"I know you don't want to waste time, but you should probably clean yourself as well. Everyone will know you're newly-turned if you go around like that, and fresh vampires tend to turn curious heads."

He wanted to argue, but she was right. There wasn't time. Nor was it wise to draw attention to themselves when that could lead Imogen and Rav straight to Alice. "Fine."

Noah hurried toward the door across from Maddie's bedroom. Swinging the door shut with what was meant to be a gentle push, it slammed with a loud *bang*. He glanced at his hand. With the amount of effort that took, he was sure he could've turned the wood to splinters with a single punch. Part of him wanted to test the theory, but he might destroy Maddie's home in the process.

"Sorry," he called.

"You'll get used to it," Maddie replied from the other room.

Noah wasted no time cranking the water on and sealing the plug in the clawfoot tub. Every second he spent wearing the crusty, ruined clothing, nausea churned his stomach more. Once everything was removed, he shoved the fabric into a bin and hoped it was meant for either the rubbish or dirty linen.

The bathtub filled quickly, and he stepped in, purposely ignoring how badly his cock ached with need. As he sank down, a groan escaped him. The warm water felt fucking amazing against his skin, his muscles, and he immediately began scrubbing. Maddie thankfully had a bath sponge and soap in plain sight, even if it did smell like cherries. He scrubbed every inch of his body, thinking about how she would have used this same sponge on her milky skin, her breasts, in between her legs… *Stop, damn it.*

When his body and hair were both clean, he settled back into the curve of the bathtub. *Only for a moment,* he told himself. He still didn't have anything to put on anyway. He thought about borrowing Ferris's clothes. The vampire was larger than him, but not so much bigger that his clothes would fall off.

A sudden suspicion crept into his mind and before he could stop himself, he called out, "Why do you keep clothes for Ferris here?"

"In case he ever got released from serving at Imogen's palace," Maddie replied immediately. "Which he now is. Or more like a fugitive."

He scowled. "So you and him aren't…" *Dating? Fucking?*

The door swung open, and Maddie bustled in with an armful of clothes. "Aren't what? Together?" She laughed as if the idea were ridiculous. "Definitely not. I've just been friends with him a long time and he risked his life to help Mouse."

Noah quickly covered his cock with both hands. "Do you mind?"

"Not at all," Maddie assured him and let herself study him from head to toe.

Noah's skin prickled at the attention, his member hardening behind his hands. A blush filled his cheeks as his gaze locked on her shapely lips. "See something you like?" he said, attempting to embarrass her into looking away, but his voice came out gruff, full of want.

She grinned. "I was only thinking you're pretty." Her eyes drifted toward his body again. "If I may…"

Noah scowled. "What?"

"It's nothing to be embarrassed about." She stared directly at his hands and Noah drew in a sharp breath. "You'll feel the lust for a few days after the change is complete, especially after feeding from the source."

"Great," he said in a higher-than-normal voice. "We can stop talking about my hard-on any time now."

"If you want my help, it will make things easier." Maddie shrugged. "Towels are in the cabinet."

Lust for days? He didn't want to go see his sister with his fucking dick hard as a rock. "Wait," he called as Maddie turned. "What do you mean by *help*?"

She walked back toward him. "If you feel comfortable, lean back and let me take care of it."

Noah hesitated. Was he really going to let her do this? Whatever *this* was? The way his veins throbbed against his cock, he knew his hand wouldn't totally resolve the issue so he consented.

Maddie peeled off her arm warmers and slowly knelt on the tile beside the bathtub. She leaned over the edge, her lips so close to his. A wave of desire pulsed through him like a second heartbeat. He wanted to rip off her ridiculous outfit, drag her into the bathtub with him, and have her lower herself onto his cock. Fuck her and fuck her hard.

Maddie wrapped her nimble fingers around his hard length, and he gasped as her hand tightened. She didn't say a word as she stroked. He leaned his head back and groaned as her pace picked up. One of his hands slid into her hair while his other gripped the edge of the bathtub. She tilted her head and lowered her lips to his neck. The scrape of her fangs against his skin sent a jolt through him. He wanted her teeth to sink into his body as he slipped his hard length into her.

Noah closed his eyes and groaned at her touch, her movements. He was so close, her hand going faster, faster, *faster.* Then one of her fangs lightly pricked his skin and he came in a hard rush, muscles tensing, body spasming, as he shouted, "Fuck!"

"All better?" Maddie lifted her head from his throat, gently releasing his length.

His chest heaved as he peeled open his eyes and he could've sworn he saw lust reflected in her gaze. But then she rose, water sliding down her arm. "Yes," he rasped.

"After you get dressed, we'll go." Then she walked out of the room, leaving him unsure what the hell had just happened.

CHAPTER NINE

MADDIE

Maddie straightened her hat as she left the bathroom with Noah remaining in the tub. Still naked… Still wet… She hadn't meant to kiss his throat, taste him with her tongue. Had only meant to rid him of his lust for a little while. But now, as she closed the bathroom door behind her, she'd created a little problem for herself. Her core thrummed with the same tightening Noah had just felt. She *needed* to purge her own lust and working on a hat would not help with this.

It wouldn't take long—she could finish the task before he even stepped foot into the hallway.

Maddie slipped inside her room and hiked up her skirt as she pressed her back to the wall. She then dipped her hand inside her panties, finding a pool of wetness between her thighs. Noah had done this to her without even a single brush of his fingers. All it had taken was the touch of his cock in her hand, the press of her lips and tongue to his neck. He'd smelled of cedar, tasted like honey. She wondered what he would've tasted like if he'd spilled himself into her mouth instead of in the water.

"Bloody hell," she rasped.

The water's swishing echoed, and she knew Noah was stepping from the bathtub, beads of water sliding down his naked form—she stroked her center. A cabinet creaked as Noah must've grabbed a towel, and she imagined him running it over his abs, his tight arse—she circled her clit. The rustling of him getting dressed reverberated—she came at that movement, imagining every hard muscle of him pressed against her softness. Her body pulsed, spasms rocking through her as she thought about what it would be like to have him inside her, thrusting, growling. Her chest heaved while taking a cleaning rag from her bedside table. She wiped her hand with the rose-scented cloth and straightened the skirt of her dress before stepping back into the hallway, just as he opened the door.

Maddie grinned, hiding the aftereffects of her orgasm that still purred within her. "Ready?"

"Are you going to tell me the exact location of the cure now?" Noah said, raking a hand through his damp hair, the muscles of his arm flexing. Ferris's clothing fit well enough, although she preferred his tighter dark T-shirt. He now wore a black, long-sleeved collared shirt with pleats across the front and arms. A single line of obsidian buttons ran up the length of his trousers from ankle to thigh. Maddie's eyes lingered on the slight bulge of his trousers before flicking them up to meet his gaze. His hair hadn't changed in color since the transition, but his eyes were an even brighter shade of green.

"Past Ivory in the center of werewolf territory, as I said. Now, chop-chop. Let's go. Grab the smaller ice chest and one of the backpacks on our way out." Maddie waved a hand in the air and spun on her heels, then lifted her bag of necessities for them.

Noah slammed the front door a bit too hard behind them and winced. The immortal would get used to his new strength eventually.

As they headed into the night, the sky was already shifting, and it would turn into morning soon. They didn't have any more time to waste, and she needed to get to Ferris. Five days had passed. Five days too long. And Ferris would be getting antsy, especially since she had planned to visit him after delivering the hat to Osanna. But then this messy immortal situation with Noah had come about.

Maddie supposed she could've left Noah and went to the safe house, but she hadn't wanted Noah to die, not after she'd turned him without his consent. She had also needed to stay with him at the cottage in case Imogen and Rav ventured back to have a chat—she'd risked enough by leaving Noah for a short while to request a donor be sent to her home for him to feed. Maddie didn't know how good of a liar Noah could be.

Since days had passed, perhaps the little deviants had grown tired with their search for Ferris and Alice and found new toys to play with. But Maddie knew better—Rav and Imogen would never stop the hunt until their bodies were discovered.

As they stepped onto the trail leading to the outskirts of the city, Noah strode beside her with his hands buried deep in the pockets of his trousers. He hadn't said a single word since they'd left, not even one of his silly questions. "Cat got your tongue?" Maddie asked.

His green gaze met hers then, a hesitant expression on his face. "Thank you," he said softly.

Maddie quirked a brow and drawled, "For…?"

"The bathroom." He scratched the back of his neck, pink staining his cheeks.

"Ah, yes." She grinned, thinking once again about her hand around his velvety length. "That. You should make it through tonight just fine. It's the least I could do after, you know, turning you."

Noah scowled, his lips forming a tight line.

Maddie didn't know what she'd said to damper his expression. "Speak, immortal."

"So, you did it because you felt guilty?"

No. If it had been Ferris in Noah's position, she would've told him to use his own hand and be on with it. "Yes," she lied.

He didn't need to discover that she'd been wanting to know what his cock felt like since he'd taken her into his lap. It was a help-help situation. Help him while helping her quench her curiosity. Although, her curiosity now led to wanting to know more. "Anyway, you had asked about a cure for Alice, so I know you don't want this life. But, I did it to save you. I wanted to allow you the opportunity to still live, albeit a different life. However, if you want me to, I can rip your heart out right here."

Noah stopped in his tracks, a look of horror crossing his face as he stared at her.

"I mean," she continued slowly. "I don't want you to die. Just, I'm sorry. I shouldn't have taken you with me to Osanna's. I thought it was safer if you were with me here in Wonderland, but apparently, you were fated to die no matter where we'd left you. But hey"—she clasped both of his upper arms and lightly rattled him—"you're not dead now!"

"Wow." He chuckled, shaking his head as he peered up at the sky before returning his focus to her. "All right... I'm not sure how to respond to *that*. You aren't so bad, though. Maybe a bit of bad luck, but you're sweet."

What? No one had ever called her *sweet* before. Even when she was a human. *Odd. Mad.* His words sent a rush of tingles straight to her chest. It was quite possible bats were flying in her stomach at the same time. With a tilt of the head, she patted his cheek. "Let's go check on you-know-who."

He lifted a brow, then his expression turned serious as they walked. "I hope she's all right."

"As I said, *he*"—she wouldn't risk saying Ferris's name out in the open—"would've let me know if she wasn't." Unless something happened to him... Unless he'd been caught. Even without a key, if Rav and Imogen knew the location, they could always find a way in.

Noah gave a brief nod.

"Now, act casual with me." She wrapped her arm around Noah's waist as they trekked through the city toward the outskirts, the red lanterns becoming dimmer as the sky lightened.

They passed a few bloodied corpses sprawled on the ground, as well as several alive immortals and humans. One couple seemed to be having a role-playing sort of day. The mortal wore fake fangs and nibbled at the vampire's neck. Some were bustling about the city, carrying baskets of goods and ice chests, while others yawned, most likely on their way home for their daily rest.

Noah draped his arm around Maddie's shoulders and drew her closer as they entered the outskirts, the lanterns lessening. "So," Noah drawled. "Since you and Ferris aren't dating, when was your last boyfriend?"

Boyfriend? Maddie had never had a boyfriend. Only lovers. "Ah, there's my questioner." She pressed her head to his arm so they appeared like any other couple to lookers. "Never. I've only fucked. There was the one time with Rav… I thought… Before I was turned. But I was foolish then."

"So you—"

"We're here," Maddie interrupted, preferring not to tell him how she'd taken lover after lover to take away the sting of Rav's betrayal. She hadn't even known the bastard for more than a day, yet his effect on her had lasted more than she would've wished. But when someone was one's first, no matter how long they knew them, they always lingered. No matter that her instant attraction to him had turned to instant hate.

Straightening her spine, she rid the memory of that tainted arse from her mind. Maddie removed her arm from Noah's waist and raised her fist to knock the secret code. Noah took his arm from her shoulders as the click sounded from the lock and the door flung open.

"I'm going to kill you," Ferris said between gritted teeth. He stood there, peering down at her with a hard stare. "Where have you been? I thought you were fucking *dead*."

"Oh, you know, just been roaming Wonderland, creating hats, and making Noah immortal." Maddie shrugged then grabbed Noah's hand and pushed their way inside past Ferris.

Ferris shut the door before whirling around to face them. "What the hell, Maddie?" His eyes widened as he scanned Noah.

"I *know* he didn't ask you to make him immortal. He was freaking out days ago."

"I wasn't freaking out." Noah rolled his eyes while resting the ice chest and backpack on the floor.

"Whatever, man." Ferris focused on Maddie. "Well?"

"There could've been a lovelier circumstance," she started. "But alas, it wasn't intentional. I promise. Imogen and Rav came asking questions at the cottage, parading a photograph of Alice and offering a reward for her. Then I had to deliver Osanna her hat and that bitch nearly killed him."

"Wait, Rav and Imogen came to your house?" Ferris's throat bobbed, and for the first time since he'd escaped the palace, he truly looked worried. "Do they know anything? If they know we're connected, they'll hurt Mouse. *Kill* her."

Maddie blocked out the images of her sister bloodied and broken, her head lolled to the side, eyes blank. "I don't think they suspect anything. They only came to see me since I was at the palace the day before. However, they didn't leave without threats."

"Fuck!" Ferris hit his fist against his leg.

"Where's Alice?" Noah asked, searching around the room, his gaze settling on the velvet settee.

Ferris rubbed the back of his neck. "That's what I needed to talk to you two about. I've been giving her blood, but she's rejecting it."

"What does that mean?" Noah stiffened. "If I'm walking about and feeling stronger than I ever have, then she should've been fine days ago."

"It doesn't work that way," Maddie said softly. "Some don't make it. Some die the night of transition. Others, days or weeks later."

Noah ran a hand down the side of his face. "I need to see her."

Ferris nodded and opened the door to a guest room for Maddie and Noah to go inside. Boxes of powdered blood took up most of the space in a corner, a stack of books in another, and a small mattress holding a frail Alice was against the opposite wall. She lay in bed curled on her side, her skin pale and sweat slicking her brow. The blankets rested in a rumpled heap on the floor beside her.

"Alice." Concern filled Noah's voice as he rushed to his sister's side and knelt beside her.

"Noah," Alice whispered, peeling open her eyes. "I'm so sorry. I didn't mean to attack you."

"You didn't." He smiled warmly. "You only tried to."

"What's wrong with your eyes?" Her gaze widened and she clenched his shirt. "You're not human anymore? What *happened*?"

He blew out a breath. "It's a long story."

This was a moment that Maddie needed to bow out from. A moment between family. "I'll leave you two alone for now." She shut the door behind her before Noah could respond.

Alice was going to die. Maddie had seen this time and time again. There had been numerous instances where she'd changed mortals over the years—some made it, some didn't. There wouldn't be any saving Alice. Not without a cure, and the cure was nearly impossible to get. Yet… A dark thought slipped into her mind. One that wouldn't make her feel guilty. It could possibly get her sister released. And Rav had mentioned a reward for Alice. Mouse had wanted Alice saved, but if the female was dying, then what would it matter?

"What are you planning?" Ferris asked, narrowing his eyes.

"Oh, nothing." She rocked back and forth on her heels.

"Bullshit."

"It's going to help Mouse, so don't you dare try to stop me." She knelt to draw out a cold blood bag from the ice chest then held it up to him and smiled. "Here, I brought you this. I know the powder is hard to swallow."

Ferris's gaze softened and he reluctantly took the blood bag. "Thanks, Maddie."

"No, thank *you*." Her shoulders hunched forward as she stood. "You're in this position because of me." Because of the foolish mistake she'd made with Rav all those years ago. Mouse,

Ferris, Noah—all except Alice led back to that mistake. So Maddie wouldn't let herself feel guilty about what she was going to do.

Ferris sighed and wrapped his arms around her, pulling her to his side. "Mouse saved me when I overdosed. The both of you are what kept me going after that. I would do anything for her—you know that." That included him giving up his humanity for only a small chance of saving Mouse. Which hadn't worked. But if Maddie gave Alice to Rav and Imogen, she could get Mouse back. It would not only help her sister, but would make everything Ferris went through worth it. She didn't know everything he'd done in the palace, what all was done to him, but she did know he had to fuck Imogen before his change and clean palace rooms with his tongue. His sacrifices wouldn't be for nothing. Maddie loved him like a brother, almost as much as she loved her sister. Once Mouse was out, she would need to figure out a way to help him find somewhere safer to stay. He couldn't remain hiding in this safe house forever. But, for now, one step at a time.

The night had already lifted and after everyone was asleep, Maddie would sneak Alice out and take her back to the Ruby Heart Palace.

CHAPTER TEN

NOAH

Water dripped against stone, the only sound in the empty room. Noah walked from corner to corner, seeing perfectly through the darkness, yet unable to find a way in or out. No windows, no doors, no air ducts.

Drip, drip, drip.

He wasn't afraid, but there was a deep sense of foreboding that grew as he continued walking around the room. Hunger prickled through him the longer the captivity lasted. He needed blood. Warm, thick, human blood. If someone were in front of him, he would sink his teeth into their neck and drink and drink and drink…

Dust rained down from the ceiling as a large crack appeared overhead. The drip of water stopped, and maniacal laughter replaced it. A boom. More dust. The crack widened.

"Baby immortal," came a vaguely familiar voice. "Bow to your queen."

Noah inhaled sharply, realizing who was speaking. Imogen. The female who'd turned his sister. "Never!" he shouted at the ceiling.

The ceiling crumbled, raining down on him in large chunks.

Noah sat up with a gasp, drenched in sweat, just before the

stone crushed him. *A nightmare.* It was just a nightmare. He dragged in a long breath then let it out slowly through his mouth, accidentally pricking himself on his own fangs. Lifting a finger to his mouth, he prodded at them. He'd desired blood in the nightmare, but he was fine now, no thirst coursing through him. How did he get the fangs to go back in without feeding? They'd simply retracted when he drank his fill at Maddie's house.

He let his arms fall back to his sides on the lumpy single mattress and sighed. With Maddie going in and out to check on Alice, he wouldn't have gotten any rest if he stayed with his sister. Not that he was getting a decent sleep anyway, but it would still be difficult now that he wanted blood. Fresh blood, like he'd tasted at Maddie's cottage. The richness of it ... the boosted strength. He felt as if he could rule the world now, more so when he fed, and he wanted— No.

His fangs finally retracted into his gums. What he wanted was to go home with his sister. Once he got the cure—with or without help—they would both take it, then never have to worry about blood or fangs or fucking vampire queens again. Despite knowing that his sense of wrongness stemmed from the dream, the thought of his sister made him desperate to see her.

He slipped out of bed and walked softly through the house, not wanting to wake anyone. Maddie had said she would nap on the sofa if she got too tired, so he didn't dare look in that direction in case she sensed his gaze upon her. If she woke, he would end up distracted.

"Alice?" he whispered as he padded into her room. With the others asleep, they could have an honest conversation without anyone else chiming in. "Are you awake?"

Silence.

And ... *fucking hell.* The sheets were flung back, the pillow dented from his sister's head. Yet there was *no Alice.*

Noah scanned the small room, but she was nowhere to be seen. "Alice?" he called louder as he left the room, not giving a shit if Maddie or Ferris woke up. She was sick. Where could she possibly have gone?

Racing from Alice's room to the living room, it quickly became clear she was no longer there. Noah's heart pounded as he struggled to remain calm. Alice couldn't have gotten far. Not in the state she was in. *Maddie.* She would know where to look. If she wasn't in Alice's room, she would be on the sofa … but she wasn't there. He stared at the empty black cushions as the truth set in.

Maddie and Alice were both *gone.*

That couldn't have been a fucking coincidence. He didn't overlook them. There'd been nowhere to hide in Alice's small space. The gut punch stole the air from his lungs. His mind immediately conjured the worst-case scenario of Imogen and Rav kidnapping them, but wouldn't he have heard the commotion? Unless they were extremely stealthy as he was certain vampire royalty would be.

"Ferris?" Noah called and hurried to the third bedroom. "Ferris!"

"What?" he grumbled through the door.

Relief whooshed from him, and he barged inside. Ferris was on his stomach on top of his covers, completely naked, with an arm slung over the edge of the mattress. Noah quickly averted his eyes from the vampire's arse. "They're gone."

"What?" Ferris mumbled, clearly still half asleep.

"Alice and Maddie, they're gone." Kidnapped, most likely, but he refused to accept that. Perhaps Alice had just needed some air… He winced at the obvious lie.

Ferris sat up and yawned. "What are you going on about?"

"Alice—you remember my sister, don't you?" Noah spoke slowly, despite the adrenaline pumping through him. Was the vampire a fucking idiot? "And the quirky, purple-hair hat maker?"

"Maddie's watching Alice tonight," he said, waving a hand through the air.

"Watching her *where?*"

Ferris rubbed his eyes. "What's all this about?"

Noah lifted a dusty vase from a table just inside the door and threw it at Ferris. "They're *gone*, ya daft pillock!"

Ferris caught the vase with one hand and gave him a withering look. "The transformation still affecting your brain? Damn. Let me get them for you."

He stood, grabbed a pair of black tracksuit bottoms and, after putting them on, brushed past Noah. Ferris wandered through the entire safe house as if Noah was the fucking moron here. Then his steps became a little less hurried as he doubled back to check the bedrooms a second time. Noah nearly screamed when Ferris sprinted into Alice's bedroom for a third look.

"Are you satisfied yet?" Noah asked.

Ferris came back into the living room, chest heaving, pupils blown wide. "They're missing," he concluded.

"No shit," Noah shouted. "Where could they be?"

Ferris paced the living room, hands clutching the sides of his head. "I don't know. Maddie offered to watch her tonight. I could tell she was upset about Mouse. It felt like she was up to something but—*oh fuck.*"

"What?" Noah demanded. "*What?*"

"It's just…" He swallowed hard. "No. Maddie wouldn't …"

Noah's hands balled into fists. He was no expert, but he'd guess there wasn't much Maddie was incapable of doing. Between hiding Alice, dragging him to Wonderland, turning him into a vampire, and jerking him off in the bathtub, *kidnapping Alice* didn't seem too outlandish. "She wouldn't what?"

"Ah, hell," Ferris snapped, and left Noah standing alone in the sitting room.

"Ferris?" he called, his voice rising along with his anger. "What's going on?"

The vampire stormed back into the room fully dressed in a black knit jumper and boots to match his trousers. "Get your trainers on. We have to stop them before they reach the palace."

"The palace?" Noah quickly collected his gym trainers from his room. They were hiding from Imogen and Rav so why the hell would she be going there?

Ferris stared at him. "Maddie had said Imogen offered her a

reward to bring Alice back."

And she thinks the reward will be Mouse's release, Noah pieced together as he finished putting his trainers on.

Ferris grabbed the key off the hook on the wall and peered outside before opening the door wide. "Let's go."

Noah followed Ferris outside, trying to even his breaths. Ferris strolled through the street at a leisurely pace, far *too* leisurely for Noah's liking. Then, without warning, he vanished down a side alley. Noah's new vampire reflexes managed to follow the movement and he rushed after him.

The city smelled the same as it had when he'd followed Maddie to Osanna's. Like blood and decay. Only now, it didn't bother him so much. The metallic scent was pleasant while the decay was more of a nuisance than stomach-churning. They avoided the red lanterns as they navigated isolated side streets, but he could see perfectly fine without the lights. The claw marks and blood spattered on the sides of buildings were as clear as day.

A discarded pair of lace gloves beside a large blood stain doubled his concern for Alice's fate. They weren't *her* gloves, but she would've worn them. And the blood smelled stale which, he assumed, meant it was too old to belong to his sister. But that didn't mean she wasn't bleeding somewhere in the palace.

It was obvious what had happened now—Maddie had taken Alice from the safe house with the intent of delivering her to Imogen and Rav. How long ago had they left? Alice could be withering away in the royal dungeons already. Or worse... He felt the blood drain from his face.

"Why would she do this?" Noah whispered. "I mean, I know why, but…"

Ferris held up an arm to stop Noah in the shadows as two vampires appeared on the street ahead, laughing hard. "Alice is dying, yeah? I'm certain Maddie wouldn't have done this otherwise," he said once they passed, leaning forward to scan one side of the street and then the other.

Noah rubbed at his chest, his heart beating out of control. She was going to turn Alice over to those two arseholes? What did it matter if his sister was dying? Noah had been planning to get the cure before that happened and then they would've been fine. "Does she really think they'll trade her sister?"

"Obviously," Ferris muttered.

After nearly fifteen minutes of walking, Noah followed him around another corner, out of the alleyways, and across the main street into a different alley on the other side. In those brief seconds when they weren't between homes or shops with slate roofs and enormous windows, he spotted a castle, aglow in red lights, perched on a cliff. Tall spires rose from the red stone structure and black stone parapets speared the sky. Light shone in the windows and shadows moved along the footbridge.

How had he never noticed it when away from the safe house? Though, he supposed he'd been preoccupied with everything going on—been distracted by Maddie on the way back to the safe house ... after she'd touched him in the bathtub.

Such a beautiful fucking deceiver.

"They won't give Mouse up, will they?" he asked, already knowing the answer.

"Depends." Ferris glared at the palace for a moment. "But my guess is they'll throw Alice in the dungeons to die alone and keep Mouse exactly where she is now."

"And Maddie?" He hated himself for asking—for caring, given the circumstances—but he didn't want to imagine her suffering. Maddie had done a despicable thing, yet no one deserved torture.

Ferris clenched his jaw shut. "It's better not to think about it."

Noah scanned every side street they passed, hoping to catch a glimpse of purple hair, but the closer they got to the looming palace, the more panic squeezed his insides.

"You're being too conspicuous," Ferris warned. "Try to move your head less when you—*damn.* There she is."

Noah's head jerked up. Maddie was talking to Alice outside a small cave at the base of the cliff. He made a quick step forward and Ferris yanked him back. "What now?" he snapped. Alice was right there. Safe, for the moment, and he wanted to keep it that way.

Maddie patted Alice on the shoulder and strode away from her. Alice shifted back until she was barely visible behind a large boulder. Noah shoved at Ferris's arm so he could get his sister before someone else saw her hiding there.

"I'll go first, grab Alice, and take her back to the safe house," Ferris whispered. "Once we're gone, get Maddie's attention and bring her back with you."

"Like hell!" He wasn't about to trust Ferris with Alice's safety now that Maddie proved untrustworthy. For all he knew, Ferris would take the opportunity to trade Alice for his own pardon.

"Shut the fuck up," Ferris hissed as a group of vampires meandered down the street. "Do what I say."

Noah fell silent, only because he knew other vampires finding them would thwart their rescue efforts. While the group took their time passing, Maddie started up a long, winding staircase carved into the stone.

"Now?" he asked when the strangers disappeared into a nearby red house. Though, once Alice was safely away, he couldn't guarantee he wouldn't shout at Maddie for her betrayal. A scene wouldn't matter much if Alice was safe, so what stopped him? He scowled at Maddie as she climbed higher and higher.

Ferris released him and moved so fast, he was a blur. One second, Alice was hidden with only a small piece of white fabric visible, the next, she was gone.

Noah took a deep breath and stormed forward. None of Imogen and Rav's lackeys knew him, so he didn't feel the need to sneak around like Ferris. He barged forward, hands in fists, and stopped at the bottom of the staircase.

"Maddie!"

"Bloody hell!" she yelled, whirling around. Then her gaze landed on Noah, and she froze. "Noah?"

"What the fuck?" he demanded.

She raced back down the steps, darting around him to peer at where Alice had been. Finding it empty, she turned and grasped Noah's shirt. "Where is she?"

"I'll tell you where she *wasn't*." He grabbed Maddie's wrists and pried her hands away from him. "Tucked safely in bed. Where she belonged."

"She's *dying*," Maddie whispered in a cracking voice. "Your sister wouldn't suffer long locked up, but Mouse will be tormented for eternity."

"You're out of your fucking mind. Are you listening to yourself? I never would've done this to you."

Maddie took three heaving breaths, eyes blazing with desperate fury, before her shoulders curled forward in defeat. "I'm sorry, but you don't understand."

"You're sorry?" Noah scoffed. He *almost* felt sorry for her, but she'd just kidnapped someone he loved. "I don't think that's quite good enough."

A male vampire passed by in a long trench coat and studied them both with a curious expression. "I'll talk to you about it when we get back," Maddie urged.

Noah didn't know what there was to talk about. She had planned on serving Alice up on a silver platter to her king and queen. *And* she was likely doing so while fully aware it wouldn't work. Noah had met Imogen and Rav once and even he could tell they weren't the sort to negotiate. Especially since they already seemed to loathe Maddie.

"Now, we need to leave," Maddie whispered. "There are guards inside the palace."

"You weren't worried about the guards two minutes ago," he snapped.

"We can't do anything for either of our sisters if we're locked up," Maddie hissed. "Don't be a fool."

Noah pursed his lips. She was right—he couldn't get the cure for Alice if he was locked in a cage. "Fine," he relented. "But this doesn't mean we're square."

CHAPTER ELEVEN

MADDIE

Maddie was caught red-handed as though she'd held a blade to Alice's throat. She just as well could've been. She knew Noah would come after her when he'd discovered Alice missing, but she'd hoped she had enough time to switch out one sister for another. However, she wasn't foolish enough to think Imogen would simply hand over Mouse. No, that wouldn't have been the heart-stealing queen at all. But with a carrot dangling in front of her, Imogen may have given in. Which was why she hadn't brought Alice with her onto the palace grounds. Imogen didn't keep guards outside her palace as they did within the mortal world. The queen only kept her slaves inside.

Maddie had hoped Ferris would've sided with her on the matter, but even then, she had an inkling he wouldn't. Because Mouse had told him to save Alice.

Clusters of large red beetles trailed beside her while she and Noah trekked back toward the safe house. As they passed through the city, a male vampire's head lay, torn clean off, beside a body, blood pooling out from both wounds. Most likely an altercation between two males over a female.

Noah pressed a fist to his mouth like he may lose the nutrients in his stomach, but he said nothing. In fact, he hadn't asked a single question, only kept those shapely lips of his in a tight line. Her fingers fidgeted with the skirt of her dress, wishing she had a needle and fabric in her hands right then.

"Look, Noah," Maddie said slowly. "Tell me what you would've done in my position. If it was *your* sister in Mouse's place, and my sister was going to die anyway."

His shoulders stiffened and his voice came out even. "I wouldn't have taken your sister."

"I don't believe you." Maddie narrowed her eyes. "Not if you knew what Mouse has been through. Not if you knew how they've been treating her in that palace. For two years, Noah! And that is only two years. This may go on forever. Do you realize *that*?"

He stopped. Turned to her. His piercing green eyes met hers then. "I get it. I do. But Alice is *my* sister, and I was only human a few days ago. Maybe you forgot what humanity is like."

Maddie sucked in a sharp breath. She didn't usually do things like this and didn't *normally* turn mortals without their consent. She knew exactly who she was. "I did save you, didn't I?"

"About that…" Noah bit his lower lip, studying her intensely. "You mentioned the cure and that it's just past Ivory in werewolf territory. I want it. For her and for me."

He was asking about that damn cure again? If Maddie could pull one out from her pocket right now, she would, but she couldn't. "There's no way you'll ever get it. Only a couple have, and they didn't go unscathed. One lost an arm, the other a leg. All the others never came back."

A look of fear crossed Noah's handsome face, and she didn't want to put it there. But he needed to understand that he would most likely die. This wasn't playing with a few bats here—these were true monsters.

"Would you risk it for Mouse?" He turned the tables on her,

just as she had done to him a moment ago.

"Yes," Maddie said simply. For her, for Ferris, for Ever, if any of them wanted to go back to being human, she would risk her life for theirs.

"Then help me, Maddie," Noah pleaded, placing his arms on her shoulders. "And I'll help you."

Help her *how*? She thought again about how she'd already tried to infiltrate the palace with Ferris. He was much cleverer than anyone she'd met, and still, he hadn't succeeded.

"My, my, my, look what we have here." Maddie froze at the sound of Rav's voice. What had the bastard heard? He slinked out from the side of a building, wiping blood from his mouth with the back of his hand.

Maddie clenched her jaw. Why did she always have to run into him? It was as though he sought her out on purpose to toy with her.

"I just came from Osanna's and was on my way to give you my condolences, but lucky me, I found you. Although, it looks as though your mortal lived." He raked a hand through his hair, smoothing out his white and red locks as he sauntered toward them. Noah clenched his fists at his sides, and Maddie screamed inside her head for him to quit showing their cards to the bastard. Rav would take notice.

"Perhaps," Rav continued, his finger stroking his lower lip as his gaze fixed on Noah's. "I can help you with whatever you need instead of Maddie. A pity you are no longer mortal, I wouldn't have minded turning you myself. After fucking you of course." His stare slid to Maddie's and he smirked.

"Sorry, I'm taken," Noah said. "I'm Maddie's." Her eyes almost widened at the sentiment, but she kept them relaxed.

"Mm. For now." Rav remained smirking as he turned his attention back to Maddie. "If Ever isn't found soon, he may end up in a cage beside your sister. Cheers then."

Maddie's nostrils flared as Rav walked away with a pep in his step, disappearing through the city. Perhaps she would rip a head off today because she wanted to rip his off right now, then cover his face in hatpins. Before she could decide to chase after him and get herself killed, Maddie stormed off in the direction of the safe house. Noah easily caught up beside her with his enhanced vampire speed. He must've seen by her expression to not ask anything because he stayed silent.

After they left the city, screams echoing in the distance, the safe house slipped into view. The night was already starting to fall as she pounded the secret code for Ferris a little too loudly on the door. He should've already made it back … with Alice.

Ferris threw open the door, a scowl on his face as his mouth opened to say something. Most likely to reprimand her.

"Not now." Maddie waved her hand in the air and skirted past him. Alice sat on the settee, her expression one of sadness. When she'd taken Noah's sister, Alice was too loopy to know what was really going on. It had almost been too easy to lure her through Wonderland. Had it been that easy when Rav had brought Alice here? She was incredibly naïve. Just as Maddie had once been. A part of her hated what she had tried to do while the other still wished she'd succeeded.

Maddie avoided looking at Alice, trudged into the room where Noah had slept, and slammed the door behind her before plopping down on the mattress.

Why couldn't it have been Imogen she'd run into today? Why did it have to be that bastard?

The door didn't remain shut for long, though, its loud creak echoing. "Ferris, I…" Her words trailed off when Noah stepped inside the room and closed the door behind him.

His expression wasn't hard as it had been earlier—it was softer, kinder. "What the hell just happened back there?"

"Rav," Maddie muttered.

"I don't understand. You mentioned him before, that you two… But there has to be more to it. Tell me." His throat bobbed as he studied her, and she felt she owed him this after taking his sister.

"Fine, I'll tell you my story and you may understand a bit more on why I don't want Mouse there a moment longer."

Maddie then explained to Noah how Rav turned her over two centuries ago, pretended he was a gentleman taking her to become a hat maker for the queen who was really Imogen, how she thought she was in love with him after a day. And how, when she got to Wonderland, Imogen didn't choose to have her as a servant in the palace and believed her too pathetic to make any hats. Maddie was tossed out in the city, starving and weak, and she'd kept walking through a world she didn't understand. Then, she'd stumbled into Ivory and met a female whom she believed was a nobody like her. But that female ended up being Ever, the Queen of Ivory. Ever had chosen Maddie to make hats for her, and only then had Imogen taken notice of Maddie.

"That motherfucker." Noah's chest heaved, angrier than he'd been earlier.

"It's fine. Rav didn't take advantage of Alice in that way."

"It's still not *fine*. He did this to you, and he did this to my sister. I want to beat his fucking arse."

"It gets worse," Maddie said. "While we want to save our sisters, he wants to kill his. The White Queen—Ever—is Rav's sister. He already turned the Ivory guards against her, sending her into hiding, so for now, Ivory belongs to Rav. He isn't really the king of Scarlet either. Imogen may say he is but the true heir, if anything were to ever happen to her, is Chess, the male you saw at the portal before we came to Wonderland. Rav isn't his real father. Ever told me how Imogen and Rav murdered Imogen's husband, the last king, his father, the same night she turned Chess into a vampire. Then she brought her immortal son to Wonderland after leaving him in England until he was an adult. The king and Imogen had given up their lives and their son to become vampires."

"Bloody hell." Noah's eyes widened. "He wants to murder his own sister? How were Imogen and Rav not arrested or whatever you do here? Though after all I've seen so far, I shouldn't be surprised. But damn…"

"Yeah…"

A tense silence spread throughout the room and her gaze

stayed trained on his. So many thoughts slipped into Maddie's mind. Her sister, what she'd done to Alice, when she'd had her hand around Noah's hard cock. For once, she had nothing to say. Nothing else to give in that moment.

"What if I offer you a trade," Noah finally said, breaking the silence.

Maddie arched a brow. "What kind of trade, immortal?"

Noah knelt in front of her, appearing as though he were her knight. "If you help me retrieve the cure for Alice, I'll help you save your sister."

"How would you help me save Mouse?" Maddie sighed, her stomach sinking.

"We'll retrieve Mouse from the palace ourselves."

Maddie tilted her head to the side and patted his shoulder. "Easier said than done. Imogen has ripped out the heart of everyone who has defied her."

"What about when you deliver her hat?" He perked up. "She'd mentioned two weeks, right? Since you've done this before, she wouldn't be expecting you to just barge in and take Mouse."

Maddie mulled it over. When she'd delivered the hats, Rav was always prowling around the mortal world. He would most likely be gone... Even then, it would be difficult. There was always the chance Chess would be there too. But what did she have to lose? If she failed, then Ferris could continue trying to save Mouse. Her sister had waited long enough.

"Perhaps we can try. I'll help you locate the cure first, but we may not make it back in time to save Alice." Maddie didn't know how much longer Alice would last. It would be a few weeks at the most.

"I want to risk it," Noah said.

"Does this mean you forgive me?" Her mouth curved into a wide grin.

Noah blew out a breath. Then a small smile crossed his face as he lifted her chin. "Would you forgive me if the roles were reversed?"

"Yes," she whispered, liking the feel of his fingers on her chin a bit too much.

"Liar," he whispered back. "Alice is safe for now, so yes, I forgive you." His hands cupped her cheeks. "But I still want to throttle you."

"You're doing mighty fine on that threat, immortal." She waggled a finger at him. Before she ruined the moment by asking if he wanted her to make him come again, she changed the subject. "Go check on Alice. I need to talk to Ferris anyway."

"All right. I'll see you soon." His hands left her cheeks and she missed the light touch, his warmth.

As soon as Noah slipped out from the room, Ferris brushed past him and entered, that scowl still on his face.

Maddie cocked her head and grinned. "Were you hovering at the door, *listening*?"

"Fuck yes, I was."

She laughed, louder than she'd intended.

"It's not funny." Ferris's scowl deepened. "You put your life, Mouse's life, and Alice's life all in jeopardy. Imogen would've killed you all."

"I knew what I was doing," she drawled. "A reward was offered for Alice, remember? Besides, Imogen never found out you were connected to me or Mouse, did she?" Maddie purposefully left out that Ferris was included in that reward. She didn't need him traipsing to the palace and sacrificing himself. He wouldn't be held in a cell like Mouse—he'd be dead. And that would destroy Mouse if she knew he'd done that for her.

Ferris lowered himself on the mattress beside her and wrapped his arm around her shoulders. "Your new plan is shitty."

"It really is."

"You're falling for that wanker, aren't you?" Ferris smirked.

"If by some Wonderland miracle we get the cure, then Noah's taking it and going back home." So there was nothing to fall for anyway, even though the feel of his fingertips on her face still lingered on her skin.

Ferris lightly shook her. "Whatever, Maddie."

She took a deep breath, her tone serious. "Watch over Alice and if something happens to me, then don't give up on Mouse, all right?"

"I'm not giving up on her or *you*."

Maddie circled her arms around him and rested her head against his shoulder. "Werewolves and Imogen, no big deal. Now, let's have some fucking bloody tea before I head out into true monster territory."

CHAPTER TWELVE

NOAH

Noah scooped Alice off the settee and tucked her into bed before mixing her a cup of powdered blood. "You have to hang on. Maddie and I are going to get something that will cure you," he told her as she shivered beneath the covers. At least, he hoped they would succeed. There was a chance the werewolves would kill them both, but he couldn't let Alice doubt. "All you need to do is survive long enough for us to get back."

"What cure?" she asked through clacking teeth.

Ferris grumbled from the other room, and Maddie's cajoling reply was muffled by the door. Noah knew this was dangerous and that Ferris didn't like it, but too fucking bad. Alice was dying and he wasn't going to let her be stuck in Wonderland forever if she did live. He glanced at his sister's frail form. An ache built in his chest and he rubbed at it. Failure wasn't an option. Not when the stakes were this high.

He sat on the edge of the mattress by his sister and tried to hand her the cup. The mixture of powdered blood smelled stale and did nothing to entice him, but it was all he had for her at the moment. "Drink this."

"No," she whispered. "It makes me feel worse."

"You need to keep your strength up," he insisted.

Alice grabbed his free hand and squeezed it, a gleam of true fear in her eyes. "I don't want to die."

"I know." He set the cup down as Maddie and Ferris continued their hushed conversation. "We'll get the cure, I promise."

Alice clung to him and rolled onto her side, burying herself farther under the covers. Noah rubbed small circles on her back and waited for Maddie to fetch him when she was ready to go. He had nothing to pack nor prepare. All he had were the clothes on his back. For everything else, he relied on Maddie.

After a few minutes Alice's breathing evened with sleep, and he stayed a long while by her side. He didn't know how much time had passed when Maddie cracked the door open. "Ready?" she whispered.

"Yes." Noah kissed Alice on her forehead and stood. He spared her a final look, offered up a prayer that she would survive until they returned, and slunk away to join Maddie.

Ferris's eyes tore into him as he followed Maddie across the living room. He couldn't blame him for being annoyed. If it weren't for Noah and his sister, Maddie wouldn't be risking her life to get a cure. She and Ferris would be on their way to saving Mouse instead. It seemed almost too easy to convince Maddie to put Alice above her own sister, but she *had* attempted to trade one for the other. Whether or not it was guilt that got Maddie to agree to finding the cure, he was grateful.

"Stay safe, Ferris." Maddie grabbed a backpack from just inside the front door and handed it to Noah, then slipped one on herself. "We should be back before the end of the week. Don't do anything I wouldn't do."

Ferris pulled her into a hug. "You better come back or your sister will never forgive me."

At least, if they *didn't* succeed, Mouse had someone left to save her. Alice only had him. He envied their sense of security. Ferris wouldn't keep fighting for Alice and, honestly, there was no alternative. The cure was her only chance. It wasn't as if their parents would come to bail them out of trouble, and no one in Wonderland owed him any loyalty. He swallowed hard, forcing down the swelling sense of dread.

"Thank you," Noah told Ferris. "For looking out for Alice."

"Mouse wouldn't absolve me if I abandoned her," he grumbled.

Noah wondered why the opinion of Mouse mattered so much to him. To Maddie, it was obvious—they were siblings and very close. Ferris and Maddie were nothing more than friends. He'd been around enough people to know when they were interested in each other.

Maddie tugged on the hem of Noah's shirt and led him out the door. His gaze fell immediately to the back of Maddie's black boots. The weight of his worry and guilt refused to let his gaze travel higher. Was it the right thing to risk Maddie's life for Alice's? Not that he truly had a choice. He would never let his sister die if he could help it, but perhaps if she gave him directions he could—*no*. There was no way he would survive this without help. He wasn't *that* naïve.

After what felt like ages, long after the cobbled streets turned to dirt paths, Maddie slowed. "He was right."

"What?" Noah jerked his head up and found they were no longer in Scarlet, but in an empty field with tendrils of blue smoke floating overhead. He sucked in a breath as he studied the glimmering wisps.

"Ferris. He said Mouse wouldn't forgive him if he abandoned Alice and he was right. My sister has the kindest heart."

Noah nodded, unable to tear his eyes away from the sky. Was Mouse anything like Maddie? He and Alice were very different, but he loved her all the more for it. Mouse had to be centuries old like Maddie. It seemed strange to think of the age difference between himself and these vampires, but it didn't *feel* like they were born generations apart.

"Alice has a kind heart too," Noah started. "Our parents became really strict as we got older, and she spent most of her time studying to please them. Then she moved in with me for university and rebelled. I was worried she would take things too far and fall in with the wrong crowd, but she never stopped being kind."

Maddie tapped her lips. "She looked very different in the photo Imogen and Rav had."

Noah turned, taking in the endless glow of the scenery. "It was an old picture. She didn't always dye her hair." Then, feeling Maddie's intense stare, he glanced down at her. "What?"

"You looked different too." She arched a brow, making no effort to hide her perusal of his body.

Noah's head fell back with a laugh. He'd hoped Maddie hadn't noticed. *Shit, that's embarrassing.* "I was the biggest nerd."

"Ah, my dear immortal, a nerd no longer. You aged quite well." Maddie smirked.

"No. I finally noticed girls and started caring about how I looked. Hit the gym four times a week, cut down on sweets, and discovered the magic of face wash."

Maddie gave a thoughtful *hmm*. "I bet the girls all fawned over you then."

Noah shrugged. He couldn't lie—it had been the biggest perk of working out. All of the hottest girls in school wanted to date him. It had been a huge ego boost for a previously self-conscious kid, but it had gotten old fast. There was far too much drama that came along with it and too many of them only wanted him for superficial reasons—looks *and* money. "I suppose. There's been my fair share of hookups, but I've only dated one person since then. That ended quite badly though."

"Only one?" She cocked her head. "What happened?"

He sighed. Were they really going to do this? Have the ex talk? "We dated for two years, then she fucked my best friend."

"You want me to stab her with a hatpin?" She patted his shoulder, her expression serious. "Not kill her of course."

"I'm better off." He exhaled sharply. "Or I was. Dying sort

of put a dent in that, if I say so myself."

"You didn't die," Maddie said matter-of-factly.

Right, right. He was technically alive, but what good was that if he was stuck in a dark world with a craving for blood? He wanted to go home. Though, if he was being honest, it was fucking amazing seeing in the dark and having super strength. "Where are we going?" he asked to change the subject.

Maddie pointed ahead. "Ivory is that way, but we won't get there for a while yet. Tonight, we'll make it to one of Ever's safe houses, then I'll give you a *lesson.*" She waggled her eyebrows at him.

His cock pulsed. It wasn't an innuendo—*was it?*—but he couldn't stop his thoughts from traveling down a lurid path. Her teaching him *exactly* how she liked to be touched, him learning *exactly* what she tasted like in every way. He shut the thoughts down, before he sported a full boner, and cleared his throat. "A lesson?"

"Let's do three lessons." She stopped and whirled toward him with an excited gleam in her eyes. "We need to test your vampire speed. Race me to that tree."

"What tree?" He squinted ahead but only more blue smoke swirled. There, in the distance, he caught sight of a silhouette so far off he barely recognized the shape.

"That one," she blurted and took off.

Noah stood there for a moment, mouth hanging open, before he raced after her. The wind whistled in his ears as he ran, focusing on the purple blur a few lengths ahead of him—Maddie. He smirked as he pushed himself harder, letting the adrenaline fuel his speed, and soon caught up with her.

"There you are," she said with a bright smile. "But you're too late."

Noah opened his mouth to ask what she meant, when she dug her heels into soft earth and placed her hand on a tree. He slowed too quickly and nearly toppled over his own feet. "Well, damn," he said with a long exhale. The tree came out of nowhere. "You're fast."

Maddie laughed and poked playfully at his chest. "Faster than you."

"Hey now." He captured her wrist and tugged her closer. "It wasn't a fair race."

She cocked her head and pretended to think for a moment. "You have longer legs, so I was at a disadvantage."

Noah chuckled and she leaned into him. A whiff of sweet cherries hit him. The air between them thickened and Maddie's gaze trailed up to his lips. They'd already done other things together, but he wanted to find out what she tasted like. Would she be as sweet as she smelled? Sweeter? How soft were her lips and would she part them for him? He lowered his head the smallest fraction as if drawn by an invisible force, about to find out if she tasted like cherries.

Maddie waved a hand in the air and quickly stepped back. "Time for lesson two."

"Oh?" Noah cleared his throat, straightened, and took in the forest. Anything to keep his thoughts from circling back to what he thought the second lesson could be. Black trunks. Gray leaves, with the occasional red one ruining the monochromatic scheme. The trees grew thicker together farther out, it seemed, but here, they appeared sparse. "What is it this time?"

Maddie slipped her backpack off, set it on the grass, and dug into it. When she stood again, a pistol rested in each of her hands, pointed directly at him. She looked between them, then up at him. "Do you have a preference?"

The fuck…? He'd never seen a gun in real life, and it instantly had him stepping back. "Where the hell did you get those?"

"There's a seller in Scarlet who brings them back from the mortal world." She held both out toward him. "So?"

"What?"

"Which would you like to use?"

His eyes widened. "Neither, thanks."

Maddie shoved one of the pistols into his hand. "Don't be a silly goose. How do you expect to enter werewolf territory without one? I have plenty of silver bullets, but we'll practice with regular ones now. They're easier to come by."

"I don't know, Maddie…" He gripped the weapon carefully, keeping his finger off the trigger. This would make going up against the werewolves much easier, though, so he'd just have to get over his reservations. "I've never shot a gun before."

"That's why we're *practicing*," she said as if it should've been obvious. "Look, it's easy."

Noah's gaze lifted slowly—or at least it felt slow. He barely had time to see that she had raised her gun. In his direction. The boom reverberated through his skull as the bullet whizzed by his head, the sound extra loud to his immortal hearing. A wave of dizziness swept over him.

What the fuck? What the actual fuck? "Did you just shoot at *me*?"

"No, I shot *past* you." Maddie lowered her arm and grinned. "My aim never fails."

"Like I give a shit about your aim? What if I'd moved?" he shouted.

"Well," she said, dragging the word out. "I suppose you'd heal then. Now it's your turn."

Noah shook the ringing from his ears, cursing his amplified hearing at the moment. "I don't know how to shoot a fucking gun. It's not like they were lying all over the place back home."

"Don't be a coward." She bent down and set her pistol on the ground, then circled around behind him. "It's simple."

"I'm not a coward. A lesson is supposed to come with instructions though." He'd much rather kill than be killed, but he didn't want to accidentally shoot the wrong thing. Like Maddie, for example.

Maddie's hand gently slipped down his arm from where she stood a little to the side behind him. "You don't want to become a meal for the hungry beasties, do you?" Her hand reached his wrist and lifted his arm up. "Turn off the safety here," she said, pointing to a small lever. "Now aim." She steadied his arm, her fingers skimming his wrists, and her breasts brushed against his back. The contact sent an immediate heat straight to his cock, but he had to concentrate. This was important. So when

Maddie's warm breath skated along his arm, he squinted ahead at his target. "Put your finger on the trigger and—"

Noah curled his finger around the trigger as she spoke and the gun blasted. His arm jerked back, his body practically humming from the blast. "Oh my God," he whispered, his heart pounding, a smile crossing his face. He hadn't expected such a power rush to come from shooting a weapon.

"Well, you weren't supposed to squeeze it yet," Maddie said patiently.

Noah took a steadying breath and nodded. Shooting was the smartest option. Quicker for everyone involved. He scowled at the gun in his hand—if only he wasn't a shit shot.

"Try again. Hit that tree over there."

Noah lifted the weapon, attempted to line it up with the trunk a few yards away, and shot. The bullet blasted through the air and completely missed its target.

"No worries." Maddie shrugged. "Werewolves will be bigger and closer."

"I'm not sure that's comforting," he grumbled. If he couldn't hit a target standing still, how did she expect him to hit one that *moved?*

"We've made enough noise for now. You can try again tomorrow." Maddie took the gun from him and slid it into his backpack before skipping to retrieve her belongings. Pulling her key ring from a pocket in her skirt, she sang, "Come along, immortal."

Noah rubbed his hands together as he plodded behind her up to the tree they'd raced to. He watched quietly as she slipped one of her keys into a crack in the bark. "What's this?" he asked curiously.

"Our safe house for the night."

With a single push, the side of the tree shifted inward, revealing a spiral staircase leading beneath the ground. Maddie ushered him inside. When he was three steps down, she came in behind him and shoved the door closed, locking them in the pine-scented safe house. He blinked twice to adjust to the darkness, but then everything was completely clear, thanks to his improved vampire vision. And by everything, he meant the smooth brown walls and matching wooden staircase.

"Go on," she said.

Noah descended the steps with Maddie on his heels to a rounded room. An *empty* room. No bed, no sofa, no nothing except for an open crate full of powdered blood.

"It'll do to keep us safe," Maddie assured him, as if she'd read his mind.

Noah slid his pack off and plopped down on the carved-out wood floor, stretching his legs. "Yes, it'll do." He wasn't going to be awake long enough to care about comfort anyway. Now that he was sitting down, exhaustion washed over him in a wave. "Sweet dreams, Maddie."

"Don't let the Wonderland bugs bite," she replied as she rifled through her bag for something. "I'll wake you when it's time to leave."

The scent of cherries invaded his nostrils. Noah wasn't sure if he'd be able to sleep with the images in his head of Maddie slipping her dress off her petite body and straddling him. He pressed his eyes shut and rolled to his side, facing away from her. *Fucking hell. Think of werewolves instead, Noah. Big beastly ones.* But it wasn't working. Not one bit. Fuck, he was in trouble.

CHAPTER THIRTEEN

MADDIE

A smidge of alabaster tulle there. A little ivory lace curved and braided between. Perhaps frosted felt entwined with chiffon near the front. Folded and shaped pearly roses of wool could be sewn into a small arch. Then at its center would rest an anatomical heart, crimson paint appearing to leak from its veins, coating the other white areas in splashes of scarlet, as though the organ were bleeding. That was it! This was the fascinator Maddie would gift to Imogen, as the perfect distraction, before attempting to retrieve Mouse. *If* they came back from this journey.

The image in Maddie's mind of the hat was one of the finest she'd come up with, one that would anger Imogen. Yet, she knew it would distract the queen for a moment, a moment where Maddie and Noah could possibly make their move. She wasn't sure what the plan would be following that, but as long as they could get Imogen's arms behind her back before she tore into their chests, then it would be a good day.

Once—*if*—they got Mouse out, where would they go? To

hide in one of these safe houses forever? To see if there was anything left in the dead Red Queen's abandoned territory? To hide somewhere in the mortal world? The mortal world may be their best option, but Maddie didn't want to constantly move every few years when humans realized they didn't age. Then to pretend she was human and hide from the sun? *No*—she liked her freedom. If they were able to retrieve the cure, and there was enough, then perhaps she, Mouse, and Ferris could also take it. *No to that too*. None of them would want that.

As Maddie contemplated the what-ifs, a strong arm folded around her middle and drew her to a firm chest. She gasped at the sudden movement, and the warmth forming in her belly. Noah nuzzled into her neck, and they were like two spoons fitting together perfectly. His hard length pressed into her, her eyelids fluttering at the contact. His breathing came out soft, even … *sleeping*. She'd been in this position many times but never while the male wasn't awake.

Noah's impish hand then slowly slid up her stomach and she stilled, wondering what was going to happen next. His palm cupped her breast and he growled into her neck, pressing harder against her. Maddie naturally arched into his touch, but she needed to wake Noah before this got too awkward for him. She didn't mind his hands on her one bit.

"Immortal," Maddie whispered, jabbing him in the ribs with her elbow.

"Mm-hmm," he groaned, somehow moving even closer, his fingers kneading her breast.

"Noah," she said louder, jabbing him harder.

His hand loosened from her breast, but remained frozen there, his entire body stiffened.

"Fuck." Noah removed his arm from around her and shifted back. "I'm sorry. I didn't—"

"No worries." With a smile, Maddie rolled to face him and placed her hand to his warm cheek, giving it a light tap. "It's natural. I told you the lust would come again." She paused, remembering her hand around him in the bathtub only a couple days ago, him enjoying it, her liking it just as much. Not only that, but it had helped him. "Do you want me to take care of you again?"

His throat bobbed as his bright green eyes studied her. "Only if you want to," he said softly. "Not out of obligation."

"I don't do anything I don't want to do."

"All right," Noah whispered. "It helped last time."

She scanned him up and down. "Let's remove your clothes, so we don't get them too messy."

Noah seemed to fight a smile as he slowly nodded before lifting his shirt over his head. Not taking her eyes from his bright green irises, Maddie reached between them and unbuttoned his trousers, then pushed them down. He kicked the material off until he was bare before her. She took in each hard muscle, his defined chest, his strong thighs and arms. This male never would've given her a second look in her past human life, and she didn't truly know if he would in this immortal life either. But they were stuck together, and she was starting to rather like having him around.

As she gripped his hard length, Noah released a deep groan and wrapped his arm around her waist. He rested his forehead in the crook of her neck when she gently caressed at first. Maddie inched closer as she circled the head of his cock with her thumb, then stroking up and down, adding firmer pressure, her movements increasing their pace.

Noah's breathing hitched—her heart pounded.

Maddie unintentionally shifted even closer, a heat spreading through her, consuming her, and she yearned desperately to sink her fangs into his throat. Not for a treat like she did with mortals, but for the pleasure that vampires gave to one another. With all the immortal lovers she'd taken to her bed, she'd never once let any of them push their teeth into her flesh though, not after Rav. Only hers penetrating them.

Her lips pressed to Noah's throat, her fangs lowering on their own accord. Maddie grazed his tender skin with her teeth, then flicked the area with her tongue, tasting his salty flesh. He shivered at her touch, and let out a delicious sound just as she pumped and stroked him even harder. She liked the feel of him, the sounds he made.

"Maddie," he rasped while his muscles tightened, his body spasming, his cock throbbing as he spilled himself.

Noah's chest heaved, her body now coiled tight, aching for a release of her own when she let go of him.

Before she could retrieve a cloth from her pack to clean them up, Noah said something unexpected, enticing, his voice curious. "Can I touch you now?"

Maddie stilled. She'd assumed she would've just taken care of herself as she had the last time. And even though anticipation stormed through her at what his fingers would feel like on her, inside her, she answered, "You don't have to."

"But I want to," he murmured, his fingers running up the length of her spine in a delectable caress.

And that matter was settled. "All right, show me what you can do, immortal."

He chuckled, then his gaze grew serious, daring. "To be fair … and less messy, how about you get undressed?"

Fair indeed. Maddie grinned. "One of my hands is already messy, so you may have to help me."

Noah didn't hesitate as he loosened the buttons at the front of her dress. Her heart beat faster, preparing to break her rib cage in half. He then reached over and peeled down the straps from her shoulders, exposing her breasts, the cool air hitting her nipples. Fangs lowering, he drew the dress down from her body, and as he reached her panties, he took them with the other material until she was naked before him.

He tossed the dress and undergarments aside and his gaze drank her in while studying her for a long moment.

"Go on," she instructed.

Noah rolled his eyes and licked his lower lip before he brought his shapely lips to her breast. She moaned when he took her peaked nipple between his teeth, sucking and nipping while his hand ventured to her center. As his fingers brushed the sensitive area, her moans grew louder—she knew her wetness was already pooling around his digits. He circled and rubbed while sliding two fingers inside her heat. Her hands balled into fists and her eyelids fluttered at his practiced movements. Noah's mouth trailed kisses up her throat, to where his fangs grazed her this time. The fear she'd experienced in the past didn't come, instead, she wished he would sink them in. And as she imagined it, as she focused on the rhythmic movements of his hand, as she thought about what it would feel like to have his cock inside her doing the same thing his fingers were, a wave of emotions pounced through her. Her body quaking and quaking and *quaking*. This was nothing like what her own fingers would've been able to do. Nothing at all.

Noah lifted his head above her, his mouth so close to touching hers. Chest heaving, Maddie pressed her forehead to his before their lips could brush. Because if she kissed him, she may just be as foolish as she'd been with Rav when she'd given all of herself to him in that forest. A kiss never mattered before, but something about a kiss with Noah seemed different.

"Next time, we'll take care of each other again," Noah said softly, pressing a kiss to her forehead before helping her back into her dress. Like a gentleman.

But all she could focus on was *next time*.

Maddie woke and stretched her arms to the ceiling with a yawn. She turned to Noah to find him still asleep on his back, breathing evenly.

He looked angelic as he slept with his chiseled features and his curled blond hair. She tapped his cheek. "Good morning, sunshine. Are you ready to find the werewolves?"

Noah's eyes cracked open, his gaze meeting hers. Crimson stained his cheeks, and she was certain he was thinking about their night before. After all, it was a memorable night.

"Come on. We'll be in Ivory soon." Maddie stood and shoved on her combat boots. She grabbed her backpack from the ground, placing the straps over her shoulders while Noah mirrored her movements.

"What's Ivory like?" Noah asked as they ascended the stone steps leading out of the tree safe house.

"Beautiful," Maddie said, opening the door to the fresh air, laced with hints of vanilla and honey. "Decorated in mostly whites and silvers."

As they entered the night, the world around them grew boisterous from creatures' activities.

"What is that?" Noah squinted his eyes as he peered around the large trunks.

"Sounds like mostly mating." Maddie paused, tilting her head to get a better listen. "And perhaps some feeding. We're in the very outskirts of Scarlet. Occasionally a werewolf will slip in."

"What the fuck?" Noah's eyes widened. "I thought they had their own territory."

"They do, but the rogue ones still prowl about. That's why most of us keep guns and silver on hand at our homes." She tapped his cheek. "But they aren't like you and me. They would be like a wolf in your world—focused on their predatory natures. Vampires like to feed, but not all of us are heartless."

"Watch out," Noah shouted, grabbing her by the shoulders and pulling her to his firm chest.

Maddie's gaze fell to where Noah stared. A group of five badgers watched them around a crimson log, their teeth razor-sharp, their skin pale and wrinkled. She laughed. "Noah, they're only a different breed of badgers than what your world has. They're harmless … well, to us anyway. Not mortals. They would drink them dry."

"They have no fur," he stated, not loosening his grip on her.

Maddie batted his arm away and crept closer to the clan of badgers. She knelt beside a smaller one with a shriveled face, then reached down to pet it, stroking its soft head. The badger let out a light purring sound. "See?" She glanced up at Noah with a smile. "Come on."

"Uh…" Noah hesitated, but then slid down beside her, shakily pressing a hand forward. The badgers focused on him yet didn't scamper away as he awkwardly petted each of their heads—if one could call it that. "These don't run like ours do," he said in awe.

"One reason why I love Wonderland." She grinned and stood, straightening the skirt of her dress. The wildlife in Wonderland had their oddities compared to the mortal world which made her feel more at home here, even if most could be deadly. But they were outcasts like she'd been. "Let's go."

They continued walking through the forest, the sounds of mating lessening with each step they took. The trees were of black and red—obsidian trunks and crimson leaves, or scarlet trunks and onyx leaves. Crows cawed above them and Noah stepped toward one near a trunk.

Maddie yanked him to her by his shirt sleeve. "Don't get near any of the birds in Wonderland—they peck out anyone's eyes who draw too near."

"Bloody hell." Noah sucked in a sharp breath. "You just told me the wildlife here was different than back home."

She shrugged. "Well, do crows try to peck out your eyes in London?"

He rolled his gaze toward the sky, a smile tugging at his lips.

Leaves crunched beneath their feet, and the trunks of the trees appeared as if they'd been braided.

"Thirsty?" Maddie asked, her throat growing drier with each passing moment.

"Very," Noah said.

"Better to eat before we get to Ivory anyway." She fished out a canteen of water, then two pouches of powdered blood and handed him one. "At least Ever's territory is more calming. I miss it."

"Why don't you still live there instead?"

"Because once Ever went into hiding, Imogen forced me and Mouse to live at the cottage in the woods. And then, eventually,

Mouse was taken."

"What a bitch." Noah cocked his head. "How long has Ever been in hiding?"

"Almost four years." Maddie shrugged and peeled open her blood pouch. She moistened her fingers and pushed them inside before bringing them to her mouth. The powder was chalky, the flavor weak, but it would do. Sometimes it was hard to swallow, so she took a swig of her water before tipping the pouch's contents onto her tongue to make a thicker, tastier liquid.

As she finished, her throat was no longer dry, her appetite satiated. Up ahead, white and silver trees poked through the slits of Scarlet's foliage.

"What is that?" Noah asked as they inched closer, taking a swig of water.

The white and silver of the tree trunks were splashed in something bright red... *Blood.*

CHAPTER FOURTEEN

NOAH

Blood splattered the silver trees. Long streaks of crimson with speckles all around, and large droplets oozed toward the white grass beneath their feet. The trails followed the lines of the bark, slipping between the cracks and making a strangely beautiful design. But it was *a lot* of blood. More than Noah felt comfortable passing off as some wild beast securing dinner. Unless that dinner was human-sized.

"Is it always like this?" Noah asked before his imagination could run away from him. She'd claimed Ivory was relaxing, but they apparently had different definitions of that word. Under different circumstances, she could've been telling the truth though. Some of the trunks were white with silver leaves, others silver with white leaves, and a light, fresh scent lingered beneath the metallic scent of blood.

"No." Maddie ran her index finger along one of the stained trunks, then inspected her red fingertip. She licked the crimson from her digit and Noah's stomach churned. "It's fresh human blood.”

Noah's brows rose. If it was fresh, then whatever did this could still be lurking around, yet she didn't seem overly concerned. Another vampire wouldn't be a threat to them unless they worked for Imogen and Rav, but he'd rather not waste time talking to anyone. "What could've done this?"

"Well…" Maddie's gaze slid from the trees to the ground and back up as she tapped her lips, thinking. "It could've been vampires, of course, or some beasties. Or the Jabberwocky."

"The what now?" The Jabberwocky *sounded* like a beastie, as she put it, but if she was making a distinction, it had to be something else.

"The Jabberwocky." She slid between trees, careful not to rub against the trunks, and steered them straight for the white dirt road ahead. "It's a horrid beastie as big as a dragon with long talons and barbed quills sticking out from its fur. Its face is dragon-like with scales and hundreds of teeth, but don't you fret! The Jabberwocky rarely comes into Ivory and Scarlet. It usually stays just past Red, but once Ever left, the creature became a little more daring. This blood most likely came about from a vampire's doing though."

Rarely was not never, but Noah chose to go with Maddie's theory. Another vampire wasn't a threat to them in the same way as some vicious beast the size of a fucking dragon. They wouldn't be hunted down for food. For other reasons, perhaps, but being a vampire removed him from at least one menu. Crazed murderers roamed all over the mortal world though, so if humans could pick off other humans, arseholes in Wonderland could do the same. The best thing to do was get the fuck out of there.

"How much farther is the swamp?" he asked.

Maddie wrinkled her nose as she thought. "If we walk all day and sleep at the next safe house, we can get there by morning."

"We can get there tonight if we don't rest then?"

"Tut, tut. We need our wits about us."

"Fine," Noah conceded. Time was ticking for Alice, but a few hours to rest could make the difference between success and failure. Facing werewolves with a fresh mind had to be for the best. "While we walk, let's go over the plan for when we get there."

"Get where?" came a tauntingly curious male's voice. Noah's pulse immediately began to race.

"Bloody hell," Maddie grumbled.

A vampire leapt down from a tree directly in front of them. Chestnut hair fell halfway down his neck, shorter pieces framing his face, and he studied them with yellow irises. He wore black trousers with a matching vest, abs on full display. This was the same male he'd seen in the park just before they first arrived in Wonderland, when Noah was under Maddie's trance. *Chess.* Imogen's son. The *prince*. Noah fought the urge to step forward and beat his arse.

Chess smiled at Maddie, fangs fully descended and a smear of blood on his lips. "Did I frighten you, little plum? I was certain you noticed me a moment ago when you looked around, but I guess you were too preoccupied with the mess I made on the trees."

Maddie shuffled slightly in front of Noah. "Weren't you searching for something before in the mortal world?"

"I'm the king of multitasking. Search for a human, search for a queen… But instead, I found a hatter and a new vampire." His yellow gaze landed on Noah, seeming to bore down to his soul. "You were a mortal last time we met, weren't you?"

Noah opened his mouth to reply just as something large fell from the same tree that Chess had leapt from. It hit the ground with a loud *thump*.

"Found a snack too," Chess said with a shrug. "Meant to tie him up there to bleed slowly, but I got carried away."

Noah peered around the flippant male and drew in a sharp breath. *A body.* The heavyset man was nearly decapitated, his skin waxy, his eyes bulging from their sockets. Noah's stomach churned at the sight. There was drinking from someone like he had at Maddie's and then there was draining people dry.

"A royal servant from Ivory?" Maddie asked, peering down at the man's dead body. "I wasn't aware those traitorous guards had left anyone alive."

Chess shrugged, all humor fading from his expression. "Where are you off to, Maddie? You know you're not allowed to leave Scarlet unless it's for the mortal world."

Maddie shifted into Noah's side and her arm circled his waist. Following her lead, he settled his arm around her shoulders. "I'm just showing my boyfriend around Wonderland. He's new, like you said, and we wanted to take a little trip. I'll be back in time to deliver your mother her next hat."

"Boyfriend..." Chess licked the corner of his lips, spreading the blood smeared there. Noah narrowed his eyes, growing uncomfortable with the scrutiny. "You know, Maddie, I never thought you were the type to sire anyone and keep them."

"It was a happy accident," she said with false cheer. "Now, if you'll excuse us..."

She tapped Noah's side, steering him away without breaking their embrace, and walked across fallen leaves. Noah released a quiet, relieved breath. He wanted to get as far away from Chess as possible, as fast as possible. But running would only make them look suspicious. Maddie hadn't mentioned not being allowed out of Scarlet before they'd left, but would it have made a difference?

Chess sidestepped in front of them and chuckled, a predatory glint in his eyes. Noah scowled, his hand tightening around Maddie's shoulders.

"Oh, Maddie," Chess whispered and tapped the tip of her nose. "You know I can't let you wander off into Ivory."

Maddie rolled her eyes. "I don't know where Ever is. Besides, you still have Mouse."

"So you keep saying, but I..." Chess prowled a step closer, forcing Maddie to look up to see his face. "Don't..." He gripped her chin. "Believe..." His eyes turned to thin slits. "You."

Noah tensed, ready to knock the prince away from Maddie. The way Chess was touching her lit his protective instincts on fire, but she wasn't even trying to defend herself. For that reason alone, he held back, grinding his teeth together to the point of pain.

Maddie squeezed his side as if in warning, rolling her shoulder slightly, and he loosened his grip on her. "You're welcome to join us then," she offered.

"I don't do threesomes." Chess paused. "With only vampires." A hiss escaped Noah without warning and Chess eyed him. "Don't sass me, child."

Noah froze. He wanted to rip the prince's face off. Tear him apart. Somewhere, deep inside, he recoiled at his own thoughts, but he'd work through *that* later.

"Now," Chess continued. "Come back to Scarlet with me like a good girl. Mother will be interested in your sight-seeing itinerary."

"Okay," Maddie said in a slightly slurred voice. Chess's grip had tightened so much that her lips puckered.

Chess stepped back and wiped his hand on his trousers. "Stay there for one moment, won't you?" He climbed the tree again without waiting for a reply, leaping and swinging on the branches like a damn monkey to reach the top.

Noah spun Maddie to face him. "What the fuck? We can't go back to Scarlet," Noah said in a rushed voice. They needed to keep going without distractions.

"We can't fight Chess either," she whispered. "He's older than I am and much stronger. Trust me and play along."

Maddie looked the same age as Chess. Immortal... Noah supposed that meant he would look like this forever. No pain, no memory loss, no deteriorating. Another perk of being a vampire.

Chess leapt down in front of them again and produced a blood-stained rope. "You don't mind, do you?"

Noah's fangs dropped. "Fuck yes, I mind."

"I was only being polite." Chess lifted one of Maddie's arms and started wrapping the rope around her wrist. "She may be weak and you may be new, but I'm far too lazy to chase you."

A growl slipped through Noah's lips as he bared his fangs, and Maddie tensed beside him. "We aren't going anywhere with you."

"You picked a feisty one," he said to Maddie, his tone somewhere between amused and annoyed.

Before he could stop himself, Noah lunged at Chess. The prince easily sidestepped him, and Noah skidded across the dirt path. He barely caught himself and whirled around, straight into Chess's fist. The force of the punch sent Noah stumbling back two steps before tripping over his own feet and landing hard on his arse.

"It seems you'll be traveling as my prisoners instead of my guests," Chess said with a sigh.

Before Noah could even attempt to stand, Chess had him flipped to his stomach, face pressed to the ground. Blood trickled from his nose where the prince had hit him, and he fought the urge to lick it away. But the urge only lasted a moment as Chess yanked Noah's arms behind his back, straining his joints. The rope cut into his circulation two seconds later.

"Chess," Maddie shouted. "He's newly-turned—don't go overboard. You know how impulsive a new vampire can be."

"Excuses," Chess grumbled. "I'm too old to deal with this shit."

"Bastard," Noah growled, and some of the white dirt found its way into his mouth. He'd been in his fair share of fights, but it had never lasted longer than a few punches. This was far more serious. He meant to tear Chess limb from limb.

Chess stood, one foot on either side of Noah's hips, and gave the rope a sharp tug. Then, to Maddie, he said, "Your turn."

Without a word, she stomped forward, a scowl on her face and her hands held out in front of her. Chess moved away from Noah and used the other end of the rope to secure her wrists together, then patted her head.

"Splendid," she sang.

"Wait here while I gather my other things." Chess stepped over Noah, purposely kicking him in the ribs as he did so. He bent over the corpse and rifled through the dead man's pockets.

"Now look what you've done, immortal." Maddie leaned down and helped Noah roll to his side. "As if escaping wasn't going to be difficult already."

Noah hauled himself into a sitting position, his arms trapped at a painfully awkward angle. "At least we're tied together."

Maddie grabbed one of his elbows and pulled him to his feet. "Insufferable," she muttered. "The both of you."

CHAPTER FIFTEEN

MADDIE

Noah just had to go ahead and muck things up and make the situation worse. Chess had stepped a few paces away, always slinking. He wasn't the brightest bulb in the box which may have been the reason Ever had been able to stab him so easily before escaping. But he was ridiculously strong.

Yet Maddie could be sneaky. She had a plan—one that now would have to come to fruition another way because of Noah's hotheadedness a few moments ago.

Chess stood near the dead man's body, the scent of metal filling the air. A heavenly smell, but she was still satiated from her powdered meal yesterday.

"Ah, here we are," Chess purred, holding up a closed switchblade that he'd fished from the man's pocket. Swiping the tip of his tongue at the corner of his mouth, he popped open the switchblade and sauntered toward Maddie. "Don't worry, little plum, I'm only taking you home." He paused. "Which means you'll owe me. But if you come back here, I'll have to get my hands dirty." The prince drew a gentle line across her throat with the blade, and Maddie held back spitting in his face while Noah glowered.

"Come on then. I've still got other jobs to do." Chess grinned, placing his hand in the middle of the rope, and tugged them forward as if leading two horses.

Maddie didn't need this delay. If he took them back to Scarlet, they wouldn't have enough time to complete their journey to save Alice before she had to deliver the hat to Imogen. She glanced at Noah and found his gaze trained on her, as though he'd been trying to silently catch her attention. Then he flicked his stare to the rope, motioning his head at it.

She frowned, not understanding what he wanted her to see. If Maddie could get closer to Noah, then she could untie him, but Chess's hand hovered between them. Noah cleared his throat and bulged his eyes at the rope, then at Chess.

Oh. She knew precisely what he wanted them to attempt. A distraction would have to do the trick first.

"What if I offer you a trade, Chess?" Maddie sang, a smile spreading across her face.

"I have everything I could ever want," the heartless prince said without looking at them, his shoulders square, his body relaxed.

"Do you?" Maddie asked.

Chess glanced back, smirking, his chestnut-colored brow arched. "Do you plan on giving me sweet Ever?"

"I told you," Maddie drew her words out slowly, "for the last time, I don't know where she is."

"Pity then." He jerked them forward and Maddie stumbled. "I may change my mind and take you to Mother instead."

The blood in Maddie's veins turned to liquid fire as she thought about Ever, what Chess would've done to her if the White Queen hadn't gotten away. Would he have slit her throat then removed her head or ripped out her heart the way his mother did with her enemies? "Yes, a pity you won't tell your mother you saw me here because then she would know you lost us."

"What are you rambling about, Hatter?" His movements stopped.

Maddie cocked her head at Noah, giving him a silent signal to do it now. With one quick jerk, the rope was out of Chess's hands, and they slammed it into his neck, backing him against an alabaster tree.

Chess seethed as Noah and Maddie both pulled on the rope from opposite sides to trap him against the trunk. Even with the rope binding Noah's hands behind his back, he had enough strength so Maddie could truly yank on it. The prince bucked and writhed so hard that Maddie thought her hands may get ripped off.

"You fuckers!" Chess's face turned bright red, spewing every curse word at them. But with each sound, she could hear him growing weaker, see it in his face. His fight lessened until his body stilled, his eyes falling shut.

Maddie released the prick from her angle and Chess slumped to the ground with a *thump* before collapsing on his side.

"Untie me," Noah rushed the words out, already in front of her with his back turned.

It took only a moment for her to unravel the knot. Noah shoved the rope from his wrists and whirled around to untie her. Not once did she remove her gaze from Chess—she didn't know how soon he would wake.

Maddie shimmied out of the rope, lunged for Chess, and grabbed his head before twisting it to the side with a loud snap that echoed through the forest.

"He'll be out for a long while." Her chest heaved as she released the prince and plucked up the rope from the ground. "Still, we should hurry."

"Why don't you just kill him?" Noah asked, Chess's switchblade now in his hand.

The thought of ripping out the prince's heart sent a thrill through her, but she had to be reasonable. For now. "We can't yet. We don't have Mouse, and if I killed Imogen's son, then she would murder my sister in the worst possible way before we could get her." Maddie lifted a finger. "However, we will revisit the matter after collecting Mouse. Now, hold up his body."

Noah easily lifted Chess and propped him against one of the thin trees. Taking the rope, she wrapped it just below the prince's rib cage. There was only enough to circle his body once—it would have to do, but she tied it tight enough so that he couldn't easily shimmy out of it.

"We'll tear off pieces from the dead man's shirt so we can bind his wrists and gag him," Maddie instructed after confirming the knot was tight enough.

Noah didn't hesitate as they ripped off two long black pieces of fabric from the dead human's T-shirt. Maddie shoved the fabric in between Chess's teeth and wrapped it around to the back of his head while Noah bound the prince's wrists together behind his back.

"If he withers here forever, then too bad." She glanced up with a grin and shrugged. "He should've left us alone."

"He's a fucking arse."

"Well, we made a great team today." Maddie straightened out the skirt of her dress. "Now, let's go since the bastard made us lose time."

Without another word, they hurried through the forest to widen the gap between them and Chess. The night was at its full peak, black and silver owls hooting from the tops of trees around them. They needed to get to the safe house before morning so they could stay on track, giving Maddie enough time to make Imogen's hat. But there was still a while before they would arrive at the hidden house. Ever had told her exactly where each safe house was located on the keyring she'd given to the Hatter. Maddie may not have been to all of them before, but Ever had shown her the ones in Ivory, long ago, when they'd both lived here.

As they pushed farther through the forest, cool gusts of air blew, and a strong scent permeated the air.

"More blood?" Noah said, his nostrils flaring as he drew in the smell.

Maddie slowed at the edge of the forest and inhaled again. Blood always tinged the air in Wonderland but it was normally a sweet odor. Ivory had never smelled like this, colder, staler. Close to four years had passed since Maddie had been here last, but not that much could change during this amount of time.

Could it?

She broke out of the forest, the city of Ivory resting before her. Tall, white structures with silver-tinted windows flooded the area. Some buildings were shaped like chess pieces, and other rectangular structures contained a single game piece in the center of their roof with spheres in the corners for decoration. A heavy quiet blanketed the city, a far cry from the peals of laughter that used to ring out through the streets. That part disturbed her most of all.

"Why's it so quiet?" Noah's eyes opened wide, his hand still clutching the knife.

"I don't know, but there isn't anything we can do about it now," Maddie said softly, wishing she could.

Farther in the distance, the Ivory Palace sat like a gothic castle that could be read about in one of Edgar Allan Poe's works. Only, it was a beautiful pearly white, its towers tall, multiple spires steepling the sky, the moat surrounding the grounds a sparkling silver. Sharp alabaster thorns covered the top along with ornate chess pieces circled with roses.

Nostalgia washed over Maddie, and she missed her home. Missed how she and Mouse would play games of chess with Ever in their spare time. Missed the celebrations the White Queen would have there, when Maddie would get lost in a lover, where Mouse would happily dance alone, while Ever would think of ways to make Wonderland better as she played her viola. Inside the palace now resided some of the guards who betrayed Ever— the others were turned unwillingly … just like in Scarlet. The kind that Ever wouldn't want. Due to their nature, Ever always said that draining a mortal dry was one thing, but turning them into something they didn't want was another.

"You all right?" Noah clasped Maddie's hand, his warmth

pulling her out of her staring spell.

Maddie shook off the feeling. "I'll be fine. Now, come on. We'll stay on the outskirts of Ivory."

They distanced themselves from the city, stalking the edge of the forest, the buildings vaguely taking shape in the distance.

Her hunger wasn't there, but Maddie forced down the powdered mixture of blood and water. Neither she nor Noah spoke too much so they could hear if someone drew too near, the way Chess had. But nothing besides forest creatures made any noise.

The darkness started to lighten and morning would arrive soon. A glistening lake slid into view and Maddie's shoulders relaxed.

"We're here." She sighed, studying the waterfall, the white flowers and pale grass surrounding it, the clusters of trees creating a canopy feel.

"This is probably the most beautiful thing I've seen here," Noah said, stepping to the edge of the lake.

"Maybe one day you'll get to see the rest of Ivory. There are much prettier lakes. Trust me." But then she remembered he was going home, and that she wasn't allowed to venture freely through Ivory anyway.

Maddie halted next to a waist-high boulder. She pressed her hands against its rough surface and pushed hard until it rolled out of the way.

Retrieving her keys from her backpack, she found the one she was looking for, then ran her fingers across the pale grass. "Aha," she sang.

"An interesting place for a safe house." Noah knelt beside her. "And smart."

"Indeed." Maddie grinned while pushing the key inside the lock and turning it with a small click. "Home sweet home for the night. If you want to take a quick rinse beforehand, now's your chance. Be fast."

Maddie stood and peeled off her arm sleeves, followed by the rest of her clothing while Noah stared up at her. "I said fast, immortal." She arched a brow.

"Oh, right." Noah bit his lip, lifting his shirt over his head, exposing his ripped abdomen. He unfastened his trousers and Maddie reminded herself that she didn't have time to sit and stare either. They needed to hurry before anyone spotted them. But she couldn't stop her mind from drifting to the night before, his fingers in her, her hands on him, the taste of his sweet flesh against her tongue.

A small squeak released from her lips when the freezing water brushed her skin. She quickly washed away the dirt and grime of the past couple days as best she could.

"Anything dangerous in the water?" Noah asked when he slipped in beside her.

"Not in this one." As she took a step, a sharp pain pierced her foot and she grimaced. "Bloody hell, I mean, yes. But not creatures. Just watch where you step."

"What happened?"

When she opened her mouth to answer, a loud noise, *howling,* not too far away, roared through the air. Then another and another, reverberating in the forest, shaking the trees, rumbling the ground.

"Well, that's it for bathing." Maddie pursed her lips and yanked on Noah's arm, tugging him to the edge of the lake. "Get in the safe house!"

They darted from the lake, not bothering to get dressed as they grabbed their belongings. Maddie threw open the hatch and they scurried inside, an earthy scent hitting her senses. She then pulled down the door and locked it, a sigh escaping her. They should've just come in here to begin with. The noises from outside weren't as loud … for now.

Silvery stone stairs glistened and led straight to a large space filled with crates stacked in the corner, holding packets of dried blood, same as in the other safe houses. Besides that, the room was bare except for a mattress—with a few folded blankets resting on it—against a wall.

Maddie set her things on the stone floor and tossed Noah

one of the fur blankets before wrapping herself in another. She plopped down on the mattress and scooted back to the wall.

"Thank you again," Noah said, taking a seat beside her. "For coming with me, even though you are, apparently, a fugitive here. If I had known you were in more danger than what we're heading toward, I would've thought twice about asking you to come."

Lovely immortal... But he still would've had to ask because he wouldn't have been able to do it on his own. Maddie waved him off, her teeth chattering. "It's fine."

"You're shivering," Noah whispered, his face concerned. "Share with me instead—body heat will help." He shifted forward and opened his blanket for her.

As her shivering continued, she couldn't deny him or herself the chance to get warmer. She dropped her own fur and let her body mold to his flesh as she tucked herself into his side, absorbing his heat. He drew her close, then leaned them both back against the wall while holding her tight.

Maddie's arm draped around his stomach, and his muscles stiffened—she knew he was getting aroused.

"What made you want to create hats?" Noah asked, fracturing the silence, as if trying to distract himself for the moment.

"Ah, a subject I could talk about all day, immortal." Maddie smiled. "It's the one thing I'm good at, and lucky for me, it's something I love. I like creating pieces that are unusual but beautiful." She bit her lip and stared up at his bright green irises. "What do you like doing?"

Noah tilted his head up and peered at the stone ceiling. "Before coming here, I made coffee, but I didn't love it. I really don't know what I want to do, if I'm being honest. I'll be finishing college soon. My parents want me to take over their business one day. It's not something I'm interested in, though. I used to want to make movies when I was younger or write books, but my parents said it was a waste of time, that it wasn't a sure way of making money."

"I would read your book." Maddie grinned. A book was an

extraordinary way of getting into one's mind, even more so than talking to them.

"Maybe when this is over, I'll help you sell your hats." Noah chuckled. "We could be hat dealers or some shit."

"A lovely plan." Except he wouldn't be staying in Wonderland, and she wouldn't be living in the mortal world. The thought made her hand slip, unintentionally brushing between his legs. She brought it back up to his abdomen, an unstoppable heat spreading through her.

"So," Noah drawled. "About last night… I haven't done anything like that in a while with anyone who wasn't my girlfriend."

Maddie's heart stilled, her stomach sinking as she thought of all the times she had. "I've never had a boyfriend. I've always just been needed when needed, I suppose."

He turned her face so their gazes met, his holding hers steady. "You deserve better than that."

Something about that one small sentence, the sincere look on his face, sent a rush of emotions barreling through her, causing her heart to flutter. Then she did the one thing she hadn't planned on doing. Her mouth collided with his. And he didn't hesitate to kiss her back. His lips tasted like vanilla, his tongue akin to sweet honey. She could drink his flavor for eternity and never grow tired of it. Not then, not ever.

Maddie hesitantly pulled back and rested her forehead against his shoulder. "Thank you for those words."

"I meant them," he whispered.

A new emotion coursed through her veins, spreading to each nerve, each fiber. An untamable desire. "Do you want to help each other again tonight?" Her voice came out husky.

"Very much."

In answer, she maneuvered herself so she was in his lap, her legs cradling his strong thighs. Her breath hitched as his hard length nestled perfectly between her slickened folds.

Maddie's heart accelerated when she pressed her lips to Noah's, his hands hugging her waist, his fingers digging deliciously into her flesh. As her tongue entwined with his, she rolled her hips forward, and her eyelids fluttered at the delectable pleasure. She continued to slide up and down his cock, releasing moan after moan. Their kisses deepened, tasting everything they could from one another. Noah groaned when her pace picked up, the friction growing stronger. One of his hands skimmed up her spine and entangled with her wet curls. He wasn't inside her, but it felt just as good—she was already too close to ecstasy and didn't want to stop.

And then a feeling rose, a sense of something she wanted to catch and hold onto. The sensation spread and built within her until everything shattered, everything becoming liquid, including her heart, at the heightened euphoria. In that moment, she yearned to have Noah feel better than good, so she took her mouth from his and trailed kisses down his throat, his chest, his abdomen, until she was at his hardened length. Maddie wanted him to come the way she just had.

"Fuck," he rasped when she took him into her mouth. His groaning turned into animalistic growls as her tongue circled the head of his cock and then let him go deeper. Slow. Fast. Faster. She sucked and licked and pumped, stroking him to his base. His hips lifted slightly while she worked him, relishing in the intimacy, until his body tightened, quaked, and he murmured her name over and over. Noah's cum tasted just as good as his mouth—every part of him did. Her fangs itched to lower, to take in the flavor of his immortal blood.

Noah drew her up, his fingers lifting her chin as he kissed her lips softly once more. "That was the best I've ever had."

No one had ever told her that before either... Not about anything besides her hats.

"Do you want me to get your clothing?" she asked, peeling herself from his body and sitting beside him.

"No," he whispered, drawing her close.

"Me neither." She folded herself around him, both of them nestled against the wall, their breaths heavy. Neither sleeping nor talking, but as she pressed her hand over his chest and felt his heart beating, it seemed to say *everything*.

CHAPTER SIXTEEN

NOAH

Growls and booming footsteps had shaken the walls of the safe house after Noah and Maddie had taken care of each other the night before. The sounds kept him up despite Maddie's assurance that they wouldn't be found, yet the noises hadn't prepared him for the paw prints in the mud outside the boulder. He froze. Dozens of them dotted the shore of the lake, each as big as his hand. With deep claws.

"What caused these?" he asked, already knowing the answer as he studied the prints.

"Werewolves," Maddie answered matter-of-factly. "Their territory isn't far now and they like to swim in the lake."

And she'd suggested he bathe in it? Well, dip into the water. He'd barely gotten wet before the howling began. "So…" He sprinted over the prints to follow Maddie. "How large are these beasts exactly?"

Maddie let out a chuckle and shrugged. "Big enough."

Noah had seen plenty of movies about the creatures but they

were very inconsistent with the lore. He wasn't sure how he imagined the ones in Wonderland. Now though? He imagined them as fucking petrifying.

"Come along," Maddie said as he subconsciously fell behind. "It's only another two miles or so. Just over that ridge."

Noah squinted into the distance where the ground rose into a slight silver crest. Without stopping, he slid his backpack down and removed the gun Maddie had given him. There was no bloody way he was chancing a werewolf encounter without it. After a quick check to make sure the safety was still on, he stuffed it into the waistband of his trousers.

As he slung the bag back over his shoulders, he caught Maddie staring at him. More specifically, at his stomach where the bottom of his shirt caught on the handle of the gun, showing a sliver of skin. "What?"

"Nothing," she said, arching a brow.

A knowing grin curled his lips as he fixed the fabric to hide the weapon. She liked the way his body looked—that much he knew—but it seemed as though she was remembering their time together last night. The way she slid her wet folds over his length nearly drove him wild with the desire for more. If the way she had moved was any indication of how she would ride him with his cock buried deep inside her, it would be otherworldly. And then she'd taken him into her mouth... It wasn't only that he enjoyed what she did with her body either. He was getting more attached. Every day she grew on him a little more, and knowing himself, it was only a matter of time before he would want more than sex. Once he and Alice were cured, he would be leaving though … he needed to remember that. Remember the way her tongue flicked over the tip of his cock, her hand pumping him, and—*enough*. He swallowed hard at the memory and forced his mind in another direction.

Monsters. Soon they would face them in order to get the cure and he had no interest in doing so with a stiff dick.

"How long do you think it will take to get the cure once we reach the swamp?" he whispered in case any enemies still lurked near the lake. They likely had heightened senses just like Noah. He was willing to bet their sense of smell was even better than a vampire's.

Maddie chewed her bottom lip before answering, "Depends."

"On…?" he prompted when she didn't elaborate.

"How long it takes to find where it is, how much interference we receive, and many other things, I suppose." She scowled. "No one has ever mentioned how far apart the landmarks are. First, we have to find the giant fang. Then we go left until we reach the floating baskets, and finally swim toward the east until we see the glowing fish. A landmass with a lake is there—the cure will be at the bottom."

Well, that didn't seem very encouraging. The last thing he wanted to find in a swamp full of beasts was a fang. "Why would the werewolves keep it hidden if they hate vampires so much? Why not let you cure yourselves?"

Maddie opened her mouth and paused, shooting him a perplexed expression. "That's a good question."

"Don't sound so surprised." He nudged her shoulder playfully as a low rumble sounded in the distance.

"We should be quiet from here on," she whispered and retrieved her own gun from her bag.

Every step closer they took toward the ridge—and the wolves living beyond that—the faster Noah's heart pounded. Random trees sprouted along the rocky landscape. Someone had arranged boulders and smaller stones into spiraling circles or, for all Noah knew, maybe they were just naturally arranged that way. It was admirable either way, and if the circumstances weren't so shitty, he would've ventured closer to check them out.

The walk didn't take nearly as long as he'd hoped, but as Maddie led him to the crest of the ridge, relief washed over him. He was so close to saving Alice.

Remember why you're doing this.

Easier thought than done.

He glared down at the pristine swampland, silver, twisting

trees sprouting from crystal-clear water. Clumps of what appeared to be white algae floated in patches, and a stagnant scent tainted with a hint of wet dog permeated the air. Noah rubbed at his nose, the odor overpowering him.

Maddie tapped his arm and motioned for him to follow her. She took quick, light steps down the incline, and he followed, the weight of foreboding growing every minute. They were in the open, wearing dark colors against the bright white landscape, without an ounce of coverage to hide in. But he needed to trust Maddie. She wouldn't risk their mission or their lives, especially if it would affect saving her sister.

When they finally hit level ground again, she leapt through the tacky mud until they reached a large, light gray boulder. They darted behind it and peeked over the top. Noah sucked in a harsh breath at the sight of werewolf homes. Or what he assumed were their homes. Twisted, woven branches formed dozens of floating domes at least eight feet tall that resembled wolf dens. In one of the nearest, a gray tail flopped out of the round opening.

A rumbling growl—of annoyance more so than warning—prompted Noah to remove the gun from his waistband. He hoped the damn beast was having a nightmare. But that was probably just wishful thinking.

Maddie nudged him again and pointed to a moss-covered path on their right that led through the swamp. She held a finger to her lips and crept out from their hiding place. Noah tiptoed behind her, his gaze sweeping side to side. From another one of the floating dens, a large brown snout, slightly open, poked out, revealing teeth as long and wide as his fingers.

Oh, we're fucked…

The beast also seemed to be asleep, heavy breaths coming out in lazy huffs, but not all of the dens appeared occupied, which meant the residents had to be lurking around somewhere. Under their feet, silver bugs buzzed where they crawled, appearing like tiny pebbles, and claw marks scarred the trees. Some were fresh, others more violent. One trunk was nearly clawed in half, the top leaning on a neighboring branch for support.

The deeper they traveled into enemy territory, the more frequently they witnessed the signs of werewolves. Bones jutted from the pathways, snapped and crushed, and a severed human leg floated in the water. A gym shoe still lingered on the foot and frayed denim clung to the rest of the limb. Slivers of flesh peeked out near the top, black by decay.

Maddie grabbed Noah's wrist and pointed excitedly to a tall tree stump, covered in old scratches. At some point, long ago, judging by how weathered the exposed innards were, the tree had been sliced in half at an angle to resemble a …

A fang.

It did look like one, even if a little lopsided. They turned left and the path narrowed. Noah fell in line behind Maddie, his heart pounding harder as he wiped the sweat from his forehead. She had mentioned the next landmark would be floating baskets, so he turned his gaze to the water. A low growl filled the air, followed by a yelp, and he clutched the gun tighter. The sound hadn't come from the immediate area, but that didn't mean the predators weren't lurking nearby.

A few minutes later, Maddie screeched to a halt without warning, and Noah slammed into her back. He swung around, searching for danger, but instead of a werewolf crouched to attack, his eyes landed on metal cages. Massive cages. Big enough for him and Maddie to fit inside together and still have room to move about. Thank fuck they were empty, though it didn't make him feel any better. If they were caught, would they end up in a cage as a snack for later? He unconsciously grabbed Maddie's hand.

She squeezed it and shifted closer to him. He caught a hint of her sweet cherry scent, and it instantly took the edge off his nerves. Next, they were meant to swim. If he hadn't seen so many fucked-up things in Wonderland already, he would've questioned the idea of these glowing fish they had to find.

As Noah lowered his gaze to the ivory, blood-stained swamp,

he second-guessed doing so. If the floating body parts weren't enough of a deterrent, the potential creatures living in the water were. He regretted not asking Maddie about that when she'd mentioned it earlier. But he would brave it regardless, for Alice, so he supposed it didn't matter.

Maddie tugged on his arm, and he froze at the worried expression on her face. "What?" he whispered.

She put a finger to her lips, then nodded at something in front of them. When he looked up, following her line of sight, he found two trees growing on a large oval patch of land. And between them, another cage. This one on the ground with only the corner peeking out from between the trunks. He tilted his head in confusion. What did it matter if there was another cage? They needed to keep moving because their luck had been *far* too good today.

An arm flopped out from between the bars and Noah jerked in surprise. *Shit.* There was someone in there.

"Hello?" a youthful voice called.

Noah shifted closer to Maddie and shook his head. It was too risky—they had no idea who was in that cage or why.

"We see you," said a second, equally youthful voice. "Please help us."

They'll call attention to us if they keep yelling, she mouthed silently to Noah.

It wouldn't matter if he and Maddie got the hell away from the cage. They had to get into the water anyway and that would mask their scent. *Maybe they're werewolves in human form,* he mouthed back.

Maddie shook her head. "The full moon was last week and that's the only time they turn human."

"Hurry!" they shouted in unison, but they didn't seem frantic. It sounded like a trap.

"Maddie, no," he whispered almost silently.

"Trust me." She pulled away from him to tiptoe toward the cage. Noah quickly glanced around and rushed after her. *The cure.* They didn't have time to be damn heroes.

When they reached the cage, they found two young boys, no older than twelve, in striped T-shirts with shaggy, matted red hair. They hadn't bathed in months, if the way they smelled were an indication. Like onions and wet dog—though the latter could be because *everything* smelled like wet dog here. Bits of gnawed bones littered the bottom of the cage as the boys—obviously twins—peered out at them.

"Shh," Maddie warned them. "What are you doing in there?"

Noah was sure that whatever put them in there was lurking in the vicinity, but he wasn't sure how far away they were. He didn't hear any rustling close or farther away.

"I'm Dee, and this is Dom," the toothless one on the left said. "We got stuck in our human form after the last moon."

Noah scowled. "So they put you in a cage?"

Maddie inched closer. "We're looking for the cure to vampirism. Do you know which way the glowing fish are?"

"Let us out and we'll show you." Dom perked up, his eyes glistening. "Please, let us out. They'll *eat* us."

Eat their own kind? Even if they were stuck as humans, someone here had to be their family. And they were young. Sure, werewolves were monsters, but this was next-level brutality. A short howl carried through the swamp followed by a slight grumble.

"Someone will catch your scent soon," Dee said.

Noah lifted his gun a little higher and glanced over his shoulder. Nothing was coming for them yet, but he didn't doubt that would change soon. "Maddie," he whispered under his breath. "We can't linger around here."

"We don't know which way to swim," Maddie told him. She then turned her attention to the twins and hesitated. "We'll let you out if you show us, then you can be on your way."

The brothers nodded, and Maddie took a pin from her hat. As she picked the lock with it, the boys exchanged a devious grin, and Noah stiffened. *Fuck.* He needed to remind himself that these were werewolf kids, not human ones. "Wait—" he started, but the door to the cage slid open.

The boys shoved each other in an attempt to escape their prison first. Maddie stepped aside and quietly closed the cage behind them. "Hurry then," she urged the twins.

"Maddie, I don't think this is a good idea." Noah grabbed her wrist and leaned closer to whisper in her ear. "I don't have a good feeling about them."

"Neither do I," she admitted. "But what choice do we have? If we left them there, they would probably have alerted someone to our presence as revenge. Be on your toes."

Noah side-eyed the twins. They could easily lead him and Maddie straight into a trap. Were they even telling the truth about being werewolves? He was pretty sure the odor would even cling to him after they left. But what if the children were bait for unsuspecting travelers? He clicked the safety off of his gun. The blast would wake every sleeping werewolf in the swamp, but if he needed to defend himself, he would.

"It's this way," Dee said. "It's time to swim."

At least they were telling the truth about that. Noah swallowed hard and waited for Maddie to go first so he could watch her back. As he eased from the path and into the water, goosebumps rose all over his body from the freezing liquid. Three steps away from land and the water drifted up to his abdomen. Maddie and the little bastards were already treading water. He followed suit, sinking into the liquid to swim while keeping the gun above the surface, then gasped when it lapped over his shoulders.

Maddie cut him a worried look at the sound, and he offered a stiff smile. Nothing about this felt right, but his sister was dying. There wasn't time to swim through the entire swamp, searching for glowing fish. He would kill whoever he had to in order to return to Scarlet in one piece with Maddie at his side.

CHAPTER SEVENTEEN

MADDIE

Maddie swam through the freezing water, her lungs aching with each shallow pull of breath. The twins, Dee and Dom, glided through the water, but a werewolf's body, whether they shifted into their beast form or not, produced enough heat to keep them warm.

After catching the twins' sneaky smiles, Maddie wanted to leave them in their cages. A werewolf, regardless of its age, was a deceitful thing. They weren't the darlings they pretended to be—she knew that. But as long as the little wolves led her and Noah to the cure, then there wouldn't be an issue.

A golden aura glowed within the water. The *fish*. Noah gave her a slight nod, catching sight of it too, while continuing to slice with his strong arms through the clear liquid.

Dee halted and treaded water before raising a hand, pointing to a landmass covered in cerulean trees with brown leaves and bright iridescent flowers. He mouthed at her, *This way*.

Maddie nodded, heart pounding, as she followed the fish's

flickering glow to the chunk of land. A scaly body brushed her ankle just before sharp teeth bit into her flesh. *Bloody hell.* She clenched her jaw to avoid making a sound and kicked at it, when another bite sliced into her wrist.

Noah growled but stopped—the demon fish must've attacked him too. She picked up her pace, shuttling past the golden carnivores.

Maddie neared the shore and peered up, her gaze connecting with Dee and Dom, standing at the edge of the shore. Pushing herself out of the water, she knelt forward to clasp Noah's hand. She dragged him to safety as a swarm of fish sailed to where they'd just been. They circled the empty water before scattering and fleeing when nothing lingered for them to attack.

Her chest heaved and water dripped down her body as she observed the area. A large glistening lake, the color and texture of milk, sat before them. No matter how hard she strained her eyes, Maddie couldn't see what rested below its surface. Curving landmasses, covered in blackened dirt, surrounded the mound she resided on, trailing to other areas in werewolf territory. Beneath her feet, brown grass shimmered like glass.

"Now what?" Noah asked, running a hand through his wet hair as he stared out at the lake. It wasn't as large as she'd expected, perhaps the size of several of her cottages stitched together.

"Go in and get your cure." Dom shrugged, propping his back against a tree and crossing his arms. His twin copied his movements, resting his head on a tree beside his brother.

"We can't see shit," Noah answered, frowning. "We don't know how deep it is."

"Go in and find out." Dee grinned, shrugging his gangly shoulders as his twin had.

Maddie narrowed her eyes at them. "We aren't both going in at the same time." She squinted, studying the area. If they both went into the lake, then no one would be out here standing watch.

"The lake's safe and you'll feel the mushrooms at the

bottom." Dee tilted his head to the side. "I would go in and retrieve the cure for you, but we did enough by leading you here already. We don't want your kind to have the cure because there's no cure for our own curse."

"It seems you're cured now," Noah grumbled. "Is that why they locked you up?"

"Our human form sickens us," Dom said with a sneer.

Dee nodded, lips curled in disgust. "We would prefer to stay beasts."

Noah arched a brow at them. He turned to Maddie and sighed. "Wait here while I go in. You have more experience in Wonderland and with weapons than I do. Besides, this is for my sister, so I should be the one to risk it. Not you."

Hesitancy coursed through Maddie, but if something happened or he didn't come back up, she could go in after him. Vampires couldn't die from drowning anyway. And from the few who survived to tell their story, their lost body parts hadn't gotten ripped off from anything inside the lake.

"Fine," she finally said. "But be quick, immortal."

Noah gave her a gentle smile and nodded, then removed his backpack from his shoulders and slipped his gun inside it. He leaned forward, softly pressing his mouth to hers. Her eyes widened as he stepped back and turned toward the lake. She placed her fingertips to her lips, her stomach fluttering.

The twins watched her as she mirrored Noah's earlier movements and took off her backpack in case she needed to dive in after him.

Once Noah had the mushrooms in his hand, they could take them back to Alice, and hopefully, after eating one, his sister would live.

Noah sank beneath the surface, and Maddie studied the twins, who exchanged smug looks. She scowled. Something wasn't right. As her suspicion grew, she peered back at the lake when a shrill whistle penetrated her ears, followed by another high-pitched noise.

Maddie whirled around, seething as she stared at the little

bastards. "What are you doing?"

"Sorry, bloodsucker." Dee giggled, pushing himself from the tree. "We needed to get back into our pack's good graces, so they'll help us get unstuck from this horrendous form."

"You, motherfuckers!" Maddie hissed, lunging forward to grip the back of their shirts as they bolted toward the swamp. But they were slippery things and ducked before diving into the water. The little chicken shits swam away, not giving a second glance in her direction.

She was prepared to go after them, but Noah still hadn't resurfaced. The twins' betrayal didn't surprise her in the least— they were werewolves, after all. At least she and Noah were at the cure's location—he just needed to hurry his arse up before something arrived and found them.

What if there were no mushrooms left at the bottom of the lake? There was always the chance there weren't any cures remaining, especially if she now knew why the werewolves didn't want vampires to have it. Maybe they'd destroyed the mushrooms themselves…

Angry growls broke through Maddie's thoughts, and she froze. Not just one or two—*many*. She jerked her head up as the land shook beneath her feet. Furred beasts, the colors of midnight, crimson, and tree bark, bounded her way, tearing across the land and swinging from trees. They hopped from landmass to landmass, headed straight for her from all directions.

Their frenzied roars grew stronger, boisterous, their shadowy shapes becoming defined as they drew closer. Maddie lifted her gun and fired a silver bullet, watching it rip through a crimson werewolf's throat. A gurgling howl escaped the beast's snout as it collapsed to the earth, its body quaking and disintegrating to fiery ash. Smoke billowed into the air.

Then she shot more and more, the savage beasts slamming to the ground. One through the eye, another the heart, the head, the stomach—each werewolf breaking into pieces. Her gun clicked—*empty*.

Maddie frantically fished out several cartridges from the front pouch of her backpack and reloaded with a click. Not in time, though, as a sharp pain pierced her back. She gasped, ignoring the throbbing and whirled around, coming face to face with an obsidian beast, its eyes the color of the orange sun in the mortal world—something she hadn't seen in so long. Blood leaked from its razor-sharp teeth as though it had come from another meal. She pulled the trigger, aiming straight through its open mouth while the beast roared, her hair flying around her cheeks. Hot blood splattered her face and she spun around, just as another werewolf swung from a tree branch and crashed in front of her. A bullet escaped her gun and struck true in its chest, blood blooming to the wound's surface before the beast fell to ash. These werewolves were about the size of one and a half of Noah—no matter how strong she was, she wouldn't be able to defeat them with her bare hands.

Bang. Bang. She continued blasting the beasts, when a splash echoed behind her. Maddie knew it was Noah by the sounds of his swimming, yet she didn't look back as she killed werewolf after werewolf.

Another gun fired from her right—*Noah*. Maddie wasn't certain if he hit his marks, but she didn't have time to check while shooting and reaching for more cartridges. She loaded and hurled bullets at werewolves on the landmasses farther away before they came nearer.

But the beasts wouldn't stop coming. It was like sewing an endless circle around and around a hat.

"We need to leave!" Maddie shouted, her heart almost breaking her rib cage as it thundered. "Those little twin bastards called their pack here. Did you get the mushrooms?"

"Yes, get in the swamp and go!"

She didn't just yet—she stayed shooting as he shoved the black and white striped mushrooms into his backpack. Maddie then grabbed her pack and jumped into the swamp, the freezing water wrapping its icy fingers around her once more, the glowing fish heading in her direction.

Maddie kicked her legs forward, dodging the bastard fish. She stayed below the surface for as long as she could until her lungs screamed for air.

Bursting through the surface, she gulped for oxygen. Noah trailed only a little way behind her, but the werewolves didn't stop as they launched their bodies into the water. Their growls reverberated across the swamp, but they were distracted by the golden fish. *Foolish beasts.* At least they were making a meal out of those for the moment, though.

She ignored the screeching pain of her back where the werewolf had struck her and glided forward, never relaxing her tight grip on the gun.

The patch from which they'd come slid into view, and she hurried to push herself out of the water as Noah followed. A werewolf leapt out from a tree and she shot, missing. She *never* missed. The beast soared toward them and, before she could pull the trigger again, Noah stepped between them. He brought his arm back and swung his fist, summoning every ounce of strength and speed he had, doubling down to do the most damage. Maddie steadied her finger on the trigger, waiting to fire. Noah's knuckles slammed into the side of the werewolf's head with a *crack.* Bright blood sprayed out from the wound as the body flew across the swamp, the beast's raging roars reverberating. Maddie fired, the silver bullet piercing the air, striking the werewolf's chest, just as its body splintered two trees in half. The beast landed in a shallow spot of water, its body convulsing before turning to smoke and ash. She didn't miss that time, but it was teamwork.

"Fuck!" Noah shouted, yanking her forward. "Let's hurry to Ivory."

She didn't know how many cartridges she had left in her backpack, but it wasn't enough to take out an entire territory of werewolves.

They sprinted down the winding path, past curving and gnarled trees, then ran through a narrow passage until just ahead, the familiar werewolf village came into view. The rows of cages glinted from the fiery posts, burning with orange flames at their tops. They slowed, treading silently behind trees so as not to draw any unwanted attention.

Her gaze fell to one of the largest werewolves she'd ever seen, bright ivory fur, its arms longer than its legs. The beast gripped two young males—Dee and Dom. Maddie grinned as the werewolf shoved the twins back into their cage. Dee scowled while Dom spouted curses.

Ah, so the little weasels didn't get the help they so desired. Maddie inwardly chuckled. The werewolf slammed the door to the cage shut, then thrashed across the ground in the direction Maddie and Noah had come from.

Once the beast was out of sight, she and Noah hurried across the land and back through the waist-deep swamp. Crows cawed from above while they trekked through the thick bog, until finally, out and away from the putrid smells, silvery trees interlacing with ivory ones appeared.

"Thank fuck," Noah rasped, placing his empty hand at his chest, the other still clenching the gun.

"The territory line won't stop all of them from entering Ivory. The bad apples will cross," she said, glancing behind her, the coast clear for now.

As the adrenaline left her veins, Maddie stumbled. She peered down at her skin, paler than usual.

"Your back!" Noah's eyes widened.

"I'm fit as a fiddle," she slurred, losing too much blood from the gashes on her back. Before she could say anything else, Maddie collapsed into Noah's arms.

CHAPTER EIGHTEEN

NOAH

"Rest," Noah encouraged Maddie. After she'd collapsed into his arms, he'd carried her back to the safe house in Ivory beside the lake in case any werewolves followed. Once she was safely off her feet, he swung the soaking wet bag from his back and unzipped it. "Blood will help, right?"

Maddie let out a weary breath. "I'm fine, really."

"If that were true, you wouldn't have nearly fainted," he said as he pulled out a sealed pouch of dried blood. Ripping open the plastic, he poured some into a half empty bottle of water. If she needed more, he would have to chance stepping outside to the lake.

The smell of the mixed blood pricked at his own hunger. After all their running and fighting, he'd built up an appetite. And the mushrooms had been *deep* in that lake. Dozens had been spread out across the mossy floor, so far apart that, once he was far enough down to reach, he'd struggled to make it from one to another. He'd spotted at least two headless human-like skeletons at the bottom from where vampires must've failed. Logically, he knew he couldn't drown, but that hadn't made the burning in his lungs any easier to bear. Most likely, the dead vampires had been killed before going into the water.

"Stop exaggerating, immortal." Maddie rolled her eyes. "My legs simply gave out for a moment."

Noah wasn't entirely sure if that were true given the huge gashes on her back. But she knew herself better than he did. As vampires, they healed differently. That didn't make him feel any better about her getting hurt so badly. It was his fault she was on this journey. He put the cap back on the bottle and shook it until the powder was fully dissolved. "Will this be enough?" he asked, handing it over to her.

"For now." She wasted no time bringing the bottle to her lips and downing the liquid.

"Maddie?" He cleared his throat. "I'm sorry."

She paused her drinking just long enough to ask, "For what?"

"Asking you to come along. If it weren't for me, you wouldn't have been injured."

She rolled her eyes as she guzzled the last few drops of blood. "Let's not waste our breath on that. More importantly, we can't stay long. If they follow our scent here, they'll leave someone near the lake to keep watch. Getting ahead of them is the only way to avoid another fight."

"As soon as you're well enough," Noah agreed. He didn't want to face the werewolves again but if they left too soon, Maddie might not be strong enough to fight or escape. However, he did have to admit using his strength to defend her and himself made him feel unstoppable. With the power to send a werewolf through trees from a single punch, was there anything he *couldn't* do?

She handed him the empty bottle and shifted as if testing her wounds. "Most importantly, you got the mushrooms."

Noah nodded and lifted them out of his bag to inspect. They were large, black and white striped, with wavy gills underneath. The stem of one had snapped—though still attached—in their escape, but the second appeared fine. Why hadn't he ignored the pain and grabbed more while he was down there? As many as he could hold. If they didn't need more than one each, Maddie could've sold the others to anyone interested and used the money to set her and Mouse up somewhere safe, somewhere far away from Scarlet.

"May I see them?" Maddie asked.

Noah carefully set the fungi into her waiting hand. "Interesting," she mused. "So frail a thing can make a vampire mortal again."

"Do we eat them like this or cook them?" he asked. Maybe there was something they needed to add in order to unlock the curing properties. "Or is there more to the process?"

"I believe you simply eat them, however, it might be hard to get them down. Solid food can be difficult to stomach. Such a change can't come without some discomfort, I suppose." She handed them to him. "You can't eat it yet though."

Noah's heart lurched painfully in his chest. "What do you mean? Alice will die if—"

"Of course, Alice needs hers right away," she amended. "We are *both* going to save our sisters, but you must wait for yours. You can't help me with Mouse if you're human again," she reasoned.

"I understand that." He wouldn't stand a chance fighting vampires unless he was one too. Being an immortal felt natural, maybe even more so than when he was human—he was in no rush to give up his new abilities. "I promise not to take it until we rescue Mouse." They'd struck a deal, and he had no intention of going back on his word. More than that, he wanted to make Maddie happy. To see her reunited with the sister she loved so much.

"Let's head out." Maddie blew out a breath and stood.

Noah eased out of his crouched position. He stretched, loosening his muscles now that the adrenaline was wearing off. His fist ached a bit from punching the werewolf, but it was worth it to save their lives. To save *her* life.

"After you," he told her with a renewed energy. Their goal was accomplished and they'd both survived to tell the tale. Now he could save Alice, too.

Maddie snuck back to the entrance of the safe house and inched the door open, sticking her head out briefly. Noah took note of the already healing wounds showing through the rips in the back of her dress. They were barely more than cat scratches now.

"All clear," she whispered a moment later and exited the house.

Noah followed her and strained his ears, listening for danger. His pulse quickened as they raced from the lake, putting as much distance between them and werewolf territory as possible. Without Maddie to lead the way, he would've gotten lost in Ivory, as he'd put too much attention into glancing over his shoulder and not enough to the path before them. So, when she stopped, he didn't notice and ran straight into her.

Maddie stumbled forward a step and tilted her head in confusion. "Look."

The trees with splashes of crimson loomed ahead, far too familiar, but that wasn't what had his brows rising. One tree in particular was worrisome—the one with torn rope littering the ground at its base and no snarky, yellow-eyed arsehole in sight.

"Fuck," he hissed.

"It was never going to hold him for long," Maddie said wistfully. "His Royal Bastard has a tendency to lurk around though."

Noah immediately peered up as if Chess would be there. He wasn't, of course, but that didn't mean he wasn't close, maybe waiting to spring a trap on them. *Let him try.* Noah just helped fight off an entire pack of werewolves—he could handle one cocky vampire. "Let's get out of here."

Maddie adjusted her backpack. "It's not too far to the safe house, so we'll stop there for a bit."

Now that they had the cure, he didn't want to wait another night to give it to Alice, but she *was* still far. After escaping the werewolves, the adrenaline wore off and his entire body ached. "Okay," he said. "But only for a few hours."

Maddie led the way back to the safe house in the tree, passing different species of Wonderland creatures, some with sharp teeth and others with curving beaks. The crows studied them as they passed but remained in the trees.

Once they reached their destination, Maddie fished the key from the front of her pack to open the door. They descended the steps, the familiar pine scent hitting his nose.

She flopped onto the ground at the bottom of the stairs with a low groan. "I could sleep for days."

"Hours," Noah insisted.

"I know, I know," she said. "And I have a hat to make."

Noah eased down beside her and yawned, closing his eyes. The urge to wrap an arm around Maddie and tug her against him rose. *Fuck*. He was never into cuddling before… His feelings for her were changing, already becoming deeper. But soon he would be leaving, right? Taking Alice and returning home as a mortal. The thought settled uncomfortably inside him as his mind drew closer to sleep.

Just when he nearly drifted off, the weight of Maddie's head pressed on his shoulder. His lips curled into a smile as he turned his head to rest on hers. It didn't matter what he did tomorrow or a week from now… Tonight, he was alive thanks to this vampire and she was beside him—apparently, with the same urge to be closer together. Noah wrapped his arm around her shoulders, letting her settle into him even more.

"Hey," Maddie whispered. "Wake up."

Noah cracked his eyes open to find her hovering over him. His pulse quickened at the sight of her, and he wanted to brush the hair from her face. Unconsciously, his hand lifted, doing just that as a warmth for her filled his chest. He wanted to pull her closer, wrap his arm around her and—reality blasted through him. "Shit." He leapt up and grabbed his bag from the floor. "How long were we asleep?"

"Three hours," Maddie said with a shrug. "Give or take."

That wasn't bad… But it had only felt like five minutes. "Is something wrong?"

"Why would something be wrong?" She cocked her head, brows lowered in confusion.

"Because werewolves are probably hunting us down and the queen's hell-spawn escaped the tree that *we tied him to.*"

Maddie laughed. "The werewolves won't follow us into Scarlet. Well, not *those* werewolves. Just the regular old renegades that sneak into the city."

Noah wasn't sure why that was any better, but they'd been fine in Scarlet so far, if he discounted his attempted murder and being turned into a vampire. He hadn't seen a single werewolf before they'd waltzed into their territory, but that didn't change anything regarding Chess. He probably had already told his mother about the encounter. They could be walking straight into the queen's guards on the way back.

"Come on." She patted his shoulder, their eyes meeting. A tiny spark lit, igniting something in him. He wanted to capture her lips with his, feel every inch of her against him. But the spell broke when she spoke again. "We need to get back before Ferris thinks we were eaten."

This time, after Maddie re-locked the safe house, Noah urged her to keep a faster pace. Hours passed before the familiar red-glowing lanterns appeared on the horizon, and he was eager to give Alice the cure.

Vampires roamed the streets in large groups, all of them wearing a variety of black lace, velvet, and dark makeup. They laughed and spoke in loud, boisterous voices, and if they weren't in Wonderland, Noah would've thought they were normal friends heading to the club. Maybe they *were* going to a club in the mortal world like Rav had when he'd found Alice.

"This way," Maddie whispered, tugging him down darker

alleys and away from the crowds. "Almost th—"

"Look who it is," a familiar voice drawled. Noah whirled around to find Chess striding up behind them. "The little schemer and her new pet."

"Ah, fuck," Noah hissed, and Maddie squeezed his arm.

The prince was a few feet away, then in the next instant, right in their faces with his fangs bared. "You tied me to a tree."

"You tied us to each other," Maddie countered.

"And I'll do it again," he sneered.

Maddie cocked her head and grinned. "How about with chiffon this time?"

"Chess!" A female gave a high-pitched squeal and he winced. "I would recognize that arse anywhere."

The prince spun on his heel. "Ari. I'm a bit busy right now."

Using the distraction to their advantage, Maddie ripped Noah out of the alley, and they ran as fast as their superspeed could take them. Weaving in and out of side streets, dodging around vampires who got in their way. They sprinted past a female vampire who had her fangs buried in the forearm of an elderly man, his head thrown back in pleasure. The scent of blood tinged the air and Noah's body tightened. His hunger surged. *Almost there*, he told himself as they made it the final block to the safe house.

Maddie banged a rhythm on the door so hard that Noah knew someone would notice. Sweat poured down the back of his neck as he scanned the streets, waiting for Chess to appear out of nowhere again. If he did, he'd punch the fucker in the face.

The door swung open and Maddie fell forward, straight into Ferris's chest. She quickly drew him to the side so Noah could leap in and slam the door shut.

"What the fuck?" Ferris asked. "You both look like hell."

"It's a long story," Maddie said with a carefree wave of her hand. "Is Alice still alive?"

Noah was already at her bedroom door when Ferris answered, "Yes." He pushed inside and found Alice curled under a heavy blanket. Her hair was plastered to her head with sweat, her teeth chattered, and her eyes appeared sunken and bruised. It had only been a handful of days, but she looked so much worse than before.

"Alice?" he whispered, kneeling beside the mattress, and set the back of his hand against her forehead. Her skin burned his palm as though she were on fire. "Alice, I'm back. We got the cure."

Maddie unzipped the bag that was still on his back and, a moment later, held out one of the mushrooms. "Here," she said softly.

"Thank you." Noah took it from her and gently shook Alice awake. She blinked her bright blue eyes open but they were dull, lifeless. She was almost gone... He could see it, *smell* it. The sweet scent of death clung to her like a second skin. "Alice, you need to eat this."

"I'm not hungry," she croaked, her glazed eyes fixed on the ceiling.

"It doesn't matter," he said, bringing the mushroom to her lips. "Just eat this for me. Please. You'll become human again."

Alice opened her mouth just wide enough to get the edge of the mushroom between her teeth. She chewed and swallowed with slow, laborious movements.

"More," Noah urged. He continued to feed her one tiny bite at a time until the mushroom was gone. An eternity passed before Alice managed to finish the cure while Maddie watched from the doorway with Ferris. Now that it was done … why was nothing happening? "Alice?"

She rolled onto her back and arched her spine with a pained groan.

Noah leapt to his feet. "What's going on?"

"I told you it's hard to keep solid food down," Maddie said. "She has to digest it."

"Can one of you get her a cool, wet rag for her head?" He wouldn't ask for a bucket, though he worried Alice might need one. If she threw up, then she wouldn't get the full effect of the cure, and he refused to accept that. His sister was not dying. She had too much life left—too many years of living without their parents' interference. Their mother's expression when Alice showed up for Christmas completely decked out in her new style would be priceless as it always was. His sister needed to survive so she could truly live.

Ferris passed Noah a damp cloth, and he hurried to press it against Alice's forehead as she writhed. "You'll be okay," he told her even though he had no fucking clue if it was a lie. "Everything will be all right."

"Digestion could take a few hours," Maddie said in a solemn voice. "Ferris and I will be in the other room if you need us."

Noah nodded and flipped the rag over, swiping strands of Alice's stray hair away from her face. A few hours felt like a lifetime, but he wouldn't leave her side until he knew if the cure worked. "When this is all over, we should get you that parrot you've always wanted." They'd never been allowed pets—not even a goldfish—but he wanted to give her something to look forward to. "We can teach it how to swear in as many languages as you want. Then we should host a family dinner."

The briefest flicker of a smile ghosted Alice's lips before twisting into a grimace again. Noah wiped the sweat from her face and neck with the cloth. "I saw that smirk," he joked.

CHAPTER NINETEEN

MADDIE

The transition from a vampire to a human would be a teensy bit more difficult than the original swap from mortal to immortal. Maddie had heard the rumors, but hadn't seen a transition first-hand. Apparently, she wouldn't now either since there was another task to complete. In only a few days' time, Maddie would deliver the headpiece to Her Royal Heart-Stealing Highness. Maddie needed to start on the delightful hat-making chore *now*, and she would finish it tonight to get it out of the way.

"I don't know about this, Maddie," Ferris said, rubbing the back of his neck as he studied her beneath thick lashes.

"Just draw me the Ruby Heart Palace's floor map leading to Mouse's cell." She patted his shoulder with a smile. "That's all I need."

With a sigh, he retrieved a notebook and pen from his room. He ripped out a sheet and sat on the sofa, then sketched a rather quick yet intricate drawing. His strokes were detailed, and she spotted the sitting room of the palace right away.

Maddie arched a brow and sat beside him. "It looks like you're good at more than drums. You never told me you could draw."

"Mouse knows. I snuck her drawings while in the palace." He shrugged before handing her the map. "Don't get your arse killed."

Maddie glanced at the closed door where Noah lingered with his sister. He seemed to be comforting Alice as she groaned in pain. Maddie had risked her life to help him save his sister. Now she would be risking his to help get Mouse. To distract Imogen, she only needed the hat, and she should've come up with a plan like this a long time ago. If something did go wrong with Noah there, she didn't want him trapped in the palace like her sister, not after getting to know him.

She pulled the second mushroom from her skirt pocket, her heart speeding up, demanding this of her. When she'd collected the one for Alice from Noah's backpack, she'd taken the second one, knowing what she had to do, what Mouse would want her to do, what Maddie *chose* to do. Pushing herself up from the settee, she inspected its stripes for a moment.

"No," Ferris said. "Not after you just risked your life for that wanker."

Maddie smirked and tossed Ferris the mushroom. He easily caught it as she said, "Give him this when he comes out and keep him safe until I return. Besides, I owe him. I did try and take Alice to Imogen." Her stomach sank at the thought of what may have happened to Alice, the torture that would've been inflicted upon her before her death. But Maddie had been desperate.

Ferris rolled his eyes and drew Maddie into a hug. "You don't owe him shite."

In case this was the last time she would see Ferris, she squeezed him tighter, more so than usual. "Remember, if I don't come back, then you'll have to find another way to help Mouse."

"I'll never stop trying," he murmured.

Maddie released Ferris and collected her things before heading out into the heavy fog. She couldn't tell Noah goodbye—it was better for him to focus on his sister. As she trekked home, the metal odor in the air was more potent than usual, and she made sure to keep her eyes peeled for Chess or Rav. Thankfully, she didn't come across either bastard, only trails of vampire blood and a couple of fingers resting in the grass, most likely more fighting. She missed the serenity of Ivory—the city needed Ever back.

The red lanterns guided her, the fog growing heavier when she reached her cottage. She unlocked her front door and slipped inside her cozy home. It felt as if she'd been gone forever. Kicking off her boots and tearing away her filthy clothing, she made her way to the bathroom and took a quick rinse.

"Much better," Maddie sang to herself as she put on a fresh dress with a poufy silk skirt, then padded into the sitting room.

Blowing out a breath, she collapsed on the chair in front of her desk. She drank a blood bag, wishing she had something warmer, but it made do for now.

Maddie collected her needle and thread, along with the supplies for Imogen's hat. Lace. Tulle. Felt. Wool. Paint. All ivory to remind Imogen of Ever, besides for the splash of crimson paint to show that the White Queen's heart bled with a revenge that would soon come. Even without Noah, the plan would still work. Once Imogen was distracted, Maddie would bind the queen's hands behind her back, tape her mouth shut, and toss her in one of the closets while she retrieved Mouse. The thought of Imogen's face as her gaze settled on the headpiece sent a rush of giddiness through Maddie.

Her fingers itched to begin when a knock sounded at the door. She sighed, just knowing it would be one of the royal bastards.

Pulling open the speakeasy, her gaze met Chess's sparkling yellow irises. "I'm not letting you in," Maddie said.

He took a step closer, his voice coming out light. "Then I'll break down the fucking door."

"Try." If he did, it would give her an advantage to easily have a weapon ready when he crashed through it.

"If I wanted you dead, I would've killed you in the forest."
He grinned. "We weren't finished talking earlier, so play nice and
open the door before I get my mother involved."

Bloody hell. Maddie could handle this bastard for a few more
days, so she let him in.

"Well, go on then. What do you want?" Maddie closed the
door behind him as he stepped inside.

Chess smirked and stopped near the settee, his gaze sweeping
across the room. "Where's your lover?"

"Finding us dessert in the mortal world." At least this time,
Noah wasn't here to put a damper in her plan and get himself in
a predicament.

"Ah." Chess tapped her nose, then whispered, "I know a
secret, little plum."

Maddie narrowed her eyes, unsure what Chess was getting at.
He always danced around the subject, so this was nothing new.
But there was an emotion in his expression, as though he *did*
know something. "I don't care about your secrets."

"Mm." He sank onto her settee, spreading his legs wide.
Swiping his tongue across his lower lip, he patted his knee for
her. "Come play for a bit."

If he wanted to chat, then he could do so as she worked, but
she would never *play* with him. "I'm about to make your mother's
hat, so if you don't have something you want to talk about then
you might as well leave."

"Oh, I have something to chat about." He lazily unfastened
each button of his vest, until he peeled it open—all of his taut
abs on display.

Maddie wrinkled her nose, not knowing what he was doing.
He'd been crude with her in the past, but she'd believed it was
all talk. Did he really think she would fuck him after their ordeal
in the woods and him admitting over and over that he wanted to
murder Ever? He never said precisely what he would do with the
White Queen, but she knew he would kill her in some sort of
horrible fashion.

As Maddie opened her mouth to tell him to mosey on out of

her cottage, he dipped his hand into the pocket inside his vest and fished something out. Maddie held back her gasp as she studied the familiar photograph in his hand. The same one Rav had shown her when he was there last.

Maddie stayed composed. "Rav and your mother already showed me this. I hadn't seen the girl then and still haven't."

"Funny thing," Chess purred, his grin growing wide. "This pubescent looks a lot like your fuck toy, doesn't he? Remove the glasses, the braces, the shitty haircut. Add muscles…"

Heart accelerating, Maddie squinted, pretending to study the photograph, and shook her head. "No."

"Liar," he cooed. "You're playing a little game to try and steal your sister away from my mother. I'm no imbecile." Chess truly was sly…

Maddie whirled around and snatched the scissors beside a stack of felt. But before she could spin around to stab him in his heart, Chess yanked them from her hand and caged her in at the desk from behind. Her chest tightened as she thought about her sister, how Mouse had been unable to escape the mortal man who'd taken everything from her. The one Maddie had slaughtered. And now, perhaps her sister would never escape her second imprisonment if Chess tipped off Imogen.

"Don't do anything foolish, or I will end your life right here," he said, taking a step back from her so she could turn and face him. "I have no qualms with your lover, and his sister isn't my top priority at the moment. Ever is. Tell me the White Queen's location and I won't tell my mother you're trying to break Mouse out or that you have Alice's brother as a pet."

A trade. Maddie would have to give him what he wanted—it was the only way. "There's a safe house in the Red Queen's territory. She's there. But I don't have the key since each safe house only has one." She then gave him the details on how to cross through the Broken Forest of Shattered Blood and to the hidden door beside the old well.

"This was your one chance, Maddie." Chess cocked his head, sliding the scissors back on her desk. "If you're lying to me, I will come after you and your fuck toy, then drag your sister back to my mother to do with as she pleases."

Maddie took a deep swallow, not wanting to think about the things Imogen would do to Mouse that she hadn't already. "What are you going to do to Ever?"

"That's a secret for another time." With those words, Chess backed away from her, buttoning up his vest before turning around.

Once Chess sauntered out the door, she slammed it shut, knowing she didn't have much time until he would return without Ever. As always, if she'd known where the White Queen was, she still wouldn't have told him. She'd sent him to the farthest safe house she knew, but perhaps she should've sent him farther out toward the Jabberwocky. Yet this would give her enough time to complete her tasks while having him off her back.

Adrenaline coursing through her, Maddie dropped onto her chair and lifted the felt to start Imogen's hat. She stitched, tore, ripped some more, all while pretending it was Imogen and Rav she split in half. Time slipped by, and her eyelids grew heavy as she worked. Her fingers turned red and raw, but she couldn't stop. The hat needed to be just right. It needed to be *perfect*.

And then the time had finally come to drizzle crimson paint onto the veins of the alabaster anatomical heart, giving it the bloody look she so desired.

Maddie reclined in her chair, taking one final look at her beautiful white and red creation and grinned. She yearned to take the hat to Imogen at that moment, but the queen allowed Maddie a specific time only. Not early. Not late.

If Maddie succeeded in rescuing Mouse, things wouldn't get easier, but harder.

A bang at the door caused Maddie to leap out of her chair. A sharp pain ran up the length of her stiff back.

As she took a step forward, she froze. Had Chess already made it back? Impossible… Maddie grabbed the scissors from her desk and yanked open the speakeasy. She gasped when her gaze met bright green eyes

"What the fuck is this?" Noah said through gritted teeth, holding up the mushroom.

Her heart thudded in her chest at the sight of him. *What is he doing here?* Setting the scissors on a wall shelf, she unlocked the door and pulled it open. "Isn't that what you wanted? Return to your mortal life?"

He brushed past her—his face drawn into a scowl. "I promised I wouldn't take it until after we got your sister back. And then you just came home by yourself with that fucking prince waltzing around."

"About him…" Maddie hurried and closed the door as though Chess were slinking around, listening. "He knows who you are, but I was able to send him away for a bit. Let me take you back to the safe house."

"No." Noah folded his arms.

She folded hers in return. "Yes. I'll take you there, then you can take the cure. The mushroom practically says *eat me*."

"No."

Stubborn immortal! A warm feeling washed over her at a thought. This male maybe cared about her if he was still willing to help her. Perhaps she was more than someone who was only used for fucks and not love. Either way, he couldn't go.

Maddie backed him into the wall, and he peered down at her with a hard stare. "I'm going on my own and not risking anyone else. Once everything has blown over, either Ferris or I will take you and Alice back to the mortal world." There was a chance she would die, but at least Rav should be in the mortal world as usual, and now, Chess wouldn't make an appearance.

"You can't tell me what to do." Noah whirled her around so she was backed into the wall this time, his hot breath mingling with hers. It sent a pleasureful feeling straight to her core—none of the fear that she'd held when Chess had caged her in was there.

"You made me this way, and I'm choosing what to do with my immortality. We'll get your sister out, then we'll be even."

"That's what this is?" Maddie frowned, realizing she'd been wrong about his motivation. "Owing each other? Like when we got each other off?" Maddie ducked down and escaped his barrier, waving her hand in the air as she padded away.

Noah drew her back by the arm, his nose touching hers. "We don't have to owe each other anything. If you want me to get you off the whole night without me coming, then fine by me. So tell me, what do you want?"

As she peered up at him, his determined expression, an emotion washed over her, taking out any fight she had in her. Maddie relented, her shoulders dropping. All she wanted in that moment was his skin pressed to hers. "For you to stay the night."

"And to go with you to the palace," he added

Maddie didn't want him to go, but she would leave whatever happened at the Ruby Heart Palace to fate. Perhaps he was meant to go with her on this final task. He could've abandoned her and eaten the mushroom, but he hadn't.

She couldn't hold back, not any longer. Her lips captured Noah's, and he kissed her in return with equal hunger. His strong arms hoisted her up, her legs cradling his waist, and he walked her to the settee before laying her against its velvet. Noah's warm fingers slid beneath the edge of her skirt, but paused just short of the place that yearned for him the most.

"Don't stop," she said softly. "If you do, I'll grab my hatpin."

With a playful smile, Noah hiked her dress up and peeled off her panties, already drenched with her wetness. Then his head was between her legs, his delicious tongue slowly gliding up her center in one easy motion. Maddie's eyes fluttered as he circled her clit, stroking, nipping. She gripped his hair as he continued working her, tasting her, devouring her. Her entire being shattered, like breaking glass as he worshipped every piece of her bundle of nerves. She grasped his hair tighter and shouted his name, listening to it echo off the walls.

Noah grinned. "How many more times do you think I can

make you feel good tonight? Should we count?"

"It doesn't matter," she said, her voice shaky from the orgasm. "I need you inside me—I want to feel you come."

"Fuck yes." Noah ripped his shirt over his head while Maddie chuckled. He loosened the ties at the front of her dress and she shoved it down her body. There was nothing cute or sweet about it as they tore away the rest of their garments. He then took her into his lap, his warm flesh against hers—she could feel every inch of him hard and ready.

Maddie lifted her body and sank onto him, animalistic growls of pleasure escaping both of them as his large cock filled her, making her moan in delight. She rolled her hips forward, and her fangs lowered on instinct. Only one thing could please her more.

"I want to taste your blood," Maddie panted, her body heating with need, *desire*. She expected him to wince, shy away, but he didn't.

Gripping her waist, Noah licked his lips. "Do it."

While grinding against him, she pressed her lips to his throat, sliding her tongue across his throbbing vein. His cedarwood scent surrounded her, his blood calling to her. She clenched his hair with both hands, tugged his head back, and pierced her fangs into his flesh, his blood spilling onto her tongue. Ecstasy washed over her as she drank and ground herself harder against him. He tasted like honey, the nectar she desperately needed.

Noah rubbed her clit, circling, until she ripped her fangs from him and gasped. He leaned down to her breast, taking a peaked nipple between his teeth. She arched into his touch, riding him harder, allowing the pleasure to draw nearer.

"Can I taste you now?" Noah whispered, peering up at her.

Maddie stilled, her gaze meeting his. "I-I...."

"Fuck. Sorry, I don't have to, Maddie," he said quickly, holding her steady, and pulled out of her.

Maddie knew he meant it, yet she *did* want him to sink his fangs into her. She lifted his face and cradled his cheeks, his green gaze meeting hers. A feeling was coming closer to the surface, one she'd wanted to avoid. Yet she couldn't in this moment…

"You can, but no one's done it since Rav. Just don't break my heart." Tears pricked her eyes. She was ruining this moment that should've been about pleasing one another, but instead, she had to open her foolish mouth. "Forget I said that, immortal."

His fingers wiped at her tears, and he gave her a soft smile. "If anyone's a heartbreaker, I think it's you. You did leave me behind, you know."

Perhaps she had, but she would do it over and over because it had led to this. In answer, Maddie claimed his mouth with hers, letting him fill her with his hard length once more. She rolled her hips as Noah trailed kisses to her jaw and down her neck to her pulse. His teeth grazed her flesh, making her moan before puncturing the skin. Noah's fangs slowly pushed into her, and she growled in pleasure, his fingers digging into her hips as he sucked and tasted. Her pace quickened as she fucked him, harder and harder. She wasn't certain what was happening anymore as crimson stars sparkled across the room.

Too soon, he took his mouth from her throat and lifted her from the settee. "You deserve the bed." She wrapped her legs around his narrow waist as he walked down the hall. "Never mind," he rasped, pressing her to the wall. "This is as far as I can go."

Maddie laughed, her lips molding to his, their kisses growing frantic, wild, as he unleashed himself. She gripped his shoulders, her nails digging in, her breasts bouncing.

Noah slid his length back so only the tip was in her, then he drove into her, hitting the base of his cock. She threw her head back in pleasure as he thrust again and again and *again*, until they both shouted in unison, their bodies drenched in sweat.

Chests heaving, they stared at one another. Maddie had never seen such a beautiful male as she did in that moment.

Noah grinned. "That's number two." He nibbled the tender spot beneath her ear, sending a wonderful shiver down her body.

Finally, he walked them into her bedroom. Pulling out of her, he gently lay Maddie on the bed as though she were a porcelain doll. He lowered himself on top of her, settling in between her legs. His lips met hers in a soft, tender kiss. Heart still beating fast, she ran her palms up the length of his chest, his back. They kissed and kissed for what felt like hours, until he grew hard once more when her mouth came to his cock, her tongue running up its length.

"Again?" he asked, his smile mirroring hers.

"Let's keep counting."

This time when Noah buried himself in her, it wasn't raw or animalistic. His movements were rhythmical, musical, as he took his time with her. She learned his body, discovered what made his toes curl with featherlight touches from her fingers, her lips, her tongue.

As though Wonderland was lit up in sunlight, bliss poured over Maddie as he spilled himself into her once more. Noah rolled to his back, bringing her to his chest and folding his arms around her.

Neither moved from their positions, their hearts pounding rapidly against one another.

Maddie had made things worse. Because now she yearned for him to stay in Wonderland, at her side, as an immortal.

CHAPTER TWENTY

NOAH

A soft sound woke Noah, and he tugged the large pillow closer to his chest. *No.* Not a pillow. It was too warm for that. He looked down to find Maddie's purple hair on the pillow beside him and his heart leapt at the sight of her nestled there. He tightened his arm around her waist. Her bare back was pressed against his chest, her perfect arse against his semi-hard cock. The events of the night before flooded through him. How they moved together, how she tasted. He smiled to himself as his length swelled even more. But more than the amazing sex, he liked waking up beside her. *Well, maybe not* more. It was equally as enjoyable though. Seeing her features so relaxed and knowing she trusted him made his chest warm.

Maddie released a soft sound and turned her head to look at him over her shoulder.

"Morning," he whispered.

"Morning," she sang and rolled to face him. Grinning mischievously, she lifted the blanket and peeked down at his growing erection. "And good morning to you."

He chuckled and traced her cheek with his thumb. "I'm tempted to suggest we make it a *great* morning."

"We have time," she said, peering up at him from beneath her lashes.

"Do we?" he asked, and quickly rolled on top of her, eliciting a surprised squeal from her. "You're not too sore from last night? I wasn't exactly gentle." The first time, anyway—the following rounds hadn't been as rough, but still…

"I liked it," she admitted and ran a hand down his chest. "And no, I'm not sore. We heal too quickly to worry about that."

"Well, in that case…" He lowered his mouth to hers and tangled their tongues in a slow, lazy kiss. His hand ran down her side, past her hip, to grip her thigh. Breaking away from the kiss, he leaned back enough to hook her leg over his shoulder and slid inside her warmth.

Bathed and dressed in a clean shirt, jacket, and trousers that belonged to Ferris, Noah held the front door open for Maddie. She spun, hair still wet as she gathered the white and red hatbox into her arms. The hat itself had been packed away before he got a good look at it. Her movements were slow and reluctant as she walked toward him, her gaze lingering on random items.

"You'll be back one day," he assured her.

"I should hope not," she said as she stepped outside, carrying a large bag with clothes for Mouse and extra supplies over her shoulder. "It wasn't ever a real home to begin with. It was just a place to create my hats which I can do anywhere. Ivory is my home."

Noah knew Maddie was right, but he felt her sorrow like a tangible thing. She loved her hats that still hung on the walls inside, but it wouldn't be safe for her to return while Imogen and Rav ruled Scarlet. They would know who broke Mouse out of the dungeons. The sisters would need to hide in safe houses for years, if not longer. So would he and Alice—but they would be hiding in their own world. He hated thinking of them alone, even if Ferris planned on joining them, and forced into hiding. While he was a new vampire, slightly impulsive, and undoubtedly a risk to them, the idea of leaving Maddie made him want to stay and protect her all the more.

"Coming?" she asked from a few paces away.

Noah shut her front door and strode to her side. They walked together in silence for a handful of streets. He took the time to notice things he hadn't before, like the goods displayed in shops. Various clothes in styles from different eras, cages with skeletal birds, and scrolling table lamps that cast elaborate shadows on the wall. Another held mirror shards pieced together along the back wall of the display, showing their selection of sex toys from every angle. Noah was torn between stopping to take a longer look and hurrying past that particular shop to avoid the distraction. If they survived long enough, he was definitely circling back if Maddie was up for it.

"This way," she said softly, noticing his distraction before they turned again.

It was early morning and few others were on the street, but Maddie was known for her hats. Carrying a box tied with a giant ribbon wouldn't be strange from the best hat maker in Scarlet, so no one spared them a second glance. Hopefully they got the same amount of attention when they went to the palace.

"I was thinking…" he started, but stopped himself. Before he could say anything about maybe staying a bit longer to help Maddie hide Mouse, he needed to see how Alice was doing. With their parents being in Leeds he might *need* to go home with her if she wasn't recovered enough to take care of herself. And that was even assuming they could return to their London flat. They might need to move to avoid Rav or Chess dragging them back to Imogen.

"Noah?" Maddie prodded.

He sucked in a breath. "Sorry, I should probably think a bit more before I open my mouth."

Maddie arched a brow and nodded. "Speak when you're ready then."

Did she even *want* him to stay? She said not to break her heart, but that didn't necessarily mean he would be welcome to practically move in with her. There were plans in place for three: Maddie, Mouse, and Ferris. His tagging along could cause problems. But he was getting ahead of himself. Alice had still been in pain when he ran after Maddie and there was no telling what state she was in now. His sister had barely overcome her agony before he left her, sleeping, to speak with Maddie.

Only she hadn't been in the safe house—she'd left the cure with Ferris. The male had wasted no time handing over the mushroom and telling him that Maddie went home. Ferris had watched him carefully after breaking the news, as if he was genuinely curious what Noah would do. He could've sworn the vampire had smiled when he left without another word. Noah winced. And then he'd spent the entire night fucking Maddie when his sister was going through an extreme transformation.

He shook the guilt and worry away. One step at a time. First, he and Maddie needed to get to the safe house. They had three days until they had to go to the palace to talk and figure out their plan to free Mouse which gave him a little time to sort through what he truly wanted.

After a quick look around to make sure they weren't being followed, Maddie led the way, slipping around the corner, graceful as a cat, to the front of the safe house. She shifted the box and rapped the secret code on the door. Ferris swung it open a moment later and ushered them inside.

"Noah!" Alice called in a weak voice.

He spun to find his sister sitting on the sofa with a plaid blanket wrapped around her shoulders. Her damp hair framed her face, and a bit of color stained her cheeks. The vividness of her blue eyes had faded, making her look almost human again. She smelled human too, but her blood held an acrid, bitter note now. "Sis." He smiled. "You look much better."

"I wouldn't go that far." She lifted a strand of hair and dropped it back down. "But an improvement, surely."

Noah sat beside her and tugged at the blanket so it covered more of her thigh. He paused. What was she wearing? A large black T-shirt and… "Where are your trousers?"

She shrugged. "Maddie's clothes are too small and Ferris is tall so his shirt fits like a dress."

"Seems like I'm dressing everyone these days," Ferris mumbled as Maddie set her box onto the small table just inside the door.

"It's not like you were using them." Maddie grinned, tapping Ferris's nose. "You didn't even know I'd gotten them from your flat after you entered the palace."

Ferris crossed his arms and stared at the box. "Is that the hat for Imogen?"

"Yes." Maddie made a small squeak of excitement and pulled off the top, lifting the cocktail hat from inside. "It's a masterpiece, if I say so myself. Far too perfect to sit on that shrew's head."

Noah turned from them as Maddie started explaining how she crafted each piece of the hat. Something tugged in his chest as he watched how her face lit up over her craft. She was … she was *adorable*. But then his gaze shifted to Alice and his stomach sank. His sister needed his attention more at that moment. "Are you feeling better?" he asked.

"Much. Everything's been hazy after I … after I attacked you." Her face turned bright red, and she hung her head, hiding behind her hair. "I know I already said this, but I'm so sorry, Noah."

"Don't be." He reached over and took her hand in his. "It wasn't really you. I'm just glad Maddie and I got the cure for you."

Alice chewed her bottom lip. "Ferris told me what you had to do to find it. You really shouldn't have—not that I'm ungrateful, but you could've *died*."

Thinking back on it, Noah was honestly surprised they hadn't died in the swamp. "I could have. You *were* going to die though, so how could I not risk it?"

With a heavy sigh, Alice settled into the back of the settee. "We should be able to go back home when the cure has finished setting us both right."

They couldn't go *home*—home wasn't safe anymore, but that was just another thing they needed to discuss. Noah shifted uncomfortably. "I haven't taken it yet," he said in a quiet voice. He hadn't wanted to talk about this the moment he walked in the door, and he would've preferred it be a private conversation. Though, if he were being realistic, no matter where they spoke inside the small safe house, Maddie and Ferris would've been able to hear.

"*What?*" She sat up straight and twisted to face him. "Why? Ferris gave it to you before you left."

"I promised Maddie I would help rescue her sister. What good would I be as a mortal?" The other reason—the part about not hating being a vampire—could come a little later. He pulled the semi-wilted mushroom from his jacket pocket. "See? I still have it."

"Eat it," she urged. "We don't owe them anything."

Noah's mouth parted in surprise. "I'm fairly certain we owe them a fuck-ton. They snuck you out of the palace, hid you from Rav and the queen, and helped me save you from certain death." Maddie *had* tried to turn Alice in for her own benefit, but that didn't negate the good things she'd also done.

"You're right." Alice winced. "I know you are. I'm sorry, it's just … I want to go home and forget this ever happened. And I need you there with me. If you stay here, you'll end up dead, and it will be my fault for dragging you into this mess."

"I'm not going to die." Noah ran a hand through his hair, hoping that was true. "It's going to be a quick rescue mission. Maddie will distract Imogen while I sneak inside with Ferris's map. By the time she finishes delivering that hat, I'll be back here with her sister, safe and sound. Okay?"

"You don't *know* that. Besides…" She paused and chewed on

her bottom lip. "What will I tell Mum and Dad? That you've run off on holiday?"

"I can come back and visit sometimes." Around Christmas and birthdays, as long as it was at night...

"Come visit?" she nearly shrieked. "I meant if you were *dead*. Are you seriously considering staying here?"

Noah felt Maddie and Ferris staring at him, but he was too cowardly to look over at them. *Fuck.* He had wanted to think this through. "I'm not sure what I want," he told her honestly. Staying in Wonderland meant leaving his entire life behind. He was torn between what he *should* want and what he *did* want. "I'm going to think about it for a couple days."

Alice grabbed his forearm with both hands. "You can't stay in Wonderland. Please, Noah, you have to come home with me where it's safe."

Safe? She was clearly in denial. But, regardless, what did he have there that was really worth returning to? A job he tolerated, another year at university to then get some new job he wasn't thrilled about? A lying bitch of an ex-girlfriend who wouldn't leave him alone? Their parents rarely made an appearance so, if he did visit once or twice a year, he would be seeing them just as much. He would have Alice, of course, but he couldn't live his life for her. He needed to live it for himself. What he needed to decide was how *long* he would live—another sixty years or forever?

"Bloody hell," he growled, not meaning to sound so angry. "I'm sorry. I need to think, okay?"

"Think about what? This is *insane!*" Alice said with wide, panicked eyes.

"I'm glad you're feeling better." Noah stood and avoided meeting Maddie's heavy stare. "If you need me, I'll be in the other room." His flat tone implied *don't need me* unless it was a true emergency. He hoped they picked up on his need to be alone for a bit. To sort through everything without outside pressure, life-or-death stakes, or a sexy hat-wearing female muddling his head.

As soon as the bedroom door shut behind him, he heard Ferris whisper, "What the fuck was that about?"

"Nothing," Maddie replied, her voice uncertain. "He's probably just tired."

He *wasn't* tired though. He should've been after all that had happened. It had been almost two weeks of jumping through mental loops and days of running through danger for the cure. His body had changed completely. But that was the thing—he *liked* what he'd become. Not the idea of drinking blood so much, but even that wasn't so bad. As a vampire, he was stronger, faster, and he felt more *right* than he ever had as a human.

Plus, there was Maddie. He hadn't known her that long, but he'd known his ex-girlfriend for years. Look how *that* had turned out. Sometimes it wasn't about the length of time two people knew each other.

Fuck. He already knew what he wanted to do. All that was left was to come to terms with abandoning one life for another.

CHAPTER TWENTY-ONE

MADDIE

Three days had passed. Maddie and Noah shared a mattress in the safe house, but he'd been quiet. So quiet. Yet she knew his thoughts weren't. It was a peaceful few days, even though she wished Noah hadn't been brooding. Before they would fall asleep in the mornings, he kissed her thoroughly as if he were trying to find an answer. But that was all they'd done. Kiss, tender and slow, as though she was stitching the finest of hats.

Maddie fiddled with her arm sleeve and glanced up at Ferris. He sat on the floor, leaning against the wall, sketching in a notepad. Noah was in the bathtub, washing himself before they headed to the Ruby Heart Palace.

A door creaked open, and Maddie turned to find Alice standing there. The vein at the girl's neck thrummed and Maddie could scent the mortal blood flowing through her. Alice hadn't spoken to Maddie since discovering Noah may possibly stay in Wonderland. But that wasn't only a surprise to Alice—it was to Maddie too. However, regardless of immortality, a shadow of their human side would always linger within the heart of a vampire. And even if Noah did stay, he may decide down the line that he wanted to go back home after all.

"Can I talk to you?" Alice asked, not moving away from her door.

Maddie lifted her chin, her interest piqued. She waved a hand in the air and patted the spot beside her on the settee. "Come on then."

Alice's gaze flicked to Ferris as her fingers dug into her oversized shirt. "Alone?"

Maddie arched a brow, curious as to what was so secretive. She stood from the settee and padded toward Alice's room. Ferris didn't stop drawing, but she knew he was listening to every word.

"Why couldn't you talk to me out there?" Maddie asked while Alice shut the door behind them.

"I can't." Alice winced. "I tried to kiss Ferris last night."

Maddie inhaled sharply. "You like Ferris?"

"No. I don't know." She nervously shifted from one foot to the other. "I mean, he saved my life."

Because of Mouse… That was why he saved Alice's life. She didn't say it out loud though—she didn't want to hurt Alice anymore. Maddie also didn't know much about his past life with mortal women, but he'd never had a girlfriend for as long as she'd known him. Only that he'd fucked Imogen to get turned into a vampire so he could become a servant in the Ruby Heart Palace for Mouse. Alice was pretty but Ferris had said he would never choose mortality again. "I'm sorry. Unrequited love is—"

"Whoa!" Alice held up her hand. "I don't love him. I just wanted to thank him and have a little fun while I was at it. At home, I still haven't really found myself."

Maddie understood that better than anyone. She'd been reckless at times, just to escape herself, her past. "You eventually will."

"Thanks." Alice bit her lip, seeming to think for a few seconds. "Please make Noah eat the mushroom."

Maddie took a deep swallow. "I'm sorry, I can't. Just as we wouldn't want to be made to do something. Even if you two both return to the mortal world, Imogen and Rav will still be alive, hunting you, regardless if you're human or not."

Alice scowled. "You just met my brother. It isn't as though he could fall in…" Her words trailed off as she stared up at Maddie, her eyes growing wide. "Do you *like* my brother?"

Maddie's heart kicked at her rib cage, screaming yes, that she liked Alice's brother very much. "He's a pain in the arse and asks too many questions."

"It's my fault for following Rav." Alice furrowed her brow. "I never should've left the club with him. I mean, how pathetic is that? All over trying to get my teeth filed into fangs."

It was a strange concept, as though she would've been dressed up for Halloween forever.

"You aren't the only one who followed Rav. And even then, you were under his influence to go down his rabbit hole or you wouldn't have gone."

Alice blew out a breath. "I never want to see a fake vampire movie, book, or club ever again."

"The clubs do sound rather terrible." Maddie chuckled, then turned serious. "Whatever you choose to do out in the world, you'll do fine, Alice. You'll discover yourself, just as I once did. As for your brother, let him decide. It's what I would do for my sister. When she wanted to turn, I didn't stop her. It was her choice in the end." But secretly, she'd been glad Mouse had chosen the path to immortality because Maddie wouldn't have to see her sister die. Yet if Noah stayed a vampire, he would have to watch Alice wither…

Alice stared at her bare toes before looking back up. "If he does stay, watch over him. He trusts with his heart too easily."

"I will." Maddie grasped Alice's shoulders, a rush of tedious guilt washing over her. "I truly am sorry for what I did. I shouldn't have tried to take you to Imogen."

"For Noah, I would've risked someone's life to save him too." Alice's eyelids flickered and she yawned. "I think I'll lie down for a little while." Hopefully soon, she wouldn't feel as drained once she regained her strength.

Maddie helped Alice to the mattress and covered her with the blanket. Alice's breaths came out even as she turned on her side. Keeping her feet light, Maddie closed the door behind her and found Ferris still on the floor sketching.

"You heard everything?" she asked.

Without looking up, he shrugged.

Unable to keep the smile from her face, Maddie knelt beside him. "So… Alice tried to kiss you?"

Ferris kept his head down, his pencil digging harder into the paper as he drew. "She's sweet but not my type."

Maddie leaned closer, catching a glimpse of his drawing. It was all done in pencil with perfect shading of a female's hand holding a caterpillar. "What made you decide to draw that?"

His body jerked and he shut the book. "Just something from when I was at the palace."

Maddie frowned and opened her mouth to speak when footsteps sounded behind her. She spun to find Noah entering, his hair wet, and him adjusting his hooded shirt.

It was time! "Ready?" Maddie asked, scooping up the hat box from the floor. "Alice just fell asleep."

Noah nodded. "I already said goodbye earlier and told her to stay safe."

Maddie grabbed the weapons that she'd gathered earlier, tucking them into different parts along her body. Scarves, to bind wrists together, went into the waist band of her skirt, a gun in a strap on her thigh, and daggers inside her boots. If she brought a backpack into the palace, Imogen would have Maddie's heart ripped out in a split second. Noah slipped a few knives into his boot and a gun, duct tape, and scarf into the waistband of his trousers.

Ferris stood with his back against the wall when Maddie spun to face him. "If I don't return—"

"Don't worry," he said. "I may have to break the world apart to get to her, but I'll do it."

Maddie grinned and patted his cheek. "That's the way to do it."

She then led Noah out into the night, the breeze blowing cold air against her flesh. Troops of bats flew above them, circling and creating their own kind of dance before darting north. A few werewolf howls tore through the darkness as they trekked farther from the outskirts of Scarlet and into the city.

"Don't worry, it's just the rogues out on the prowl tonight. You have your gun just in case." Maddie produced the floor plan that Ferris drew for the Ruby Heart Palace and shoved it into the back pocket of Noah's trousers. "When it's time, follow the path to my sister and look for pink hair and violet eyes." Once Mouse turned immortal, her chestnut strands had turned magenta, her brown eyes to violet, making her appear even more ethereal.

As she turned a corner, Noah grabbed Maddie by the elbow and hauled her to the back of a tall black building with scarlet windows. "Look"—he raked a hand through his blond locks— "I want to stay."

She figured he would want to remain by his sister's side, which was why she'd originally made an alternative to go to the palace by herself. "If you want to go back to Alice, then you should go."

"That's not what I mean." He sighed, pressing closer, his intoxicating scent enveloping her. "I want to stay in Wonderland after making sure Alice is safe."

Noah still needed time to think about it, but perhaps he'd had enough time to do so in the safe house. "We'll talk about it once we get out." She grasped his hands and intertwined their fingers. "*If* we live, that is."

Noah drew her to his chest, brushing his lips against hers. "I should've kissed every inch of your body last night."

"Whose fault is that?" She laughed and tapped his nose as she pulled back.

He rolled his eyes.

"Come on. I'll keep that pretty heart of yours protected as best I can." Perspiration gathered in Maddie's arm sleeves as she held onto the hatbox. She kept her eyes peeled for Chess. The prince would be due back sometime today … once he figured out Ever wasn't where Maddie had said she would be. There'd been no sign of Rav slinking around either, and she prayed he was in the mortal world, per usual, at this time.

The palace loomed high in front of them as they approached its crimson glossy outer walls, its obsidian towers. Red roses filled the entire garden along with several gray gazebos stained in blood. Imogen would stick the hearts of those she felt deserved death on pikes inside the marble structures.

Maddie took the scarlet glass steps to the entrance and tapped the wooden door's anatomical heart iron knocker. A few moments later, Rine answered. She was one of the servants who Imogen had kept around for years. Most likely because she was ruthless like the queen.

"Ah," Rine said, her pale pink irises settling on Noah, "who is this?"

"My guest, Rine," Maddie sang. "We come bearing Imogen's gift."

The vampire clucked her tongue. "You were almost late. Go sit and wait." She spun on her heel and sauntered up the curving checkered staircase, her dark hair swishing behind her back.

Maddie motioned Noah to the plush black settee in the middle of the room. She followed his gaze around the cozy area as they took a seat. Red and black checkered tile rested beneath their feet. Anatomical hearts were painted across the walls, and in between hung ornate roses. Always red roses or hearts. Maddie should've brought a bouquet of ivory roses to shove in Imogen's face.

Heels clicked against the marble steps and Maddie peered up as Imogen descended the stairs. Rine never followed, always stayed behind to do whatever it was she did. The queen's fiery curls flowed down to her waist, the hem of her black and blood-red silky gown trailing behind her. She was dressed fancier than when Maddie had seen her last. The queen always wore trousers when out in the city, but inside her home, she dressed extravagant, *dramatic*.

"What is this?" Imogen cooed when she crept closer to them. Her gaze locking on Noah, a wide smile playing across her ruby lips. "How do you like being immortal? Osanna told me the glorious details." She turned to Maddie. "Pity she has to find a replacement for Robin, though."

Anger coursed through Maddie, but she held it back as she went to stand.

"Stay seated," Imogen snapped, fishing out her deck of cards from inside her dress. Lazily, she ran her fingers across the deck, shuffling them. "Pick a color, Hatter. If you're wrong, I'll keep your lover here with your sister."

Maddie bit the inside of her cheek, knowing she needed to play along. *Don't get anxious, Maddie.* Fifty percent chance she would be right since there were only two colors in her deck. "Black," she sang.

Imogen drew out a card, moistening her lower lip with her tongue as she flashed a black five of spades. "It seems to be your lucky day." She stuffed the cards back into her dress and straightened. "But we'll see if your luck is still here next month. Now, first thing's first before we move on to other matters— show me my hat."

Maddie's heart pounded, *slammed*, against her rib cage as she handed Imogen the box. The queen's lithe fingers slowly unraveled the silky bow, peeling it away. And then she lifted the lid…

"What the fuck is this?" Bright crimson crept up Imogen's throat, her face, pure fury as she took out the hat.

Maddie tensed up, preparing to strike just as Noah was grabbing the tape out from his waist. She then jolted from the settee, barreling Imogen to the floor. Noah rushed beside her and slammed a piece of duct tape to the queen's mouth just as she was about to scream. Imogen bucked and wriggled but Maddie flipped the queen to her stomach. Maddie held Imogen's wrists behind her and pressed down on the queen's body. Noah took out the silk scarf from his waist and wrapped it around

Imogen's wrists before tying it into tight knots.

"Go!" Maddie hissed once the queen's wrists were bound. "I'll take care of the rest." They didn't have any time to fiddle around. It would be better if they could both go and retrieve Mouse, but they couldn't drag Imogen down the hall with the guards and they couldn't leave her here alone. Besides that, even if she tossed her into a closet, Maddie would be recognizable without a disguise, and they would know she wasn't supposed to be there. However, Noah would blend in with the queen's newly-turned vampires. Maddie was also stronger and better equipped to fight Imogen.

Noah's throat bobbed as he stared at her, as though he wanted to say something, but then he nodded and took off down the hall.

Maddie drew out the silk cloth from her waist and tied Imogen's ankles together as she continued to buck and make strangled sounds. She didn't know how long the silk would hold, but she wouldn't have been able to sneak in chains or rope.

Gripping Imogen's upper arms, she tossed the queen into the chair across from the settee before taking a seat in front of her. With a satisfied grin, Maddie leaned back against the plush material of the settee and crossed her legs. She waved a hand in the air. "How about we discuss the different kinds of teas? Let's begin with Earl Grey, shall we?"

CHAPTER TWENTY-TWO

NOAH

Bloody fucking hell!

By some miracle, Noah and Maddie had just tied up the queen without getting their hearts ripped out. It felt as if the organ was going to pound out of his chest now though. He forced himself to walk slowly through the hallway to avoid drawing attention. Leaving Maddie alone with Imogen made him more than uncomfortable. Even tied up, the female was a threat due to her paranormal strength and the decades she'd had to hone it, but there was no other choice. He swallowed hard and flexed his sweaty hands. How had he gone from making coffee to breaking someone out of a dungeon?

The mission. He needed to focus on his whereabouts.

Ferris's map was detailed enough that, after going over it days earlier, Noah was able to easily recognize the turns he needed to take without bringing the folded paper out to check. He knew if anyone saw him standing around, examining a map, it would draw suspicion. The anatomical heart décor seemed to flow throughout every hallway with only slight differences. The material of the hearts hanging on the walls switched from metal wire to a variety of cog wheels to thread and nails. One smaller heart he found appeared to be made from real flesh, but he wasn't going to stop and examine it to be sure. *Sick bastards.*

His vision narrowed on a suit of armor with a black spade painted on its chest. There were two on the map, one with a spade and one with a diamond. Was it the spade where he was meant to turn left? He envisioned the map in his head, seeing the path Ferris had drawn, and he became sure it *was*, before rounding the corner. A dazed human with puncture wounds on her neck exited a room ahead and stumbled past him without looking up. His breath caught at the scent of fresh blood, but it smelled diluted, as if she barely had any left.

Shaking the thought away, he looked for the painting of dodo birds. It was large enough that the frame nearly touched the ceiling and floor. The artist had used heavy brush strokes to depict six of the feathered beasts seemingly dancing around a small fire. *Wait.* Noah sniffed. That wasn't paint … it was *blood.* He scowled and turned again. A few yards later, he went right at the stained-glass window of bloody red roses, down the stairs across from a velvet chaise tucked into an alcove, and through a hidden door behind a tapestry of a mortal woman on horseback.

The farther he went, the more his fear increased. Someone had surely noticed the queen was in danger, Maddie was in trouble, and soon they would be coming after him. But he had to save Mouse. That was what Maddie wanted and he owed her for helping save Alice—he couldn't slip up and get himself caught beforehand. He'd already passed by a few servants. Thankfully none had given him a second glance.

He slowed his steps, listening intently for guards. Ferris had told him one or two always lurked in the dungeons, but Mouse was kept away from the other prisoners. Her constant ramblings apparently made the guards stay far from her door. They would pass by once in the morning and again in the evening with blood bags. He and Maddie had timed the escape to avoid both. It didn't mean he wouldn't run into anyone on the way.

Creeping from the dark tunnel, he lifted the edge of a tapestry showing the image of a moonlit lake and entered the path behind it. Noah hurried to the left to find a hallway full of metal doors. Each had a metal slat near the top with iron mesh covering it and a locked slat halfway down which, he assumed, was how they passed blood to the captives. His heart hammered in his chest as he looked inside the first door. *Completely empty.*

Noah shook his head, ignoring the urge to open the door to make sure no one was there. Curiosity would get him killed. It didn't matter who was inside these cells—only the one Ferris specified on the map. He kept his steps light and moved as quickly down the hallways as he dared. The scent of piss, stale blood, and death permeated the air, so he kept his breaths shallow—not an easy thing to do when his adrenaline was soaring through his entire body.

"Did you see the new servant Rav brought in yesterday?" a distant male asked.

"Which?" replied a feminine voice.

The male laughed, the soft pad of their boots coming closer. *Damn.* Noah needed to get the hell out of sight, but the only place to take shelter here was an unlocked cell. *Fuck…* Without any other choice, he slipped into the nearest one, shutting the door with barely a *click.*

"He'll present her to the queen later today if you want to take a look. Luke is keeping an eye on her in the south wing," the male said.

Noah held his breath and plastered himself to the wall as the duo's footfalls brought them near his door. They continued speaking but he couldn't make out the words over the fear humming through him. Once they continued past the cell he was hiding in, he waited until their voices were too far to be heard before slipping back into the hall.

His hands shook slightly as he took the map from his back pocket and doubled checked his route. This was too important a mission to fail—Mouse's life was in his hands. With a steadying breath, he continued through the dungeon. A right, a left, straight, then another right. This hallway was different than the others. The walls were seamless black stone for at least three meters with a single door straight ahead. Soft, gentle singing carried through it.

Mouse. It had to be, judging by the door the sound came from.

He rushed forward and wasted no time pressing his face to the mesh, his gaze landing on a female with a long, pink plait. Mouse sat crossed-legged in the center of a thin mattress, the worn skirt of her black dress stretched tight over her knees. On the taut fabric, a bright blue and yellow caterpillar swayed side-to-side with her song.

"Hello," she said, ending the song abruptly, her violet gaze flicking up to meet his. The resemblance to Maddie was uncanny. "You're new."

Noah smiled. *He'd found her.* "Your sister sent me." He moved back and examined the door for the handle. Three large bolts slid through metal bars and into another set attached to the walls on either side. All he had to do was slide them the opposite way.

"Maddie sent you?" she asked, her chin tilted up as she glared at him. "Where is Ferris?"

There would be time for questions later. He quickly shoved each bolt free, leaving him with only a lock to pick. He pulled out the paperclip Ferris had given him while they'd planned this and got to work.

"He's waiting for us," Noah answered. The lock clicked and he released a breath. He stood and wrenched the door open just as Mouse screamed, "Wait!"

But it was too late—it was wide open.

"Oh, bollocks," Mouse said with a wince. Then, to the caterpillar sitting in her palm. "He's really done it now, hasn't he, Des?"

Noah's brows rose. "Done what?"

"Triggered the silent alarm," she said as if it were obvious. She raced to the flat mattress on the floor and yanked out a stack of papers tied together with twine. Noah easily recognized the artwork as Ferris's after staring at the map for days. "They installed them only last week after Ferris helped a girl escape."

"Fuck!" He leaned into the room and grabbed Mouse's hand.

She ripped herself free. "How do I know I can trust you?"

Maybe because he was breaking her out of prison? He pulled the map out and unfolded it for her to see. "Ferris really sent me. Now, we have to *run*."

Mouse offered no resistance after that as he took her hand and they bolted back the way he'd come, taking the same staircase up two flights. The secret escape Ferris had told them about was nearby—only one turn away after they emerged from the tapestry depicting the mortal woman. He'd been hoping they wouldn't need it—the ten-meter drop into a garden of thorny rose bushes didn't sound like a pleasant experience. He'd take it over death though.

"Come on," he urged, practically dragging Mouse around the corner when she stumbled.

Mouse glared at him suspiciously and repeated, "Where's Ferris?"

Before he could answer, shouts and racing footsteps echoed behind them. The guards would catch up in no time at this rate, but Mouse was gasping for breath. He spun and scooped her up, her body nearly weightless in his arms, before doubling his speed. The steel, industrial refrigerators looked exactly like the ones Ferris drew with double doors and padlocks. Behind the third one rested the tunnel they needed.

Quickly setting Mouse down, he yanked the refrigerator away from the wall, but it was stuck on something. "Shit," he hissed, giving it a hard yank. It didn't budge. He scanned the machine and an idea formed. "Climb over," he told Mouse, cupping his hands in front of him, knowing she was too short to reach without a boost. "There's a tunnel on the other side."

"How are they running these without electricity?" she mused. "The guards mentioned generators—is that true? It seems like a lot of energy to run these."

"Seriously? *Now*?" He couldn't give two fucks about how the refrigerators worked in this place. The boots were close enough that the guards were probably at Mouse's cell now. His heart pounded painfully against his sternum.

Mouse set her foot in his hands and leapt up, then slid behind the steel machine. Noah followed, but the space wasn't wide enough for him, trapping him between the coils of the refrigerator and the wall. *No!* Mouse's hands wrapped around his ankle and pulled hard.

He felt his ribs crack from the pressure, but there wasn't time to completely register the pain before gravity took hold. He slid down a tunnel at an alarming speed.

Mouse squealed in fear as the faint moonlight glowed at the end. Stomach in his throat, Noah closed his eyes and hoped he wouldn't land on top of Mouse, crushing her. He could only tell they'd exited the tunnel from the distinct lack of stone digging into his back. Wind whistled in his ears as he dropped.

And dropped.

And dropped.

A *thunk* sounded—what he assumed was Mouse hitting the ground—only seconds before his hip smacked into something solid. It sent him careening sideways and his eyes flew open to find a blur of red roses. "Fuck!" He brought his arm up just in time to shield his face from the thorns as he slammed into the bushes.

He sucked in one breath. Two.

"Hey," Mouse whispered, hugging the stack of artwork to her chest. "Are you conscious?"

"Unfortunately," he grumbled as blood trailed down his arm from a deep cut.

His entire body hummed with shock, and he felt dull pain that he was positive wouldn't remain that way once he calmed the fuck down. He shoved himself up, ignoring the bleeding scratches and throbbing in his hip. Glancing over his shoulder, he took in the palace. Red light flickered over the glossy stone walls as figures inside moved past windows. Maddie was still in there…

"We can't stay," Mouse said, clutching the caterpillar gently in her hand. "Take me to Maddie and Ferris."

She was right—they couldn't stay. Every second they wasted made their capture more likely, but … *Maddie*. He shook his head. They had to leave her. That was always the plan—to escape and she would catch up to them. He had to trust in Maddie's own strength and do his part.

He tightened his jaw and nodded. Telling her Maddie was in the castle might make her run back in, and he couldn't risk it. "Come on then."

CHAPTER TWENTY-THREE

MADDIE

Ginger? Mint? Hibiscus? Maddie mulled the different teas over in her head before settling on chamomile. "Back in London, this was my favorite tea. Even now, I'll put a hint of it in the blood I'm drinking while creating a hat. It enhances the flavor. Silkier. Sweeter." She paused and smiled, staring into Imogen's raging yellow eyes. "You should try it sometime."

The queen jerked out of her chair and lunged for Maddie. She easily grasped Imogen by the shoulders, then pushed her back down into her seat.

"Tut, tut," Maddie sang in a hushed voice. "Do that again, and I may have to take you outside."

A hard kick came to Maddie's stomach and she gasped. Her gaze fell to the queen's freed ankles, the bindings torn and resting on the checkered floor. Imogen rammed her leg forward again, but Maddie stepped around the chair, holding the queen's shoulders firmly against the velvet back.

"A pity," Maddie said, observing the shredded cloth on the

floor. "But alas, make another move, and I'll rip your head off after stabbing you in the throat and heart. Understand?" She released Imogen and drew out two switchblade knives from her boot, then shifted back in front of the queen.

Imogen narrowed her eyes but didn't lift from her seat again. Even though Maddie's heart pounded ferociously, she held her casual expression as she set her switchblades on the settee beside her. There wasn't much time left until she needed to go back to the safe house. She'd told Noah she would give him fifteen minutes to retrieve Mouse, then she would meet him there. And if he wasn't there, then she would return to the palace. But she wouldn't make it far, not with Imogen still alive, knowing what Maddie had done to her. If Maddie killed her though, it would only make matters worse. She would be hunted harder, and if Mouse was free, her sister and Noah would be as well.

Maddie was about to move on to discuss the dainty flavor of lavender tea when loud stomping stormed down the stairs. She glanced up, stilling as she saw Rine's hair swishing around her face, the female's lips curled into a snarl.

"The alarm, my queen," Rine shouted to the back of Imogen's chair. "Mouse has escaped."

Noah did it. Maddie couldn't contain a grin. He'd gotten her sister out. Relief didn't wash over her yet though—she was unsure if they were out of the palace and safe.

Maddie grabbed a switchblade from beside her and stood, preparing herself.

"What is this?" Rine's eyes widened as she stepped farther into the room. Her gaze focused on Imogen, her duct-taped lips, her bound hands. Vicious sounds emanated from the queen's throat, her words trapped inside her mouth.

Before Rine could attack or free the queen, Maddie hurled herself at the female and thrust the switchblade into her chest, a squishing sound emanating. Maddie grasped the female's head and twisted hard to the left, tearing it from her body, the crack of her spine filling the room. Rine's body thumped to the floor, bright crimson pouring out from the gaping hole and pooling near Maddie's feet. She took a step back, making sure to not get blood on the bottom of her boots—she didn't want to leave a trail behind. As she dropped the head beside the body, more blood splattered the floor.

"If only this could've been done without getting messy." Maddie shrugged and spun to face Imogen with a grin. "Now, I must apologize about Rine, even though she always was a nasty little thing, but I do have to go. Our time is up. Ta-ta."

As Maddie's eyes shifted to the settee to collect her other knife, she froze. It was *gone*.

The tear of fabric came and in a split second, Imogen was standing, her hands free, the tape off her mouth. *Idiot, Maddie. If Rine hadn't distracted her…*

"You shouldn't have done that, you crazy bitch," Imogen seethed. "I'm taking you to the dungeons where you will wait and watch as I kill Mouse, then I will bite the flesh from your bones, piece by piece. You'll suffer for a long, *long* time before I rip your heart out, Hatter."

Well, that didn't sound pleasant in the least.

"Not today," Maddie said, waving her hand in the air. She lunged for the first object she could find, grasping a metal vase from a shelf on the wall, just as Imogen came forward. The queen growled, her fangs sliding out, and knocked the vase from Maddie's hand.

With a grunt, Maddie whirled to the side and caught the object just as it was about to crash to the floor. She didn't need the loud sound reverberating. As Imogen swiped again, Maddie struck the queen's hand with the heavy metal.

"Now now, we were having a much more relaxing time discussing teas." Maddie darted around the chair and tossed the vase in its seat. All she needed to do was get to the front door, but Imogen blocked it. She patted her dress for a weapon—the gun would be quick but too loud.

"Hatter, I've played enough games over the years and I always win." Imogen hurled the switchblade forward and a sharp pain pierced Maddie's shoulder.

Maddie held back a scream as she yanked the blade out. She ground her teeth together against the pain while hot blood oozed from the wound. But it would heal quickly, and she didn't have time to waste. Imogen shot toward her and Maddie dove for the other side of the room. Spinning around, Maddie hurled her knife forward and it lodged in Imogen's chest, but the queen didn't falter.

"Bloody hell," Maddie hissed, her fangs dropping. She'd missed the heart.

Imogen ripped the blade out and tossed it back, this time striking Maddie's other shoulder. She clenched her teeth at the deep ache.

"Thank you for giving it back." Maddie grinned, staring at the door. If she played this game a little longer, she could eventually draw closer to the exit.

"I've had enough! Guards!" Imogen yelled.

Oh no. This will not do.

"Just wait until you watch what I do with your sister," Imogen purred, her lips pulling into a cruel smile.

Anger coursed through Maddie, and she launched the knife forward, driving it into the queen's heart. Imogen's eyes rolled back, and she lurched to the side. Maddie felt fulfilled as she watched the evil shrew try in vain to suck in a breath. This was for Mouse. The queen swayed and crumpled to the floor.

Maddie stared at the door—this was her chance, her escape. Only Rine had seen Maddie thus far. A thought spun in her head, something dark, yet a necessity that would make this a bit easier for everyone. She didn't know if she could be quick enough before the guards got there, but she had to try. Maddie jolted forward to Imogen's still body and thrust her hand into the queen's chest, shattering her rib cage. She clenched Imogen's bastard heart and yanked it out, crimson splattering the floor.

Maddie's hand shook as she held the bloody organ, squeezing it. She liked the feel of the wet heart, one that had brought so much torment to her and her sister, in her hand.

The distant clomp of boots reminded her of where she was,

what she'd just *done*. Now that she'd killed the queen, she knew she'd truly made a mess of things. A servant dead was one thing, but Rav and Chess were still alive. Rav might not know Maddie was responsible for her death, but Chess would.

Imogen being dead wouldn't make things easier—it would make them *worse*.

Footsteps drew closer, and she looked at the door, which was directly across from the hallway. *Hide.* Her gaze fell to the large statue of the queen from a chess board in the corner. She collected both her switchblades from the two bodies, along with the hat and box she'd brought, then rushed to the statue with light steps and ducked behind it.

"What are you yelling about now, Mother?" Chess said, his tone bored. He lazily strolled in with his vest unbuttoned while rolling his eyes at the ceiling. His gaze dropped to his mother's body, and he came to an abrupt stop. Maddie's heart slammed so much she feared it would burst, and her hands trembled as the prince studied Imogen's torn-open chest, her empty gaze. Chess's arms dropped to his sides, tears streaming down his face, as he stared at Imogen for what seemed an eternity, as if he was waiting for her to stir.

"Mother!" he finally shouted and fell to her side, scooping her dead body in his arms. Blood smeared his bare chest as he held Imogen close.

Maddie covered her mouth with her shaking, bloody hands. Did he love her? Imogen was his mother, but she didn't think Chess was capable of love. Then again, Imogen had loved Rav and possibly Chess as well.

Glancing toward the door, Maddie didn't know if she would get the chance to escape. Just as Chess lifted his mother's bloody heart with his free hand, boots pounded down the hallway.

"Imogen, Mouse escaped!" Rav screamed. He stopped in his tracks as he rounded the corner of the hallway in front of the stairs. *Damn it, they're both here.* His breathing hitched as he studied Chess holding Imogen. "What the fuck have you done?"

Chess's face paled and he opened his mouth, but no words

escaped.

"You killed her!" Rav roared.

Maddie sucked in a sharp breath.

"No, I didn't," Chess stuttered. She'd never heard him sound so weak, so small. But she couldn't feel sorry for him, not after he'd tried to kill Ever. Not when he'd threatened to hurt Mouse. Yet still…

Three guards rushed in from the hallway and halted.

"Seize him," Rav growled. "He killed the queen."

The guards glanced at each other for a moment, then two came forward and grabbed Chess by his arms while the other gently returned Imogen's body to the floor.

Chess didn't fight back, only whispered, "I didn't do it."

"Then, who did?" Rav took a step forward, his fangs down, eyes wild.

Chess licked his lips, his eyes narrowing as he seemed to piece something together. "I don't know. But you have no purpose here now. Go back to Ivory, and I'll handle my mother's death."

"The murder of the queen does not make you king, regardless if you're the heir. You're now a traitor. I will come to you in the dungeon soon enough."

Chess didn't say another word as the guards hauled him out of the room and down the hall.

Why was Chess protecting Maddie? Then she realized he *wasn't* protecting her. He was making sure he was the only one who knew she was a traitor. If Chess ever found her, he would kill her.

Rav peered down at his dead wife, then fell to his knees beside her with a sob. "I know he's your son, and I know you wouldn't want me to kill him. But for this, he has to die." He ran his hand over her hair and pressed his lips to Imogen's.

He then stood and grabbed a heart vase from a shelf on the wall and threw it against the floor, shattering it to pieces. Maddie clenched her jaw, remembering everything he'd done, not just to her but so many innocents, turning them without their consent.

She remembered what he and Imogen had both done.

Rav's cheeks reddened as he ripped paintings from the wall, snapping them in half and throwing them across the room. He drew closer and closer to Maddie. She quietly fished out her gun, knowing she wouldn't miss his heart, even though the entire castle would hear the fateful shot.

As he stepped in front of the chess piece statue, one of the guards from earlier crashed into the room. "My king, the prince has escaped."

Rav whirled around. Maddie couldn't see his face, but she could hear every vicious word in his voice. "What kind of guards are you if everyone keeps escaping? First, the girl and Knave, then Mouse. Now you allowed Chess to murder Imogen before fleeing himself!" Rav shot forward and buried his teeth in the guard's throat, shredding it until the spinal cord split in half.

Dropping the guard, Rav straightened and wiped the blood from his lips and chin as he looked at his queen. "I suppose everyone will have to die since we can trust no one."

Maddie swallowed deeply while Rav stormed down the hall, seeming to prepare himself for a killing spree. Screams echoed, loud and shrill, and faded. This was it. Her opportunity. She dashed for the door and peered down the hallway where Rav had left. Bloodied bodies littered the area—crimson stained the walls. Slowly opening the door, she slipped out into the cool breeze and ran out into the night.

Maddie hoped Noah had made it home with Mouse because if Chess escaped the palace already, she didn't know what he would do next. But as she ran through the rose gardens, passing the marble gazebos, and entered the outskirts of the city, she didn't see a sign of Chess anywhere.

Still, she had a sinking feeling that the prince was somewhere out there lurking, watching her.

CHAPTER TWENTY-FOUR

NOAH

In all his life, Noah never thought he would slide out of a palace tunnel and land in a damn rose bush. All that lingered of his wounds now were dried blood and a dull ache in his hip. His heart hadn't stopped racing since he and Mouse had run from the queen's gardens. He was sure guards would catch up to them at any moment, yet no one chased them through the streets of Scarlet. Someone had to have seen them running from the garden…

Noah rapped on the door using the rhythm Maddie had taught him. It immediately swung open as if Ferris had been standing there with his hand on the knob. *Thank fuck.*

Shoving Mouse over the threshold, straight into Ferris's chest, he slipped inside behind her and slammed the door shut. They were either safe or they had led the enemy to their doorstep. He slunk along the wall, tuning into his vampire hearing to see if he could pick up on anything suspicious outside. The only thing audible was muffled chatter and laughter.

"Ferris!" Mouse shouted. Noah turned around just in time to watch her leap into his arms.

For the first time since he met the vampire, Ferris's face softened into a smile as he caught her. "Good to see you again, luv."

"You did it," Alice said, rushing from her room, straight for Noah. He stepped forward and pulled her to him. "I was so worried."

"I told you I'd be fine." And he'd never been more relieved to be right. When he'd told her that lie, he wasn't sure of anything at all. Neither he nor Maddie had voiced it, but he knew she felt the same. He stepped away from Alice and looked around the safe house. The most important person was missing. "Maddie…?"

"She's not back yet," Ferris answered in a low voice.

Her part had been easier than his. Keep an eye on the queen—that was all she'd had to do after they tied her up. Unless the alarm he'd set off while rescuing Mouse had blared through the entire palace, sending guards to warn Imogen. He swallowed hard. Maddie wasn't back yet. She wasn't fucking *back*. He couldn't wait another minute. Mouse and Alice were safe. He had to go back, had to—

Someone pounded on the door, making him jerk Alice behind him for protection. It took a moment to recognize the secret knock. Ferris must've realized it sooner than Noah did, because he cracked the door enough to let a body slip through. *Maddie.* A weight lifted from his chest to see her alive and in one piece, despite her rumpled clothes and mussed hair. Then he noticed something that made his breath catch when she dropped the hat box on the floor. *Blood.* Slick crimson covered the tips of her fingers all the way up to her elbows, saturating the arm warmers. More splotches were on her face. "What—"

"Maddie!" Mouse cried and brushed past Noah to get to her sister. Maddie flung her arms out wide to welcome Mouse into her embrace.

Noah dragged in a harsh breath. He didn't want to ruin their long-awaited reunion, but he needed to ask. "What happened? Are you hurt?"

Maddie looked up at him from over Mouse's shoulder. Her expression was tight as she shook her head. "It's not mine."

"It smells like the queen," Mouse whispered.

"What did you do?" Ferris asked in a serious voice that made Noah's heart beat even faster. Why would the thought of Imogen bleeding put Ferris so on edge?

"She's dead." Maddie eased away from Mouse and took her hand, leading her sister to sit on the settee. "I don't know what happened precisely. I planned on leaving her knocked out but then something came over me."

Ferris ran a hand down his face. "What did you do with the body?"

"Oh, they know she's dead," Maddie clarified. "They just don't know I did it."

Noah's brows rose. He and Maddie were the last two to be alone with Imogen. It didn't take a genius to put the pieces together. "Who do they think murdered her then?"

"Don't worry, Noah, I killed Rine first, so you're in the clear." Maddie held her stained hands up in surrender. "Chess *may* know it was me, but Rav and everyone else think that the prince is the culprit." She bit her lip. "Chess escaped but I'm confident he didn't follow me."

"We're all safe at the moment," Mouse piped up. She shuffled closer to Maddie on the sofa. "That's the most important thing right now. That we're safe and together."

Alice slipped her hand into Noah's and squeezed. "She's right."

Mouse took a long inhale of the air, her eyes fluttering, her canines lowering. Her gaze landed on Alice and the tip of her tongue darted from between her lips, licking as if she were hungry. "She's mortal again?"

"Yes," Noah replied, shifting to partially hide Alice behind him. "She's my sister."

"I'll get us all something to drink," Ferris announced, his

worried stare still trained on Mouse.

Noah protectively inched backward into his sister, remembering all too clearly how Alice had lost control of herself and attacked him in this very room. Given how long Mouse had been in captivity and knowing what he did of Imogen, she was likely starving for fresh blood instead of bagged. He turned to Alice and ushered her toward the bedroom. "Why don't we let them have some time alone? They haven't seen each other in two years."

Alice appeared to take the hint and went straight into the other room. "We should probably talk about going home now," she said the moment the door was shut.

"She won't bite you," Noah assured her. "No one will let her."

Alice scowled. "I trust you, but I can't stay here. I just … I really want to go home."

Noah flopped onto the mattress and sighed. He knew she wanted to go home and that it needed to happen as soon as possible, but not tonight. Now that the adrenaline was beginning to wear off, the ache in his hip throbbed. It was probably shattered, or at the very least, cracked. He was sure it would heal like everything else, but until it did, he just wanted to lay down. The exhaustion hit him like a truck.

"Tomorrow," he promised her. "I need a little rest now."

Alice mumbled something to herself and plopped down beside him. "Don't fall asleep until you drink some blood, okay? It will make you feel better."

"I feel fine," he lied. Alice smelled *mortal* and his gums tingled, fangs threatening to descend. But he would *not* bite her—even if his instinct for blood told him to. So he would drink whatever Ferris brought to ensure Alice's safety, then he would sleep with one eye trained on the door.

"You were limping." She lightly smacked his arm. "Don't argue with me."

Noah smirked. "I wouldn't dream of it."

When Noah opened the bedroom door the next evening, he found Maddie nervously weaving a needle and thread into some sort of cloth. Mouse's head was in her lap as she slept, but it looked as if Maddie hadn't gotten an ounce of rest. He'd meant to have a chat with her after finishing the blood Ferris had brought him, but he'd fallen asleep as Alice listed out options for returning to London. Or *outside* of London, since they couldn't risk Rav finding her again.

"Give me a minute?" he asked over his shoulder to Alice.

"Sure," she whispered, shutting the door at his back.

Maddie silently slipped out from beneath Mouse's head and nodded toward the other side of the room. Ferris had taken the second bedroom, and they couldn't ask Alice to wait near Mouse, so it was as private as they could get. Noah followed her into the corner and cast a glance back at Mouse to make sure she was still asleep before turning fully to Maddie.

"Are you okay?" he asked, brushing the stray hairs from her face. Flecks of blood had dried in a few places.

She wrapped her arms around his waist, burying her face in his chest. "Thank you."

Noah hugged her back, soaking in the feel of her against him, and placed a kiss on top of her head. Warmth stirred inside him at her sweet scent, and he tightened his arms slightly. "For what?"

"You got Mouse out." She pulled back and looked up at him with a bright smile. "She's safe now because of you."

"Not because of me. Because of *us*. You, me, and Ferris." Noah may have physically broken Mouse out, but he never could've done it alone.

"It feels a bit like a dream to be with her again after all this time."

He could only imagine. But, he supposed, he wouldn't have to wonder for long. Once Alice was back in the mortal world, there wouldn't be a day that went by where Noah wouldn't wonder if Rav had found his sister. Still, Alice was smart and he liked to believe that she would make sure to cover her tracks.

Maddie's smile faltered as she peered at him, seeming to notice something in his expression. "Are you taking Alice home now?"

"We thought it best to get it over with." Before anyone figured out it was Maddie who killed Imogen and came looking for her on the streets. One of the guards could recognize Noah from when he had wandered the halls looking for Mouse. Or worse—Chess.

Maddie's gaze fell as she stepped back, nodding. "You're probably right."

Noah tilted his head, studying the way she bit her lip as if she were fighting with herself not to speak. "I'm coming back," he told her. "I know we haven't gotten the chance to hash everything out, but I want to be here."

"Why? It could potentially mean a life in hiding."

It would also mean a life with *her*. He tilted her chin up with the tips of his fingers so she met his eyes. "I think it would be nice to stick around and get to know you a bit more. Besides, we won't have to hide forever."

She scowled. "We could literally be doing just that … *forever*."

"No," he said with conviction. "At some point, we would have to fight back, but I want to do that with you too."

"Fine, immortal, fine." Maddie grinned and stretched up to kiss him, her lips pressing against his. Noah tugged her closer so their bodies melded, her heat warming him. A primal part of him didn't want to give her up, even though he hadn't known her long. But did it fucking matter? She was different. The world here felt more like home, the immortal body he was in now felt more like his than it ever had before. He wanted to learn everything about this place. And to see Maddie's smile and determination when she created the hats she loved so much, to know what new things they could do with their mouths, their bodies. They fit together too perfectly and he wanted *more*. He slipped his tongue between her lips, reveling in her sweet taste.

Someone cleared their throat and Noah groaned as he pulled away. Mouse sat on the settee, rubbing her eye. "Maddie, I think you left a few things out last night," she said with a sleepy grin. "You said he was a friend."

"He *is* a friend. And maybe a few more things," she admitted as Ferris joined them. "Noah's taking Alice back tonight."

Ferris nodded. "We should get out of Scarlet too."

"Hang on." Noah wasn't sure what the vampire thought of him exactly, but Ferris needed to hear he wasn't planning on abandoning Maddie from his own lips. "I'm coming back. Don't leave until I do. I'll only be gone a few hours."

Ferris looked between Maddie and Mouse and gave a shrug. "That'll give us time to pack all of our essentials, but we can't wait longer than that."

"We'll wait for you," Maddie told him, casting Ferris a hard stare. "You'll be less noticeable if I stay here, and I don't want to leave Mouse alone just yet."

"Stay. It will be faster this way, anyway." He took a deep, fortifying breath and glanced at his sister. "Alice, it's time to go."

The door opened and his sister poked her head out, her gaze landing immediately on Mouse. When the pink-haired vampire didn't move to attack, Alice stepped into the room. Ferris held his hand out to her and they exchanged their final goodbyes.

"Is there anything you need me to bring back?" Noah asked Maddie.

"Just yourself." She leaned forward and pressed her warm lips to his once more, then flicked her hand in the air and gave Alice a curtsy. Noah arched a brow as Maddie sang, "Stay safe." It was a very Maddie goodbye, but one that made him want to come back even more.

"You too," Alice said. She studied Noah and nodded toward the door in a silent plea to leave.

"All right then." He took his sister's hand and headed for the door. On one hand, he was eager to get Alice back to the mortal world where she was safer, but on the other, he hated to leave her. "We won't be long."

Their flat in London had been ransacked. Tables were toppled and sofas torn to shreds. The stuffing littered the floor along with glass from shattered photos. Noah took note of the broken frame that once sat on the mantle, displaying the family photo Chess had somehow taken from Rav. The entire contents of the kitchen cupboards were scattered about and the mattresses in the bedrooms had been flipped.

"What a mess," Alice muttered, nose wrinkled as she stepped over a piece of her broken bedframe.

Noah grunted in agreement. There wasn't anything he truly cared about that had been destroyed—it was just … stuff to him. Things his parents had bought because of how the objects looked, not because there was any attachment or because it was comfortable. In fact, the sofa was like sitting on stone, but it was more the audacity Imogen and Rav had to destroy everything because his sister escaped them. And that they so easily found where his sister lived since Rav had taken Alice's purse. *Arseholes.*

Alice would have to break the news about the flat to their parents—perhaps it could be part of why she needed to leave London. Someone broke in and scared the living shit out of her, she fled before getting hurt, and … something. Alice would be the one to maintain the lie, so he would leave the details up to her. As for his absence, he was granted a last-minute opportunity to study abroad. Sure, his parents would be pissed he didn't inform them and that he left Alice alone, resulting in her being endangered by the robbery, but what could they do? Ground him? Cut off his allowance? He was twenty-two years old for fuck's sake.

"Only grab what you need," Noah said. Their parents would make sure she had a new wardrobe and whatever else, so she wouldn't truly need anything. But that didn't make up for the things she loved that were ruined.

The hair on the back of Noah's neck suddenly stood on end. He tensed, sensing someone behind him. Tuning into all his heightened senses, he took in their nearly weightless footfalls and the lingering hint of metallic in the air. Not a concerned neighbor checking on them then. He moved to the console table in the hallway and made a show of pretending to look for something while he curled his fingers around the silver letter opener.

A floorboard creaked just behind him, and Noah whirled around, grabbing the vampire by the front of his black hoodie. The male was young—at least he had been when he'd been turned—with a gap between his teeth. But the only thing that mattered were the fangs. Noah shoved the letter opener into the side of his neck and ripped it out before the male could make a sound. Hot blood splattered across his face and the wall.

Noah carefully dragged the vampire into one of the spare rooms and laid him down so as not to alert Alice with a loud thump. *Fuck.* Rav must've had the place under surveillance. He grabbed the vampire's head and set a foot on his chest, holding him in place, then easily ripped the head the rest of the way from his body. They didn't need him recovering and telling Rav that Alice had come back. He'd simply have to return and deal with the body after sending her off.

He quickly left the space, shutting the door to hide the vampire, and climbed through his disaster of a bedroom. After sparing a moment to switch out of Ferris's bloody outfit, he yanked some of his favorite shirts off their hangers, stuffing them into a bookbag, along with other necessities.

"I'll need to buy a new phone," Alice said from his doorway. Noah flicked a quick glance in the mirror to make sure he didn't have any blood left on his face. It was clean. "Mine was in my purse so Rav probably still has it."

Noah nodded. He wasn't keen on the idea of her traveling alone, especially at night, and definitely not without a phone. His old one was somewhere at Maddie's cottage. "Grab one as soon as you can, yeah? We'll get you settled in a hotel tonight, and you can head out in the morning."

She hoisted an oversized bag over her shoulder and sighed. "All my credit cards and money were in my purse too."

"No worries." He tossed her a pair of his folded socks.

"What's this?"

"My emergency fund." He'd been saving up for his own flat so he could live independently from his parents' money, but he wouldn't need it now. Not in Wonderland.

Alice unrolled the socks to find a neatly rolled stack of bills. "Bloody hell, Noah."

"I figured I might need to bail you out one day. Thought it would be from jail, but hey…" He laughed. "Come on then. There's a place a few blocks over."

Alice shoved the socks into her bag and followed Noah from the flat. "Will I see you again?" she asked when they hit the sidewalk.

Noah put his arm around her shoulders. "Of course you will. There are plenty of portals and it's not as if I'd miss the holidays. I'll just be there a bit later to avoid, you know, burning to death."

"But you'll be fugitives."

"True." Noah sobered. That part would definitely be shitty, but it wouldn't be forever. They would make their stand against Rav eventually, and Chess too when he resurfaced. "I might miss a few holidays, but don't worry, sis. After all I did to save you, I'm not about to vanish from your life."

Alice thought for a moment, a line forming between her brows, before she relaxed under his arm. "That's true, I suppose. But Noah, I'm really sorry about … everything."

"Sorry?" He smiled. "Don't be sorry. I wouldn't have met Maddie if it wasn't for you, and I actually *like* being a vampire."

Alice uncomfortably shifted on her feet. Noah could tell she still felt both guilty and grateful by the way she studied him, but he didn't want that. He wanted her to heal and live her life, knowing he was living his.

"Just don't come looking for me," he warned, his tone joking, though he was serious.

Alice chuckled, the sound thick with unshed tears. "I don't think you need to worry about *that*."

Noah laughed with her to distract himself from the mounting pressure behind his own eyes, but then he winced at the thought of anyone else searching for him. "Don't let Mum and Dad worry about me. Maybe buy a second phone since I lost mine and text them as me once in a while."

"I can do that," she whispered.

Noah caught the scent of the blood flowing in her veins again. He held his breath for a moment, pushing down his urge to feed. "Good. Then you'll need to remember a few important things to make it look real. What was I going to uni for?" he quizzed.

Alice jabbed him playfully in the side with her elbow before answering correctly. Noah asked her several more important questions, sprinkling in a few smaller things to keep up appearances.

"When in doubt, be vague or ignore them. It's what I would do," he suggested as they reached the front of the hotel. "I'll walk you in."

"No." Alice sighed. "I'm not the best at goodbyes, so let's say them now."

Noah swallowed hard. "Are you sure you'll be okay?"

"Positive." She gave him a strained smile, her eyes filling with tears. "Thank you for saving me."

Noah sighed, wrapping her in a fierce hug. "What are big brothers for?"

"I mean it," she said into his shirt. "Thank you."

"You're welcome." The words came out tight around a lump in his throat. He didn't want her to see him cry, but *damn* if it wasn't hard to hold back. Even if he would see her again, he didn't know how long it would be or if she would be safe until then. "I love you, sis."

"I love you, too." Alice pulled back and adjusted the bag on her shoulder. "Go on then. Keep yourself safe."

"I will." He nodded at the hotel. "But I'm not leaving until you get inside."

Alice rolled her eyes, tears slipping from the corners, and turned away from him. "See you soon."

"See you," he called as she entered the brightly-lit lobby, hoping *soon* would be the truth. But, for the time being, he had to figure out how to clean blood out of carpet and dump a body in the Thames without being seen.

CHAPTER TWENTY-FIVE

MADDIE

"We can't wait forever," Ferris said as he zipped up his bag.

Maddie shot him a glare. "It's been less than twenty-four hours."

"It's been precisely twelve hours," Mouse pointed out, her pink plait falling across her clean lacy black dress. The gown she'd arrived in hadn't even been fit for a rat. The gothic frock she now wore fell between her knees and ankles—it was her usual dark and brooding style.

Her sister had been quiet most of the time since she'd been back, except for when she would hum to herself. She'd never sang before being captured, but she must've had to entertain herself somehow.

"He's taking his sweet time." Ferris walked out of the room and Maddie rolled her eyes at his back. He wasn't usually this impatient, but she knew he wanted to get Mouse farther away from Scarlet as much as Maddie did.

Mouse hummed while fishing something out of her front

pocket. Something that wiggled, curled. Maddie squinted at the blue and yellow thing in her sister's palm. A caterpillar. What in all of Wonderland? It slowly crawled along the center of Mouse's hand.

"Why do you have that?" Maddie arched a brow, watching as the caterpillar stood on its hind legs, seeming to sway to Mouse's song.

Mouse let out a breath but didn't take her gaze from the small creature. "She's my friend and kept me company while at the palace. Her name is Desdemona, but I call her Des."

Maddie's lips tilted at the edges. Her sister always did love a good Shakespeare piece. There wasn't a single one she could recall that her sister hated. "Othello is still your favorite play, I take it?"

"It is." Mouse watched the caterpillar, her expression unreadable. Maddie waited for a smile to cross her sister's face like it always had, but there was nothing. Only a solemn look that Maddie wanted to wipe away and see her laugh instead. As she studied Mouse's hand, the caterpillar—something inside her mind clicked.

It wasn't a random hand or caterpillar that Ferris had drawn … it had been her sister's and Des. A memory from his time spent at the Ruby Heart Palace...

"Do you want to release Des outside?" Maddie asked softly. "Since you're both free now?"

Mouse jerked her head up, a horrified expression crossing her face. "No."

"What happened to you in there, Margo?" She hadn't used her sister's real name in so long. It was reserved for dire situations. After facing Imogen in the palace, Maddie should've been stronger. She should've attempted to rip out Rav's heart when he'd been alone.

Mouse's gaze grew haunted, her lower lip wobbling. "Nothing. I was treated fine." She straightened and shrugged, her eyes becoming distant once more. "I've been through worse."

She was lying. Mouse may have survived a horrendous act when she was human, but Maddie believed something worse occurred in that palace. Her sister had never looked like this before. Since she'd been back, Mouse hadn't really spoken much after their hug when her sister had arrived.

Maddie circled her arms around her sister and held her close, breathing in her gardenia scent. "Just talk to me when you're ready."

"I'm tired," Mouse mumbled into her shoulder.

Taking a deep swallow, Maddie rubbed her sister's arm. "When we get to the next safe house, you can sleep for as long as you want."

A familiar knock at the door sounded and Maddie's breath hitched.

He'd come back.

Maddie took her arms from Mouse and went to answer the door. Her heart sped up as she cracked it, peering out into the street, worried it was Chess or someone from the palace, but it wasn't.

Noah stood there, his blond locks falling at his brow. He no longer wore Ferris's oversized clothing, but a tight solid black T-shirt and jeans that showed off his muscular arms and legs.

"Maddie," he murmured, his green eyes brightening as his gaze fastened on hers.

"Noah." She grinned.

"You're back," Ferris grunted from behind them. "Good, because we need to leave."

They really did. Maddie knew that no inch of Scarlet would be left unsearched as Rav hunted down Chess for supposedly killing his queen. She was pretty sure Chess hadn't followed her because she would've already been dead if he had. Once Rav found Chess, she didn't know how long it would take before the prince voiced his suspicions that Maddie murdered his mother.

Earlier, she had taken a quick rinse to wash away any traces of Imogen's blood so no one would scent it on their travels. As Maddie scooped up her pack, she decided not to worry about

Chess now. She needed to focus on the others and get them to a safer house.

The group headed outside into the cool breeze of the bare streets. Not a single bat flew in the air as Mouse and Ferris walked ahead. He took Mouse's bag from her, then hoisted it over his shoulder. Neither one of them talked but Mouse shifted closer to Ferris, her humming stopping as though he was her cure.

Maddie realized then that her sister had grown even closer to Ferris in the past two years. Her stomach sank—she knew she'd missed two years of her sister's life, but she hadn't realized that Mouse wouldn't want to confide in her. Perhaps she could with Ferris though.

"Are you all right?" Noah asked, his deep voice relaxing her a fraction.

"I'm perfectly peachy." Besides having to leave all her hats behind at the cottage, but she couldn't risk going there. She was almost certain Chess would be sitting on her settee, with his legs spread open and his vest unbuttoned, lazily waiting for her to arrive so he could remove her heart like she had his mother's.

"You don't look it."

"How was Alice?" Maddie asked, changing the subject.

"She's safe. Our flat was in shambles and one of Rav's goons showed up. I had to dump him in the Thames and ruined my favorite jeans. Yet I'd have to say I'm perfectly peachy too."

Maddie sucked in a sharp breath. She should've known Imogen and Rav wouldn't have left his flat unwatched. "I should've come."

"You can't save me every time." He grinned. "I'm an immortal in training."

"Ah, that you—"

Mouse stopped, sniffed the air, her eyes growing wild as she gazed around the tall stone buildings. It was almost as if she was a new vampire... "I need to eat."

Ferris grasped her shoulders. "Hold Des and I'll get you a packet."

With a nod, Mouse held the caterpillar. She took the powdered blood and water from Ferris.

Something wasn't right here. Ferris's gaze met Maddie's and he shook his head, telling her not to question it.

As they kept to the shadows, Mouse seemed to perk up a bit yet still focused on Des, who was crawling up her arm.

"What's with the caterpillar?" Noah asked. "She was singing to it back in her cell."

Maddie shrugged, but her chest tightened for her sister. "It's her friend from the dungeon."

She kept her eyes peeled as they ventured away from the city. They walked for hours until they reached the same white and silver trees that she'd traveled past only days before with Noah. All remained quiet as they drifted deeper through the outskirts of Ivory, staying clear of the city. The abandoned lands of the Red Queen would've been the ideal place to go, but Chess knew the location of its safe house. She feared he would try to return there at some point to look for them.

As they entered the opposite side of Ivory, Maddie scanned the trees, searching for the trunk with a mark across its belly. Some thin and wide, others gnarled or drooped. Her gaze fixed on a curving line in the middle of a mossy trunk. *Aha*! This was it.

Maddie drew out the key from her skirt and shoved it into the thick trunk. A soft click echoed and she opened the door, allowing everyone entry. When she stepped inside, the smell of flowers and fresh rain snared her senses.

Closing the door behind her, she ascended the white marble flight of stairs. All around her, the room was entirely white, its surface giving off a glittery sheen. Down below, an ornate dinner table surrounded with high-backed alabaster chairs took up the open space. When she hopped down the last step, she peered up at a chandelier, covered in pearl beads, hanging above her. In the center of the table rested a chess game that looked as if it ached to be played. Six doors surrounded the room, and Ferris opened each one. Five bedrooms and a bathing area. It was almost like a miniature palace underground compared to the other safe houses she'd spent nights in.

"I think I'm going to lay down for a bit." Mouse yawned and padded into one of the rooms, leaving the door wide open. Maddie's stomach sank at the thought that her sister didn't shut it because she feared being caged in again.

Ferris's brow furrowed as he studied the room where Mouse had entered.

"Was she like this when you were there?" Maddie whispered to him.

"Sometimes." He ran a hand across his strong jaw.

"Watch over her tonight. I think she'll confide in you more than me."

"Of course." He set his and Mouse's bags on the floor and walked into the room.

Tomorrow would be a new day. Each day her sister was gone from the palace would get better for Mouse—it would have to.

A warm body slid up beside her, reminding her she wasn't alone in the room. This male, who'd become immortal not too long ago, had decided to stay in Wonderland, to remain a vampire.

To be with her.

She turned to face Noah, her chest swelling as she studied each of his chiseled features, his bright eyes. But she wished she could pull back each of his layers and see everything that rested inside him too, including his tender heart. It could be considered morbid, but she just wanted to see everything that ticked within him, what made him caring, determined, loyal.

For the first time in her life, she wasn't sure what to say, what their next step would be, or how long they would stay there hiding. Yet the most important thing had happened—both their sisters were safe for now. Ever was still gone, but Maddie knew she would meet up with her again one day.

Her gaze flicked to the chess game on the table, studying each of the black and white pieces once more. Her fingers twitched, wanting a challenge.

"So," Maddie said, adjusting her hat and taking elegant steps toward the table. She then picked up the white queen piece and whirled around. "How about a game? Winner gets to choose what we do next."

Noah smirked, sauntering up to her until his broad chest pressed against her breasts, his arms caging her in at the table. "You want to play chess?" His deep voice was like silk caressing her ears.

"Of course," Maddie sang, ducking down and out from his cage. She then ran the tip of her finger along his jaw and traced his soft lips. "Unless you're afraid I'll beat you, immortal."

Noah pulled out a chair and took a seat, stroking the black king as he studied her. "I highly doubt it. I was the best player at my school when I was twelve."

She wanted to pat his head and congratulate him on that rather cute remark. "Ah. You forget I have many more years than you playing the game."

"You want to play by the rules and go first?" Noah continued to brush the king, and she couldn't help thinking about his long, lovely fingers or how good they felt pressing into her flesh.

"White always goes first, but I suppose I'll allow you to." She drew out the chair opposite him and sank down, resting her elbows on the table. This was just the distraction she needed from Imogen, Rav, Chess, Mouse, Ever...

"I'm glad I met you, Maddie," Noah murmured. Her heart drank in that comment and before she could reply, he straightened in his seat, growing serious. "Now, let's focus."

Maddie grinned wide. "Let's do this."

Noah went first, both of them staying quiet while they played, as though they were at a tournament. The game came naturally to her because of Ever's past lessons. Maddie moved. Noah slid. She jumped. He swiped. She took. He claimed. But in the end, she still won. However, he was incredibly close to conquering her.

Maddie set the pieces back into their proper places and stood from the chair, rounding the table until she was beside him. "We can play again tomorrow. Should I go easy on you next time and let you win?" Maddie teased.

"I already won." Noah pushed the chair back from the table and pulled her into his lap as she gasped.

Taking a deep swallow, she studied his hooded eyes, his dilated pupils. Butterflies swarmed in her chest and neither uttered a word. Instead of trying to discover what words were, she brought her fingers to his face, like before, and cradled his warm cheek.

Noah leaned into her touch and whispered, "I know I'm being needy, but damn, I can't control myself around you." His mouth captured hers and she wanted every inch of him.

If she was a needle, then he was her thread, and together, they would figure out the next step, and the next, and the next after that. But, for now, she wanted more of his lips on hers.

CHAPTER TWENTY-SIX

NOAH

Noah lifted Maddie, her legs encircling his hips. Their lips remained sealed as he carried her into the nearest bedroom and kicked the door shut behind him.

"Ah, aren't you the eager one, immortal?" Maddie grinned against his mouth without pulling away. "It was me winning the chess game that turned you on, wasn't it?"

"Exactly that." He nipped her bottom lip and set her gently on the plush fur blankets covering the bed. A gilded mirror hung above the headboard, matching the simple yet elegant room. With the floors and walls both glimmering white, the two small dark tables beside the ivory bed, were a stark contrast.

Maddie twiddled her thumbs, her grin growing wider. "Well, are you going to kiss me?"

Hell yes, he was. Purple curls spread around her head like a halo on the white quilt, her hat askew. The way she looked at him made his heart pound faster than it ever had. Noah slowly crawled over Maddie until he caged her in. He leaned close, only a hair's breadth from his lips touching hers. "I want to kiss every damn inch of you." He ran the tip of his nose up her lips, inhaling her enticing cherry scent, then pressed his lips gently to hers.

Her fingers fell to the edges of his shirt, and he let her lift it over his head and toss it somewhere on the floor. They had pleasured each other several times now, but this was the first time he felt in control of his lust since turning. He wanted to take his time. Explore her thoroughly.

Noah sat up and placed his finger at the top button of her dress. Teasing them both, he slowly unfastened each button, all the way down to her navel. He then peeled the fabric back over her shoulders, exposing the perfect swells of her breasts. She bit her lip as she stared up at him, and he couldn't control himself when he took her perfectly peaked nipple into his mouth. As he circled it with his tongue, he drew down the remainder of her dress while she moaned.

He then pushed up from her, his gaze meeting hers once more. "I'm going to continue kissing you."

"Where next, immortal?" She grinned.

He smiled wide as he crawled down her body until he was off the bed and standing in front of it. His eyes raked her in, wearing only a pair of see-through purple panties that didn't hide any inch of her.

Dropping to his knees, he grasped her legs and tugged her to the edge of the bed with one swift movement. She laughed as Noah smirked mischievously and placed a kiss on the side of her knee. He hooked his fingers beneath the sheer fabric and shifted back only long enough to slide them off, his gaze never leaving her glistening core. Then he returned his lips to her flesh, just above the knee, dragging his mouth across the soft skin of her thigh, biting at her gingerly. Maddie sighed as he traveled to her other leg and repeated the motions. Only, this time, he kissed higher and *higher*. His chest swelled with an intense emotion. The other woman he *thought* he'd loved ... how wrong he'd been. *This* was what they wrote books about—this was the beginning of their story, and he wanted to see where it would lead.

"Are you going to kiss me?" Her voice came out breathless, with a tinge of craving … for him.

"Yes, right here," Noah whispered. He leaned in and flicked her sensitive clit with his tongue. Her gasp made his hard length throb. *Patience*, he urged himself, and lowered his mouth to her. His tongue circled and flicked until her hands found his hair, entangling, gripping, driving him wild. Hooking one of her legs over his shoulder, he plunged his tongue deeper into her before slipping a finger inside.

"Noah," Maddie begged, growling.

"Hmm?" he asked without pausing. She tasted so damn good—he could kneel in front of her like she was his queen and drink her like this forever.

"More." Her voice was low, and Noah's breath caught in his throat. How could he deny her that? Deny her anything? As he gazed up at Maddie, her eyes glazed, she was the prettiest thing to ever grace this world—*any world*. He added a second finger and her legs shook. Increasing his speed, he pumped and licked, relishing in her quiet sounds of ecstasy, until she shattered with his name on her lips. A sense of pride filled him as he took in her flushed face and lowered eyes. But he wasn't finished with her yet. Sitting back on his heels, he wiped her arousal from his face.

"Stand up," Maddie whispered, trailing a finger down her side.

Noah tilted his head and did as she instructed, his body anticipating her next touch. She slowly sat up, her fingers grasping his belt loops and tugging him to her.

"Come here," she whispered, peering up at him from beneath her lashes. That emotion was there again as they studied one another. Neither said a word, their eyes doing the talking, as she slowly unbuttoned his trousers, the sound of the zipper filling the room, and shoved them to his knees. His hard length pulsed with need as she wrapped her hand around him. A deep groan escaped him when her warm tongue ran from the base of his cock to the tip.

Noah swept the hair away from her face so he could watch

as she took him between her lips. With a moan, he tilted his head back, committing the sensation to memory. *Damn.* In that moment if she were to ask him for anything, he would do it. Even if it was bringing her the fucking moon itself.

Her mouth left him a second later, her hand continuing the pace she'd set as she trailed kisses up his chest, to his neck, to right behind his ear, her fangs grazing the flesh. "That's enough of that," she sang in his ear.

Noah's eyes fluttered as she pumped him and he couldn't help smiling at her words, her adorable and sexy oddness.

"I agree." Using his newly-acquired speed, he scooped her up with the intention of setting her down gently. Instead, he forgot his trousers were still around his knees and they flopped sideways onto the mattress. Maddie covered her mouth as she laughed, and Noah quickly kicked off the denim.

"Found that funny, did you?" Noah climbed over her, settling between her legs. Biting his lip, he tucked a curl behind her ear. He never thought he would be in this position again after his disastrous breakup, but here he was. With the immortal who saved his life, faced a pack of werewolves at his side, and took down an evil queen to save her sister. The same immortal who'd stolen his heart with her peculiar hats and bright soul.

Her eyes glittered with amusement as she shrugged. "Maybe I did."

Noah's heart gave a warm, pleasant *thump* and he dove in for a kiss. Their lips collided, tongues dancing to a perfect symphony. Everything about her was perfection. And he would worship her for all eternity.

"You're beautiful," he mumbled and kissed her again. His hand cupped her breast, the pad of his thumb rubbing her nipple. Without warning, his own fangs dropped.

He slid his mouth down her neck, kissing, licking. A soft, satisfied sound left Maddie when he traced her vein with his tongue, the saltiness of her skin hitting his taste buds. It spurred him to graze the same spot with his teeth and her hips rose to meet his cock.

He lined himself up with her entrance and paused to admire the expression on her face. The look that mirrored his—needy, dazed, flushed. *Fuck.* He placed a lingering kiss on her throat—

Then he sank his teeth into her tender flesh at the same time he slid into her heat. The taste of metal flooded his mouth, coating his tongue, as her delicious folds took in his length.

"Noah!" she growled, arching in pleasure.

Her nails dug into his back, her legs quaking as she wrapped them around his waist. He drew her blood into his mouth with a gentle suck, and she moaned quietly, a hand over her lips to stop Ferris and Mouse from hearing.

Forcing his fangs from her skin, he started to move within her. Slowly at first, shifting his hips in a circular motion, learning every inch of her. Which movements made her gasp hardest, which made her back arch off the bed, and which had her shifting beneath him for a new angle. Finding one spot that made her nails dig into his back deeper, he skimmed his hand down from her breast to rub her bundle of nerves. *Shit.* He wasn't going to last long.

"Keep doing that," she murmured. "But faster."

Noah groaned and thrust harder. Faster and faster, just as she requested. His eyes fluttered while trying to fight the urge to spill into her, but he wanted one more orgasm from her first. Just. One. More. She deserved to come many, *many* times. He ground his teeth together in an attempt to hold himself back, but his rhythm turned more frantic. More desperate.

Maddie's finger traced his shoulder as she buried her face in the crook of his neck. She gave him open-mouth kisses, her tongue flicking the sensitive area. A moment of intoxicating pain flooded him when her fangs pierced his flesh and bright stars floated in his vision. His release barreled out of him without warning at the same time her walls squeezed with her own release.

"Fuck!" he growled as he rode out the pleasure.

When he finally stopped moving and the flutterings of Maddie's second orgasm abated, she drew her fangs from his neck. He rolled off her, distrusting that he had the strength not to crush her. That was the most intense pleasure he'd ever experienced. His cock was already growing stiff again, wanting *more*. And not just physically. He wanted more of Maddie's laughter, her bravery.

"Thank you," Maddie whispered.

Noah turned his head to stare at her, their noses almost touching. "You don't have to thank me for good sex," he teased.

"No, silly." She grinned. "Thank you for coming back."

A smile spread across his face. How could he have stayed away from this alluring female who constantly made his heart race? "You don't have to thank me for that either. It was the only logical choice."

"You could've taken the cure," she reasoned, a guarded look slipping into her features.

"No," Noah said firmly. He wanted to erase that look from her face forever, wanted her to know *why* he'd come back. "Becoming a vampire wasn't something I could've predicted, but I've never felt more like myself than I do now. You're here and I think… I mean, I *know* that I'm falling in love with you, Maddie."

Her lips parted as though she must've misunderstood what he said.

"Bloody hell, after all we've been through, I might as well just say it. I love you, all right?" He rolled his eyes and smiled.

She blinked rapidly for a moment, a tinge of nerves building in his chest while he waited for her to say something. *Anything.* Did she not feel the same way? It was okay if she didn't—they could work up to that if she gave him the chance.

"How could I not love you, too, immortal?" Maddie finally said, her honey-colored eyes brightening as she took his face between her hands. Warmth spread through him while she pressed her lips to his forehead, his nose, his mouth, his neck, just before whispering in his ear. "Now, how about you help me make a new hat and ask me more of your wonderful, inquisitive questions."

"Only after I make love to you one more time."

"Fine, immortal. Fine." She laughed as he hauled her into his lap, then her laughter was replaced by beautiful gasps of pleasure when he sank into her once more.

He would never get tired of her sounds. He would never get tired of *her*. She was something unexpected, but somehow he knew, she was his messy, unpredictable, wondrous, immortal match, nonetheless.

EPILOGUE

MADDIE

A hat was still like a heart.

But now Maddie's heart was full of more than her love for hats, her sister, and Ferris. It had opened up to something new, *someone* new, something wondrous. A new kind of love. With Noah.

She didn't know what was next, though. The four of them were still hidden below ground in Ivory. As for Alice, she was safe. Noah had snuck out once, only briefly, to check on her in Leeds.

Maddie glanced up from sewing and leaned into Noah, who was reading a book. Mouse sat beside Ferris on the floor, playing a game of chess with him. Her caterpillar, Des, rested at the edge of the board, silently watching them. Ferris hated the game, but he did it for Mouse. After a month away from the Ruby Heart Palace, her sister still hadn't smiled like she used to.

One day, she will again.

Maddie brought up her scissors and cut out several Queen of

Night tulips that she'd drawn into the thick fabric. She was making a hat for her sister in an effort to cheer her up. For weeks, Maddie made do by using fabric from one of the beds and breaking it apart over and over again to reshape. Then while checking on Alice, Noah had retrieved materials for Maddie to make a few hats. After that tiny gesture, Maddie had given him the utmost pleasure. He'd returned the favor—her body unintentionally heated at the reminder of that night.

"Do you want me to help you with that?" Noah whispered in her ear and set down his book.

Maddie tilted her head. "You want to do it right here in the open?"

His cheeks pinkened, but his eyes still sparked with desire. "I meant with the hat."

"So boredom made you turn to hat-making then?" She grinned. "Take this." Pressing a needle in between his finger and thumb, Maddie placed the fabric in his other hand.

He lifted her and sat her in his lap, making her laugh. Together, she helped Noah weave in and out of the fabric, even though he didn't need the help—she just wanted to keep touching him.

A knock sounded at the door, echoing throughout the house. Everyone stilled. Ferris stood, grabbing the gun he kept beside him.

Maddie leapt off Noah and grasped hers from on top of her backpack while Noah retrieved his from the bedroom. Weaponless, Mouse padded toward the stairs, unafraid.

Then another knock came, familiar. A knock Maddie *knew*. The same one she and Ferris had shared at the safe house back in Scarlet.

Jolting forward, she raced past Mouse, in case it wasn't who she believed it to be.

Maddie held her gun tightly, aiming it upward, as she swung open the door to a female with black hair and brown eyes, wearing jeans and a raggedy old Dracula T-shirt.

"Is that the way you greet a friend?" Ever arched a brow, her gaze focused on the gun pointed at her face. "Next time"—her long fingers touched the tip of Maddie's weapon and brought it to her chest—"remember to aim for the heart."

With a grin, Maddie lowered the gun and yanked the White Queen inside before sealing the door shut. Maddie then folded her arms around her friend and squeezed her tight, inhaling her lily scent.

Ever took a step back and smiled. "My attire is rather drab, isn't it?"

"You look positively human," Maddie said. She'd never seen her friend not wearing something white and lacy.

Ivory's ruler placed her hands on her hips and blew out a breath. "Do you know how many safe houses I had to visit before I found you?" She took the wig from her head, exposing her white hair pulled back in messy pinned-up curls, while descending the stairs. The queen's shoulders relaxed as she peered around the room, her gaze landing on Mouse. "She's safe." But then Ever cocked her head as she gazed at Noah. "So it seems all of you are wanted in Scarlet. But I don't know you."

"That's Noah. I'll explain it all." Maddie shrugged while Noah studied the new guest with a furrowed brow.

Ever walked to the middle of the room, removed her backpack, and took a seat on one of the chairs at the table. "I heard from my spy that Imogen is dead, but my bastard brother still isn't. I would've come back from the mortal world sooner if I'd known they'd had Mouse. After hearing of Imogen's death, I knew it was time, but it shouldn't have taken me this long to return. I was also informed that not only are you all wanted, but my dear, precious, Prince *Chess* is." Her lips curled up into a smug grin.

Even if Ever had come back sooner, she likely would've been dead before she'd found Maddie anyway.

"Do I have the story for you," Maddie sang. "But first, what were you planning to do next?"

Ever reclined in the chair and peered up at the ceiling. "The time has come for me to reclaim what is mine and intimately acquaint my brother's heart with a stake."

BOOK TWO

CHESS

CHAPTER ONE

CHESS

BEFORE

Everything in Ivory was so … *pristine*. White and silver and sickeningly clean. Every time Chess crossed the border from Scarlet, he was overcome with the desire to soil it, even in some small way. Now, he was sullying a set of satin sheets. The vampire riding him—*what was her name again?*—moaned as he grabbed handfuls of her tight arse.

His gaze shifted from her perky breasts to the ceiling of her home and how the plaster had been artfully molded into scallops spreading away from the simple chandelier. *Fuck.* If he was noticing the décor, he wasn't into this. Accepting the invitation into this female's bed had sounded like a good idea at the time, but he'd only just finished drinking from a donor's neck. The feeding had fueled his lust as the blood had powered his body, and the voluptuous brunette had made the offer at the precise moment.

Now, boredom stirred.

Not bored. Preoccupied, he decided as the female made slow, grinding circles on top of him. He needed to finish this so he could do the job he was tasked with. The one his mother—the Queen of Scarlet—had given him. He scowled. Best not to think about his mother at the moment unless he wanted to leave with aching balls.

Chess growled and flipped the female over, setting her on her hands and knees. She gasped, then groaned as he slammed back inside her. Holding her hips, he pumped into her over and over, harder and faster, until his release barreled through him. He squeezed his eyes shut and thrust one final time, emptying himself into her, with a low grunt.

"Already?" she asked, peering over her shoulder at him in disbelief.

He snorted. They'd been at it for over an hour, and though he could last twice as long, he was running late. "Sorry," he said, sounding every bit as insincere as he felt, but he didn't give a fuck. "Things to do, places to be."

Climbing off the bed, he gathered his clothes, stopping only long enough to step into his black trousers, before heading for the bedroom door. She huffed in irritation as he slipped into the hallway, but by the time he reached the female's front door, she was finishing herself off, if her moans were any indication. At least she hadn't bothered to ask him to stay.

Chuckling to himself, Chess made it to the street. The home was nestled between a bakery, meant for the mortal donors who either lived in or visited Wonderland, and an art studio. All of the buildings on the block were white marble, veined silver, with large frosted windows and steep roofs. In the distance, he could barely make out the peaks of the Ivory Palace. Unlike the one in Scarlet that loomed over the city from atop a cliff, Queen Ever's residence was only a short walk outside the city.

He hummed to himself as he meandered back to the place where he'd hidden his attire. The white suit and silver tie would help him blend in with the citizens of Ivory as they readied for the royal ball, and the mask he'd chosen was a silver-plated cat. Since it covered nearly half his face, no one would recognize him. Especially with his hair pulled back and brown contacts hiding his yellow eye color. Not that his mother cared if anyone knew who he was. It mattered to Chess, though, but only because it would make it easier to blend in at the palace if he looked the part. He'd always lived by the motto: *work smarter, not harder.*

The fast-paced violin notes drifted around him from streets away as he changed quickly in an alleyway, tucking his black vest and trousers behind the same planter where the costume had been. Finally, he hid the dagger he would use to take Ever's heart inside his jacket. Then Chess slipped silently back onto the empty alabaster streets. Most vampires seemed to already be at the palace given the lack of souls in his sight. Shops were shuttered and windows dark. Before, when he'd joined the female at her home, the city had been bustling with costumed bodies and laughter.

Soon, they would all be subjects of Scarlet. The Queen of Hearts had waited nearly a year for the opportunity to have Chess sneak into the enemy's lair. She'd plotted and schemed with Rav while Chess ... well, his *plan* was a simple four steps.

One—*Attend the party.*

Two—*Find Ever.*

Three—*Kill Ever.*

Four—*Flee.*

He was no coward, of course, but he wasn't a fool either. Murdering the White Queen in her own palace would bring every guard down on his arse—at least the ones who hadn't turned on their queen already. Once Ever was dead, her prick of a brother could step right into the role of ruler. Rav was the next in line to rule after she was gone, which meant the hostile takeover of Ivory would have a peaceful transition. Hypothetically. Rav didn't necessarily want to sit on the throne—he just wanted Ever to shut the fuck up about human consent before they were turned.

But none of it mattered to Chess. As always, he was just along for the ride. His mother, Imogen, had disappeared when he was eight years old, only for her to drag him to Wonderland once he'd turned twenty-two. *Following* her and Rav's murder of his father, who had become King of Scarlet after abandoning Chess as a baby. Losing his shitty mortal life and his shitty life prospects wasn't a hardship. He'd never felt anchored to anyone or anything before, so he embraced the carefree lifestyle in Wonderland. Feeding, fucking, and exploring until his heart was content, all for the small price of murdering a few of his mother's enemies. His mother would rule alongside the white-haired fucker and Chess would play. It worked well for everyone.

As he finally reached the edge of the royal grounds, he paused to study the exterior for plausible escape routes. Any of the rounded first floor windows would give him easy access to run, but jumping from the second and third floors could result in minor injuries as each pane of glass was capped with tiers of carved spikes. Together, they appeared like silver vines climbing up the sides of the building. Beautiful and deadly, just how Chess preferred. The most stunning things in Wonderland had both qualities and he made it his mission to track them down. Fuck them, study them, sometimes kill them…

The most troubling obstacle he faced was the silver moat surrounding the grounds. If he didn't get back across the drawbridge in time, he would have to swim. He would never admit it, but water was the one fear he hadn't been able to overcome after turning immortal. When a bunch of older street youths had tossed him into the Thames at twelve, he'd nearly died. Sure, he'd figured out how to swim that day, but he never looked at water the same again.

Adjusting the cat mask on his face, Chess took one step onto the drawbridge, then another and another, ignoring the gleaming water on either side of him until he was finally across. The prince released a small breath and entered the bustling castle through the rounded doorway. Marble floors shone underfoot and a massive chandelier with sconces shaped like lilies dangled above.

Delicate violets hung in garlands around the ceilings to add a splash of color to the otherwise monochromatic space.

It wasn't his first time inside, but when he'd visited with his mother for *negotiations*, all had been still. Now the sound of chatter, laughter, and pleasured moans joined in with the orchestra's classical tune. Masked vampires filled the entire entry, spilling into rooms on either side. There were foxes and wolves, full-faced masks and half-masks, silver and white. A female with purple hair—Maddie—skipped across the room beside her pink-haired sister, Mouse, both wearing elaborate hats in addition to their masks.

Chess ignored the Mad Hatter and her Dormouse of a sister by plucking up a goblet of warmed blood from a tray as a servant passed. He then inhaled the wonderful metallic scent. Where had Ever come up with enough fresh human blood to serve so many? Not quite the humanitarian as she pretended to be. Only turning willing humans to serve them—*fah*. Immortality was a gift. It was only fair that the newly-turned had to serve the one who gave it to them. Murdering mortals, however, seemed to be acceptable. It would take fully draining at least five dozen adults to give everyone a single glass, unless they only took a small amount from hundreds of donors.

How, Chess wondered absently, *did Ivory have so many willing mortals living in a city that feasted on them?* At the Ruby Heart Palace, there was no confusion about where humans stood. They were food, not servants or friends.

Brushing away the thoughts, Chess slinked farther into the palace in search of Ever. He moved along a wall of full-length mirrors and sterling busts of former Ivory monarchs. Bodies swayed around him, knocking his goblet more than once. Blood sloshed over the sides, sliding down the backs of his fingers. He switched hands and licked the precious liquid off.

"How do you like the vintage?" came a soft, regal voice.

Chess spun to find a female smiling brightly at him from behind a silver lace mask, her eyes a deep brown. *Ever*. The queen's white hair was plaited and artfully woven with a diamond crown atop her head. Her silver gown shimmered in the candlelight, hugging her perfect curves and highlighting her assets. Chess didn't bother to hide his perusal of her body. *A damn shame he didn't have a chance to fuck her.*

"An elderly woman, if I had to guess," he mused.

"Perhaps," she answered, swirling her own goblet. The blood clung to the sides. "There were many donors." She looked him over and cocked her head. "Who are you?"

"I could tell you, but that would take all the fun out of wearing a mask," he whispered with a smirk.

A wide grin crossed her face. "Ah, so does that mean you don't know who I am?"

"Perhaps I don't," he teased, sipping at his drink. "How about you give me a tour and we can chat more? It's my first time attending one of your balls."

Ever plucked the goblet from his hand—her warm fingers brushing his, sending a heat straight to his cock—and set them both down on a nearby table. "I don't normally give tours, but for you, I suppose I will." She leaned in and murmured, her hot breath hitting his mouth, "But only because you're wearing a mask of my favorite animal."

"Does that earn me a *private* tour?" Chess purred, imitating a cat, and Ever trailed a hand down his arm, tantalizingly slow.

"Oh, indeed. A very *personal* tour." She smiled coyly and backed up three steps before turning with the unspoken order for him to follow.

Chess watched the Ivory queen sashay through the crowd, his eyes studying her bare legs as she nodded at those who caught her attention. Alas, there wouldn't be time for him to tear the gown from her body, slide his hands down her curves, explore the swells of her breasts, and fill her with his hard length. She smelled of lilies and, he was sure, would taste just as sweet. He'd wasted too much time fucking around earlier. *Ah, well.* There was plenty of hot arse back in Scarlet, and the prince had no trouble filling his bed at home.

Sliding between party-goers, he followed Ever from one

white and silver room to another. Each resembled the last. Colorless, soulless. Even the room with a variety of stringed instruments was bland with its white and silver violins and cellos. They needed to add more than the splash of color the violets gave in the entry way—the palace needed paint, fabric dye, and richly stained woods. He could solve those problems once Ivory was absorbed by Scarlet and make this place less of a mausoleum.

When Ever finally opened a door near the back of the palace and disappeared into the garden, he smirked behind his mask. It seemed she found him just as attractive… Perhaps a *little* time to play first wouldn't hurt—there were countless places he could fuck Ever without being seen. Against the pillars of the gazebo, bent over one of the granite benches, on the edge of the large fountain. Shit, he would even take her on the ground amidst the blooming flowers since none of them had thorns like the rose bushes back home.

"Such a lovely garden," he murmured as they ventured to where they were alone. There were hydrangeas and hyacinths, tulips and lilies. No roses, though, and he wondered briefly if that was because Imogen was so fond of them.

"Isn't it?" Ever hopped up to sit on the edge of a low, ivy-covered wall. Flowers budded among the foliage, promising future white blossoms.

With a chuckle, Chess prowled closer, toying with her. Ever reached out and took his arms, tugging him closer, then ran her hands up to his shoulders. Her light lily scent became stronger, intoxicating, his mind clouding. Chess leaned down so she could wrap her fingers around the back of his neck. He set his palms on both sides of her hips and studied her plump lips.

"So tall," she murmured and leaned toward him. Her palms skimmed his neck and down his chest, his eyes fluttering. "And so *strong.*"

Chess licked his lips, bringing them a breath away from hers while she continued to explore his body with exquisite movements. His cock stirred as she glided her fingers lower, to the button of his trousers, then dragged them back up, teasing him.

"How about a kiss?" he asked, surprising himself. What the fuck was he doing? Kissing was usually the last thing on his mind and he never bothered to ask with words.

In answer, she pushed him back and rammed her knee into his groin.

"What the fuck?" he groaned, doubling over in pain.

Ever shoved him sideways so he tumbled to the ground, her form looming over him. With a knife in her hand. "Did you think I wouldn't learn about the assassination planned for tonight, Princeling?" She threw the knife into the air, the blade spinning, and she caught it.

He chuckled despite the ache radiating through his groin. He should've known she hadn't singled him out so quickly and gotten him alone out of lust. Ever was said to be a virgin queen, but he didn't believe that one bit. *Thinking with my cock again.*

But he wouldn't fail in his task.

Steeling himself, he pushed away the pain and leapt at her, grabbing her wrists. Fighting her so close to the palace was bound to get him caught. If the wrong guards noticed, he was fucked, so he began dragging her farther into the garden, holding her tightly so she was unable to use the knife.

Ever twirled away, ripping herself from his grip, her dress whirling around her, and brought her arm up. The blade—*a second blade*—pierced his chest. Pain flared through him, hot and sharp. *Sloppy,* he chastised himself just as the metal cut through flesh and scraped at his bones. Chess grunted and fell back into the grass. Ever glared down at him with icy brown eyes.

"Guards!" she shouted.

Fucking hell. There was a good chance the guards who had heard her would haul him off to the dungeon. He wasn't about to let himself be caught. Ripping the knife free of his chest, he took a garbled breath.

"Tell me, was this your mother's idea or my brother's?" Ever asked curiously as a flurry of movement caught his eye.

When six familiar guards surrounded them, a smug grin

tugged at the corners of Chess's mouth. "Wouldn't you like to know?"

"Arrest him," Ever snapped, seemingly at the end of her patience.

Only the guards didn't move toward him. They moved toward *her*.

"Rav may be an arse," Chess said as he tucked Ever's knife into his belt, "but he has an equal claim to your throne." The bastard hadn't wanted it before, choosing Imogen over the crown, but now the couple felt no need to choose between territories. Why would they when they could have it all? "I guess you didn't know that he still has friends in Ivory."

A flash of panic crossed Ever's face and she whirled, fleeing back into the castle. Chess held up his hand to stop the guards from following her. "I never turn down a game of cat-and-mouse," he said, pulling his feline mask away from his face. She wouldn't get far and it would—dare he say it—be *fun* to chase down the proud queen. *Run, mouse. Run.*

CHAPTER TWO

EVER

PRESENT DAY

A queen didn't always wear a crown because she wanted to. Sometimes the world required it.

Ever never asked to be the White Queen of Wonderland. Never chose it. But she fulfilled the duty nonetheless because she wanted to keep humans safe. Not from her bite, or her kill, but from becoming immortal if they didn't choose it. Being a vampire wasn't a natural sort of thing, so forethought was necessary, the decision conscious, just as both she and her twin brother, Rav, had chosen. Before the Red Queen murdered the former White King and White Queen, the royals had waited until the siblings were ready to turn them. But karma came to the Red Queen when she met her own demise from a murderous beastie. *Thank you, Jabberwocky, for that glorious and vicious kill.*

Ever peered around one of Ivory's rather ridiculously large

260

tree trunks, her gaze settling on *him*. Chess. *Surprise, surprise, Princeling. I do believe I owe you your death.* He was hiding from the Kingdom of Scarlet after being accused of murdering his mother, Imogen, the Queen of Hearts—who'd ripped the bloody organ out of so many.

She watched as he stood in front of the glistening silver lake, the gray of the world growing darker as night descended, and peeled his black vest from his broad shoulders. He shook his head, his chestnut hair framing his chin and neck. She rolled her eyes. Who was he trying to impress with no one else around? The water? Apparently, he assumed the lake that would be running its liquid hands up his chiseled body needed to be impressed by his presence. Conceited prick.

Time to die.

Ever tiptoed in his direction until she was close, so close that her digits could easily brush his bare back before digging her fingernails in to tear off his flesh.

The wind blew past them and Chess tilted his head back, inhaling the air without turning around. "You found me."

"That I did, Princeling. I won't ask for a kiss as you did with me, I'll just get on with it instead." This time she didn't use a dagger to stab him in the chest. She thrust her hand forward, breaking through his rib cage, gripping his still-beating heart, and ripped the warm organ from its home.

Ever spun him around to face her. His lips were parted, his eyes wide as he stared at the thick crimson sliding down her arm and dripping to the ground.

"I didn't miss your heart this time," she cooed. Chess's knees buckled and his body collapsed to the dirt with a *thump*.

A rustling stirred at the edge of the forest. Ever dropped the heart and darted away from the prince's still body to duck behind a tree. Out from the tall silver and white bushes came a male, shoving his long white hair with red tips behind his shoulder. *This is the perfect day.*

Rav—her twin—stopped, hovering over Chess's dead body, but she couldn't focus on the fact that he was her brother…

He was now her enemy, especially after turning her own guards against her in the past. Before she could surrender to her thoughts of thinking of him as family, Ever leapt out from her hiding place and slammed her feet into his back while her hands gripped the sides of his head. She used him for balance as he shouted curses at her, but his words ceased, became trapped in his mouth, after tearing his head from his body in one easy motion. Rav fell to the ground beside Chess. *Glorious.*

"Dear, deceitful brother." She grinned as blood leaked from Rav's neck wound, pooling at her feet. "Goodbye."

"You did it, Ever, but you weren't the one to rip out my heart as you'd dreamt about, were you, darling?" Imogen purred, appearing out of thin air in front of her. The dead Scarlet queen's crimson curls hung down her back, and she wore a silky red dress with a low v-cut that went past her navel, exposing her milky skin.

"Bloody hell," Ever growled, pushing away what had been a wonderful fantasy until Imogen had rudely invaded it. Couldn't she remain dead in someone else's daydreams?

Ever lifted the white queen chess piece that she always carried in her pocket for luck. She'd been toying with it for what had to have been hours while lying in bed, unable to sleep, only thinking of things she wished would come to fruition. It had been a while since she'd rested in a proper bed, not since she lived in the Ivory Palace.

Nearly four years had passed since Ever had stepped foot inside Wonderland. She had spent most of her time tucked away in the mortal world, hidden inside a safe house like a coward. Until recently, when she reconnected with an old friend and discovered the Queen of Hearts had been murdered. Come to find out, it had been Maddie who had done the marvelous deed.

There was so much Ever had missed, and if she'd known her friend Mouse had been taken, that Maddie had been banished to a cottage in Scarlet, she would've returned sooner. *Should've checked in on them.* But there was still the part of her that didn't want to face her brother because that blasted piece of her still loved the fool. Wonderland hadn't changed him. He'd changed himself. He'd never cared about ruling before, but from her old friend, she learned he was planning on joining all of Wonderland's territories since he was the only ruler left.

Ever squeezed the chess piece, to the point that if she pressed any harder, her strength would break it. She wanted revenge against Rav, but she also wanted Chess.

In the past, the prince had never once approached her. He'd always watched her when they'd been at parties, just as she'd watched him. She'd waited for him to slink up and attempt to woo her, and on the night of her masquerade ball—when he tried to retrieve her heart—was the moment she'd taken matters into her own hands. Because she'd expected betrayal from him, she was prepared to stab the prince, but then she'd been caught off guard when her staff had taken her brother's side. She should've ripped off Chess's head or tore out his heart before escaping.

Releasing a huff, Ever sat up and pressed her back against the ornate headboard. She was safe once again, and she was tired of it, tired of not doing anything. Lingering in her Wonderland safe house wasn't the answer. Her friends were safe, and she wouldn't risk them.

Ever shoved the silky sheets aside and pushed up from the bed. Most of the safe houses only had the necessities, some more, but this one was like a small palace underground.

Grasping the edges of her lacy white nightgown, Ever drew it over her head, knowing she couldn't parade across Wonderland wearing anything ivory in color. She tugged on the blue jeans from the floor, followed by her *Dracula* T-shirt—that made her smirk—and a pair of checkered Vans.

She scooped up the black wig and shoved her hair into its bothersome depths. The thing was itchy and hot and, eventually, she would set fire to it.

Ever tucked the chess piece into her pocket and lifted her backpack. As she pulled open the door, the main glistening, white room sat empty for everyone except for one immortal at the table in the middle of the area.

Ferris.

She blew out a breath, alerting him to her presence. Ferris's hand stilled on a notebook he was sketching in and he hurried to shut it. His brown gaze peered up at her and an eyebrow arched. Since she'd seen him last as a mortal, he appeared mostly the same. Some vampires inherited different hair colors, eye colors, but he'd gained neither. For her, it was her hair, which had become white as snow instead of the deep murky brown it had once been.

"You're not sleeping?" Ever asked and stepped toward him.

He ran a hand through his short, dark hair. "Nope, not today."

Earlier, Ferris had been mostly quiet, but his eyes had drifted to Mouse every so often. Always drifting to Mouse, even back at the club before Ever went into hiding. When he'd been human, after Maddie and Mouse brought her to a run-down club, Ever had drank from him with her friends. He'd had a heavenly taste, but she'd seen the truth in his blood, the pain, something only a few royals could do. After that, she didn't want to drink from him, didn't want to see his suffering again.

Ever sank down in a chair beside him and took out a pack of blood and her canteen of water. She figured she better get her strength up before leaving.

"How do you like being a vampire?" Ever asked to break up the silence.

"It's better than being human." He paused, and bit his lip, his eyes meeting hers. "You never told them what you saw?"

Ever shook her head, thinking about him at nineteen … the car wreck … his pregnant girlfriend dying. At the club, he'd seen the pity in her eyes when her gaze had unintentionally latched onto the promise ring he'd worn on a chain around his neck, the one he'd given to his dead girlfriend. He'd somehow known what she'd seen and an understanding had passed between them in that moment. "It's not my place."

Ferris let out a relieved sigh. "Thank you."

"No thank you needed." If he wanted to tell Maddie and

Mouse more about his tragic past, then he could. But the past was the past. No, that was a lie. Sometimes the past did require a bit of betraying. Chess… Rav…

A low, groggy moan came from one of the bedrooms where Mouse was sleeping. "How is she?" Ever glanced back at Ferris. He'd been with Mouse at the palace for two years as Imogen's Knave, while she'd been in a cell. Ever also learned Imogen had taken him to her bed, then fucked him before turning him into her vampire servant. He'd done it all to protect Mouse, to try and help her escape. If anyone was a damn prince, it was Ferris, especially since she'd known through his blood that he'd never wanted to get close to another female again.

"She's a fighter," he said softly. "The palace wasn't good for either of us, but even with some of the shitty things I had to do there, I'm glad I was with her."

The former White King and Queen had never mistreated Ever or Rav. The twins had been made into a prince and princess after falling into Wonderland, but the royals' servants had always had a choice before becoming immortal.

"I need you to do something for me," Ever finally said.

Ferris threw his head back and rolled his eyes at the pearl chandelier hanging above them. "Bloody hell, don't tell me you're leaving already."

"Promise me you'll watch over them while I'm gone."

His gaze fell back to hers and understanding was there. "I will."

Ever finally mixed the blood and water, then drank the thick concoction down. Ferris's fingers tapped against his closed notebook, and she wondered what was inside. But she didn't ask, didn't want to know if his demons were in there like they'd been inside his head.

"Do you miss the drums?" She smiled, remembering the one image he'd held that helped him through his past before Mouse had saved him from his overdose.

Ferris nodded, giving her a curious look at the sudden change in subject. "I do."

"When I return to the Ivory Palace one day, you will come and bring a new set with you." She needed new guards anyway.

His lips tilted up at the edges. "They'll be fucking loud."

"Good. I'm sick of quiet." Ever smiled and stood from her seat to bid Mouse and Maddie goodbye before returning to the mortal world.

Ever adjusted her backpack, then left Ferris to himself. Mouse's door was still wide open and the White Queen walked in, finding her friend lying asleep in bed, her breaths even. Instead of the serene expression her face normally held in the past as she slept, a scowl sat in its place. Ever wondered what she was dreaming, or perhaps, what the nightmare was about. Her stomach tightened at the thought that she was the reason this had happened to Mouse … and to Maddie.

She stepped farther into the room toward the bed—the area was similar to where she'd slept, except the bed and wardrobe were both obsidian, while everything else was a glossy white. Mouse's pink braid rested over her shoulder, and on the bedside table, her blue and yellow caterpillar, Des, lay atop a bright green leaf, fast asleep too. Maddie had told Ever that her sister acquired the creature while a prisoner inside the Ruby Heart Palace. A caterpillar in Wonderland wasn't destined to become a butterfly as in the mortal world. They didn't have those insects here, so instead, it would remain a beautiful wingless creature for all eternity.

"Mouse," Ever whispered, lightly shaking her friend's shoulders, and Mouse jerked forward. "I wanted to tell you goodbye, but I'll only be gone temporarily."

Mouse blinked, her violet eyes glazed, and let out a small yawn. "I can come."

"No, you will not. You still need time to heal." She didn't mean the physical wounds. In the past, Ever wouldn't have minded her coming, but not this time, not after the suffering Mouse had endured at the hands of Rav and the Queen of Hearts. She bent forward and kissed the forehead of her friend, who still smelled of gardenias like she always had.

Mouse nodded, but her lips pulled into a tight line, hesitant, as she laid back down. Des lifted her small head and peered at Mouse, as though checking to make sure she returned to sleep all right. Mouse's breaths were already even so Ever padded to the next room, then knocked lightly on the door. It only took a moment for Maddie to answer dramatically.

When Ever arrived earlier to the safe house, her friend had appeared just the same as the day the White Queen escaped the palace—purple curls, the tilt of her hat, her attire. They'd been friends for over two hundred years. She'd found her in Wonderland, lost, starving. Ever had pretended to be a normal female since she'd been acclimated to vampires using her because of her title. And when she'd revealed herself to be a queen, Maddie had treated her the same, never differently, always honest. Then she'd brought her sister, Mouse, to the palace, and like that, Ever had found true family again.

"You're leaving already?" Maddie asked, pressing a hand on her hip, her honey-colored eyes meeting Ever's. Her usual violet attire was replaced with a long black shirt that must've belonged to Noah—the human Maddie had turned immortal due to a wretched incident where he'd almost died at the hands of Imogen's friend, Osanna. Ever hated that bitch.

"Rav's heart awaits my stake," Ever said with a smile.

"That bastard deserves two stakes," Maddie sang. Her expression turned serious as she cocked her head. "Let me come with you."

"We discussed this earlier, and you agreed to wait. We can't show all our cards at once, so it will be only me for now. However, if I don't return in a month, then that means something's wrong. You can't stay in hiding forever or as long as I did … like a coward." Ever gritted her teeth at how long she'd been gone, how much time had been wasted.

"You're not a coward. If something does happen to you, we will murder your brother with all the hatpins in Wonderland." Maddie wrapped her arms around Ever and held her tight, her comforting cherry scent enveloping them. "Now, let me at least walk you to the door."

"I wouldn't mind that at all." Ever released Maddie and headed toward the stairs. Ferris was already gone from the table and must've silently slipped back into Mouse's room to watch over her.

They walked up the glistening white steps together in silence, and when Ever grasped the door handle, she glanced back at Maddie. "You know this, but don't open the door for anyone unless you hear my knock. Even then, remember to aim your gun at the heart."

"Or my sewing needles." Maddie grinned and patted Ever's shoulder. "Now, go kill that bastard and reclaim your kingdom. But if you need us, we shall be ready."

They were all wanted. Mouse for escaping, Maddie for hiding her, Ferris for fleeing with Noah's sister. She assumed Noah might also be since she'd recently learned Rav knew he'd been turned by Maddie. It wouldn't be hard for Rav to put two and two together. However, Rav didn't seem to know that it was Noah and Maddie who'd helped Mouse escape.

Ever smiled and gave Maddie a small wave as she ventured out into the night, knowing exactly where her first stop would be.

CHAPTER THREE

CHESS

The inside of the London cab smelled like old cigarettes and peppermint, nearly blinding Chess to the scent of the driver's blood. He was wrinkled, bald, and at his age, probably full of prescription drugs to keep him alive, so he wouldn't be on the menu anyway. Chess enjoyed the occasional drug-riddled human, but the sort who would give him an enjoyable high—not thin blood or lower cholesterol. They made the blood taste downright atrocious.

Brick buildings flickered by the window. Hedgerows, street lights, and all the *cozy* trappings of a mortal life. He hated it. All of it. The flower boxes, the warmly lit rooms in the homes. Perfect family cohabitation. It was much better when everyone lived their own lives, did their own thing, and relied on themselves. Like him. Imogen was his mother and he had loved her, but they hadn't truly *needed* each other. The image of her heart in his hand flashed through his mind, and he shoved it away as he always did before an unwanted emotion could swallow him whole.

"Turn here," Chess instructed.

"Have a destination yet?" the man asked in a raspy voice, taking the turn.

Chess had flagged him down near a train station and simply told him to drive when he climbed into the backseat an hour ago. There was nowhere to go—at least nowhere he felt safe. Every club he knew in London played host to vampires from Scarlet and they would undoubtedly turn him into Rav. It was bad enough he was slumming in the basement of an abandoned home outside the city, but he needed to feed. There hadn't been time to gather supplies when he'd fled Wonderland and the bleeding bastard who currently ruled Scarlet, so he'd had no powdered blood to sustain himself. He hadn't dared return to Wonderland either.

"No," he replied, weariness settling into his bones. "Just keep going."

The driver shrugged and continued on while Chess turned his attention to the streets. They passed people in groups of two or more but none alone. How was he to lure someone into an alley for a bite this way? He could compel an entire group, but it took more energy than he had. He could manage two humans at most tonight, and one of them needed to be his driver because shockingly enough, he had no money. He scowled, knowing there were hundreds of pounds sitting in his dresser back at the Ruby Heart Palace in case he wanted to play with mortals without compulsion. Buy their drinks, buy them dinner, play the long con... He sighed. The only ones getting conned now were the vampires and mortals in Scarlet.

Everyone would believe Rav when he claimed Chess murdered their queen. It wouldn't even be that shocking, given how ruthless Scarlet could be. Yet, as callous as Chess was, she was still his mother. Sure, she had abandoned him when he was eight years old. But his father had left them both when he was only a baby to become Scarlet's king, meaning his upbringing was less than ideal, sleeping on the streets, pick-pocketing, or worse—whatever he'd needed to do to eat. To survive. But that was in the past. Imogen had killed the father he'd never met and come back to give Chess the best gift of all: eternal life. He'd forgiven her easily after that. She'd loved him enough to come back for him, after all, but he'd had no desire to wear her crown.

Maddie didn't seem the type to want it either, though, and she'd slaughtered his mother. Granted it was likely to save her sister… If he hadn't left to track down Ever, he might've been there to stop it from happening. He'd trusted the Mad Hatter. Trusted that, in exchange for allowing her to save Mouse from the dungeons, that she would give up Ever's true location. He'd traveled for days, searching up-and-down the Red Queen's territory for this elusive safe house, only to return empty handed … to find Imogen dead. He hadn't told Rav because he was the one who wanted to find Maddie, and he hadn't wanted the bastard to discover that he was partly the cause by allowing the Hatter to retrieve her sister. Guilt twisted in his chest, and he rubbed the sensation away.

First, he needed to deal with the back-stabbing arse. Then he would take care of that purple-haired twat.

No—first he needed to feed.

Rolling the sleeves of his white dress shirt, Chess sighed a second time. "Take me to the closest club outside of London."

"You got it," the driver said, sounding relieved to have an end to this trip.

Chess settled into the backseat and stared at the cab's roof. What was Rav's game? Did he *really* think Chess had killed Imogen? After centuries together, even while barely tolerating the other, the accusation felt like a betrayal. Surely, he knew Chess better than that? And if he *did* know the prince hadn't murdered his own mother, what was his motive? Even if Rav was desperate for a crown, he had one waiting for him in Ivory once Ever ran from her kingdom. Right after she'd stabbed Chess… He rubbed at his chest, thinking about the old wound, that night, her face… Since then, he'd wanted to find her *desperately*.

"Like sister, like brother," he grumbled to himself.

Ever had at least had the decency to stab him in the chest with a real blade. He had to respect her for that anyway. Before he fled, he'd thought she was a coward for hiding, but he understood now. It wasn't about being a coward, it was about being strategic. There was no path to achieve revenge if one was dead. And, before he met his final end, Chess had every intention of burning Rav alive.

"Here we are," the driver said, pulling the prince from his thoughts.

Chess leaned forward and met the man's eyes in the rearview mirror. "Thank you for the ride," he cooed, infusing his voice with his vampiric influence, letting the power smooth his tone. "I've had a rough night, so you won't charge me for the trip."

"No, I won't," the mortal agreed jovially, as if it were his idea. "You have a good night."

"You too," Chess said with a smirk and slipped out of the cab. He stood in front of a large gray building with darkened windows. The loud, thumping music from inside promised a bloody good time, so he approached the line of humans standing outside. The hunger growing in him was a stark reminder that there was no time to waste waiting alongside them. He cracked his neck and with a quick burst of speed, entered the club, unbeknownst to the muscular bouncer.

Dozens of humans packed the dance floor. Smoke swirled around their ankles while neon lights flashed overhead in time with the bass. A woman with two twisted knots atop her head stood on a raised platform, headphones pressed to one ear, tweaking the music on her turntables. Chess inhaled, closing his eyes for a moment to revel in the sweet scent of her blood, though faint since it was still in the vein. It only made his mouth water more. *Fuck*, he was hungry.

He opened his eyes and met the piercing blue gaze of a man across the room. The way the blond mortal sucked on the straw in his drink sent a rush of heat straight to Chess's cock… It had been way too long since he'd sank his fangs into someone's soft flesh. Chess grinned and prowled straight for his conquest, avoiding the sea of dancing bodies.

"Hey there." He reached the area near the bar, resting an elbow on a tall table, and stood in front of the delectable mortal. Smudged glitter shone across both of his cheekbones under the flickering lights. "You alone tonight?"

"Not anymore." The man stood a little straighter and scanned Chess up and down. "What's your name?"

"Charles," Chess lied.

"Alec," he said and stepped closer, sliding a calloused hand up Chess's arm. "Want to dance?"

Chess plucked the drink from Alec's hand and set it on one of the high-top tables along the wall, then flicked a glance at his lips. "I have a much better plan."

The twinkle in the mortal's eyes told the prince that he understood exactly what he meant. Chess leaned in and inhaled Alec's scent across his neck, the delicious blood lingering beneath his flesh. Playfully nudging the man backward, Chess soon had him up against a wall where he slowly ran his tongue up Alec's skin, tasting the salty sweetness. The mortal was practically begging to become Chess's personal drink. The prince kissed his way up the mortal's throat to his shapely lips. His fangs threatened to make an appearance as he tasted him further, twisting their tongues together. He held himself back, warming Alec up so the influence would be easier to apply. Not that it was a hardship. The human was an expert with his tongue, slipping it between Chess's lips, sliding and sucking. When he felt the bulge in Alec's trousers press against his leg, his fangs dropped of their own accord.

Heat coursed through Chess, as he was starved for more than blood…

Chess grabbed the back of Alec's neck to steady himself and to keep him from pulling away as the prince trailed his lips across the mortal's cheek to reach his ear. "Let me feed," he said, using the last bit of influence that his strength allowed. If anyone at the bar or on the dance floor noticed, they would never know what he was *really* doing.

Then he sank his fangs into the human's soft flesh—hot, metallic liquid burst over his tongue. Chess moaned, his eyes fluttering as the warm crimson glided down his throat. Mouthful after mouthful of utter bliss. The prince's cock grew painfully hard when Alec groaned, not in pain, but in pleasure. Drinking a final gulp, Chess flicked his tongue over his bite marks and retracted his fangs, power coursing through him.

"Thanks," he whispered while grinning.

"Shit," Alec breathed. "I don't know what that was, but it was fucking hot."

"Oh?" Chess quirked a brow. What sort of club was this exactly? He turned to take a second look at the clientele, but Alec tugged him, spinning him so his back was against the wall. The desperate look of *need* on his face sent a thrill through Chess. *"Oh?"*

Alec lunged forward and captured Chess's lips again, this time with more force. Chess would let the mortal have his fun, believing he was stronger, more dominant. If things continued, he could show him just who the alpha was later—*in private*. Alec's hands roamed the prince's chest, and soon, his mouth ventured to explore more of him as well. Nibbling Chess's ear, unbuttoning his shirt as he licked down his neck…

Chess's glazed expression drifted to the dance floor. The masses moved against each other, grinding, swaying. It hypnotized the prince as Alec sucked at his neck. *Damn,* he needed this. They were going to have to find an empty bathroom or dark alley soon so they could please each other properly.

A figure entered the dance floor. Two figures. One with obsidian hair and a short, black lacy dress, showcasing long legs, and the other, a dark-skinned male with his braids tied back. The couple danced along with the crowd yet there was *something* that caught his attention about them. The graceful movements, perhaps. But the hair on his arms now stood on end.

Vampires.

Fuckity-fuck. He had been so preoccupied by blood, so damn

hungry, that he hadn't bothered to do a sweep of the club. They didn't seem to notice him, or, if they had, they didn't care. Still, it was better if he got out of there, just in case.

"Sorry," he said, extracting himself from Alec. "It's been fun."

Alec said something in protest, but Chess was already making his way toward the door. If the couple hadn't recognized him yet, he didn't want to tempt fate. Sparing them a last look before reaching the door, he froze. He squinted, his gaze stilling on the female's features. That heart-shaped face, those deep brown eyes, that pouty mouth he had asked to kiss, had wanted to kiss before taking her heart…

No.

It couldn't be … could it? Almost four years had passed since he'd seen the White Queen, but he'd seen her twin nearly every day for centuries. It was *Ever*. He didn't recognize the male with her, but who the fuck cared about him? He'd been searching her out for *years* and now he just *happened* to run into her? It wasn't like him to look a gift horse in the mouth.

"The enemy of my enemy…" he said to himself. With a grin, he buttoned his shirt as he backtracked to the bar, sitting on the stool to watch and wait. To plot how best to use this opportunity to his advantage.

CHAPTER FOUR

EVER

Silver trees with ivory leaves surrounded Ever, and the branches rustled violently, creating an interesting melody. It wasn't only her friends she'd missed over the years, but Ivory, more than she could've imagined.

After trudging through the forest for a long while, the grass rippled as the wind picked up even harder. Sharp rain fell from the dark sky, where the moon sat full and the stars shone brightly.

"Of course, it would storm at this moment," Ever grumbled, shaking her fist at whatever vampire gods might've been looking down on her.

Ivory's trees thinned, giving way to Scarlet's red and black ones. She picked up speed, traveling a good distance before her ability lagged, requiring her to stop. *Damn.* She wished the speed would've lasted longer so she could've gotten to her first destination quicker. The wildlife stayed hidden among the trees, peering at her as she passed. She caught sight of a crow, studying her, seeming as though it wanted to peck her eyes out. If she drew too close, the little bastard would try, but she would be faster.

"Yes, it's a lovely day, isn't it? Even though I'm a soggy mess." She couldn't help grinning at a bald squirrel baring its sharp teeth at her in a smile.

As Ever entered the kingdom of Scarlet, screams filled the air of the city. She didn't know whether it was a brawl, lovers role playing, or someone getting slaughtered. It was the usual dark melody of Scarlet accompanied by the scent of blood and decay. Tall black and red glossy stone buildings surrounded her, and ruby lanterns led her way to the specific house where she needed to stop for a moment. A three-story building with gargoyles perched at each corner of the slate roof and crimson curtains hanging from the large arching windows.

Bringing the tendrils of her dark wig forward to cover her face, she ascended the six steps, then lifted her hand to use the hideous snarling wolf knocker. Ever schooled her features but mentally rolled her eyes at the décor. It took a few moments before the unlatching of the lock sounded. The door swung open to a tall female staring at her with a pristinely arched green brow. Her long emerald hair matched that pompous brow perfectly, and her golden dress with a popped collar brushing her cheekbones made her look even more haughty.

"What do you want?" Osanna asked in a bored tone, barely scanning the White Queen over.

"So, you haven't found new help yet?" With a bit of grace, Ever moved the locks of her wig aside and lunged forward just as Osanna's eyes widened in recognition. Her hands easily grasped the vampire's head, and she ripped it off in one swift motion, a loud crunching sound echoing delightfully. Blood spilled down the throat of the headless body, the scent of metal filling the air, as it slumped to the ground with a perfect thump. Smiling, Ever tossed the head beside the cunning bitch, brushed her hands together, patted her lucky chess piece in her pocket, and whirled around before continuing through the city.

That was for Maddie and her new lover, Noah. Osanna had

nearly killed him, leaving Maddie no other choice but to save him. Of course, there had been another choice … to let him die. Which was what Ever would've done by allowing nature to take its course, but perhaps, this once, she could agree that Maddie made the best decision she could in the situation, especially since the Hatter hadn't had the White Queen to confide in.

The rain slowed to a light mist, but Ever kept her head down as she passed several vampires carrying ice chests. Another vampire was fighting with a male over a mortal female. His hand shot forward, tearing open the male's chest while the woman screamed. Ever really needed to fix this calamity of a city. Things could be bloody without being so damn violent. Her wet hair hung in her face until she arrived at a portal leading to the mortal world. She would meet with her spy soon.

Beneath a gnarled, bat-infested scarlet tree, was a completely exposed dirt hole. In the mortal world, the portals were always hidden. She remembered the day she'd stumbled upon the one with her brother centuries ago. It had been in the woods behind their parents' home, and she'd slipped through while Rav had hurried to stop her from falling. However, they'd both fallen.

Most of this was her fault. If Rav had never gone down the hole with her, he would've never hurt Maddie—she wouldn't have been taunted by him all these years. But Maddie was happy, content, with Noah now, and Ever would hold onto that.

As she dropped to her knees and crawled through the dirt, a tingling sensation coursed through her. Bright green and red beetles scurried around her, their scuffing noises echoing.

At the end of the tunnel, bushes blocked her exit, and she pushed them back as she crawled the remainder of the way out into the night. Ever hoisted herself up to stand in a park surrounded by trees and a playground that looked as though it hadn't been used in quite some time. Brushing off her hands, she ran the short distance through the trees to her safe house near a lake.

A hidden door was buried at the base of a walnut tree farther away from where Londoners routinely ventured. Ever shoved her key in the lock of the camouflaged door and lifted the lid, letting the earthy smell caress her nose. She scurried inside and locked the latch, then trotted down the few steps to her small space. There wasn't much besides a mattress, pouches of dried blood, her viola, solo games, stacks of clothing and wigs, and a few other necessities. The past few years, she'd played solitaire so many times that she'd lost count, plucked the strings of her instrument just to hear any other noise besides her thoughts, breathing, and the mortal world's creatures above.

But tonight, there wasn't much time if she wanted to meet her spy. Pulling off her wet clothing, she rushed to get dressed for her mission: to begin taking back what was long overdue.

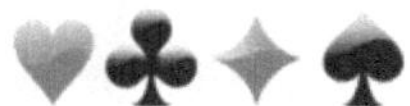

Ever adjusted her tight, sleeveless black dress and ran a hand through the dark locks of one of the new wigs from her stash. The other one was practically rubbish after the rain so she'd tossed it into a bin along the way to the club. It was easy to get things from the mortals—just influence them and they would give a vampire anything. But she tried only to take what was necessary, which had been more so lately.

Outside the gray, windowless building, loud beats from the music drifted on the breeze. Over the years, she tried and failed to appreciate most modern sounds. She preferred violas, violins, and the piano. Anything classical. Bach, Beethoven, Mozart. However, she did like the way Yo-Yo Ma ran his bow across his cello strings. It had been decades since she last went to one of his concerts.

Ever passed several women who appeared tipsy as they stumbled from the club. She entered the stone building, sweat and alcohol hitting her senses, along with something even more delicious. *Blood.* And *plenty* of the heavenly liquid. It had been years since smoking was allowed in establishments, and that was a good change because the odor had always wreaked havoc on her.

Ever's gaze locked with the bald bouncer's, and she used her influence to avoid paying and to gain access into the spacious room ahead of those waiting in line. He didn't hesitate as he let her pass, a distinct huff echoing from behind her. Neon lights flashed around the dark room, which was filled with warm bodies. So many mortals, the blood pumping in their veins, made her mouth water. Even though she'd drank plenty earlier, she wanted more, just one taste. But there wasn't time for it. She searched around the room, her gaze falling to a busy bar with a female bartender wearing a black bow tie, then to a male toying with the sound system as Ever looked for her vampire spy.

"Hello, beautiful," a deep voice said from behind her, wrapping his strong arm around her waist, "care to dance?"

"Sure." Ever smiled and turned around, finding a broad male in front of her with beaming dark brown eyes. His long braids were wrapped in a bun at his nape, and he wore tight trousers with a sleeveless shirt that showed off his ebony skin and bulging muscles.

March. Her spy and friend.

"Did you find what you were looking for?" March asked as he took her hand and led her into the middle of the club where people were drinking, grinding, kissing, and touching in secret places. She trusted March because she'd sired him long ago and knew his heart from what she'd seen in his blood. He was loyal to her, always had been. And she'd wished that he'd still been a servant in the palace when her guards had turned on her. Yet he'd left Wonderland years ago to live in the mortal world, and she hadn't reconnected with him until recently, when he'd told her about Imogen's death, Mouse being held prisoner, Chess accused of his mother's demise, and Rav's new plans for Wonderland.

"It took me a while, but I did," Ever said, biting her lip.

He brushed a lock of her wig over her shoulder. "I was about to come searching for you."

"Don't ever do that."

March used to attend the tea parties that Maddie and Mouse hosted at the Ivory Palace. He'd always yearned for more from Ever, but she couldn't give him what he wanted. They'd given each other oral pleasure a time or two, but even then, Ever refused to give herself to anyone fully. It wasn't that she didn't want to have sex with someone—it was that she couldn't trust most individuals. Not after having numerous vampires sent to her to get information, whether it had been from the Red Queen, the Queen of Hearts, her own damn brother, or just random vampires who'd wanted her kingdom for their own. But with March, she didn't want to hurt him by not feeling the same way, even though she had considered giving her body to him at least once.

"I discovered something new." He paused, drawing her close, his hand caressing her lower back. "Something you may find interesting."

"What do you know?" she asked, swaying side to side with him to the beats of the music.

March leaned in so his mouth was just below her ear, his lips brushing her neck. "He's using humans as servants now."

Rav. Ever inhaled sharply, her eyes widening. "What do you mean?"

"He's not changing them as he did before, but keeping them influenced instead."

What the hell? Ever pulled back and took a deep swallow. "Like actual slaves?" Rav had all the guards and servants in the world, had *her* guards. Or not, since March had told her he'd murdered every single one of his guards and servants in Scarlet after Imogen died. But for some unknown reason, Rav had gotten her guards to turn on her.

March spun her in a circle. "Yep. He's not taken his beloved's death well, it seems."

Could her brother be any more of a bastard? Before, the vampires he and Imogen sired were given no choice physically, but at least they weren't slaves mentally. Just when Ever didn't believe things could get worse, they sure as bloody hell did.

"Anything else?" she asked.

"There might be something, but I need more time to figure it out." He bit his lip. "I just need to do this once more with you." His lips crashed to hers in a fierce kiss. She didn't hesitate as she kissed him back, her tongue dancing with his, her tugging him closer by his waistband so she could feel his hard length against her. Sparks didn't course through her veins from it, or vibrate through her heart, but it felt good nonetheless.

"I'll meet you again soon," Ever whispered near his ear—no mortal would be able to hear it, but a vampire's senses were far more superior. "In three days."

March gave her one last kiss before walking away, his arms flexing as he ventured through the crowd and out of the main room. She wished she could make herself feel something more for him because he was a good male, but she just … couldn't. She didn't think she would ever feel love for anyone. Not how Maddie practically glowed when she'd discussed Noah. But it didn't matter. She had herself and Wonderland to focus on, and that was good enough.

She allowed the music to fill her ears, let her body move to the intense beats. For once, she truly absorbed the sounds and didn't compare it to the music she preferred to hear, somehow finding it not as tedious. But that might have been because of the intoxicating scent of the blood around her, enveloping her, getting her high from the enticing odor.

With a smile, she brought her gaze down from the ceiling and focused on the bar across the room, her gaze connecting with a lithe male sitting on a stool. She stilled, her lungs frozen.

The prince of Scarlet.

Chess wore attire that he never would've donned before—a white dress shirt with the sleeves rolled up, his chestnut locks pulled into a low ponytail, several layers loose and framing his face. He stared straight at her, his arms folded over his chest, and a smirk on his villainous face.

CHAPTER FIVE

CHESS

The color drained from Ever's face the moment she recognized Chess, and his grin grew wider. There she was, finally noticing him. Even though she was dressed in all-black attire, she was still as beautiful as a white rose. When he'd seen her last, she had been confident as she led him through her masquerade ball, into the garden. Confident as she kneed him in the groin and stabbed him in the chest. But then, her expression had shattered as the guards turned on her. It was good to see she hadn't forgotten him or the threat he'd brought—even if he was no longer working on his mother's orders.

The memory of his mother's body flashed through his mind. Her blood pooling across the marble floor, her chest gaping open, broken. The feel of her heart in his hand. Warm. Heavy. How her eyes had stared, lifeless and dull, up at the ceiling. The scene played out in his mind over and over ever since he'd walked in to find her dead, his body frozen in shock for the briefest of moments. A flood of grief threatened to swallow him.

He shook off the memories—they would do him no good at the moment.

Seconds stretched between Chess and Ever, each feeling longer than the last. The impulse to tackle her right there in the crowded club and drag her home warred with the urge to let this play out. Bringing her back to Wonderland could potentially clear his name—*prove* he was still loyal to Scarlet and hadn't desired his mother's death. If he gave Rav everything he had planned to give his mother, perhaps he wouldn't try to frame Chess for her murder. If that was, in fact, what Rav was doing. If Chess knew whether the arse really believed he was responsible, things would be a lot easier to sort out. But, if Rav wanted the prince dead, he might spin the situation so it looked like Chess was working with Ever to murder Imogen.

Fucking bastard.

He needed to make a decision and make it quickly. Attacking Ever in the middle of a public, mortal space wasn't an option, but he knew she would never leave with him willingly. He sat on the bar stool and studied her every little movement. He ran his thumb across the seam of his mouth as he took in her lips, still parted in surprise, and the few strands of white hair sneaking out from beneath the dark wig.

Beside him, people called out drink orders. Liquid sloshed into glasses and ice clinked behind the bar, each tiny sound putting him more on edge. Ever had to be running through different escape options at the moment so he needed to act. Now—before she slipped through his fingers … *again*. He didn't have another four years to waste searching for her.

He sauntered toward her, the music booming around him, yet he heard every breath escaping her pretty mouth. Panic swirled in her eyes for the briefest moment before her expression smoothed. At least she wasn't bolting…

"Your Highness," he said with a small bow.

Ever straightened, pulling her shoulders back, her creamy skin flawless, the swells of her breasts begging to be touched. "Princeling," she replied through gritted teeth.

"I've been searching for you," Chess purred, skimming his index finger across his lower lip.

Her eyes narrowed. "I'm sure you have."

"My mother would love to have a chat with you," he said, testing her knowledge of recent events. Imogen wouldn't have wanted to talk to Ever and they both knew it. Given the chance, she would've attacked the White Queen so fast that she didn't see it coming.

"Mmm, yes, I'm sure she would have…" She paused and raised a brow as she inched closer to him. "If she were still alive."

"There are little birds singing in your ear then, eh?" He figured as much. There had been a vampire dancing with her—he could've very well been the one to have told her. Most of her own guards had turned on her, but that didn't mean Ever had no friends in Wonderland after Rav killed those still loyal to her. The crazy Hatter was long suspected of being a spy and, after she killed Imogen, Chess had little reason to doubt it despite Maddie's insistence that she didn't know where Ever was. *Liars and sneaks.*

A man in a mesh T-shirt stumbled into Ever, spilling his beer and knocking her into Chess. He caught her by the waist and they both stiffened, her breasts pressed firmly against his chest. The White Queen's lily scent drifted to his nostrils and, before he could draw the smell in further, she shoved him away. With lightning-fast reflexes, he latched onto her arm, taking her back three steps with him.

"Well, that wasn't very nice," Chess chided, his gaze locking onto her brown eyes.

"Let me go," she hissed.

Chess tightened his grip on her arm. "After nearly four years, I think you owe me a conversation at least. You did stab me, remember?"

"I owe you *nothing*. You deserved it." She fisted the front of his shirt and paused, seeming to remember they were in a mortal club, surrounded by humans. "And you took my throne."

Chess chuckled. "Did *I* take your throne?" He leaned down,

his nose brushing the tip of hers. "As I recall, it was your brother who stole the allegiance of your guards. Whether or not my mother asked me to take your heart the night of the ball, your time as queen was over. You chose to flee that night instead of fighting to keep your crown, so don't push the blame onto me."

Ever was rather pretty when she was angry, despite the hideous wig. Color filled her cheeks and her eyes sparkled under the flashing white lights. It was much more attractive than her false seduction at the ball—just before she kneed his family jewels. As a betting male, he was willing to guess she was a spitfire in bed when she was upset. Under different circumstances, he might've even offered a good hate-fuck.

Alas, he was wanted in Wonderland, his mother was dead, and he had three scores to settle. If he played his cards right, Ever could lead him straight to Maddie, then help him destroy Rav. Followed, finally, by Ever's destruction. He owed it to his mother for failing to stop her death. Without any living monarchs in Wonderland, war would eventually break out, but what the fuck did he care? Chess had always enjoyed traveling through Wonderland and doing his own thing instead of playing at politics. Let the courts implode.

Ever opened her mouth to reply when the burly, tattooed bouncer from outside the door stepped up to them. "Everything okay here?"

"Yes," Chess and Ever answered in unison. Nosy mortal. Everything would be perfect once he convinced her to help him get revenge.

The bouncer looked between them for a moment. "You better take the argument elsewhere."

"We're finished," Ever assured him, twisting her arm from Chess's grip as she released his shirt. She shot him a scathing look and stalked toward the door.

"Wait, darling," he called, flashing the bouncer a smile. "I have the keys to the flat."

Without wasting another second, he darted after her. He would be damned if she vanished again after all this time.

Stepping to her side, he hooked his arm through hers and held tight as they exited the club. The line of humans waiting to get inside nearly wrapped around the side of the building now and a new bouncer had replaced the one who had interrupted them inside. Ever's features tightened, her teeth grinding as they passed beneath a softly lit street light. He felt her arm muscles flexing with the desire to rip him off her, but there were still too many humans.

"We need to talk," he said in her ear. "No fangs, no fights."

"Just words?" she snapped, keeping her gaze straight ahead to a narrow, dark alleyway across the street.

"Exactly." The violence would come later … after she helped him accomplish what he wanted. He didn't fail at the tasks his mother assigned him, and just because she was dead didn't mean he wasn't going to fulfill her wish to see Ever killed.

They stepped from the pavement, and she tightened her arm around his, her fingernails digging in to his flesh. "Like I would ever believe a word out of your mouth, Princeling."

He chuckled. Of course she wouldn't—just as he wouldn't believe her—but that didn't matter. They could tell each other beautiful lies all the way back to Wonderland for all he cared. Perhaps a hate-fuck could be in the cards after all.

Speeding up their pace, Chess practically dragged Ever into the shadows between two shops. Rotten food and piss permeated his senses, but it offered the privacy they needed. He hauled her to the other side of the industrial bin before releasing her. She took a step back and let out a loud breath.

"We can help each other," he offered without preamble. He would keep the fact he was wanted for matricide to himself. If Ever already knew, she would've rubbed the information in his face, and it would work to his advantage if she thought he still had the full privileges of being a prince.

Ever laughed, the sound incredulous. "Us? Help each other?" She shoved him again, both hands slapping his chest. "Be serious, Chess. The only help I will be giving you is to the grave."

Fuck this. She wasn't going to believe him. He didn't even blame her for it because he would've had the same reaction. Letting her race back into hiding was *not* an option, however. "Don't say I didn't try to do this the nice way," he said with a sigh.

And lunged.

Chess didn't want to have to do it, but she'd left him no choice. His hands wrapped around her neck, squeezing. Once she passed out, he would take her back to his basement where she would eventually wake as good as new. She would be just as trapped as him when the sun rose, leaving them with ample time to come to terms. Ever kicked at him while he lifted her off the street by the neck, pressing her against the brick building. He shifted to take each blow to the legs instead of his groin. Once was enough.

Ever's fangs lowered and she took a gasping breath—*tried to*—as she reached out to claw at his face. Couldn't she just pass out already? Chess slammed his eyes shut to avoid getting them scratched and took those blows too. He would heal before the night was over. All he had to do was get—

Palms landed on either side of his head. *Ever's palms.* Chess's eyes flew open and he met her defiant gaze. A grin spread across her lips as she tightened her grip on his head and then—

Crack!

CHAPTER SIX

EVER

*C*ocky prick.

Who the hell did the bastard think he was? Chess was no prince of anyone's heart. Ever was easily able to wound him again—this time making him unconscious, his lying words trapped away. She should rip his heart out right there, relish in spilling his blood.

Not yet, the tiny voice of reason murmured in the back of her mind.

"Fine," Ever huffed. Chess was the one who had lived in the palace the longest. He knew Rav best. Better than her. Ever only knew the old Rav before they'd come to Wonderland, or the one who she'd lived with inside the Ivory Palace's walls. Even then, he'd always been full of lies and secrets. It had been centuries since he'd truly been her brother. Chess had been right under his mother's wing, performing deeds for her and Rav. No one else still alive had been that close. According to March, all of Rav's other guards and servants were dead. Too bad it couldn't have been the Ivory guards who'd betrayed her. It would've served those bastards right.

She peered down at Chess as she stood above him. After she'd twisted his head, breaking his precious little neck, he'd tumbled to the ground in a heap. It was nothing less than what he was trying to do to her—she had just used a more expedient method to render him unconscious. The Princeling wanted a chat? She supposed he would get one. But it would be her way. Not his.

Heavy footsteps sounded behind her, and she whirled around to find a short man wearing tight trousers and a silky plaid shirt.

"Shit, sorry," the mortal mumbled when he discovered Ever and ran his hand through his shaggy red hair. "Just needed to take a piss. That line isn't moving at—" His eyes widened when they landed on Chess. "Is he all right?"

"He's fine." Ever waved her hand nonchalantly in the air. "Just passed out drunk as usual. I really can't bring him anywhere."

The man blew out a breath, hesitantly approaching her. "I know it's not my business, but sometimes it's best to leave people like that. They need to want to help themselves first."

"Oh, I know." She shrugged. "We won't be together for much longer." Before the mortal offered to help or waste more time, Ever thought of the perfect plan. Her gaze met his and she focused on him, swaying him with her influence. "You will drive us back to my home."

The mortal's dark irises glazed over as he nodded. Ever could easily scoop Chess up and carry him to her safe house, but it wasn't every day a female toted a male around in the mortal world. With a closer look from prying, immortal eyes, even with her disguise, she would be recognizable, and Chess even more so.

"First, help me take my boyfriend to your car," Ever instructed, unable to contain her smirk at what she was about to do.

Without a word, the man lifted Chess on one side while Ever

held him on the other, the prince's feet dragging across the pavement as they walked the short distance. The vehicle was an older model with chipped green paint and a dent on the passenger side door. Above them, the full moon shone brightly while most of the stars were hidden from the light pollution. Back in Wonderland, the werewolves would be in human form on this night, but it was rare they would slip out in the mortal world. However, she still kept a gun with silver bullets in her safe house just in case.

The man unlocked the door, and they propped Chess in the backseat, his head leaning against the window. He shouldn't wake any time soon, but if he did, she needed to have the advantage, which she wouldn't have if she slipped into the front, so she slid in beside him. No one had seemed to pay them any mind since it wasn't unusual to see someone drunk or passed out from the club. This was positively perfect.

The mortal remained quiet as he sank down into the driver's seat and started the engine. He stayed focused on the road after she gave him the instructions on how to get to the old park.

"Put it on a classical station please," Ever said, needing a bit of calm after this tedious night.

A harder melody with fast bow movements across cellos came through the car stereo and she relaxed in her seat. She peered up at the ceiling with a smile while moving her index finger side to side as though performing her own symphony to the music. Imogen was dead. Ever had Chess in her clutches. And her brother would come soon enough. It was like the notes of a song, falling splendidly into place.

After about ten minutes, the car stopped in the crumbling parking lot of their destination. Not a soul was inside the park and only a few cars passed down the dimly lit street.

Ever leaned forward as she spoke to the mortal in an even tone. "After we shut the door, return to the club, and if you were planning on meeting someone, tell them you're late because you forgot something at home." She then opened the door and wrapped her arms around Chess's waist, yanking him from the vehicle, before hoisting him over her shoulder. With a grunt, she adjusted his lithe body and shut the door using her foot. A pleasant aroma of pine and rain radiated from him, and she held her nose, brushing the smell away for a second.

"Come on, Princeling," she whispered as the mortal drove away. "You get to come to my home sweet home."

A light breeze with the scent of earth blew around her. An owl hooted in the distance, and the branches of the trees rustled. Ever walked past the dilapidated playground, then used her speed to hurry through the trees to the safe house—she didn't want to hold Chess a moment longer.

The gnarled walnut tree came into view, and Ever fished out the key from her small cross-body purse. She held onto Chess's legs as she knelt to the ground, pressing the key into the small lock. If it weren't for her vampire sight and knowing the precise location of the keyhole, she would never have been able to find it. After lifting the door, she carried Chess down the ladder.

As her feet hit the bottom, she scanned the small space and thought about where she should rest her new *guest*. The mattress or the floor? *The floor it is*. Ever dropped Chess's body on the wood with a thump and retrieved a few items from a crate in the corner. Rolling the prince to his stomach, she drew his arms behind his back and circled them with a heavy metal chain, then used another to tightly bind his ankles. He wouldn't easily escape those since he would have to be a magician to tear through the metal.

Smiling, Ever stood and brushed her hands together, silently thanking her lucky chess piece for this. She then removed her heels and picked up her viola and bow. With a satisfied sigh, she sat atop her mattress, running her bow across the strings of her instrument as she waited for the villainous prince to wake.

"Mmm," Chess groaned, rolling to his side, facing her.

Ever stopped playing her viola and perked up, finding the prince's eyes still shut. She arched her brow when he let out another deep groan, the edges of his lips pulling back into what looked to be a smile. It didn't sound like a painful awakening as she'd expected, or wished for, but as though he was having a *pleasureful* dream. She gripped her viola in one hand and her bow in the other, then stood from the mattress in front of him.

Chess's spine arched while he tossed his head back. "Right there," he whispered. "Fuck. You're so good at this. Keep sucking. Harder, faster."

She snickered to herself. "What a fool."

"Don't think you aren't getting a turn, sweetness," he purred. "Let me taste you now, Ever."

Her eyes widened. What the fuck? He was dreaming about *her?* About *tasting* her?

"Damn, you taste like sweet nectar."

Ever cleared her throat and kicked him in the ribs with her foot, not wanting to think about *where* he was performing this act with his mouth. "That's quite enough of that."

Chess's eyes jerked open, his yellow gaze meeting hers. He blinked while staring at her, as though he couldn't believe she was standing before him.

"What were you dreaming about?" Ever cooed, holding up her viola and running the bow across its strings to play a melody.

The prince lifted his head and shook his arms behind his back when he seemed to finally come to a realization. "What the fuck is this?" He jerked his chains, writhing like an insufferable snake. However, his movements did go along well with her music as she continued to play, like a cobra being mesmerized by a charmer performing a song on a pungi. "Stop playing the damn violin!"

She cocked her head, her movements pausing. "It's a *viola*."

"What the fuck ever." He clenched his jaw, still rattling the chains on his ankles as he pushed himself up to a sitting position. "Release me."

"I don't think so, *Princeling*. You're lucky I didn't kill you." She knelt in front of him so her nose was incredibly close to brushing his. "You wanted a chat? Well, here we are. We do it *my* way. Not yours. You're the one who betrayed me in the first place. Trying to play the role of the Huntsman in *Snow White*. You know what happened at the end of that story? She won. The Evil Queen died." Ever clucked her tongue—the dig was specifically about his wretch of a mother. "Refresh my memory … what happened to the Huntsman?"

Chess narrowed his eyes, his nostrils flaring. Her gaze unintentionally drifted down to his pouty lips that had been tasting her in his pathetic dream. But the little voice at the back of her mind wondered briefly what that would feel like, those plump lips between her thighs, flicking his devilish tongue slowly up her center. *No. No. Bloody hell, no.*

"Unbind me and I'll be a good little boy," he purred. Her gaze slid back up to his, thankfully clearing her horrendous thoughts.

She sat across from him, slowly plucking a string on her viola. "Name the song I was playing and perhaps I will."

"Simple." He grinned, his lips spreading wide so each of his perfect teeth were on display, his fangs bared. "'Fur Elise.'"

Damn. She should've chosen a harder song. "I'm still not untying you, Princeling."

"We can work together," he said, confidence lacing his words. "We both want the same thing."

What could they possibly both want that was ever the same? They had nothing in common besides liking the taste of blood. "And what is that?"

"Your brother dead."

Ever held her gaze steady, keeping her features neutral. She knew Rav wanted him for the murder of Imogen. But she'd believed before that, they were the perfect devious trio. After all, he was the only father Chess had ever known. "And why does it matter to you if he's dead?" she slowly asked. "Aren't you Scarlet's new king? You can do with him as you wish. Send him back to Ivory. I can then return to my home, reclaim my throne, and kill him myself." She arched her brow, seeing if she could get him to admit his lie or not.

He gritted his teeth. "I can't."

"And why ever not?" She smiled, waiting for him to admit that he was wanted in Scarlet for the murder of his mother.

"Because Rav is the king at the moment."

Ever laughed then, the heaviness of the sound spilling out from her throat, so much her eyes watered. "Of course he is. Did you really think my brother would hand over Scarlet to you, even though you're the rightful heir? Look what he did to me, his own sister." She paused. "My contact did say Rav seems to have narrowed his search for Imogen's murderer, but we still don't know who ripped out her heart."

"Who's your *contact?*" Chess asked, his voice suspicious.

She bet everything on it that he was thinking her contact was Maddie, but he couldn't know she'd recently met up with her. "He's here in London. I haven't been back in Wonderland since I ran from the ball. I only recently emerged from this *fabulous* home of mine and reconnected with an old friend."

Chess leaned toward her, his heavenly scent caressing her nose. "Your *lover?*"

"That's none of your business," she spat.

"Help me become king and I'll help you return to being queen." His gaze focused on her hair. "And take off that wig. It looks like shit."

"What a way to entice me into working with you," Ever said dryly but drew off her wig, letting her long white locks fall down her back.

Chess's eyes widened for a short moment before returning to their normally cocky stare. "Ah, there's the White Queen in all her glory. I don't think I've ever seen you with your hair down." He ran his tongue across his lower lip. "If you unbind my wrists, I promise to play fair."

He was such a lovely liar. But she was too. "Perhaps another day." She lifted her bow and returned to playing a song, just for him, on her viola while he seethed.

CHAPTER SEVEN

CHESS

Chess had never needed the luxuries that palace life offered, but he sure as hell appreciated them. Especially now that he was lying, tightly bound, on the floor of Ever's...

He wasn't sure it could be called a *home*. It was a literal hole in the ground with added creature comforts. It was no bloody wonder he struggled to find her safe houses in Wonderland all these years. If they were as well hidden as this one was, it was going to be nearly impossible, and Maddie was undoubtedly locked away in one of them right now.

He'd just have to smoke the Hatter bitch out. Right after he took care of Rav and cleared his name because, otherwise, searching Wonderland would be a nuisance.

Turning his attention to Ever, he studied her face. She'd fallen asleep on her mattress hours ago with the viola tucked under her arm. The worry had drained from her features as she slumbered, making her appear younger. Her lips were parted, her breaths soft. The wig she'd worn the night before and the fancy up-dos he'd seen her wear previously didn't do her justice. Her white hair looked softer than his sheets back in the Ruby Heart Palace. Sheets he would do nearly anything to fuck her on if the situation was different…

"Oi," Chess called to Ever. He couldn't get distracted right now. Despite his many, *many* attempts to free himself, he was still just as confined as when he'd first awoken and he was over it. "Oi, Queenie. You going to sleep all day?"

Ever's eyes cracked open and she smiled with a yawn. "What else should I be doing, *Princeling*? Entertaining you?"

"Oh, I would like that very much. I'm sure you know all sorts of ways to keep a male *entertained*," he said with a coy smirk. "But unchaining me would be a good start."

"Hmm, let me think about that…" She closed her eyes again, her smile widening. "No."

"No?" Chess threw himself up into a sitting position and scooted up to the mattress, chains clinking. "I can make this very uncomfortable for you as well, you know. Unless you plan on murdering me every day?"

"Perhaps I do," she mumbled.

Chess held back a growl. He had no intention of staying like this any longer—he was no one's prisoner. Getting caught was his fault. He'd been too sure of himself in the alley outside the club, but he should've known the queen of Ivory wouldn't go quietly. Temporarily killing her was the only way he was going to get her back to his basement. Going straight for a pseudo-death was much faster and more efficient than dragging her off while awake, though a raging headache did accompany it after.

Not quite as uncomfortable, hm? Chess would need to play a little dirty, he supposed. With a smile, he dropped his fangs and slinked forward. Ever's arm hung off the mattress, her lily scent caressing his nostrils. She didn't even open her eyes as he neared, then he drove his teeth into the exposed flesh of Ever's forearm as hard as he could. Her blood burst in his mouth and he lost all sense as her flavor—the richest he'd ever tasted—sent a wave of ecstasy through him.

Ever screeched and, grabbing a handful of his hair, ripped him off her. "What the hell are you doing?"

Chess grinned as a trickle of her warm blood flowed down his chin. "Tit for tat."

"I never bit you," she snarled, throwing him away from her.

He fell on his side with a *thunk*, unable to use his limbs to stop himself. "Unchain me and maybe I'll let you."

Ever stood over him, wrinkling her nose. Blood trailed down her arm from his bite, dripping off her fingertips, but the puncture wounds were already healing. "Don't flatter yourself. I'd rather drink from a dead man."

She moved to step around him, and he raised his chained legs into the air to block the path between himself and the mattress. "We both know that would kill you."

"And yet"—she stared at his legs hovering before her—"I stand by my statement."

"Such a brutal white rose, you are." He chuckled. "I could make you feel more alive than any feeding could. Would you like me to prove it?"

She picked up her viola from the mattress behind her and ran a bow across the strings. She tilted her head as if listening for something. "Mmm, the notes seem to say *no*." Ever kicked him in the ribs, forcing him to lower his legs as he curled in on himself just long enough for her to get past him. Silently, she picked through a pile of neatly-folded clothes and selected a long-sleeved jumper with three old musician faces across the front with the words *I listen to dead people* above them. *Dead composers*, he thought, but had no idea which. Then she slipped inside a side door and the sound of water sloshing in a bucket filled the room. A few moments passed before she came out again smelling of soap, dressed in her fresh jumper, and her white hair was tucked beneath a curly brunette wig.

"I'm going out," she announced.

"What?" Chess rolled to his stomach, pushed onto his knees, and managed to stand. Fuck his hurt pride, the indignity, the embarrassment of being captured. She was so sure he wouldn't get out of this place that she was prepared to leave him alone? Without talking things out first? What if she was caught by someone else tonight? What if she— His anger immediately deflated as fear coursed through him instead. What if she was going to tell her spy she'd caught him? What if she learned the truth that he was a wanted male and turned him over to Rav in exchange for Ivory?

"Afraid of being alone?" Ever asked sarcastically.

"We need to talk," he said, serious.

The tone of his voice must've gotten through to her because her body stilled, her eyes narrowed in thought. He was seldom outwardly serious—even she had to know that. His reputation always preceded him as the untroubled prince.

"About what?" She angled her head to the side. "I'm not releasing you."

"Why not? You don't think you could snap my neck a second time?" He almost winced, knowing the jab might curb her willingness to listen. "I can help you get your throne back."

"And why the hell would you do that?" She crossed her arms over her chest. "It's your fault I lost it."

"It's Rav's and my mother's fault technically, and as you said, she's dead." Pain scratched at his insides as he said the words, but he knew they were necessary to prove his point. "I don't give a flying fuck who rules Ivory or Scarlet, and I never did."

"It sounds like you care now," Ever drawled, her lips curving into a smile.

Chess opened his mouth to deny it and paused. Did he care now? Not about Ivory, no, but was he going to let Rav rule Scarlet? It was rightfully his—Imogen never crowned Rav. If she had wanted him to rule when she was gone, surely she would have made him king? Did that mean his mother *wanted* Chess to rule? He didn't have any interest in wearing the crown but Rav had just set the entirety of Wonderland against him. Betrayal colored his vision red for a moment. Chess *would* rule Scarlet, as was his birthright. To keep Wonderland the playground he knew it to be, yes, but also to spite Rav.

"I care slightly more than before," he finally admitted, shrugging one shoulder, the chains digging in. "If you need your brother's head, I certainly wouldn't mind giving it to you."

Ever laughed. "How kind of you. And what would you be getting out of this arrangement?"

Maddie, dead. But he couldn't admit that to Ever when the two females were such good friends. Chess needed to play the game with the White Queen. Make her trust him. Eventually, the murderous Hatter would appear. As an immortal, all Chess had was time. He could be patient if he had to.

"I suppose you've got me there," he said with a smirk. "Rav was never made king, which means the title belongs, rightfully, to me. I've never been good at sharing. Unless of course it's in bed. If you'd ever like to introduce me to your lover from the club, I'm sure we could work something out."

Ever's fingers rapped a rhythm on her arms as she studied him. He wished he could read every thought flickering through her head. While her face remained passive, the conflict flashed through her eyes. Belief. Disbelief. Back and forth between the two.

"Prove your usefulness to me first," she said, completely ignoring his invitation to a threesome.

That might be tricky if it included waltzing back into Scarlet. "How?"

"Tell me everything Rav's been doing." She lifted her chin in challenge. "Starting with the day of my masquerade ball."

Chess grinned. "Done. But first," he purred, "unchain me."

Ever scowled. "I'll unchain your legs but not your arms."

"I'm losing feeling in my fingers. They'll be no good to you if they shrivel and fall off," he said, winking.

"Everything you say only makes me want to leave you bound. Take the offer or leave it, Princeling." She shrugged.

"You drive a hard bargain, but I suppose you leave me little choice. I am at your mercy, oh majestic queen." He would get his arms free soon enough because he couldn't run like this if a situation arose where he needed to flee.

Ever dropped to her knees in front of him and pulled a key to the padlock from her back pocket. When she looked up at him from beneath her lashes, those pouty lips parted, a bolt of desire stormed through him.

Fuck me, that was a sight. Now if only his hard cock were between those full lips—sucking, licking, tasting—as it had been in his dream. His fingers threading through her ivory hair while he groaned. Ever's delicate hands working him instead of the metal lock near his feet. Her gaze shifted to the growing bulge in his trousers and she inhaled sharply before turning her attention back to the chains.

When the lock was finally removed, she unwound the chains from his legs, the links clanking together, echoing, as she gathered more of it into her hands. It only took her a minute to complete, but by the time she was done, the air practically crackled between them.

"There." She sighed, sounding slightly breathless, and stood. Their bodies pressed close, only an armful of chains between them.

Chess could've sworn her body shook slightly when their eyes met, and his cock throbbed painfully, wanting nothing more than to make her scream his name. "Thanks," he said in a husky voice. What would she do if he drew her close, claimed that pretty mouth with his? He'd asked last time in her garden and received a resounding *no* with her knee to his groin, but she didn't seem to loathe the idea so much now with her hooded eyes.

Stepping back, Ever tossed the chains into a corner. "Don't make me regret it."

"Of course not," he promised. Not yet, at least. He stretched his legs, shaking the feeling back into them, before lazily sinking down on the edge of Ever's mattress. He peered up at her with a wide grin. "So, your brother…"

Two nights passed as the White Queen questioned every aspect of Rav's life. Chess shifted uncomfortably where he sat on the floor, his arms still chained, as Ever lifted a bottle of mixed powdered blood to his lips. The weak solution scratched at his throat, and he released a small cough. Ever lowered the bottle without glancing at him, instead plucking absently at the strings of her viola.

"How did you know I liked my meals half-dissolved?" he asked.

"A wild guess," she mumbled.

When she flicked a glance at him to raise the bottle again, she gave a small sigh. She set the instrument aside and Chess drank in her bare legs as her dress slid up. Every curve was visible beneath her tight black dress, the skirt barely covering her firm arse. Not that he'd felt it himself but he'd gripped enough in his lifetime to know just by glancing. She looked so good in the damn scrap of fabric that he almost didn't mind being her prisoner. *Almost.*

The backs of Ever's cool fingers grazed the corner of his lips where a trickle of blood escaped. He felt her touch all the way to his cock when she wiped it away, but she gave no indication that she wanted him. No increased heart rate, no catch of her breath…

Infuriating, honestly.

When had he ever spent so much time with a female and *not* had them want him? He'd never talked this much either. Ever knew everything about her brother now. His feeding habits, his relationship with Imogen, their political policies. Everything Chess knew, she now knew. Except, of course, that Rav had ordered for Chess to be thrown in the dungeons.

"I need to meet with someone," Ever said, pacing the room. She'd been plaiting and unplaiting her dark wig. "You'll have to come with me."

He *had* to? Interesting. She'd been fine with the idea of leaving him alone before, when his legs were chained. "I promise to be your perfect guard." He winked, though he wasn't sure if that was the truth. They had a tentative truce, but the flight response still lingered inside him. He could trust her just as much as she could trust him.

"No." She cast a glance at the chains in the corner. "I could chain you again, but you've held your end of the bargain. If we're to take down my brother together, we need to try having a little faith in each other."

Chess scanned her over, his brow furrowing. "Who are you and what have you done with Ever?"

She snorted, unamused, and took another key from her pocket. "Turn around."

Chess turned slowly, half expecting her to bash him over the head, but she quickly unlocked his chains and peeled them away. He groaned as blood rushed back into his fingers. Rolling his shoulders, stretching the muscles, his bones *cracking*, felt painfully good. "Bloody hell." He moaned deeply to himself and looked over his shoulder at Ever.

At the sight of her dilated pupils, he swallowed a sarcastic comment he wanted to make about not letting her tie him up again in the future. In fact, he would probably beg her to do just that if it got them to share a bed. Or a table. Or literally any surface. Her riding him. Him fucking her with maddening, lustful thrusts.

"Do you like it when I moan?" he said with a smirk.

Her gaze snapped to his, losing the lustful stare. "Excuse me?"

"If you want to hear it again, I know just how you can accomplish that." He rolled his shoulders once more and turned to face her fully. "A variety of ways, in fact."

"You're absolutely incorrigible," she huffed. "Maybe I *should* leave you here."

Chess laughed at her annoyance, but he had no real desire to stay behind in her safe house. Leaving with her would be safe enough. While he didn't trust the White Queen, she'd avoided being seen for nearly four years, so he knew their destination would be clandestine. That only made him want to go more.

"I'll be on my best behavior," he vowed, placing a hand over his chest. "Prince's honor."

After hesitating for a long moment, she headed up the ladder. His gaze fixed on her arse and he cursed at how stretchy the fabric seemed, hiding any glimpse of what was beneath. He suspected she knew as much or she wouldn't have climbed the ladder first. They both knew he was too much of a scoundrel not to look.

Just before pushing up on the hatch that would lead them outside, Ever arched a brow at him. "Princeling, you should understand this: you need to *have* honor in order to swear on it."

CHAPTER EIGHT

EVER

The prince's cock had hardened at Ever's touch, the bare brush of her fingers had ignited something within him while unlocking the chains near his ankles. But that shouldn't be difficult to believe since he was known to fuck anything that walked. She wouldn't be surprised if he'd been with a werewolf in his past— while the creature was in beastly form. Perhaps he wouldn't go *that* far, but still.

Though what made Ever pause for a second, a *very* brief one, was that an extremely small, *foolish*, part of her wanted to see what hid beneath those tight trousers of his, see what had everyone so eager about it in her world. Wondered how it would compare to the others she'd stroked, had in between her lips.

Ever! she scolded herself. *This is what you get for remaining a damn virgin for centuries.* Queen Elizabeth was known as The Virgin Queen back in her day, but everyone knew she was no such thing and took lovers into her bed. Ever should've coupled with March at some point in the past, but again, she knew that wouldn't have been fair to him. And she wouldn't be selfish just to lose her maidenhead.

She and Chess walked from the park to the pavement, the wind barely blowing, the moon only a sliver of yellow resting in the night sky.

"So," Chess drawled, rolling up the sleeve of his dress shirt. "Who are we meeting this fine evening? Your lover from the club?"

"Yes." Ever pushed the braid of her dark wig over her shoulder as several cars passed them on the street. Tonight, she'd chosen to wear another short black dress but with a pair of knee-high leather boots instead of the heels. In truth, as mundane as it was, she would've rather worn her checkered Vans, jeans, and another T-shirt since she couldn't very well parade around in her white attire.

"How long have you two been fucking?" Chess smirked. "Since before or after you left Ivory? I don't remember anyone by your side at the masquerade ball."

"It's none of your business." Ever lifted her chin, still thinking about when he sank his teeth into her arm. It had been a snaky move but something she would've done. She looked him over, and he'd readjusted his short ponytail. The front locks hung deliciously at his chin. *Pathetically*, she'd meant. "What I do remember from that day at the ball was you trying to murder me."

"Are we going to rehash this every time we speak?" Chess asked, his long fingers toying with his hair. "I'm sorry."

Ever knew that was a downright lie. "For?"

"Trying to take your heart." He placed a hand over his chest and sighed. "Your turn."

"What?"

He circled her as though she were his prey before coming to a stop in front of her. "Say you're sorry for kneeing me in the groin and stabbing me."

What a spoiled prince he was. Did he think she would bow down and apologize after everything he'd done, especially in light of his own flimsy apology? "Are you serious? You're insufferable. And I don't accept your insincere apology."

He didn't deny he'd been false about the sentiment, yet the past was the past. That didn't mean she trusted him though. He would betray her in an instant if a better opportunity arose—and vice versa—but for now, this was the best resource she had for taking down her brother.

Ever spotted a black taxi, waved her hand, and the car slowed to a stop in front of them. They were headed to the same club from a few days ago where she would meet up with March. Sometimes he was early and sometimes he was late, but he was always there.

Chess opened the door to the taxi and motioned her inside. "My lady."

Ever released a very unladylike snort and slipped into the car, sliding over to the window. The taxi reeked of old food and possibly sex. Chess took a seat beside her, a little too close, and shut the door.

"To Serenity nightclub," Ever said, using her influence on the young mortal driver. He barely looked old enough to drive, his head shaved and pale skin covered in acne. "First, put it on the classical station, please."

"Of course," the boy said, changing the radio station until violins and flutes filled the car before driving down the low-lit street.

"You're really into this stuff, huh?" Chess asked. "At the ball, I thought the music was just for the occasion."

"Well," Ever said slowly, "if you had gotten to know me instead of trying to *kill* me, then maybe you would have learned some things."

"You wound me with that response." His fingers seductively tiptoed across the seat toward her but not daring to touch her. "So why the viola? Why not the violin?"

Ever thought back to when she was younger, when she'd still lived with her parents and brother. When Rav had simply been Ravon. Her twin who'd followed her everywhere, even fallen with her into Wonderland. In truth, she'd wanted to play the violin at first. The instruments hadn't been around the mortal world that long, but when her uncle from Italy brought them as gifts for Ever and her brother, she'd laid eyes on Rav's viola and had to have it once she'd heard its sounds. Rav wanted the violin just as much so they'd traded.

"I like the lower notes and its larger size," Ever informed him.

"You like larger, huh?" Chess grinned, biting his lower lip.

"*Very* large," Ever said slowly, "and I'm certain it's not something you would know much about."

Chess chuckled. "You can find out any time you like." He then paused, locking his yellow gaze with hers. "You play well." His voice seemed sincere for once.

"Do you play anything?" she asked, unable to stop herself. But she was always curious about those who could play music.

"No, my father left for Wonderland when I was a baby, and my mother was too busy trying to provide for us. Then she abandoned me, too, and I was left to myself at eight years old. Years later, my mother came back and turned me, then brought me to Scarlet. By that point, I didn't care to learn about anything that didn't involve my new world."

Ever's stomach sank at his words and she didn't understand why. She shouldn't have felt sorry for anything he'd said. But he'd raised himself, then his mother had shaped him into what he was today. "A pity Rav didn't teach you," Ever said, wondering if he had ever played again. Once they'd fallen into Wonderland, he'd stopped.

"Rav was preoccupied with fucking my mother and being an arse. So, I found my own entertainment."

"By turning mortals unwillingly?" Her eyes narrowed.

Chess frowned for a minute, thinking. "Only in my younger years, when my mother wanted me to learn how the process worked."

Ever didn't understand how he could worship the ground his mother had walked on, especially knowing that she'd murdered his father even though he'd been a good male. But Ever wasn't going to discuss more family matters with him now. He'd told her plenty of information about her brother, how he often slinked to the mortal world to bring a new human home to toy with, how he and Imogen fed from them, turned them, enslaved them. Then, most of the time, they killed them shortly after when they displeased Imogen in even the slightest way.

The car slowed to a stop, and Ever leaned forward. "Forget you drove us to the club and go where you were planning to before." They then stepped out of the taxi and headed for their destination.

Outside the building, cars lined the street, more than the previous night. Mortals strutted toward the entrance, some with plenty of skin on display. One woman wore a long vinyl jacket over fishnets, while others had on black lingerie, miniskirts, tight leather trousers, and harness bondage.

"Seems we're underdressed for the occasion." Chess leaned in and whispered, "Or should I say, *overdressed?*"

Ever blew out a breath and rolled her eyes as he brushed his hands down the front of his button-up shirt and dark trousers. The line outside the club was much shorter than last time, and she assumed most of the people were already inside.

"What's going on tonight?" Ever asked when they approached the bouncer. It was the same man as a few nights ago, his shirt tight across his bulging muscles.

"It's Kinky Tuesday," he answered, his expression serious.

"Let us in," Chess said silkily. The bouncer's eyes instantly glazed over, and the man gestured for them to go inside.

They walked down the narrow hall to the main space where the music blasted through the speakers. Heavy, techno beats drifted to Ever's ears and heavier white smoke surrounded the mortals dancing in the room under the flashing bright lights.

"I know what we're doing tonight." Chess's voice came out playful.

Ever followed his gaze across the room, her brows lifting. A man wearing strips of leather over his lean body cracked a whip as a female in a thong and bra wrapped rope around a woman in a tight pink corset.

In another corner, couples, ball gags in their mouths, thrust against each other in several large metal cages. Everything about this night was sinful as partners grinded, arousal filling their eyes.

Ever had seen her fair share of couples seducing one another, but she couldn't help being in awe of their movements, the atmosphere.

The scent of lust, blood, and sweat enveloped her, and she peered at Chess, who swiped the tip of his tongue across his lower lip. And she knew he was feeling it too. She could control it, but she was still fighting the urge to tear throats apart and drink as thirst stormed through her.

Ever peered around, searching for March's braids, his tall frame. But she didn't spot him anywhere. At the bar, several people who looked as though they were trying to be vampires, with light contacts and fake fangs, flirted while sipping on beers.

Glancing up toward the large rectangular window above them, she tugged on Chess's sleeve. "Let's try upstairs." Sometimes March waited for her at one of the tables there.

Chess nodded and they broke through the crowd, past sweaty bodies. She let the prince lead her up the metal stairs. They may be on the same side for now, but that didn't mean she trusted him enough to allow him to walk behind her in this place.

Pictures of what looked to be old musicians hung across the red-painted walls. At the top of the stairs, the room opened up to a large space cluttered with pleather sofas against the walls, black tables and chairs in the middle, and several dancing couples.

She glanced at faces and found a male with braids sitting at a table, but it wasn't March. Her gaze flicked toward the bar across the room and she scanned the seats, then froze.

White hair, red tips.

Her brother faced the bartender, chatting with him. Four other female vampires stood beside him, wearing tight, short crimson dresses. Long red locks cascaded down one's back, another orange, and the other two with dark braids. Even from behind, she would notice the bastard anywhere—that hair, his build, the relaxed way he stood. Chess, the fool, didn't seem to notice as he started to walk in the direction of the bar.

Just as Rav turned, Ever shoved Chess onto a sofa beside them and climbed into his lap, straddling his narrow hips while blocking his face. Chess's mouth parted and his eyebrows rose before his normal cocky expression fell back into place. When he opened his mouth to speak, she muffled his voice by crashing her lips to his. Her mouth skated across his—he didn't hesitate, thoroughly returning the kiss, his fingers digging into her hips. She plunged her tongue into his mouth, caressing, tasting his damn luscious flavor, finding herself *liking* it. Gripping his hair tight, she rolled her hips forward. He let out a low groan as she did it again and again, knowing she should stop but not wanting to. It wasn't even him doing this—it was all *her*. His length hardened against her softness and instead of this being a distraction from Rav, it was turning into something else. Something that she didn't want to end. She yearned to tell herself that she didn't know who she was grinding against, wanted to pretend it was someone else, but she knew exactly who she was riding. In that moment she didn't care.

Chess's hands left her hips, trailed her thighs, then reached up her dress to grasp her buttocks.

His lips drew from hers, leaving her hungry for his taste. "Do you want me to take you right here or somewhere more private?" he rasped in her ear. "I'll do whatever the fuck you want."

"I-I..." Ever couldn't formulate words as she inhaled his pine scent. And she was *liking* who she was doing this with? As his hand cupped her breast, she halted her movements, grasping what she needed to say. "My brother is at the bar with four females. I didn't want him to see us. Slowly look up and tell me what he's doing now."

Chess's jaw clenched at her confession, his eyes hardening. He leaned forward, his breath hot at her ear, tickling her neck. "He's not here."

Ever jerked her head up and flicked her gaze toward the bar. Rav wasn't there. She jumped from Chess's lap and peered around the room. He was nowhere in sight and neither were the females he'd been with.

"Downstairs. Now." She grasped his hand and tugged him with her so they could avoid Rav until they formulated a proper plan. They were five against two. She didn't feel up to her full strength and she was sure Chess wasn't either after sitting underground for days while not having enough blood to drink.

The room was foggier than before, and even with her vampire senses, she could barely make out anything besides the outline of bodies, their intoxicating odor.

"This way." Chess clasped her hand and pulled her through the crowd, the smoke thinning. The prince then drew her to a sudden stop. "Dance with me." He pressed his fingers to her lips before she called him a fool. "To the door."

Instead of fighting him, she gave into his touch once more. But she told herself it was all for show because she truly hated him and they needed to get the hell out of here.

Yet she couldn't stop feeling his earlier hardness beneath her, the way her body had molded to his.

CHAPTER NINE

CHESS

Even in a room full of alluring blood, Ever's lily scent consumed Chess. The only thing keeping him from taking her into the bathroom, locking the door, and ravaging her until she screamed his name was the looming threat. Rav was somewhere in this club and that wasn't something he could lose sight of—even if he hadn't laid eyes on the male himself.

"I'll make sure he doesn't spot you," Chess whispered in her ear. He gripped Ever's hips, nuzzling her neck as they moved slowly toward the door. Too slowly, but they had to keep from being noticed. Running straight for the exit would undoubtedly draw attention, even if they did it quickly enough not to be seen by the other dancers. It was too crowded to avoid running into them all and Rav would know what a trail of humans, seemingly fallen over themselves, meant. It wasn't necessarily Chess and Ever who had fled, but it was evidence that *someone* had.

So Chess swayed to the beat, Ever against him. Tantalizingly close. Now that he knew her lips tasted of wild berries and her blood blissfully rich, it was all he could do to focus on the faces visible through the manufactured fog.

Where is the fucking git?

Ever had said four females were with Rav at the bar, but they seemed to have vanished too. Dividing and conquering…

Ever grabbed onto the sides of his already-wrinkled shirt, shifting him slightly to peek over his shoulder. Chess's attention snapped to her. "Are you all right, Queenie?"

"Positively lovely," she hissed. "I adore playing a game of spy the arsehole."

"Does that mean you like my help?" he purred.

She snorted.

He couldn't help thinking about their moment upstairs. Her riding his cock over his trousers, the scent of her arousal. It carried similar notes to the light lily coming from her skin and the boldness of her blood mixed with a sweetness he would do almost anything to taste. His mouth watered at the idea of running his tongue through her desire.

Rav. Not fucking. Focus on Rav. "I don't see them anywhere," he said, doing his best to sound unaffected.

"Perhaps he found another poor soul to fuck and enslave." She wrinkled her nose in distaste, then released her grip on his shirt and flattened her hands on his sides instead, poised to push him away.

It was entirely possible that was why Rav had come, but this club was out of the way, farther from the entrance to Wonderland than most vampires traveled. Not to mention that he usually hunted alone. He wound an arm around Ever's lower back and tugged her tightly to him. "It may be safer to take you back upstairs. I wouldn't mind having you in that position again."

She inhaled sharply and Chess was sure she was about to tear out of his arms when a figure appeared beside them. Chess's grip tightened, his body tensing. "Who the fu—"

"March!" Ever breathed in relief, pushing away from Chess. She latched onto the male's arm and leaned into his touch. "I was starting to worry about you. Rav is here and he's not alone."

Chess realized he'd seen him before—it was the same male she'd been dancing with the last time they were here. Her lover, most likely, since they had also kissed. His lips pressed into a hard line.

"I know," March said quietly. "They're scouting outside. I barely made it past them—" The male's eyes narrowed as he focused in on Chess. "You're with the *fucking prince of Scarlet?*"

"Do you think they know I'm here?" Ever tugged March's arm, ignoring his comment about Chess, and they drifted away from the prince. She didn't even gift him a glance over her shoulder.

I don't think so.

Chess started after them as they wove through the moving bodies. Was she really walking away from him? Didn't she know there was nothing stopping him from running outside and telling Rav that Ever was inside? Well, other than the fact that Rav probably wanted Chess *more* than his own sister at the moment, but she wasn't aware of that. Yet.

He jerked into motion, following Ever and March. If the male tried to tell her about Chess's predicament, the prince would be forced to act. *Fuck.* What was he going to do? He couldn't kill Ever's acquaintance in the club while blending in *and* keeping her as an ally.

"Woah now," Chess said, slipping up to Ever's other side. "Who's this handsome piece?"

The male flared his nostrils as his eyes locked on Chess. "What are you doing with him, Ever?"

"It's a long"—she cast a withering stare at Chess—"*long* story."

"The Scarlet Prince, though?" March stepped sideways, putting space between her and Chess. "You know what he tried to do to you."

"March," she snapped, peering over her shoulder as she steered them toward the bathrooms. "Sorry, but they could come back inside at any moment."

March looked between Chess and Ever with wide,

disbelieving eyes. "Make this make sense," he said in a stern voice.

Chess slid in front of them, walking backward, through the swinging men's bathroom door. He stood aside, gliding his arm out with a flourish so they could join him. "Leave," he told a stocky man washing his hands. The mortal's blue eyes glazed over, and he hurried back to the dance floor without turning off the tap. With the room free of mortals, Chess leaned his back against the door and folded his arms across his chest as he studied March. "It makes sense, cupcake, because I am the only one close enough to her brother to help her kill him."

March barked a laugh. "You? But you're—"

Ever elbowed March and they exchanged a wordless warning that Chess couldn't understand. Finally, March let out a long breath. "Fine," he conceded. "You're still my queen and I trust your decision."

Ever reached out and gave March's hand a squeeze. The affection between them rankled in a way he'd never experienced before. How she'd turned away from Chess toward March as if he were her savior. Sure, Chess hadn't proven himself to be a white knight in the past, but he hadn't acted as her enemy in the last few days. *Not precisely, anyway.*

"I'll explain later, but we have to leave," Ever told March. "We need a plan and our weapons before we move against my brother."

March chewed his bottom lip. "Are you sure? We're evenly matched now and—"

"Evenly matched?" Chess's brow rose. "Did your mother never teach you to count?"

March puffed his chest and stepped forward with his hands in fists. Ever flung an arm out in front of the vampire, bringing him to an immediate halt. "Those females with Rav are nothing special," March growled.

Chess rolled his eyes. Rav didn't travel with others, but if he *were* to bring anyone with him, they would not be *nothing*. He likely plucked the strongest females from the royal guards. But why—for *who?*

"Enough," Ever demanded. "We need to feed and get out of here unseen."

"Are you out of blood again so soon?" March asked.

Ever narrowed her eyes in Chess's direction. "My house guest is a bottomless pit."

"Please." Chess snorted. "You hand-fed me every drop and you *liked* it."

Someone pushed on the door. Chess met Ever's gaze and smirked, stepping away. The man pushed a little harder and stumbled. Chess just managed to catch him by the forearm as he fell inside. "Oh look." He kicked the door shut again. The short, pale mortal was extremely unappetizing, in his opinion. Blood was blood, but he had a habit of eating with his eyes. Convenience was key at the moment though. "Dinner."

"Chess," Ever warned.

"What the fuck?" the man snapped, attempting to tug his arm from Chess's grip.

"Allow us to feed," Chess purred to the man, letting his words sway him into compliance. The man relaxed and Chess lifted the mortal's arm to his mouth. He latched on without another word, blood flooding his mouth from where his fangs punctured. Ever could complain all she wanted but he knew she didn't disagree. Humans lived amongst vampires in Ivory—they were treated with respect for the blood contributions—but that didn't mean they weren't viewed as cattle. Humans cherished chickens, would even decorate their kitchens with them, and yet, most ate them without hesitation.

Chess pulled in a few long mouthfuls, allowing the thick metallic liquid to slide down his throat, before pushing the man toward Ever. His body hummed with new energy. "Your turn."

Ever glowered. "I'd rather not take your leftovers."

"And yet, you will." Chess licked the blood from the corner of his lips, feeling March's heavy gaze on him. "You too, if you're hungry."

"I ate earlier." March gritted his teeth. Then, softer to Ever,

"I hate to say it, but he's right. You need to feed to keep up your strength."

"I know." She sighed, kneeling on the floor beside the mortal as her fangs lowered. She then lifted the man's other arm, sinking her teeth into his flesh.

Chess watched her suck and swallow, her eyes filling with pleasure, and the smirk faded from his face. Damn, he wished in that moment she were sucking on something else. *And swallowing.* March cleared his throat and Chess ground his teeth together. Now was not the time for fantasizing when Rav was just outside. Waiting to drag him home and imprison him.

"All right," Ever said to the man after she took her fangs from his arm. "Go into the cubicle and stay there until we leave."

The man turned robotically and strode straight for the first cubicle, shutting the door behind him.

"Now," Chess drawled. "Let's get out of here."

"Why don't you go on ahead and distract them," March suggested. It sounded innocent enough but Chess could see the challenge in his eyes. "He's your *stepfather*, after all."

Like hell he would leave Ever alone with this asshat. Give him the chance to tell Ever that Rav wanted Chess locked in the dungeon? Fuck that shit. "Alas, I have no interest in returning to Scarlet so soon."

"If you're going to help me get Rav's head…" Ever spoke slowly, seeming to weigh her words as she spoke them. "It might be beneficial for you to be by his side."

The prince crossed his arms over his chest. "Fine," he said reluctantly. He would distract them … but not with his own body. The stakes were much too high for that. "But I'll need help."

Ever and March both chuckled at that, then exchanged a look, sobering. "You're serious?" Ever asked.

"I am *always* serious, my prickly white rose." He cracked his neck and straightened. "Now, you"—he waved a hand in March's direction—"will take a human out back and feed. The scent of blood will draw their attention. I'll wait nearby to intercept them before they reach you and Ever will leave through the front."

"Why would I need to lure them out back?" March asked.

Chess huffed. Must he explain *everything*? Bleeding idiot. "Because we need all five of them to leave the entrance to the club unattended. Unless you'd like to chance one of them not giving a shit about my appearance. Believe it or not, if a vampire doesn't enjoy males, they won't lose sight of their mission and ogle me."

"*Wow.*" March shook his head in disbelief. "Could you be more self-absorbed?"

"Confidence," Chess corrected, motioning to himself. "It's called *confidence.*"

"So, March lures them to the back of the club with the scent of blood, you stop them before Rav gets to March, and I sneak out the front," Ever summarized, bringing the conversation back on track.

"Bingo." Chess bopped the air between them as if he were touching the tip of her nose. It was a decent plan considering there was no time to plan anything better, even if he wasn't going to fulfill his part of it.

March's eyes narrowed as he considered the plan. "Ever?"

"It should work," she conceded.

Should? It would. If Chess had any intention of following through on his part. March had no reason to avoid Rav and his minions. Chess had never heard his name uttered in the Ruby Heart Palace or as a suspected cohort of Ever's. He seemed smart enough to think on his feet so, when Rav approached him, it would be easy to spin a lie. An average vampire, taking a jaunt into the mortal world for dinner. And what did it matter to Chess if the lie wasn't believed? Ever wouldn't need to know he left her spy on his own.

"Of course it will work," Chess promised. "Go straight back to the safe house and I'll meet you there."

"How do I know you won't lead them back there?" she inquired. "Or run off?"

Fair question, but that was a lot of extra work. "If I wanted to hand you over to your brother, I would have. And you didn't seem concerned about my scampering off when you left me standing on the dance floor alone."

Ever hesitated then nodded and gave March a quick hug. "I'll see you again soon."

"Ever, are you *sure* this is a good idea?" The male pulled away to meet her gaze. "We can think of something else that doesn't require you leaving, by yourself, with the same male who tried to assassinate you."

"I'm not at all sure," she admitted. "But I've been alone with him for days and he hasn't tried anything."

"Well, you *did* have me chained," Chess quipped.

"You're not helping," she growled. Then, to March, "Trust me."

"Anything you say," March agreed. The tick in his jaw said otherwise, but he was apparently smart enough to know his place. "Now, hurry before they decide to come back inside the club."

Ever raced from the bathroom without giving Chess a second glance. March glared at him from across the bathroom as Chess smirked, a silent war waging between them. With stiff shoulders, narrowed eyes, fangs dropped, Chess waited for him to attack. To warn him away from Ever. Seconds ticked by. Five. Ten. Thirty. If March didn't get outside, neither Ever nor Chess would escape.

"If you hurt her—"

"You'll rake me over the coals, yes, yes." Chess waved a dismissive hand in the air. "I'm terrified."

He took two rapid breaths. "You're not *my* prince and I have no reservations about killing you."

"No one does," Chess admitted with a laugh. And it was true. He had many enemies and no close friends back in Scarlet. The only thing stopping people from trying to kill him—besides his renowned skills—was his mother's wrath.

March cursed under his breath and swung open the cubicle

door. The man stood, staring at the wall with a blank gaze. Gripping his jaw, he turned the man's face so he could make eye contact and influence him. "Come with me."

The dazed human stepped out behind March. Chess slid sideways to allow the pair to exit the bathroom and took a few deep breaths. *All right, Chess. Time to do some sketchy shit.*

The prince slunk back to the dance floor just in time to see March escort the man outside through a back door. Giving the club a once-over, he saw no trace of Rav or female vampires. Only Ever. She stood near the exit, close enough to a group of girls to appear like one of their friends, and when the door opened to allow more people inside, she sniffed the air. The next moment, she slipped outside.

And, a few steps behind her, so did Chess, wearing a smug grin.

CHAPTER TEN

EVER

Even if Rav had been alone at Serenity, would Ever have sought him out and given him the death he deserved? Once her brother was dead, she swore to herself she would play a song over his body. One he would hear even from his grave. It would be a song not only for him but for her.

After Rav's death, Chess would certainly claim the throne destined to be his, even though he should've been king already. But could she separate herself from Scarlet and let him rule as king? He didn't seem to turn mortals unwillingly, yet that didn't counter the fact he'd tried to take her heart—kill her. Perhaps he wasn't as villainous now that his mother was gone and he was wanted by Rav, but she also knew he most likely wanted Maddie dead for what she'd done. And if the prince chose to pursue Maddie, Ever would easily end his life without a thought.

The coast was still clear of vampires, except for an annoying prince. Slinking farther behind her, Chess moved like a shadow. If Ever didn't already know that the prince was secretly following her from the club, she wouldn't have been attuned to it. He was quiet, nimble, yet she could feel his presence, like silk to flesh. She bet he was even gloating, grinning, thinking he'd gotten away with his lies.

He was a cocky nuisance who she would be glad to be rid of soon. Even after drinking the delicious blood from the mortal in the bathroom, she could still feel the taste of Chess's tongue on hers.

Ever hadn't gotten to discuss the prince's situation with March, but the male seemed to understand what she had wanted to tell him. Keep quiet about anything on Chess.

The night was out in full force, the lights lessening as she padded down streets and cut through trees to avoid having Rav potentially spot either one of them on the main road. Ever may have been disguised well, but Chess still looked himself. She should've made him wear a damn wig, and she would the next time they ventured out, even if it meant she had to cut one of her own to suit him.

It wasn't that late and the way home wasn't dreadfully far, but she still would've preferred taking a taxi. Ever hadn't hailed one, though, because she didn't want to distance herself from Chess too much, just in case he decided to go rogue and plot something else. Like skulking away to Rav and confessing where Ever was staying in exchange for a pardon.

The trees grew thicker around her as she entered the woods, their branches creaking with the wind. A pale moon shone through the limbs, and a few hedgehogs scampered about. She approached the tree in front of her safe house, then sank down to the ground, propping her back against the trunk. Chess's shadow lingered several trees away, but she didn't look in his direction. She waited outside to see how this charade of his played out.

After ten minutes of Ever's thoughts bouncing back and forth, hoping March was all right, Chess stepped from the trees, making his presence known with heavier footsteps. What a cocky fool.

"There you are, Princeling." She smiled, lifting her head, pretending only then to notice him. Even in the night, his yellow eyes shone like a cat's. "I thought I was going to have to hunt you down."

"Aww, were you worried about me, Queenie?" He smirked as he stopped across from her, fiddling with the edge of his shirt sleeve, rolled at his elbow. "All went well at the club. You should thank me."

Ever inwardly rolled her eyes as she stood. She reached into her dress pocket to take out the key when a leaf crunched behind Chess. Snapping to attention, she watched as a female wearing a short, skin-tight vinyl dress stepped into view. Her orange hair fell in thick curls behind her back. It was one of Rav's vampire friends from the club.

Ever's fangs lowered and she prepared to leap forward when the female spoke to Chess. "I knew that was your arse I saw leaving Serenity." The female chuckled, barely sparing Ever a glance. "I lost you for a while but finally found your booted tracks in the woods."

"Ari..." Chess offered her a flirtatious smile. Did the fool not realize the vampire had been with Rav? But then again, Chess hadn't seen Rav or the other vampires he'd been with. "What are you doing here?"

"I was with the king back at the club." She shrugged.

"With Rav?" Chess asked, arching a brow. "Since when do you frequent the mortal world with him?"

"Since he asked me to. He needed vampires he could trust to assist, so he asked me, Anna, and a few others who Imogen considered friends." She pressed closer. "He wanted to recruit Osanna to help find you, too, but found her dead. He suspects you may have had something to do with that as well."

"I'm a little busy right now." Chess's voice came out clipped.

Ever hid her smile, liking where this was headed and waiting to see what Chess would do. Then Ari's focus latched onto Ever. "Who is this?" Her brow furrowed before her eyes widened in recognition. "You did it—you finally found the bitch? I'll bring her back to the king and tell him you found her, unless you want to kill her first?"

A pity that things had to turn south so quickly. Chess and Ari seemed to be friends, so it looked as though Ever's time with Chess had to come to an end. The White Queen readied her hands, her fangs still lowered, prepared for their attack. But when Ari launched forward, Chess moved faster, gripping her head and ripping it off with one fatal yank. The female's body slumped to the ground, crimson pooling from the wound.

The prince stared at Ever, his chest heaving as he held Ari's head. Blood dripped from her severed neck to the ground.

For a moment, Ever thought he may have killed his friend to ensure her safety, though she would have easily torn out the vampire's heart. Yet she knew the true reason why he'd done it— Ari was a threat to his lies.

"She was your friend?" Ever asked.

"Not exactly, but my mother's," he said softly. "Yet she did come to my bed on several occasions."

Ari hadn't tried to drag him back to Rav so Ever believed the vampire had considered him to be more than *not exactly*. The female must've thought taking Ever to her brother would pardon Chess, perhaps even lead to them having another tumble after. She briefly wondered what it would be like to take a lover to one's bed when they weren't friends. And then an image slid forward—she shoved away the thought of her sitting in Chess's lap back at the club, on top of his cock. There had been a *reason* for that.

She needed to discuss other things, not think about her pretend tryst with the prince at Serenity. Ari had mentioned Osanna, so Scarlet knew she was dead. But Ever didn't seem to be a suspect. She needed to continue playing her part, making it seem as though she knew nothing. "Who do you think killed Osanna?"

He scowled. "I don't know, but Osanna had many enemies."

The Hatter being one. And she bet with what recently happened with Maddie's boyfriend, Noah, that Chess believed there was a strong possibility the Hatter had killed Osanna. Yet Ever couldn't tell him that it was her who murdered the twat because he wasn't supposed to know she'd returned to Wonderland.

Ever peered at the tree trunks, wondering if Rav or one of his other female vampires was going to break through the foliage. But no one came.

"We need to take the body to the nearest lake," she finally said. They couldn't leave the body there in case one of the vampires tried to track Ari down before she turned to ash in the morning.

Chess nodded and handed Ever the vampire's head, then lifted Ari's body. The lake wasn't too far away, and they used their speed to get there, easily ducking beneath low-hanging branches.

After tossing the remains in the murky water, Chess washed the blood from his arms and hands, but crimson still stained his shirt.

They then slipped into the woods, heading back to the safe house. Ever lifted the door and allowed Chess entrance before locking them both inside. The prince unbuttoned his shirt and slowly peeled the fabric from his lithe body. As he turned to face her, she averted her eyes from each taut ab. When he'd come to the Ivory Palace with his mother, he'd always worn an open vest so it wasn't something she hadn't seen before. But a flame ignited in her chest anyway.

Taking a steady breath, she blew out that flame and lifted her viola from the mattress. She let a Chopin song fill the space around them as her bow slid across the strings.

Chess lowered himself to the floor on his stomach, his hands tucked beneath his head while he studied her. She waited for him to tell her to quit playing the damn instrument, but he didn't. Instead, he murmured, "You're quite lovely with that thing." Then he closed his eyes, his breathing growing even. It wasn't anywhere close to morning for them to be tired, but she knew he hadn't slept well in days.

Ever halted her playing. This was her chance. She thought she may have needed to knock him out again, and perhaps she should, but she chose to let him sleep.

With light steps, Ever crept up the ladder and opened the door. She turned the lock with a soft click after shutting it. Thunder rumbled in the distance, but no raindrops fell yet. Using her speed, she bolted through the trees to the park near one of the private schools. There were still hours before the sun rose, but this wouldn't take long.

On a picnic table across from a pair of swings lay a male, peering up at the darkened sky.

March.

Back at the club, Ever had given him the one finger hand signal, telling him to meet her at this park sometime tonight.

Another crack of thunder came as she stopped in front of him at the table.

"The prince?" He sighed, his gaze meeting hers. "Really?"

She sat on the table's bench, resting her elbows beside him. "I don't trust him, but he's going to make things easier. And he doesn't think I know he's wanted by Scarlet for his mother's death."

"I kind of figured that out." March chuckled.

His earlier clothing still appeared intact, no sign of a fight with any other vampires. "Did you see Rav at the club since we knew Chess was lying about intercepting anyone? One of the females followed Chess, but he killed her."

"Actually, good things may have come from this night." March rolled to his side and propped his head in his hand.

"Oh?" Her interest was piqued. "Details."

"Your bastard brother did stumble upon me, and we feasted on the human together." His grin grew wolfish. "He offered me a position to be one of the guards at the Ivory Palace. Seems he's scouting the mortal world for rogue vampires who may want to side with him since he took out most of Ivory's guards who he didn't trust."

Her eyes widened. "Rav trusted you that easily?"

"I do turn on the charm when necessary." He paused. "But I don't believe he trusts me, just that he needs a few more hands there until he joins the territories. Apparently, he's still picky about who stays with him in Scarlet, though." Her blood boiled at the thought of the guards who betrayed her and wondered which ones remained in Ivory. They would all have to die regardless.

"Are you going to take the position?" This was like a dream come true. She would have him spy inside her palace in Ivory. He could then feed her necessary info about guard rotations and number of enemies so they could break into the palace, then take control of it.

"Of course. I'm headed there tomorrow." He peered up at her, his expression turning serious. "Be careful."

"I've been careful for nearly four years." It was time Ever used her carefulness for other things, like trying to take back her kingdom.

"I mean, with the prince."

Ever's heart pounded at his words and she took a deep swallow. "Don't worry. He's just a tool and once he betrays me, I'll rip out his heart as he'd planned to do with mine." And she would then feed it to the werewolves afterward. It wasn't a question of *if* he would turn on her but *when*.

March trailed a finger down her arm. "If you need me to do it, just give me the signal."

As she mulled over the wonderful news, the plan finally fell into place. "In a few days, I'll head to the Ivory Palace. Meet me at the lake on the eastern side of the castle and we can go over anything you've learned." There was plenty of foliage in that location to keep her hidden as they discussed matters.

"I'll gather everything I can."

"Thank you." She placed a hand on his cheek. "If you decide to stay in Ivory after this is over, you always have a place inside the palace."

"Not now. But if you change your mind about me, I will in a heartbeat." He scooted closer and pressed his mouth to hers, dipping his tongue in between her lips. But all she could think about was when Chess's mouth had been on hers, the way his soft lips felt, the way he'd gripped her hips, the way his heart had pounded.

"I wish I could, but I can't." Not looking at what expression his face held, she pulled back. "See you soon."

"Until we meet again."

Ever hurried back to the safe house, being extra careful to make sure no one followed her. The next night, they would need to gather a few more weapons and get Chess some new clothing.

Once she was home, she locked the door behind her and found Chess still on his stomach, his lips parted, his chestnut hair covering his face. A tiny piece of her wanted to brush the strands from his eye. However, she did no such foolish thing and lifted her viola instead.

As she played a soft melody, her gaze lingered on his form, his naked upper body, her attention unable to fix on anything else. But he wouldn't have to know that.

CHAPTER ELEVEN

CHESS

Over the next several days, Chess had gone with Ever for supplies three times but never for more than an hour. It was too risky with him having killed Ari. Chess couldn't say he was sorry for murdering her—she'd been friends with his mother and was a decent fuck, but she'd also clung to him like bad cologne, always wanting more. More attention, more pleasure, more *him*, though he wasn't sure if she ever actually liked him or if she liked his position of power—as small as it was. Either way, he didn't have to worry about her anymore. He *did* have to worry about Rav trying to hunt her down now though. With Ari gone, he would be searching for her and whoever made her disappear. And he wouldn't be alone. Apparently, he'd recruited his mother's friends, including Anna. Anna who could've passed for Imogen's sister. Chess knew if he saw her it would stir up memories of his mother that he'd rather leave buried.

"Don't think too hard. I wouldn't want you to hurt yourself," Ever quipped from where she sat on the floor, recounting their supplies. Guns had been impossible to find on short notice, but they had retrieved one more dagger for her collection and raided the blood bank.

Chess snorted, twisting the strings of the hoodie he'd stolen, and watched Ever carefully as she loaded her backpack, not sparing him a glance. He couldn't help thinking about the way Ari's appearance made him feel. Nervous, yes, because maybe Rav was right behind him, and then pissed because she could have blown his lie out of the water. But it was the rush of adrenaline urging him to protect Ever that irritated him. He'd hunted her for years to kill her. *Protect her?* Never. He huffed and turned his attention to the supplies still spread out neatly on the ground.

Seventeen blood bags, the three guns Ever already owned with a box of silver bullets, and four daggers. She'd packed two wigs into her backpack already—one with brown curls, another a dark bob—plus a change of clothes for them both.

"Are the costumes really necessary?" he asked.

"They're *disguises*, and do you really need to ask? Ari spotted you easily enough."

"Point taken," he grumbled. Ari had followed him with no trouble because he was so focused on Ever. *Damn.* He really needed to step up his game.

"Here." Ever tossed a blond wig at him. "I cut this into a style just for you."

Chess snatched the wig in the air and scowled. "I don't think this is my color."

"It's fit for a vampire prince." Ever grinned, seeming to know that the wig looked like shit. "Try it on and stop complaining."

"Demanding thing, aren't you?" Chess purred, slipping the wig over his chestnut hair, not bothering to tuck any strands beneath. "What do you think?"

"It will do." She pursed her lips in what appeared to be an attempt not to laugh.

Chess reached for a hand mirror beside the mattress. Looking at his reflection, his eyes widened in horror. Stringy strands hung down his neck and back while choppier spikes rested on top. "What the fuck is this atrocity?"

"I believe the mortals call it a mullet."

"No." Chess ripped the wig from his head and glowered at it. "I've seen stylish mullets and *this* … this is an insult."

Ever batted her long lashes innocently at him. "No one could ever accuse you of being unstylish, Princeling, which makes it the perfect disguise."

"Yeah, fuck that," he grumbled and lunged for the scissors on the other side of the room.

"Don't you dare," Ever shouted, and leapt onto his back. "The whole point is to make you look different. Remember *you* were the one who was spotted the other night."

He grunted as her weight shoved him to the floor on his stomach. "Trust me, I'll look plenty different with this baggy-arse hoodie. The bad mullet is vetoed, Queenie." Everyone had their limits and he wouldn't be caught dead wearing that wig.

"We don't have time for you to fix it," she huffed, her warm breath brushing his ear. He shivered inwardly at the soft caress of it.

Chess rolled beneath her so she was straddling his abdomen, his fingers at her hips. It closely reminded him of the position they were in the other night. He imagined himself slowly slipping into her heat as she rolled her supple body forward. "We have time," he rasped. "Plenty of time, in fact, if you're interested in finishing what we started on the second floor of the club." He lifted a hand from her hips and traced her lips with his fingers, surprised when she didn't shove him away.

Ever drew in a sharp breath, her eyes flicking to his mouth. Then she snatched the wig from the floor and pushed herself up. "Time to go, Princeling."

Chess missed the weight of her on top of him. Damn, he needed a release—preferably by her hands. Or better yet, her mouth. Those perfect lips would undoubtedly feel like bliss running down his hard shaft. He eased his upper body up to lean on his elbows and watched her shove everything into her bag with a smirk on his face. She had considered his offer to continue, if only for half a moment. Which meant she had to want him too … wanted him to taste every inch of her, touch, tease, fill her up and wring out every drop of pleasure. The question was how much? Enough to have a tumble despite the loathing she harbored for him? The possibility felt a little closer every day they spent together. For once, he was glad he failed at assassinating her in the past.

Ever swung her bag over her shoulder and fished the key from her pocket. "Up, up," she urged, motioning for him to stand. "We're losing the night."

Chess's grin widened. "It's barely midnight."

"Yes, well…" She blew out a breath. "We're leaving. That's an order."

"Oh?" Chess was on his feet the next moment, moving fluidly until he was standing an inch from her. Taking her chin between his fingers, he laughed. "You may be a queen, but you are not *my* queen. Unless, of course, you'd like to be. Once I reclaim Scarlet, of course."

She stilled, her lips parting, her eyes widening at his words. They stared at each other for a moment too long before she batted his hand away and scurried up the ladder.

Chess stayed rooted to the spot. Had he really just suggested she become his wife? He'd meant to make her uncomfortable, to put her in her place and show how she couldn't control him. But he would *never* take her as a queen—in fact, he would never take a queen at all. There were too many souls out there left to ravage in his bed to let just one vampire lay claim to it. He shook his head. She took it as intended—as a bad joke.

"Chess!" Ever called from outside of the safe house.

He scrambled up the ladder and pulled himself out into the cool evening air. "Don't get your panties in a twist, Queenie."

She sighed heavily before closing and locking the hidden door again. "This is a mistake, isn't it?" she asked when she stood beside him.

"Care to be more specific? There are a lot of things that could be considered a mistake lately." Kissing each other, cohabitating with the enemy, murdering old acquaintances…

Ever began walking, her steps sure and brisk. Chess followed beside her while scanning the area in case any of Rav's spies were lurking about, but they seemed alone. Once they were back in Wonderland, vampires would be nearly everywhere, so he'd enjoy it while he could.

"So," Chess drawled to distract himself from the idea of his highly-probable impending capture. He wasn't quite ready to face Wonderland again, knowing his mother was no longer part of it. Knowing that everyone likely thought he was the murderer. "This mistake you spoke of. It's leaving your violin behind, isn't it?"

"Viola," she corrected. "Quit being a fool, you know what it is. But alas, it's too large to carry around with us so I'll come back for it later. The mistake is bringing *another* large, unnecessary thing instead."

Chess scanned her over, finding nothing that matched her description. Everything they had fit inside her one bag.

"You," she said slowly when it became obvious that he didn't understand. "I meant bringing you, of all people, with me to reclaim my throne is undoubtedly going to fuck me over in the end."

"I can fuck you any time you'd like." He flashed a playful grin, but her words rang true.

"You never stop, do you?" She leapt across a small stream and kicked aside a prickly bush, revealing a hole. *A portal.* "Try and take my heart again, and I'll take yours first, understand?"

"I'm content with your heart right where it is," he said with a laugh. One day, that might change, but for now, her company was growing on him.

Ever then motioned toward the portal but Chess hesitated. "Are you waiting for a written invitation to my kingdom?" She cocked her head.

No—he was actively trying to justify returning to Wonderland when everyone would be hunting him down like a rabid werewolf. How would he hide the truth for long when he couldn't be seen? "If you have one," he answered. "Perhaps on embossed cardstock? With a little gold leaf on the invitation to make it *pop*."

"Bloody hell," she mumbled, grabbing hold of his hand.

"Well, if you wanted to touch me again all you had to do was ask." Chess looked to the night sky, taking in the stars, and released a resigned breath.

Ever then yanked him forward, making him lose his footing. He stumbled into the hole and took one step forward through the mirror-like portal. White, glowing bugs crawled around the edges like a living frame. Vibrations ran along his skin, sending a shiver down his spine, but it ended in seconds as he stepped into a monochrome forest.

Most of the landscapes in Ivory were a mixture of white and silver, but there was none of the latter here. The bare trees were so white that they seemed almost fake, and the short grass blended into one giant blanket covering the ground. Even the dead leaves on the grass were pure alabaster. Like always, the pristine land brought the urge to ruin something. Chess wanted to dig in his heels, crush up the dried foliage and scatter their dust about. Instead, he scuffed his shoes on the ground, hoping there was something really nasty lodged into the soles.

"I hadn't realized we were so close to a portal into Ivory," Chess said. His voice was quiet, the atmosphere demanding their silence. It was oppressive here—the forest almost requiring perfection of anyone who laid eyes upon it. He recognized the staleness to the air, though, the coldness. The smell had taken over Ivory shortly after Ever disappeared.

Ever shrugged. "Why *would* you know?"

Because he'd traveled all through Ivory and Scarlet over the centuries, portals were one of his favorite things to discover. "The world is my oyster. I make a point of knowing where all the pearls are."

Ever released a quick breath. "We'll go to one of my safe houses next to the rendezvous point until it's time to meet with

March."

"How would March know to meet us here?" Chess asked as she sauntered away from him. He quickly caught up with her and drew her back by the wrist.

She smiled wide. "Oh, did I forget to tell you? While you were getting your beauty rest the other night, I met up with March and he's to be one of Rav's shining white knights at the Ivory Palace."

Chess arched a brow. "Hold the fuck up. I'm going to ignore the fact that you snuck off into the night without me, but Rav is just inviting anyone to be a guard in Ivory now?"

"Seems so."

Bastard. Chess wasn't sure if he meant the thought for Rav or March, but it fit them both. After Imogen spent years planting spies, bribing Ever's guards, and plotting the White Queen's assassination, Rav was tossing any random bloke in the castle to protect it? And March… He was sure the male would come through on Ever's behalf, but Chess didn't relish the idea of seeing him again. "You're sure he'll meet us there then?" he asked, hoping to avoid it.

"I'm sure of my friends," she said without hesitation.

Chess glanced at her from the corner of his eyes. If she kissed all of her *friends* like she'd kissed March at the club, the rumors of her lack of experience wouldn't have spread. But if she claimed they weren't lovers, he would believe her. Because, honestly, it didn't matter to him. He'd personally fucked a good portion of Wonderland himself.

Following Ever through Ivory, Chess continuously scanned their surroundings, but not a single vampire appeared to be in the forest where they entered. It was no wonder Chess had never stumbled upon the portal—there were only trees, trees, and more trees, none with leaves, as if this were a wasteland. The animals lurking about made it clear that there was plenty of life here though. Silver foxes with red eyes slunk into their den as they walked by, and albino birds watched them curiously from the bare branches. Angry squirrels with bared fangs chased each other through the dried leaves covering the ground, chittering back and forth.

When silver began to creep back in, breaking up the blinding white land—first as a handful of leaves still clinging to the branches, then as entire, glimmering trees—his heart beat a little faster. This was the Ivory he knew.

The ivory teeming with vampires.

Ever stopped at a small creek. Silver water flowed over opaque rocks with white tadpoles racing between them. The trees ended on one side and, on the other, were rolling hills. White grass and silver rocks as far as the eye could see. An ear-piercing screech filled the air, high-pitched yet brimming with power. Chess jumped—though he would've fully denied it if Ever pointed out that fact.

"The Jabberwocky," Ever said solemnly. "What's it doing here?"

Chess released a small chuckle. "At least something scares you more than my mother. Once Rav is dead, looks like you'll still have a nemesis to conquer."

"Your mother didn't scare me." Ever took a leaping step over the creek and walked softly down the path leading between swells of land. Chess hurried after her before she could disappear between the hills. Once he was at her side, she continued, "I didn't run because I was afraid. I ran because it was the smart thing to do. There would be no reclaiming the throne from the grave."

"If you say so, Queenie." He cringed as another screech rang out. At least it sounded farther away. The Jabberwocky was a problem neither of them could've planned for, but, even if they could've known the beast was traveling out of Red, he wouldn't have agreed to crossing its path. "For the record, I was scared of her on occasion myself."

Ever tilted her head to study him and opened her mouth when a shout rang out.

"Fuck!" an unseen male bellowed from farther down the path. "Fuck, fuck!"

"Calm down, Garrett!" a female hissed almost as loudly.

Movement fluttered at the bend in the pathway ahead. "You'll attract its attention."

"Don't tell me to calm down, Dinah. We need to get out of here. If anyone was hiding around here, the Jabberwocky will have beat us to them."

Chess recognized those fucking voices. Vampires from Scarlet. He'd even enjoyed them both, separately, once or twice. *Dinah and Garrett.* They weren't part of Scarlet's guards—they would've been dead if they were, apparently—but they had been good friends with his mother. *Fuck this.*

Chess bolted up the side of a hill and pressed himself tightly against the wide trunk of a white tree, leaving Ever alone on the path. At least she had her disguise.

He grimaced. Maybe he should've worn her damn wig after all. If they attacked Ever, he'd be forced to step in to end things, but leaving a trail of bodies wasn't what he'd consider stealthy.

A stocky female wearing red leather trousers and an even stockier male with a metal bar pierced through the middle of his nose rounded the path and came to a dead stop. "Hello," Garrett called. "Are you lost?"

"No." Ever shifted her weight between her feet, keeping her head down. "Just taking a short cut."

They prowled closer, circling her like she was prey, taking slow, purposeful steps as they eyed the White Queen over from head to toe. Ever stood perfectly still, looking far too relaxed for Chess's liking, but her calmness would likely save her. The pair had been fleeing the Jabberwocky a moment ago and her lack of obvious fear would send them on their way without much fuss.

Dinah smiled, baring her fangs. Chess tensed. That was *not* a good sort of smile. "All alone? A sweet thing like you."

Ever shrugged. "The Jabberwocky seems too busy tracking you at the moment to worry about me."

As if on cue, the beast let out a different sort of cry. One that shook the trees and the ground beneath Chess's feet. Judging by the excited—*terrifying*—note in the call, the Jabberwocky had picked up on the scent of its dinner. Dinah shared a petrified look with Garrett before speaking again. "Off you go then. Be sure to report any sightings of—" Another roar, closer this time. "Fuck it. Let's go." But Garrett was already fleeing from them. "Ya bleeding coward," Dinah shouted, and took off after him.

Chess loosened a breath and counted to ten before peeling himself away from the tree and scrambling back down the hill to Ever's side. "We should probably go too," he suggested.

Ever crossed her arms, smirking. "What's wrong, Princeling?"

Was she serious? The Jabberwocky was tracking Dinah and Garrett … who just happened to run straight past them. Something large, angry, and loud as shit. "Is there a problem with your hearing?"

"No, but I thought there was something wrong with my eyesight for a moment. Why did you hide?" she asked, almost smug.

"I may have fucked them. Both, if that was unclear," he said truthfully. It was clearly not the reason he didn't want to be seen, but he couldn't tell Ever that they were likely hunting *him*. They wouldn't be like Ari—they would certainly try and hand him over to Rav. He turned his gaze to the sky, expecting to see a beastly shape soar overhead. "It would've been a tad awkward."

Ever scowled. He could see it in her eyes—the knowledge that Chess would never find running into an old lover to be awkward. But then the Jabberwocky cried out again, saving him from her questions.

A loud *whoosh* of wind whipped around them, and Chess latched onto Ever's hand just as a shadow passed over them. He knew without looking what it was. He knew and he stared up anyway.

The Jabberwocky.

"Move," Ever snapped, and tore down the path, dragging Chess along with her.

CHAPTER TWELVE

EVER

Ever's heart was two seconds from exploding out of her chest.
And no, she wasn't being melodramatic.

The Jabberwocky had never ventured into Ivory in the past.
But perhaps with the Red Queen dead and the White Queen
being gone for so long, the curious beastie was a bit more
adventurous. Generally, it was only the rogue werewolves who
attempted to slip into her territory and stir up problems.
However, her guards had always shot them down before they
could wreak havoc on her city.

Above them, bats flew from the trees, their wings pumping
violently as they banded together in the air. The Jabberwocky
tore toward them, the beat of its leathery wings shaking the trees,
the entire forest. Ever's wig whipped around her head from the
wind.

The Jabberwocky appeared the same as when she'd seen it
last in Red, just before it had gobbled the hellion Red Queen up.
Its massive bat-like leather wings cracked, its gnarled and curved

340

talons ready to swipe a meal. Dark green, almost black, fur covered its entire body, thorns ran the length of its elongated tail, and thin spikes sprouted down its head. Barbed quills poked out from its fur—the creature's size could best compare with a dragon. Opening its large mouth, with rows of sharpened teeth, even wider, the creature shot forward, not leaving a single bat in the sky. The Jabberwocky then circled the air, swooping downward.

Ever yanked Chess toward the nearest tree, slipping behind several silver hanging vines that barely concealed them. Turning, he pushed her back against the bark, caging her in. She couldn't tell if the prince was trapping her in or *protecting* her.

Above them, the Jabberwocky continued to loop, cracking its tail like a whip as it searched for more prey. Ever clutched the front of Chess's shirt and didn't take a breath while his warm body held her still. With a shrill shriek that pierced her eardrums, would have shattered them if they'd belonged to a mortal, the creature darted away, the beat of its wings fading.

Once they were out of danger's way, Chess's chest heaved against hers as she finally took a breath. Then their eyes met, mischief shining in his yellow irises. A smirk crossed Chess's face as he peered down at her hand still grasping his shirt. "You're not pushing me away," he drawled.

Ever didn't want to shove him back like he expected her to do. So with a smirk of her own, she released his shirt and slowly trailed her finger down his chest, his taut abs, halting at his waistband. She partially dipped her digits inside, brushing warm skin, while toying with the ties of his trousers by using her thumb. "Do you want me to touch you?"

The prince's throat bobbed and his eyes became hooded. "Fuck yes."

"Nah, we don't have time for that, Princeling." She laughed, then playfully shoved him away. But a part of her yearned to see and feel what so many in Wonderland had, even though the thought should've revolted her.

Chess hauled her back to him, a wicked grin spreading across his face. He lowered his head beside her ear, a fluttering forming in her stomach, warming. "Perhaps if it's me touching you?" He paused, his voice deep with his next word. "Fingers, tongue, or cock. Your choice. Either way, I'll make you come like you never have before, Queenie."

The place that yearned for him to use all three of those tightened at his alluring words. Betraying her. She wanted him to touch, to circle, to lick, then to press inside her. Damn it.

"Who do we have here?" a female voice cooed from a gnarled tree across from them. Ever and Chess broke apart, her fangs lowering, as the two Scarlet vampires stepped out from behind the trunk. Dinah and Garrett. They must've hidden as well, knowing they couldn't outrun the beast.

"The traitorous prince and the cowardly queen." Garrett chuckled, pressing his fist to his mouth. "Together? Our king's been looking for you, Chess. And for what you did to your mother, you're going to pay dearly."

"You really will fuck anyone, won't you?" Dinah shook her head, wrinkling her nose in disgust. "It's now obvious why you killed your mother. Because you're the White Queen's lapdog. You'll turn on anyone."

Before the queen or Chess could speak, Dinah released her fangs and lunged for Ever. The queen whirled around her, then thrust the vampire against the trunk. She slammed her boot into Dinah's upper back. The female released a growl, but she was much weaker than Ever. The queen gripped the female's head and yanked it to the side, giving Dinah an extra rush of pain before tearing it from her shoulders. Hot blood sprayed the queen's face and shirt. Ever then tossed the head beside the body as thick crimson oozed down her hand.

She turned to Chess, who stood gripping Garrett's bloody heart in his hand, the vampire's body dead on the ground. The blood *drip, drip*, dripped while the prince stood frozen like a fool, not peering up at her, but studying the heart. An unreadable expression rested on his face.

"Tastes like victory." Ever swiped the tip of her tongue

across the blood on her palm, wishing she could see into vampires' memories the way she could with a mortal's. Then maybe she would've been able to get some insight into Rav.

"The last time I held a heart," Chess whispered, "it was my mother's."

Ever's thoughts turned to Maddie, her friend telling her how she'd killed the queen. How Chess had come into the room and lifted his mother's dead heart, how tears had streamed down his cheeks. How Ever had believed the bastard prince didn't know how to cry.

A boisterous roar sounded, interrupting Ever's thoughts. The Jabberwocky was coming back. It must've smelled the blood that Ever and Chess had spilled, and if it didn't, then the beast surely would soon.

Thankfully the safe house wasn't too far away from their location. So the Jabberwocky wouldn't track them, Ever tore off her bloody T-shirt, leaving her wearing only her bra. She then ripped the heart that Chess was still holding out of his hand and tossed it beside the corpses.

"Come on, you idiot," Ever shouted, grabbing his hand.

The words must've drawn him from his thoughts because his legs started to move faster while she dragged him along with her. They skirted around trees, avoiding as many leaves and twigs as they could. She yanked Chess to the right, letting her enhanced speed take them across the rolling hills and through the luscious landscape.

The shimmering stream slid into view and she ran even faster. They came to a stop in front of the flowing water, sucking in gulps of air. She quickly washed the remaining blood from her arms, face, and neck as Chess did the same.

The Jabberwocky's sounds had vanished, but Ever still hurried to take out her key and unlock the secret door in the ground beside the stream. She didn't know what enemy might make an appearance next—there had been a few too many already in their brief time back in Wonderland. For all she knew, Rav would slink up soon since two of his Scarlet lackeys were here … and now dead.

As Ever opened the door, she motioned Chess inside. "Go."

Ever slipped into the safe house and closed the door behind them, locking them in. Her heart continued to beat wildly as she walked down the stone steps into an almost bare ivory room that held an earthy scent. A few blankets rested atop a mattress against the wall, and a wooden chair tucked into a small table, with a crate containing packets of dried blood atop it, sat in the corner. She fished out a clean shirt from her backpack and tossed her wig to the floor before sliding the fabric on.

"Told you we would need spare clothing," she said as she ran a hand over her pinned-up hair.

Chess peeled off his blood-speckled hoodie and lowered himself on the mattress, not glancing up at her.

"What is it?" Ever asked. "Cat got your tongue?"

"It's got a lot of things actually." For once, his voice wasn't assured while he stayed peering at his clasped hands. "About what happened back there, about what they said, it's not—"

Ever had wondered if he was going to say anything about his mother's death first. She folded her arms over her chest and took a step toward him. "Don't try and lie. We're past that and this part of your game needs to come to an end. You think I'm a *fool*? You believed that March really wouldn't know about what was happening in Wonderland? That he wouldn't tell me Rav killed his guards and how he's now recruiting your mother's friends to replace them? That he isn't turning mortals into vampires anymore but leaving them in a trance? And that every vampire knows you're wanted by my brother for the murder of his queen?"

"I didn't know any of that and I *didn't* murder my mother." His gaze met hers then, his voice steady. "At first I thought Rav blamed me on purpose, but it seems he really believes it was me. It wasn't."

"I know it wasn't," Ever bit back. And she knew the mistake as soon as she said it, but she hadn't been thinking about Maddie.

"You know?" He eyed her suspiciously.

"I know because, back there? When you were holding Garrett's heart, I know why you stood so still. You were thinking about your mother. You loved her."

"And you hated her," he accused, his voice bitter.

"I did." Anger coursed through her veins as she started to think about that bitch, truly think about all she'd done. "For her sending you to kill me. For hurting my friends. For turning mortals without a fucking care. For murdering anyone who wouldn't do what she wanted. I understand that you loved her, because I still love my brother, but I can see when my own flesh and blood is a monster." She slapped her hand to her chest, right over her heart. "We may be monsters, too, but your mother was the greatest one of all. She abandoned you as a child, then showed up in your life years later, turned you, and hauled you back to Wonderland without your consent. Did you even *want* to be a vampire? Don't you care that she murdered your own damn father? He was a good male who wanted to give you a choice of what life you wanted. Instead of giving you that opportunity, she murdered him with my fucking brother's help, then dragged you to her hell."

"Shut up," he whispered, his nostrils flaring as his fists shook.

"No." She gritted her teeth and knelt in front of him. "I will not. My brother is a bastard and I know it, so how can you not see it? How can you not have feelings about what she's done?"

"I see it, damn it." His jaw tightened, his hand slamming against the mattress. "I know what my mother was. But she loved me. Who the fuck else ever would?"

Even though her stomach sank at what he'd spoken, she had to continue. These were words she'd held inside her chest for years. Words she should've spewed at him in that garden instead of fleeing. "She did in her own way, but to her, you were *her* tool. Would she have still loved you if you had told her no? What would she have done to you if you'd refused to take my heart?"

"And isn't that what I am to you right now?" he seethed. "A tool?"

"Don't." Ever held up a finger. "Don't pretend for a second

that you weren't trying to use me." She needed to get up and walk away before she said something worse, before she admitted that Maddie had been the one to kill his mother and she was glad for it.

Ever stood and padded halfway across the room, when Chess's hand clasped her wrist. He tightened his grip, then backed her into a wall so his firm body was once again pressed to hers. "You're a fool." He narrowed his eyes at her, then lowered his face, his nose brushing hers. "After everything, after our past, you turned your back on me. If I'd wanted, I could've easily ripped your fucking heart out."

"Is that your end game?" she spat. "Tearing it out because you didn't get the chance to before? Even after all you've done, when I could've easily killed your foolish arse a hundred times in the mortal world, I didn't." *Not to say I won't.*

The prince's chest heaved—the vein at his jaw feathered, the one at his neck thrumming harder. She was prepared to spew more spiteful words with whatever asinine reply that came out of his mouth next, but instead, he brought her to him and folded his arms around her, his body trembling while he cried.

Ever's eyes widened, and she didn't know what the bloody hell was happening as her head rested on his chest. She knew she could've been anyone in that moment, but he apparently just needed this. Over the past several days, she hadn't hated him as she should've, yet she didn't think she liked him either. Perhaps she did a little, though, because she lifted her arms around him, holding him as he cried. The prince of Scarlet, who always had a smirk on his face, was vulnerable for once.

After a long while, when he stopped shaking, she took a step back from him. Her gaze locked onto Chess's, his eyes red-rimmed from crying. "Now that your lies are out in the open, you can continue with me or go back into hiding. If you decide to leave, I promise I won't tell my brother I saw you. Unless you turn on me, that is." There was one thing he still wasn't telling her—he knew Maddie had killed his mother. But Ever would never put her friend at risk by admitting that.

"Rav has to die, and the only way it will happen is if you and I continue to stay aligned." He paused, eyeing her warily. "However, I'm not much of a prince at the moment."

In response, Ever could have said so many awful things, yet she chose to speak the truth. "No, Chess. You're the king of Scarlet. Its rightful heir. And if my viola were here, I'd play us a song to prepare for our destinies."

CHAPTER THIRTEEN

CHESS

Chess followed Ever along the crest of a ridge toward a sparkling silver lake where they were meant to meet March. Four white gazebos with scrolling silver iron railings were spaced around it and a dock reached a few feet into the water where a canoe was tethered. He imagined parties took place here in the past.

But now, despite the beauty, it felt lifeless. As if no one had visited in ages. He couldn't put his finger on why it felt that way—perhaps it was that the air was too still or the temperature was cooler than it had been when he and Ever had exited the safe house moments ago. Or maybe it was all in his head.

Since he'd broken down and cried the night before, the whole world seemed off. Just slightly—like someone had tilted the earth a degree or two—but there wasn't time to get his footing. He'd fucking *cried*. In front of Ever, no less. *Bloody idiot.* He'd learned on the streets at a young age not to show his feelings or weaknesses. Then no one could use them against him. Now his enemy held that power.

Well... He glanced down at Ever as she walked beside him. The curls of her brunette wig bounced gently around her cheeks, and the urge to brush them away filled him. *Maybe she wasn't exactly his enemy.* There had been a subtle shift between them. An unspoken understanding after seeing another side of each other. Chess vulnerable and Ever comforting. It was strange and yet he didn't loathe it. He sure as hell didn't understand it, but it wasn't unwelcome. Why had he hated her for so long?

Because of his mother...

"I'm surprised they haven't torn any of this down," Ever whispered as they reached the nearest gazebo. Marble benches ran along the interior walls with a small, empty brazier at the center. "This used to be one of my favorite places. The music from my viola traveled so well here and everyone would sing and dance the night away."

"Even the humans?" Chess asked, genuinely curious. In Scarlet, no one danced unless it was in someone's blood.

"Sometimes." Ever sank onto the bench and looked out over the lake. "Most of the time they were ... *busy* after feeding a vampire."

Chess smirked, knowing exactly what sort of activity usually followed. "At least Scarlet has something in common with this place. A good fucking after a good feeding."

Ever snorted. "No, Princeling, both the feeding and the fucking in Ivory are never simply *good*. They're always amazing. What sort of court were you running?"

"To be fair, I wasn't running anything. If I had been home more often, maybe I could've saved those poor souls from mediocre pleasure." He winked as he sat down beside her and scanned the area, looking for any sign of vampires, finding none. As much as he would love to tell Ever tales of his prowess and watch her reaction, they were there with a purpose. "Your friend is late."

Ever drew in a steadying breath. "March will be here."

If he wasn't discovered. Or killed. Or a traitor.

Ever said she trusted the male but she seemed to trust Chess too. Obviously, she was mistaken with Chess since he planned to betray her by killing Maddie, so she could be wrong twice. He looked at her again and sucked on his bottom lip. The thought of seeing her dead—or worse, alive and aware of his duplicity— made him shift uncomfortably on the bench. His blood warmed in shame. Was he really going to go through with it? Ever wouldn't forgive him once he killed Maddie, but that was the only reason he could think of for continuing down this path. They both wanted Rav dead and, once he was, his gut told him that they would be able to rule their respective kingdoms without too many issues. Maybe if he gave up his revenge…

Don't go getting soft, he warned himself. Imogen had been a shit mother, sure, but she still needed to be avenged. Even if she had forced immortality on him—he liked it now, after all—and lied to him. Ever said his father had been a good male, wanted Chess to have a choice about immortality, while his mother only ever disparaged the male. It was too late to know for sure now that he was dead. His mother had been his only blood relation for centuries and that counted for something.

Right?

Regardless of what he decided to do about Ever, the truth was he might not get the chance to double-cross her now that she knew the truth about him. Apparently Ever knew the *entire* time. She'd been playing with him, letting him spin his lies. She must've just *loved* that. Allowing him to look like a fool. Embarrassment burned beneath his skin, but the fact that she hadn't actually cared about his predicament cooled him slightly. She hadn't treated him any differently now that the truth was out. In fact, the wall he had created seemed to have crumbled, allowing them to see each other over the ruins. Somehow. He scowled. Was that normal? During his long life, he hadn't bothered to connect with anyone on an emotional level…

"He's here," Ever whispered.

Chess sat up straight and shifted a bit closer to her. A blur of motion came from the other side of the lake, a quick flash of red.

Then March stood before them in his guard uniform, crimson with black piping along the front. They were very different than the stark white ones Chess had seen at the ball four years ago.

"Your Majesty," March said, bowing slightly, his braids slipping over his shoulders. "It's so good to see you."

Ever leapt up from her seat and hugged him tightly. When he returned the hug, Chess gripped the edge of the bench to keep himself seated. "It's good to see you too," she said with so much sincerity that Chess rolled his eyes.

"All right, all right," he snapped from his seat. "Enough with the touchy-feely. What information do you have?"

The two broke apart and March glowered down at him. Chess gripped the marble harder—he would *not* give the male the satisfaction of knowing how agitating his presence was. Though agitated might be too mild a term for the growing emotion inside of him. The sight of March's hand still on Ever's waist woke a territorial part of Chess that he hadn't known existed.

"I don't take orders from you," March said calmly.

"Who *do* you take them from, then?" Chess arched a brow. "Your queen? Or have Rav's cohorts put you under their spell yet? I know from experience just how alluring it can be to strive for Scarlet's ideals. All that gorging on blood, the death, the carefree—"

"Chess," Ever said in a flat tone. "Not now."

He narrowed his eyes at her and, reluctantly, snapped his mouth shut. It wasn't like him to take orders from anyone—especially her—but the faster they got March's intel, the faster they could get away from him. Leaning back into the gazebo's railing, he motioned to March for them to continue.

"I have to be quick in case I was followed. They're keeping a close eye on me since I'm new," March said in a low voice. No one outside of the lake area would be able to pick up on his words. "As we already knew, Rav took out a lot of the guards here."

"How many are left of the ones who betrayed me?" Ever

asked.

March cast a wary glance at Chess and hesitated before speaking. "Three, that I know of. They're the ones in charge of the new vampires Rav's been sending as replacements. One of them is on duty at all times. The good news is that the rest of us aren't trained as guards—we're given uniforms and told where to stand watch. The bad news is that the palace is now run by cutthroats with no morals and have no problem murdering citizens if they look at them sideways."

Ever's expression turned stony. "How many guards in all?"

"Twelve." March took Ever's hand and tugged her a few steps away from Chess, toward the opening to the gazebo. "Are you *sure* he should be hearing this?"

"He's fine," Ever assured him with a distracted wave of her hand. "What's the best way to get inside?"

"The—"

Chess leaned forward, resting his elbows on his knees and tilting his head as if this answer were particularly intriguing. It wasn't—he was simply along for the ride on this part of their journey—but he knew it would make March squirm. And squirm he did. The vampire leaned closer to Ever, wrapping a protective arm around her shoulders, and positioned her so they could flee together. As if Chess would suddenly decide to murder the White Queen after all this time when she had back up.

"Go on," Chess urged with a vicious smirk. "Tell us how to get into the castle, pretty boy."

March sneered and his fangs dropped. "I can't do this, Ever. How can you trust him? I'm about to tell you the greatest weakness to the castle's defenses *in front of the enemy*."

Ever released an exasperated sigh. "What do you think he'll do, March? Run and tattle to Rav? Do you think my brother will let him live long enough to tell him our secrets?"

"Technically, he's only ordered my arrest," Chess said with a shrug. Unless Rav had upgraded the order from throwing him in the dungeon to lopping off his head. "I'd have *plenty* of time to wag my tongue. And I'm good with my tongue, aren't I?" He licked his lips suggestively, eyeing Ever, knowing full well that March would misunderstand. Then, from their earlier conversation, he added, "Some would even say *more* than good, despite my being from Scarlet."

Ever turned toward him, meeting his gaze straight on with an icy stare that seemed to say *don't lie just to rile him up*. But he couldn't help himself. March made it too easy. If the male had only hugged Ever, clung to her hand and whispered in her ear, he would've behaved. Mostly. But Chess wasn't one to lie down and take personal insults from anyone, let alone someone as inferior as—

Ever opened her mouth, but before a word could pass through her lips, March lunged forward. Chess leapt from the bench and met him midair, fangs dropping. Together, they landed, slamming into the brazier, the metal clanging as it flew out from beneath their bodies. Everything that happened next was a blur of fists and fangs.

Chess took a particularly solid punch to the jaw that knocked his head into the edge of the bench. Stars burst behind his eyes. He shook his head to clear his vision, but before he could, March's fangs were lodged in the side of his neck. *Fuck.* He leaned into the bite so March couldn't rip the flesh from him and rolled, dragging March closer to the fallen brazier.

Grabbing a metal leg of the brazier, Chess swung the entire firepit at the back of March's head. It slammed against his skull, jostling him enough for Chess to free his throat. Hot blood flowed down from the wound. With a hiss, he lunged for March, mouth open, ready to tear out his throat.

A forearm suddenly appeared between them. It was too close for Chess to stop himself before chomping down on the flesh. Blood burst in his mouth, rich and … familiar. He unclenched his jaw, removing his fangs from Ever, and fell backward onto his arse, chest heaving.

"Enough," she growled, her gaze darting all around. "Not only are you two completely out of line, you're putting us in danger. Do you *want* us to get caught?"

"Sorry," both Chess and March mumbled, and shot scathing looks at each other.

Chess stood gracefully and wiped Ever's blood from his lips. "I—"

"I don't want to hear it. Play nice—end of story," she snapped at him before rounding on March. "Now, I'll ask again. How do we get into the castle?"

March got to his feet and straightened his uniform as best he could. "There's a loose grate hidden behind some bushes that leads into the cellar baths."

"Perfect. And when is the next shift change?"

March balled his hands into fists and flexed them again. "Two hours from now."

"We'll meet you in the baths in two hours then," she said with a note of finality. "Go before someone notices you're missing."

March gave a stiff bow. "Be careful around him," he warned before stomping out of the gazebo and racing away from the lake.

"That was eventful," Chess said once they were alone. Ever folded her arms over her chest, drawing his attention to her breasts instead of her pursed lips. The fabric of her T-shirt was taut, showing the swells perfectly behind the graphic of a skull that read *dead inside*. He couldn't help wondering what the tempting globes would feel like in his hands, against his tongue, the sound she would make when he sucked her nipple into his mouth. A rush of heat soared through him, straight to his cock. "You know, the only thing better than feeding and fucking is fighting and—"

Ever placed a finger to his lips, her skin soft, her lily scent caressing his nostrils. "Don't finish that sentence. If you screw this up for me when I'm finally close to regaining my castle, I won't forgive you. I already shouldn't after that ridiculous scene."

A grin grew on Chess's face. "I can think of a few ways to make it up to you."

"I'm in no mood to talk about your cock right now, you arse," she snarled and stepped out of the gazebo.

Chess licked the last traces of her blood from his lips and watched her hips sway as she stormed away from him. *Damn.* She had no business looking so fuckable when she was pissed. "Wait for me, Queenie," he called, chuckling to himself.

CHAPTER FOURTEEN

EVER

"**A**re you going to talk to me yet, my prickly white rose?" Chess purred from a tree limb directly above Ever.

She peered up at him in his crouched position and cocked her head. "Why are you hovering in the branch like a cat?"

"I can see all from this angle." He dropped to a hanging position from the branch, swinging with a smirk on his face before dropping and landing on his feet in front of her.

After the "brawl" between Chess and March, Ever had been frustrated, not only because their plan was put at risk from their foolishness, but because she'd been aroused by the way Chess's lithe body had moved, even when ridiculous words had poured out of his mouth.

Ever's fingers, restless, wished to play the viola to release her emotions instead of squeezing the chess piece in her pocket. Once they took out the guards in the palace, she would retrieve her favorite viola from under her bed. Unless Rav had cleared out her room and given her things away, which was most likely the case. Still, she hoped her prized instrument was there.

"So how long have you and March been lovers?" Chess asked, plopping down beside her and ignoring personal space. They had seemed to have passed that point a while ago, though.

She sighed. "Enough of that. March isn't my lover."

Chess perked up like a flower under sunshine, his grin growing wide. "Do tell. He clearly adores you."

Ever didn't know why she was telling him any of this, but perhaps she owed him more truths after his revelations the night before. "March wants more than I can give, so we aren't together in a pleasureful way anymore."

"You were literally kissing each other at the club," Chess pointed out.

And at the park when she'd went to secretly meet him. "There won't be any more of that."

"A pity for him." His grin grew even wider as he took a lock of her wig and twirled it around his finger. "So, who's the better kisser? Me or March?"

"Seriously?" She smacked his hand away from her hair.

"It's me." He chuckled. "If it were March, you would've easily said it."

"Bloody hell, you're a pest." A smile tugged at her lips as she found herself laughing too.

"Trust me, I'm no pest." He leaned close, his warm breath mingling with hers.

Ever fought against the desire to press her lips to his and pulled her thoughts together into a coherent sentence. "We need to go—we don't want to be late for our *very* important date with the guards."

"Ah, yes, a blood bath it will be." Chess stood and drew her up from the ground. Her eyes widened, but she didn't say anything.

They then skirted around trees and slinked out of the forest. The ivory garden came into view, its flowers overgrown—it clearly hadn't been wandered through, even by guards. Their steps remained light and their eyes stayed peeled for guards passing by in the grime-covered windows. The untrimmed bushes near the back of the castle were only a short distance away so they used their enhanced speed to get across. Ever pushed the daisy bushes aside and located the silver grate March had mentioned. When she'd ruled here last, it had been sealed, or at least she believed it had been. Her previous guards' words were no longer trustworthy.

She lifted the loose metal, revealing a hole big enough for them to fit through. Chess didn't hesitate and slipped in first. Keeping as quiet as she could, she climbed in next, then shut the grate behind her before her feet lost purchase against the stone and she fell.

Her heart pounded and she prepared to hit the hard floor, but two waiting hands caught her.

"And you consider me a villain." The prince smirked, his yellow gaze dancing.

"That's exactly what you are," March interrupted as he walked toward them.

Ever leapt from Chess's arms and peered around the cellar baths. It looked much more unkempt than usual—the sparkling white stone floor was covered in muddy boot prints and dirty guard uniforms were piled around the room. The silver walls, ivory clawfoot baths, and several ornate wardrobes that were once filled with towels and scented soaps still appeared the same, though the fur rugs resting in front of each bathtub were covered in brown stains.

"So where are we starting?" Chess asked, rubbing his hands together in anticipation.

"The only door leading out of here," March said with sarcasm, pointing to the wooden door at the opposite side of the room. He then turned to Ever. "Two of your original traitors are just outside this door, Sonny is in the back, and the other nine newer guards are scattered throughout the palace."

"That's good. We should be able to easily pick them off one by one." Ever shrugged. She couldn't risk what occurred last time to happen again. Soon, she would have to rebuild a new guard on her own, one that wouldn't deceive her again.

"I like when you're bloodthirsty," Chess purred in her ear.

March's eyes lingered on Chess a beat too long before motioning them forward. Ever opened the door and Chess bolted through it first. She was going to hiss at him to hold the fuck on, but he already had her old guard Kopa's bloodied head in his hands. When the other bastard guard, Leslie, shot across the room, Ever stepped between her and Chess.

"I bet you weren't expecting us to meet again," Ever seethed at the surprised guard's face, thrusting her hand into the vampire's chest with a sickening squelch and tearing out her beating heart.

The door flew open and two male guards wearing Scarlet uniforms came barreling in. Their gazes widened when they landed on the bodies and blood on the floor, leaving enough time for March to shoot forward, muscles flexing as he swung his sword, cutting cleanly through their necks. Blood sprayed the walls and Chess gave quiet applause.

"Not yet, Princeling," she said, tossing down the heart and rushing up the stairs to the sitting room. Chess and March's feet echoed behind her.

The door at the top of the stairs was locked, but March used his key and shoved it open with a bang. A female guard growled and leapt at March, but her head was already gone before she could touch him, blood oozing like a necklace down her chest.

Ever's pulse raced as they hurried down the narrow hall filled with dead flowers in vases on the walls. They cut through two more empty areas, the silver and white furniture covered in dust. Three guards darted into the sitting room as soon as they entered, hissing and pausing when they spotted Ever and Chess. She didn't think it would be an advantage for her and Chess to be seen together, but apparently it was quite the game-changer.

Ever tore the head from a stocky female, most of the spine coming away with her prize, blood dripping from the bones. A hand gripped her shoulder, but when Ever turned around, the head was gone, the body buckling and falling to the floor beside

March and his bloody sword. The third, Chess had already taken care of. A guard flew down the steps and Chess moved like a tiger as he leapt over the handrail and snatched the heart from the male's chest, the rest of the vampire rolling down the stairs to the floor, the sounds building like a crescendo.

Three more left.

As if in answer, two more barreled down the stairs, a female and male, looked at Chess drenched in blood, then started running back up them like cowards. March and Chess went after them as Ever caught her eye on the last living betrayer, Sonny.

Her old guard walked through the door and paused, a smile on his tan face. "Look who's back," he grunted, "but not for long."

Too bad Ever knew all her guards' moves since she'd watched them train over the years, so with him alone, she could do this. She ducked as he reached for her head and she kicked her leg out, tripping him. He fell flat on his stomach with a low grunt and before he could push up, she was on his back, pulling his head toward her. A loud snap reverberated through the room.

Ever landed on her back from the hard yank, the guard's head in her hands, blood drenching her clothing as her chest heaved.

Victory. Or so she hoped.

She hurled the head, then hurried to see if Chess and March needed help, but they stood at the bottom of the stairs. March wiped his sword on his uniform and Chess was polishing his nails against his bloody hoodie as in a job well done.

"So, that was entertaining," Ever said with a small laugh. "And a bit satisfying. Now you may clap, Chess."

"We need you to play your viola as well." Chess winked at her and March frowned at him.

"Perhaps later if it's still here." She smiled and focused on March. "Do you mind staying here as a guard, at least until Rav's dead?"

"Of course. I wouldn't leave you in a predicament without any guards here."

Ever caught Chess rolling his eyes and she ignored him.

"For now, we'll dispose of the bodies in the cellar," she instructed.

Chess nodded, stacking several and carrying them out of the room. Ever drew March back by his arm. "Tonight, I'm going to tell Maddie we reclaimed the palace and have them come here to help you once Chess and I leave."

"Are you telling him what you're doing?" March whispered.

She shook her head. No, she couldn't put Maddie's life at risk.

"Good," he said and scooped up a dead guard.

They then dumped all the bodies and bloodied pieces down in the cellar before March offered to clean the scarlet from the areas. She wasn't going to let him do it by himself, so she grabbed some cloths to help.

Chess looked at them both while they cleaned as if he'd never done a chore in his entire life. He probably hadn't, at least not since becoming immortal.

"You're not too good, Princeling. Come on." She threw a wet rag at his face and he caught it.

He puckered his lips but sank down beside a pool of blood then started on the task, although he moved much slower with it.

Once everything was spotless, Ever bid March a goodnight and led Chess up the spiral staircase to her room.

"I never had the royal tour of your palace before." He trailed a finger across the rail as if he just needed to always be touching something. "So where are we staying?"

We… "The royal quarters." She held up a finger. "But it's split into two rooms, so you get one and I get one."

She'd been gone for nearly four years and it looked it, without having any servants around to clean and dust. Same as before, pearl chandeliers hung from the ceilings, white chess piece statues rested in the corners, but her famous paintings of musicians hanging across the walls were gone. At the top of the stairs, the portraits of the old king and queen still remained. Her heart sank at the sight of their warm smiles—she still missed them, but it was good to see their faces again.

Ever opened the door, a flowery scent hitting her nose, and locked it behind them. The room was now bare of any of her musical decorations, only white and black walls, like a checkerboard, the floor a sparkling white and the ceiling a glistening obsidian. Her looming wardrobe rested across from the canopy bed covered in silky black sheets, the desk clear of all her notebooks.

She opened one of the two other doors in her room and glanced at Chess, who was studying her bed. "This is an adjoining door to Rav's old rooms. It hasn't been used in a while, unless the Scarlet guards slept there, but you can get some rest in here. A bathroom is attached inside for you to get cleaned up." He was covered in as much blood as she was, yet maybe even a little more.

"You know we can share a bath," he cooed, leaning against a doorframe and gazing at her beneath hooded eyes.

"And what filthy water that would be. We would hardly get cleaned." She chewed on her lip and took a step toward him. "Thank you for your help today. It might have taken me a teeny bit longer to do without you."

Chess chuckled and shrugged. "It was necessary." He turned on his heel and glanced over his shoulder at her with a big smile. "The door to my bathroom will be open, though."

She rolled her eyes and shut the door between them before heading into her own bathing chamber. Not surprisingly, all her things were gone, the counters bare, yet towels hung from the hooks on the wall.

Tossing her backpack in a corner, she peeled her bloody clothing from her body as she let the warm water fill the bath. With a sigh, she sank into the liquid and washed every part of her skin clean with a lavender soap bar until the water was no longer clear. She wondered what Chess would be doing after his bath, most likely lazily sprawled across Rav's old bed. Naked? She shook away the thought of his lithe body, his toned abs, his beautifully sculpted face…

Stop. That.

Ever left her wet hair hanging down her back as she wrapped a fluffy towel around her body. A giddiness filled her that she hadn't felt in a long while. Maybe, just maybe, one of her lacy dresses would be left behind. She opened her wardrobe and blinked. Her clothing wasn't gone—it was all still there. But every piece of fabric was ripped and ruined. A sinking feeling washed over her as she slammed the wardrobe shut and dove for her bed. She lifted the bed skirt and reached beneath it, expecting to touch emptiness. Except she didn't. She sighed as her hand brushed wood, but when she drew her beloved instrument out from the bed, horror filled her.

It was smashed and broken, covered in dust. This was her first instrument, a gift from her Italian uncle, the viola she'd traded with Rav, the one she loved so much. She reached under the bed again and took out the bow … snapped in half. Tears pricked her eyes. Had Chess come in and done this after she fled? Had one of the guards? Or Imogen? She shoved open the door, finding Chess with a towel around his waist, digging through Rav's full wardrobe of unruined clothing.

"Do you know who did this?" Ever stuttered, hating the sound of her voice as she held up her broken instrument. "Did *you* do this?"

Chess whirled around to face her, his brow furrowed while studying the viola in her hand. He then shook his head. "I remember Rav said he was going to take care of some of your things, but I didn't know what that meant. I thought he was just clearing them out." That would have been better. If she'd found the instrument gone, like she'd thought it was going to be, that would have been better than this. But Rav had wanted to hurt her, in case she ever did try and come back. And he had.

Ever sank to her knees, the instrument clacking to the ground, as she held her face in her hands. She didn't want to cry, not in front of him, but she couldn't control it. "My brother knew how much this meant to me. I can get new clothes, I can build a new palace, but this viola will never play again. I can't get this back. It was what reminded me of home, my parents, a gift from my uncle." Sobs escaped her and she couldn't get them to stop.

Ever waited for Chess to make a joke but he didn't. Instead, he crouched in front of her and tucked a lock of wet hair behind her ear. "I'm sorry."

"It wasn't you who broke it," she whispered.

"No, but I should've tried to kill Rav a long time ago." For the first time, something like guilt crossed his expression.

Ever clasped his face in her hands, drawing him close, taking in the smell of pine. "You're going to do it now, and so am I." She then pressed her lips to his and she told herself she was a fool and to stop. But she didn't want to stop, not as he kissed her back, not as his tongue slipped between her lips and danced with hers, and not as he drew her into his lap.

Chess's lips left her mouth, trailing flames of desire down her throat while he kissed and nipped. She could feel the soft graze of his fangs drifting over her flesh. His fingers fell to her towel, dipping in to remove it, his gaze meeting hers, asking. She nodded and he took the layer of fabric from her skin, exposing her to the cool air of the room. His eyes hungrily roamed over her body—he then lifted her so she could wrap her legs around him, absorbing his warmth. She glided her lips across his again, drinking the sweet nectar that was all him.

Chess lay her gently on the bed, his hand lightly venturing over her breasts and down her stomach to between her thighs, where he cupped her mound. Her heart accelerated at his touch and she moaned when he drew a nipple into his mouth, softly sucking. His fangs then grazed her flesh, following to where his hand rested. They stopped at her inner thigh and he sank his teeth in, her body arching in pleasure. He flicked his tongue over the spot he bit before kissing his way to her core. She moaned as he licked his way up her center before pushing a finger inside her, then another. It had been so long since she'd been in this position with someone, but she couldn't remember it ever feeling like this. His movements were practiced yet tender and wickedly delightful as he caressed with his lips, swirled with his tongue.

A blissful feeling swam through her and she grasped his hair when her body quaked beneath his mouth, her fangs sliding out. He grinned that maddeningly wide grin of his while he crawled up her, caging her in and she *liked* that too. Especially the feel of his hard cock against her, but even the layer of his towel was too much.

She reached for the fabric and unraveled it, then grasped his velvety cock, pumping and stroking, her thumb circling his tip. The prince's head rested on her shoulder for a moment before he sank his fangs into her while she continued her movements. His bites were delectable and she wanted more when he drew back, his breath warm and tickling her neck.

Chess groaned, his body spasming as he spilled himself. "I don't … fall in love," he rasped, his breaths ragged.

"Good." She smiled, trailing her finger up his spine. "Because neither do I."

Chess chuckled, his lips softly kissing hers. He lifted her chin, peering into her eyes. "Just give me a minute and I'll make it so any past lover will be ruined for you."

Ever was tempted, so very tempted. She wanted to feel him slide his hard length into her heat, feel what it would be like to be fucked into oblivion. But she remembered what she'd always told herself because betrayal was always an option. "I don't go past this point. Ever," she breathed.

"Excuse me?" Chess's eyebrows flew up his forehead.

"I don't do more than this," she said, cocking her head. "With anyone. I never have."

He sucked in a sharp breath. "It isn't just a rumor? You're a virgin?"

"Yes. Is that an issue, Princeling?" She smiled at his dumbfounded expression.

"For *centuries?*"

"I've had plenty of pleasure in other ways, and I know how to take care of myself too."

"It's just, you're so … beautiful." His throat bobbed. A

second later his expression turned back into a sly one. "Well then, I can show you other ways of pleasure the next time, if you wish. I just never imagined you and I…"

She laughed and tucked a lock of hair behind his ear. "We're quite a mess, aren't we?"

A knock came at the door leading to her room and she jerked up. Ever shoved Chess away and leapt from the bed, grabbing her towel and shutting the door between their rooms. She wiped Chess's pleasure from her hand against the fabric as she wrapped it around herself and hurried to the door.

March stood there, wearing a fresh Scarlet uniform, his eyes widening as he studied her. He took a whiff and she knew he could smell Chess all over her. "I heard noises and just wanted to see if everything was okay."

"It is. Thank you," she said, not meeting his gaze.

"I'll see you soon," he whispered, his shoulders sagging as he turned away.

Ever nodded and shut the door. Guilt washed over her and she didn't understand it. She wasn't with March, and he knew she only wanted to be his friend. But it wasn't only that. Guilt was there because of Maddie. What would she think of what Ever had just done? With someone who wanted her friend dead, who had tried to kill Ever…

A part of her wanted to open the door back to Chess's room and see what would happen next. But she might do something even more foolish. Yet she couldn't stop imagining what it would feel like for him to press inside her and thrust until she could barely remember her own name.

She didn't open the door between their rooms though. There were bigger things in the works than quenching her physical curiosities. Instead, she would wait for him to sleep and once he was, she would leave.

CHAPTER FIFTEEN

CHESS

Chess laid beneath the down-filled duvet, trying to fall asleep in a strange bed, for hours. Not that he hadn't slept in dubious places before, but this was the heart of Ivory. The soft mattress and lingering scent of lilies wouldn't allow him to forget that fact, so he'd noticed when Ever's soft footfalls paced her room. Felt her gaze when she'd cracked the door to peek in on him.

Part of Chess wondered if she was simply having trouble sleeping in case anyone snuck in to assassinate her, but his intuition told him there was more to it. The air was full of static, crackling with distrust. Things hadn't been that way between them since they'd first been forced together in the mortal world safe house. But maybe he was imagining things…

Should I check on her?

If all she needed was a little comfort, a *distraction*, he was more than willing to comply a second time. By spreading those creamy thighs, tasting her, bringing her over the edge over and over. She'd been so responsive when he'd licked her slit and had tasted so fucking good. Both her sex and her blood. Sweet. Like how he remembered candy tasting when he was a mortal. It would be no hardship to have her hands on him once more. Ever may have been a virgin, but that didn't mean she didn't know what she was doing. If she ever granted him the honor of taking her fully, he wasn't sure they would ever leave a bed again.

Unless it was to fuck in the bath or on a table or against a wall … *oh* the things they would do together. They could explore each other all night until March came searching for her *again*—because he undoubtedly would. Clingy bastard. There were many other things to do now that Ever had reclaimed the castle and they couldn't afford to lose momentum by reveling in their victory. Rav could show up at any moment for all they knew. They'd killed his guards with a glorious swiftness, but the news was bound to get back to him soon. March could busy himself with that instead of worrying about Ever.

But perhaps March was right to worry about her. The gut feeling that she was up to something only increased along with the padding of her feet.

Chess purposely evened out his breathing and snuggled into the pillow to appear as if he were asleep. It only took ten minutes of pretending for him to get his answer. The soft *click* of her door shutting in the adjoining room told him everything he needed to know—Ever was sneaking out.

But to where? Why?

Chess eased from the bed, threw his clothes and boots on, and slipped into the hallway. Ever was already out of sight. He cursed silently and listened closely. Her rapid footsteps came from the right, descending stairs, if he was hearing correctly. Light on his feet, Chess followed.

He kept his distance, not allowing himself to get closer than to see a blur of deep brown hair in the dark, as she traversed the castle. She'd put on a black skirt and a light blue T-shirt, though he much preferred the towel. When she snuck out a side door, he did the same.

Outside, the night swallowed them both. There was no

moonlight tonight, but he could still see everything clearly. Bats flew overhead, swooping through the air, and the rustle of feathers floated down from the trees. Most importantly, he followed Ever's silhouette with ease. *Where the fuck are you going?* She wouldn't abandon him in her castle, would she? He could imagine March's reaction to *that* in the morning—so her destination couldn't be far.

They passed through the palace gardens and patches of forest. He couldn't stop to examine the surroundings as he needed to make sure he didn't lose sight of the White Queen, but if he didn't know any better, he'd say they were heading toward Scarlet. He narrowed his eyes at the figure weaving between trees. His stomach sank. No way would Ever have made a deal with her brother, even if it was to rid herself of Chess's presence. Only hours ago, she'd let him between her legs for fuck's sake. She had her castle back so what was left for Rav to barter anyway?

Then what—

Not more than a five minutes' run from the castle, Ever glanced over both shoulders before raising her hand to knock on an old, mossy tree. She rapped out a rhythm and stepped back. A few moments later, a door swung inward, expertly disguised to look like bark. Chess's eyes widened and his jaw clenched at *who* stood before Ever.

The mad, violet-haired twat who murdered his mother. *Maddie.*

Chess's vision went red. *Kill her* echoed through his head. *Kill her like she killed your mother.*

Fuck yes. She needed to die. *Now.* Before he could think better of charging rashly into the situation, Chess barreled from the trees at full speed. He knocked both Ever and Maddie down a staircase inside the hidden safe house before either of them could see him coming. They tumbled down in a heap, Ever's wig sailing past him in the process, and struck the edges of stairs. Chess's arm gave a sharp *crack*, but he ignored the blast of pain as he scrambled to get his hands around Maddie's neck. He still wasn't able to manage it before they landed in a pile at the bottom of the staircase. Ever was trapped face down beneath Maddie's body, Chess on top of them both.

The purple-clad vampire let out a shriek—part surprise, part fear—and snapped her fangs at his face. She clawed at his arms, raising her shoulders to protect her neck from his hands. The sound of a door slamming open and hitting a wall barely registered as he snatched her wrists. Chess hissed, spittle flying. He would rip her head off. Lick the blood from his lips. Send her heart back to Rav so he knew vengeance was had—just before Chess did the same to the bastard.

A muscled forearm pressed into Chess's neck from behind and ripped him off the female. He snarled and snapped while clawing at the arm hoisting him up until it bled freely.

"Don't kill him!" Ever yelled. Pins were slipping out of her white hair, the braids falling from where she had wound them against her head.

"Fucking prig!" Ferris shouted.

What the fuck is the Knave doing here? Not that it mattered. He drove his head back into the asshat's nose with a satisfying *crunch*.

"Fuck! Noah, grab his legs," Ferris growled.

Noah—Alice's damned brother—hurried forward, leaping over Maddie and Ever. Chess brought his legs back and kicked him square in the chest the moment he was close enough. Noah sailed into a glittering, white marble room with an ornate dining table. The force of the kick sent Ferris backward where he stumbled on the stairs, loosening his grip just enough for Chess to twist free.

His gaze went back to his prey. Maddie helped Ever off the ground, trusting the males to keep Chess away from her. *Foolish murderess.* Nothing would stop him from avenging his mother, no matter what she'd done to him as a child. *Nothing.* "You will *die* for what you've done!"

"No!" Ever shouted, and shoved Maddie behind her. Chess met her steely gaze, feeling irrationally betrayed that she would stop him. "You will not harm her."

"I will make it quick," Chess spat. It was all he could compromise on. Maddie deserved hours—no, days—of torture before she met her end, but for Ever, he would make it fast. There was no other option given the circumstances.

A figure moved in the open doorway behind the two females and Mouse stepped out, grabbing her sister's arm. The next moment Maddie was gone—inside the room, the door slammed shut. That was fine—there were no windows underground. He would simply need to finish off the vampires out here first, then rip off the fucking door and end the fucking she-devil. No problem. His eyes flickered to Ever. Perhaps a *slight* problem. But the males were completely dispensable.

He whirled around to face the Knave. Noah had joined him again and nervously bounced on the balls of his feet as if he was just *waiting* for the signal to attack. "You're an *infant*," Chess warned the new vampire. "Come at me and I will tear you apart."

"Maybe," Noah conceded. "But I like our odds."

Chess snarled. Noah was likely remembering the time he and Maddie managed to tie him to a tree on the edge of Ivory. But he failed to realize that Chess wasn't allowed to kill them at the time—or at least Maddie. His mother needed her to lead the way to Ever, and killing Maddie's boy-toy seemed detrimental to earning her cooperation. Now? He would see them both dead.

"There should be some reinforced handcuffs in the trunk at the foot of my bed," Ever said, her voice low. "Noah, if you wouldn't mind…"

He nodded and stepped out of the room, leaving only the Knave in front of him. "Your Highness," Chess said without turning around. "You never mentioned being so kinky. I would've happily obliged when we were together earlier … naked. My tongue—"

"Shut up," she growled in warning. The Knave's brows shot up as he looked from Chess to the queen. Ever kicked at the back of his knees and Chess buckled, catching himself. Ever huffed. "Incapacitate him and put him in one of the rooms. I don't want to see his face right now."

"With pleasure," Ferris said, his lips curling into a vengeful grin.

He leapt forward, but Chess sidestepped him. The Knave leapt again with the same result. Chess let out a small laugh as they seemed to dance with one another. Circling, ducking, sliding his feet against the marble floor to avoid the attacks. It was too easy. And he quickly grew bored of it. Maddie was right on the other side of that door. His revenge was so close and he wouldn't be denied.

"Enough," Chess snapped. "There is no quarrel with you, despite how you betrayed my mother. I just want the Hatter."

"She did all of Wonderland a favor by ripping out her heart," Ferris said spitefully.

Well, *now* there was a quarrel… His upper lip curled and he tensed for his first counter attack. The jangle of metal was his only warning before something heavy slammed into the back of his head. Chess's vision blurred and he stumbled.

Ferris took the opportunity to attack. He grabbed the sides of Chess's head and snapped his neck.

Chess jerked awake. Pain sliced up the back of his neck and his temples throbbed with a headache. He tried to raise a hand to his forehead but found them tightly bound behind his back. Cold metal dug into skin. And not only his wrists, but his ankles too. One side of each handcuff was attached to him, the others locked around the legs and back rungs of a steel chair. *Fucking bastards.*

He blinked the drowsiness away and scanned the room. A bed with messy, wrinkled sheets took up a majority of the space with two narrow tables on either side and a pile of clothes on the floor. The black wood of the furniture was carved with dainty lilies, and an empty vase sat on a long, thin table against one wall. Everything else was as white as the forest outside. Chess gave a sniff. It smelled stale, but a light scent of lilies lingered. How long ago had this space been used?

The door creaked open and Ever stepped inside, kicking the door shut. Strands of her hair stuck up at all angles. The pins were gone from around her face and her messy braids now hung over each shoulder. "You're awake," she drawled.

"This place seems a step up from the one in the mortal world," he said, purposefully glancing around. "You should've stayed here instead."

"You followed me," she accused matter-of-factly, ignoring his comments. But Chess didn't miss the hint of pain in her voice. "But this was where I stayed the night you tried to murder me in my own gardens. I gathered what I could and formulated my plan to stay in the human world right in this very room." She stalked around him, trailing her hand across the footboard as she passed the bed. "And now I get to come up with a new plan."

"You knew, didn't you? You knew she killed my mother all along and played me like a fool." His chest heaved.

"I knew, all right." Her nostrils flared. "What do you want me to say? She's my best friend. Of course, I would protect her."

"If you're trying to figure out how to let me kill your friend without shouldering the blame, I assure you, it will be *all* my fault. So, if you could just undo these cuffs…"

Ever whirled on him, eyes blazing. Her hand soared toward his face, cracking against his cheek. "How dare you do this? After everything? I don't know how, but something … something along the way changed between us."

"Between *us*, they have," he admitted. Though he wasn't sure what that meant exactly. He was fond of her, lusted for her, and for whatever forsaken reason, wanted to keep her safe. If it was anyone but himself, he would say *feelings* had developed. The type he'd never felt before and had no desire to experience now. Nevertheless, it was true. Murdering Maddie had nothing to do with how he felt about the White Queen though. "This has nothing to do with you. She killed *my* mother."

Ever leaned closer until her face was a breath from his. "Maddie took out the greatest threat to Wonderland and we should be *thanking* her for it."

Chess inhaled sharply. His mother was a vicious bitch with more problems than he could count but… "She. Was. My. Mother."

"That's all you have to say for yourself? You defend your actions even now that the moment of passion has passed?" She searched his face, perhaps hoping to find some sliver of remorse.

"If…" He swallowed hard. The fucking organ beating in his chest would be the ruin of him. "If my actions have hurt you, I *am* sorry for that. But I can't say I won't try again."

Ever stiffened and stepped back. "I'm sorry to hear that. Wait here while I talk to the others."

Chess tugged at his chains with a rueful smirk. As if he had a choice…

CHAPTER SIXTEEN

EVER

"**W**hat in all of Wonderland is going on here?" Maddie waved her hand in the air as she took a step toward Ever after the queen came out of Chess's room. "When you were here last, you said the time had come to reclaim Ivory and that Rav's heart would be intimately acquainted with a stake. I had assumed Chess would come next—I never thought you would *protect* the prince if you encountered him. He tried to *murder* you."

Ever hadn't expected any of this either—in her past, she'd thought of every single way she could kill Chess, viciously and slowly. She peered at the table where Noah pretended to observe his hands, Ferris watched her like a hawk, and Mouse played with her caterpillar.

"A lot has happened..." She pressed a palm to her forehead, not wanting to deal with this conversation. The way Maddie needed her hats when she was nervous was the way Ever yearned for her viola, but there wasn't one around and there wasn't time to think about music or symphonies to distract.

"I would say so." Maddie arched a brow. "When you left, you hated Chess, and now? Now…" She covered her mouth with her hand as though coming to some sort of realization. "You *like* him? He's becoming your *friend?*"

Ever thought about earlier, how he'd run his tongue slowly, expertly, up her center, how he'd kissed her mouth with delicious hunger, how she'd wanted to do more than stroke his alluring cock. "It's a long story." She sighed, wanting to keep those moments that she should've regretted, but didn't, locked away for now. Forever.

"I'm pretty sure we have time for it," Ferris piped up, studying her as though he could read her thoughts, the way she had seen his history in his blood.

"Then afterward, I'm pretty sure he'll need to die," Noah added, running a hand through his thick blond hair, no longer able to hold his tongue. "When we were on our way to get the cure for my sister, we ran into Chess in Ivory. He tied Maddie and me together and was going to haul us back to Scarlet."

Ever blinked, her gaze locked on Noah's bright blue eyes. "To have you *killed?*"

"Well, no," Maddie sang. "Only because I wasn't 'allowed' in Ivory." She air-quoted, then adjusted her dark hat on the side of her head. "But we escaped and tied him to a tree after I knocked him out."

Ever would've done the same thing. She had also only learned that Maddie and Mouse hadn't been allowed in Ivory when she'd first arrived at the safe house after being gone for so long. Another reason why she wanted to hurt her brother, for keeping them away from their home and holding Mouse in a cage like an animal.

"Tell her," Mouse said, glancing up at Maddie, her voice barely audible. A mortal would not have been able to hear her soft words.

Maddie wrinkled her nose, staring at her sister in confusion. "Tell her what?"

Mouse stayed silent, letting Des crawl from one hand to the

other before she spoke again. "Tell her how you were able to get me out from the Ruby Heart Palace."

"Oh, I already told her how I created this miraculous hat and—"

"No," Mouse drawled. "About the prince stopping by your cottage before you and Noah came to the palace."

"Oh yes, I did forget to tell you that part. The weeks have been a blur." Maddie shrugged. "So, Chess came to my cottage, somehow piecing together a part of my plan with Noah to get Mouse back. Instead of killing me or reporting it to his mother, he allowed me to hatch the plan..." The Hatter frowned as though she were uncomfortable admitting this.

"And?" Ever prodded when her friend stopped talking.

Maddie rolled her eyes. "He agreed to keep quiet in exchange for your hideout's location. I, of course, led him on a wild goose chase to Red." She cocked her head. "I suppose I can see why he's a teensy bit angry."

Chess was more than angry—he'd been livid when he'd stormed toward them, causing them to take a vexing tumble down the stairs. He could have been less brash and dramatic about it. Ferris had moved fast, and if she hadn't spoken up in time, Chess would've been like the damn Headless Horseman, except dead. Even though *he'd* attacked them, the thought sent a sinking feeling to the pit of her stomach.

As much as she loathed Imogen, Maddie had killed his mother. Although the bitch deserved it, she could see why Chess would be upset. By allowing Maddie to go through with her plan, he was part of the reason his mother was dead, and guilt had to be filling him.

Ever glanced to Ferris, who had been around him for two years, *lived* with him. "How was the prince at the palace?"

He groaned, glancing up at the ceiling. "A spoiled prince who fucked and fed constantly."

That wasn't surprising, but then her heart lodged in her throat at a thought. "Was he like Rav and Imogen? Dabbled in their disgusting hobby with mortals?" She'd discussed the turning of humans with Chess, yet this was a dire situation and there could be no more lies.

"No." Ferris shook his head. "He did the tasks Imogen assigned him, but the unwilling turning of mortals was a sick game between her and Rav only, as was your brother's experiments with them."

Rav had always enjoyed being some sort of deranged scientist. She didn't know what he had done with the unfortunate souls and preferred not to imagine the cruel things he concocted. Before Ever could ask another question, Mouse interrupted, "Chess would visit me at my cell."

Maddie whirled on her sister, her eyes wide. "For *what*?"

"To ask questions about Ever of course." Mouse set Des on the table, the caterpillar's head perking up as though it were listening too. "But, he would bring leaves for me to feed Des after he saw her with me one day."

Chess had brought Mouse leaves for her caterpillar to eat? Something was off about that. The only reason he would do that would be to get something in return. Information on Ever.

But that had been before. Before all this...

"A few leaves for your caterpillar doesn't erase everything he's done," Maddie said.

"He grew up differently than us." Mouse furrowed her brow. "People can change."

"I hate to say it," Ever started. "But Chess actually helped reclaim my castle, although his presence has been mostly accompanied by lies. He did come clean recently though. Of course, after being caught." She then went into more detail, discussing his lies, how he'd helped kill the vampires in the Ivory Palace, and how they both wanted Rav dead.

"You have the palace now?" Noah asked.

"Yes." Ever nodded. "My spy—March, who Maddie and Mouse are acquainted with—is there now. I had only come here to tell you the news, but since Chess now knows everything, I would like you all to come to the palace now. I trust you to help protect it, and I have to be more careful in the guards I pick this time. But if you choose not to, I understand."

"And Chess?" Maddie plopped down onto Noah's lap, one of his arms snaking protectively around her waist. "What are we going to do with him? I don't care what he wants to do to me, but, again, he tried to murder you."

He had. But from all their recent days together, he hadn't attempted to harm her. He'd been nothing but aggravating, yet he'd also been … caring? "I know he did. However, I have something to ask of you, Maddie. If you agree to come with me, I want to allow him an opportunity to join us. Will you allow it?"

By how red Noah's face was, she could tell he wanted to shout *fuck no*, but he waited for Maddie to give her answer.

"Only if I can personally escort him to your palace with his hands cuffed," she sang with a grin.

"Deal." Ever laughed. "Now, I need to have a word with the princeling." She gave a final look to Noah. "I also killed Osanna for you."

"One less vampire we have to kill." Maddie grinned.

Ever then left the group to themselves, Maddie patting Noah's cheek and telling him to calm down about the prince while Ferris watched Mouse scoop Des into her palm.

Pushing open the door, Ever found Chess still seated in the chair with his ankles cuffed to the legs and his wrists bound behind his back. Even then, he lazily rested his head against the back of the chair. He lifted his head, a smirk on his face as his yellow gaze met hers, as though he were tempting her to come closer.

Ever shut the door behind her and entered the room, taking in the black and white walls, the obsidian wardrobe, the dark bed, the steel chair that made the prince look like a seductive devil luring her in. And bloody hell, she wanted to be lured in.

Focusing, she shook the blasted thought away. "I assume you were listening," she snapped. It may have been more at herself than him because she should've been wanting to rip his head off for trying to murder her best friend, and in turn, knocking them down a flight of stairs like a fool.

"To every word," he purred. "Osanna was always a cunt, so you taking her out doesn't bother me in the least. Now, what would you like to ask me first?"

"Why did you bring Mouse leaves for her caterpillar?"

Chess clucked his tongue and straightened. A line rested between the prince's brows, questioning. "Out of everything, that's what you're curious about? Ah, Queenie, I think you can do better than that."

"Just answer the question," she huffed.

"Poor little Mouse, all alone in her cell," he cooed. His gaze left hers and he studied the ceiling, as though, if he looked at her longer, she would discover the emotion he wanted to keep hidden. "I wanted her to think I was charming so she would tell me more about you. *Confess* where you were hiding."

"That's not the whole story though, is it?" Ever inched closer to him, then leaned forward, ignoring his lovely scent. He didn't speak as she pressed her hands to his warm cheeks, drawing his face to hers. She would keep his gaze focused on hers so he couldn't hide behind his lies.

The prince's yellow irises blazed, his breath hitching. "I had planned to toy with her like I did with Maddie. The Hatter was fun to get a rise out of, but Mouse… She was different. Always humming. Even when… Even when…" He paused, his nostrils flaring. "Even when Rav and my mother would bring her out for her *interrogations*."

The blood in Ever's veins boiled and she was about to slap him, but then she remembered how he'd allowed Maddie to save her. A realization struck her—it wasn't only the leaves.

"You gave her the caterpillar, didn't you?" she whispered, her thumb stroking his cheek.

"And why the fuck would I do that?" he murmured.

"So you could bring her the leaves."

Chess stayed silent for a long moment before relenting. "Fine, I did. But don't believe for a second I was being a hero or that it was all out of the kindness of my heart."

"Yet the caterpillar was one of the things that helped her

survive." And Ferris, but that wasn't a conversation to have now.

"The caterpillar helped me over the years, too, even though I was a bastard." Chess blew out a breath. "I told the furry little worm to crawl into a lonely vampire's cell and keep her company. Mouse doesn't know I gave the caterpillar to her."

Ever's brows shot up over the good deed, no matter if there was a bit of selfishness behind it. She'd bet anything that Mouse and the others had been listening and now knew what he'd done too.

"What would have happened if you'd found me in Red?" she said, changing the subject before she could think too much on the good deed he'd done. "Be honest."

"Don't slap me." His lips tilted at the edges. "I know I riled Maddie up on many occasions by testing her patience about you. But I never would've tortured you if I'd found you." His smile dropped, his throat bobbing. "If I'd discovered you, I would've taken your heart to my mother, just as I would've at your masquerade ball."

It wasn't a surprise, and for some reason, her stomach didn't drop at the words. That was the past, and what was more important was the present, the future. "Would you still now?" Her palms left his cheeks, his eyes questioning. "If Imogen were still alive, would you rip out my heart right now and give it to her."

"No," he whispered and shut his eyes for a brief moment. "I would hide you from her for an eternity if I had to."

Her heart pounded harder. She believed him, completely, wholly. This wasn't one of his lies. Everything was out in the open now, yet there was one thing he would have to agree to if they were to continue on their path. "We need to work together. *All* of us. But you must tell me now, Princeling, will you leave Maddie alone? Deep down, you know, that for Wonderland, it was for the best. As much as you loath what Maddie did, as much as it hurts inside here"—Ever placed her palm against his wildly beating heart—"it wasn't planned on her part, but somehow fate intervened and it happened. She did what needed to be done, for our world, just as it pains me to do the same thing to my brother. I know you loved your mother, yet you're free now because of it. You didn't deserve for her to make you jump through fire in order to remain in her good graces. You deserved to be treated like her son." She paused, taking a deep breath. "Let the hate and guilt go."

Chess bit his lip and remained quiet.

He wouldn't do it—he couldn't see what Ever wanted him to see, what she hoped he would believe. She took her hand from his chest and straightened. Letting out a sigh, she padded to the door before he called, "Wait."

Ever turned around as a loud squeaking echoed, finding Chess trying to move the chair toward her.

"I understand what you're saying, but you have them." He nodded toward the door where her friends all waited. "And I have no one. I only ever had my mother in Wonderland."

She moved back toward him until she was just as close as she'd been before. Peering at him, she understood that he was never a heartless prince—he'd just been lonely and hurting. And now, the heart could mend. "You have me, Chess. We're on each other's side."

The prince studied her for a long moment, as though battling something within himself before finally speaking, "For you, I promise I won't hurt Maddie." Then he couldn't help himself and smirked. "Unless she tries to hurt me first."

"That's good enough, but know this—if you do, I'll have to kill you." Ever smiled. "I suppose we can uncuff you now but please play nice."

As she took the key from her pocket, he leaned forward and whispered in her ear, his breath warm on her neck, making her shiver. "Or we could leave them on a little longer. Let them hear how I made you feel at the Ivory Palace."

Heat flooded her cheeks as she unlocked his handcuffs at his wrists and ankles—wondering if her friends had heard his seductive words. "Let's not be hasty now." She then whirled around with Chess chuckling behind her.

CHAPTER SEVENTEEN

CHESS

Ever's gaze locked onto Chess when he sauntered out of the bedroom. Mouse watched on with her big eyes, while the caterpillar Chess had sent her way inched along her forearm. Maddie glowered from beneath her black hat, and fresh-faced Noah's scowl looked wrong on him. Then there was Ferris who appeared just as broody and suspicious as he had at the palace. How hadn't he noticed the Knave was a spy? The expressions of hate directed at his mother—the ones she mistook as lust, and how he skulked around places he had no business skulking. Not that it mattered now...

Chess gave them one of his cocky grins and held his hands up in mock surrender. "Consider me subdued."

Maddie tilted her head and studied him from where she was perched on Noah's lap. "Where are his cuffs?"

"About that..." Chess brushed past Ever and lazily sank into one of the empty chairs. Placing his elbow on the table, he wove his fingers together and cleared his throat. Ferris swiveled in the chair beside him and tensed. "I heard about your condition for me to return with Ever, Hatter, and there will be no more cuffs. At least, not for me. Well"—he gave Ever a seductive grin—"not under these circumstances."

Maddie rolled her eyes. "Ever already agreed. If you want to come—"

"The fuck if I care what was *agreed*," he growled, all traces of humor dissipating. "You killed my mother. You will not further insult me by parading me through Ivory like a prisoner when I've done nothing wrong." His gaze drifted to Ever. "At least, not lately."

Noah's grip tightened around Maddie's waist and Ferris's stare dug into him, but it was Mouse who spoke next. "You're selfish," she said softly. "But not incorrect, in this instance."

"Mouse," Maddie whispered, her lips set in a tight line.

"It's true. And we can all be selfish at times." She shrugged. Des perked her head up from the table, nodding in agreement. It was a name he wouldn't have chosen for the caterpillar, yet it somehow suited her.

"All right," Ever said in an even voice. "Now that this is settled, everyone will behave themselves. We all want the same thing—my brother dead. Gather what you will and we'll head to my palace. Home."

Slowly, Maddie slid from Noah's lap, taking his hand and leading him into one of the bedrooms. Ferris's chair scraped against the floor when he followed suit. Mouse, however, remained. "They're prickly for a reason, but you have a reason too." Her gaze softened for a moment before glaring, her voice coming out quiet. "Thank you for your kindness with Des at the palace. However, if you attack my sister, I will rip your throat out." She scooped Des off the table and patted his shoulder as though she hadn't threatened him. Maddie's sister was a strange little thing, but his heart lurched when he thought about what his mother and Rav had done to her over and *over*.

Ever grinned at Mouse, seeming proud of her. Once the female shuffled away from the table, Ever grabbed Chess by the ear. "You can't hurt my friends."

He offered a small smile. "No, but you never said I had to be *nice*."

"Taunting them into attacking you so you can defend yourself isn't allowed either."

"So many rules." He *tsked* and brushed her hand away. "You can only ask so much of me, Queenie. I won't attack them nor will I change who I am to appease them. Their anger management is their own problem."

Ever narrowed her eyes, studying his face. He wasn't sure what she found there, but he was determined not to budge a step further. Maddie murdered his mother *and* the queen of Scarlet. He wouldn't mind if the Hatter fell off a cliff and died, but he wasn't going to hurt her. The problem was that Rav would still want to end her life. Or, at least he would if he learned the truth before Ever killed him. There was still a chance someone else loyal to Imogen would solve the problem on Chess's behalf.

"We're ready," Maddie chirped.

Ever turned from Chess and nodded. "Come on, then."

Maddie adjusted her hat and fell behind Mouse, Ferris, and Noah as they climbed the stairs. Chess stood and followed behind the White Queen, keeping her between him and the others. There was no sense in tempting anyone's control by accidentally getting too close. Besides, he liked being behind her. Not only for the view of her arse in that black skirt, but he felt better knowing nothing would attack her from a blind spot. She'd protected him from her friends, had trusted him enough to let him be in the same room as his mother's killer. That thought warmed something inside him.

The Hatter halted in front of Ever and spun to look at him. "We have a truce then?" she asked hesitantly.

"For as long as Ever lives." Chess shot her a strained smile, forcing himself not to snarl instead. If anything happened to Ever, all promises were null and void.

"Best keep me alive then," Ever said, her tone trying and failing to sound lighthearted. She nudged Maddie toward the stairs. "March will worry if I take too long."

Maddie bit her lip, casting a final wary look at Chess. He raised one brow in silent challenge before she said something he wasn't expecting. "I still loathe you, but thank you for giving my sister Des." She turned on her booted heel and rushed up the stairs.

Did … she just *thank* him? That was unexpected. Chess wasn't sure how to feel about that.

Pinning her hair back into place and forgoing the tangled wig, Ever followed wordlessly behind the Hatter, and Chess trudged after the group. Just what he needed … more people who loathed him. Was he *so* unlikable? He chuckled silently. *Certainly.* But perhaps he could change that one day and be slightly less antagonistic. On occasion. At least a few times a year, anyway.

As soon as he stepped out of the safe house, Ferris slammed the door shut and locked it back up with a key attached to a large ring. His nostrils flared at Chess's proximity which only made him want to step closer to the Knave. The male hadn't exactly been treated well by Imogen or Rav, but Chess had never touched him.

"I'm guilty by association, eh?" he said quietly to Ferris while the others started back toward the palace.

"Don't act innocent. Everyone knows who you are and that didn't change just because you helped Mouse," he snapped and brushed past Ever to walk at Mouse's side. The pink-haired vampire cast the prince an unreadable look over her shoulder.

"Are you joining us?" Ever asked when Chess didn't move. "You're welcome to go your own way if you choose."

He didn't want to go his own way—he wanted to stay with Ever. But the others…? Things were about to change. He could feel it in the air. Ever would withdraw as his presence drove a wedge between her and her friends, leaving him alone. Again.

"What do you prefer I do?" he asked softly.

"I want you to come." The corners of her mouth lifted. "And go back to being your cocky self."

He released a relieved breath, turning it into a chuckle to hide that he'd been worried about her answer. "I would have come regardless. Do you think it'll be that easy to get rid of me?" Leaning down to whisper in her ear, he added, "You taste too good for me to walk away now."

Ever drew in a sharp breath and he quickly nipped at her ear before straightening. Her widening eyes made his grin grow into a knowing smile. She remembered the pleasure he gave her just as well as he did and, if he wasn't mistaken, wanted another round. *Soon.* First, they had to get back to the castle and their conveniently adjoined rooms.

Chess nodded toward the group and started sauntering away. He knew the Knave and Maddie, had spent time with Mouse, but Noah was a stranger. While he seemed to listen to Maddie, Chess would need to watch him closely to make sure his newly-turned control was stable. The last time he'd seen Maddie and Noah together, they were walking through the forest in Ivory. He'd wondered where they were going when he'd found them, but their answer hadn't mattered much. Whatever their cause had been, his mother would've expected Chess to deliver the pair for questioning. Since he was Alice's brother, he probably knew where she was—possibly cured already from what he'd overheard while cuffed, not that he gave two shits anymore.

"Did you hear that?" Ever asked under her breath as she stilled, grabbing his arm.

Chess perked his ears up, listening hard. Everyone stopped moving. For a moment, all Chess could hear was his own breath. Then—

Snap.

They weren't alone in the forest, but there was nothing to be afraid of in Wonderland for six vampires. Except the Jabberwocky, of course, but it never came this far into Ivory. Chess scowled. He hadn't thought it would be in Ivory at all until they'd arrived on the outskirts, but the Jabberwocky wouldn't lurk about, snapping twigs. Perhaps it was one of Rav's spies. A low, rumbling growl filled the air.

Or a fucking werewolf.

"Not again," Noah said, tensing.

"Our bullets are low after our last werewolf situation and we don't want to attract more unless we have to," Maddie said.

He hadn't brought a gun from the palace and by the looks of it, Ever hadn't either. Perfect. Not that they would've trusted him with a weapon anyway. "Better get running then," he said, scanning the forest for any sign of the beast. Fighting a werewolf with his bare hands wasn't at the top of his bucket list.

A large black blur shot out from the shadows of the trees and tore straight for them. It was smaller than most, nearly as big as Chess. An adolescent that likely strayed too far from pack territory without realizing. *Fuck*. They were almost worse than the adults. *No, they* were *worse*. Hunting vampires down for sport, tearing them apart without bothering to eat them. Regardless, the adults would come looking for it, if they weren't already. Which meant they would get to deal with an arsehole child and an overprotective parent.

The werewolf released a deep roar and eyed its prey.

Eyed *them*.

Then its footsteps pounded against the ground, shaking the trees, its body snapping branches as it barreled past them.

The Knave lifted Mouse over his shoulder and dodged out of the werewolf's path. Noah and Maddie had already disappeared into the trees while Chess was focused on the charging beast. He bolted after them, following a flash of white that had to be Ever.

The thunderous rumble of galloping paws pounded behind him as he pushed himself faster, closing the distance between him and the queen. Only … it wasn't Ever. The white he'd seen was a shirt hanging out of Noah's backpack. Chess took a hard left behind a tree as the werewolf raced by. *Where the fuck is she?*

Doubling back, he frantically searched the woods for any clue to where Ever might be. Had she followed Ferris and Mouse instead? "Ever!" he shouted. Fuck the risk—he was faster than the werewolves. "Ever!"

"Shut up, Princeling," she snapped.

Whirling around, he nearly knocked her over. His heart caught in his chest and he pulled her to him. "I couldn't find you."

"I was running toward the castle, you big idiot." She pried herself out of his grip and took his hand. "Hurry."

Another growl came then, this one deeper, *angrier*. And from behind them. Ever took off toward the castle a second time, pulling Chess alongside her. A parent had come for their offspring and smelling vampires near their child would only make things more dangerous. They moved as fast as they could, weaving between trees, with the werewolf on their heels.

From nowhere, the young werewolf leapt in front of them, releasing a vicious roar that showcased its rows of sharp teeth. Ever stopped so fast that she fell forward. Chess's hand slipped from hers and she landed on her stomach. The younger werewolf chose that moment to surge forward. Chess bolted sideways in hopes the beast would follow.

And it did.

But the second werewolf had caught up—a female, judging by the narrower frame. Chess looked over Ever's shoulder just in time to see the adult beast yank her white hair and roll away. "Hey!" he shouted, turning on his heel. "Over here!"

The older werewolf's lips curled at the same time the younger pounced. Chess dug his feet into the ground and brought a fist back. "Get the fuck out of the way," the prince growled. He swung his fist upward, connecting with the underside of the younger werewolf's jaw. The teeth clacked together as the beast's head swung backward with a loud, pained yelp.

Ever thrashed, fangs exposed, clawing at the adult's snout when it snapped its head toward Chess. The werewolf released a deep growl, rattling the branches. At the sound of her offspring's agony, a malicious glint shone in her eyes. Dragging Ever by her hair as though she were a ragdoll, she sprinted toward Chess.

"Fuck," he hissed under his breath. How was he going to fight off two of them *and* save Ever? He jumped toward the nearest tree, scrambled up the trunk, and flung himself onto the first stable branch. Ever screamed, bucking her body wildly, when the adult stopped near the adolescent. The younger werewolf shook his head violently while Ever swiped at his mother to break free.

"Drop her, mutt," Chess warned the adult. *Fucking arse.* He was just toying with the werewolf now before he found a clean shot and went in for the kill.

The younger werewolf padded forward, head hung low, tilted to the side as if in pain. Even then, the adolescent's hungry gaze was focused on Ever. *Shit.* He was out of time. With a deep breath, he dropped from the branch and landed on the younger one's back as hard as he could. A bone snapped in its back under the impact—nothing that wouldn't heal—but the adult dropped Ever in response.

Ever scrambled to her feet with her hair a wild mess. Her gaze flicked between him and the beasts. *Run*, she mouthed.

"You first, Queenie," he said, climbing from the collapsed body, edging slowly away from the prowling werewolf. Ever hesitated as Chess sidestepped closer to her. "Any time now."

She bolted, but the werewolf must have anticipated it because she lunged, maw open wide. Chess didn't think—didn't question what he was about to do. He simply acted. Jumping in front of the werewolf, he shoved Ever out of danger's path.

A crushing pain burst in his shoulder and he cried out wordlessly. *Fuck!* The werewolf had his entire shoulder in her mouth. Her teeth carved through his shirt, the flesh, and crumbled the bone. Stars burst behind his eyes.

Boom!

The blast rattled his ears. And then … nothing. Silence rung through his head. The werewolf didn't shake him like she had Ever. Didn't gnaw on him or use her paws to rip at his body. He shook his head to clear his vision and found himself kneeling on the forest ground. Ever was in front of him, lightly slapping his cheeks.

"If … you wanted to hit me…" He tried to smirk but failed. "You could've saved it for the bedroom."

"Bloody hell, I think my ears are bleeding from that statement," Maddie scoffed from his side. The boom… She'd shot the werewolf. For him.

"Did you just *save me?*" Chess asked the Hatter as Ever helped him to his feet. Specks of fiery ash burned on the ground—all that remained of the werewolf.

"Someone needed to end our lovely feud. It was either that or shoot your arse," she sang, waving her hand in the air. "We waited for you at the edge of the forest and doubled back when it took too long for you to show up."

The queen wrapped his good arm around her shoulders. "Let's get you some blood."

"We need to move before more werewolves show up to investigate all this noise," Ferris called.

Chess glanced farther into the woods and found him waiting with Noah and Mouse. Noah approached the incapacitated werewolf. It whimpered where it lay.

"Leave him," Chess told Noah. It was only acting on instinct and was no danger to them in that condition. Coming into Ivory was foolish but he was young and had lost a mother as a result. That was enough punishment—he knew first hand. "If another werewolf comes, they will haul him home instead of chasing us down."

Noah lowered the gun and looked to Maddie who nodded. Chess released a breath. He cast the werewolf a knowing glance as Ever led him back toward the castle.

"That was really foolish of you," she whispered.

Chess chuckled. "I do a lot of foolish things." His chest warmed as he studied Ever's heart-shaped face and her deep brown eyes. The way they bantered, the way he felt when she touched him… Realization struck him like lightning, his heart pounding as if there were thunder beneath his rib cage.

He was falling in love with the fucking Queen of Ivory.

CHAPTER EIGHTEEN

EVER

Chess had saved Ever's life—the prince who'd once tried to murder her had risked himself. For *her*. Maddie had then killed the werewolf and saved Chess's life, even though she could've easily killed the prince instead. But she hadn't, and Ever knew it wasn't because she was a queen—it was because they were friends.

Yet if Chess had harmed a single hair on Mouse's head in the Ruby Heart Palace, a very different fate would've occurred by the Hatter's hand. Mouse had told Maddie she'd been treated fine in the palace, but after hearing Chess's confession, that wasn't the truth. Her stomach sank at what Rav and Imogen could've done to her during the "interrogations," but Mouse wasn't ready to talk about it and she wouldn't push her to.

"Thank you," Ever murmured to Chess as they came to a stop further away from the werewolf. Her scalp still ached from where her hair had been yanked, but it was quickly dissipating. "Truly."

The prince licked his lower lip. "It was nothing, Queenie." It wasn't nothing. It was something.

Maddie handed Ever a scrap of blue silk from her backpack to wrap around Chess's torn shoulder.

The prince eyed the fabric as though it were poison, and shrugged it off. "It's just a bite and is already healing," he muttered, his voice weak.

"Just take it, Princeling." Ever sighed as blood continued to blossom across his shirt.

With a smirk, he took the silk and placed it over his wound. "Only because you said it oh-so-nicely." The smile left his face and he stumbled, beads of perspiration sliding down his forehead.

"Quit wasting energy," she reprimanded, then peered around the group. "Can someone get me some blood?"

Noah fished out a pouch and poured the contents into his canteen, shoving it into Chess's face. "You owe me," he grunted to the prince.

"Staying under the same roof shall be fun," Chess taunted, taking the canteen and chugging it down as though he'd never drank before in his life. He wiped a drizzle of crimson creeping down his chin and drew his shoulders back, grinning.

Maddie rolled her eyes and Ever nudged him forward. Even though they were tucked in the woods, she didn't want to linger so close to the fresh blood, especially with everyone in the group being wanted by Rav.

It wasn't long before they reached the palace and crossed the bridge toward the door, the silver water of the moat rippling from the wind. The smell here didn't seem as cold as before, but that may have been in her head. Ivory remained quiet as though the vampires in the city hadn't wanted to leave their homes.

That would change soon.

"Finally, home sweet home," Maddie sang after Ever unlocked the door and they entered the palace. "Hmm, it seems we will be redecorating." The Hatter studied the bare walls, the unkempt areas, and dirty furniture. A hint of blood from the dead guards still drifted through the air.

March rounded the corner, no longer wearing Scarlet's uniform but dark leather trousers and a tight white T-shirt. His eyes widened at the group, obviously not expecting Ever to have brought everyone home, then a bright smile formed on his face as his gaze settled on Ever, Maddie, and Mouse.

"It's been a while," he said to Maddie.

"Indeed, it has." The Hatter laughed and skipped to him. "But we can resume our tea parties now that you're back. Although, there will be a few new guests." She motioned to the side. "This is Noah and Ferris."

March's stare flicked to Chess, who'd been lingering behind them, and he scowled. "You're supposed to be in your room."

Chess smirked, slinking past the two males and stepping next to Ever. "I had a few things to take care of."

March shook his head. "You're a nuisance."

"I'm still royalty," Chess purred, picking at invisible lint on his tattered shirt.

"He did protect Ever from a werewolf," Mouse whispered, her caterpillar crawling up her arm.

March quirked a brow at her. "Did everyone forget he tried to *murder* her? He's one of the reasons you ended up in your cell, Mouse."

Ferris drew in a sharp breath and shifted protectively beside her. "That was Rav and Imogen's doing. Chess never touched her or he'd be dead," he said, his jaw clenched.

"If we're playing a game of forgiveness," Chess cooed. "I forgive Noah and Maddie for choking me until I passed out, then leaving me tied to a tree. Where I could've *starved*." He glanced at the duo with a wide grin.

"You tied us together first," Noah grumbled, balling his fists at his sides as though he wanted to punch the prince in the face.

"Unimportant detail." Chess shrugged. "As delightful as this day has been, I'll retire to my quarters. The one attached to the *queen's* bedroom." He winked at Ever. "See you soon, Queenie."

Ever pursed her lips, knowing he was trying to rile everyone up as he turned around and sauntered up the stairs without glancing back. *Cocky bastard.* Yet she couldn't help but watch how his arse flexed in his tight trousers.

"You can't be serious." Maddie's voice rose an octave. "Sleeping in *your* room?"

"It's not *my* room. It's the adjacent room." Ever paused. "To keep an eye on him."

"Mm-hmm. We heard everything at the safe house during your conversation with him," she pointed out.

Before more questions ensued, Ever straightened, becoming the queen she needed to be. "March, will you discuss with Ferris and Noah everything that's been going on while I take Maddie and Mouse to their old rooms? Then you can assign shifts to guard the palace until we can locate trustworthy vampires who hate my brother."

March nodded, gesturing for Noah and Ferris to follow him while Ever led Maddie and Mouse up the stairs. Mouse remained quiet, her face expressionless, her eyes haunted, as though her mind were somewhere else, fighting something dark. Ever's heart sank at seeing her friend this hollow.

Mouse had always been quiet though, seeming as if she would never hurt a single thing, but that had never stopped her from taking lives when needed. If a problem arose, Ever knew, underneath it all, Mouse could easily become vicious. Helping guard the palace wouldn't be an issue for her, yet Mouse also didn't seem like she was in the right headspace, which was why Ever brought her and Maddie up together, as not to single the younger sister out.

At the top of the stairs, they turned down a hall opposite from Ever's. White and silver tile still covered the floor, only now, booted footprints marred the marble. The palace needed a thorough cleaning at some point.

No longer did Maddie's white and silver hats decorate the wall—instead, only nails poked out where they had once been.

They came to a halt in front of the sisters' old rooms that were across from one another, the obsidian handles covered in dust.

Ever broke the silence. "Are you two up for guarding tomorrow? I wouldn't ask this of either of you after all you've been through lately, but we're short on staff, as you can tell."

"What's tearing off a few more heads if I need to?" Maddie shrugged, studying the area from floor to ceiling.

"I'm fine," Mouse said softly, sounding anything but fine. "I'll do whatever you need me to."

"For now, rest." Ever placed a hand on her small shoulder. "I need to talk to Maddie about a few things."

Mouse nodded with a yawn and opened the door to her room, leaving it cracked.

Maddie smiled while sighing. Mouse had been sleeping with the door wide open, but maybe this was a step in the right direction, that she was feeling more at home, could start to heal.

Ever followed Maddie into her friend's mostly-empty room. The Hatter's bed was there, still covered in black and purple blankets, and the ornate obsidian wardrobe hugged a corner. Beside it rested her desk and chair where she'd created hats, but all her belongings were gone. Not even a needle lingered.

"Of course nothing I need is here," Maddie huffed. "Those fuckers probably sold my creations across Wonderland to make a few coins. When Mouse and I were taken to the cottage, Rav and Imogen barely let us gather anything before I had to slave away at making the queen a hat every damn month."

Ever took a deep swallow at those words, guilt washing over her. She couldn't change the past, but she could alter the future. "Eventually, you can return to the cottage and collect what you would like. All your hats." Not until her brother was dead though.

"Although I do love a good discussion about hats, this is not the conversation we need to have." Maddie cocked her head and dropped on her mattress, patting the spot beside her. "Now, what is going on with you and Chess exactly? Please deny there has been heavy petting of any kind."

Ever ran a hand down the side of her face, avoiding eye

contact as she sank down on the bed. "Something foolish."

"Oh dear," Maddie groaned. "Did you fuck him?"

"No," Ever drawled, yet thinking how close they had been to that point.

"That sounded more like 'not yet'." She wrinkled her nose. "I may not like the arse, but he's different than when I saw him in Scarlet last. Still cocky. I can't put my finger on it though... Perhaps not selfish? No, no, he will always be that, but maybe less so."

"We'll see." Ever smiled. However, she'd seen it. Thus far, she'd seen a change in the prince.

"Something else I noticed," Maddie sang. "March seems to be a tad bit jealous. I don't think he'll ever stop carrying that blasted torch for you."

"He knows I don't want more than friendship with him." Eventually, he would move on, find someone who felt the same way. One day.

"March never was the right one for you..." Maddie looked as though she wanted to say something else on that matter, but she changed the subject. "I should probably go chat with the others and start preparing in case some devious bastards show up."

"I'm glad you're here." Ever grasped her friend's hand and gave it a gentle squeeze. "Unfortunately, I'll be leaving for the Ruby Heart Palace soon. And speaking of devious vampires, it won't be long before Rav discovers what has happened here. Whether he makes an appearance himself or sends new guards as he did with March, I'm unsure."

"We'll be ready"—Maddie tapped Ever's nose—"then have bloody fucking tea afterward."

"That's the spirit." Ever laughed. "I don't know much about Noah, but he seems a good match for you."

"He does, doesn't he?" Maddie grinned. "Who would've thought?"

Ever bid her friend goodnight and headed toward her bedroom. A strange feeling washed over her as she padded down the hall alone. In the past, there would always be a human or vampire servant around, cleaning. None were ever mistreated who served in the palace.

As Ever opened the door to her room, her gaze fell to Chess sprawled out on her bed, back against the headboard, his hair wet, shirt off, showing his chiseled abs. His shoulder was now almost fully healed with only raised pinkish marks. Once again, his trousers hung low, showing a patch of dark hair leading underneath the fabric.

She pushed down the heated feeling blooming inside her, pulsing harder, and placed her hands on her hips. "What are you doing?" Her voice came out more breathy than irritated.

"Being your knight for the day." He leaned forward, propping his elbow on his knee, his yellow eyes smoldering as he studied her with a seduction that must've lured half of Wonderland into his damn bed. For the first time, jealousy roared through her at the thought and she shoved the bothersome feeling away. "I did protect you earlier, didn't I?"

Ever took a step forward. "You could've gotten yourself killed."

Chess was off the bed in a split second, standing in front of her. "None of this would've happened if you'd told me the truth, Queenie." He pressed a warm finger to her lips and she hated that she was tempted to run her tongue up it instead of yearning to bite it off. "But I understand why you kept quiet about your rendezvous. Things are all out in the open now and we're one big happy family in your palace."

"That's a stretch." She laughed, a high-pitched sound that caused him to smile, only this smile was beautiful, captivating. That expression didn't make her want to push him away but pull him closer.

Chess must've sensed what she felt because he hoisted her up, then backed her against the wall. She squeaked in surprise, her legs betraying her and wrapping around his narrow waist. "Oh, Queenie," he murmured, "I wouldn't say that. I believe you like me plenty. Kiss me, then deny it."

She wouldn't deny him any damn thing right then.

His cock hardened in the precise place where she wanted it. Her eyes fluttered, and she inched closer, his breath mingling with hers.

"I'll play however you want tonight," he said, brushing the tip of her nose with his.

That shapely mouth of his wouldn't stop calling to her, and she was the first to give in, pressing her lips to his, gentle at first, then hungrier with each movement, each taste, until the hunger was all-consuming. His hips steadily rocked into her, making her moan in both pleasure and the need for more.

"How do you want me to touch you this time?" Chess purred in her ear. "With my fingers, my tongue, my lips, my cock? Tell me and I'll fucking do it. I won't stop until you come as many times as you damn well wish."

It was as though Ever could feel his invisible hands everywhere, touching her, devouring her, readying her. "All of them," she rasped, her fingers at the waist of his trousers, unfastening the button. He shoved them down and hiked up her skirt, drawing her panties to the side. His velvety cock slid against her warmth and she groaned in ecstasy, her fangs lowering. "I want to taste you this time," she breathed. At that moment, she could hear the symphony she would play for him, feel the way her fingers would press the viola strings, the way she would stroke them with her bow before she would let him glide slowly, deliciously, in between her lips, against her tongue.

He didn't hesitate as he carefully lowered her to her feet, their eyes meeting, something sparking. She was about to drop down to her knees, an act she thought she would never do with this male, when a sharp knock came at the door.

Ever froze and Chess growled in frustration but didn't tell her to ignore it. If it was important, then she had to take care of the matter. Yet disappointment stormed through her, her heart still pounding from what was happening between them.

She smoothed out her skirt and answered the door to March. His gaze narrowed as he glanced just past her to Chess, who was adjusting his trousers by the sound of the rustling.

"I'm sorry to break up whatever is going on here." March sighed. "But I have something important to show you, and it isn't good."

CHAPTER NINETEEN

CHESS

*F*ucking March.

If there was an award for impeccable timing, he would win, hands down. Chess scowled as he tucked his hard cock back into his trousers and adjusted himself as well as possible. There was no hiding the massive tent, but it wasn't as if March couldn't tell what he'd interrupted. The sweet scent of Ever's arousal filled the room from where she'd been rubbing herself up and down his cock. March had just apologized for interrupting a moment before, but he was a dirty liar.

Ever tensed. "What happened?"

"It will be easier to show you," the male said.

Ever nodded once and glanced over her shoulder at Chess. "Wait here."

Chess clenched his jaw. If there was a problem, he could help solve it, but she was the queen here. There would be things she had to deal with on her own that were none of his business and, as curious as he was, he had to accept that.

"Sure," he said with a sly grin. "We can finish what we started when you come back."

March clenched his jaw as he put an arm around Ever and ushered her out the door, murmuring that they needed to hurry. The door shut with a hard thud, leaving Chess alone. His lust was no longer an issue, but the image of Ever almost sinking to her knees lingered in his mind. He pushed the sensual budding image away—it was more important to deal with royal business, especially if Rav was on his way.

Oh shit.

What if it *was* Rav? Was Chess just supposed to sit around like a fool and wait for the bastard to storm the castle? He paced the room, his fingers flexing at his sides. Wait for Ever to be captured? Then find him lazing about in the bedroom as if there wasn't a care in the world?

"Maybe I should alert Mouse," he mused to himself. She loathed him the least and could pass the information along to the others. But what if it wasn't Rav? He didn't want to create a panic over nothing. Then Ever would be exasperated with him and her friends would trust him even less, if that were possible. There was only one solution…

Chess cracked the door open and slipped from the room. Fading footsteps came from the right so he sprinted in that direction, pausing at each corner to listen. His own steps were silent as he prowled closer and closer in the darker halls. They hadn't gotten as far as he expected which was odd. If March had something important to show Ever, they wouldn't have been taking their sweet time strolling through the palace.

Neither of them had spoken, but—finally—their steps increased with some unspoken urgency as they reached the first floor. Was there something he wasn't seeing?

"Out here," March said.

Chess pressed himself against the wall and peeked down the adjoining hallway. March opened the large glass door to a square courtyard. Ever stepped over the threshold, followed by March, who conveniently left the door open. *Imbecile.*

Sneaking closer, Chess made out the details of the courtyard. An oval water fountain sat at the center—either not turned on or no longer working—and silver ivy climbed the walls to a terrace that ran around the second floor. Numerous flower pots were scattered across the brightly-colored mosaic floor, some broken, others turned over, spilling soil. Purple and ivory flowers still rested in larger pots, their leaves draping over the edges.

"What am I supposed to be seeing?" Ever asked, searching the courtyard.

March led her to the far side of the courtyard, drawing her closer. "Shh. I heard something."

Ever whirled around, scanning the terrace, but what March must've heard was Chess—though he hadn't moved then. Sighing, Chess stepped into the courtyard and shrugged, arms stretched outward. "Extra security," he purred with a smirk. Turning his gaze to the terrace, he did a quick sweep for danger, just in case.

Ever released a breath, shoulders relaxing. "I told you to wait in the room."

"And I decided not to listen," Chess cooed, sauntering up to the fountain and scooping out a handful of dead leaves, scattering them to the ground. "What's so wrong that couldn't wait until later?" He kept his voice light, curious, but a cloying sense of wrongness descended upon him. It wasn't the disrepair of the floral arrangements that had March's panties in a twist, so what was it? He rounded the fountain, trailing his fingers around the stone edge while scanning the space. Above them, the moon was bright, casting long shadows across the ground.

"Chess." Ever cocked her head.

"What?" he asked innocently. A shadow moved and his eyes snapped up. Was it the ivy moving? But there was no wind… "I think we should get back inside." Then, so as not to let March or any potential intruder know he was onto them, he added in a more serious tone, "And finish what we were doing before."

Ever's brow furrowed, ignoring Chess's innuendo per usual. "March, what's so important? Quit dallying around here."

The shadow slid along the wall, elongated limbs reaching out, creeping forward. It wasn't the ivy—ivy didn't bloody well have arms. Or *swords* for that matter. "Ever, now!" he snapped.

She blinked at Chess in surprise. March still held her elbow from when he'd guided her farther into the courtyard, tugging her closer. She scowled up at March, then her gaze flicked back to Chess and she opened her mouth to speak.

Before a single word could pass her lips, six figures dressed in all black leapt from behind the columns of the terrace. Swords rested in their hands and black fabric covered their heads so only the skin of their faces showed. Chess bolted toward Ever as they fell toward the courtyard in unison.

Horror painted her face when the intruders surrounded him, blocking him from reaching her. It was the only clue Chess had that he was completely fucked before a blade drove into his lower back. He stumbled forward and Ever struggled to pull herself free of March.

That bastard planned to have her killed.

Chess bared his fangs and punched the black-clad vampire in front of him. "Ever, run!" he urged as the others descended upon him.

The blade struck through his back once more, the agony spreading through his body. Again and again. Three, maybe four blades pierced him at once. An arm, a leg, his chest—all seemingly missing vital parts on purpose. He choked down the agonized scream. If they had wanted to cut off his head or slice through his heart, there was no doubt in Chess's mind they would've done it already.

Chess fell to his knees and another blade slammed into his calf, pinning him to the ground. "Fuck off," he snarled as they crowded him, blocking his view of the queen and March. "Ever!"

"Let *go!*" she shrieked. March released a harsh bellow the moment she finally tore herself free. The male directly in front of Chess was shoved aside and Ever ripped the sword out of his hand. She swung the blade, cutting off the male's head in one motion, crimson splashing the White Queen's face.

"Ever, stop!" March shouted.

Chess reached behind him for the sword pinning his leg to the ground, ignoring the other blades still shoved into his body. The taste of his own blood flooded his mouth and he spat it to the ground. This was going to hurt like a bitch.

The hilt of the sword was too high and too angled for him to reach, so he grabbed the blade. It sliced through his hand as he pried the steel upward. He ground his teeth against the pain radiating in his calf, yet it had barely moved at all before one of the attackers flicked a coiled whip toward him. The braided leather looped around his neck and the female yanked him forward. Chess gasped for a breath, but the whip was too tight for the oxygen to reach his lungs.

Ever screamed her fury wordlessly, backing toward Chess, holding her sword up in his defense. "March, what the fuck is this?"

"You were blinded by him," March said in a sympathetic voice. As if Chess had somehow manipulated her into giving a shit about him. "He's a danger to you. To all of Ivory. Your brother has accused him of murdering their queen and he needs to pay for that, at the very least."

"He didn't kill his mother!" she growled. "Now stop this."

"I knew he would follow you again." March stepped toward Ever and she pointed the sword at him so he held his hands up, placating her. "Don't you see how treacherous he is? If he'd listened to his queen's command, he wouldn't have walked into a trap."

"If *Chess* listened to me?" she screamed from where she stood in front of the prince. "*You're* not listening! Call them off."

The five assailants still remaining hadn't moved to further attack. Chess was pinned to the ground with a whip around his neck—trapped, his vision slowly growing fuzzy. They weren't sent to kill—they were sent to capture. He would be back in Scarlet tonight and at Rav's mercy. Ever wouldn't be able to stop this attack alone.

"What the actual fuck?" Ferris roared from the doorway.

"Bloody hell!" Maddie screeched, her violet curls bouncing as she pushed her way around him and raced to Ever's side. "We heard you screaming. What is this?"

The whip tightened and Chess swayed. *Fuck.* Far too many vampires had to be enjoying the sight of him so powerless. He clawed at the coil around his neck but it was too tight, biting into his skin.

"We didn't agree to fight the White Queen," one of the male assailants called to March. The others stood, stiff and ready to attack on cue from the one who spoke. Their leader, Chess assumed.

March scowled down at Ever and spoke to the leader. "Take him and go. No one will stop you."

"Like hell," Mouse chirped from the doorway. "No one deserves to be in the dungeons in Scarlet."

"Ever," Chess attempted to speak, but it was impossible. Darkness was creeping into his mind, his vision fading as Ferris stepped into the courtyard.

A moment later, a throbbing pain pulled Chess out of the darkness and he sat up with a gasp. Blood covered the mosaic floor of the courtyard. Ever was still before him with the sword, but March was now on his knees, head lowered. Ferris and Mouse were dragging a headless body toward the door and… Where the fuck were the rest of the attackers?

It hadn't only been a moment, Chess realized, though he had felt it was. He'd been unconscious long enough for five vampires to meet their demise—or flee—and March to surrender. He flicked his tongue against his parched lips and tasted his own blood.

A flash of purple approached from the side and Maddie bent down to speak in his ear. "I'm going to pull the sword from your leg now."

"Don't enjoy it too much," he said in a hoarse voice.

"Hmm." She grinned. "I can't promise that."

Ever glanced over her shoulder at him, healing scratch marks marred her cheek on one side, speckled blood on the other. Her breath came in heavy pants, but she offered him a weak smile anyway. Chess swallowed hard, bracing himself for the pain Maddie was about to inflict as she freed him. Guilt bubbled inside Chess. Ever's friend had betrayed her because of him, but March had never been a true friend if he was willing to do this. He hadn't wanted to be her *friend* at all. March wanted Ever as his lover, but Chess had taken that title as his own.

"Ready?" Maddie drawled.

He took a deep breath. "Not reall—"

The sword was yanked free and Chess cried out as a deep pain shot through him. Blindly, he fell to his side and rolled onto his back where, thankfully, the other weapons had already been pulled out. "Fucking hell," he grunted.

"You're welcome," Maddie sang. Then she tossed down the sword and approached Ever. "Are you okay?"

Ever's hands shook where she held the sword. "Is Noah still following the one who escaped?" she asked, ignoring the question.

"Yes, he'll catch him," Maddie assured her and motioned to March. "Do you want me to…"

"No." Ever drew in a shaky breath. "It's my duty to deal with traitors."

She was going to kill March. He deserved it, in Chess's opinion, but that would leave a mark on Ever. Killing friends always did. Not that Chess personally knew as he lived his life without getting close to anyone, but he'd seen it happen to those around him for centuries. Though she was killing him for betraying her, she could regret it later.

"Ever," he rasped. "Don't."

March's head snapped up to glare at him and Ever released a shocked laugh. "What?" she asked.

"Lock him up and think about this before you kill him," Chess urged. "He won't be any less dead if you wait a day or two. Besides, what if Noah doesn't catch up to the escapee? You should learn about everyone willing to betray you."

"I know my decision," Ever said. "Maddie, Ferris, can you

please put March in the dungeon and I'll meet him there soon."

"Of course." Maddie took the sword from Ever and kept it pointed at March. Ferris walked around Chess and hoisted the male from his knees, leading him from the room.

Ever turned to loom over Chess, her hand gripping her hair. "Let me get you some blood before I have to deal with this. Wait here."

"This time, Queenie, I don't think I have any choice but to listen."

Ever shook her head and left him on the ground with only Mouse, who hovered near the entrance with the blue and yellow caterpillar in her hand.

"You all right over there?" Chess asked her. She had always been overly quiet when he visited, but it was no less worrisome outside of the dungeons.

Mouse met his gaze and something feral swirled in her eyes. "Hungry," was all she whispered.

CHAPTER TWENTY
EVER

The metal scent of the prince's blood permeated the air, but his wounds were slowly healing. He needed to drink to speed up the process, though. Ever handed Chess a basket holding a bundle of dried blood pouches and a couple of canteens. She then set the large jug of water beside him. He picked out a pouch and passed it to Mouse, who appeared hungrier than the prince did as she gnawed at her lip with her fangs. Ever studied the female for a long moment, but as her friend drank, a ravenous expression remained on her face. She wasn't certain how often Mouse fed when trapped in the Ruby Heart Palace, but it was clear that her friend would need a mortal to feed from soon.

In the distance, a blond head caught her attention. Noah. He picked up his pace and was beside Ever in only a few seconds.

"It's done," he said, chest heaving, his clothing covered in bright crimson. "I killed the last attacker and hid the body."

Ever didn't know Noah well, but she already liked him, as long as he treated Maddie like a queen. "Stay with them. I'm going to settle things with March."

Wiping her hands against her skirt, she headed inside the palace. She looped around the back, walking through hallway after hallway until she reached the ornate oval door leading to the dungeons. Her steps echoed down the stairs, the narrow walls seeming to close in on her before she came to the circular room filled with ivory cells. Above each one rested king and queen chess pieces that had represented the past royals before her. Ever had never removed them because she'd wanted parts of her caregivers to remain throughout the castle in their memory.

Maddie and Ferris stood near the back of the room, anger written across both their faces, her lips pursed and his set in a snarl. Ferris hadn't known March well, but Maddie had.

The cells here had never been filled like the ones in Scarlet—Ever's enemies were killed immediately and she didn't place humans in them either.

"Noah's back," Ever said, then glanced at Ferris. "I think you need to find Mouse a human to feed on. Sooner rather than later."

He bit his lip while nodding and slipped past her. Ever could see in Maddie's face that she agreed by the way her expression fell.

The Hatter handed Ever the bone key that usually hung on the wall. "I'll wait outside the door." She placed her palms on the queen's shoulders. "Be careful. I'm on your side, no matter your decision." Maddie was a good friend, ever since the day the Hatter had stumbled into Ivory, lost and broken, not knowing who Ever truly was.

"Thank you." Ever watched as Maddie shut the door, then turned to face March, who stood in the corner of the cell, his mouth set in a tight line. The only item in each cell was a dusty silver mattress on the floor.

Ever didn't say a word as she unlocked the door to his cell. She shut it behind her, this time prepared if he attempted anything deceitful.

March was the first to break the tense silence as his warm gaze latched onto her. "After everything that bastard did, we can't trust him."

"I know better than anyone what he's done, some of it right in my own garden, but I believe he can be trusted now or he wouldn't be alive." Ever took in a breath, flexing her fingers. "He didn't kill his mother." She wouldn't tell him it was Maddie who'd done the deed because that was irrelevant.

"It doesn't matter." March paused, his eyes pleading for something she couldn't return. "I love you."

Ever sighed, her heart lodging in her throat. "And I love you, you know this, but as a dear friend. Even when we pleasured each other, you knew this." She couldn't give him more now, just as she couldn't then.

"But this *bastard?*" March's fists clenched at his sides. "I've seen you with others, and I would be content if you were with anyone else. Forgive me if I can't get past him trying to murder you."

"It isn't something for you to get past or to forgive." She placed a hand on his chest, his heart beating rapidly against her palm. "It's for me. *My* decision. If he'd been the one to betray me before I got to know him, I wouldn't have been surprised, but it was you who did. The one male who was supposed to be on my side. You knew what I faced with my past guards, and yet—and yet—" she stuttered, fighting the emotion brewing in her chest. "You may not have physically tried to rip out my heart, but it was just the same."

"Rav doesn't know yet," he whispered. "I never would've risked him knowing you were here, alive. I only collected the few vampires who I could trust to bring Chess back to Scarlet."

"And what if Chess hadn't followed me outside?" She threw up her hands. "Then what? Would you have tried to play another game to see if he would listen?"

He hung his head. "No, they would've taken him from inside the palace."

"Damn it, March!" she snapped. "I wouldn't even give Chess

a second chance if he'd done this tonight instead of you. How can I trust you won't do this again?"

"You can't. I trust you with my entire heart, but I won't ever accept him," March said softly, placing his hand against her cheek. "You made me a vampire because I wanted it. And I had asked because I loved you, even then. I left Wonderland to stop these feelings, yet in the mortal world, all those years away from you, I couldn't end the yearning. So kill me. Kill me before I make another mistake."

Her stomach sank, her eyes widening at his words, even though she'd been prepared to kill him if he'd forced her hand. "March, no…"

"Your mission is to let humans choose what they want. Do the same for me, and be the one to end my life. That's all I want."

"Is … is this what you really want?" Ever's heart pounded wildly, the blood rushing in her ears.

"It is." His voice was resigned, his shoulders falling. This was what he wanted, *needed*.

Taking a deep breath, she tried to steady her shaky hand on her friend's chest, his gaze fastened to hers. She didn't want him to suffer any longer, and perhaps it would've been better if she'd never met him, if she'd never turned him, yet she didn't want to take their friendship back. Because she did love him.

Tears slid down her cheeks, as he lowered his mouth to hers, a goodbye kiss that held everything they'd shared. Him dancing with her inside the palace, her walking with him outside in her garden, them laughing, sharing blood at the tea parties with Maddie and Mouse. So many blending together like a fading rainbow.

Then she thrust her hand into his chest, shattering his rib cage to get to his beating heart. A relieved gasp ripped from his throat as she tore the organ from his chest. She caught his body before it fell to the floor, then carefully lowered him to the mattress while she cradled his heart.

Ever didn't want to release it, and she held the organ until the warmth was gone, until *he* was gone. She wouldn't toss his heart down as though it meant nothing, so she tucked it back into his broken rib cage and kissed his forehead. Pressing her clean fingers into the pocket of her skirt, she fished out her lucky chess piece and placed it into his hand before leaving the cell.

Maddie stood outside the door, her expression solemn. "I'm sorry," the Hatter said.

"March wanted it this way." Ever wiped the tears from her cheeks. "Have Noah take his body to the mortal world. He would want the sun to turn it to ash instead of being buried here."

"We'll take care of everything. Go rest. You can't go to Scarlet like this."

Maddie was right. As much as Ever hated it, as much as she wanted more than anything to tear her brother apart, if she went like this, she wouldn't be able to save her kingdom or Chess's.

She nodded and headed toward her bedroom. When she opened the door, she found no sign of Chess, who was most likely still drinking blood.

Blood.

March's blood was still on her damn hands.

Stripping out from her clothing, she filled the bath and washed the blood from her body. Washed and washed until her skin was raw, until blood was no longer there. Tucking her knees into her chest, she sobbed, remaining in the water until it turned cold, just like March's heart had. She didn't even have an instrument to play her friend a goodbye song and that made her sob again, breaking her apart on the inside.

The door to her room opened and she didn't peer out into her space to see that it was Chess—she knew it was by his familiar scent, his movements.

"Are you all right?" he asked, stepping to the open door of the bathroom.

"No." Ever stared down at the swirling scarlet water.

Being Chess, he didn't leave her alone, yet stepped inside, their gazes locking. He was no longer covered in blood and ripped clothing but clean, his hair wet, his shirt off. The prince's wounds were still healing, pink lines decorating his skin.

"I killed him. He wanted me to," she whispered, trying to fight the uncontrollable sobs that still managed to escape her.

Chess didn't say anything, just scooped her out of the bath and held her to him. She cried into his chest as he took her to the bed and laid her down, covering her with the thick blankets.

"Sleep," he said softly. "I never promise anything, but I promise I won't ever betray you."

The prince lowered himself on top of the blankets, resting his back against the headboard. He ran his fingers through her wet hair, and Ever closed her eyes at the comforting touch. She then tried to sleep, even though the nightmares would take control, playing an angry melody inside her head.

Ever didn't know how long she'd stayed in bed. But it had been longer than she'd liked. *Days.* As she cracked open her eyes, Chess handed her a cool bag of blood. "Maddie got this for you, and Ferris was able to retrieve a human for Mouse to feed on." The prince wore one of Rav's old black vests, but it fit him better than it ever did her brother. It had been so long since she'd seen Chess in his usual style, but it suited him well.

"How is Mouse?"

He shrugged. "Not as hungry." *Good.*

"I'm surprised the others didn't give you a hard time for staying in here."

"What can I say? I do have an aura that makes everyone come around eventually, including a certain White Queen." He gave her a wide grin.

"You're so cocky." Ever rolled her eyes, then straightened, thinking about more important matters at hand. "Tomorrow morning, we leave for Scarlet. Only you and me. The others will guard here."

"Aw, you want to be alone with me some more, Queenie, is

that it?"

"You're insufferable."

"Am I?" Chess arched a brow.

Holding the blankets to her chest, she leaned forward and grabbed him by the arm with her free hand. His lips parted in surprise as she pulled him beside her and pressed her mouth to the prince's. "Truly." Her forehead rested against his. Over the past few days, he'd stayed with her as she sulked, as she wept, and had brought her blood. It was different, and she couldn't thank him enough for sticking beside her.

He inched his body closer, capturing her lips with his, his tongue slipping inside, flirting with hers. Her heart accelerated, turning frenzied.

The kiss deepened, becoming more than the simple kiss she'd planned, and the way he was kissing her was different than before. He was gentle with her, his hands entwining in her hair. A heat spread through her, making her heart pound harder, thirsty for more, hungry for him. She pushed the blankets away, inviting him in. Her body was still bare from her bath, ever since he'd taken her from the bloody water and tucked her safely into bed as he guarded her, even though he'd been the one who had needed protection.

She unbuttoned his vest and drew it off. Her hand trailed down the length of his chiseled chest, taking in every sculpted curve. Her fingertips drifted to the laces of his trousers and loosened them, allowing him to shuck them the remainder of the way off.

Chess scooted closer, his lips slanting over hers, claiming them. Their bodies were now flesh to flesh, igniting a fierce warmth, not a single barrier between them. Ever rolled him to his back, trailing open-mouth kisses down his throat, his chest, his abdomen, then his thigh, wanting to explore every piece of him. Her fangs were eager to come out, and she sank them into his salty flesh, the way he had with her. She relished in the euphoric growl that escaped the prince as she tasted him, as her fingers skated to his cock and pumped him thoroughly.

While drinking in his metallic flavor, her body tightened, his growing taut. Ever released him, then slowly ran her tongue up the base of his length to the tip before taking him fully into her mouth. His hips slightly bucked in rhythm with her movements. She continued to lick, to taste, to stroke, to devour until he writhed beneath her, spilling himself onto her tongue.

With a smile after she swallowed, she glanced up at him, his yellow eyes pinned to hers, blazing with lust.

As they stared at one another for what seemed like an eternity, she knew this was what she'd saved herself for, *who* she'd saved herself for.

"I've never given myself to anyone," Ever breathed, "but I want to with you. It doesn't have to be today, it doesn't have to be tomorrow, just whenever you're ready."

In one swift motion, she was resting in his lap, a laugh escaping her as he purred, "Oh, I'm ready, Queenie." His lips crashed into hers, growing desperate, ferocious. She mirrored his movements, her hips rocking into his until he was hard once more.

Chess gently lay Ever on her back, kissing down her chest, her breast, flicking a peaked nipple with his tongue before sucking it between his teeth. Her back arched and her eyes fluttered at every single one of his licks, his touches.

The prince's fingers drifted between her thighs, circling her clit as he kissed his way to her ear. "Tell me if you need me to slow down," he rasped.

She cradled his face, bringing his mouth to hers again, never wanting it to leave. "Don't you dare. I want you inside me."

A wickedly delicious smile crossed his face and he did as she asked, sliding into her with one exquisite motion until she was full. It was harder than he would've moved with a mortal, but the perfect amount of force for what a vampire could handle. A slight ache burned, making her gasp, yet only for a moment before her body held a new sensation.

Chess's body shook as he slowly moved inside her, and she knew he was holding back, for her. "Faster," Ever said. She dug her fingers into his back and drove her fangs into his shoulder. In answer, his pace picked up, his thrusting growing harder, faster, exactly what she'd asked for and more. He was fucking her and she *liked* it, *loved* it. "More."

He flipped them both so she was in his lap, his fingers gripping her hips, then her arse, urging her to move faster this time, harder, while he sank his fangs into her neck.

The world was filled with music, as though all the musicians of the past and the present had come together, performing the loudest song she'd ever heard. One she wanted to be a part of, one she never wanted to end while it pulsed within her heart. And then the cymbals struck, a rush of ecstasy rolling through her, and she moaned Chess's name over and over again.

She rode him even harder, wanting him to feel the way she did. It only took a few pleasureful moments before he groaned, his sounds reverberating in the room.

Ever collapsed against him, their chests heaving. He wrapped his arms around her as he murmured in her ear, "Ah hell, Queenie. I suppose slow and gentle wasn't meant to be for your first time."

She smiled in the crook of his neck. "I wouldn't have wanted it any other way, Princeling."

CHAPTER TWENTY-ONE

CHESS

The scent of lilies greeted Chess as he stirred from sleep. A smile lifted the corners of his mouth before he opened his eyes. He shifted closer to Ever and inhaled deeply. Not only lily, but his pine scent mixed with the headiness of their late-night fucking. They'd stayed up nearly all day, exploring and enjoying each other's bodies. It wasn't until Chess was too exhausted to move that he'd drifted to sleep while Ever idly traced the lines of muscle on his stomach.

Chess cracked his eyes open and studied Ever's face. She looked at peace in a way she hadn't before, awake or asleep. She nuzzled closer and his heart thudded. The sensation of her skin brushing against his had his cock rising. She was so soft against him, so smooth. And she'd chosen him to give herself to. It was an honor he never thought much of before but, with her, it was different. After everything he'd done in the past for his mother, Ever had not only forgiven him, she'd *chosen* him. The sudden urge, that *need*, to be inside her again swept over him.

Chess rolled her onto her back and hovered over her, nipping at her ear to wake her. When she stirred, he ran his tongue along her neck and pressed a kiss at the hollow of her throat. Ever let out a small laugh, then spread her legs to allow him to settle between them.

"Good morning, Your Majesty," Chess whispered with a crooked smile.

"I could say the same to you," she replied, shifting her hips beneath him. "Is this how I should expect to be woken from now on?"

Chess's breath caught. Never once had a female expected him to linger before. Plenty of females had hopes of keeping him in their beds—for power or status or the multiple orgasms. Or all three. But he'd never wanted them for more than their bodies. This was different. Chess wanted Ever and that made him vulnerable. Honestly, he didn't hate that fact as much as he thought he would. Though how the fuck he managed to fall in love was beyond him.

"You should, yes," he said, lifting himself enough to look down at her. "Unless you object?"

"I certainly do not." She laced her fingers behind his head and drew him down to her.

Their lips met with tenderness, pressing softly, moving with reverence. Chess rubbed his hard length against her slick opening, eliciting a moan from his queen. He chuckled and trailed his kisses down her neck. Ever tilted her head back to allow him better access.

"Do you want me to bite you?" He nipped at her throat, but his fangs hadn't descended yet. "Or fuck you?"

"I think you know the answer, Princeling."

"Both then." His fangs dropped and he pierced her flesh at the same time he pressed inside.

A growl left him as his urges took over, sucking gently, fucking hard. She ground herself against him, met him thrust for thrust. Her moans were delicious, her fingernails biting against his back. *Fuck.* He wasn't going to last. Not when she was so fucking perfect.

"Chess!" she cried as her orgasm squeezed around him.

He pulled his fangs from her throat and kissed her fiercely as he came. Panting, he rolled off her a moment later and grinned. "It's unfortunate we don't have time to go again."

"It is unfortunate, but we would have to wait another day to murder my *beloved* brother…" She sighed and sat up. Chess's gaze focused on her flawless breasts and he fought the desire to lean forward, take a peaked nipple into his mouth while ravishing her with his fingers between her thighs. "We will have a concert to celebrate his death."

"Ah yes." Chess pressed his eyes closed for a moment before meeting her stare. "Shall we go kill the bastard then?"

Ever nodded silently. "Let's get washed up and say our goodbyes. I don't want to linger and risk him knowing I'm here. Surprise will be our greatest advantage."

Chances were high that *somehow* Rav already knew Ever had retaken the castle, but she was right not to want to wait. If Rav traveled to Ivory at the same time they journeyed to Scarlet, they might miss each other. The bastard wouldn't expect Ever to bring the fight to him after hiding away for nearly four years. While Chess knew she wasn't a coward, the rest of Wonderland wouldn't necessarily agree. They would remember a queen who'd fled her home, who'd abandoned them.

"I'll meet you here in thirty minutes," Chess said. That would be enough time to bathe and gather whatever weapons might be useful.

Ever slipped from the bed. He watched her arse as she walked away and gave a satisfied smirk. It quickly fell from his lips as he realized they were about to return to Scarlet. Where he was wanted for his mother's murder. Killing Rav wasn't going to make the accusation magically disappear, but it would be a start. If he made it that far…

Ever waltzed back into Chess's bedroom with a dark, curly wig on her head. She wore a clean pair of acid washed jeans and a plain black hooded jumper. Nothing she had on would draw attention, but she still looked delectable. The way her jeans hugged her thighs, the swell of her breasts beneath the jumper…

Ever cleared her throat. "Are you ready?"

Chess peered down at himself. Blue jeans and a white tunic weren't his style at all, but that was fine. He was trying not to be recognized and the black vest was too much of his signature outfit. "No wig for me?" he asked. As much as he'd teased with her about them before, he wouldn't deny wearing one now that they were going back to Scarlet.

"Sorry," she said, her lips growing into a wide grin. "We could give you a haircut before we leave. Maddie is quite talented with scissors."

"Something tells me different colored hair or a new style wouldn't make much difference," he admitted, slowly twirling a piece of his hair around his finger. Too many vampires knew him. Loved him, loathed him. No matter their feelings, turning him in now was likely to get them a huge bounty. Especially since Ever would be included in it. "I was thinking about how we should get to the Ruby Heart Palace."

Ever tilted her head thoughtfully. "Go on."

"Let's go back to the mortal realm and use the portal into the palace basement. No one will see us unless they're skulking around the park in London. And even if they are, the only ones allowed to use the portal into the palace are Rav, my—" He caught himself before he could include his mother. "And myself."

The lower tunnels were always clear of guards because Rav didn't want anyone in his business, but past that point was where they lingered, prepared to throw anyone in the dungeon who ventured down. Any intruder would have their heart ripped out by his mother or become Rav's next experiment, which was enough deterrent to keep the castle safe.

"Great minds think alike." Ever trailed the tip of her finger across his bottom lip, and bloody hell, he wanted to suck on that too.

"Are you trying to take credit for my plan?" he asked with a chuckle.

"Technically it was my plan first—you just didn't know it yet." She laughed. "Now, come on before the mortal night fades."

Chess swiped his gun off the bed and strapped it to his boot, then followed her down the hallway. The others were waiting for them in the banquet room just off the main hall. Mouse was reading a Shakespeare play quietly to Des at the head of the table while Ferris and Noah played a game of cards. Maddie had acquired hat making material and the remainder of the table was strewn in ribbons and lace.

"Ever!" the Hatter chirped and held up a swath of sapphire satin. "What do you think of this shade of blue?"

"It's lovely."

Maddie nodded thoughtfully. "Mouse requested a hat that matched Des. I wasn't quite sure if this was better than the cobalt silk."

"The sapphire." Ever smiled at her friend, but it slowly faded from her face. Clearing her throat, she announced, "Chess and I are leaving."

"Only to kill her brother," he explained when the room remained silent.

Ever arched a brow at him, then looked to her friends once more. "I won't let Ivory be taken over again."

"We won't either. This is our home too," Maddie started. "But what about you, what if something happens to *you*?"

"We won't think about that now, will we?" Ever smoothed the front of her shirt and straightened.

"Do you need anything before you go?"

"Some blood, perhaps?" Mouse asked without looking up from the play.

"No, thank you." Ever cocked her head and smiled at

Maddie. "Perhaps a hat for when I return."

"Ah, that I can do," Maddie sang.

Ever moved around the table to hug Maddie, then Ferris and Mouse. Noah, she simply ruffled his hair. "Stay safe."

Chess backed away from the room while they each offered Ever well on the journey and exchanged how much they cared. The emotions swirling in the air made his skin crawl. He never used to care if he had friends like that … or he hadn't *thought* he'd cared. Maybe he'd convinced himself he didn't need it, but seeing it now, he had to admit he wanted the same. Someone to miss him, to worry about him. Without all the verbalizing, of course— he didn't want to hear it, but *feel* it. Though, he supposed, he would need to start behaving slightly less like an arse for that to happen. He wrinkled his nose at the thought. *Not sure it's worth it.*

"I'm about to show you another secret portal, Princeling." Ever smiled, joining him in the hallway. "Tell anyone of it and you may lose a precious body part."

Chess perked up. "Go on."

Ever grabbed his hand and led him through the heavy front doors, into the dark, starless night. They paused on top of a large, silver stone medallion in the middle of the pathway. "Trace your finger over the crack in the wall."

Chess studied the castle entrance and found a fissure in the doorway. At first glance, it looked like a vein in the marble but now that he was paying attention, he could see it was more. He tilted his head and did as she instructed. The moment his finger reached the end, the floor shook. A rumbling filled the air just before the stone gave out beneath them. He sucked in a breath of musty air as they fell straight down into a portal, swallowed up by the silver, mirror-like surface, and were spat out in the middle of a cemetery.

The old, worn headstones were packed tightly together, some tilting, others cracked. Fog caressed the ground and an owl hooted overhead. Ever climbed to her feet and adjusted her wig. The corners of her lips curled in amusement as she cast a glance at Chess, who was still on the ground.

"You're not going to sit there all day, are you?"

Chess pried his boot from between two stones and stood, taking her chin between his thumb and finger. "You enjoyed that, didn't you?"

"I don't know what you mean." She grinned.

"You'll pay for that later." He chuckled and fuck it, he gave into quick temptation and drew her close, capturing her mouth with his. Just because he could. Just because he was the bloody prince of Scarlet. And just because he damn well loved her, even if she didn't know that. He'd bring her to the edge of pleasure again and again, and only let her fall off when she begged him for it. "Though, you'll probably enjoy the punishment far, *far* too much."

"You talk a lot." Amusement danced in her eyes, and he'd bet anything that between those pretty thighs of hers, she was aroused. "Lead the way to your portal into the Ruby Heart Palace."

Chess swallowed hard, knowing he needed to leave the distraction at this cemetery. There was no point in delaying the inevitable any longer. If his time was over, there was little he could do to change fate. He would die in Wonderland though— not in this forsaken mortal world. Wonderland was a brutal place, but at least they didn't hide that fact like the mortals did. As a child, he'd experienced more ill-intention hidden behind kind smiles than he'd care to admit. "Keep up," he said with a wink, and raced through the peaceful London streets.

Ever was right behind him the entire trip to the tree where the portal into the palace basement was. The entrance rested at the tree's base, hidden by leafy shrubs. She said nothing as he pulled aside the brush covering the opening and motioned her inside. Without hesitation, she hopped down into the hole. His pulse raced as he glanced over his shoulder to make sure they were alone, then he leapt down beside her.

Once they crossed into Scarlet, Chess would be hunted down like a bleeding human in a city of starving vampires. Ever, too, though she might be better at talking her way out of a death sentence than him. Rav might be willing to cut a deal with her with the right terms. But if they managed to kill Rav, Chess could live in relative peace … as soon as he cleared his mother's murder from his name, at least. He could easily blame his mother's servant, Rine, who had been dead in the same room, and claim he'd killed the female for the injustice.

"And the concert begins," Ever whispered to him.

He nodded.

They stepped through together and Chess drew in a deep breath. A mixture of scents—blood, hot summer air, and sulfur from the portal—filled him with a sense of home, but the Ruby Heart Palace didn't quite feel the same. The slate tunnels were so familiar yet less endearing.

"Are you all right?" Ever asked under her breath.

"Smashing." Chess swallowed hard as centuries of memories assaulted him. Some good, some bad. All tainted now. He led her down the black slate tunnel, then turned down another.

"Did ya hear that?" a bloke called from the far end.

"Hear what?" another male replied.

Chess froze. *Well, fuck me.* Rav had the guards in the lower tunnel levels now instead of at the top? What kind of shite was that? He glanced at Ever, whose fangs were already dropped, and he gave her a nod. They could easily take out two guards, then finish with their plan.

A loud sniff from the second guard, followed by an annoyed grunt as the strong sulfur smell must've reached them. "It's probably the king coming back," the first male said.

Chess's gaze snapped to Ever. Rav wasn't even here? *Bloody hell.*

"I thought he was staying in the mortal world for a few days." The male's voice jarred Chess's memory. If he wasn't mistaken, it was a vampire his mother turned about a century ago. *Michael? Micah?* Something like that. "Maybe he's coming back early with one of those groupies?"

"Nah, I overheard him mentioning Apex which is one of them fancy clubs."

"No shit?" The second sounded impressed, though given that Rav was king, it didn't seem that strange. "I've always wanted to go there."

Ever tugged at Chess's shirt and motioned for them to go back the way they came. He followed reluctantly. There was no getting in unannounced and Rav would simply find them when he came home if they didn't get out of the tunnel. If he had to fight Rav in the mortal world, so be it. At least he wouldn't have an entire palace worth of guards at his disposal.

CHAPTER TWENTY-TWO

EVER

Ever and Chess kept their feet light as they raced down the slate tunnels until they reached the portal. She hurled her body through, the barrier tickling her flesh, and stepped out into a small, dirt cavern. Six feet above her, moonlight shimmered down from a round opening. Chess stepped through behind her and lifted her by the hips without hesitation, thrusting her toward the mortal park. She dug her fingertips into the dirt around the edge of the hole and hoisted herself up. A grunt escaped her mouth—going up was more tedious than dropping down.

"I like my view right now, Queenie," the prince called up, and his smile translated in his tone. He said the most ridiculous things at the most inappropriate times.

Ever rolled her eyes as she threw herself from the hole, the fresh air hitting her nose. She stood and turned, smiling as she grabbed Chess's hand and drew him out. "Have you ever thought when we crawl out of these holes at night that we look like the zombies straight from the mortals' movies?"

"Ah, but aren't we the monsters of their movies?" Chess purred, brushing a lock of hair from her face. Her gaze focused on his gleaming yellow irises, and she remembered how he traced her entire body with delicate fingertips, how his lips moved slowly, *seductively*, up and down her flesh. How he thrust inside her from the front, from behind, then her riding him into bliss, him driving her into madness. She'd never felt something so … so … she couldn't grasp onto the words. Her damn fingers ached for a viola to draw the things from her mind.

Swallowing, she drew herself from those thoughts. "Some of us. But we need to get out of here before the guards investigate who used the portal."

"Those fools didn't sound the brightest."

She highly agreed with that statement.

The club awaited and more than a little blood would be spilled. Ever just prayed it wouldn't be her or Chess who ended up without their heads and hearts.

A bird cried out in the distance and the flap of another's wings tore through the air. The moon rested high in the sky, its color a pale silver as it cast its light upon the park. Ever and the prince jolted forward, barreling through the foggy area.

They wouldn't need to hail a taxi tonight since Rav's portal was an easy walking distance to the club scene. As they approached the road, a flood of cars passed, the night still being young.

Ever grasped Chess's hand and they continued at a casual pace once they reached the opposite side, as not to draw in any unwanted attention. Bright lights flickered from buildings just ahead, and chatting and music clashed together while they passed. She could pick out precisely who was going to the clubs by the flash of their clothing and the pep in their step.

As they turned down a sidewalk, a faded white building, covered in graffiti paintings, stood at the corner of the road. This was it … the club the guards had mentioned where Rav was staying, though there were no guarantees he would be there. This wasn't a new club to Ever—this was where Rav had met Imogen.

Back then, they'd known of the Queen of Hearts, who she was, how she was married to a kind male. But this was where Rav had been lured in by her, or perhaps it was her to him.

The front glass door of the club opened and music boomed louder as two men, their arms draped around one another, walked out kissing while one reached for the button of the other's trousers.

If they couldn't find Rav tonight, then they would have to either wait here, go back to her brother's palace the following night, or go home. The last choice wasn't an option.

Chess held the door open for her and she walked inside, catching a whiff of blood, sweat, and something smoky. A tattooed woman at the front desk, wearing a black crop top, started to open her mouth when Ever met her gaze. She let her influence seep into the woman, grasping and tightening.

"Let us in," Ever demanded.

The young woman nodded, her red ponytail bobbing.

As they slipped through the hallway leading to the dance floor, the blood, as always, called to her, sending an intoxicating thrill deep into her bones, her marrow. Bodies gyrated around her, grinding, on the brink of pleasuring one another, but she didn't catch sight of white hair.

"I'm going to scout upstairs," Chess said. "Check around here for him, and keep your eye on the bar. He has the tendency to always show up near one."

"Be careful," Ever whispered. She didn't want to separate, but if Rav slipped past one of them, the other could catch him.

He winked and slinked away, his arse flexing against his tight jeans, just as Chess knew how to do best.

Pushing a lock of her wig forward, Ever covered her face a bit better while she searched the crowd. Blue and green lights flashed as a new hip-hop song poured out through the speakers. The club scene reminded her of the times she'd met March, but she placed the memories into a hidden box for now. He was gone because of her. *Because he'd wanted it*, she reminded herself.

Her gaze drifted through the crowd, searching, and found

nothing. But then her heart picked up, her lungs pumping harder as she spotted someone who had once been dear to her. Farther ahead, near the edge of the crowd, long white hair wandered away, like a rabbit begging to be followed. Rav moved the same as he always did, silkily. She wanted to get Chess, but she also couldn't lose sight of her brother. Keeping her hand near the knife in her pocket, she broke through the crowd. She turned down a bare brick hallway, then another, finding two couples against the wall kissing, their hands roaming over each other's bodies.

Ever thought she had lost him, when her brother rounded the corner. Her shoulders fell—it wasn't Rav. The hair matched his, only it wasn't tipped with red. Something was off about him as he studied her with bright blue eyes and a knowing expression—he was a vampire, but that wasn't all...

Just as she drew out her knife, the couples—*vampires*—shoved off from the walls and locked onto her wrists, another with a blade at her throat. One of the vampires ripped the knife from her hand and Ever dropped her fangs as anger rolled off her in waves.

A mortal would've screamed. She knew what happened when one screamed while in the grips of a vampire—they wound up dead, and any mortals nearby would be influenced to forget.

"Rav's been looking for you," a female cooed, her dark braids pulled up into a bun atop her head. Ever recognized her as one of the females from the night she'd seen Rav at the club.

"Then take me to him," Ever demanded. She would try to find a way out of this, but if she didn't, at least she wasn't hiding away in a hole in the ground any longer.

The five vampires led her to the end of the hall and unlocked the door before bringing her down a flight of metal stairs. Blood and sex permeated the air of the room. The answer as to why came when her gaze drifted to three naked females wrapped around a male with white and red-tipped hair... Her brother.

"What is it?" Rav panted, his fingers digging into the waist of the female atop him, guiding her as she rode him, her breasts bouncing. The other two were taking care of each other, stroking between their legs, their opposite hand caressing Rav's arms. Ever wanted to spit in her brother's face.

"Seems we found a White Queen," the dark-haired vampire said.

"About fucking time," Rav groaned with ecstasy. "I'll see my lovely sister in a few moments."

Ever clenched her jaw, ignoring the sounds of her brother's growls, the females' moans. Once he shouted a long curse, he peeled his sweat-slicked body from the females to slip on a pair of leather trousers and approach her.

"I've been trying to find you for a very long time." Rav cocked his head, his brown irises pinned to hers. "Why would you stay hidden from your own brother for so long?"

"Stop with the games," Ever spat, the blade at her throat digging in further. "You turned my guards against me."

"It wasn't difficult." He shrugged. "You shouldn't have put your nose in Scarlet's business."

There was no use discussing how it was wrong to turn mortals without their consent. He knew her feelings on it, and he didn't give a damn. "If you're going to kill me, then just do it."

Rav removed her wig before patting her down, searching for her hidden weapons. He fished out the gun within her boot. As he lifted it, he glided a finger down the barrel. "Let me guess, you were going to try to shoot me from afar like a coward? Then rip out my heart? How cliché of you, sister." He swiped the tip of his tongue across his lower lip and chuckled.

She clenched her teeth. "Just repaying you for what you not only tried to do to me, but what you did to my viola."

"Ever, Ever, *Ever*." Rav trailed a finger down her cheek, drew close so his hot breath touched her ear. "I left you scraps of your instrument. I could've easily burned it. But I now know you reclaimed your palace, just the way I wanted."

She stilled, her breathing hitching. "What?"

"I knew once you heard word of Imogen's death, along with

Mouse and Maddie now hidden somewhere, that you would come crawling out from your cowardly hole." He paused, his brown gaze boring into hers. "You're not the only one I want. I also want the one who has been obsessed with you. The bastard who killed my queen." Rav glanced past her, a vicious smile spreading across his face. "And right on time."

Two broad male vampires carried Chess through the door with three more females behind them. After murdering all his guards, it hadn't taken her brother long to find a whole new set.

Chess didn't show any of his cards as he smirked. "Pleasant seeing you again, *my king*." His eyes met hers and she looked away.

Rav ignored the prince, studying Ever with his lip curled in disgust. "I smell his arousal all over you. Chess has been obsessed with finding you for years. Honestly, his infatuation was ungodly. He killed Imogen after releasing Mouse to get you out of hiding. His obsession drove him to kill his own mother. *My* Imogen." Spittle flew from his mouth, red staining his face.

That was what her brother believed? He'd conjured up this reason for why he'd found Chess that day holding Imogen's bloody heart. She knew her brother's mind, when it got scientific, when it went elsewhere—he would build on a hypothesis and not shy away from it. In his mind, he was always right.

"I didn't kill her," Chess said through gritted teeth. Even now, after all they shared, she shouldn't have been surprised that he didn't confess the truth about Maddie, but she still was.

Rav continued to ignore the prince as he spoke to Ever, "I don't want you dead, sister. That's old news now."

What a pretentious bastard… "What do you want then? All you ever do is ramble on."

"Oh, Ever, you know I'll never stop that." He took a step back, fastening the button of his trousers. "You're my sister. You made mistakes. I made mistakes. We should make amends."

She wrinkled her nose. "Amends?"

"I'm uniting the territories and you will be my loyal subject, as it should've been to begin with. In the mortal world, I would've been the rightful heir. When we return to the palace, you'll have to earn your way back into my good graces. Be grateful—the little prince won't have the same chance as you."

She sucked in a sharp breath, but he continued, "I want my sister back. Do you agree to the terms?" His eyes, matching hers, stared at her, pleading.

Rav… He wanted her back as a sister? After everything he'd done? She remembered them as children, trading their instruments, laughing, playing, then as adults having tea with their parents, when they were mortal and everything was different.

Ever thought and thought, her mind spinning, her heart beating wildly, calming, focusing. "With pleasure," she finally said.

A shouted *no* poured out from Chess's lips, just before a female snapped his neck.

CHAPTER TWENTY-THREE

CHESS

A groan slipped from Chess's lips as he roused. *Fucking terrible nightmare*. Ever turning on him, Rav capturing him. His head throbbed with the aftereffects of having … died. *Fuck!*

Chess bolted upright, only to be jerked to a halt, his muscles aching. Metal cuffs bound his wrists over his head and heavy chains held his ankles in the lower corners of a table. If this were any other situation, he may have been excited to be bound, but then his predicament slowly sank in. "Oh, fuck no," he growled. Based on the stone ceiling and the blood splattering the walls, he was in the dungeon. Not to be unexpected, given the situation, but it was this particular table that had his pulse racing. He wasn't keen on the idea of having his limbs slowly torn off like the others who had been there before him.

"You're awake," Rav sang as he burst through the solid metal door and kicked it shut behind him. His white, red-tipped hair was pulled back in a ponytail and the sleeves of his black tunic were rolled to the elbow.

"You put me on the rack?" Chess seethed. "Is this the best you can do?"

Rav *tsked*. "We don't want to start with the big guns and ruin all the fun."

"I didn't kill my mother!" His roar echoed off the walls as he tugged at his bindings. Logically, he knew there was no getting out of them. Even if one broke, three more held him down. Rav would have the problem fixed before he could break free again. Same as it had been with other vampires Rav had toyed with in the past.

"There's no need to admit it." Rav strolled to the wheel positioned beneath the ledge of the table, out of Chess's sight, and gave it a turn.

The metal tugged at Chess's ankles. It wasn't painful—not yet. It was only a warning of what was to come when Rav inevitably stretched the prince's limbs to their breaking point. At least Rav wasn't using him in any of his science experiments at the moment. He'd seen vampires cut apart and allowed to heal around new appendages. Eyes plucked out, fucked with, and reinserted. Torture was definitely preferrable to any of that and the effects were only temporary.

"Don't you want to destroy who *actually* killed my mother?" Chess asked. He wouldn't give the Hatter up, not only because of how much it would hurt Ever, but because Maddie hadn't been the one to betray him. Ever had. He winced. *Fuck*. It didn't matter. For some reason, he still … loved her. "It wasn't me," he said again, quieter this time.

"Chess." Rav chuckled humorlessly. "I walked in on you holding her heart."

"I picked it up, arsehole." He lifted his head and let it slam back to the table. "She was the only one who gave a shit about me—why would I rip out her heart?"

"Because I've always known you to be an ungrateful bastard. And your mother? She said you reminded her too much of your father." He scoffed. "We should've ripped out your heart like we did him, but I'll remedy that soon enough."

Chess released an exaggerated sigh. "Yes, by all means. Use your toys. Break me apart. I still won't be guilty. Ask your sister—she knows the truth."

"My sister has agreed to align with me and believes you're guilty." Rav spun the wheel a few more clicks until Chess's joints were stretched, *burning,* then he circled the table in quick, predatory steps. When Rav stopped near the prince's head, he leaned down and whispered, "She's turned on you, it seems."

But she had claimed to believe him innocent. *No, she knew I was.* Maddie had done the deed… Which was why it made perfect sense for her to proclaim Chess guilty to Rav. Ever had betrayed Chess. Taken his heart and stomped on it. Perhaps it would've been better if he had remained alone and miserable. Whatever physical torture Rav planned to inflict was nothing compared to the invisible stake in his chest.

"Always the liar, you are," Chess quipped. "Given your exceptional skill, I would think you'd be able to tell when other people were being truthful or not."

A blade sliced Chess's cheek before he could even register one rested in Rav's hand. He hissed at the sudden sting, yet it didn't matter—he'd been through worse and it would heal in moments. The blade cut again, this time his neck.

"Before the fun begins, we need to bleed you a bit," Rav explained as if he were bored. "Can't have you healing too fast."

Starving while being wounded would be physiological torture. Each new cut or break would drive him closer to the brink of madness. Chess had seen a few torture sessions in the past and found them rather unnecessary. The repeated stabbings, acid baths, fang extractions… There was no reason not to kill them and be done with it. Though, he supposed, some did deserve it. The mortals who had mistreated him after his mother left for Wonderland would have earned themselves some time in this dungeon.

Rav began humming "Waltz Of The Flowers," starting the melody low then higher, a deadly edge to it as he cut and cut *and cut* again. Warm blood trickled from the slices, gliding over the skin on his face, neck, and arms. He fought against the bindings, struggling to break free, despite knowing there was no escape.

He would die there.

Perhaps not on the rack or even in the dungeon if Rav decided to make his execution public, but what did it matter? Ever betrayed him. His mother was gone. All of Scarlet thought he was a traitor and everyone in Ivory loathed him. He was alone for the third time in his life, and he wasn't sure if he had the same strength he'd summoned as a child. The same will to survive.

Fucking hell.

What was he thinking? Chess was *not* going to accept his own death. That was the heartbreak talking and that was not like him. A smirk tugged at his lips. All he had to do was wait until Rav thought he was weak enough to remove him from the rack. Once he was transferred to the next torture device, he would make his move. Kill Rav, find Ever… Deal with her somehow. He wasn't sure what he would do when he saw her again, if anything, but he would fight his way out of this damned place, fang and nail.

"You won't find this amusing for long," Rav warned. He stared down at Chess with a malicious glint in his eyes. Then he slit Chess's throat.

Chess tried to drag in a breath. Blood filled his mouth instead of air and it sprayed outward when he coughed, splattering across his face. The room spun, but not for long as he succumbed to his second death that day.

When he woke again, his throat was drier than chalk. Chess shifted on the table only to, once again, find himself strapped to the rack. How had he forgotten that bit? His shoulders ached from being stretched upward, while the metal dug into his ankles. The dried blood from Rav's cuts itched his skin. He let out a sharp breath and tried to focus on the stone ceiling, but the details were fuzzy.

Hunger consumed him, ravenous, as his head throbbed, his veins pulsing. "Fuck," he rasped.

The door opened as if someone had heard him speak. He rolled his head to the side expecting to see Rav returning for another bloody round. Instead, a female with vibrant red hair, spilling down her shoulders over a lacy black gown, approached. His heart leapt in his chest.

"Mother?" he croaked.

As she inched closer and leaned over him, her face took shape. It didn't have the familiar angles of his mother but was round, soft... Of course. Because his mother was dead. He squeezed his eyes shut and shook away the delusion.

When he opened them again, the female gave him a lopsided smile full of pity. "Sorry, Prince. It's just me."

"A—Anna?" he asked, barely remembering her name. She had been one of his mother's friends who lived outside of the inner city and only came to the palace for the parties. "What are you doing here?"

"Rav asked me to come," she said in a soft voice. "He wanted vampires he could trust around him after Imogen's death."

"Oh, right." Ari had mentioned that before he killed her. Chess tried to clear his throat, but the motion only made it worse. "I suppose you're here to exact a bit of revenge for yourself then? Should I be expecting all of my mother's friends to stop by?" Wouldn't that be just like Rav? To let everyone have a piece of the murderous prince.

"I hold no ill-will for what you did. We are what we are." She brandished a large ice pick. "However, I did come here to help Rav and I've been instructed to kill you again."

"Of course, though for the record, I didn't murder her." He grunted. "Before you carry out your orders, how long has it been?"

"Since they brought you here? Two days. Most of it, you've spent dead and bleeding." She patted the top of his head. "This should be the last false death for you. Next time you wake, I imagine you'll be weak enough for Rav to do what he wishes."

Torture him. Ruin him. Kill him.

"And Ever?" He swallowed deeply.

"The White Queen and her brother are getting along well. With any luck, they will unite the kingdoms in no time." She smiled as if Rav was actually doing something beneficial for Wonderland. Chess knew better—anything his mother's lover did was for his own benefit. But what was he getting out of reconciling with Ever? She wouldn't give him Ivory.

Shit. His mind was too muddled to think clearly. Who was telling the truth? He supposed it wouldn't matter once he freed himself and killed Rav. Then the only truth that mattered would be his own. All he had to do was hold onto enough strength. Not impossible… Not probable, but this was life or death.

"You better get on with it then," he said with a smirk.

Anna lifted the ice pick and adjusted her grip. "Apologies," she said and drove it into his chest.

It was the scent of blood that woke Chess next. Fresh, and from the source, based on the richness. His hunger roared to life. It clawed through him like an angry beast, demanding he partake in the feeding.

His limbs jerked against the chains as he lurched upward. A feral snarl ripped from his chest. Rav stood at the foot of the table, fangs deep in a mortal woman's neck. One of the slaves who stayed in a trance, Chess assumed. Their gazes locked and Rav smirked as he drank. A stream of crimson flowed down the column of her neck when she leaned into Rav's chest, her head thrown back in pleasure.

Chess pulled harder against his shackles, which, if he wasn't mistaken, had been drawn tighter. The pain radiating from his shoulder made him think it was dislocated already, but fuck if he cared. The metallic scent wafted through the air, caressing his nostrils, luring him in to the seductive odor. He zeroed in on the blood pulsing beneath the female's dark flesh. As his cravings increased, he would do anything for a simple taste, even if it meant gnawing off his arm.

"Now, brother. That's just selfish," Ever said from the doorway. Her white hair was carefully pinned like a crown around her head and she wore a stark white, formfitting dress that hugged every curve. His cock stirred in anticipation, not only for a meal but for a pleasureful fuck.

A hate-fuck.

Rav dropped his fangs, letting the woman slump to the floor with a dazed expression on her face. "Isn't it?" He laughed and turned to leer at Chess. "Come, sister." Ever stepped into the room, keeping her gaze averted, and up to her brother's side. He wrapped an arm around her shoulders and licked the blood from his lips. "Are you ready to dole out a bit of justice?"

Her gaze pierced Chess and his pulse spiked. A deep growl vibrated through the room as his hunger fed his fury.

"I am," Ever said, her lips curling into a vicious smile.

CHAPTER TWENTY-FOUR

EVER

"**S**tab him in the heart with this," Rav said, shoving a lock of hair over his shoulder. He then handed Ever an obsidian dagger encrusted in ruby jewels from his boot. "I think he deserves one more false death before we bring him to Imogen's gardens. I don't care how weak he is."

"Wouldn't want him to struggle even a little now, would we?" Ever grinned, taking the blade from her brother. She turned to Chess, looking straight into his yellow irises. He didn't say a bloody word as she drifted closer, rotating the dagger in her grasp while inhaling his pine scent. Lifting the blade in both hands, she plunged it directly into his heart with a sickening squelch, just as she'd always planned to do, right before ripping out his heart.

Only, Ever hadn't ripped his heart out as she'd dreamt about for almost four years. Not yet. Her pulse pounded feverishly, and the thought of what she'd just done brought her no pleasure, only a sickness swirling in her stomach. Yet she excelled at hiding her true emotions—that was what a royal was always taught to

441

do. She continued to neutralize her expression as she wiped the prince's blood on the ivory skirt of her silk dress. "Now what, brother?"

Rav took the blade from her and shouted, his deep voice booming off the walls, "Guards!" The door opened to the familiar vampire with red hair, loose curls cascading down to her waist. Four other guards stood behind her. Lifting a long finger, Rav motioned at the female. "Anna, undo the traitorous prince's bindings." He stepped beside Ever, tucking the dagger back in his boot. "Now, sister, we need to discuss what will happen after the kingdoms are united."

Ever folded her arms, a line forming between her brows. "Are you going to continue the unwilling turning?" She knew if she agreed with him on everything, he would see through her. Rav was no fool though—that was why he'd kept her in the dungeon these past few days instead of allowing her to walk around the palace freely. While being held as a prisoner, she wasn't completely treated as such. She was fed properly, given new attire, and guarded by the red-headed vampire, Anna, who had remained silent, even when braiding Ever's hair into a crown. Even the blankets in her cell were made of silk while the other prisoners had none at all. Yet her brother had only visited her briefly each day since, she assumed, he was busy torturing Chess or fucking his female vampires.

"No," Rav finally answered. "I do believe if we are to start fresh, I'm going to have to make a change myself. Instead of turning mortals unwillingly, I will focus more on my sciences and toy with the humans, do more than leave them in a trance. Perhaps I'll come up with new theories and hypotheses about vampire creation and alteration. Maybe even *create* something new altogether." His eyes grew wild as they did when they'd been children, when he would experiment with dead animals.

Ever took a deep swallow. He was sounding positively mad, like one of the doctors from a mortal's horror book. This was even worse than turning an unwilling mortal into a vampire.

Before she could speak, Rav snatched her by the wrist and

drew her to him, squeezing her flesh roughly. "After Chess is murdered, you'll retrieve the Hatter and her sister, then bring them to me. The prince helped Mouse escape and that means you know where they are. They'll be executed next. We shall give them a swift death and then, finally, we'll hunt down Imogen's bastard Knave, for betraying her. Since we never found the newly-turned vampire he helped escape, we'll need to get her location out of him before he dies. Our slates will be wiped clean, and you and I will start anew." Rav's eyes beamed, a dysfunctional sort of gleam. He still didn't know that Ferris was connected to Maddie and Mouse, and he hadn't discovered that Alice was human again or Noah's sister either.

"The prince is untied, Your Majesty," Anna said, bowing her head before standing in line with the four other vampire guards.

Rav released Ever and grabbed Anna by the chin, inspecting her face. "I never noticed before, but you look a lot like Imogen, especially in that black dress. Tonight, you'll put on one of her gowns and stay in my bed."

"My pleasure." Anna bowed again, but Ever could've sworn she'd seen the vampire curl her lips in disgust. Ever continued to keep her expression blank as Rav hoisted Chess's limp and bloody body over his shoulder. Even though his only visible wound was the one she created, she would never forget hearing his growls of pain through the wall beside her cell as Rav tormented the prince. Ever loathed herself for not standing up to her brother sooner, for getting caught at the club before killing him.

The guards led them through the palace hall, two vampires in front of them and three behind. Several of the entranced human servants paced up and down the halls, causing Ever's chest to tighten. All the décor had been taken off the walls from when she'd been there last, and in its place were anatomical hearts, *hundreds*, painted across the entire surface. It looked more like an obsession than a decoration. By the fresh smell of paint, they were added not long ago. She was surprised Rav hadn't covered the walls in Imogen's portraits that the Queen of Hearts had commissioned to be painted every year. The palace's attic was full of the finished pieces, where Ever assumed they'd been collecting dust.

Over the past several days, Ever hadn't slept, not once. It had felt just as it had the last time she fled her castle, like she was powerless. As she mulled things over again and again while walking down hall after hall of anatomical hearts, she wasn't certain how to get out of this blasted situation, how to save Chess. Even if she were to confess the truth about Maddie murdering Imogen, Rav wouldn't believe it—he would think she was admitting that only to save Chess. At this point, she needed a damn miracle, and she didn't know if she would be blessed enough to gain one of those. What she did believe was that Chess would die hating her, thinking she'd betrayed him, and that she'd pleasured him just to get him in this position.

A stocky guard with blue dreadlocks opened the door outside. The warm breeze rumpled Ever's hair and dress as they trudged through the rose gardens. A whiff of the overwhelming flowery scent tickled her senses. Thick crimson vines, with obsidian thorns, wrapped around the gazebos, and near the one in the center, stood two vampire guards.

They stopped in front of the garden structure, dark red blood staining most of its gray color. By the rich smell mixed with decay, some of the blood was fresh.

"Tie him up," Rav demanded, handing Chess to two females. They grabbed the chains attached to the poles on the gazebo and cuffed his arms, then stretched out his legs to bind them to the chains at the bottom, his body appearing in the shape of a hollow star.

The prince looked pitiful, so helpless, nothing like his cocky self. "What now?" Ever asked, breaking the tense silence.

"Rouse him with your viola." Rav clapped his hands and Anna grabbed a brand-new viola from inside the gazebo, its wood-stained cherry red. Too beautiful. Too perfect. Too new. All it did was remind her of how Rav had broken her old one. Not meaning to, her expression slipped. Anna caught it before

Ever masked it, but the vampire didn't say a word, only handed her the viola and bow.

"The prince has been enjoying 'Waltz Of The Flowers,' so let's give him what he wants." Rav grinned, his teeth bared wickedly in delight.

Focus, Ever. A little longer. But for how long? She didn't know what the hell would come after this. Her fingers trembled, yet she did what she knew how to do—she played, letting the notes flow from the strings, low and gentle, growing bolder, stronger, filling her heart, her blood, her soul. With everything in her, she tried to play it differently, so it wouldn't remind Chess of what he'd experienced while hearing it.

She didn't know how many times she'd played the song before Chess's eyes peeled open, his gaze meeting hers, no one else's. A smile tugged at his lips, then it fell away as he must've remembered where he was and everything that had happened to him. She didn't know all Rav had done…

The prince lifted his arms and they fell back into place. Even through his weakness, his usual smirk made an appearance. "What's wrong? Not ready to say goodbye to me yet?"

"You deserved everything you've gotten, you piece of shit," Rav spat, taking a leather holster of daggers from one of the guards and stepping beside Ever. "I was going to have my sister start with cutting off your legs, but I'm growing bored of your voice so we'll have her carve out your vocal cords instead." He paused. "Perhaps this first though."

A dagger tore toward Chess, whistling with the wind, before striking straight through his left thigh. The prince sucked in a sharp breath, then released a grunt as another pierced his right leg. Blood bloomed to the surface as two more cut through the air, each landing in one of his arms.

"Fuck you!" Chess snarled, his eyes igniting a fire of their own.

"Is that any way to talk to your king?" Rav taunted. "Your father loved you, you know. But he was naïve as fuck and believed your mother loved him. She was only ever with him because she conceived his child before marriage."

Chess didn't take the bait, only drew up his lips in a small smile.

Rav halted before throwing another blade. "I suppose I won't throw a dagger at your cock, but if you give me another one of your pathetic smirks, I'll rip it right off, Prince."

Ever had to think fast and think now. If she tried to kill her brother at that precise moment, the vampires would end her life before she could set Chess free.

"Now, forget the vocal cords, cut out the bastard's heart, Ever." Rav handed her the same dagger from his boot that she'd used on the prince earlier. "Once that's done, we'll drain his blood so I can use it in my lab."

Ever wanted to dig her nails into her brother, rip off his flesh piece by piece and use *that* for an experiment. Her lungs were thirsty for more air—she felt as if she couldn't breathe, but she kept it as steady as she could and nodded. She set down the viola, then padded toward Chess, avoiding his brilliant eyes so she could think, calculate.

Taking a breath, she stopped in front of him, finally peering up at his eyes. He watched her, several emotions burning there. Disbelief. Hate. Melancholy. But something else, something bright, strong, something like … love.

Trust me, she mouthed and stabbed him in the chest, the soft squish echoing. She slowly carved in a circular motion, tears filling her eyes while he groaned. A horrid thought washed over her because the next step was ripping out the heart. This was going farther than she could've ever imagined and time had run out—she couldn't think of a way to save him. Even though Wonderland depended on her, even though the vampires of Ivory and Scarlet did too, she wouldn't push herself to do the next step of this. Maddie, Mouse, Noah, and Ferris could continue what she'd started. If something happened to her, they could finish Rav.

Perhaps she was a coward.

Perhaps there were better vampires who could've been

queen.

But she was who she was and that was what she'd come to accept.

Whirling around, Ever hurled the dagger, and just as it was about to penetrate her brother's heart, the vampire with dreadlocks jumped in front of him, blocking the blow.

That was her one chance, and she knew it had been a long shot. Ever lunged forward, fangs bared, but her brother was stronger, faster, knocking her to the ground on her back. A groan escaped her as pain radiated up her spine from the impact.

"You weren't supposed to do that, sister," Rav growled. "Perhaps you're just as obsessed with the traitorous prince as he is with you."

"No!" Chess croaked. "Don't hurt her!"

Rav slammed his hands on the sides of Ever's head, a pain shooting through her from his crushing. Then when her neck started to crack, a sharp cry ripping from her throat as she writhed, his body slumped on top of hers. Her brother's hands fell from her, and the world spun, but she didn't hesitate to shove the bastard's body off her. Ever pushed to her feet, ignoring the spasms in her neck as she stumbled, her wild gaze connecting with Anna's. The vampire's hand cradled Rav's bloody heart, a neutral expression on her face.

A slender female guard lunged forward, tearing Anna's throat out with her fangs, blood spraying across the already red roses. She tossed Anna's body to the ground, then spun to face the White Queen. But it was too late, Ever had the vampire's head between her hands, kicking her foot against the female's chest, and ripped it from the shoulders.

"Don't you dare touch the White Queen!" Chess spat to the rest of the vampires who stood there, watching, his eyes wide while Ever waited to see who she would need to murder next. "I'm your true king and I swear on all of Wonderland that you *will* obey me."

"Why would we obey someone who killed our queen?" a dark-haired male shouted.

"Bloody hell! For the last time, I didn't kill my fucking mother. The vampire who did it is dead and I didn't give her a pretty death either. Rav was a delusional piece of shit who lied to you. Things need to change around here and the White Queen and I will be part of that change," he panted. "Well, once she gets me down anyway." With how badly he needed to feed, Ever was surprised he'd been able to get all those words out and not faint.

The guards stood there, silent, questions swirling in their gazes, but they didn't make a move toward them.

"Get him some blood. Now!" Ever shouted, unsure if anyone would listen.

But then the male with dreadlocks stormed in the palace's direction, while Ever went toward Chess, not turning her back on the vampires as she removed each of his chains.

"I thought you betrayed me, Queenie," Chess whispered.

"I'm a pretty good deceiver, aren't I, Princeling?"

"Ah, I'm not sure you can call me that anymore since I'm king now." A smirk crossed his face, then his body slumped as she unfastened the last chain. She easily caught Chess, letting him lean on her as she brought them both to their knees, his chest heaving against her.

Ever wished she could've thanked Anna—she didn't know her at all, but perhaps she was tired of what Imogen and Rav had been doing too. Or perhaps it was something as simple as she hadn't wanted to dress as Imogen in Rav's bed. Whatever it was, she'd helped save Wonderland.

The guards continued to watch, their lips parted as they must've come to the realization that there was more between Ever and Chess than Scarlet and Ivory working together. And in that moment, she realized what it was too, what she'd been feeling.

Love.

"Ivory and Scarlet united," Ever called out to all who were listening as she held tightly onto Chess, protecting him fiercely.

"United," the guards said in return, sinking to their knees

before them, their heads bowed.

It was a true start.

A new beginning.

In more ways than one.

CHAPTER TWENTY-FIVE

CHESS

The carriage clattered over the cobbled streets as it made its way out of Scarlet and onto the bumpy dirt roads that would take Chess and Ever to Ivory. It was not the fastest route nor the most comfortable, but it made a statement. Bringing out the royal carriage said they were in no rush. Just a couple of royals, traversing their lands in style, all while the grind of the wheels announced their presence and made it clear they weren't afraid of shit.

Two days after defeating Rav, both the King of Scarlet and Queen of Ivory needed all of Wonderland to know they were untouchable. Thankfully, Anna had been the one to kill the fucking bastard in front of witnesses, but Chess would never be free of suspicion over his mother's death—there would always be *someone* who believed the lies. He wasn't foolish enough to pretend that couldn't lead to problems in the future. And then there was Ever, who had hidden herself away for four years. Her reputation would be rebuilt, but it would take time and effort.

They had stayed in Scarlet long enough to send the enslaved mortals home and see Rav's body burn in a royal funeral, though he hadn't deserved it. Even Ever had appeared conflicted over the honor. The vampires in Scarlet seemed appeased enough afterward that Chess felt comfortable leaving guards in charge so he could escort Ever back to Ivory. As rightful heir to the throne, he didn't think anyone would try to steal it already, but he wouldn't risk an ambush as Ever left his territory. If he didn't see her safely back to her doorstep, he wouldn't be able to focus on a damned thing.

"We should've sent the carriage to Ivory without us in it," Ever grumbled as it bounced violently over a rock in their path.

Chess rubbed the side of his head where it had slammed into the carriage window. "I think we've earned a little rest."

After all, he had been starved, repeatedly murdered, and stabbed in the chest by the female he loved. As for Ever, she'd been a moment away from having her head ripped off by her brother, a moment where Chess had nearly broken apart. She'd played Rav as well as she played her instruments, and that brief time when he believed she'd joined her brother was almost as painful as the torture. The helplessness he felt toward the end, before Anna saved the day, still lingered. He imagined it would for a while yet, but he couldn't bring himself to admit that out loud.

Ever grabbed his chin playfully. "This is not restful, Your Majesty."

He chuckled and wrapped his hand around her wrist, drawing her closer. Their lips nearly touched as he nudged her nose with his. "I know more exciting ways to make the carriage rock."

"I thought you wanted rest?" she pointed out, arching a brow.

More than rest, he needed to get closer to her. To forget everything and focus entirely on the one good thing in his long, wretched life. Chess grinned and hoisted her onto his lap in one fluid movement. A beautiful laugh escaped her shapely lips, her deep brown eyes latched onto his. The skirt of her white lace dress rode up to her hips as she straddled him, her heat settling against his growing length. Fuck if he cared whether the coachman heard them or not.

"I do," he agreed and kissed her neck. His hands slid up her thighs and around to grip her arse. "But why rest when there is fun to be had?"

Ever tilted her head aside to give him better access to her neck. His lips roamed over her skin. One hand left her arse to tangle in her neatly pinned hair and the other tugged the top of her dress down her shoulder. He rained kisses across her collarbone, savoring her, and felt her center moisten against the fabric of his trousers. A low growl left him as he shifted to unbutton himself.

The carriage jolted again, sending Ever's chest straight into Chess's face. He looked up at her and smirked. "I rather like the carriage, actually."

"Hmm, you would," she whispered. "Though I must admit, it might have its benefits."

Her hands went between them to help pull his cock free. When her soft fingers wrapped around his length, he closed his eyes with a grunt. She pumped him slowly, sliding her thumb over his slick tip. Her touch was unlike anything he'd experienced before. She seemed to know exactly how to move, how fast, how hard, as if she were made for him. Perhaps she was.

"Damn, Queenie." He pulled her hand away gently when he felt his release start to build. As much as he would've loved to come, he had every intention of bringing her pleasure first. Quickly, he slid her panties to the side. Their eyes met and a sense of *rightness* flooded through him, making his pulse race.

"Chess," she pleaded.

"Go on then," he dared.

Ever drew in a sharp breath and lined his hard length up with her folds. Sinking down slowly, she shared her heat with him. When she'd taken him fully, Chess gripped her hips tightly to hold himself back. His body wanted to move, to please, but he gave her every ounce of control instead. Ever ground against him, shifting her hips in small circles. The most exquisite moan slipped from her mouth, and he growled in response.

"*Chess*," she breathed, this time against his lips just before she kissed him. Their mouths collided, their tongues dancing together. Ever wrapped her hands around the back of his neck and rocked her hips. Chess felt every inch of her as she moved languidly on him, making him practically vibrate with pleasure.

As the carriage continued to bump and jostle, Ever's pace grew faster, harder. Chess shifted his hips up to meet her, his heart accelerating with the friction. His breath turned ragged and he broke the kiss, trailing to her neck once more.

Fuck. He would never get over how perfect she was. How perfect she felt. Tasted. His fangs dropped at the memory of her sweet blood. She shivered against him as he dragged them along her neck, then moaned when he sunk them into her tender flesh. Her blood flooded his mouth and stars flashed behind his eyes while she slammed down on him again and again. When he pulled away with a deep breath, Ever smiled at him, her fangs on display.

Chess tilted his head to the side in invitation and held his breath in anticipation. The moment her fangs broke into his neck, he knew he wouldn't last. She drank deeply. Fucked beautifully. His heart nearly exploded with the combination of love, happiness, and utter bliss.

"Ever," Chess roared as his climax rushed through him. Ever cried out when she met her own pleasure, fluttering around his cock.

"Fuck," he breathed. "I love you, Queenie."

Ever settled her head into the crook of his neck, still drawing deep breaths. "I love you, King of Scarlet."

Hearing those words from her mouth was what he'd been waiting for his whole damn life, and he hadn't known it. "I told you that I know *many* ways to make this trip more exciting," he said, smirking against her ear.

She laughed. "Hmm, you may have to show me in order for

me to believe you, *Your Majesty.*"

"Naturally." He chuckled, and spun her around so her back was flush with his chest. Guiding her legs together, he widened his own. "Hold onto something."

The carriage slowed to a stop and Chess flicked aside the deep red curtains. The Ivory Palace loomed outside with its spires and parapets. Chess released a silent sigh. He wasn't ready to bid the White Queen goodbye yet—not ever. They would reunite, of course, but that didn't make leaving any easier.

"You're home," he sang, letting the curtain fall again.

"Already?" Ever shifted on the bench and patted at her mussed hair.

Chess chuckled. "You're a mess, my queen."

"I suppose I should thank you for that." She gave him a wink.

"No thank you necessary." He leaned over and nibbled playfully at her creamy neck. "I'm willing to repeat the process any time you wish."

She turned in her seat to face him fully and took his cheeks in her hands. "Soon."

Chess studied her face and found something he couldn't recognize there. He saw her affection for him, her love, but there was something else. Something he didn't like—not one bit. "What is it?"

"Nothing," she whispered.

"Liar." He nipped at her lips. "Tell me."

"It's nothing. Things just feel like they'll be different now." She rubbed her thumbs along his cheekbones. "So I suppose I'm soaking up the moment."

"I'm not leaving you," he insisted. "Things will be different, but that was the point of all of this, wasn't it?"

Ever nodded. "You're right."

Chess understood then that she was mourning her brother.

Now that the danger had passed, now that she was back home, the reality was descending. Anna had murdered her brother and, while they both had needed the bastard dead, she had loved him once. There was no shame in it. He wasn't exactly looking forward to going back to Scarlet and picking up the pieces his mother and Rav had left. And to do it alone… At least Ever had friends by her side.

"Come on," he said gently. "Let's get you settled inside."

After a lingering kiss, he opened the door and held his hand out to help her down. She placed her hand into his palm and stepped onto the grass, sparing a nod to the carriage coachman Chess had commandeered from the garden at the Ruby Heart Palace. The main doors banged open and Maddie raced across the drawbridge with a wide smile, leaping at her friend in a flurry of purple fabric. Ever slid one foot back to take the impact. The two females wrapped their arms around each other and laughed. Chess turned away to give them their moment and found Noah, Ferris, and Mouse hurrying toward them.

"Ever!" Mouse said with a smile. "We were so worried."

"It's done," the White Queen assured them. "Rav is dead."

The group descended into conversation. Or more like an interrogation, as far as Chess was concerned. A thousand questions swirled through the air about what happened. Ever barely got the answers out before a new one was asked.

Chess made an exaggerated sigh and pushed his way back to Ever's side to save her from an endless bombardment. "Enough with the questions," he said, rolling his eyes. "Play inquisition later after we've had a bath."

"Ignore his insufferable manners," Ever said, "but I do need a bath. We'll get into all the details tomorrow, Maddie."

"We'll have a tea party." Maddie grinned.

Ever laughed, then threw a wink at the foursome before heading toward the castle with Chess. "They just want to know what happened."

"And *I* just want to clean up in the bath, preferably with you." He kissed the top of her head. "Call me selfish, but there will be plenty of time to fill them in after I leave."

"Oh, you are certainly selfish." Her lips tugged upward at the corners. "But I'll forgive you this time."

"You better."

It wasn't until Ever was fast asleep after a bath, fucking twice more, and another, longer, relaxing bath, that Chess slipped from her bedroom. They had both needed to distract themselves with each other's bodies, but reality couldn't be avoided forever. Before he left to start things anew in Scarlet, he wanted to make the first step toward a life partially in Ivory.

"Prince," Maddie drawled when he poked his head into one of the drawing rooms. Her brow arched at the sight of him and Noah tensed beside her on a small settee. In front of them, a fire crackled, casting the room in a warm glow. "Where's Ever?"

"I'm a king now. And she's sleeping." He smirked, stepped into the room, and folded his arms across his chest. "I actually wanted to speak to you, Hatter."

She wrinkled her nose. "Why?"

"I was hoping we could have a civil conversation." He glanced at Noah. "Alone."

"Fuck no," Noah said.

At the same time Maddie let out a suspicious, "Ooo-kay."

"Maddie, I'm not leaving you alone with him," Noah whispered urgently.

"I'm *right* here," Chess scoffed.

"It's fine," Maddie assured him, although she still eyed Chess. "Could you please give us a moment?"

Noah hesitated, glancing between them, before stalking toward the door. "I'm waiting right outside. If I hear anything—"

Chess groaned his annoyance. "Yes, yes. If she screams, please do rush back in."

"You really shouldn't goad him." Maddie cocked her head. "It's very unnecessary."

"Many things are *unnecessary*." He shuffled farther into the room and lifted a dusty book from the mantelpiece. "Yet, they are still done."

She leaned against the back of the settee and blinked, staring at him as though trying to read him. "What do you want?"

"To make peace. For Ever's sake," he added. He didn't give a shit otherwise. "It looks like we'll be around each other often, even if we both hate it. So, I figured, it might be beneficial to have more than a tentative agreement not to murder one another."

She shrugged, her fingers skimming the brim of her hat. "If it weren't for Ever, I would gladly use your skin as a pincushion."

He offered half a smile. "And I would strangle you with the ribbon from your own hat."

"That settles it then," she sang, a small grin on her lips. "You may leave."

He laughed, then quickly sobered. "I…" It was so easy to admit this to Ever, but in this moment, he was exposing himself to someone he should hate. "I love Ever."

This time when she blinked, it was rapid. But then a huge grin took up her whole face. "The heartless prince somehow found a heart."

"Well, let's not go getting crazy now," he said with a raised brow. "I'm leaving for Scarlet soon, so I wanted to ask you to stay with her. I know you've likely got your own life to start now that my mother isn't holding Mouse hostage and—"

"I'm not going anywhere," she interrupted. "This was my home long before my cottage was, though I'm keeping that too."

Chess set the book down and held his hands up. "No one will touch it."

"Good. I had to leave behind many hats."

"I'm sure." He chuckled. "Ever is lucky to have you. All of you."

"We are lucky to have each other." Maddie waved a hand in

the air and studied him. "Fine, *King*. You've talked me into it. We'll be friends."

"We'll be … friendly," he amended. Though he hadn't asked for friendship from her, he found he didn't entirely hate the idea.

She stood and offered her hand. "Ah, once you've had my special tea, you'll change your mind. Friends, it will be."

Tea sounded horrible, if he was being honest. It had never tasted good to him, but especially as a vampire. Still, he smiled and shook her hand. "Make sure your male gets the memo, yeah?"

"I'll pass it along, but I make no promises." She pulled her hand back and adjusted her hat. "Now if you don't mind, we were having a bit of a romantic evening."

Chess spun on his heel and slinked away. *There.* That was settled. He grinned at Noah on his way out of the room. "Do continue, lover boy."

A featherlight touch along Chess's nose woke him. He grinned, knowing without opening his eyes that it was Ever. "You should do that a bit lower," he breathed.

"Hush you." She laughed and playfully smacked his shoulder. "It's morning."

"And I must leave," he said, voicing the unspoken part of her sentence. He opened his eyes and stared up into hers. His reluctance to leave her was mirrored in her expression. "Though I'd much rather stay right here."

Ever smiled. "I'll keep the sheets warm for your return."

Chess rolled on top of her and kissed her fiercely. He really did need to get back to Scarlet but the longer their lips touched, the harder it was to pull away. In all honesty, he shouldn't have left immediately after Anna murdered Rav, and it was imperative he get back to stake his claim. Weed out traitors. Set new laws. He was exhausted just thinking of it all.

"I'll miss you," he mumbled against her lips. "But not for long."

She sucked in a breath.

"Because I'll be back before the sheets even have time to cool." He pressed a quick kiss to her forehead and slid from the bed before he could talk himself into staying a *little* longer.

"We'll both be kept quite busy," she offered. "Which means we'll be preoccupied."

Chess buttoned his trousers and swiped his vest off the floor. "Not preoccupied enough."

He put one knee on the bed and leaned over for one last kiss. Their lips touched, lingered, caressed, for only a moment, but Chess committed the entire feeling to memory. "You taste sweet," he said as he leaned back. "Stay here and rest. Don't see me out or I might change my mind about going."

Ever settled back into the soft pillows, only a sheet covering her naked body, and studied him. With her white hair tumbling over her shoulder, she looked every bit the goddess she was. "Be safe and hurry back."

"One week," he vowed. That was as long as he thought he could manage without laying eyes on her again. "Even if it's for one night, I'll be back next week."

Ever's eyes lit up. "If not, I may have to take another journey to the Ruby Heart Palace."

EPILOGUE

EVER

Ever paced back and forth in her lily garden, the trees around her blooming with bright silver and white flowers, as she glided her bow across the viola's strings. This time, she chose to play a modern song she'd heard in the mortal world at a club once, letting the bow kiss and meld against the strings, the deep notes surrounding her while she got lost in the melody's richness. She smiled at the way she was changing it to fit her own classical edge.

Two weeks had passed since a Scarlet vampire had ripped out her brother's heart, two weeks since Ever had realized she loved Chess, two weeks since they'd last brought each other to bliss, two weeks since he'd left the Ivory Palace, and two weeks that she'd missed the damn princeling with every aching fiber in her… Kingling just didn't have the same ring to it, so he would just have to get used to the nickname.

Some days Ever thought that perhaps, since they were kingdoms apart, Chess had concluded that he'd only wanted her because she'd been convenient. They'd needed each other to succeed before and now that they'd both gotten their kingdoms back, she didn't know if he'd changed his mind since he was late. Then she peered at the instrument as she continued to bring it to life through her movements, the song. The viola was a gift sent to her, an instrument that had belonged to the famous musician Carl Stamitz. It had been accompanied by a short note that still made her heart full.

Queenie,

I went to a lot of trouble stealing this from a museum. This may not be your first instrument, and I wish dearly that I could've mended the other one for you, but I hope this will please you.

Your Princeling

Ever glanced back at the palace, where Ferris was inside training the new guards she'd collected from the city. Ever still had to learn to trust the new staff, but they seemed relieved she was back in Ivory, that Rav no longer had control. Even the air had slowly started smelling sweeter as it once had, not stale and cold. The vampires of Ivory had been welcoming, bringing gifts to the palace, but she still feared they would always wonder if she would abandon them again.

Ever wouldn't. And she would continue proving it.

The song ended and she played another, this time "Clair de Lune," a slower classical piece that would never get old. Though her brother had to die, she still missed the damn bastard at times. Then she would think about what he'd done to Chess, as well as the harm she'd caused to the prince, and it made her heart plummet to her stomach.

But Wonderland would now become better because of all they'd faced, all that had happened. A piercing roar wailed in the distance, shaking the trees—the Jabberwocky. Fear crawled through her at the sound, and she stumbled over a chord. The beast had already been in Ivory before—what would stop it from returning? She prayed it wouldn't, but she would need to prepare in case it did.

Two arms circled her waist and Ever gasped, then she inhaled Chess's lovely scent. She returned to her song, creating music while he nuzzled her neck and pressed tender kisses just below her ear.

"You're late," she said, leaning into him.

"It seems Scarlet needed more help than I'd anticipated. Don't stop playing," he whispered in her ear, pulling her even closer so she was molded perfectly against him. Her breathing increased, her heart pounding in desperation for him, yet she finished the song for them both.

With a smile, she set the instrument down, then whirled around and backed him against a tree trunk. He looked like himself, his hair hanging freely around his chin and neck, his dark vest tight against his chest, showcasing each of his sculpted abs. It made her smile that he wasn't in hiding any longer, that she wasn't either. "It's strange, isn't it?"

"What is?" He brushed his nose against hers, his gaze hooded with burning desire that mirrored hers.

"You once failed to take my heart." She cradled his cheeks, a wary expression crossing his face as if he were worried she would break his. "Yet you ended up claiming it anyway. It's yours, Princeling."

Chess's body relaxed, then he grasped her by the waist and drew her to him, gently caressing her hip bone. "And mine is fucking yours." He smirked, his fingers deliciously skimming down her thighs.

"I'm tired of our homes being separate already. I wish you didn't have to leave." Ever turned in his arms and unbuttoned the first two buttons of his vest as he stroked her over her panties, sending tingles through her.

"You have no fucking idea how much I've missed you," he rasped.

Ever had thought about something else over the past two weeks, something that needed to happen. "My brother did have one thing right.”

Chess stopped his movements and arched a brow, blinking as he waited for her answer. She knew he believed Rav had done nothing right, but there was a small seed he'd planted that had potential.

“To unite the territories.” She unfastened another button of his vest, her lips tilting up at the edges. “I was thinking perhaps you and I could build a palace in the center of Wonderland?”

Chess chuckled, his familiar grin growing wide. “Queenie, are you asking me to be your king?”

She rolled her eyes. “You will forever be infuriating, but yes, I am. We can look after Wonderland together.”

“I'm more interested in looking after you at the moment, but I agree.” Chess hoisted her up, her legs wrapping around his hips. He took them to the ground, sitting with his back against the tree.

“Good.” Ever pressed her forehead to Chess's, her gaze locked on his as they studied each other, taking in this moment, *them.*

As she skimmed her fingers down his chest, a strong metallic scent filled the air. *Blood.* Ever leapt from Chess and whirled around, her fangs exposed.

A small form walked through the garden, her dark dress billowing in the wind—bright crimson painted nearly her whole body. Even her pink hair was mostly red.

Ever took a deep swallow. “Mouse?”

“Are you all right?” Chess asked, his voice concerned as he moved to stand beside Ever.

Mouse's lips were drawn into a tight line while she held her caterpillar close. “I did a very bad thing. Don't tell Maddie.”

BOOK THREE

KNAVE

CHAPTER ONE

FERRIS

BEFORE

Do something enough times and the body remembers. Brushing teeth, putting on a shirt, tying a shoe—all of it was accomplished without thought. For Ferris, that list included playing drums.

One. Two. Three. And four.

He counted beats in his head, even though he didn't need to. It was just something to fill his thoughts as his arms moved across the drum set in front of him. Sweat dripped down the back of his neck, and flashing lights illuminated the bar. Dozens of people crowded the stage, rocking out to the loud music. The heavy drumbeats, the quick guitar notes, the screaming vocals.

One. Two. Three. And four.

The heart-pounding song poured from him in sync with the rest of the band, Death Remedy. Perfect. Well-practiced. All body memory and no conscious thought. Without his arms knowing the movements, the beats, he wouldn't be able to play anymore. His mind was numb. Empty. Except for the counting…

One. And two. Three. And four.

Ferris's lifeless eyes followed the studs on the back of the lead singer's jacket as he moved energetically across the stage, riling up the crowd. The man had to be sweating his nuts off since Ferris was in a tank with torn-off sleeves and still dripping. Dark hair fell across Ferris's slick forehead and stuck, whereas Oliver kept his short, so at least he had that going for him.

That and the lack of anxiety over getting another hit. Oliver had been suspicious that something was up with Ferris and had searched his stick bag earlier, discovering the dwindling coke stash. Ferris had hidden it in there before the show, deciding to wait until after the gig to take more and relying on hard liquor to get him through the performance. There would be a fight later. Another one. Which only made Ferris need the high all the more. Needed it so he could fucking forget. Forget *everything*.

What the fuck did Oliver care anyway? Ferris had his addiction completely under control. It was *fine*. He just needed something to take the edge off the pain. His bandmates didn't understand—*couldn't* understand. And they were no saints either. They'd all experimented at some point and he'd never given them shit.

One. Two. And three. And four.

Shit. That was wrong. Lucas, their bassist, shot him a sideways look as Ferris stumbled to catch up with them. Maybe he needed to stop counting and just let his body do all the work. Let his mind shut down.

Ferris squeezed his eyes closed. If only it were that easy. Thoughts circled through his brain endlessly, reminding him, blaming him. That was what the drugs were for: *forgetting*. The cymbal *crashed* against his stick and he flinched.

Images of *that* night came between flickers of the strobe light. Metal crunching. Tires squealing. Flashing blue police lights. Blood. Everywhere … blood. The heat of it streaming down his forehead, into the corner of his right eye. And—

The drumsticks fell from his hands. "Fuck!"

"You okay, mate?" Lucas asked as his fingers kept plucking the string of his bass. Oliver's singing never faltered and Johnny didn't miss a chord on his guitar.

Ferris could barely hear the question over the music. Or perhaps it was the ringing in his ears. The phantom *whoop whoop whoop* of the ambulance as it took away everything important to him. He turned his head just in time to avoid puking all over his snare.

Lucas jumped back as the vomit splattered the stage next to the bassist's custom rainbow-checkered Vans. "Ferris! The fuck?"

Ferris shoved up from his stool and tripped, falling forward. He crashed into the drums, sending them flying, and slammed face first on the old wood floor. The song screeched to a halt. Every eye in the godforsaken room landed on the drummer, the silence deafening, as he struggled to get back on his feet. Embarrassment flushed his face. *Just fucking perfect.* Oliver met his gaze, his eyes hard. Ferris winced.

"Fuuuck," Ferris groaned when he was finally standing again, swaying. He reached for something to steady himself, but found his crash cymbal. The moment he put weight on it, the metal tilted, dumping him back to the floor again.

"Shit," Johnny said as he hurried to catch him.

And failed.

Ferris rolled onto his back and closed his eyes with a disgruntled *hmph*. He could hear his friends now—*loser!* And his family—*such a disgrace!* First, he'd gotten Ellie pregnant before marriage, and now he couldn't function without shooting up. He couldn't function *with* the fucking drugs either. He was too far down the rabbit hole and there was no climbing out. He didn't *want* to climb out. But this… He closed his eyes against the shame and let himself pass the fuck out.

Whomp, whomp, whomp. Ferris groaned, clutching his head as his pulse thrummed in his ears, echoed in his mind. The sounds of the bar boomed, muted, through the walls of… Where was he? Squinting, he took in the off-white metal interior of the van plastered with different band stickers. The band name *The Swingers* carved into a pineapple, a red snake circling a skull, an angry, zombified teddy bear, and on and on. Collected from all the bands that Death Remedy had played with over the years. Some from concerts he and his friends had been to before they'd became popular. And, now that they were popular, the band was phasing Ferris out.

"Fuckers," he wheezed. His band members had dumped him in the back of their van and… He listened harder. And went back to playing? The twats. "See how good you are without a drummer, arseholes," he shouted to the stickered ceiling.

Rubbing his face, Ferris forced himself to sit up, kicking empty beer cans away. His palms were sweaty, hands shaking, and he ground his teeth against the urge to scratch his face. He needed his fix *now.* Oliver could go fuck himself. Except… *Damn.* His stick bag was inside with the rest of the equipment.

He stared at the stickers above him and focused on the one of a penguin holding an iced coffee. Stars rested in its overly large eyes and a smile lingered on its beak. *Ellie.* His girlfriend had been just as excited, just as happy, as that stupid bird. About nearly everything. It was what made Ferris fall in love with her when they were sixteen and stay in love with her for the last four years. Her optimism was contagious, her smile more addictive than the drugs his body now craved. If he could, he would trade anything to hear her laugh again. Give up his damn soul to bring her back.

But he couldn't.

No one could.

Because she was dead. And their unborn daughter had been ripped from the earth along with her.

Ferris and Ellie had danced in the rain on their fourth date, then cuddled in the van when lightning struck at the park. She'd seen the band's paltry sticker collection at the time and fished out the penguin from her purse. When he'd asked her why she was carrying it around, she said she'd bought it on a whim that morning. Where she randomly found it was a mystery and he regretted not asking her, not that it really mattered. He was sorry he hadn't asked a million things over their three-year-long relationship. Little things he would never know now, things that anyone else would call irrelevant. But when someone died, *everything* was relevant about them—it was just too late to realize it.

Pressing the heels of his hands against his eyes, Ferris willed away the building tears. It had been eleven months since the accident. The one where *he* had been driving. Where *he* hadn't swerved in time to avoid the car driving down the wrong side of the road. Eleven months and thirteen days.

Every day since had been a complete and total spiral into hell. "Damn," he croaked.

He needed to get high before his thoughts went any further. Like to the list of baby names in Ellie's handwriting that he still carried in his wallet even though they'd eventually decided on Luna, or to the plant she'd kept in their shoddy flat that was now withering because he was apparently shit at keeping anything alive.

No. He scrambled to unlatch the back door and flung it open, practically falling to the pavement. Drugs were exactly what he needed to forget *them.* The fact that they were gone. He needed—

"Ferris!" a deep masculine voice called.

He squinted down the alleyway, catching sight of someone he'd painted houses with a couple years ago. Roger? Or Richard? Something like that. He looked the same as he did back when he was sacked for showing up to a job while tripping. Ferris grinned.

"Hey, man." He stood up straight and smiled. *Raymond!* That was it. "How you been?"

"Good, good," Raymond said. "Looks like you're having a

rough night, though. Did you hit your head up on stage?"

A wave of shame washed over Ferris but vanished as quickly as it had come. "Nothing a little pick-me-up wouldn't fix."

Raymond smiled knowingly. "I thought as much. You got cash?"

Ferris stumbled up to him, hands shaking with need, and cast a quick glance over his shoulder to make sure they were alone. Pulling his wallet from his back pocket, he drew two fifties out—his last banknotes—and handed them over. "What will this get me?"

"What's your poison? Pills? Powder?"

"Coke." Ferris licked his lips, aching for a hit.

"For a hundred?" he asked, brow raised.

"Come on. As you said, it's been a rough night." First Oliver finding his stash, then the stress of the impending fight, and the whole falling over his own drums…

Raymond studied him for a moment. "I've got something new tonight. Not sure what it's cut with, but it should do the trick."

"I'll take it," Ferris blurted. As long as it made his mind shut the fuck up.

His old acquaintance dipped his fingers into his pocket, taking his sweet time as Ferris's heart beat anxiously, then reached out to shake hands. "Have fun, mate."

Ferris glanced down at the bag of white powder. His needles were in the stick bag, but that was fine. Tapping a messy line out on the back of his hand, he quickly snorted it, then repeated the process. The burning inside his nostrils faded to numbness. Ferris sighed, eager for the full effects of the high to kick in, and stumbled through the backdoor of the bar.

The world spun for a moment. Florescent lights in the hallway became starbursts and it felt as if the ground tilted beneath him. Ferris collapsed to the dingy floor with just enough time to realize how badly he'd fucked up.

Soft lyrical voices drifted around him. Dreaming. Dying. Images of Ellie floated across the back of his eyelids. Her long blonde hair danced around her oval face, her dark eyes glittering as she smiled. She cradled the baby bump that grew beneath her shirt and held her hand out to him. He stretched to grasp it...

Pain lanced his arm and he tried to pull back, but couldn't. His fingers twitched, unable to reach Ellie with his free hand or move the other away. A scream built in the back of his throat, trapped, captured by his unconsciousness. Then the pain faded. Pleasure replaced it.

Every inch of his body hummed with life. His skin tingled, a warming sensation spreading through him, through every cell, just right. He imagined himself floating. Up, up, up. Toward something better. Something sublime.

The smile fell from Ellie's face and the image of her blurred. Faded. Disappeared. He fought to pry himself away from the pleasure clouding his thoughts, anchoring him. To follow Ellie and their daughter.

Let me go, he pleaded.

Let him join them, wherever they may be. He wanted the pain to stop, to end it all. Overdosing like this had been an accident, but maybe it was for the better. Then he wouldn't be such a burden to everyone around him. He wouldn't have to suffer this loneliness anymore...

Come back, he begged Ellie. *Don't leave me here without you.*

"Is it working?" asked a woman.

An intense pressure came against his arm as someone sucked. He gasped and his eyes fluttered open. The pale-yellow walls were bright, too bright, around him. The tiles too hard. His arm lowered on its own.

No. Not on its own. Someone gently placed it on his stomach and patted him. "There now, you're all right."

Ferris forced his eyes to focus. A woman leaned over him, her head haloed by the ceiling light, her face in shadows. He dragged in a ragged breath. The woman shifted to where her face was visible. Delicate features with a spattering of freckles across her nose and cheeks. Violet eyes and soft lips. A pink plait draped over one shoulder. He'd never seen anyone so beautiful before

… so *inhuman*. Perhaps he was dead after all.

"Are you an angel?" he rasped.

The young woman blinked, a smile slowly spreading across her cheeks. "Me? Gracious, no."

Ferris sat up slowly, his head throbbing, body shaking. Another figure with purple curls and a bowler hat atop her head moved behind his angel. The second woman looked similar, except her features were a bit sharper. A sister, maybe. "Looks as if this is your lucky night," she sang, grinning as she adjusted her hat.

Sure, if bad luck counted as luck… Ferris thought for a moment, letting what had happened sink in. He'd had a horrible reaction to whatever Raymond sold him, had been dying, had *wanted* to die for a moment. Because Ellie was… He swallowed hard. Somehow, he was awake now. Not only awake but clear headed.

"I…" His body ached with a soreness that ran bone-deep. "I think we have different definitions of *lucky*."

"He looks like a newly-hatched baby bird." The purple-haired one poked his arm.

"At least he's sober now," the angel replied.

Sober. When was the last time he'd been that way? *Eleven months and fourteen days ago.* "I don't understand." Ferris lifted his arm, his gaze locking onto two puncture wounds with a trickle of blood running from each. What kind of strange ass shit were these two into? "The fuck?"

"I drank the poison from you," the angel said softly.

Did she say *drank*? As in pierced him with something, then drank his *blood* to sober him up?

"Good thing, too. You'd be dead if Mouse hadn't found you." The purple-haired woman waved her hand in the air.

Dead. Yes, he'd been dying, but hearing someone else speak the word was jarring. Ellie and their daughter were gone, but he wasn't ready to join them. Not really. Not yet.

The angel—Mouse—knelt beside him, a comforting gardenia scent drifting around him. What sort of name was Mouse, anyway? As she leaned in to whisper, Ferris forgot the question.

"You look as though you need a friend. And perhaps I can help you, if you help us. If not, I can make you forget."

Ferris arched a brow. He wouldn't easily forget this night, no matter how much coke he snorted in the future. "What do you mean exactly?" The ache in his temples throbbed harder, distracting him from gathering proper thoughts.

A faint smile twitched at Mouse's lips as she drew closer, caressing his ear with her voice, her warm breath brushing his skin. "You want a high and we want to feed. So would you like to make a deal with a vampire?"

CHAPTER TWO

MOUSE

PRESENT DAY

A mouse was a quiet thing, one that hovered, listening, waiting for its moment. Although small, the creature wasn't helpless—it could terrify if it so chose.

And waiting was precisely what Mouse was doing.

Waiting for her moment to strike.

Loud techno beats boomed around her while white lights shimmered through the smoke inside the mortal club. Mouse easily blended in, wearing her black gothic frock and dark platform boots, her pink plait resting over her shoulder. She sat at the bottom of the stairs, peering out at the crowd as the mortals' bodies gyrated. Their blood called to her, pulsing, *slamming*, in their veins, begging her to rip their flesh open and take her fill.

Breathe, Mouse.

The front pocket of Mouse's dress wiggled. "Just a little longer, Des," she said over the loud music, lightly patting her chest. The caterpillar had been with her each night, calming her, keeping her from massacring innocents, the way she'd done that day in the donor building in Ivory when she'd murdered twenty mortals. The donors were supposed to be safe in Wonderland. But she'd been so incredibly *hungry*.

Since returning to the Ivory Palace after Ever reclaimed her throne, Mouse had been feeding on humans—those who deserved it—almost every night. Her hunger never satiated. Her sister, Maddie, didn't know about Mouse's appetite, and she couldn't either.

A warm body, smelling of cigarettes and luscious blood, sank down beside her on the stairs. The rows of steps stretched across the back wall in the dance room, and at the top rested a stage with several tables and chairs. On some nights, bands would play up there but tonight it was couples drinking, kissing, and groping.

Mouse ignored the mortal, but the brazen male shifted closer so his arm was pressed to hers. She again inhaled his intoxicating scent buried within his flesh when he finally spoke, "What's a pretty girl like you doing here?"

"I've come to satisfy my appetite," she said, not meeting his gaze.

His index finger brushed her hand, delicately stroking, and the urge to rip it off flowed through her. Bold, touchy mortals didn't sit well with her. Not since that day long ago when a mortal man forced Mouse against a library shelf, hiked up her skirts, and had his way with her. Even after fighting against him, she'd been silent through it all, until she'd gotten home and finally cried, truly screamed.

"You look a little young to be here," the man purred in her ear.

Mouse clenched her jaw as she met his dark irises. He wasn't unattractive—his chestnut hair was parted on the side and his chiseled cheeks were sharp under the lights. He wore a black fishnet shirt and dark trousers with too many buckles. She'd been twenty when she was turned, but the majority of humans believed she was much younger.

"Do you *like* young girls?" she cooed, then bit her lip, setting the trap.

He grinned, wolfish, his white teeth shining too brightly. "That depends."

"I'm sixteen," she lied, waiting to see if he took the bait.

"That's older than I'm used to."

Rage filled Mouse, her veins throbbing hot. She wanted to rip off this mortal's head, tear out his heart, break him into pieces, lap up all his blood. "Follow me to the back alley," she said softly, calmly, "and I'll do anything you'd like."

"Maybe you should get my name first." He licked his lower lip. "I'm Liam."

"I'm Margo." She used her real name most of the time with humans because she didn't want them to have the one that felt more like her.

Liam stood and Mouse led the way through the dancing crowd toward the back door. She tried not to breathe too much as the bodies pressed against her, begging her to taste them.

Outside, lamps along the building lit up the area. Several people lingered, smoking and laughing. Mouse glanced over her shoulder when Liam's hand clasped her arm. Her rage only intensified at his touch. Since having her virginity ripped away, she hadn't allowed a male or female to get close to her in a sexual sense, not even a kiss besides pressing her lips to a throat, a wrist, a thigh, to sink her teeth into their flesh to sate her appetite.

They walked to the side of the building and entered a dark, damp alley that reeked of the rubbish bin.

"You said you would do anything I like?" Liam's breath was hot on Mouse's neck as he backed her into the brick wall while unbuckling his trousers. "Suck my dick."

Mouse blinked and pressed her lips into a tight line. "Bollocks, I changed my mind." She leapt forward, slamming his back against the opposite wall. Her fangs dropped and she pierced his throat as he sucked in a sharp breath. Before he could feel any pleasure from her bite, she tore out his throat and drank. The thick liquid against her tongue tasted like the richest of heavens. So good, so *good*. Mouse couldn't stop, not even to rip out his heart and drink that dry too. She wanted more and more, and *more*. Wanted it to block out *everything* that had happened at the Ruby Heart Palace…

After every speck of the mortal's blood was inside her, she dropped his body, letting it collapse against the ground. Another murder that would go unsolved. A well-deserved one.

Her pocket wiggled once more, and Mouse sighed, taking out her blue and yellow caterpillar. Des, head tilted to the side, peered up at Mouse with beady black eyes.

"He deserved it, and I think you agree because you didn't try to stop me as you did in the donor building."

The caterpillar wrapped her body around Mouse's index finger, giving it a hug.

Mouse glanced down at herself, soaked in scarlet. She needed to stop making a mess out of her meals, but she wanted it to hurt. However, now she couldn't very well go traipsing into the club looking like an axe murderer.

Placing Des back into her pocket, Mouse darted out from the alley and away from the club, using her immortal speed. Rav's old portal was the nearest one, but she hadn't been back to Scarlet since her escape. Chess was there, preparing for the new palace that he and Ever would share on the border between Scarlet and Ivory. The construction had already begun, yet it would still be a while before they all moved in.

Gripping the skirts of her dress, Mouse bolted into the woods. She ran through the night, unable to ignore her unwanted thoughts that always managed to slip in. In that blasted Queen of Hearts' palace, every weapon imaginable had pierced Mouse's heart. Numerous blades had carved bloody smiles across her throat. Thorned whips had flogged her back, tearing her flesh over and over again. Her head shoved into a bucket full of water, in and out, in and out, until she drowned. Bled dry with Rav's scientific contraptions. After tortures such as those, a vampire needed fresh human blood to fully heal on the inside, but Mouse had never been given any. Only the same cold blood bags day in and day out. It caused her cravings to intensify, and the effects lingered. Maddie couldn't know—Mouse didn't want her sister to feel any more guilt. The Hatter had been through enough.

Mouse had always been a bit vicious when it came to her appetite. Unlike Maddie, she had killed some of her prey. Liked it. *Loved it.* But those humans had deserved it, just as her mortal abuser had when Maddie slowly killed him with hatpins and knives. Regret still haunted Mouse that she hadn't been the one to break him apart all those years ago.

Instead, she'd recently killed the twenty donors.

Rav had created a monster.

Her.

Mouse shoved that day away, the humans' screams, the way her teeth had plunged into their throats, shredding them, how she'd sucked every drop of their blood from her fingertips.

A light fog covered the cemetery and cracked headstones littered the area, not a fresh grave in decades.

Mouse knelt by one of the trees and crawled through the gaping hole. Before her, a mirror-like surface appeared, a glistening sheen reflecting her image. She pressed a hand forward, and a floral scent ignited as she was tugged through then spat out in the middle of a pathway, the stone medallion now across from her.

Rising to her feet, Mouse dusted off her hands. In front of her, the Ivory Palace loomed, beautiful and gothic, its towers massive with a silvery moat surrounding the castle. Once the new castle was built, she would miss the Ivory Palace dearly. But maybe she could still return here sometimes when she needed an escape.

The white daisies were in full bloom and a troop of bats beat their wings overhead. Mouse hurried around the palace to the back and slipped inside with her key.

Mock, a guard with dark irises and yellow hair just past his shoulders, stood at the foot of the stairs beside Didi, a newer guard. Her silver and orange locks were drawn back in a bun, and she smiled warmly at Mouse.

"The coast is clear." Mock grinned, seeming to have noticed how she preferred sneaking in.

Taking a breath, Mouse nodded while staring at the floor, then bounded up the stairs to her room before someone else could round the corner. She didn't want to answer questions, and she shouldn't have to either.

Mouse should've been at the Ivory Palace, but she'd snuck away, claiming she was still tired. However, the truth was she hadn't been able to sleep, not in months. Maddie always believed herself to be the strange one of the sisters, but perhaps it was Mouse because with each passing day, she'd found it harder to know what to say to anyone.

Except for the once-Knave of the Ruby Heart Palace. Her friend, Ferris.

Yet, she'd kept recent things from him too. She wasn't ashamed—she didn't know what she was. Most certainly she wasn't that female who'd saved his life back at the club. The one who would dance to his music, the one who would laugh at his sarcasm. Two years in a prison cell could change someone, but two years tortured by Rav and Imogen would make a monster out of anyone. Even though she'd already been one.

But she was *fine*.

Mouse left her door cracked open as she'd been doing since leaving her prison cell. On her bed rested a pale-yellow envelope. Mouse's heart inflated at the sight, and with a smile, she scooped it up. She opened the envelope and fished out the paper. A rosewood scent drifted to her nose, and she inhaled the comforting smell as she unfolded it. Drawn across the page was a feminine hand holding several gems. At the bottom was a single sentence: *You're stronger than any diamond.*

She smiled at it. *Ferris.*

Mouse refolded the paper and stashed it with the others beneath her bed. He'd snuck her drawings while she'd been in the prison cell and continued to give them to her afterward. She set Des on top of a green leaf on the bedside table then went inside her bathing chambers to wash.

The warm water calmed her until it turned cold—icy like it had been in the Ruby Heart Palace when Rav would poke and prod her with needles, drawing her blood.

Clenching her teeth, trying to forget those memories, Mouse toweled off and put on a fresh dress. She then padded to her bed and slipped beneath the silk covers.

It was still night and she shouldn't be lying in bed, but all she'd been wanting to do was feed and rest. Des lifted her head for a moment before falling back asleep on top of her half-eaten leaf.

Imogen digging her nails into Mouse's flesh, then shoving her head into a bucket filled with water drifted through her mind. Mouse hummed to make it stop, to go *away*—it was something she'd started while inside the prison cell. She couldn't breathe, the water filling her lungs.

Shakespeare. Shakespeare. Shakespeare. She thought about his plays, as she always did in times like these. Des had been named after Desdemona, after all. But Mouse had always felt something for Ophelia from *Hamlet.* What would have happened if Ophelia hadn't killed herself? Sometimes Mouse thought about going to the mortal world and waiting for the sun to rise to see if she truly would die.

A light knock came at her cracked door, and Ferris's hulking shadow crept up the wall. "Mouse?"

"Come in," she whispered, inhaling his calming rosewood scent as he approached. Ferris looked striking, dressed in the white and silver Ivory guard uniform, the clothing hugging his strong arms, chest, and legs. His short dark hair was swept back, and his brown gaze latched onto hers.

"Hello, luv." Ferris smiled softly. She loved that smile, loved seeing it on his handsome face. "Maddie returned from Scarlet."

Her sister. She still didn't know Mouse had slaughtered the donors. Ever and Chess had agreed to keep what she'd done a secret, as long as it didn't happen again. "I'll meet with her later."

She bit her bottom lip. "Thank you for the drawing."

Ferris shrugged and stepped forward. "Do you want company?"

Mouse knew what that meant—he needed company but didn't want to ask it of her and put pressure on her. Neither of them liked asking for things, yet she did want the company, *his* company. She nodded, opening her arms to him. "Are you having a tedious day too?"

He took off his boots and his large frame slipped beneath the covers beside her. "It's better now."

She circled her arms around his neck and held him close. Ferris was her best friend. For centuries, it had always been Maddie and Ever—she'd never wanted to let anyone else in. Not until him.

As she breathed Ferris in, she remembered the days at the club when she would feed off him, giving him the high he needed, giving her the food she craved. Since the day they'd met, they'd never talked about their pasts, only the present, the future. But back then, Mouse had known he'd wanted to escape his demons, just as she'd needed to feed. The day she'd found him, almost dead, there was something about him she'd wanted to save. He'd thought her an angel while most mortals had believed her to be a demon.

As she listened to the rhythmic sound of his pulse, her fangs threatened to drop at the thought of what his blood would taste like in his vampire state. What would the high feel like to each other now that he was a vampire? She'd never tasted the blood of an immortal since being turned by Maddie. The hunger swirled in her stomach, her eyelids fluttering.

The sound of his voice snapped her out of the moment. "Are you all right, luv?"

"I still feel everything from inside that palace." She rested her head in the crook of his shoulder, her chest heaving, not wanting to discuss how she craved to taste him. That would be another of her secrets, one that would have to go away.

He ran a hand through her wet hair. "I know. So do I."

CHAPTER THREE

FERRIS

"Ferris?" Mouse whispered.

Ferris stirred from sleep and cracked open his eyes to find a halo of pink hair framing Mouse's face as she looked down at him. She'd come into his room this time, which she did whenever she needed him. "What's wrong?" he asked, his voice thick with sleep.

"Nothing really." She set her head back down on his pillow and snuggled closer.

A sheet was between them, kept there so his naked flesh touched no part of her body. Mouse knew he slept without clothes and never once tried to crawl beneath the blankets. An unspoken agreement between them so their nights together didn't get awkward. It was especially important now that he couldn't stop wondering what it would be like to settle between her legs. To have her naked body beneath him. Ferris shoved the thoughts away before blood could rush to his cock. This was *Mouse*.

"Nothing?" he repeated.

"I just wanted to hear your voice," she replied quietly.

"Ah." Ferris draped an arm over Mouse and tugged her closer, giving her what she needed. "Should I tell you a story to help you fall back asleep?"

She sighed against his chest, relieved. "Yes, please."

Ferris set his chin atop her head and thought for a moment. "Have I ever told you about when I learned to play drums?"

A gentle shake of her head.

"Well, I was only ten when I begged my mom for lessons, but she was dead-set against it because it would be a racket. My dad though? He only winked. A week later there was a drum set in my room when I came home from school. My first lesson wasn't until later in the month, but of course I was too impatient to wait. I wailed on those things, smashing the cymbals as loud as I could. It was complete chaos. My mother nearly went mad listening to it.

"But once the lessons started, I practiced everything I'd learned over and over. Which, I'm fairly certain, only made things worse." Ferris chuckled, remembering his mother's exasperated stares. "Soon enough, I understood how to read music and the noise became songs. It took a while for them to be *good*, but at least they were recognizable."

On and on Ferris went. Talking about his different drum sticks, about the first time he'd played through one of his lessons without any mistakes, his mother's growing acceptance of never having a moment's peace. The story wasn't riveting by any means, but it wasn't meant to be. It was simply a way to soothe Mouse and, he supposed, relive a memory or two.

Once Mouse's breaths were soft and steady again, Ferris slowly slipped from the bed. He was no longer tired, and he ached to play the set Ever had given him. He glanced wistfully at the drums in the corner. It was far too late to play now unless he wanted the whole palace to wake up.

Instead, he grabbed a pair of loose gray sweatpants and settled into the chair beside the bed with his sketchbook. The pencil was still between the pages where he'd left off, the last drawing of a rose bush covered in blooms that made him think of Mouse. Not quite as beautiful as her, but delicate, soft. And her hair matched the petals almost exactly.

He quietly pressed the pencil tip to the next blank page and began drawing the outlines of Mouse's face. Her features were smoothed in sleep, her plump lips parted slightly, her long lashes caressing her cheeks. A few strands of pink hair slipped over her temple and down her cheek, over her chin to rest against her neck.

The drawing took shape slowly as he tried to capture her essence with a simple piece of lead. He erased, retrying parts until his muscles ached before setting the book and pencil on his lap to stretch his back. The pencil fell to the carpet and, as he bent to reclaim it, the book followed. When he opened it again, it was to a sketch of Ellie, and his chest tightened. He didn't have the heart to tear the image from the spiral binding, but he'd made a point of *never* looking past a certain point in the notebook.

Practically flinging the sketch pad back onto his bedside table, he grabbed a black T-shirt from the floor and left before he could wake Mouse. He needed to expel some energy and, if he couldn't play drums, he needed to do something else. But what? What could *possibly* stop the memories from overwhelming him? Swallowing him whole?

Ellie. Their daughter. The crash. Crunching metal. Flashing lights. Sirens. A funeral.

Ferris shook his head violently to rid himself of the thoughts building without permission. There was only one thing that had ever helped him cope. *Two things.* But he could never ask Mouse to feed from him now. He knew what happened when two vampires indulged in sharing blood—a practical fuck fest followed. After everything he and Mouse had lived through in the Ruby Heart Palace, he didn't want to use her like that. Not that he didn't think she was the sexiest vampire in Wonderland.

"Shite," he swore under his breath. Some time away from the palace might do him good, help him clear his head. And maybe he needed a little bit of help managing it. He scribbled a quick note to leave on his bedside table in case Mouse woke up to find him gone, then he fled the Ivory Palace.

When he stepped through the main doors without running into anyone, Ferris breathed a sigh of relief. The cool air filled his lungs but did nothing to help the frantic edge building in his head. He needed to go … just *go*. What he needed could only be found in the mortal world.

Ferris ran his trembling finger along the crack in the outer wall and dropped through the portal, landing unceremoniously on his knees in an old cemetery. He stared up at the night sky, purposely avoiding looking at any gravestones, and stood. A heaviness thumped in his chest in time with his heart. The sorrow of losing Ellie and their unborn daughter had never left him, but sometimes it was easier to live with the pain. He could've lived without the reminder of death at the moment though.

Rushing from the cemetery, he let his feet carry him away from the portal. A slight drizzle fell from the sky, just enough to make everything damp and smell musty. He'd missed this place, though he didn't want to admit it. But Wonderland was his home. It was where he could be himself, live his life without judgment—at least now that he was no longer forced to slave away for the Queen of Hearts. He had played his part as the love-struck Knave well, but he'd always belonged to Mouse. Saving her was worth the torment he'd suffered. He'd do it again in a moment if he had to, but sometimes he still felt like a true knave for not telling Mouse about his past. The death of Ellie and their unborn daughter, Luna, set off a chain of events that led to him in the back hallway where he'd nearly died.

His mother and father had refused to speak to him for months after he'd gotten Ellie pregnant. They were strict Catholics and he wasn't married. Even after Ellie died, things remained strained with his parents. So, he'd tried drugs to cope with Ellie and Luna's deaths and found they worked—almost too well. Ferris had only ever been an embarrassment to his parents. And his bandmates…

After Mouse saved him, he'd refocused, found a new high to thrive on—her bite. Getting clean was enough for his bandmates to forgive him, but that hadn't meant they'd trusted him anymore.

He slowed to a walk once he reached a sketchy, run-down bar and stuffed his hands into his trouser pockets. The cold, misty rain landed on his face, clung to his hair. Inside, the stench of alcohol assaulted him. His trainers stuck to the dirty floor, each footstep going *scritch* until he plonked himself down on a stool at the bar. He'd been here before. Knew the bartender, Ken, would have what he needed.

"Hey," Ken said, peeling himself away from a couple of older women at the opposite end of the bar. "Haven't seen you in a long time."

"I've been busy," he grumbled. "Do you have anything?"

Ken nodded once. "Not been out of town at rehab, have you?"

Ferris snorted. If only that were true. "What does that matter to you?"

"It doesn't." Ken shrugged. "Just trying not to personally kick anyone off the wagon."

"Ken," Ferris said, compelling him. "Give me the coke on the house and, when I walk back out of this bar, forget you ever saw me."

With stiff, robotic movements, Ken fiddled around beneath the bar and finally slid him over a can of beer. Beneath it would be the hit Ferris desperately needed. Using his vampiric speed, he snorted the white powder before anyone could notice. The burn was instant, faded quickly, and was replaced with the tingle of a high.

Only it stopped there.

His body no longer reacted the same. Mouse and Maddie had spoken about how drugs didn't affect vampires, but he hadn't really wanted to believe it.

"Fuck," he growled to himself.

"Something on your mind?" Ken asked, tossing a cloth over his shoulder. "There's got to be a reason you came looking for a hit tonight."

"Sure there is," Ferris said through his teeth. "I remembered my girlfriend and daughter are dead. I just spent two years groveling to the power-couple from Hell, plucking body parts off monsters to be used in horrible experiments, and falling asleep to screams of tortured souls. Also had to fuck the bitch and pretend I wanted to do it again, when I hated myself for doing it at all. Of course, the reason was worth it, but I'd only ever been with Ellie before that and—" He dragged in a deep breath. The fuck was he doing, spouting off like this to one of his old drug dealers, of all people? But he couldn't seem to stop himself now. "I finally got out of that toxic as fuck palace, only to hide away with some newly-turned female who asked *why* more times than a damn toddler. But at the end of the day, what good was I, really? I saved Alice, sure, but I had to let Mouse be tortured for two years. I couldn't even help kill the arseholes who'd held her captive. I'm as useless as an old fucking shoe."

"Wow." Ken grimaced. "I don't understand a single thing you just said. Are you sure you should've taken another hit?"

Another. He thought Ferris was already high and speaking nonsense. "I'm fine," he mumbled and let out a long breath. Just saying that out loud made him feel better. Or did he feel worse now? Calmer, either way. Resigned to his life and the fact that he needed to pull himself together without reverting to old habits. "See you around."

Having lost his appetite, Ferris returned to Wonderland and strolled the streets of Ivory instead. Since becoming a vampire, he'd never really gotten the chance to explore this part of his new world—though Scarlet was as familiar as the back of his own hand after all the sneaking about he'd done during the last two years. Over the past couple months, he'd been getting to know the city around the Ivory Palace. A few streets here, a few more there, unwilling to get himself completely lost but enjoying that he wasn't trapped in the Ruby Heart Palace or running from safe house to safe house.

Vampires and humans roamed the streets together, laughing, talking, kissing, feeding. Art shops beckoned him closer with the brilliant works in their display windows, but he kept walking. A new café had even opened that served human food alongside blood so anyone could enjoy a meal together. Good timing too, as the donation center was still temporarily closed. That didn't stop other vampires from keeping their own private donors in Wonderland or bringing them over for a night, of course. Ferris still wasn't hungry after his trip to the mortal world, though he would force down a bag of blood when he returned to the palace to keep himself from regretting not eating tomorrow. He nodded to a young woman as she exited a clothing boutique on the arms of a male with a green streak in his hair. Mouse might like checking out the place once she was feeling up to an outing. Update her wardrobe a bit since it had been years.

The castle rose at the edge of the town and Ferris stopped in his tracks. He wasn't ready to go back, fake a smile for Mouse's sake so she didn't worry about him. Avoid Maddie's questions. Play a round of cards with Noah. Ever would ignore his current mood as she was always busy with her queenly duties or Chess.

Instead, he turned around and walked back down the streets. Past white and silver store fronts, through waves of jazz music spilling from open windows, and away from the hubbub of the crowd. When a glittering silver lake appeared before him with pearly white gazebos, he smiled to himself. The clearing was scenic in the moonlight as crickets chirped. Eager to see something new, his pace quickened.

Mouse would definitely like to see this, he thought as he rounded the lake to one of the gazebos. It was quiet here. Peaceful. She had probably already visited, though, since she'd lived at the Ivory Palace before. Ferris wanted to show her something to help pull her out of her own head a bit. Distract her. Help her heal.

Ferris wandered through one gazebo, then the next, taking in the feel of the lake. The drums would sound amazing here. Maybe he could put out a notice for other musicians and start up another band here in Wonderland. One just for fun—nothing serious like Death Remedy.

Something to enjoy without the pressure of earning enough money to pay the bills and booking gigs. His lips spread into a grin. *Absolutely going to happen.*

Hopping onto the marble railing, Ferris spread his arms wide and closed his eyes. The light breeze blowing off the lake brushed against his body while the fresh scent of Ivory hit his senses and—

His eyes flew open.

And blood.

Slightly stale blood.

Fangs dropping, he leapt off the railing and darted straight for the metallic scent. It became stronger, overwhelming, as he neared the furthest gazebo. Straining his ears for any hint that he wasn't alone, he prowled closer. A splatter of rust-colored blood decorated one of the pillars holding the gazebo roof. Ferris slowed his steps, casting a glance at the white and silver tree line for danger, before turning his attention back to the blood.

More of it dotted the white grass. Along with a severed finger.

Ferris took another step and froze. The rest of the body was scattered around the ground in a giant pool of dried blood. Or what was left of it. A foot, still wearing a black stiletto, another finger, and a clump of ... *fucking hell.* Was that part of their intestines?

Occasionally fights resulted in a severed limb or two, but vampires didn't eat flesh. So where was the rest of the body? Whether the victim was an immortal or a human didn't make any difference. No. This was no vampire attack. A werewolf maybe. They'd been in the woods of Ivory when the group had left the safehouse, though he saw no signs of the beasts here. No beastly footprints in the blood.

A long strand of black poked from the dirt a few yards from the gore. Ferris skirted around the mess and plucked the object from the ground. *A quill.* Did Ivory have porcupines? If it was a porcupine, it was fucking massive, given the quill was nearly as long as his arm.

Twirling the quill between his fingers like one of his drumsticks, he took in the carnage again. Ever needed to know about it. It was too close to the palace grounds not to say anything and he didn't know what could've caused this. Ferris rushed back to the palace, shoved his way inside, and nearly barreled into someone.

"Woah," Chess said, stepping back just in time to avoid the collision. He wore a black vest, his chestnut hair tied back with a cord, and reeked of sex and Scarlet. "Something chasing you, boy-o?"

"What is this?" Ferris asked, ignoring the jab at his youth, and held up the slightly bloodied quill.

"That—" Surprise flashed across the king's face and he quirked a brow. He snatched the quill away and studied it before speaking again. "*That* is bad news. Where did you find it, Knave?"

"Near the lake." Ferris wiped the flakes of dried blood from his hands. "Someone was torn apart there."

"Torn apart?" Chess asked in a low, curious voice. "You saw the body?"

Ferris shrugged. "Parts of it."

Chess snorted. "I'm surprised. The Jabberwocky doesn't usually leave leftovers."

"The Jabberwocky? It rarely ever comes to Ivory and Scarlet." At least, that was what everyone had told him. That, and how loud the beast was, always letting its presence be known. He'd always pictured it as having scales instead of quills, though.

"Ah. This is true." Chess bopped Ferris on the nose with the narrow end of the black quill. "But as you know, Ever and I saw the beast in Ivory when we returned months ago. The lake is too close for comfort though, isn't it? And no one heard the beastie?" Chess gave a sharp *hmm* and dropped the quill into a tall decorative vase in the hallway. "Keep this between us until I speak to Ever. We don't want to create a panic when your female is still recovering from our latest tragedies, do we?"

"I'm not lying to Mouse," Ferris said in a low voice. He'd heard enough stories of the Jabberwocky to know this was no light matter.

"It's not lying if you simply say *nothing*. Consider it a royal secret and keep your mouth shut. I'll tell Ever and she can arrange things on her end as she sees fit." Chess spun on his heel and disappeared down the hall.

Mouse would be pissed when she found out Ferris knew and didn't mention it. Of course, she would. But…

Maybe Chess was right, as much as he hated to admit it. Mouse was still sleeping with her door open, and she was barely speaking to anyone except her caterpillar. Not about important topics, anyway. Nor was she sleeping properly. He wasn't going to give her anything new to fear unless absolutely necessary.

CHAPTER FOUR

MOUSE

Two days had passed since Mouse sated her appetite at the mortal club. She wanted to see how long she could wait to drink fresh blood, but, already, the hunger stirred within her, beating at her like the sound of Ferris on his drums, reverberating through the hallway from behind his closed door. Mouse had remained in her room, and since Maddie had come home, the Hatter hadn't disturbed her besides slipping leaves for Des into the room when she'd pretended to be asleep.

Mouse couldn't keep avoiding her sister, though. She knew if she didn't seek her out today that Maddie would come to her. When her sister returned from the Ruby Heart Palace, Mouse should've gone to her, like she always would've in the past. As much as she was relieved Imogen and Rav hadn't taken her sister, a part of her wondered why they hadn't. Had they believed Mouse didn't love Maddie as much as the Hatter did her? They'd seemed to think both had known where the White Queen had been hidden. But Maddie was Mouse's weakness just as much as she was her sister's.

Straightening the skirts of her obsidian dress, Mouse descended the marble staircase with Des sleeping in her pocket. Footsteps echoed from below and she caught sight of long white hair flowing down the Queen's back with a plait across the front. A viola case rested in her hand and a short lacy dress with sleeves to her wrists cloaked her slender form. She normally wore her hair up except for when she was around the king of Scarlet. A hint of a smile crossed Mouse's face that Ever was happy, but it vanished when two male guards walked into the room carrying luggage cases.

"Are you leaving for a while?" Mouse asked.

Ever's head jerked to Mouse, a wide smile spreading her lips. "You're so quiet that I didn't even hear you. It won't be that long. I need to help Chess with a few things. He's already left to check on the situation in Scarlet. It's getting better, but occasionally there is a stir of trouble. Everyone needs to know we are truly aligned and that uniting the territories is best for Wonderland."

Mouse nodded and approached her friend. "I can help."

"Once the new palace is built, I will accept your offer. For now, focus on you." Ever stepped closer, a concerned expression forming. "Do you need to talk? I can leave afterward."

Mouse shook her head. She didn't want to make Ever waste time on her over something so important. The queen and Chess had spent enough time apart and she didn't deserve to be wrapped up in Mouse's troubles. Not when there was nothing that could be done.

"It's not good to keep everything bottled inside," she whispered so only Mouse could hear. The guards stood at the front of the room, not seeming to be interested in the conversation. They were committed to Ever and nice enough, but Mouse wasn't ready to let anyone else in. Not even those closest to her.

"I'm fine," Mouse murmured.

Ever released a breath and circled her arms around Mouse. "Take care of yourself and if you need me, come to the Ruby

Heart Palace or I can come back. However, please at least see Maddie. She's worried about you."

"I will." Mouse held Ever tight and rested her head on her friend's shoulder. "I'm glad to see you happy again."

Ever drew back and lifted Mouse's chin. "I want to see *you* happy, Mouse. Healing works differently for all of us. I don't know everything that happened to you in that palace, but I believe your feeding habits will return to normal."

Mouse shrugged.

"How about when I come back, we have a game of chess, then I'll play the viola and you can dance like old times?" Ever's deep brown eyes held Mouse's.

"I would love that." It was a lie, but she didn't want to hurt Ever, not with the hope sparking in her friend's gaze. Before being held prisoner, dancing would've been precisely what Mouse would've wanted. But not now. Most likely not ever. Lying was all she seemed to be doing these days. Inside she was screaming, *crying*, but she didn't want anyone to hear it. No one but her.

Mouse bid Ever goodbye, then ventured through the palace toward the drawing room.

Didi turned down the hall, carrying two pouches of blood. "Just grabbed Mock and me a snack." The guard's smile was warm again.

Mouse nodded as usual and focused her gaze back on the marble floor. It wasn't that she was trying to be rude to Didi or the other guards—they were quite lovely—she just couldn't force a simple hello. Perhaps because as they learned more about her, they would see her for what she was. Broken.

The drawing room's door was wide open and a fire crackled. She peered inside, her eyes meeting black combat boots hanging off the side of a chair.

Mouse padded inside and Maddie jerked forward, her purple curls bobbing, a dark hat pinned to the side of her head.

Maddie grinned as she continued to work on a felt beret. "Hello, sister, so lovely for you to join me on this glorious occasion.”

“What’s the occasion?” Mouse asked, taking out a chair and sinking down at a table for two. A metal chess set rested on top.

“Why for our chess game, of course,” Maddie sang, tossing her sewing things on the cushion before plopping down across from Mouse.

“I haven’t played you in a while, only Ferris.” Even then, she hadn’t done that since they’d all been hidden in the safe house together months ago.

“He’s shite at the game. You need a real opponent.”

Mouse’s lips tilted up at the edges. “All right.”

“Tea?” Maddie asked, already grabbing a porcelain set and an ice chest from beneath the table.

Mouse took a deep swallow. Once she’d had a taste of fresh blood after being held prisoner, she hadn’t wanted to drink any other sort. “Not at the moment. Where’s Noah?”

“He’ll be back soon. He’s visiting Alice.”

His sister—the girl from the palace, the one Mouse had told Ferris to save after Alice had unwillingly been turned into a vampire. He’d stopped by Mouse’s cell with Alice in his arms before he was supposed to bring her to the dungeon. Mouse had just gotten lashed earlier that day and she’d heard Imogen’s favorite, Rine, laughing about the things she was going to do to Ferris, followed by what else she would have him do with his tongue besides clean the rooms. Mouse would’ve wanted Ferris to save Alice anyway, but it had been an opportunity to get him out of the palace since she hadn’t known how much longer Imogen would keep him alive. It was a chance for him to be unchained to the Queen of Hearts. He’d been more than lucky the memories she’d seen in his blood hadn’t included Maddie and Mouse or he would’ve been dead.

“Your move first,” Mouse said as Maddie poured herself a cup of blood. The smell drifted to Mouse and her eyelids fluttered at the scent, but the cravings pulsing through her veins weren’t for that, but something warmer.

Maddie inched a white chess piece forward, then Mouse went

next. With each move, Mouse lost concentration, her thoughts focused on leaving the palace and heading to one of the mortal clubs again.

"Another round?" Maddie asked, taking a sip of blood.

"Perhaps tomorrow."

Her sister sighed. "You can't go on like this forever."

"Oh, I think I can." Mouse blinked, not looking at her sister. She wasn't sure what aspect Maddie meant, and she didn't want to ask either because that would mean discussing it.

"Ah yes, we are immortal." She waved a hand in the air, then reached to softly grasp Mouse's fingers. "I want you to heal at your own time, but with each passing day, you're drifting further and further away."

Mouse drew her hand back, biting the inside of her cheek until it bled. "I'm fine, Madeline."

"You're not." Maddie furrowed her brow, her lips set in a tight line that was very unlike her sister. "I know you weren't treated fine in the palace. You used to tell me everything. I know … I know this is my fault and it should've been me with Imogen and Rav. Not you. Never you."

Mouse's heart lodged in her throat at those words because she never would've wanted her sister in there. Not with Imogen and especially not with Rav. Her sister wouldn't have survived him. "Imogen would come by my cell," Mouse finally said. "Flash me her pathetic cards, predict my future with them, ask me where Ever was. Rav would taunt me about how he would see you, how you were so easy to give yourself to him when you two first met. There, satisfied?"

Maddie let out a breath. "I'm glad those fuckers are both dead, but there's more to it than that. You won't feel better until you talk about what happened. It doesn't have to be with me, just someone."

Biting the inside of her cheek harder, she stood from her seat. "I'm hungry now. I'm going out. Thank you for the game."

"Mouse," her sister pleaded, rising from her chair.

"I love you, Maddie. You don't have to worry about me. Be

happy with Noah. You deserve it. I'll play another round of chess with you tomorrow." Mouse walked out of the room, tears pricking her eyes. She ventured down several hallways, humming to herself, staring at the floor, not wanting to meet anyone's heavy stares. As she rounded the corner, she bumped into a broad, *naked*, chest, his abs perfectly sculpted. "Bollocks."

Without glancing up, she knew it was Ferris by his comforting rosewood scent. Not only that, but the raven tattoo he'd designed on the left side of his stomach and the chain necklace with the white gold ring dangling. He only wore his dark jeans slung low, paired with his black boots, just as he always did when he wasn't on guard shift and practicing his drums.

"Why hello there. Fancy running into you here," he teased, grinning as he tilted her chin up, his dark irises meeting hers. "You should keep your eyes up when you walk, luv."

She wrapped her arms around him, holding him, squeezing him too tight. Ferris's heartbeat echoed in her ears, that alluring rhythm drawing her in. With his bare skin pressed to her cheek, his scent became stronger, and as on the previous night, her fangs threatened to fall. There was a need, a drive, to tear into him. His throat, his wrist, then unbuckle and slide down his jeans ever so slowly so she could pierce his thigh with her teeth. She just wanted to taste him, his blood.

What the bloody hell was wrong with her? He wasn't mortal anymore, his blood wouldn't satisfy her hunger. Perhaps it was a different sort of craving she yearned for… She wanted to discover what else rested beneath his jeans. He was so tall, and she wondered how big his length was, how it would fit inside her mouth, slide against her tongue… Horrified at the thought, she drew out of Ferris's grasp—her *friend*—and backed away from him. "I gotta go."

"Mouse, wait—"

Before she could hear the rest of what he was going to say, she dashed from the hallway, past the stringed instruments hanging on the walls, and ran out the back door of the palace. She'd always loved feasting on Ferris, but she hadn't thought about tasting him like this before. This was Rav and Imogen's fault. *Steady, Mouse. You just need a human to drink from.*

Mouse didn't pause as she darted around the daisies and leapt into the mirror portal leading to the mortal world. It spat her out onto her stomach in the cemetery and Des wiggled in her pocket. The night was pitch black with a sliver of the moon in the sky— not a single owl hooted, but a rustling of one stirred in the tree above her. Pushing herself up from the damp grass, she checked on Des, finding her back asleep, before hurrying in the direction of the clubs.

On this night, she would slip into one where mortals pretended to be vampires. Once she made a vicious kill at a club, she would wait a bit before returning to it.

She thought about Ferris, when he'd first come to the palace, how surprise, anger, relief, and fright filled her at seeing him there. He shouldn't have risked his life, shouldn't have bedded Imogen to become a servant at her palace. Mouse didn't deserve what he'd done—she hadn't deserved that sort of friendship. Then there had been the drawings he'd snuck to her, ones that she looked at over and over after each threat, each beating, each death.

As she crossed the street toward the clubs, Mouse dropped her fangs. She could be her immortal self and easily blend in at the mortal vampire club.

She opened the door to a sleek black building and a broad man with auburn hair to his waist greeted her. "ID," he grunted over the loud music and adjusted his septum piercing.

Cocking her head, Mouse locked gazes with the man, letting her influence seep into him. "I'm old enough. Now let me in."

Eyes glazed, he nodded and she walked down a hall, decorated with framed vampire posters, into the main room where bodies danced against one another. A heavier song took over, its beats pounding like a rapid heart. Blood pulsed in tune inside the crowd's veins, and she wanted to taste each precious throat. A monstrous side of her wanted to shred them apart, drink them dry until nothing was left.

Mouse tightened her fists, steadying her breaths while scanning their attire. Several wore fangs, white or black contacts, bat wings, cloaks, leather, bondage, vinyl.

Her mouth was dry, and the thirst took over. She studied the room, then the bar, deciding who she would feed on tonight. A young man sat at the bar and she was about to just take him when a woman behind him, wearing a leather miniskirt and a fishnet shirt over a black bra, poured a clear liquid into a drink without the mortal seeing, then handed it to him. Mouse's brows rose. She hadn't seen a woman attempt to roofie a male before, and it looked as though it would be a death tonight instead of a feeding.

Mouse took the cup from the man's hand before he could drink from it. "Go dance," she said, persuading him out of his seat with her influence.

"Excuse me, bitch?" the woman spat, her fake fangs exposed.

Mouse stilled, the blood in her veins pulsing hot. Her voice came out quiet, deadly. "I think I've experienced worse than name-calling before. Come with me outside."

The woman's eyes glazed over and she nodded. It wasn't as fun this way, but the mortal wouldn't have followed her outside like the man had the other night.

Tonight she'd planned to feed on numerous mortals until her thirst was quenched, but draining one who'd done wrong would be more fulfilling.

When they got outside, Mouse led the mortal to the back of the building where only the rubbish bin lingered, its decaying stench drifting in the air. She released her influence on the woman to see the horror on her face, then lunged forward, shredding her throat apart as she fed, lapping up the taste, the *feel*, of the blood on her tongue.

"What is this?" a man stuttered.

Mouse jerked her head up to a mortal holding a bag of rubbish. His eyes widened at the blood covering her mouth, her dress. *Monster*, he thought—she could see it in his expression.

His blood caressed her nose—she couldn't control herself and leapt forward, knocking him to the building. Mouse pierced his throat with her fangs, yearning for only a taste.

She needed to stop.

But she was unable to stop.

She tore into him the way she had the woman, drinking all of his essence, relishing in the moment. His body was limp in her arms and she drew back, shaking. Des stirred in her pocket, fully alert. Since the donor building, Mouse had promised herself no more innocents.

What had she *done*?

CHAPTER FIVE

FERRIS

Ferris hadn't intended to follow Mouse. After she ran into him in the hallway, he'd gone back to his room and gotten dressed with the intention of finding himself a meal, but something felt … off. It almost felt like she was nervous to be near him, though he *knew* that wasn't true. Which meant either he'd done something to unintentionally upset her or something else was wrong. Once he found Mouse, he would either join her or go about his night, depending on whether she was all right or not.

Since Mouse had gotten a head start, Ferris used his enhanced speed to track her down. He'd already gone into two clubs that he knew Mouse enjoyed, finding a handful of vampires but none with pink hair. At the third establishment, he stopped dead. The hint of fresh mortal blood tinged the air. The metallic smell didn't mean Mouse was there, of course. It could've been any vampire, but there was only one way to find out.

As he rounded the back of the building, the scent became stronger. Ferris's fangs dropped without warning as the rich, metallic scent practically danced over his tongue. The odor was far *too* strong. This was no simple feeding. He ignored the urges pumping through him to *feed, feed, feed,* and approached the alley with silent steps.

And came to a dead stop.

Mouse held a man with flailing limbs against the building, feasting at his throat, a hand over his mouth. Surrounded by rubbish. She drank and drank as his movements slowed to a near stop, the body limp in her arms as she drew back, trembling with apparent hunger. Her grip on him tightened, and she leaned back down to lick away the remainder of blood still oozing from him.

"Mouse?" Ferris breathed. He'd never seen her like this. So wild. So … *starved.* Just behind her laid the lifeless body of a woman in a mini skirt. She'd drank two mortals to death and still craved more? It was too much. "Mouse!"

She raised her face from the man, her trembling ceasing as a savage glint flickered in her eyes, the dead mortal falling from her arms. Blood ran over her lips, dripped down her chin. And she snarled at him. The sharp twist of her mouth turned her sweet face into something foreign. Something feral.

"I beg your *fucking pardon?*" Disbelief coated his words. What the hell was happening right now? Had he walked into *The Twilight Zone?* Mouse had *snarled?* At *him?*

Her monstrous expression dissolved as recognition settled in. She stumbled back, furiously wiping at her face. "Ferris?" she squeaked. "What are you doing here?"

He took a tentative step forward, his eyes holding Mouse's terrified violet ones, until he reached the man's side. Kneeling in the pool of blood, he felt for the man's pulse, even though he already knew he was dead. There was nothing he could do here. Not for either of the victims. The woman was beyond help, her throat torn as if a ravenous beast had shredded her apart. He'd seen vampires do worse, had seen Imogen rip out hearts, Rav string victims out in the garden that he would break and cut. But not Mouse. Never had he seen her do something like this. She'd always been sweet when she'd drank from him, her touches light, her tongue delicate across his flesh.

"Ferris, I..." Mouse stumbled over a few consonants as she pulled Des from her pocket before falling completely silent. The caterpillar's head lifted to peer from Ferris to Mouse, worried.

"It's okay." Ferris stood and stepped over the man, taking Mouse's scarlet-coated face between his hands. More blood soaked into her dark clothes, leaving wet patches where the splatter had landed. "It's okay, Mouse. We need to feed, yeah?"

"But he was innocent," she whispered. "I couldn't stop myself."

"You didn't mean to, right?" he said in a consoling voice. While he knew she'd been struggling with her inner demons lately, he didn't want to believe Mouse killed without reason. She'd never been one to murder her way through a crowd before.

"Only *her*." Mouse's lips pursed, her nostrils flaring as she studied the dead woman's body.

Ferris froze. He was no stranger to killing. Of course not— he'd spent two years in the Ruby Heart Palace. Mortals had come and gone, either to their grave or onto immortality. But Mouse? *His* Mouse? The same female who had found him nearly dead and saved his life... It was hard to believe she'd murdered the woman just because she'd felt like it.

A rustling came from not far away and Ferris stepped away, grabbing Mouse's slick hand. "Come on. Let's get out of here."

Without waiting for Mouse to agree, he led her through the club, pausing only long enough to compel someone into taking a smoke out back so the bodies were found. After a quick stop in the bathroom to clean Mouse's face and hands—there was nothing they could do about the stained dress—the pair made their way through the gyrating bodies and techno music. It was a den of temptation. Even for Ferris, the scent of their arousals and promise of warm blood made his gums ache as his fangs almost descended. It would be worse for Mouse, who was still licking the corners of her mouth when she thought he wouldn't notice. He should've led her around the building, but they couldn't walk around with blood all over Mouse's face and hands without raising a few brows. At least the crimson-soaked dress wasn't as obvious. It blended well with the black fabric.

Outside, London greeted them. A dark sky, cobbled streets. Brick buildings with flower boxes lined the sidewalk, and people sat at tables set up outside a pub. Ferris held Mouse's hand as they walked, not fully trusting that she wouldn't try to make a beeline for a portal. If they went back to Wonderland, their conversation could be overheard by Maddie or Noah, but here, they had complete privacy.

"Would you like to go home?" he asked anyway, knowing he would never force her to divulge her secrets.

"Not yet. I … can't." Mouse's chest heaved, and he swore he could hear the desperation in her heartbeat.

"Okay," he soothed. "We don't have to go back yet. Let me take you somewhere else."

When she gave him a relieved nod, Ferris led her through streets lined with bars and clubs and down a narrow alley that ended in a small courtyard. Stone buildings rose up around an open-aired space with a dozen folding chairs tucked into rectangular tables. The windows looked into a dimly lit café and the shop door was held open in invitation by a stone. A tall woman with wiry hair popped out of one of the side doors and halted, a smile lighting her face.

"You're right on time!" she said brightly in an American accent. "Take a seat. I was just about to bring out our canvases."

"Oh, I…" Ferris had been expecting a quiet little alcove to talk to Mouse but, according to the sign he'd missed at first glance, he had led them to a paint and sip. *What the fuck is a paint and sip?* "Sorry, we didn't—"

"Oh, please stay!" She rushed forward, hands clasped under her chin. "It's my first-time hosting one and only three people signed up. *Three*," the woman emphasized. "And I'll do half price."

"What is it?" Mouse perked up, peering inside the door.

"A paint and sip." She motioned to the table set up in the small courtyard. "I have all the supplies and they'll bring us out the wine soon. We're painting the magnificence that is the night sky today, hence the late hour. Which, now that I think about it, might be why so few people are coming…" She bit her lip and Mouse squeezed Ferris's hand, her fingers digging in. He cast a glance at the vampire, finding her eyes locked onto the woman's neck. "I'm Linda, by the way."

Ferris drew in a breath. "I don't think—"

"Let us participate for free," Mouse said, using her influence on the mortal woman.

"Of course." The mortal's eyes glazed over. Another couple walked into the alleyway, their arms draped around one another, and drew Linda's attention. "Have a seat," she urged them before going to greet the newcomers.

"Let's go," Ferris whispered at the same time Mouse said, "Let's stay."

He blinked down at her. After she'd killed two people in a back alley, she wanted to stay and paint? There was blood on the knees of his jeans and splashed across her black dress, though it was hard to see on her. And, he supposed, his jeans could look mud-stained in this lighting.

Still, he said, "I'm not sure that's a good idea." He'd wanted to take Mouse somewhere more private, away from small spaces full of humans. Because, while she'd calmed down significantly on their walk here, there was still a slight glimmer of hunger behind her gaze.

"I'll be good," she promised, perking up, and slipped into the nearest seat.

With a silent sigh, Ferris joined her. He couldn't believe they were doing this together, that she was doing something—anything—other than wandering the Ivory Palace like a ghost or lying in bed humming. It almost felt like old times when they would meet in a club before slipping away so she could feed from him. Then they would hang out and talk for hours or watch old movies on his cracked leather sofa. She seemed almost *relieved* to be sitting there with him at the moment, which tugged his lips into a slight smile. Maybe she was thinking the same thing…

"You came after me tonight?" Mouse asked as Linda led the others to the opposite end of the table.

Ferris leaned back in his chair and shifted slightly to face her better. The light freckles sprinkled across her nose and cheeks made him want to trace patterns in them, and the curve of her lips held his attention, possibly for a beat too long. "You ran away from me at the palace as though I'd hurt you or something. I wanted to make sure you were all right."

"I'm fine," Mouse whispered. "I'm always fine."

"Sometimes we're not fine." He leaned in closer, lifting her chin, as her gaze locked on his. "Sometimes we have to talk about our demons to someone. You can talk to me, luv. Always." Her gardenia scent caressed his nose and a warm feeling washed over him. Something raw, growing bolder.

Mouse opened her mouth to say something when Linda returned, along with an older woman who sat down opposite them, and began handing out a canvas and paintbrush to everyone. Ferris blinked, dropping his hand from Mouse's chin.

He'd wondered at times where she'd been going so frequently, but he didn't own her, and it wasn't his right to ask. But maybe she'd been visiting a particular mortal for feedings. Like she had with him. Only, maybe *unlike* him, they would've done more than feed. *Fucking.* A chill of jealousy crept through him and he frowned. "Next time you have an ache to run off, you can ask me to come. I'd go anywhere with you, luv."

"All right. But if I don't ask, don't follow me." She furrowed her brow as though thinking deeply about something.

"So…" He glanced carefully around at the mortals who were all preparing the paint Linda had set into the center of the table. Mouse grabbed a few tubes of blue and set them down between them. Ferris picked up the cerulean and worked the paint from the end, rolling the tube. "What happened back there?"

"Nothing I'm not used to," Mouse answered matter-of-factly.

Ferris arched a brow. They were vampires, so of course she'd killed before, but she hadn't been the Mouse he knew when she snarled at him so viciously over her prey. "I don't know what that means."

She let out a breath. "You don't know everything about my past."

Linda appeared at the end of the table and handed Ferris two small pallets for the paint. "Here you are. Is everyone ready to get started?"

Ferris passed Mouse her pallet and they both silently squeezed a dab of each paint color onto the wood. Mouse and the single woman exchanged tubes once they were finished, giving them all two different shades of blue, black, white, and yellow.

Linda set up her own canvas and started discussing how to make the paintings their own. She was only there to guide them, but they were free to use whatever inspired them about the night sky. As she went on about mixing colors, a waiter brought out a tray with glasses, half of them full of red wine, the other half with white.

"Thanks," Ferris muttered as he and Mouse took theirs. They wouldn't drink them, but they wanted to at least *seem* like they would. As a mortal, he'd drunk enough wine—and vodka and beer and rum—to last ten lifetimes. Any alcohol he could get his hands on after Ellie died. He drank and drank until he blacked out or vomited his guts out.

Mouse tapped the end of her paint brush against her lips in quiet contemplation. They were still a little pinker than usual from her scrubbing the blood away with paper towels in the club bathroom. A little fuller, even. Ferris lifted a hand to smooth out the crease between her brows but stopped himself.

"What?" she whispered, apparently noticing how quickly he'd dropped his hand.

Clearing his throat, he pretended to pluck something from her hair. "You have some lint."

Mouse glanced sideways at him. "Do you know what you'll paint? You know how to get fancy with this sort of thing while you've seen my scribbles. Perhaps I should just follow Linda's instructions."

Her art skills weren't the best, he would admit, but he loved her attempts anyway. Once, when he was still human, she'd found one of his drawings and asked him to teach her. "Fine, luv, but only if you don't tell your sister. I don't need the whole world asking me for lessons," he'd teased.

Mouse had come to his flat for her first and last lesson. The pencil strokes were too light as if she were afraid to make a mistake or commit her vision to paper. In the end, she had a blob that was meant to be a mouse. They'd laughed together, the first full laugh he'd had since he'd lost Ellie and their daughter. Then Mouse had fed from his wrist, his fingers tangled in her hair, while he relished in that high, in her friendship. Ferris had kept that drawing. Hidden it in his room in the Ruby Heart Palace for two years and taken it with him when he fled with Ever's set of keys. Right now, it was tucked into one of his old sketchbooks back in Ivory.

"Let's do what we feel," Ferris said. "And we won't peek at each other's until the end."

"Mmm, so like a present to one another." Mouse smiled and nudged his shoulder with hers, then shifted in her seat so she could hide her canvas better. Ferris grinned and mirrored her movements. They spent the next two hours working on their art as Linda led the group in replicating her own painting. The mortals laughed and drank as they moved their brushes. He and Mouse stayed focused, his gaze every so often sliding to the milky skin of her face, her neck, her shoulder, stirring something within him that had been hidden for so long.

In the end, Ferris had created a sky of blues and blacks. Stars flecked across the landscape where he ran his thumb over the brush, to splatter white paint in a fine mist. In the top corner, he crafted a full moon and spread a cloud over the bottom half. Two more wispy clouds cut across the image. It was his perfect sky—one meant to be gazed at from below in wonder.

"Ready to share?" he asked Mouse.

She remained quiet.

"Mouse?" He shifted to face her. "Do you need more time?"

She shook her head and slid her canvas toward him. Ferris peered down to find the entire square painted black. The paint was thick, the brush strokes choppy and sharp, as if she tried desperately to force the canvas to become even darker. "You said to paint how we feel," she explained.

Fuck. Ferris dropped his canvas to the table and scooped her out of her chair. They needed to get back to Wonderland and away from the prying eyes of mortals. Then she needed to talk to him, tell him exactly what was going on and how he could help her. Doing nothing was obviously not helping. Sleeping beside her. Offering her distractions with games and books. Comforting her. None of that was enough. He needed to do something more, be someone better, to help *her.* More than ever, he was relieved he'd listened to Chess and kept the Jabberwocky quill a secret. She didn't need added pressure.

"What did I do wrong?" she squeaked as he raced away from the pub, heading toward the portal back to Ivory, with her tucked against him.

"Nothing. You did nothing wrong, luv," he whispered. "We should go home now and I'll draw you a bath. Then we're going to leave the Ivory Palace together for a while."

CHAPTER SIX

MOUSE

If Shakespeare were still alive to write Mouse's story, she wondered if it would end up a tragedy or one of his rare, semi-happily ever afters. As the wind rumpled her hair, her face planted against Ferris's strong chest while he ran her home from the paint pub, she took in the darkness behind her closed eyelids. Black. Black. Black. Just as she'd painted across her canvas at the paint pub Ferris had taken her to. Her life, she decided, was leading toward a tragedy, one that Shakespeare's ghost may rise from the dead to write at that very moment. *Woe is me.*

Mouse finally forced herself to open her eyes, pulling herself away from the black oblivion. She peered up at Ferris, his determined gaze focused straight ahead, his hard muscles flexing against her flesh as he moved. The floral scent of Ivory washed over her and a murder of crows cawed high in the night sky. Over the course of her life, she'd been saved on numerous accounts. First by Maddie who'd turned her into a vampire, then by Noah who'd rescued her from her prison, and now by Ferris who'd helped too many times to count. Even in the mortal world, centuries ago, Maddie had always been there to get Mouse out of trouble, except for the one time she wasn't… The thing was, Mouse didn't mind being saved. What did it matter if one wasn't a savior? Did that make them any less worthy in life? In a story? In Hamlet, even though Ophelia was a tragic heroine, that didn't make her *nothing*. Everyone was something.

But Mouse didn't want Ferris to think she *always* required rescuing—he had his own inner demons he needed to face.

"I can walk," Mouse whispered, staring at the hard lines of Ferris's handsome face. She'd always thought him pretty with sharp angles and chiseled features.

As though attuned to her low words, Ferris halted, not arguing as he lowered her to the pale grass. "I didn't mean to go all caveman on you there, but I just wanted to get you home," he said, his chest heaving.

"If I didn't want you taking me home, you would've certainly heard it from my lips." The palace rested ahead, its gothic physique appearing ethereal beneath the moon's glow. "Let's go through the back. Ever's gone, but I had a slight argument with Maddie earlier and I don't want to see her just yet."

"Mmm, so avoid the Hatter. Done." He smirked, grasping her hand and leading her to the back of the palace. They passed tall white daisies that danced with the breeze. A few guards stood in the windows, peering out at them, and gave a brief nod.

Mouse took out her key and unlocked the backdoor. They slipped inside, finding Didi guarding near the stairs. "Good evening," the female said, bowing her head.

"Hey, Didi, hope you're staying out of trouble." Ferris grinned as they passed and Mouse studied the floor. She should finally say hello, too, be friendly, invite her to one of Maddie's tea parties like she would've in the past, but she just couldn't. There weren't tea parties for Mouse any longer.

"Oh, you know me, just making sure no bastards take over Ivory again," Didi said.

Noah's deep voice echoed down the hall and Mouse hurried

up the ivory staircase before he could relay to Maddie that her sister was back. Not that she would shame him for it, but Noah didn't keep anything from Maddie, not after their journey to save his sister … and Mouse.

They ventured down the silent hallway, neither saying a word until they stepped into her room. Mouse left the door cracked open behind her and turned to Ferris, the skirt of her dress swishing. "I'm sorry," she rushed the words out.

His brow furrowed. "What do you have to be sorry for, luv?"

Mouse rolled her gaze to the ceiling. The way she'd acted when she'd first seen him behind the club—it was as though she wasn't herself for a second, as if she didn't recognize him. "Snarling at you earlier. Then we were having a pleasant time at the paint pub and I made more mistakes. Perhaps I should have just painted the night sky or *sunshine* instead."

He bent his knees, lowering himself so they were eye to eye. "Snarl at me and I'll snarl right back," he teased. "And I think we both hate sunshine, so that would've been a horrific choice. As for the canvas, you painted how you felt. You could've hidden it and not shown me. Instead, you let me in. That's fucking brave."

Mouse didn't feel brave. As she stared into his eyes, a curious emotion washed over her. She wanted to know what was hidden behind those dark irises of his—his past—as she'd always reveled in the here and now with him. Yet right then, standing in this room, she wanted to know what had ailed him and how he'd faced those demons. How they could exorcise the gruesome things they'd both dealt with at the Ruby Heart Palace. Perhaps together?

"I'm going to draw a bath for you," Ferris said, "then we can talk."

"I can start my own bath, you know." Her lips tilted up at the edges.

"Not the way *I* can." He smiled and leaned in close. "There will be lots of bubbles."

She couldn't help laughing. A warmth spread through her as

Ferris exited toward the bathing chamber, glancing one more time over his shoulder at her before going in.

Her smile faltered as she mulled over the talking part… Ferris was going to dig like Maddie. Dig and dig until there was nothing left to find but her melted, ruined heart. The brokenness. Some vampires murdered relentlessly—she'd killed over the years when she felt the ache of what Mr. Taylor had stolen from her, but what she was doing, what she was starting to become wasn't her—it was Rav's monster. His creation.

Running water echoed from the bathing chamber and Mouse lowered herself to the soft bed. She removed her boots before fishing Des out from her dress pocket.

The caterpillar cocked her head at Mouse, her furry body completely blue, not a sign of yellow in sight. This meant her mood was down too.

"I know. I know, I did a very bad thing tonight. Again." Mouse couldn't get the image of the man she'd killed out of her head. She wanted to believe that he was an awful human being, but most likely he wasn't. What if he had a wife? Children? *Stop it, Mouse. It's done.* A part of her still believed that walking outside into the sun would be the answer, but what came after that? She didn't know if she would end up in a true hell, where Rav and Imogen were.

Des wrapped her furry body around Mouse's finger, giving it a hug.

"Thank you, friend," she murmured, then placed the caterpillar on top of a fresh leaf on the bedside table. Blood lingered on Mouse's dress, the metallic odor brushing her senses. Her body trembled, remembering not only the man's face tonight but all the donors she'd slaughtered in the building. Her teeth diving in, her strength tearing off limbs as she'd fed, blood spraying her flesh…

Humming escaped Mouse's lips while her heart pounded faster, her throat turning dry. Ferris's heavy footsteps behind Mouse drew her out of her bloody reverie. She stood to face him, his eyes growing wide.

"You're shivering." He wrapped an arm around her, the heat radiating from him making her eyes flutter, her body tremble less.

"I know. The bath will warm me up," Mouse said, keeping her voice light, even though she didn't feel cold anymore next to Ferris. "Don't go yet." She walked past him, inhaling his comforting scent once more.

Lavender enveloped her as she kept the door cracked behind her, the bath filled with endless bubbles. The edges of her lips tugged up again, and Ferris was right—he did know how to make a bath. One fit for royalty. She peeled the clothing from her body, unplaited her hair, and stepped into the water. A low moan poured from her mouth as she sank into the bath's depths.

"You can come in now," Mouse called after she was settled beneath the foam.

Ferris cleared his throat and the door opened fully, but she couldn't see him or even his hulking shadow.

"I said come in, Ferris." She laughed, amused. "I'm up to my throat in bubbles and you wanted to talk." As she studied him, her thoughts turned in an unexpected direction—Ferris slipping into the room, her pulling him into the bath with her, clothes and all, his large hands skimming up her naked body, cupping her breasts, then dipping his fingers into her heat.

He stepped inside, yanking her from her not unwanted thoughts, and raked a hand through his dark hair, his eyes darting everywhere but on her. "We do need to talk, but we don't have to talk in *here*."

For a brief moment, the humming left her lips like earlier, just as it had in her prison cell, just as it would when wandering the Ivory Palace halls. She wanted to keep her thoughts inside her, not bombard anyone, but she couldn't. Not any longer.

"I don't want you to see me differently..." she whispered, twirling her finger through the bubbles.

"I see you, Mouse. *You.* Only you. That won't change." Ferris's gaze trained on hers as he sat on the floor, propping his back against the pale cabinets.

"You know that Rav and Imogen would bring me behind

closed doors for interrogations," she said slowly, taking calming breaths. "It wasn't only chatting or taunting—it was more than that. They would break me apart. Whip me, drown me, remove my eyes, drain me of blood. So much and too much. And the times when I would see you in my cell, I wanted to forget, and I did. By you being there, it was as though everything was fine."

"They *what?*" Ferris inhaled sharply, his hand covering his mouth. "You didn't tell me any of that. I thought—"

"You thought it was bad but not this bad. Chess was there sometimes and—"

"That fucking bastard." Ferris pushed himself from the floor. "I'm going to kill him."

"No." She leaned forward, holding a hand up. "No. You know he helped me with Des."

"But he did *nothing,*" Ferris growled, his fangs dropped.

"He did the best he could and he's done so much now." Mouse paused, taking a deep swallow. "I haven't told anyone. Not even Maddie. And it wasn't only me who faced Rav and Imogen's wraths—you did as well."

Ferris gripped the back of his neck, his face twisted in pain. "Mouse, it was hell for me there, but nothing like that. Imogen's taunts about my past? Cleaning the palace with my tongue? Rav being an arsehole? Seeing all that awful shit? That is nothing compared to this. I would spend a damn eternity doing all that for them not to have touched a hair on your body."

Ferris was being a savior, but perhaps she was, too, because she would've dealt with it for an eternity if he was safe. "We can't compare our experiences. They were both equally life-changing. It's why I had to get you out of there."

Ferris narrowed his eyes. "What do you mean get *me* out of there?"

Bollocks, he wasn't going to like this. "It's why I told you to save Alice."

"Motherfucker." He clenched his jaw. "I should've known."

He wouldn't have saved himself, otherwise. "It all worked out," she said, cocking her head, the frown still on his face but slowly dissolving.

"But what if it hadn't?"

"It did, though."

"You have the best heart, you know that?" He inched closer to her.

"No, Ferris, I don't." Mouse reclined in the water, leaning her head against the back of the bathtub as she stared at the ceiling. "Once I was free, everything hit me at once. The memories. The hunger. To go without feeding straight from the source while enduring Rav's abuse did *something* to me. I'm just so blasted hungry all the time."

"You have been feeding more than normal. But it will have to level out soon, right?" It sounded more like a question, one that she had no answer to.

"There's something else you don't know about me," she said softly. "Because of something in my past, I kill mortals differently. Over the centuries, when I feel the hunger stir, when I'm having a rough day, I venture out into the mortal world and take someone's life who I believe deserves it. Today it was the woman you saw—she'd been trying to drug another mortal. But recently it's become more frequent, less controllable, and I … I did something awful not long ago."

"Go on." Ferris knelt at the bathtub, not a single sign of fear shining in his eyes. He wasn't as old as her and had only been a vampire for two years, so he would have a much stronger human side than she did.

"I'm the reason the donor building is temporarily closed. I killed everyone inside with my bloodlust." Tears pricked her eyes and she wanted to sink beneath the water, drown herself for a second before her breaths returned, but she kept her gaze locked on his.

His brows rose, his throat bobbing. "That's why it's closed?"

"Yes, only Ever and Chess know."

"Chess again?" Ferris said between gritted teeth, the muscle feathering along his jaw.

"He was with Ever when they spotted me returning here

drenched in blood. Since that day, I sometimes lose control of my hunger and I'm trying not to unravel. But I don't know what's happening."

"I promise I'll help you, luv, and I won't tell anyone." Ferris's soft gaze turned hard. "If Rav wasn't dead, I would murder the fucker. Piece by piece. Over and over."

Mouse could feel the ghosts of Rav's needles piercing her flesh, taking and taking and taking not only her blood but her essence. She couldn't confess anymore, not right then. "Can we talk more tomorrow?"

Ferris nodded, pushing a lock of wet hair behind her ear, and her stomach fluttered at the gentle movement. "Get some rest and we'll decide our next step then."

Mouse watched him leave, keeping the door cracked behind him, and a little weight lifted off her chest after her confessions. But as she sat in the bath for a long while, hours passing, the weight started to build back on her lungs, her bones, like an anchor wanting to tug her below the freezing water's surface. Her breathing came out quick, her body shivering from the cold water, and she needed to see someone. It had to be Ferris because she still couldn't go to Maddie and talk about everything again. Not right now.

Mouse threw on a long black skirt and silky shirt, then padded down the hall to Ferris's room. She just needed to slide in bed beside him and hold onto him.

As the door creaked open, her gaze settled on a muscular form resting on the bed. Smooth, naked tan skin. Mouse blinked and blinked. Ferris was usually under the covers… But not now. He lay face down, his firm buttocks on display, his taut back covered in the tattoo she'd always been drawn to. A piece that made it look like his skin had been peeled away, revealing a mechanical system beneath the layers. He'd sketched it himself for the artist to tattoo the design on him. Her eyes drifted back down to his arse, lingering on the delectable curves of it. Why couldn't she take her eyes from that body part? Her fangs threatened to drop, to sink into his taut muscles.

Ferris stirred, rolling over, his gaze meeting hers. "Mouse? Shit, let me get dressed."

Mouse spun around from him, but not before she caught a quick peek at his length—thick, long and perfect with a shiny silver piercing at its tip. "I know you thought you wouldn't see me until tomorrow…"

"No, it's fine." The rustle of clothing sounded.

She studied the poster on the wall, a black and white scene of a drum set covered in fog, trying to distract herself from what she'd just seen. A heat spread through her, drifting lower, and she liked it a bit too much. She thought about Maddie and how her sister would use sex in the past to take away her pain. For the first time in her life, Mouse truly wanted to give in to that lust, trail her tongue down Ferris's abs, then run it up his cock. Mr. Taylor had taken that want from her. He'd been courting Mouse and they'd done things … but she'd wanted to wait until marriage to make love and the bastard hadn't. But this wasn't about covering up pain. She wanted to see what it would feel like for Ferris to slide himself inside her.

No. He's your friend. Emphasis on friend. A friend she wanted to—

"You can turn around now." Ferris's voice came out thick with sleep.

She slowly spun to face him, finding him now dressed in only dark trousers. "I was just seeing if you wanted to take a walk." There was no way she could lay beside him at the moment, in a bed, where she would either be thinking of what it would be like to sink her teeth into him to taste his blood or what it would feel like to have his length inside her. *What in the world was happening?*

"Of course, wake me up for a nightly stroll any time."

Or a nightly fuck. Mouse's eyes widened at her own inner thought, but she schooled her features and nodded.

As they walked out of the palace, the fresh air circling her, Mouse was starting to feel back to herself instead of focusing on Ferris's naked body.

"So, luv, should we discuss our top-secret plan to curb your appetite?" He waggled his brows, making it so she knew he was there for her, despite what she'd done.

"Ah yes, the lovely plan." She smiled, nudging his arm with hers. "Do tell me more about it."

"Imagine this." He smiled wide, tiptoeing his fingers across his palm. "We get the fuck out of here for a week and—"

In the distance, a piercing wail reverberated, interrupting Ferris. They both stopped and Mouse squinted, catching sight of arrows soaring through the sky from the city. The next roar shook the trees, followed by blood-curdling screams. And then she saw the creature darting through the sky, its leather wings cracking like thunder.

The Jabberwocky.

CHAPTER SEVEN

FERRIS

Mouse tensed beside Ferris as the massive beast circled closer, practically overhead, its leather wings beating so hard the wind whipped the branches of trees. He could practically feel the predatory gaze scrape against him where they stood on the far side of the moat outside the palace. It sent a shiver down his spine and he reached out to touch Mouse, to remind himself she was beside him and safe. Knowing she was okay allowed him to steel himself against the danger. To be the guard he was trained to be.

This is the Jabberwocky. The roaring beast could be nothing else—especially with the quills poking out from its fur. The same as the one he'd found near the lake.

A volley of arrows soared through the sky from the palace turrets just as screams rose up from the streets. The Jabberwocky tilted, avoiding being hit, and dove for the center of the city, landing with a boisterous thud. Ferris remembered the quill hidden inside the large vase just inside the main doors.

Remembered and regretted listening to that bastard Chess. Ferris had seen what happened to someone who was killed by the creature. Seen that practically nothing was left of them with bits and pieces strewn about the blood-soaked grass.

"We have to stop it from destroying the city," Maddie called, bursting from the palace and racing across the bridge to them.

As Ferris looked again toward the hideous beast with its deep green, almost black, fur, quills, rows of sharp teeth, talons, wings, and barbed tail, he had only one thought: *How?* He'd seen many things in the Ruby Heart Palace. All sorts of torture. Brutal murders. Everything in between and beyond. But he'd only heard tales of the Jabberwocky—and everyone seemed to agree on one thing. If you see the legendary monster of Wonderland, run … and hope your friends are slower than you.

"Mouse!" Maddie cried and swept her into a quick hug. "I'm sorry for earlier, but we have other matters to deal with as you can see. Here."

Ferris forced his gaze away from the monster to find Maddie handing Mouse a bow and arrows. "Do you know how to use that thing?" he asked.

"Of course." Mouse swung the quiver of arrows over her shoulder. "I should already know, but what weapon are you best with?"

"Preferably a gun." Swords and arrows were fine, but he was more of a modern-weapon guy.

Maddie produced a gun, having seemed to suspect his answer, and held it out to him. "Silver bullets won't save our arses like they did with the werewolves, but they'll still hurt like hell."

Ferris took it from her and flicked off the safety. The weight felt good in his hand, powerful. Deadly. When he looked up, he noticed Maddie and Noah each held a matching gun as well.

"Hurry," Maddie urged the group.

Guards were already filing from other palace entrances, swords drawn, arrows nocked, and Maddie and Noah raced after them. Didi and Mock led the group, their bright white uniforms soft in the moonlight. Following suit, Ferris took off for the city where screams seemed to rattle the windows. The sound mingled with the monstrous roars and his racing pulse, creating chaos inside his head.

"Come on, slowcoaches!" Didi yelled back at them, and Mouse smirked.

Running against the crowd, Ferris pivoted and jumped to avoid colliding with those fleeing. It was every vampire for themself as they tore down the streets. A blonde female fell and curled onto her side when a male stepped on her chest. More feet pummeled against her lithe body, marring her white suit. Ferris shifted between vampires with the intent to help her up, but she beat him to the punch the moment a pocket formed between citizens. Blood trickled down her forehead, the sweet copper scent quickly filling the air, but she wasted no time disappearing between shops.

The ground vibrated with another growl when Ferris and his friends neared the city center. Quills poked above the tops of buildings as the Jabberwocky reared up. Its wings stood high and proud. And the stench… *Bloody hell, the smell.* A mixture of wet dog and rot permeated the air, burning his nostrils. Ferris drew in a shallow, steadying breath. *Damn.* The beast was even bigger up close.

When they reached the edge of the town center to fully face the Jabberwocky, Mouse released an arrow. The projectile hit its back leg and bounced away, but the Jabberwocky didn't even flinch. Just turned slowly, eyes narrowed, and slammed a taloned furred foot down on the granite fountain.

A loud *crunch* sounded as the stone crumbled to dust. Water flowed between the cobblestones, carrying away rivulets of blood that dripped from a mangled body clutched in the beast's talons. He hadn't noticed it until just then—the top of the head was barely visible between the beast's claws, strands of dark hair trailing over the beast's fur.

Another arrow flew, singing through the air as a dozen more followed from the guards that had caught up. All projectiles hit.

All bounced harmlessly away. Mock aligned two arrows onto his bowstring at once and let them soar. "This isn't working," he called out.

"Bollocks," Mouse mumbled. "We need something stronger."

"Fuck," Noah hissed.

Mock was right—the Jabberwocky didn't even seem to care they were attacking it. They were no match against this bloody thing. Not without better weapons, not without strategy. He raised the gun Maddie had given him. Aimed. Shot.

The blast echoed through the city center, vibrations running up his arm, and the Jabberwocky whipped its head to face them. A low growl rumbled out from between jagged teeth, its foul breath carrying all the way to them. But its fierce orange eyes only flickered over them as if they were fucking insects. Instead, the monster turned its gaze to the surrounding buildings. The streets. The sky. Its nostrils flared, quills bristling. It was almost like the beast was searching for something…

"Fuck this," Didi shouted, shoving her plait over her shoulder. She bolted forward with her sword raised and released a battle cry.

The Jabberwocky spun, its body a blur. It was much faster than Ferris expected something its size to be. One second, Didi was racing forward, the next, she was between its teeth. She didn't even have enough time to scream. With one grinding *crunch*, Didi's lower half fell to the ground with a wet *thwack*.

Mock screamed her name and Ferris's breath caught in his throat. Didi … was dead. His eyes had witnessed it happen, but his brain rejected the idea. She was too full of life for it to be snuffed out so easily. They'd only just become friends…

Fuck this, Didi had yelled. And Ferris couldn't have agreed more. He raised his gun as the beast chewed. Fired his weapon again and again. One of the bullets slammed into the Jabberwocky's soft upper lip and a small spot of blood shot outward. The Jabberwocky reared back, half-howled, half-screeched, and threw the unknown dead body from its talons at

Ferris.

Leaping backward, the mangled, dark-haired corpse splattered at his feet. The head was completely flattened, making it impossible to know who it might have been, and a large hole pierced straight through their chest cavity, exposing snapped ribs and torn intestines.

"Fucking hell," he breathed. Images of Rav's experiments flashed through his mind. The bodies Ferris had to dispose of. The brain matter he had to mop up…

Mouse sucked in a sharp breath and he snapped his gaze to her, hoping she wasn't thinking about the same thing. *Rav's room of horror.* But no, it wasn't that, not as something darker filled her eyes—*hunger.* Her fangs dropped, piercing her bottom lip where she'd bitten it, and she shifted her feet back. Whether it was about stepping away from the vampire's body or away from the Jabberwocky wasn't clear, but Ferris grabbed her arm to steady her as she swayed.

The Jabberwocky scanned the city center once more as Mock fired uselessly at its face, screaming his rage. Then, Ferris could've sworn intelligence flickered in the beast's eyes. Throwing its head back, the beast released a high-pitched screech and leapt into the sky. The Jabberwocky pounded against the air to gain momentum for its massive body, dipping a few times before soaring away.

With the crack of the Jabberwocky's wings fading, silence descended, heavy and cloying. Ferris tucked the gun into his waistband and turned to Mouse. Her eyes were wide as she stared at the blood on the ground, her breaths coming too fast. "Luv," he said slowly. "Let's get you back to the palace."

She jerked at the sound of his voice and lifted a hand to hide her fangs. "I'm fine. We need to clean up the city."

Ferris took in the carnage, the crumbled fountain, pieces of debris knocked from surrounding buildings. Shattered glass lay in front of windows, their awnings in tatters. Shingles from roofs littered the ground. But none of that mattered. Either the guards or the people who lived in the city could take care of it. It was more important that Mouse didn't lose her self-control and attack a guard. Worse yet if she tried to drink the blood from the cobblestones. She was considering it—he could see the thought in her eyes as her gaze flicked back to the blood on the ground.

"We can handle it," Maddie said. Her tone was strained, her shoulders stiff, but she offered Mouse a comforting smile. "I'll see you in a little bit, all right? Ever is already being summoned to return."

"I can help clean up," Mouse insisted.

"No," the Hatter said with a sigh. She looked over her shoulder and sighed a second time at the sight of Noah holding Mock back from Didi's half-corpse. "Please, go inside. We'll take care of Mock, but you need to take care of yourself."

"Fine." Mouse relented.

Ferris released a breath and guided her away from the gore. Vampires were already creeping back from their hiding places. *Cowards.* Not that Ferris blamed them. It wasn't fair to ask most of Wonderland to take up arms when they weren't trained to fight. A chill ran down his spine as he thought about the massive wings, claws, and teeth. The damned thing was built to kill.

"Are you all right?" Mouse asked when they entered the palace through the main doors.

Ferris furrowed his brow. "Me?"

"You look a little horrified," she said.

"Well, yeah," he admitted. "But what about you?"

She bit her bottom lip. "I'm … hungry."

"I know." He gave her a small smile and turned them toward the storage rooms where the blood was kept. Aware that Mouse craved it fresh from the source, he wasn't sure how much good the powdered stuff would do to take her edge off. There was little to be done about that tonight, though. Anyone she fed off of would probably end up like that bloke behind the club. *Dead.*

"The Jabberwocky has never attacked anyone here before," Mouse wondered aloud, seeming to speak to herself.

Yes, it has.

"I'm going to get Des," she added before scampering up the

nearby staircase.

Ferris opened the door to the small kitchen where meals would sometimes be cooked for human visitors. Pops of blue in the tile backsplash accented the gray quartz countertops and white cupboards. A small sink, narrow icebox, and gas-powered burner made it functional. He ran his hands down his face and released a sigh. Things couldn't be calm for two fucking seconds? He had to jump right back into the fire and lie to Mouse on top of it?

Mouse entered the kitchen, steps light as air, and took a seat on one of the tall barstools along the peninsula. She set Des on the cool marble in front of her. "So, what do you think could've changed? To bring the Jabberwocky so far into Ivory, I mean."

"Damned if I know," Ferris muttered. He poured some of the powered blood into a water bottle, shook it, and guzzled it down to ward off the hunger that always followed a battle.

With Imogen and Rav dead, and Chess and Ever merging territories, it was possible the upheaval set the beast off. Ferris set about collecting a few packs of powdered blood and water bottles, his mind wandering. The Jabberwocky had been at the lake, so very near the palace, only days ago. Had killed someone then too. Chess had a point about not creating panic over the quill Ferris had found, but now? The Jabberwocky had done that all on his own.

Ferris ran a hand through his hair. "Mouse?"

"Yes?" She eyed the red liquid he'd absentmindedly prepared, and he slid it toward her.

"I need to tell you something."

CHAPTER EIGHT

MOUSE

"The other day I—"

Ferris was cut off when two sets of loud footsteps echoed down the marble hallway and Mouse turned from him to find Ever and Chess rushing toward them.

"Are you two all right?" Ever asked, her nostrils flaring and her plaited hair disheveled. "One of the guards came through the portal to Scarlet as soon as he heard the Jabberwocky, but it seems we're too late. I shouldn't have left." She sighed, flexing her hands.

"No," Mouse whispered. "The guards were prepared, but the Jabberwocky hasn't been in Ivory since the day when I…" Slaughtered all those innocent donors. Lost control of herself instead of continuing to fight it.

Chess let out a low whistle, observing his nails, then arched a brow at Ever and Ferris. The queen pursed her lips and Ferris's throat bobbed while they all exchanged a knowing look.

"What is it?" Mouse stepped toward Ever as she gently

placed Des in her pocket. "I should've been more observant, been ready if the Jabberwocky had returned. But perhaps I didn't expect for the beast to do something like this since it hasn't made an appearance in months."

"The Jabberwocky has been here recently," Ever said slowly. "Once for certain. And made a kill."

Mouse tensed, her gaze drifting from face to face. Her chest tightened as their knowing looks seemed to make sense. "No one told me?"

"About that..." Chess ran his thumb across his lower lip, glancing over his shoulder down the hallway. "After the Knave found a quill from the Jabberwocky, I ordered him to stay quiet about it until I spoke to Ever."

Mouse glanced at Ferris and he narrowed his eyes at Chess.

"So Maddie didn't know either?" Mouse murmured.

Chess scratched the side of his face while peering at Ever. "This is going to get a bit messy now, Queenie."

"No, Maddie knows," Ever said. "I informed all the guards before I left for Scarlet."

Mouse's heart sped up, the white room seeming to pulse in sync with her blasted organ. "But I saw you before you left, and I went to Maddie right after that. *No one* said anything to me."

Ever placed a hand on Mouse's shoulder. "We felt it was best not to until we learned more. We didn't believe the Jabberwocky was an immediate threat, and not only did I leave Maddie in charge while I was away, but I prepared guards to warn me if I needed to return from Scarlet immediately. You've been going through a lot. More so lately. It just didn't feel right to make you worry."

Inhaling a sharp breath, Mouse drew out of Ever's grasp. "So is everyone going to tiptoe around me? Hide important matters from me? We talked about the Jabberwocky months ago in the garden. You didn't mind then."

"That's because you'd heard the beast," Chess pointed out. "You were outside, remember?" Outside and covered in the donors' blood...

"Hush." Ever elbowed him in the arm.

As Mouse opened her mouth to speak, more footsteps sounded, vibrating across the floor. She glanced toward the hallway just as Maddie and Noah entered the room with a few guards behind them, including Mock. Their clothing was spotted with a mixture of blood and dirt, the reek of death. She pushed away the alluring metal odor that started to overpower the rest.

"Wait." Mouse held a hand up and focused back on Chess. "Did Noah know the Jabberwocky was here before you left for Scarlet?"

"Not from me—Maddie's boy toy has a big mouth. But after Ever told the Hatter…" Chess trailed off.

"I did tell him." Maddie skirted around Chess while biting her lip. "But he's—"

"I don't care if he's one of the guards. He's been in Wonderland for barely any time at all." Mouse balled her hands into fists, then pointed at herself. "*I've* been here for centuries, *Madeline*. I don't care if you think I'm the actual *mad* one—I deserved the truth. I deserved to be warned."

"Mouse, you need to understand," Ferris said, his voice pleading.

"No!" Mouse cut him off. "You're the worst one of all." Even though it may have seemed childish to everyone there, she turned on her heel and raced from the room, darting up the stairs with her sister shouting behind her as she followed.

She pounded down the hallway, wishing she had chosen to flee the palace instead. But there was nowhere in this direction left to go except for her room. She didn't want to see anyone, feel the embarrassment rising around her when she looked at their faces, knowing they were walking on eggshells around her.

Maddie caught her by the arm and spun Mouse around. "You're being unreasonable."

"*I'm* being unreasonable!" Mouse shouted. "You want to be secretive just because I haven't confessed my truth to you on my own terms? Fine! You want to know what I experienced so you can have as many nightmares as I do? Fine! Fine, fine, fine! Every week in the Ruby Heart Palace, I got to have my bloody fun with Imogen and Rav. Her, with whips to my back or drowning me. Him tearing me apart from the inside out or bleeding me dry. You name it, they did it. And ever since then, I've been growing hungrier, more ravenous, wanting to eat and tear apart every human in sight. So much so that I murdered everyone in the donor building. It was *me*! *There*, damn it!" Her voice cracked on the last word as spittle flew from her mouth.

A horrified expression crossed Maddie's face, tears filling her eyes while she slowly released her arm. "Mouse, I—"

Mouse shook her head, batting her sister's arms away when they reached forward to draw her into a hug. "No, I don't want your pity. Because no matter what mindset you were in, no matter how much you felt like you were drowning, I would've warned you about the Jabberwocky, about *danger*. That would be *protecting* you. Not keeping it a secret, which in turn, could've destroyed me. If I had known, I could've been helping instead of being caught off guard like I was today."

Maddie took a step forward, not looking at her any differently. "It's just … you're my little sister and—"

"*And* you're my sister. Nothing can change that, but for now, leave me alone." Mouse gripped the knob to her room and opened the door, then slammed it behind her, closing herself inside.

Mouse pressed her forehead to the door and ran her hand against the wood. Even though Maddie didn't call out for her, Mouse knew she was still there, heard the rustling of her sister's dress as she must've lowered herself to the floor and the press of her back against the door. Always her big sister. Always her protector. Mouse had said exactly how she felt, so why did shame, regret, and guilt wash over her at once, pleading with her to apologize for her words?

Slowly backing away from the door, Mouse sank down on the edge of her bed and drew Des from her pocket. The caterpillar rested in the palm of her hand, lengthening her body upward so their eyes met.

"Am I?" Mouse asked in a hushed tone. "Am I being unreasonable?"

Des cocked her head side to side as if she wasn't sure who to agree with. The caterpillar was still entirely blue, not a speck of yellow visible. Perhaps it was her moods that had made Des this way, perhaps she was better off before befriending Mouse too.

Mouse placed Des atop her leaf on the night table, then stood from the bed, pacing back and forth. The day crashed into her … the Jabberwocky's destruction. She hadn't known the beast would be there today, but Ever had informed the guards about its previous prowling. Didi would've been informed. And even then, the caring guard had died. A guard who had been nothing but kind to Mouse every time she passed her in the Ivory Palace's halls, even though Mouse had been aloof, staring at the floor instead of the vampire's eyes, not able to say a simple hello. What the bloody hell was wrong with her? And now she would never be able to. She would never get to invite Didi to a lavish tea party.

"But there are no tea parties for me anymore," Mouse reminded herself.

And then she looked at the door … the *closed* door. Her hands trembled and her body quaked, hot tears like lava pricking her eyes. All she had to do was walk to the door, turn the knob, and pull it open. But her body stood frozen, trapped, trapped like she'd been in her dank, dark prison cell. Blood. She could smell all the blood that Rav and Imogen had stolen from inside her. So much spilled from the whips, the slices, the—

Mouse dropped to her knees, releasing an ear-shattering scream as she rocked against the hard marble. "Maddie, I'm sorry!" she cried, her body racking from her sobs. The door flew open and a tall form rushed in, scooping her into his lap.

"She left to clean herself up so she asked me to keep watch," Ferris said softly. "She'll be back, I promise."

Mouse thrashed, fighting him. She didn't want him. He'd hid important things from her. And she was mad at him most of all because she'd believed he was the one person who would never lie.

"You didn't tell me!" she screeched, shoving at his hard chest.

"I know," he whispered, his dark eyes locking on hers. "I was fucking stupid and shouldn't have listened to anyone, much less Chess's dumb ass. But I was about to tell you before the whole troop burst in there and made everything worse."

"You could've told me sooner." Mouse stopped fighting, her body relaxing slightly as she grasped the collar of his shirt. "I told you so many things today. You were the first I told about what went on inside the palace..."

"I know, luv," Ferris rasped. "I know." Their gazes locked, and his lower lip trembled. For the first time, Ferris truly looked afraid. Was it of her?

"I overreacted," she said, her chest heaving. "It's been happening a lot lately. I'll make it stop." Fear crawled through her that she could lose him, that he would get exhausted of her antics.

"No, you didn't." He brought her plait over her shoulder and toyed with the ends of her hair. "I-I had a girlfriend."

Mouse furrowed her brow, a sinking feeling churning within her stomach. "What are you talking about?"

"She … Ellie died," he whispered. "It was when I was nineteen, before I met you. She was pregnant with our daughter, Luna. There was a car crash, and I was driving. It wasn't my fault, but it felt like it was. Still does at times. That's why I started using drugs. Even after nearly a year with her gone, I just couldn't deal with life. Not until I met you."

Mouse took a deep swallow, letting his words echo in her mind. She'd known Ferris for a little over four years and they'd never talked about depressing aspects of their pasts, yet this… He'd lost not only a girlfriend but his unborn child too. She couldn't imagine losing two things so dear at once.

There were a handful of people she could never live without, including the one holding her now. Mouse thought about if something horrific were to happen to him, if he were to die. What if the Jabberwocky had gobbled him up or chewed him in half like it had with Didi? Her lungs ached, and she couldn't breathe, couldn't find the air she desperately needed. She cupped his beautiful face, his soft cheeks, and pulled his mouth to hers, their lips molding together. That was the only thing that could save her in this moment, the air she needed.

Mouse closed her eyes and allowed her lips to move against his, drinking him in, his breaths calming her as he kissed her back. Slow and gentle, his hands drifted to her hips, holding her steady.

Safe.

Ferris was her safe place.

Mouse drew back, finally opening her eyes, his meeting hers, both of their gazes wide as they studied one another. A smile played across his lips and she mirrored it as she rested her head against his chest, then wrapped her arms around him, not regretting the first real kiss she'd had in centuries. Her smile fell as the world came back into focus. "I'm so sorry, Ferris. I'm so sorry you didn't get your family and now you're stuck being a babysitter to me in this life."

"You have nothing to be sorry about. I would follow you anywhere, to *any* life, luv."

She wished she could go back to the days at the mortal club. Happy. Carefree. Listening to Ferris on his drums while dancing to the music.

Yet this felt more real than anything, especially with her lips still tingling from their kiss. A comforting kiss from one friend to another.

But her heart told her otherwise, that it was more than that, as did the heated warmth spreading through her, traveling lower and lower. Her fangs dropped, begging her to taste him, to taste every inch of him. Because she would follow him anywhere too.

CHAPTER NINE

FERRIS

Mouse's fangs scraped over Ferris's neck, ending with a light nip. It didn't break the skin, but it *did* send a shock straight to his cock. Her weight shifted on his lap. And then she was straddling him, a knee pressed against either side of his hips. His pulse sped at the sensation of her breath on his skin. Her fangs. The slip of a tongue as if she were tasting him.

Shit. He wanted that tongue somewhere else. Somewhere lower.

The thought snapped through him and his grip tightened on her hips, bunching the black fabric of her dress. They were friends… *Just* friends. So he shouldn't be imagining her licking his cock, the sounds she would make if he ran his own tongue up her core. Mouse moved her mouth up his neck to skate along his jawline until she found his lips again.

Fuck it. There was no reason they couldn't indulge each other a little. Was that his dick talking? Probably. But two years of hell in the Ruby Heart Palace left him with a need his own hand couldn't satisfy.

He pressed his lips to Mouse's, met her tongue with his own, careful not to prick himself on her fangs. One of his hands drifted higher. Up her back. To her hair. Gripping her plait gently at the base of her skull and holding her close.

A moan filled his mouth—*her* moan. A sweet, seductive sound that had his cock straining in his trousers. Then she *moved*. Slid herself against the bulge beneath her. Tentatively at first. The layers of fabric separating them were a damned curse. Ferris wanted to feel her. Wanted her to feel him. She must've sensed his desire as their tongues slid over one another because the next time she moved her hips, it wasn't shy. Her mound ground against his length and he groaned.

Mouse broke away from his mouth with a gasp, pupils blown wide, and kissed his neck again. Ferris let his head fall back to give her better access. His breaths turned shallow as she explored his chest with her hands. Somewhere deep in his mind, he wondered if he should stop her, but—

Fangs settled against his artery. He froze as the air took on a slight edge. There was nothing wrong with a bite and a fuck—in fact, it sounded damned amazing. He wanted to experience it himself, preferably with Mouse, but not when she was having control issues.

"Stop," he whispered.

He tugged her back where he was still holding her hair. The space between them crackled with arousal and he wanted nothing more than to indulge but … not right now. Not until she was better in control of her hunger. If she took too much and killed him, he knew Mouse would never forgive herself.

"I should…" He swallowed hard. "I should go take a shower."

A crease formed between Mouse's brows, but she nodded slowly before climbing from his lap. He sat a moment longer to try to compose himself, but his length was too stiff, too demanding, to even think about waiting until his hard-on was gone.

He nearly groaned when he stood and walked from the room. The piercing at the ridge of his cock pressed at an odd, almost painful angle against his zipper. *Shit.* He rushed into the bathroom and removed his trousers with a relieved huff.

The relief didn't last long, however. His hard length swelled, begging for attention. Grinding his teeth, he turned on the shower, removed the rest of his clothes and stepped under the warm spray.

But he could still feel Mouse's mouth on his, her tongue on his neck, the way she moved on top of him. Phantom sensations that throbbed through his veins had him gripping himself. Ferris stroked his cock and rubbed his thumb over the tip. The barbell piercing had two small silver balls at the edge of his head. One above the ridge. The other just below, next to his shaft. He stroked again and set his forehead on the glass door, his heavy breaths fogging it.

Holding back a groan, he imagined Mouse doing this instead. Imagined her on top of him exactly like she had been, her clothes gone. With her wet folds gliding over his length. He moved his hand faster. Harder. Ferris squeezed his eyes shut and imagined her gripping him, guiding him to her soaked entrance. Sinking down on him.

"Shit!" he growled as his cum spilled against the glass door. His legs trembled slightly when he pushed himself upright again and angled the showerhead to wash away the evidence. Just as he shoved away the pang of guilt he felt for thinking of his best friend riding him.

She *had* initiated it though. Kissed him first. Straddled him. Teased his neck with her fangs. Still—better not to tempt fate and ruin their friendship because he was horny as fuck. Maybe he needed to get out of the Ivory Palace for a bit. Out of *any* palace and learn who he was as a vampire. He hadn't gotten the chance before becoming Imogen's toy. And it would help clear his head. But he needed a purpose. A goal. He didn't want to wander aimlessly around Wonderland.

The Jabberwocky.

It was perfect. The beast needed to be stopped and no one knew how to achieve that. He could find out. Fueled by his new idea, Ferris quickly washed himself and made his way back to his bedroom in only a towel.

To find Mouse sitting on his bed with an empty bottle of blood.

"I ate," she whispered, seeming to have followed his gaze. "Sorry about almost biting you."

He smirked. "It wouldn't be the first time. And I never minded before, did I?"

She shook her head and Ferris slipped on a pair of loose black shorts before tossing his towel over the back of a chair. "Are you going to wear those to bed?" she asked with a tilt to the head, her gaze trailing down his bare chest. "I can turn around if you'd like to get under the covers and be comfortable."

"I'm not going to bed yet," he admitted. As Ever's guard, he would need permission to leave his post. The sound of her viola music drifted through the palace so he knew she was still awake and he'd like to leave as soon as possible. "I need to talk to the queen."

Mouse looked up at him in surprise. "Why? Is something wrong?"

"No." He hesitated. Mouse wouldn't like him risking himself alone… "I want to go to Red and see if I can find anything to help us fight the Jabberwocky."

"What?" The word was a mere breath. "You're leaving?"

"I hope to," he said as he rummaged for a T-shirt.

"What do you want to find in Red?" Mouse pressed. "There's nothing left. It's a wasteland."

The royals were dead and the citizens had either moved to Scarlet or Ivory, but that didn't mean *nothing* was left. "Some sort of clue might still be there. Or I'll go to the library—I heard talk about one inside the Red Palace. Maybe there's a painting on a cave wall or something, I don't know. But I should try, shouldn't I? Before more vampires get hurt."

"It doesn't have to be you," she said after a long, thought-out moment.

"It doesn't have to, no. I would like it to be, though." He needed to do *something* other than roam the hallways.

"Then I'm coming with you." Mouse stood and squared her shoulders. "We'll talk to Ever together."

"No," he said, slightly harsher than he intended.

"What do you mean, *no*?" She scowled at him. "I will go wherever I like."

He released a sigh. "You should stay here with Maddie."

"I love my sister, but that doesn't mean I need to be attached to her every moment for all eternity." She folded her arms. "I'm coming."

"You need to feed," he reminded her. "Red is a wasteland. What will you do for blood?"

She scoffed and held up the empty bottle. "I *can* survive off of this, just like you can."

Just more of it. *A lot* more, that they would need to carry with them. And what if she snapped? Ferris didn't want to have to pin her down until the bloodlust ceased. "No," was all he said, and brushed passed her into the hallway.

"Before the Jabberwocky rudely interrupted, you were planning to take me somewhere for a week anyway," Mouse said, following on his heels, feet practically stomping as they followed the quiet, complex melody of Ever's viola to the empty ballroom. She stood in the center with the instrument up to her chin, eyes closed, looking regal and every bit the queen. Decorative pillars lined the room, carved with climbing ivy, and a massive crystal chandelier hung overhead. The white grand piano in the corner gleamed.

"Hello, Ferris," she said without stopping the song. "Mouse."

"I didn't mean to intrude," he started.

"You're not." She lowered the instrument and looked over at him. "Chess is still taking note of the damage in the city, so I thought I'd try and relax with a song while I waited for him to finish." Ever tilted her head. "What brings you two here?"

"Grant me permission to go to Red," Ferris blurted.

Her brows rose. "Red? It's been a desolate wasteland ever since—"

"The Red Queen died, I know," he said. The stories he'd heard of the monster's murderous rampages in Red had sounded terrifying as fuck when he'd first arrived in Wonderland, and he didn't want Ivory to become like that. "Everyone left because of the Jabberwocky, but that's exactly why I need to go."

"I'm not sure I understand," she replied slowly.

He took a deep breath and let it out, glancing sideways at Mouse. "That's where the Jabberwocky is from, right?"

"We want to see if we can find any clues on how to defeat it," Mouse chimed in.

Ever glanced between them. "I'm already gathering a group of guards to travel to Red for that purpose. I want to know how to kill it, but I'm just surprised the two of you want to take on the task."

"It killed Didi," Mouse said quietly.

"And I need some time…" *Away.* He kept the last word to himself, but he could see the understanding in Ever's softening expression. Clearing his throat, he continued, "The Jabberwocky is a one-of-a-kind monster which has to mean something. If Red dealt with it for centuries, there has to be something. Someone must've documented it." Like Bigfoot back in the mortal world, with conspiracy theories and all that shit, only real.

Ever studied them for a long moment. "I agree to it. It will draw less attention if the two of you go in place of an entire group of guards first anyway."

"Mouse should stay," Ferris added firmly, though he couldn't stop the wince. He knew Mouse would hate him making choices for her.

"I'm going," Mouse snarled.

Ever played one long, drawn out note and stared at Ferris. "Will you leave her here alone?"

He couldn't distract himself, couldn't run from his problems, if they followed him. He wanted to kiss her again. Sink his fangs into her, drink her blood, see what she tasted like, the way she used to taste him when he was human. Touch her. Listen to her moan his name as he— *Shit. No.* Friends. They were *friends.* "She won't be alone. You and Maddie are here."

"Yes, but it's not me or Maddie who she creeps in bed with almost every night, is it?" Ever raised a brow in challenge, then focused on Mouse, color filling her cheeks, before the queen looked back at him. "I think she should go. Getting out of Ivory might be good for her bloodlust. Besides, I know what a strong fighter she is, how vicious she can be, how smart, and how well she can help you hide if you encounter the Jabberwocky."

Ferris clenched his jaw. Ever had a point though—Mouse was strong and clever. "All right," he agreed.

Mouse raised her chin and stared at him with an unreadable expression. *No.* Perhaps not unreadable. Part pride, part hurt. Part something else.

Ever smiled and ran her bow across the strings, playing another song, deep and hopeful. They left the queen there to play and he forced his thoughts away from being completely alone with Mouse on a probably-perilous journey as he jogged up the stairs. Mouse moved slower, taking the steps one at a time.

If there wasn't a fresh mortal to feed from, it wouldn't really be good for her problem, but Ever had known Mouse longer than him, had been a vampire even longer than that. He would trust that she knew what she was talking about.

"We should get a good sleep in before we leave." Ferris rubbed the back of his neck, unsure if Mouse would want to join him in his room now that he'd pissed her off. He wanted her to—he *always* wanted her to. He was even willing to keep his clothes on tonight. After their kiss, he didn't want to sleep next to Mouse naked. Though maybe she wouldn't mind it. Maybe she wouldn't even mind crawling under the covers with him now… Damn it, *no.*

"I'll pack in the morning," she said in a cool tone. "We can talk about our strategy as we travel."

Ferris nodded and Mouse appeared pacified as she strode around him, into his room. He hesitated in the hallway, the memory of her grinding against him flashing through his mind.

"Coming?" she called from inside the room.

"Yes, sorry," he replied as he walked toward his doorway. *Though, not in the way I'd like to be coming.*

CHAPTER TEN

MOUSE

Red was a deserted wasteland that Mouse had only ventured to a handful of times. Neither Ever nor Imogen had been interested in claiming that part of Wonderland as their own, but now that Ever was working with Chess to unite their territories, that might change one day. However, they didn't want to revive the desolate territory if the Jabberwocky was constantly a threat. The Jabberwocky needed to be eliminated for the safety of all of Wonderland, but how could one destroy a beast with a body like iron?

A mystery indeed.

A mystery that was in dire need of being solved.

What Mouse needed were the witches from *Macbeth*. If witches were real, she would have one cast a spell on the Jabberwocky or at least offer a prophecy on how to kill the wretched monster.

Mouse hummed lightly while she finished packing her bag with a few changes of clothes, dried packets of blood, a few canteens of water, and daggers. She'd gotten plenty of sleep with Ferris and she was supposed to meet him at the palace's entrance once she finished. But she tried not to focus on what had happened the night before—his hot mouth on hers, the way she'd ground her hips into his, how delicious his flesh tasted against her tongue, how his hard length had nestled into her softness, even with clothing on. If he hadn't stopped, she knew she wouldn't have. And she wished he wouldn't have either.

Pushing away the heat that was spreading to her center, she slipped her gun in her boot, then straightened. The main reason Ever had agreed for Mouse to journey with Ferris was because the queen didn't want to keep her trapped like Imogen had. It was one thing for Ever to say she wasn't ready to be a guard, but a whole different matter to forbid her to go somewhere entirely. Ferris hadn't wanted her to go at first, but she'd forgiven him since he hadn't fought her on it again.

A nagging sensation tugged at Mouse—there had to be something valuable in Red, some sort of clue that would hint at a way to destroy the Jabberwocky. The Red Queen had been a vicious twat from what Mouse had heard over the centuries, even Imogen and Rav had agreed on that. What was suspicious, though, was why such a tyrant allowed a terrifying beast to live in her territory if she'd possibly had a way to destroy it herself?

Mouse peered at Des, who lay curled on top of the mostly-eaten leaf, her mouth parted as she lightly snored. Selfishly, Mouse wanted to bring her good luck charm on the journey for her own comfort, but she needed to learn she couldn't drag the caterpillar everywhere, especially since she wasn't certain when she would return. The only one of their group who had been to Red in recent years was Chess, back when Maddie led him on a wild goose chase in search of Ever. But he'd returned just fine, not even spotting the Jabberwocky while there, so Maddie shouldn't get her panties in a twist when Mouse informed her what she was about to do.

Adjusting her backpack, Mouse then scooped up Des's sleeping form, tucking the caterpillar into the front pocket of her dress to bring to her sister.

Mouse stepped into the hallway and walked to Maddie's room and knocked on the door. Her sister didn't answer, so she headed downstairs to the drawing room where she found her sister asleep on the chaise, thread and felt in her lap. Maddie's purple curls were mussed and her black and white striped hat rested on the velvet cushion beside her head.

Mouse's heart ached at the sight. Before she met up with Ferris, she needed to discuss a few matters with Maddie. She couldn't leave Ivory after the last few outbursts she'd had with her sister—she needed a clear conscience so she could focus on the task at hand.

Kneeling beside the chaise, she cupped Maddie's cheek. "Big sister, wake up."

Maddie's eyes flew open, her honey-colored irises shining from sleep. "Mouse." She sat up, patting the cushion for her hat.

"I have to tell you something," Mouse whispered. "Remember the stories Mama used to tell us when we were younger? You always wanted to be the hero and I wanted to be saved?"

"Ah, yes, Mama's glorious tales." Maddie grinned, placing the hat on her head. "It made our roleplaying decisions easy."

Mouse folded her hands in her lap. "I don't want to be the hero of this story, but I do want to make it easier for you and the others."

Maddie furrowed her brow. "I don't like the sound of this, Margo."

Mouse studied her sister's concerned face and she couldn't hold back her emotions. She threw her arms around Maddie, squeezing her tight. "I'm sorry for earlier. I'm sorry for the past few months."

"You don't have to apologize for anything," Maddie murmured, brushing a loose tendril from Mouse's plait behind her ear. "If I had known what that sick bastard had done to you, I would've left the safe house and slaughtered his arse myself. Stabbed him with a thousand hatpins, then cut him into the smallest of pieces before setting them on fire.”

“That was one reason I didn’t tell you—I didn’t want you to risk yourself again. But most of all, I thought it would be easier to keep everything inside, that it would go away.” Things never truly went away, though—they just lessened over time. Even after Mr. Taylor ripped away her virginity, she was still haunted by the good times they’d had when he’d courted her. And she *hated* that.

“Think of a hat,” Maddie said. “There is only so much fabric and pins you can place on and in it before it will tip over and bleed to death.”

“I love your analogies.” Mouse smiled softly. “That would be quite the bloody predicament.”

“The bloodiest,” Maddie sang, then she drew back, her expression serious. “Now tell me what you’re planning. I assume I won’t want to throw a tea party in celebration of it.”

Mouse stood and adjusted her skirts to avoid her sister’s staring, then took a seat on the chaise. “You certainly won’t. But I need you to do me a favor.”

Maddie pressed closer to her sister. “No more beating around the bush,” she sang.

“I need you to take care of Des.” Mouse took the sleeping caterpillar from inside her pocket and placed her in the center of Maddie’s palm. “I’m going on a little adventure with Ferris.”

Maddie’s lips tilted up at the edges in delight, one of her eyebrows quirking as she tucked Des into the pocket of her skirt. “A sexy adventure? It’s about damn time. This will be good for you, sister.”

“*What?*” Mouse shrilled, her blood coursing through her veins, straight to her heart where the blasted organ was *agreeing*. “Ferris is my *friend*.” A friend who she liked kissing. A friend whose salty skin she wanted to feel her teeth on. A friend who she wanted to see naked on his bed again. Or preferably her lips on his *while* he was naked, then pleasuring one another, taking him in between her lips, her tongue swirling around that piercing of his. *Oh, heavens…* Her body was growing warm, too warm.

Maddie cocked her head, her eyebrow still arched, disbelieving.

"I'm going with him to Red!" Mouse hissed.

"Red!" Maddie screeched back. "No. No, no, no. Are you mad?"

"Maybe we're all a bit mad here." Mouse laughed softly and lifted a brow in return.

"This is no laughing matter, Margo! The Jabberwocky is venturing wherever the hell it wants to now. It isn't as if the fucker is nestled away like before!"

"Then it may not even be in Red." Mouse shrugged. "Besides, Red's a big place. We've been there together, *remember*? Before Ever sends guards in search of the beast there, I want to see if we can find a hidden way to kill it so they don't get themselves slaughtered. It would be beneficial for the guards to remain here for the time being after the recent attack anyway."

Maddie scowled and Mouse could see in her sister's gaze that she knew she was right about the guards. "Wouldn't someone have found an answer already if one existed?"

"I don't believe anyone has *looked* before." Mouse folded her arms. "Remember when we had a tea party in the abandoned palace? You, me, and…" Her voice trailed off before she could say March's name. He'd asked Ever to kill him and she had to accept his decision.

"Ever was so mad!" Maddie laughed.

"Yes, mad we didn't invite her," Mouse pointed out. "Anyway, we never thoroughly searched the palace. Maybe there is something hidden?"

"You know what? You're right." Maddie waved a hand in the air and stood from the chaise. "I'm coming with you."

She then spun on her heel and Mouse hauled her back by the arm. "You will do no such thing."

"And whyever not?"

"You went to werewolf territory to save Alice, where hundreds and *hundreds* of snarling beasts live. This is only one monster. Let me do this alone with Ferris. I know how to hide well. The more people go, the more chance of being spotted." She held up a finger. "And hush. You will not go with Ferris. *Me*. I'm going to meet him at the entrance now. This might be a way to find myself again. Not sit in the palace and dwell or drink blood in the mortal world day after day."

Maddie pursed her lips while holding Mouse's gaze, then relented. "Fine. You deserve to do this, to make your own choices. But you do need to be careful since you've been craving fresh blood even more so lately. When you return, if you want me to come with you while you feed, I can make sure you don't get carried away. I'm your big sister and I'm always here for you."

"I would like that." She released a breath. "But I'm going to drink powdered blood every day, and Ferris is going to have cold bags right when we leave." Mouse ignored the hunger churning in her stomach at the thought of blood.

"If you start feeling unwell, please don't push yourself." Maddie tugged Mouse's arm. "Let me at least take you to Ferris."

"Thank you."

Mouse walked beside her sister down the halls leading to the stairs near the palace's entrance. Mock lingered at the door in his white uniform, his yellow hair pulled back, and his eyes no longer red-rimmed but still puffy. Beside him stood Ferris with his backpack strewn across one arm. He looked positively delicious wearing a tight dark T-shirt and jeans that hugged his thighs perfectly. Mouse's heart accelerated as she met Ferris's heavy stare. Did the blasted thing always do that at the sight of him before?

"You might want to give into temptation," Maddie whispered in her ear.

Mouse shot her sister a glare. "Quiet."

Maddie drew Ferris and Mouse into a hug on each side. "You watch her with your life," her sister said to Ferris, then glanced back at Mouse. "And you watch him with yours. Once you find the beastie's secret, I'll go after it with the others."

"That's fair," Mouse agreed. "Don't forget Des likes the leaves from the trees near the lake."

"She won't be a happy caterpillar when she wakes."

Des would understand. Mouse couldn't stop her stomach from sinking as she peered beneath her lashes at Mock. "I'm sorry about Didi." Her voice came out louder than usual.

Mock's brows shot up, his eyes widening. "Thank you, Mouse." It was the first time she'd spoken to him, and it was a start.

With a final goodbye, Mouse and Ferris walked outside, the cool air rustling the ends of her plait.

"Here you go," Ferris said, handing her two cold blood bags. She drank the first one down in seconds, then forced herself to go slower with the second.

Mouse noticed his empty hands and he didn't have any for himself. "Drink some?" She held it out to Ferris. When he didn't take it, she said more firmly. "I demand it."

"Well, in that case." He smirked, taking it from her hands, his fingers brushing hers. Again, the butterflies swarmed in her stomach at the contact.

As she watched him drink from where her mouth had been, his tongue licking the tip clean, she shoved down the urge to press her lips to his, to taste not only the blood there but *him*, just like she had last night.

Mouse turned her focus to the portal as they approached, and the flowery scent hit her senses when they crossed through the barrier to the cemetery in the mortal world. There wasn't a portal directly to Red that she knew of—the queen had somehow kept those a secret, even after her death. But there was one not far away from the cemetery that would take them to the edge of an Ivory forest, next to where Red's territory began.

"Would you have truly wanted to go to Red without me?" Mouse asked.

"I think you know that answer, luv." Ferris winked.

She wanted to talk about what they'd done the night before, but that would mean she would need to discuss how badly she'd wanted to taste his blood too. Her gaze fell to the chain around Ferris's neck, and her chest tightened when she realized what the ring was for. It had to have belonged to Ellie, not just an heirloom or to wear for fashion…

"How about you teach me?" Mouse said as they walked through the cemetery, her gaze trained on his hands to avoid the necklace.

"Teach you what?" he asked, his voice raspy.

Her breath caught, unable to stop the images crawling into her mind of him doing *other things* to her with his hands. "Drums," she finally answered.

He grinned, bumping his shoulder with hers. "You want to learn? I'll teach you any song you'd like."

"How about that AC/DC song you once played for me at your place?" She could still see how fast his hands had moved, hear how the heavy beats had sounded, watch how he'd bit his lip when he closed his eyes, relishing in the music.

"'Riff Raff?'" He chuckled, his infectious laugh echoing through the cemetery. "You know how long it took me to play *that?*"

"I'm a fast learner."

"I bet you are." The edges of his lips stayed tilted up as his gaze trained on her mouth.

An urge to draw his face to hers, run her tongue across the seam of those shapely lips, tugged at Mouse. Her hunger was craving both his blood and his body, and she chewed on the inside of her cheek to tame the lust-filled sensations down. These thoughts were becoming out of control, but more so, welcoming…

Mouse walked beside him in comfortable silence, though her body was still coiled tight, as she led him through the woods and the city until they reached the closest bridge over the Thames. "There." She pointed downward as cars sped past them.

"The river, luv?" Ferris asked. "Where our bodies will collide with water? Are you sure a portal is there?"

"Follow me and find out," Mouse taunted. With that, she leapt from the bridge while Ferris cursed above her. A sparkling white light flashed, the portal sucking her inside, her body falling through glittering darkness. Mouse's stomach rose to her throat as she plummeted, the adrenaline rush singing in her veins until the portal opened, spitting her out on the soft white earth of Ivory.

Ferris grunted when he landed on his stomach beside her. "That was fucking awful."

"Saved us time though, didn't it? Another good reason I came." Mouse smiled, pushing herself up from the ground. She brushed off her hands on her dress and stared straight ahead to where silver and white trees turned to ones of red. But not like the trunks in Scarlet. These were a deep red that was almost black with not a single leaf growing from any of their gnarled branches.

"So, this is Red? It looks positively lovely," Ferris said with sarcasm.

"It is, isn't it?" She laughed softly.

As they crossed into the forest, the scent of rain enveloped her. It was known as the Broken Forest of Shattered Blood because it was where the Red Queen had brought whoever she desired to die. She would break them into pieces, then hang their body parts in the trees as decorations. In many ways, the Red Queen was like Imogen.

The ground below their feet was a sandy red texture and squished as they walked. Up in the branches, bald owls hissed, their beaks filled with sharp black fangs.

"Well, aren't *they* friendly?" Ferris rolled his eyes.

"They're like the crows in Scarlet. Leave them alone and you'll be fine." She shrugged. "Otherwise, they'll peck away and eat your flesh."

The rainy scent of the forest changed to something else… A metal smell wafted through the air, caressing her nose. *Fresh.* A mixture of vampire, human, and werewolf.

Mouse's fangs dropped on instinct and when she peered at Ferris, his were too. They took a few steps forward while surveying the area. A rustling came behind her, accompanied by a deep growl. She yanked out her gun from her boot, whirling around just as Ferris's went off. The werewolf thrashed, its obsidian fur turning gray and orange as its body disintegrated to fiery ash. Another growl sounded, shaking the trees surrounding her.

A twig snapped to Mouse's left and she pulled the gun's trigger, blasting a white-furred werewolf with its fangs bared. Its form changed to ash just as another came barreling from her right. But Ferris gunned it down, its body quaking to the ground while falling to pieces.

"Should've expected rogue werewolves to slum it up here," Ferris grumbled.

Mouse listened closely for a sign of any others. Werewolves weren't ones to stay hiding—if there was a threat, they would all come. But only bugs and small animals made any noise. Through the silence, the scent of blood became stronger.

She walked a few steps behind Ferris as they padded past thick tree trunks to where several piles of bones rested, licked clean of any remains. Blood splattered the ground, a vampire's head on its side, but the rest of the body was gone.

A gurgling sound caught her attention and she crept behind a tree to find a male form beside another pile of bones. He was without one arm and both his legs had been ripped off. *Human.*

By the sounds of his uneven breathing, he wasn't going to make it. Mouse's hunger stormed through her veins, her eyes fluttering.

Ferris lowered himself and whispered in her ear, his hot breath tickling her neck, "Go on, luv. We are what we are." Her eyes fluttered more, but for a different reason. He then gently nudged her forward. "The mortal won't make it anyway."

Taking a deep swallow, Mouse nodded and peered down at the human, his wide blue eyes. His words came out garbled and she couldn't make out what he was saying. Her hunger grew ravenous as she knelt beside him, but she attempted to rein it in, to control herself. Not be Rav's monster and tear the mortal apart even more.

"Sleep. There will be no more pain after this," she murmured, then lowered her teeth to his neck, piercing his flesh, giving in to her instincts. Warm blood flooded over her tongue and she drank, giving the man what he needed.

Death.

CHAPTER ELEVEN

FERRIS

When vampires referred to Red as a wasteland, they weren't full of shit. Burnt patches and brittle, dead brush dotted the red clay. Even the distant sky was tinted red with the amount of dust the wind blew into the air. Ferris, with a hand on Mouse's lower back, steered her around the skeleton of a large cat-like creature while reveling in her warmth, wishing he could take more of it. But Mouse assured him that they were almost at the palace and he needed to focus. *Skeleton,* he thought to himself, staring at the dead animal to keep his mind on track. These weren't the first remains they'd come across—small birds had been littered about too. Even a human—or a vampire—curled up against the trunk of a decaying tree. Mansions had caved in on themselves while other buildings were completely gone, leaving nothing behind but their foundation.

Despite the obvious disrepair of the entire territory, Ferris wasn't prepared for the sorry state of the palace. He paused, Mouse beside him, and they stared at the polished red sandstone.

What *used* to be polished, anyway. Now it sat in crumbling heaps and gold flecks glittered up from the larger chunks. Two stories still stood with what looked to be at least two more having partially collapsed.

Shattered glass crunched underfoot as Ferris picked his way through what once must've been a glorious courtyard. Bricks in varying shades of red were laid in massive overlapping circles with the base of a huge statue at the center of the largest. The base was carved from black stone and only three marble feet were left attached to it. One woman's heel and two old-fashioned men's shoes with broad buckles. Whoever the statue was of—likely the dead king and queen of Red—had been reduced to pebbles. The king had died long before the queen, so Ferris absently wondered if this was her monument to him or if it was created before his death.

"Do you think there's anything worth salvaging?" Mouse asked quietly.

Ferris scowled at the palace. It wasn't like Red was overrun with bandits. Everyone was dead or gone, but there was no telling what happened as soon as the royals had died. If the grounds *were* raided, it would've been for jewels or other nice ass shit—not conspiracy theories about the fucking Jabberwocky.

"Only one way to find out," he answered.

Mouse slipped her hand in his and his heart gave a little jump. The memory of holding her hips as she ground on top of him rushed to the surface. The urge to have her on top of him again pulsed through his body. He wanted his mouth on hers, to feel the weight of her breasts in his hands, to slide into her. To thrust. Hard. *So* hard that she would know how much he wanted her. *Needed* her.

He swallowed, pushing away his reckless desire, and gave Mouse's hand a squeeze before leading her to the main entrance. There was no longer a door, but a round opening where it would've been. The entrance chamber was blacker than sin, not that it mattered much with their ability to see in the dark. He'd seen much more terrifying shit done in brighter places while inside the Ruby Heart Palace. Red's castle smelled stale and dry with the sweet hint of death.

"We should try to find the library first and any rooms along the way," Ferris mused. "If that doesn't turn up anything on the beast, we can search somewhere else."

Mouse scowled, then nodded once. "There's a private library that belonged to the king and queen. If they held secrets about the Jabberwocky, they might have kept them hidden there."

"I wonder why they didn't send someone to kill the monster." Ferris peeked inside the palace and found it empty, save for the layer of red dust. The floors were made of the same sandstone as the walls, the stones laid in a careful herringbone design. The gold flecks in the material were dulled but still visible. Overhead, strands of chains linked five chandeliers made of antlers. Black candles were still imbedded on the points, dried wax running down the bone. "*If* they knew how to kill it, I mean."

He'd wondered about this as they traveled to the palace, but hadn't brought it up because it would mean this might be a wild goose chase. It made no sense to keep the Jabberwocky alive if they could've rid themselves of it. Unless killing it was a lot harder than living with it…

"We can worry about that later," Mouse whispered, seeming to feel how he'd tensed. "Follow me. I think I remember where the library was, but it's been a while since I was here."

Ferris let Mouse take the lead, pulling him down dark hallways by the hand. Even the simple contact, her skin on his, had his body buzzing with desire. Dragging her into the nearest bedroom was a looping thought, but they had a job to do. Jabberwocky first. Fucking second, if she wanted to. So, he studied his surroundings in a desperate attempt to get his dick to behave.

The walls of the palace were all bare—whether it was because any artwork had been stolen or if it was a style choice, he wasn't sure. Dust, leaves, and bramble had blown inside through the open doors. Tattered shreds of fabric clung to the empty window frames and splintered pieces of wood were shoved against the wall under a layer of dust.

They passed by rooms in disarray, finding nothing of use there—chairs toppled over, tables missing legs, chandeliers dangling precariously from the ceilings. Doors hung from the hinges, if there were still doors at all. Rust-colored blood stains splashed against paneled walls and on porcelain tile.

A skeleton sprawled in the middle of a large sitting room caused Ferris to slow his steps. The skull, however, was displayed on an iron sconce hanging from the wall. Judging by the powdered wig still framing the face, it had been a male.

"Interesting décor," he joked.

Mouse followed his gaze, giving a snort, and led him away from the display. A few more rooms down, Mouse stopped in front of a set of open double doors. "We're here," she said and hesitated before stepping into a massive library.

Shelves were toppled, books spilling from them, loose pages scattered about. A pair of green sofas still sat across from each other with a round table between. Directly above was a domed ceiling made of glass with cracks webbing across it. In its glory, this must've been fucking badass. Even Ferris might've considered reading there. *Nah.* But maybe he would've dragged his drum set in.

He gave Mouse's hand another squeeze and dropped it. "Where should we start?"

"This side? We can work our way across," she suggested while chewing on her lip.

Together, they made their way to the far left and scanned book titles. Mouse used her fingertips to trail over them, pushing the ones on the shelf until they sat in even rows. He imagined those fingers trailing over him instead. Starting on his chest, skating down. Tracing the lines of his abs and down the V to unbutton his jeans. Those fingers wrapping around his cock. Stroking him. Ferris drew in a deep breath and let it out slowly. He ran his knuckles over the rows of books to even them, knowing it would please Mouse to see his shelves in proper order too. And also as a distraction to tamp down his damn lust.

The Balance of Life.

The Ballad of a Lady.

Bartholomew's Theories.

Ferris ran a hand through his hair. The titles were arranged, seemingly, in alphabetical order but with no thought to what they were about. Romance novels were beside scientific tomes and poetry. He glanced over at Mouse, holding a weathered black book in her hands, opened to a diagram. She sucked on her bottom lip as she studied it, and he stared at her perfect mouth. Remembered how it felt on his. The way her lips moved over his neck. Holy shit, they had searching to do and all he could focus on was pleasing her and his dick.

"What do you have there?" he asked, clearing his throat, pushing himself to fucking *focus*. The old sketches on the page were too hard to see from where he stood.

Mouse jumped and snapped the book shut. "Nothing."

Before she could place it back on the shelf, Ferris plucked it from her hands with a laugh. She bounced onto the balls of her feet to try getting it back, but Ferris held it over his head, curiosity piqued. The spine of the book was too worn to read so he flipped it open to find page after page of sketches with notations at the bottom.

Sketches of people fucking, their bodies in various sexual poses.

"This is definitely *something*," he said with a grin.

Mouse sighed and crossed her arms. "I only looked inside because I couldn't read the name of the book."

He glanced at her, his grin widening. That might've been why she opened it, but she was most definitely interested in the contents based on how hard she'd stared at the pages a moment ago. "This one looks fun," he said, and held the page open so she could see.

The woman laid on her back with one leg wrapped around the man's thigh, the other draped over his shoulder, as he fucked her. A basic position, but given the year this book was made, maybe it was more intriguing. Still, it *was* a fun one, and he felt himself stiffen slightly, throwing all his focus on searching out the damn window.

"Maybe add a blindfold to the mix for a little extra spice," he suggested, watching her carefully. Their eyes met and he imagined having Mouse beneath him just like the drawing. Her pink plait wrapped around his hand, his cock sliding inside her, the sounds she would make. When he spoke again, his voice was husky. "He should be kissing her, at least. Showing her breasts a little love."

When a blush tinged her cheeks, he closed the book and set it on the shelf behind her. She didn't move as he leaned closer to do so. Only held her breath. He breathed her in, the light floral scent going straight to his cock. Ferris lowered his hand to tuck her hair behind her ear and she let out a small gasp.

"I liked what you did the other night," he whispered. They were friends—adding benefits could fuck everything up. Especially since he *knew* feelings were involved on his end. But damn, he wanted more. He wanted to slip into her heat and fuck her like every single one of those pictures, make love to her so she would be ruined for anyone else, so it was only him tearing orgasm after orgasm from her. "How you kissed me. How you *moved*."

"Ferris," she breathed.

His pulse sped, his cock stiffening even more at the thought of tasting her again. Of plunging his tongue into her mouth to dance with hers. He wanted to lift her off the ground, wrap her legs around his waist, and fuck her against the broken bookshelves. Feel her quiver around him. *Fuck*. He was getting ahead of himself, but the idea of it made him crazy.

"If I wanted to kiss you right now, what would you say?" he rasped in her ear.

"N—no." Mouse spoke in the smallest of voices.

Ferris's chest tightened and he ripped himself away from her, his desire fading. "Fuck. I'm sorry. I didn't mean—"

"It's not that I don't want to kiss you. I enjoyed the other night too," she added quickly, and turned to face the shelves instead of him. Her hand shook as she resumed lining the books up perfectly.

Shit. He'd done something wrong. Was he too forward? Had she wanted the other night to be a once-off? "I'm sorry," he said again.

This time Mouse shot him a sad smile over her shoulder. "If you had asked me in any other room, I would've had a different answer."

Ferris frowned. So it *wasn't* him—it was the library? "I don't understand."

"Did Maddie ever tell you about my past? I doubt she did, but maybe…?" She looked slightly hopeful at the idea, yet when Ferris shook his head, she sighed. A long silence filled the room as Ferris watched her fidget with spines. Finally, she whispered, "It happened in a library."

A crease formed between his brows. He stepped closer and she tensed, so he moved back to his side of the row. "*What* happened?"

"When I was still mortal, my neighbor, Mr. Taylor, courted me." Her voice was emotionless, dead. "We were friends growing up and got along well. He spoiled me, actually. Buying me trinkets and picking wildflowers for my hair. His family had a lot more money than mine, yet it never mattered to him. Our families were even talking of us getting engaged soon. It wasn't a love match, but back then, we were lucky to marry someone we genuinely cared for. Maddie had been missing for a while, and they wanted me to be well taken care of in life. Mr. Taylor seemed to check every box."

Ferris reached unconsciously to play with Ellie's ring hanging around his neck. He was an idiot to think Mouse had never been in a relationship before—she was hundreds of years old. *Of course* she'd been with men. Maybe even women for all he knew.

"What happened?" he asked gently when she didn't continue.

Mouse shifted nervously. "Well, we did things together. You know? Kissed and touched. We even used our mouths on each other a few times. None of it was like I'd expected it to be, but no one really talked about sex back then. It was taboo. Something to be done between a man and wife and never spoken about in good company. But he wasn't my husband yet. Our families hadn't even come to an actual agreement that he would *ever* be my husband. It was still being discussed…"

Ferris curled his fist around Ellie's ring, his chest twisting uncomfortably as he realized where things were likely going with this story. Anger rose, hovering just beneath the surface, waiting for her to confirm the worst. "What did he do to you?" he growled.

Mouse's body shook slightly as she stopped fussing with the books. "One night after dinner, he wanted to show me something in the library. Our fathers had gone off to smoke cigars and our mothers were distracted, so we snuck off alone. Something told me there wasn't anything he wanted to show me, but I figured we would do what we'd always done. I told him I wanted to save myself for marriage, but… He demanded more than I wanted to give."

Ferris's fangs dropped. "He took you unwillingly?"

Mouse hesitated, then slowly nodded.

"I'll fucking kill him," Ferris snarled. His vision went red, his pulse roaring in his ears. *How dare that man?* How *dare* he take that from her?

"He's dead, Ferris," she said matter-of-factly. "Maddie killed him."

"Then I'll dig up his grave and kill the fucker again." He lunged forward and pulled Mouse against his chest in a tight hug. "I'll grind his bones to dust and scatter them in the sewer."

Mouse laughed. Actually fucking laughed. How could she be laughing when he was being consumed by rage? His mind was swirling with ways to resurrect a corpse so he could torture the fucking shit out of it. Now he understood why she fed off of and killed those who hurt others.

"Ferris, you're squishing me." She patted his arms.

"Sorry," he snapped without meaning to. His anger wasn't

directed at her in the least bit. "Sorry!"

"It's fine, but let me breathe," she said with another small laugh.

Ferris loosened his arms and inhaled her scent. It filled him, calmed him. He held her until his fangs retracted. Until he could see straight again. Then placed a kiss on top of her head.

"I'm sorry that happened to you," he whispered.

"Me too," Mouse murmured. "But it was a long time ago and I don't like to dwell on it. I just wanted you to know, it's not you. It's the library. That's the only time I'm truly bothered by it anymore."

Ferris stepped away from her, and she glanced up at him. His heart gave a painful thump when their gazes met. Brushing a loose tendril of her hair behind her ear again, he offered a soft smile. "You never have to explain your *no* to me, luv."

"Well," she bit her lip and blushed. "I do, if it's *not* a no. It's just a *somewhere else*."

"Right now?" he asked. After a revelation like that, he wasn't sure it was right to be lusting after her. But, if she wanted it, he would worship her like the queen she was.

Mouse quietly took the book of sexual positions off the shelf and headed for the door, leaving him to follow.

CHAPTER TWELVE

MOUSE

As soon as Mouse stepped out of the library and into the hallway, relief washed over her. She'd wanted to believe she'd gotten over her fear of libraries after Mr. Taylor, but deep down, a shadow of that night still lingered inside of her, just as the acts inside the Ruby Heart Palace did. Both places always would, but she needed to face her fears. One step at a time. Shakespeare had helped her in the past, during the dark moments, when she still had to live next door to Mr. Taylor, when her mother had held her, comforting her but had also told her to be quiet about it. Back then it was different.

But now, she didn't need the protection—she didn't *need* a Shakespeare play for distraction, or for Des to be her comfort companion, or for Ferris to be her savior. She wanted them because she *chose* them, just as she was tired of trapping her desires away, pretending as if she didn't want anyone, when she sure as hell yearned for Ferris.

"We don't need this." Dropping the book of sexual desires,

Mouse whirled around and leapt into Ferris's arms. He caught her and crashed back into the wall. Her instinct was raw, driven. Lust burned within her, waiting to unleash.

"No, we don't," he rasped. "I can make you feel so good, if you'll let me."

"When did you first see me differently?" Mouse asked, her heart accelerating.

Ferris spun around so she was planted against the wall, his hard cock deliciously pressed against her. "When you were taken by Rav and Imogen, I realized what you meant to me. Then once you were safe, I let myself wonder… And now, I fucking want you like I've never wanted anyone. I don't know if that makes me a piece of shit because of my past."

"It doesn't, and I want you just as much. You're the first person I've ever truly wanted." She ran her hand down his cheek, and he leaned into her touch. "You don't need to be careful with me and you don't have to worry about being too rough. I want it all with you, Ferris."

His lips came to her neck, trailing kisses to just below her ear, his fingers digging into her hips. "If you ever want me to stop or slow down, just say the word."

"Likewise." Mouse skimmed the tip of her finger across his plump bottom lip. "Now, let's go to a room. I don't care how filthy it is." It didn't matter if they were in a crumbling palace—they were together and that was all she needed in that moment.

"Let's see what we can find, then." He chuckled, holding her close as he started walking down the bare hallway.

She loosened her arms around his neck. "I can walk if it's easier on you."

"No, I like you right where you are." Ferris grinned, the tip of his tongue moistening his bottom lip. He halted at a door that wasn't all the way shut and used his boot to kick it open. Before she had a chance to peek in, he spun around, and started walking again. "We don't need an audience."

She laughed louder this time, glimpsing the skeletal remains over his shoulder. "I suppose we could've just turned the guests around if we had to.”

“Mmm, we may have to if we can’t find anything better.” Ferris chuckled.

Broken items littered most of the rooms on the second floor, and black smudges and cracks covered the walls. Due to the rotting wood, the rail around the interior balcony looked like it would collapse to the shattered marble below at any moment.

Ferris opened a crooked door that was falling off its hinges. He carried Mouse inside the mostly clean room and sat them both on a torn chair. The room wasn’t as eroded as the main areas of the palace, only layers of dust clinging to everything. A large bed, lower on one side than the other, was pressed against the wall, an empty wardrobe rested in the corner with its doors missing, and the two chairs were beside a writing desk, where a stack of worn books was collected on top.

Mouse studied Ferris’s pretty features, her heart still beating like the drums he played. He knew the darkest parts of her that had remained hidden and he didn’t look at her differently, just as he hadn’t when she’d confessed to him about her past in the Ruby Heart Palace and her visits to the mortal clubs.

She pressed her forehead to his. “You truly don’t see me differently now? I don’t want you to think of me as broken.”

“No, luv. We’re all broken pieces just trying to find a way to fit back together again. And our jagged edges line up perfectly.”

Mouse grinned and crashed her mouth to his. He didn’t hesitate to kiss her back with equal hunger, his hands sliding down her sides to her hips, urging her to move against him. She rolled her hips forward, picking up where they’d left off the other night. He growled and she liked the taste of that sound, the way his tongue dipped into her mouth, flicking against hers.

Ferris trailed kisses down her jaw and whispered in her ear, “Even when I left your room the other night, I couldn’t stop thinking about you.”

A thrill shot through her. “What did you do?”

“Do you really want to know?”

“Every detail,” she said, grinding against his hardness.

"I fucked my hand," he said in a gruff voice. "I pretended it was you stroking me, your mouth sucking, me thrusting inside you." His hands drifted to the curve of her buttocks, and she ground harder into him. "How wet are you now?"

A heat spread through Mouse, sinking lower and lower, her body coiled tight. "Very." She hadn't touched a cock since Mr. Taylor's, and her thoughts turned to Ferris when she'd found him naked in his bed, how much she wanted to see his length again, only this time, *hard*. Ferris wasn't prim and proper the way men were back in her century, and she liked that he was both sweet and daring.

Mouse wanted to be adventurous too, wanted to show her bold side. For now, she would start by making him feel good. "Stand up and show me how you took care of yourself the other night," she murmured.

"As you wish." Ferris grinned seductively and Mouse helped him peel his shirt over his head. Her heart pounded as he lifted and placed her into the chair before rising in front of her. He kicked off his boots, then she unfastened his jeans and drew them down, freeing his large cock, the silver piercing at the tip shining. Hunger swirled in her as she studied his broad chest, his defined muscles, the raven tattoo on the left side of his stomach.

Ferris brought his hand to his hard cock, stroking, and a pearl glistened at the head. The bead seemed to beg for her to lick it away, see how good he tasted.

"What are you thinking?" he rasped as his hand moved at an enticingly slow pace.

She pushed up from the chair and stepped closer, her gaze locked on his. "That I want to sink my teeth into you."

"Then do it, luv."

Mouse's body grew hotter at his words, her heart slamming against her ribs. She stood on her tiptoes and pressed her lips to his collar bone, her fangs dropping. But she didn't want to pierce him there—she wanted the place she'd been thinking about for a while. It had always been his neck and wrists in the past.

Mouse kissed down his chest to his nipple, circling it with her tongue before gliding her fangs lightly across his flesh, all while he continued to stroke himself faster. Her hand met his and they pumped his cock together, his breaths ragged. Lowering herself to her knees, she took over for him.

She ran her free fingers up his thigh, then sank her teeth into his salty flesh there. A rush of euphoria swept through her as his blood burst onto her tongue. *Heavenly.*

"Fuck," Ferris growled. "That feels so damn good."

Mouse's eyes fluttered as she drank in the taste of him. A part of her wanted to drink him in forever, but she fought that ravenous appetite of hers. Her desire for blood turned toward the need to taste something else. She drew her fangs from his thigh, then shifted her position to collect the pearl from his tip with her tongue, tasting the delectable saltiness. A quiet moan left her and she leaned in to lick from the base of his length to the crown. She circled the warm metal of his piercing before taking him into her mouth completely.

Mouse gripped his buttocks, and he gently thrust into her mouth while his hands fisted her hair. She liked this, the being in control, and she worked him in between her lips, loving how he felt in her mouth. Then his cock pulsed. It had been so long since she'd done this, but it felt natural—all of it.

"I'm about to come," Ferris groaned. But she didn't leave his velvety cock, only continued to take her fill until her name fell from his lips on an inhale and he spilled himself inside her mouth.

Mouse swallowed his delicious flavor, then rose off her knees to stand in front of him. He lifted her chin, his chest heaving. "Tell me what you want now."

"For tonight, I just want to feel your fangs inside me." Mouse unbuttoned the front of her dress and drew it down her shoulders, letting the top fall to her waist, so her breasts were exposed. "And for your hands and tongue to touch me here."

In one swift motion, Ferris hoisted Mouse up, making her laugh while carrying her to the bed. She sat in his lap once more, her legs cradling his hips. His hand slid up her spine as he leaned down, bringing her closer to his face. His warm tongue circled her peaked nipple, then he took it into his mouth, his hand kneading her other breast.

She moaned as he released her nipple and trailed his tongue to the top of her breast, his fangs brushing her skin. Ferris sank his teeth in to the crook of her neck and she arched in pleasure, his fingers caressing her skin as he drank her. Mouse's eyes fluttered and she wanted more. More. More. More. "More," she demanded, her voice breathy.

He flipped her onto her back, caging her in. A loud creak came from the bed before it collapsed to the floor. Mouse squeaked and Ferris's shoulders quaked with laughter.

"I think that's our cue to search the palace like we're supposed to be doing." Mouse smiled.

Ferris smirked, licking the blood from his lips. "We'll continue this *soon*." He crawled off of Mouse and helped her to her feet.

She had never felt this way about anyone, the anticipation flowing through her. For the first time, she wasn't distracted by the need to feed, even though it swirled in her stomach. After searching a little longer, she would drink from their provisions.

Ferris slipped his clothing on while Mouse buttoned her dress, neither removing their gazes from the other.

She bit the inside of her cheek. "We do need to go back to the library since we didn't finish searching it."

Ferris lifted her chin, his dark eyes fastened to hers. "How about in the morning? That will give you time to prepare for it. If you want, I can even search it myself. For now, we can check other rooms in the palace."

Mouse let out a relieved breath. "I like that plan."

As they explored the palace, there were so many rooms to go through, and her eyes started to close as tiredness swept over her. But she wanted to look a little longer since they were almost finished with this wing.

Mouse opened a door that led to a large chamber and she knew right away that this had once belonged to the royals. The bed was large enough for four people and the faded artwork painted across the walls gave it away, along with the words *Bitch Queen* written everywhere. A potent metal smell enveloped her as she entered. Even centuries after the royals had died, the stench of blood still lingered in the bedroom.

Most of the room appeared to have been raided at some point, not a single jewel was anywhere in sight and near-empty dresser drawers were strewn on the floor.

"Looks like the Red Queen was rather popular," Ferris said sarcastically and slipped inside the bathing chamber.

Mouse crept beside him, peering down at the bathtub filled with black sludgy muck and two dingy skulls at the edge. A rib cage rested on the floor in the corner, dried blood beneath it. The mirror was broken with shattered pieces on the cracked marble.

Imogen was known as the Queen of Hearts for her passion of taking hearts while the Red Queen was known not only for hanging body parts in the forest, but for basking in blood.

"If you didn't know already, the Red Queen liked to bathe in blood like Elizabeth Báthory," Mouse said.

"So, Elizabeth wasn't the first to actually do that then?" Ferris arched a brow.

Mouse sent him a sly look. "No, the queen would've easily bathed in Elizabeth's blood."

He smirked. "Check the floors in the other room for loose secret compartments while I go through them in here."

Mouse nodded and went to the desk in the bedroom. Even though the drawers were on the floor, she pressed her hands inside the open slots of the desk, patting around for anything unusual. Besides a few quills that had fallen to the bottom, it was empty.

The wardrobe was empty as well, but she stepped into the large space, feeling over the ornate wood, looking for a sign of uneven texture. Yet she found only smooth surfaces.

Mouse lifted a decaying rug from the floor, but no secret compartment rested there. She shoved the bed to the side, searching beneath. It would have been rather cliché for the queen to have kept anything there, but it was commonplace.

A gut feeling coursed through her as though she was missing something. Mouse glanced at the wardrobe again, frowning, then she pushed it to the side and knelt on the floor. Biting the inside of her cheek, she knocked along the marble until a different, hollower, sound answered.

Eyes wide, she dug her nails into the thin edges of the tile and lifted it. Inside rested an old black book and a velvet crimson bag. "Jackpot!" Mouse yelled.

"You found something?" Ferris asked, rushing into the room.

"We'll see." Mouse handed Ferris the velvet bag while she flipped through the yellowed pages of the book. A musky odor invaded her nostrils while she read over the pages, discovering it did indeed belong to the Red Queen. There weren't many entries inside as if the queen had gotten bored with writing in it.

No longer tired, but wide awake, Mouse settled in, poring over the pages. Most of the entries were about how the Red Queen hated her king and how he'd fucked females behind her back. Her jealousy of the White King and White Queen grew because of their genuine love for one another. She found a way to kill her king and make it look like an accident by feeding him to the Jabberwocky. Her last entry was how she'd plotted to kill the White Royals and had succeeded.

"Well, now we know the queen had a secret about her king," Ferris said.

"There's nothing else about the Jabberwocky in here besides the one mention." Mouse shut the book and sighed.

"You'll be really intrigued by what's in the bag," Ferris purred.

"What is it?" She perked up, finding a small yellow scroll in Ferris's palm.

He cleared his throat and straightened, then changed his voice to a proper accent as he read it aloud. "I cut off pieces of my king before feeding him to the Jabberwocky so he couldn't touch another properly, even in death."

Mouse blinked, waiting for more. "That's it?"

"No. Wait for it." Ferris smirked, then emptied the bag on the floor. Ten bone fingers clacked against the marble.

"And still"—Mouse pursed her lips—"she didn't seem as awful as Rav and Imogen."

"Definitely second place for Wonderland's psychopaths."

Mouse opened her mouth to speak when a boisterous rumbling filled the palace.

CHAPTER THIRTEEN

FERRIS

The palace shook, the king's finger bones rattling against the floor. Glass clinking against glass followed by a shattering in the distance. Booms echoed in a steady rhythm—a drum beat, slow and even. Then a guttural roar ripped through the air, too loud for a werewolf. It sounded more like … *the Jabberwocky*.

"It's the fucking Jabberwocky," Ferris whispered.

Mouse tossed her plait over her shoulder and tiptoed to the window. "It certainly sounds like it."

A low chuffing reverberated from the opposite direction—through the doorway, muffled. "It's coming from over there." Ferris crept out the door and glanced down to the first floor from the railing that overlooked the front entrance. A large shadow passed outside the main doorway, the dark silhouette spilling into the palace. "Oh, shit."

"What?" Mouse asked, peeking over his shoulder.

"It's outside." He snuck down the hallway, his back against the wall. When Mouse followed, he extended an arm in front of

573

her, so he could easily pull her behind him if anything attacked, and peered over the balcony railing.

The shadow moved again, the tip of a tail swishing across the dusty ground outside. Then a sharp, surprised roar echoed into the broken palace. Ferris froze, pressing Mouse against the wall beside him. A furred, darkened snout shoved into the doorway. Nostrils flared on a long inhale. Once. Twice. Then its lips wrinkled into a snarl. Razor-sharp teeth bared. A low growl burst through the front entrance carrying the stench of death.

Fuck.

The beast withdrew from the doorway and replaced its snout with a large furred foot. It reached inside, dragging its talons along the floor with a resounding *screech* that left cavernous gouges in the stone. Ferris swallowed hard. Why hadn't he kept a weapon on him? Not that they were very helpful against the monster back in Ivory, but he needed to make sure Mouse didn't fucking die.

After moving its clawed foot around in search of something that wasn't there, the Jabberwocky growled, deep and guttural, before pulling back. The cracking of wings reverberated, piercing Ferris's ears. He let out a long breath and dropped his arm from in front of Mouse.

Ferris listened hard to the sound of wings as they drifted farther away. Searching the rest of the palace wasn't as important as safeguarding their lives and he wouldn't let anything happen to Mouse. He took her hand in his. "Come on."

Mouse followed close behind him as he led the way down the stairs to the main floor. They needed to find a safe place to hide. Somewhere they wouldn't be seen, heard, or smelled until the Jabberwocky left.

A heavy *boom* came from the roof. He froze as dust rained down from the ceiling, his body tense, waiting. Scrapes and thuds echoed through the palace. As if someone—or some*thing* was punching the ceiling.

"Ah, fuck," he hissed. They were no match for this thing alone. "Do you know if there's a basement?" If they could close themselves off below ground, it might hide their scent long enough for the beast to leave in search of another meal.

"Tunnels, like in … in the Ruby Heart Palace," she said with a wince. "Maddie and I found them when we snuck in for a tea party once."

He ran a hand through his hair and released a short breath. "Okay, I'm sure there are other places to hide. Do you—"

"It's fine. Rav never took me down there to…" Mouse trailed off as the Jabberwocky let out a frustrated screech overhead, the palace walls shaking. "I only know about the tunnels because I visited Imogen with Ever before and… And that's how Rav brought me to his palace the day he locked me up."

Ferris shook his head. No matter the time she'd spent in the tunnels, he didn't want to remind her of that damn place. Didn't want to remind himself of it either, though he knew he could disassociate from it long enough to keep them safe. He'd become an expert at it over the last couple years.

"Ferris, it's okay. If it's safest there, let's go," she said softly.

"All right, luv," he conceded. A portal might even be hidden down there which could get them the fuck out of here. They could check in with Ever and come back later.

Mouse jogged down hallways, glancing inside doors and taking turns with hesitation. Ferris kept an eye on the ceiling as the stone fractured overhead. The Jabberwocky seemed to be following their movements on the roof, but that would be impossible since it couldn't see them. Maybe it could track their footsteps. A *crack* filled the air, stone splitting, and the hair on Ferris's arms stood up. He lifted his gaze upward. They were out of the main part of the palace and the ceiling beneath the roof wasn't visible.

"Are we getting close, luv?" he asked, attempting to keep his voice steady, but he was sure the Jabberwocky was making progress.

"Here!" Mouse called and bolted through an open doorway, down a narrow staircase with spiderwebs crisscrossing.

Ferris glanced over his shoulder as a series of louder cracks tore from above. Then a moment of silence filled the air before chaos descended. The booms and crashes of falling stone and glass. The victorious cry of the beast. A single heavy beat of its wings. Quick, heavy footfalls as it barreled in their direction.

"Fuck!" Ferris shouted, and squeezed into the stairwell.

Mouse made it to the bottom of the steps just as the stench of the beast wafted down behind him. It was far too narrow for the monster to follow, but if it could break through the ceiling, what was stopping it from going through the floor?

Ferris joined Mouse, wrapping an arm around her and propelling her farther into the cavernous room. "Where are the tunnels?" he asked, scanning the circular room.

The walls were rough red stone, just like the floor, but there was no exit. Above, thick metal bars made a tight grid over the ceiling with a large, unlocked padlock dangling over what looked to be a gate.

"Mouse, where are the tunnels?" he asked again when she remained quiet.

Still, she didn't answer. He turned her to face him and froze at the horror in her expression. Eyes wide. Mouth parted. Breaths coming too fast.

"Shit." He took her cheeks in his hands. "Luv, look at me."

Her violet gaze lifted to his. "I was wrong."

"It's okay," Ferris soothed. He knew the tunnels would be a struggle for her, but now there was something on the ceiling that reminded him of the bars of a cage. She wasn't wrong about being able to handle it, though—she was stronger than she knew. And he was going to get her out. "I'm right here. We're fine, yeah? Not trapped. You just need to tell me where the tunnels are and I'll get us out of here."

"No." The word wobbled between them and she looked over his shoulder to where the Jabberwocky now snarled down the stairwell, clawing at the walls with its thick talons in an attempt to fit its body through. "I was wrong, Ferris. These aren't the tunnels."

The muscle in his jaw tightened. Looking around again, his

gaze fell on something white. *Bones.* Scattered across the ground, gouged by teeth and claws. He registered the old, faint scent of blood. The pile of dead leaves and sticks off to the side and the scattered trinkets.

"Okay." He inhaled slowly, trying to keep his concentration despite the beast clawing its way into the narrow stairwell. The Ruby Heart Palace had a few places like this too. One where Rav dumped the remains of his experiments, which were then carted outside by unlucky guards. Another that had held humans before they were brought up to feed vampires during parties. They had been tossed inside from a chute at the base of the palace. "It's okay. Trust me. Tell me where we are and I'll figure a way out of this."

"There's no way out." Her voice cracked, barely audible over the continued roars of the beast hunting them. "I've heard tales about this that I didn't believe were true, but I think this is where they kept the Jabberwocky when they managed to trap it."

"Trap it…"

"The Red Queen had supposedly caught the Jabberwocky once long ago, kept it in this lair to try to tame it but it escaped. The tale Ever told me said the Red Queen wasn't able to trap it a second time, but she had fortified it just in case." Tears welled in Mouse's eyes as she stared up at where the beast was. "There's no other way out."

"Fuck that," Ferris growled. He ran his thumbs over her cheekbones, wiping away the tears. "There's always more than one way out."

"There's not." She grabbed onto his wrists. Held on tightly. "There's not, Ferris. I know there's not. I… I can't…"

There wasn't another way out of her cell. He pulled her close and held her against his chest. "We aren't there, luv. I'm here with you and we *will* get out of this. I've got you."

"Ferris," she sobbed. "Please."

His heart cracked, his head frantically searching for a solution. He'd punch his way out of this place just like the animal threatening them if he had to. Mouse would never be trapped or feel this way again. Not if he could help it.

"Shh," he whispered into her ear. "It's okay."

It was not okay. But he would take the burden of knowing that from her.

The door to the lair flew down the stairs as if the Jabberwocky was calling him a liar. Mouse shook in his arms while the beast slammed into the stairwell over and over. *Fuck.* He saw nothing. No way out. *Think, think, think.*

A low, frustrated grunt poured out from the monster. Then stone blew inward. Blasted down the stairs. And the Jabberwocky tumbled into the underground room, the floor shaking.

Ferris shoved Mouse behind him and pushed her back. Kept himself between her and the beast.

"Shit," he hissed. They were so extremely fucked. "Mouse, hide," he urged. She could disguise herself in the leaves, maybe. Or when the Jabberwocky attacked him, she could run back up the stairs and escape. His pulse thundered, but he held onto the rhythm of it, letting it lead him into the readiness of battle. "Leave me as soon as you get the chance."

"I'm not leaving you," she said, clutching the back of his shirt.

He opened his mouth to argue when the monster rose to its full height, its hulking shadow crawling across his body. Ferris backed away and it advanced. Snarling. Thick saliva dripped from its jagged teeth.

"Nice monster," he tried. "You don't want to eat us."

It opened its jaws wider, as if to say it *very much* wanted to devour them, and took one step closer on those massive furred feet. The ground shifted. Another step. Prowling. The ground cracked beneath its weight. The beast paused and narrowed its orange eyes.

Something was wrong. The lair was built to trap it and yet…

Ferris sucked in a breath. The royals had fortified it to keep the Jabberwocky *better* trapped. What if this wasn't the real lair? What if they'd set this up with the trinkets and the nest as bait?

What if the real lair was beneath…

"What's wrong, pretty beastie?" Ferris taunted. He could be wrong—very wrong—but if he was, they weren't any less fucked. "Not so hungry after all?"

The Jabberwocky snarled and took two more slow steps. The ground caved in with a loud crunch, dragging it down. Panic flashed in the Jabberwocky's fiery orange eyes as it fell, clawing at the air to save itself. Ferris sucked in a shocked breath, expecting the creature to fly back up at him and Mouse. But crumbling chunks of stone smacked against its wings, preventing them from opening to save itself.

Ferris breathed a sigh of relief and turned to Mouse. An unreadable expression filled her wide eyes. "We have to get out of here," he said. They could skirt around the gaping hole in the floor and flee before the beast freed itself. With any luck, they could be halfway to Ivory before the fucker escaped.

Mouse nodded and he spun, holding her tightly by the hand. The ground wavered with each careful step they took, threatening to crumble. Then, before it could truly register in Ferris's mind, the threats became reality as a crack ripped through the room.

The floor gave out beneath him, tearing him away from Mouse. He shouted for her, but she was falling too. Spiraling. Both of them tumbling through the air. He stretched out in a desperate attempt to reach her, but she was too far.

"No! Mouse!" His body slammed into the bottom of the rocky cavern moments before hers, then boulders smashed down between them like a wall. "Mouse! Mouse, can you hear me?"

He shoved up from the ground, feeling every broken rib, as he pounded at the rubble. Behind him, the Jabberwocky stirred.

Motherfucker!

At least Mouse was safe.

But she was trapped. And he refused to let her stay that way.

The beast shook off the stones, its back to Ferris, and shuddered. Pebbles and dust flew outward, slapping Ferris in the face. He winced and pressed himself against the rocks. But the Jabberwocky simply spread its wings and flew out of the pit without noticing him.

Probably gone off to lick its wounds, yet he didn't doubt the beast would be back. They were easy prey now.

"Mouse!" he called again. "Please! *Mouse!*"

CHAPTER FOURTEEN

MOUSE

"*Ah, there's the pretty mouse," a deep voice purred in Mouse's ear, his hot breath tickling her neck, sending chills up her spine. She kept her eyes closed, hoping he would get bored with her, would go the hell away. But no one ever answered her prayers when she silently begged and pleaded, not when the lashings came, not when the drownings occurred, and not when he'd torn out her eyes.*

"Don't play coy. I know you're awake and ready to play." Rav lifted one of her lids, and her gaze met his light brown eyes, the tip of his tongue licking at his lower lip in anticipation of his sick game.

Mouse's pulse spiked, her heart pounding, making the blood rush into her ears. She held back spitting in his face because it would only make things worse, so much worse. When she'd done it last, he peeled off the flesh of her arm with a carving knife and she hadn't known if he would ever stop. She'd once been strapped in a bed next to one of Rav's victims, privy to watch as he stripped away the vampire's flesh until there was nothing but bone. Then he broke the skeleton into pieces, saving the decapitation of the skull for last so the vampire could feel it all. Mouse could never get those screams out of her head—they haunted her every night in her prison cell.

The door opened and the click of heels sounded. Mouse curled in on herself, yanking at her bindings, but she was strapped down to Rav's laboratory table.

"She truly is quite exquisite for such a little thing," Imogen cooed as she leaned over Mouse, the queen's long, crimson hair spilling over one shoulder. "Perhaps I should keep her in a cage in our room. She can be our precious doll."

Terror coursed through Mouse's veins, panic sewing its way into her heart. Please no. *That would be so much worse than her secluded prison. Ferris couldn't sneak into Imogen's room, and Mouse wouldn't be able to hide Des or the drawings she kept beneath her mattress.*

"No, she would probably get too much pleasure in watching us fuck." Rav smirked, swiping a lock of his red-tipped, white hair behind his ear.

"That reminds me, come to bed when you're done. I want you to fuck my mouth." Imogen's gaze turned hungry and she cupped Rav's length over his trousers, her lips coming to his in a seductive kiss that made him groan. Mouse held back her nausea, staring up at the ceiling. The queen finally pulled away, peering back at Mouse. "But don't stop her lesson too soon."

Rav watched his queen as she swayed her hips, her black and red silk dress swishing behind her. He went and shut the door, then grabbed the chair from his desk, where stacks of paper with drawings of scientific torture designs were strewn across.

Settling into the seat, he placed his chin in his hands as he rested his elbows at the edge of her mattress. His hair brushed her arm and she clenched her teeth to fight the disgust stirring inside her.

Without a word, he studied her for a long while, as if she was his project. Which she supposed she was, as she had been, over and over again. The monster to his Frankenstein.

"You know how easy it was for me to fuck your sister?" Rav finally asked.

Not this again… *"You've told me."*

"Well, let me tell you again." Rav arched a brow, seeming to dare her to try and stop him. "After our very brief exchange, she let me fuck her. I didn't even have to use my influence on her. How pathetic." He paused, perking up in his chair while leaning closer to her. "Here's a secret you don't

know. I studied the two of you in your mother's hat shop, deciding who I wanted to take to Wonderland. You were my first choice, but then I knew you wouldn't have been much fun, would've wanted me to court you until marriage before we fucked."

Mouse took a deep swallow, her past creeping in. Mr. Taylor. Him slamming her up against the library shelves, the books crashing to the floor.

"Ah, do you have a secret I don't know about, pretty mouse?" A wicked grin spread across his face. "Perhaps I'll find that out another time." He collected a large silver knife from the drawer of his desk and started sharpening it, the metal scraping metal echoing in the room. As he worked, he hummed a song Ever would sometimes play on her viola. "Dance Of The Sugar Plum Fairy." Except he hummed it darker, viciously.

"Now, let's begin." Halting the movements of his blade, he looked down at her before a sharp pain spread through her leg as he thrust the tip into her thigh.

Mouse jolted, her body shooting upward, the room spinning. A small cry escaped her mouth as a piercing ache traveled through the back of her head and up her spine. She couldn't stand, even though she could feel herself healing. Her breaths came out rapid, her chest heaving, as she searched for Rav. He wasn't there. She wasn't back in his horrific torturous palace. He and Imogen were both dead, and Mouse was in Red with Ferris.

Darkness cloaked Mouse, and even though she could see well without light, she still had to squint. Red sandstone walls surrounded her except for one where large boulders blocked her way out. Mouse's very real dream came back to her once more— her strapped down on the table… The Ruby Heart Palace where her prison cell bars prevented her from escaping...

Mouse's chest tightened and a scream built in her throat, sticking there when a scuffling stirred from the other side of the boulders. Her eyes widened, the dizziness fading, as hope filled her.

"Ferris!" she tried to shout, but it came out a rasp as if she hadn't drunk anything in a while, which she supposed she hadn't. But she didn't know how long it had been since she'd fed from the man in the forest.

"Thank fuck! I thought you were dead. It's been two days!" Ferris whisper-shouted. "Talk as quietly as you can, though—I don't know if the Jabberwocky is coming back. I've been trying to move these boulders ever since we fell down here."

Two days? "I can't stand yet," Mouse started. "Something in my back is broken, and I think I cracked my skull which may have been why I was passed out for so long. I need blood and we don't have our damn bags." Their backpacks with their blood provisions were still in the library… Her stomach let out a small growl, realizing the same thing.

"It's okay. Save your strength. I'm going to get you out today."

Mouse tried to stand again and a gasp escaped her mouth as agony shot through her spine. Rav's song from her dream played inside her mind and she couldn't get it to stop. The walls seemed to close in on her, the smell of Rav's room coming back to her, so she softly hummed a different song as she'd started to do in her prison cell. It was the only way to stop her from hearing the bastard's awful melodies, to push away the memories of what he'd done to her.

Hours passed and Mouse stopped humming. The only other noises that had accompanied her was Ferris grunting, cursing, and hitting things. She didn't think he'd slept at all.

Mouse's spine still wasn't fused. It was healing slower than it should've since she'd been without blood. Her stomach ached, *needing* to feed, but she thought of anything else to push the hunger aside. Maddie. Ever. Des. Home. *Ferris*…

As if hearing her thoughts, a loud clang reverberated from the other side of the boulders. "Ferris?" she said.

"I'm here," he answered in a gruff voice. "How are you doing, luv?"

As long as she continued to talk to him, not focusing on the fact that she was trapped or ravenous, she would tell herself she was fine. "I'm alive."

"Always a good sign." He chuckled.

Mouse closed her eyes, pretending she wasn't in the small

space as she spoke to him. "I think you need to leave, save yourself. You don't know if or when the Jabberwocky is coming back."

"Do you really think I'm going to fucking leave you here? I left you behind once at the Ruby Heart Palace upon your request. I'm not doing it again," he said, finality in his voice.

"But if you're dead, I'll still be trapped anyway."

"Don't care. I'm not leaving."

"Stubborn male." She sighed, but her chest warmed at his words. "At least rest a bit. You're wasting strength."

"Not doing that either, luv." He slammed his weight against the boulders and dust rained down from the ceiling.

Bollocks. If her spine would hurry and heal, she could help instead of feeling like a useless slug on the ground, covered in dust and debris. "So," she said. "Once we get this tedious step out of the way, what will we do next?"

"Well, we won't be able to climb out, I'll tell you that," he grumbled.

Mouse couldn't see the opening now, but she thought about the fall, how far down they'd gone, the smoothness of the walls. She would need a miracle to scale walls like that.

An ache thrummed in her stomach, clenching, her throat parched. She craved a drink, desperate for the taste of blood, *any* blood. Most vampires could go for much longer, but not her, not anymore. She remembered the donor building, the victims she'd slaughtered, how good they'd tasted, their warm blood sliding across her tongue. That was what she needed now—throats ripped apart so she could consume the liquid faster.

Stop! Mouse bit the inside of her cheek until it bled, just so she could taste her own blood. She needed a distraction—she needed to be able to *walk*.

Mouse thought about her and Ferris's time together earlier, his length in her mouth, his lips and tongue on her breast. Their fangs inside one another's flesh. This was what she needed, him with her. "Perhaps," she said slowly, "when we do find a way out and are safe, then we can finish where we left off?"

"Please don't make me fucking hard right now," Ferris growled, his voice deep, seductive.

She laughed softly. "I suppose we can do something different, then?"

"Oh, we will certainly be fucking," he drawled. "We deserve it after this shit, but we need to feed first."

"Feed first," Mouse agreed, her smile widening across her cheeks. But as she peered up at the ceiling, images of the Ruby Heart Palace came back in a rush and she closed her eyes, pretending she was out in the open, not trapped.

And then she hummed once more.

Mouse had fallen asleep at some point, and as she cracked open her eyes, she went to sit up, her spine not hurting any longer. She'd never healed this slow, not even when she was in the Ruby Heart Palace. But her spine had never been broken before. She'd had her neck snapped plenty of times, but even then, she'd healed in less than a day. Yet she'd never fallen this far before either.

As Mouse pushed up from the ground, hunger gnawed at her insides, coursing through her.

"Are you awake?" Ferris asked.

"Yes, and I can finally stand," Mouse whispered.

"Good, because I'm almost there." A scraping sounded, then a small opening appeared as he removed a stone. Mouse walked up to the space and found a dirty, sweat-stained Ferris grinning at her and her stomach dipped at the sight of him.

"Hello, luv." His grin widened further. "I bet you've been dying to see my pretty face, huh?"

"You have no idea." She inhaled his intoxicating scent and wanted to break the rock wall apart to get to him, to pierce her fangs into his flesh. Mouse tightened her fists, digging her nails into her palms to control her urges.

"Let me work on this one." He slipped his hand inside the hole, gripping the boulder, and pulled to create a thin slit.

"Move back," Mouse instructed. Gathering what strength she had, letting her hunger drive her, she lunged forward, shoving her body against the boulder, blowing it wide. Rocks collapsed behind her, but she didn't glance back.

She caught another whiff of Ferris as he stepped in front of her, stronger, alluring. The urge to *devour* him pulsed within her. Mouse's body moved of its own accord, no matter how loud she screamed at herself to not do it. Her fangs dropped and she barreled forward, knocking Ferris to the ground, burying her teeth deep into his throat.

CHAPTER FIFTEEN

FERRIS

Pain shot through Ferris when Mouse knocked him to the ground on the uneven rocks. His vision went black for a moment before the familiar sting of her bite tore into his neck. She buried her fangs in deeper, sucking brutally as she writhed on top of him.

"Mouse," he groaned, arching in to her touch, part pain, part pleasure.

Normally he would welcome the rough treatment, would let her have any control she damn well pleased, but he'd just spent days breaking down a fucking wall without a drop of blood to quench his thirst. Still, his cock responded. How could it not when she gyrated so skillfully against him, teasing him with a hint of what she could do if he were inside her. Circling her hips, sliding along the length of him. As though under her spell, he gripped her hips, tugging her tighter to him. She snarled as she drank from him. The softness of her lips on his flesh and the caress of her tongue pulled a possessive, animalistic sound from his throat.

"Mouse," he growled. As much as he wanted her, as much as he wanted to show her what it was like to be fucked with rawness, with tenderness, to give her what she wanted, *needed,* they had to stop. If she took too much, they'd be screwed. He would pass out and, with no way to replenish himself, they'd never make it out of this shit hole. And there was no telling if or when the Jabberwocky would come back. The bastard hadn't returned for days, so they had no idea if it was even in Red anymore. "Control yourself," he said gently, and reached up, placing a hand to her warm cheek.

She snarled again and clamped her jaw tighter, but slowed her drinking. No longer was she pulling more blood into her mouth, but simply enjoying what was already there. Her tongue slowly lapped up what had oozed from beneath her fangs, enticing him toward something *more.* And he was more than willing to oblige. One hand slid from her hips up to wrap her plait around his fist and his other trailing up her thigh, beneath her dress, reveling in the feel of her smooth skin. She drew in a deep mouthful of his blood and his breath caught.

"Damn, luv," he choked out. Her fingers met his, guiding them to her panties. As she released his hand, he skimmed his digits over the silken fabric, finding her aroused, *wet.* "Bring those beautiful lips of yours to mine."

"Touch me," Mouse whispered, her jaw loosening slightly. Her hips shifted over him, seeking friction. Ferris slipped his fingers beneath the fabric, brushing her bundle of nerves. Her breath caught as he pressed against her core and rubbed slow circles.

"Relax," Ferris urged, picking up his pace. He tightened his grip on her plait and her moan skated along his neck, her fangs gently scraping his skin as if she was fighting not to bury them back in. Her hips found a rhythm with him and he shifted to better feel her. His cock strained to be set free of his jeans. To be stroked and licked and fucked. To be inside her, to feel her heat, to make her scream his damn name.

"Ferris," Mouse begged, voice full of lust. Her tongue swiped the place she'd bit, but she didn't resume sucking his flesh, her attention moving to the other sensations.

"Come for me, luv," he rasped, adding more pressure, dipping two fingers into her heat.

Mouse cried out against him, hips jerking. Her fangs threatened to pierce him as she rode her orgasm out on his hand. Ferris lifted his groin up, desperate for more. When Mouse reeled back with a gasp, he released her hair. When it was safe, he would let her drink and drink from anywhere on his body, feed on him as much as she liked. But he *needed* her to be safe.

"You with me?" His voice was husky with desire, his gaze meeting her violet irises.

She stared back at him with wide eyes. "Ferris, I'm so sorry. I—"

"Hush." He leaned up on his elbows and captured her lips with his. He tasted his own blood on her mouth and hunger rumbled through him. It was important he feed soon, but first, he needed to sate his other appetite so he could focus on getting Mouse out of there and not how hard he was. His kisses grew harsher, his mind clouded by desire.

Mouse dragged her nails down his chest and fumbled with the zipper. When her hand wrapped around his length, he thrust into her touch. *Shit.* Her grip tightened and he was lost to the feel of her. Their lips coasted over one another, their tongues caressing, as she used long strokes up and down his cock, her thumb circling his pierced tip. His release built at the base, his balls tightening.

"Fuck, luv. You feel so good," Ferris growled against her mouth.

His release barreled through him as Mouse continued her perfect pace. "Bloody hell," he groaned. Stars burst behind his eyes. It felt like he came for ages before she let him go.

Muscles aching, he slowly tucked himself away and sat up. A trail of his blood still ran down Mouse's chin. He reached out and wiped it away with his thumb. Even in his wildest dreams, he never expected to experience this with Mouse. She'd drank from him so many times and, though it had turned him on, he'd never explored it with her. Only used his hand over and over again. Now, he wasn't sure how he'd ever resisted asking her if she would want more than blood.

"Are you all right?" His chest heaved.

Mouse nodded, her eyes filling with tears. "I'm a monster. I'm sorry."

"You're not. You were stuck behind a wall of rock for days, luv." Ferris pushed himself to his feet with a pained grunt. He helped her up and lifted her chin, leaning in close. "We both needed it to continue. Besides, I enjoyed it. I *like* it rough."

Mouse's cheeks pinkened. "Still, I shouldn't have attacked you like that."

His lips tilted up, giving her a soft smile. "We'll work on your control, yeah? But we should get the fuck out of here in case the Jabberwocky returns."

Mouse looked up at the broken floor above them and shivered. "Any idea how to do that?"

Ferris blew out a breath. He'd been so preoccupied with getting to Mouse that he hadn't bothered to search for an exit. Without Mouse, he hadn't planned on leaving, so breaking down the wall had been his only priority. It seemed they'd fallen into a cavern of sorts, though. Water dripped onto the newly-fallen debris from stalactites and the walls funneled to one passageway. The ceiling was too high to jump out, the walls smooth and slick, and there was nothing to climb.

"It looks like we only have one option," he said.

"Appears so," she agreed, squinting through the darkness. "Though it seems like a trap, if I say so myself."

Ferris brushed the hair from his face and shrugged. "Seems to me like we already fell into the trap. If the Red Queen had planned to keep the Jabberwocky down here, she would need access to the beast, right?"

"Perhaps." Mouse picked her way around large fallen boulders toward the passage. "But perhaps not, if she wanted it to wither and die down here instead of train it."

Ferris followed behind Mouse, holding her steady as they crossed over the rocky ground. This all seemed fucking ridiculous if the dead queen only wanted to trap the beast. There was a nest and bones in the original lair which meant the royal cared somewhat. Either way, they needed to at least find where this path led.

They made their way into the dark tunnel and Ferris hoped it would take them to the others. In the Ruby Heart Palace, all the underground tunnels intersected at some point. There was no reason to think they wouldn't do the same here or at least offer an emergency escape. Though there was no reason to think they *would* either.

Keeping quiet, they walked straight ahead. Ferris cocked his head as they traveled down the tunnel, listening harder in case the Jabberwocky made a bloody unwanted return. There was no way in hell its massive body would fit down this pathway, but the beast had already proven itself capable of breaking down walls. Still, he wanted to be clear of this damn place.

"When we find a way out, we need to return to the library," Mouse said after they'd been walking for maybe fifteen minutes. There were no twists or turns to the tunnel. All the debris had given way to smooth stone floors with small puddles of water collected from the dripping ceiling.

"I don't know if we'll find anything there, luv," he admitted. If the Red Queen had gone through all the trouble of trying to capture the Jabberwocky a second time, then maybe she'd wanted to tame it since she didn't know how to kill it.

Mouse shrugged. "We should still check. Besides, our backpacks are there and we need to drink blood."

"All right." There was nothing to lose by checking, but if he heard so much as a single growl or the beat of wings, they were heading straight for the portal at the edge of Ivory. He would tell Ever they didn't uncover a damn thing, admit their failure. The queen wouldn't give them a hard time as long as they both returned. She had originally planned on sending more vampires anyway. But if they didn't find answers on the Jabberwocky, an entire army might not be enough.

Pausing, Mouse sniffed the air. "Do you smell that?"

"What?" Ferris inhaled and was greeted with warmer, fresher air. His lips curled into a smile. "We're close to an exit."

Mouse sprinted ahead and he easily caught up to her. He scanned the slick walls for any hint of a door, but it was Mouse who saw it first. She skidded to a halt in front of him so fast that he nearly ran into her. Grabbing her waist to steady himself, he glanced over the top of her head.

The tunnel ended with a large grated door. On the other side, another few feet of tunnel stretched with hazy red sky beyond. Ferris slid past Mouse and grabbed onto the metal bars. He shook them and the sound echoed down the path behind them. There were no hinges to know which way it should swing open and the space between the bars was too small to fit between.

"I think it lifts up," Mouse said, pointing at the ceiling.

The rock had been carved out, the metal disappearing inside. Ferris adjusted his grip and pulled upward. The door creaked, tiny pebbles falling. But it was too damn heavy to gain enough space.

"I might need your help," he told Mouse. After days of breaking through a stone wall, then having Mouse feed from him, he wasn't exactly in top form at the moment.

She stepped beside him and latched on. Together, they picked it up inch by inch until there was just enough space for them to squeeze beneath. His muscles quaked under the weight of the gate, coupled with the hunger brewing inside himself, aching.

"Go!" Ferris urged. He couldn't hold the door forever and he wasn't sure she would be able to keep it up alone. But as long as she escaped, she could bring back reinforcements to get him out. If she knew that he was willing to stay behind, she'd never fucking leave—and she needed to be free.

Mouse let go, elongating her body as she rolled beneath the door, then grabbed onto the bars from the other side. "Come on," she said with a relieved smile.

"Can you hold it alone?"

Mouse's smile faded. "It's only for a moment."

If she couldn't hold it, he'd easily be crushed. Then he would be trapped there while she got help, a sitting duck for the Jabberwocky to devour. "Maybe you should go back to Ivory."

Mouse narrowed her eyes. "You didn't leave me and I'm not leaving you. Trust me to hold it long enough. I can do it."

The shaking in Ferris's arms increased and for the first time in a long time, he doubted himself. He never once doubted himself while he was with her in the Ruby Heart Palace, not when they were in the safe house after Mouse's escape, and not even when he was removing the boulders to get to her. But she looked so sure of herself. *Fuck.* He needed to feed and he couldn't hold this piece of shit thing forever. "On the count of three," he said. "One…"

Mouse widened her stance. "Two."

"Three." Ferris used every ounce of his vampire speed to slide under the door.

The sound of Mouse's strained grunt as he passed beneath the heavy metal made his breath catch. But he shoved himself to his feet before it slammed shut. Mouse jumped away from the door, covering her mouth with her hands.

"Bloody hell." Ferris sucked in deep breaths, chest heaving. If the gate had fallen on him, fuck being trapped, he would've been cut in two. "Now I expect you to help save my arse every time." He chuckled softly as he drew her to him, kissing her temple.

Mouse leaned into him for a moment. "I told you I could do it."

"You sure as fuck did." He set his chin on top of her head and willed his heart to slow. There wasn't enough blood in his veins for it to race like this. He had control of himself for now, but he didn't want to test it either. Mouse had been through too much with Rav and Imogen for him to blindside her with a bite. "We need our bags."

CHAPTER SIXTEEN

MOUSE

Hunger clawed within Mouse but not like it had before she'd drank from Ferris. Back in the alley at the club, she'd *almost* lost control with him. This time she had. It was something she could never let happen again, yet part of her had known to drink from him slowly, savoring his taste, instead of ripping apart his throat.

As they entered the palace through a large hole in the castle wall's side, Ferris's eyelids fluttered. There was no sign of the Jabberwocky or any other danger for that matter. A good thing. But if the beast returned, Mouse would have to do her best to carry Ferris—she didn't think he could make it much farther.

They traveled down several crumbling hallways, then to one with shattered glass littering the floor that opened to the main entrance of the castle. Mouse wrapped her arm around Ferris's waist, searching for a place to hide. *Aha!* A small crevice rested beneath the stairs, the perfect place for Ferris to remain out of view in case danger struck again.

Ferris had saved Mouse, pulling her back from the brink of

madness, had touched her in a way that made her see stars. It was more than a distraction from feeding on Ferris, more than him just trying to help her.

She guided him to the stairs and found his gaze trained on her neck, the tip of his tongue sweeping across his lower lip. If Ferris didn't feed soon, he would attack her, the same way she'd done to him. Any other time, Mouse would hold out her wrist, but if she gave him what he wanted in that moment, the monster within her could rise once more. And this time she might not be able to hold back from tearing out his throat. If she did, life wouldn't exist for her any longer.

"Wait under the stairs," Mouse whispered. "I'll collect our backpacks, then we'll drink and get cleaned up at the lake before searching the library." They were both covered in sweat, blood, and grime, and they needed to make certain the Jabberwocky couldn't sniff them out as easily if it did return.

"No," Ferris swayed, his gaze never leaving her throat. "I'll grab them. You shouldn't have to go into the library by yourself."

"I'm fine and can do it quicker." Mouse held both his arms, steadying him as she brought him to a sitting position beneath the stairs. He was too weak to argue with her about it. "Save your strength or we may murder each other, and neither of us wants that now, do we?"

"You smell so fucking good," Ferris slurred, his fangs lowering. He shook his head, sobering himself. "Go and be careful."

Mouse was hesitant to leave him, but she nodded and raced up the staircase, not wanting to waste a drop of any more time. Her movements stayed quiet, her feet barely touching the floor as she used what energy she had left for her enhanced speed. When she came across the library doors, her stomach sank. Pushing away the anxious feeling, she snatched their backpacks and left.

Heart pounding, she stormed to the main entrance just as fast, wishing for the Jabberwocky not to show its monstrous face.

It had only taken her a few seconds to reach Ferris, yet it seemed like an eternity passed. His skin was paler, perspiration dotted his brow, and he clenched his stomach as his breaths came out ragged.

"Hold it together for a little longer," she said quickly, unzipping his backpack first to fish out both his canteens of water.

"I've never been this damn hungry before," he rasped. "I've gone much longer without feeding."

"You've also never worked yourself like this." She opened a pouch of powdered blood and poured it into one of the canteens. As the delicious metal smell struck her nose, she held her breath or else she would pour the powder directly into her mouth. She wouldn't care about the chalkier taste or how much harder it was to swallow—she *craved* it.

Steady, Mouse.

She slowly inhaled as she shook the canteen to mix the powder and water.

"You drink first," Ferris demanded, even though he looked half dead.

"No." She shoved the bottle into his hand.

"Stubborn vampire." He smirked but put the mixture to his lips, growling as he drank, deep and lusty.

Taking a swallow to push away her burning desire, she took the other canteen and poured in the powder. The liquid was warm when it hit her tastebuds, a moan escaping her mouth while the blood slid down her throat, strengthening everything inside of her. Her tiredness dissipated, the hunger lessening.

"Let's drink another," Ferris said, appearing more like himself, his eyelids no longer fluttering and his voice steady. "Just in case we run into some shit again."

"Smart idea." Mouse fixed them both a drink in the last two canteens from her bag, then they finished them off. Only a tiny hint of hunger buried itself in her stomach, and she hadn't felt this full in a while, but with Ferris's blood pulsing in her veins along with the provisions, it should hopefully hold her over for a bit.

"Let's hurry to the lake while the coast is clear." Ferris crawled out from beneath the stairs and rose to his full height. He helped her up and led her to the front door, where he peered out, then waved her to follow. "No sign of the beast."

Her shoulders relaxed and she walked out the door beside him. A light breeze rustled the hem of her dress and the sky was darkening, the half-moon high up in its depths. Above the castle, a large bat flapped its wings while gliding through the air.

As they passed barren trees and the deteriorating statues, Mouse listened for any sign of the Jabberwocky, the crack of its leather wings, or the pounding of its heavy footsteps. But nothing sounded. She prayed the creature wasn't back in Ivory or Scarlet either. If it were in werewolf territory, that would be a dream come true. It could feed on those awful creatures forever.

A dead garden came into view, not a single leaf bloomed from any of the bushes, and they skirted around it. It would take a lot of work to revive this territory, but the potential was there, especially when they rounded the castle to the back. Her gaze settled on a low decorative stone wall that ran around the edge of a glistening crystal-clear lake, forming a walking path along it. Tall trees that weren't completely barren sprouted a few deep purple flowers.

"This area doesn't seem so bad," Ferris said, kneeling in front of the lake to fill up his canteens.

Mouse mirrored his movements with her two, then placed the bottles in her backpack. She zipped up her bag and stood, finding Ferris's gaze trained on her, his dark irises shining.

"Turn around so I can undress," she said softly.

Ferris arched a brow and smirked.

"What?" Mouse placed her hands on her hips.

"You do realize you've seen me naked more than once now, and I've seen you pretty damn close to being so." That deep voice of his pulled at her, making her skin tingle.

Again, the way he'd touched her came to mind, that rush of heat spreading through her veins. But they needed to get cleaned up and hurry back inside the castle. Even though the Jabberwocky had been inside, it was still safer than milling around out in the open.

"Well," she drawled. "Then you can wait until later to see me fully. Now, turn around."

"Until then." He smiled seductively, facing the opposite direction as she took out a black dress from her pack.

Mouse glanced at Ferris's back, her gaze drifting to his buttocks, the way his tight jeans hugged the curve of it, how they showed off his muscular legs. As butterflies swarmed in her stomach, she pulled off her dirt-covered dress and kicked her boots away before slipping naked into the warm water.

"All right, come on," she called, unraveling her plait.

Ferris turned around, his dark gaze studying her as he crossed his arms.

Mouse tilted her head to the side. "What?"

He lifted a finger and slowly spun it in a circle, that perfect digit which had brought her to bliss so easily. "Now, *you* look away, luv."

Fighting a smile, she rolled her eyes and did just that. Even though she couldn't see him, she couldn't stop listening to his every movement, the way his clothing rustled as he peeled them from his body, how the water sloshed against his flesh when he moved through it, *toward her.*

"You can look at me now," Ferris said, his voice gruff.

A blush crept up her face as she found his hair already wet, the beads of water glistening against his strong arms and broad chest.

Neither spoke as they scrubbed the dirt from their bodies, but her gaze continued to drift toward him as if he were her beacon. Smiling to herself, she glanced toward the castle where a pristine balcony rested. Not a single crack or missing piece marred the stone. A trellis woven with dead vines hung beside it, reminding her of the balcony in *Romeo and Juliet*, and how Shakespeare had written the scene so splendidly.

"Are you thinking about Shakespeare?" Ferris asked, running

his hands through his wet hair, his lips tilted to one side.

"How did you know?"

"You have that look when you read his plays or talk about him. Should I be jealous?" His grin widened.

"Hmm." She pretended to mull it over. "If the master of plays were alive today, you might have a bit of competition there. He does have a way with words," she teased.

Before she knew what was happening, Ferris's hands were around her waist and her legs circled his hips. "I can have a way with words," he purred in her ear.

"You really like getting me in this position, don't you?" she said, pressing herself into him.

"I do." He tightened his grip on her, somehow bringing her even closer, her softness pressing into his hardness. "And didn't I say we would fuck after we fed?"

As she parted her lips to give into temptation, a roar tore through the air, followed by the cry and howl of a werewolf in the distance. The Jabberwocky must've found a meal…

"Maybe not this second though," Ferris growled, carrying her out of the lake and placing her on her feet.

Mouse shoved on her clothing and boots, not worrying about plaiting her hair. At least the Jabberwocky was taking care of a rogue werewolf so they wouldn't have to use loud bullets again.

Snatching their backpacks, they bolted for the castle, keeping as close to the trees as possible. Once inside, they darted up the stairs and down the hall toward the library. Her heart slammed against her rib cage, her chest heaving as they reached the room. She bit her lip, staring at the doors of the library for a moment before deciding on shutting and locking them. With the doors closed, it would give them a little more time to hide if they had to.

"You don't have to shut them," Ferris said gently.

To give them more time wasn't the only reason she'd done it. Mouse also needed to face her fears, and perhaps it was being trapped behind the boulders that had done it, or knowing that while being with Ferris, he would always try to get her away from danger. Either way, she now knew she could survive inside a room with the doors shut. They'd been wide open when she'd first left the Ruby Heart Palace, then cracked, and now this was the final step. As for the library, it wasn't the same one where she'd been hurt—these weren't the same books that had surrounded her, and this man … this man was nothing like the one who had broken her. She grasped the strength within her, taking even breaths. "I'm all right. I have you with me in here and I trust you, Ferris."

"I trust you too, luv."

But then she remembered how she'd attacked him, which was more recent—one memory that wouldn't easily go away. "Maybe you shouldn't," she murmured. "I'm still unpredictable."

He cocked his head and blinked at her as if she were mad. "Do you feel like you want to attack me now?"

"No," she said slowly.

"Maybe you should." He took a step toward her, pushing a lock of wet hair behind her ear. "It led to good things, didn't it?"

"Ferris!"

"Shh!" He put his finger over his lips while smiling. "This conversation is over. We have work to do."

Mouse rolled her eyes but couldn't stop grinning as she pored over the spines of decaying books. She didn't know if the queen, king, or both of them had read the tomes, but most were mundane and about building things. A bright blue spine caught her attention with the words *Beast of Wonderland* written on it in gold cursive. She wiped the dust from the cover and flipped through the yellowed pages of the thin book, filled with mostly drawn pictures of the Jabberwocky. Badly, she might add. Her finger followed the lines as she read over a few facts about the creature. The beast had first been spotted in Wonderland centuries ago and was the only one of its kind. It had been caught once by the royals, but was untrainable, even when provided vampires or humans to eat. The Red Queen wanted to use the Jabberwocky against other territories, but the attempt had failed.

So, the Red Queen had truly caught it once then…

"It doesn't make a lick of sense." Mouse wrinkled her nose, showing him the page. "How can the Jabberwocky be the only one? It still had to be born from somewhere, right?"

Ferris shrugged. "Scotland has the Loch Ness Monster. The States have Bigfoot. And Wonderland has the Jabberwocky."

"The what?" She frowned, not understanding what in the world he was talking about.

"Right. You're *older* than me." He smirked. "And you haven't hung around the mortal world enough to hear about those cryptids. But I guess the Jabberwocky wouldn't be considered one anyway since it's proven to be real."

"Our next quest when this is over will be for you to teach me about what a cryptid is," she pointed out, smiling to herself as she returned to scan through the remaining pages. "Bollocks, there's nothing useful in here!"

Mouse went to slide the book back on the shelf, but then the urge to make the row even nagged at her. One of the tomes at the edge of the row continued to stick out a centimeter and she shoved it in when a click sounded. Scowling, she pulled out a stack of books and found what looked to be a small silver key inserted into the inner wall shelf. The metal was about the size of her fingernail and matched something on the back of a wind-up toy.

"There's something here." She beamed, brushing her fingertips against the metal and cranking it to the right.

A grinding noise filtered into the room and the shelf shook, the tomes rattling. Mouse took a step back, the bookshelf opening toward them like a door. Her eyes widened as she met Ferris's gaze.

He rubbed the back of his neck, a satisfied smile on his face. "Let's hope we just struck fucking gold."

CHAPTER SEVENTEEN

FERRIS

Darkness swallowed Ferris and Mouse. The secret door only spilled light into the passageway for so long before they had to rely on their vampiric eyesight. Cobwebs hung down from a white ceiling, crisscrossing along their path. Deep green and gold foil wallpaper lined the walls and a matching carpet softened their footsteps.

"How far do you think this goes?" Mouse asked when they'd been walking for nearly three minutes.

It was impossible to tell which direction they were going anymore—if the floor slanted up or down, made gradual shifts to the right or left. The outline of the door leading back into the library had vanished from view. For a moment, he found himself eager to make it to the other end—not because he was afraid, but because exploring the palace was becoming more like a treasure hunt by the hour. "That's a very good question."

Mouse thought for a moment, sweeping away cobwebs from where they looped across their path. "It almost feels like we're going to the pits of Hell…" She wiggled her fingers in the air and smiled.

"Except without fire." He grinned, plucking another web from her hair. Nothing had ventured down this hallway in ages, judging by the amount of strands weaving across the passageway.

She paused and stepped back from a particularly thick cluster. "I hope there are no living spiders in there."

Ferris chuckled. "You have a caterpillar at home and you're afraid of some spiders?"

"There aren't any spiders—these webs are old." She poked him playfully in the side. "But don't compare Des to them. She doesn't leave a clingy mess behind."

"Sure, luv. I'll go first," he said, laughing again. "Come on."

Ferris entered into a large sitting room and took in six glass cases full of strange objects resting on velvet pillows. One wall held shelves and, on them, what looked to be journals bound with strips of leather. In the middle of everything was a round table between two red armchairs. He paused just inside, Mouse right on his heels, and scanned for threats.

"Seems safe enough," he said. "No skeletons either, which is always nice."

Mouse stepped in front of him and reached up onto her toes. "Let me."

She gathered dusty cobwebs from his face and hair with featherlight touches. He drew in a deep breath, remembering her naked in the lake. Pressed against him. Her soft skin brushing along his. *Shit.* Now was *not* the time for his mind to take a side trip into the gutter, but he couldn't help it. Not when her hands ran down his chest, collecting more webs from him. He wanted to touch her too, wipe her clean … then make her dirty again.

Mouse looked up at him with a coy smile as if she knew exactly what he was thinking. "There you go. Handsome as ever."

"I'm glad you approve," Ferris said in a husky voice and placed a kiss on her forehead. "Now, let's see what goodies we can find." He rubbed his hands together and waggled his eyebrows at her.

Mouse spun around to face the room and gasped. "This looks fun."

Soft, glowing yellow lights flickered to life when they stepped farther into the room. Ferris tugged Mouse back in case they'd triggered a trap. Imogen had them in the Ruby Heart Palace, strategically placed anywhere she didn't want prying eyes. Orbs floated near the ceiling, circling each other and spanning out again to create simple swirling patterns. Shadows danced along the walls from the light but nothing else stirred. No trap doors opened and no arrows soared toward them.

"What is this?" Mouse asked in awe. She lifted a hand toward them, too short to reach, and wiggled her fingers in their light.

"Hell if I know. Let's see what the rest of this shit is." Ferris walked forward carefully in case anything more than orbs appeared, but when he made it to the table unscathed, he released a breath.

Mouse moved around the perimeter of the room, fingers skimming the thick wallpaper. "I wouldn't exactly call this *shit*."

Ferris followed her gaze to the middle display case. Inside was a wide belt inlaid with dozens of gem stones. Large and small. Marquee cut, square, round, pear, princess, all of them gleaming as if the sun were shining brightly overhead. "It's strange," he said quietly.

Mouse inched closer and set her hands on the glass, her lips parting. "It's … humming."

"Even fucking stranger," he said, stepping back. The last thing they needed was to set off a trap. Everything in here was undoubtedly worth a fortune—otherwise, why hide it? A secret door that any vampire could've stumbled upon wasn't likely to be the only security measure in place.

"What do you think this one is?"

Ferris scowled when she ran a finger over the next glass box. Folded red fabric took up a majority of the top shelf. Gold trimmed the edges and a large medallion clasp held the neck together. An overcoat of some kind, he guessed. But it was more than that. The air around the display was thicker, heavier, and scratched against his skin. It didn't hurt but was definitely an uncomfortable sensation. Iron bars surrounded the seams of the glass with engravings in an unknown language. Three pearls were nestled beside it—one blue, one pink, one white. The next shelf contained a golden hourglass encrusted with rubies.

"Oh, a dagger!" Mouse had shifted to the smaller display at the end while he was distracted by the mystery object. "This is what I imagine the dagger would look like that Juliet takes from Romeo to end her life."

Ferris joined her, partially to be near her, to make sure it wasn't rigged against would-be thieves. It *was* a beautiful blade. The point appeared razor sharp, the edges expertly tapered. Halfway up the top of it was harsh serrated edges and a floral design etched along the center. The hilt was gold, inlaid with diamonds and emeralds, scrollwork snaking around it. At the base, the gold flared out into a flower. Another large emerald sat at the center.

"Unless you think it can kill the beast, let's keep looking," he said.

Mouse tsked. "You're no fun."

"Am I not?" He raised a brow. "I'm fairly certain you were singing a different tune when we—"

"We should rest," she said quickly, her cheeks turning pink. "I think it's safe enough in here."

Ferris glanced around the room for any potential triggers he might've missed—a plank that didn't settle right or an item perfectly out of place. Nothing set off alarm bells. "Let's finish looking around first."

"Ferris," Mouse chided. "You spent days breaking down rocks to free me. Sleep so you can think more clearly."

He reached out and lifted a strand of her pink hair, admiring how soft it was. "I would gladly suffer sleepless years, bloodying my hands, to protect you. You should know that by now."

"I do know." Her breath hitched when he let her hair fall back to her shoulder and traced a line over her neck. "And you should know that I would do the same for you. I'll settle for making you rest though."

He gave her a soft smile. "I'm not sure I'd be able to sleep yet. My mind is too busy."

"Oh?" Mouse bit her bottom lip. "Maybe I can help with that."

Mouse stood on her toes and pressed her lips to his. He slid his hands into her hair and tilted her head back to gain better access. She tasted sweet with the faint hint of blood. His hunger was sated with the powdered drink, but he wanted to taste her. To drink *her*. But neither of them were strong enough for that at the moment.

Her tongue slipped between his lips and Ferris's grip tightened in her hair as he thrust his tongue to meet hers. She tasted like bliss—*his* bliss—and he needed more. He fucked her mouth with his tongue, wishing it was his cock. But he couldn't pull himself away long enough to see if she would drop to her knees for him. Her lips were too delicious, too soft, but he needed *more*. Mouse tilted her chin, forcing his kisses to skate down her neck instead.

"Should we be doing this right now?" he asked against her skin. Everyone was counting on them back in Ivory.

"Probably not," she breathed. "You're not going to be able to help them if you don't rest though."

"And this will help my mind turn off," he agreed. It usually worked when he managed the task alone.

His fangs dropped and he dragged them gently over her skin, eliciting a moan. The sound went straight to his cock, making it hard as fuck. She'd gotten him off when she'd fed from him after being trapped in the cave, but he was nearly desperate with the need to feel her touch again. His hands shook as they drifted from her hair to slide the collar of her dress down.

Mouse inhaled, pressing her chest toward him while he kissed his way across her bare shoulders. "Ferris," she breathed.

"Yes, luv?" He trailed his tongue slowly along her collarbone, hoping to drive her just as mad as him. When he nipped gently at the upper swells of her breasts, she drew her bodice down to expose her peaked nipples. He grinned at her. "So impatient."

"Just making up for the lost time we should've been doing this," she said as desire flickered in her eyes. "Besides, I can lose a little sleep so let's not wait any longer."

Ferris chuckled. "I'm going to teach you the perks of delayed gratification."

"Ferris," she warned. Her hand fell to his, and she guided it up her stomach, ever so slowly until she enfolded it around her breast. "Make me feel good."

Ferris gripped her chin with his free hand, his gaze trained on hers. "Your orgasms are mine now."

"Are they now?" she asked with a wide smile.

Ferris leaned in and sucked her bottom lip between his teeth, careful not to draw any blood. When he released her, he trailed kisses along her jaw to her ear, then whispered, "I want you to touch yourself in front of me, the way I did for you."

Mouse shivered from his words, her heart thrumming with what had to be the same lust that matched his. Playful defiance shimmered in Mouse's eyes as she took a step back. She peeled the dress from her hips, taking her panties down with it, until the fabric pooled at her feet. His pulse thundered as he raked over every glorious inch of her naked body. The curves that led to her perfect arse, the soft swell of her beautiful breasts. Her arousal filled the air and he clenched his fists at his sides to keep himself from going to her, from taking her into his mouth right then.

"I've never touched myself in front of anyone before," Mouse whispered. She looked hesitant at first, and he was about to tell her she didn't have to when she dragged a hand up her abdomen to cup her breast. Her thumb grazed the tight nipple as she backed up, maneuvering around a display case, toward the red armchair. She sank down onto the cushion with hooded eyes. Her free hand wasted no time skimming between her thighs, finding its target.

Spreading her legs wide, Ferris got an unobstructed view of her gleaming core. His hands balled into fists in an effort not to reach out and touch her himself. She was so damn sexy. Every inch of her.

Mouse slid her fingers between her folds. Up and down, teasing herself. Then she pressed against her clit and arched into her own touch. Ferris groaned, moving toward her, desperately wanting his tongue everywhere she was touching. She circled the bundle of nerves with measured strokes before dipping the same digit inside. His cock throbbed and he stalked around the display case.

"Enough," Ferris growled.

He knelt in front of her, threw her legs over his shoulders, and stood. She gave that sexy squeak of hers, and her ankles locked around him, pressing between his shoulder blades, as her hips shifted toward his face. He walked them three steps to the wall and held her against it.

Gripping her thighs, he looked up at her. "I want to taste you so fucking badly."

"Then why aren't you?" Her fingers tangled with his hair, guiding him to her and that was the only push he needed.

They both groaned when he ran his tongue along her slit. Her sweet flavor was better than any blood he'd ever tasted. He didn't know how he'd survived so long without feasting on her. Closing his lips over her, he sucked her clit into his mouth and swirled his tongue over it, drinking in her sweet flavor like it was fine wine. Again and again and again as she ground against his face. He fucking loved it, loved that this vampire could make him so wild with desire just from the sound of her gasping as he pleasured her. He wanted her for the rest of his fucking life.

His tongue slipped away from her clit and drifted downward. Her body quaked, and his name came out as a breath from her lips when her orgasm shattered. Ferris grinned against her core while she continued to writhe against his face, his fingers digging into her thighs.

When her grip on his hair relaxed, he gave one more lick, to taste the remainder of her arousal. Her legs relaxed and Ferris shifted away from Mouse to help her down. She brought her left leg over his shoulder at the same time he moved her right. Mouse slid sideways with a gasp, grabbing an elaborate picture frame to steady herself. Ferris pressed her against the wall again to stop her fall, the lengths of their bodies pressed together.

He chuckled into her neck. "Sorry about that, luv."

His own arousal met her wet center through his trousers and he moaned. But he didn't want to take from her. He *did*, but he also enjoyed giving with nothing in return. So he backed away, setting her gently on her feet.

"Am I still no fun?" he asked, his voice low.

Mouse smiled. "You're almost as fun as I can be."

She stepped toward him, eyes trained on the bulge in his trousers, when the picture she'd fallen into slipped from its hook. Ferris lunged for it, knocking it out of the way before it crashed into Mouse's head. It smashed into the nearest glass case and a small crack skated across the surface.

"Ferris?"

He looked up to see what had Mouse's voice sounding so curious. A large hole had been bashed through the wall. Jagged edges of stone and bricks hung around the opening where the ripped wallpaper frayed.

"Well, fuck me." Ferris squinted into the dark hole, seeing nothing but stone walls. "This place is full of surprises."

CHAPTER EIGHTEEN

MOUSE

Mouse's chest heaved as she stared at the peeled green and gold wallpaper, the opening in the center, not knowing where it would lead next. She drew on her clothing and Ferris helped her fasten the buttons of her dress. His fingers fumbled on one as exhaustion swirled in his gaze. He'd been through so much in a single day, *days*, long ones where he hadn't even slept as he fought to save her from behind the boulders.

"Thank you," Mouse said softly as he buttoned the last one. They smiled at one another and she stepped around him to peer inside the hole within the wall. Heavy darkness cloaked what looked to be another tunnel, and she let her eyes adjust to the dull black brick surrounding the space. The end seemed to curve, leading to the unknown. She had no idea how far it would go or if it would take them anywhere worthwhile.

"It's a tunnel," Mouse finally said, stepping back so Ferris could take a look. "How about we check it out first thing in the morning? You've had practically zero sleep in days and we don't

611

know where it will even take us." Besides that, she needed to recover for a moment, catch her breath, not only from everything she'd been through the past few days, the past few *years*, but from Ferris giving her the release she'd needed. She'd never thought she would be so bold as to touch herself in front of another. But she trusted Ferris, trusted him with her life.

He pressed his hands to the wallpaper and scanned the area. His rosewood scent enveloped Mouse as he inched closer to her, and her gaze naturally took in the hard muscles of his arms, the tight trousers hugging his buttocks.

Ferris furrowed his brow as he moved backward. "Are you sure? This might be the final place to search before we return to Ivory."

In reality, she wasn't certain if they should take a break to rest because the Jabberwocky had ventured to Ivory twice recently, yet they knew the beast still lingered in Red from when they'd rinsed themselves in the lake. She didn't know if the beast would go back any time soon or continue to terrorize the rogue werewolves here. But Ferris really needed to recover or he wouldn't be good to anyone.

"Yes, we will rest," Mouse started. "And I agree about us leaving after this. We've found a whole lot of nothing on the Jabberwocky so far, but we've also discovered other things." She closed the door to the room and locked it in case anything tried to come for them from the secret passage.

Ferris arched a brow, a smirk on his face. "The king's fingers in the bag? Is that our prize to take home?"

"I think Chess would be the most amused to learn that the queen saved his bones after feeding the rest of him to the Jabberwocky." Mouse grinned. She settled on the stone floor, resting her back against the wall, and patted the spot next to her. "Besides that, there are these treasures here that Ever and Maddie can examine to see if they might mean anything."

Ferris tossed his backpack beside her and used it as a pillow while turning to face her. "Unless the dagger can be used to penetrate the Jabberwocky's flesh, then they're just some old relics." He placed a palm on her thigh and butterflies stormed in her stomach at his touch. Mouse thought about the way his tongue had trailed up her center, how he'd used it with such perfect precision as if he was drawing the night sky and all its constellations with it.

She ran her fingers through his hair while looking at the different items they'd rifled through. The belt, the key, the hourglass, the pearls, and much more. It was strange. They looked like nothing she'd ever seen in Wonderland or the mortal world. Most of these things seemed to have come from a storybook. Wonderland had swords and daggers, but nothing of this nature as if they held some sort of power.

"Perhaps the weapons can. We should take a few," Mouse said, staring at the dagger in the glass case, then at the collection of the others near a dusty iron sword on the wall. Even if they couldn't harm the Jabberwocky, she wanted to take them home to show Ever and Maddie. "Ferris?" She looked down at him when he didn't answer her, but his eyes were shut, his lips parted as he slept, his breaths even.

Mouse smiled softly, trailing her fingers from his hair down his face, to his plump lips, the curve of his neck, stopping as her digits brushed the metal chain. The necklace he never took off. She drew it from beneath his shirt and studied the ring that she now knew to be a promise to Ellie. Mouse wondered what she'd looked like, what Ferris would be doing now if she'd lived, if their baby had lived. Her chest tightened, not because she was envious of this ring, or his former love, but because of what it had meant. He would've been a wonderful father, would've had a different life. She could see him teaching his daughter how to play drums, teasing her, tossing her in the air then catching her as she giggled. But that life was gone, just as her old one was. And even though centuries had passed, she thought about what would've happened to her if Mr. Taylor had never ripped away her virginity. Would she have still discovered Maddie had been watching her? Would she have chosen to become a vampire? Leave the mortal world? There was no point in wondering because both of their lives had taken a different path, one where their worlds collided, her heart pulling toward his.

Tiredness no longer lingered within her, her mind spinning with too many thoughts. Perhaps because she'd slept for days.

Mouse tucked the ring back beneath Ferris's shirt, then stood and walked to the glass cases. She used her strength to break the seal on the first case and collected the dagger, along with the others resting on the shelf by the sword, then placed them inside her backpack except for one. A clear blade that looked as if it was made of glass, but it wasn't precisely that. It seemed to hum against her hand and she held it up to the light illuminating from the orbs. The glass reflected in a way she'd never seen before. A strange inscription in an unknown language was written on the handle.

"Where were you created?" she murmured.

Mouse looked toward the hole in the wall. Her thoughts turned to her sister, Ever, Des, Noah, and Chess. Even to Mock who had lost Didi. She wondered what they would do if they were here now, if they would explore the new tunnel or try to force themselves to rest. So far, nothing too dangerous was found in this hidden area, but Ferris wouldn't approve of her going alone. She glanced at him, watching his chest slowly rise and fall—she didn't want to disturb him.

Curiosity nagged at her and she chewed her lip as she weighed the choices. She would be quick. The door was locked, protecting Ferris, and if she heard anything she would run straight back to him. Mouse slid the dagger into the belt loop of her dress, then grabbed the gun from her bag. Ducking her head, she stepped through the splintered wood of the wall and entered the dark tunnel. A musty odor invaded her nostrils, heavier than in the previous room. Only a few cracks marred the faded stone of the walls.

The hallway led her down a curving path that turned into another room. Her heart pounded as she took in the circular area where six dark concrete coffins stood upright. Sets of three lined the walls across from each other, and if she were to step inside, they were tall enough to house two of her.

In the center of the wall between the two sets stood a door, this one looked to be heavy steel with multiple locks running up its length. The Red Queen and all her secret doors. But Mouse knew she was getting closer to something, a giddiness filling her.

When she'd been to the Red Palace last with Maddie and March for their tea party, she now wished they had thoroughly searched the palace. But even then, it was fate that had led her and Ferris to this secret place. Perhaps no one had believed the library would hide things of value since the jewels hadn't been kept there.

Tucking the gun at her waist, Mouse gripped the lid of a coffin and slid it to the side. The scraping sound echoed off the walls. She blinked at what rested inside, expecting to possibly find something useful. Instead, iron chains coiled within the empty space. One by one, she opened the five other coffins, discovering only chains and nothing useful, and a disappointed sigh escaped her.

Perhaps the Red Queen had brought vampires down there and placed them into the coffins, but why? From what she knew, the Red Queen would just murder them and hang their pieces in the forest. But maybe she had done what Rav and Imogen had done to her—punish them to get answers.

Mouse's heart thundered, pushing away memories of the Ruby Heart Palace attempting to surface. She focused her attention on the bolted-up door, her fingers itching to unlock it. Mouse pressed her ear to the cool steel, but nothing stirred from within. She started at the top, undoing each bolt with a grinding click. As soon as she released the last one, she leaned into the steel door with her shoulder and shoved it open, inch by inch. A new smell wafted out—decay, sickness. Nausea swirled in her stomach and she clutched it, hoping to not expel the contents from her last meal.

Mouse had come too far to stop now, and she took a tentative step into the room, then halted. Bones littered the floor, no two pieces still connected. Her gaze settled on part of a skull, the jaw ripped off and vampire fangs protruding. But then she found something else that made her suck in a sharp breath. These weren't normal vampires. *Wings* and claws curved from their fingers were scattered about. Thousands of scratch marks marred the black walls, along with deep gouges and small holes.

Bollocks, these were the *ancients*. Wonderland originally had six who'd wreaked havoc long, long ago. Well before Ever, Rav, and Imogen had ever stepped foot here. Older than even the Jabberwocky. It was believed they had vanished, but the Red Queen must've contained them here. For what purpose? But deep down, Mouse knew, it was to bend them to her will. The Red Queen had been one of the first to ever be turned and survive them.

The tales claimed that their blood ran black, their hearts of the same color, and that was why they had created other vampires, so they could feast on them whenever they chose. And it looked as though they had certainly had to feast on each other here.

But...

She held her breath, counting the skulls, and frowned. There were only five...

A rustling came from above and she didn't release her breath as she slowly glanced upward, her eyes widening. A single naked male form hung along an iron rafter from a domed ceiling. His alabaster skin was stark against the dark stone, his wings leather and obsidian. The vampire's bones jutted out, his stomach sunken, and his flesh tight against his frail form as if it could tear away at any moment. He stared down at her with golden eyes, deep crimson hair hanging in greasy clumps around his head. The vampire cocked his head and cracked his massive wings, hunger swirling in his gaze, his long black tongue licking his thin lips.

Mouse gasped, pulling herself from her staring spell. She bolted out the door, putting her weight against the steel to shut it. Her hands trembled, making her fingers fumble as she reached for the locks. Before she could slide the bolt in on the first one, the vampire rammed its body against the door, knocking her to the floor. The gun fell from her hand, skidding across the floor. And she cursed herself for not shooting at him inside the room.

She pushed up, lunging for her weapon, and snapped it up. But the vampire was already there, shoving her back to the floor. His claws dug into her flesh as he flipped her over, her fear spiking when he pinned her to the floor, trapping her. A reeking smell, like death and body odor, invaded her senses. "Ferris!" she screamed. "Run!"

The ancient vampire snarled, gnashing his sharp teeth at her. He then bent toward her neck, sniffing up her skin, speaking in an old language she didn't know. Her fangs dropped, her body writhing as she continued to scream to get this thing off of her.

Heavy footsteps pounded and the creature jerked back, hissing, giving Mouse enough time to pull the trigger at the ancient's heart. The loud shot pierced her ears, yet the ancient barely moved backward, the bullet unable to knock it out as it would any other vampire. He smacked the gun from her hand before barreling toward Ferris, but he ducked just before the vampire tore into his flesh.

The ancient moved too fast, caging Ferris in against the wall, sliding his fangs into his shoulder. Ferris growled, shoving against the vampire.

"No!" Mouse darted forward, a few centimeters away from thrusting her hand into the vampire's rib cage to retrieve his blackened heart.

But the vampire whirled around, releasing Ferris and grabbing her by the upper arms. He flapped his wings, the wind they created rustling her hair as he lifted her toward the ceiling.

Mouse jerked, drawing on all the strength she had, but he still overpowered her, holding her to him tightly, *squeezing*. The way Mr. Taylor had… Dread coursed through her and tears stormed down her face. She didn't want to be helpless again. But that was precisely what she was in that moment. And she screamed, screamed as loud as she damn well could, even though it didn't do a single thing.

The ancient didn't lessen his grip on her, only speaking words in that old language of his, then buried his fangs into her throat. The pain from his bite tore through her, not a single ounce of pleasure radiated within her—it was as if her skin was on fire, burning past muscle, blood, and deep into her bones. As he drank, ripping farther into her throat, she peered down at Ferris, who was shouting frantically, climbing on top of the coffins to try and get to her.

As the vampire planted her against a wall, his body pushing harder into hers, the dagger she'd taken dug into her hip. It was her only chance. Eyes fluttering, her fingers shook as she drew the blade out. She was unable to reach his heart to see if it would knock him out, so with all the strength she could muster, she thrust the dagger into his stomach, slicing to the side.

The vampire screeched, his hold on her releasing, and she fell, her body crashing to the floor, pain flaring, bones breaking, the room spinning.

Mouse took one last ragged breath, finding Ferris off the coffin and lunging toward her. "I love you. Now *run*," she rasped, her eyes falling shut.

CHAPTER NINETEEN

FERRIS

Run? Fuck that. Ferris would sooner throw himself at the fucked-up vampire than let him touch another hair on Mouse's head. And that was exactly what he did.

Ferris barreled into the vampire as the male dove through the air for Mouse. The vampire looked ancient, emaciated, with bat-like wings and rows of sharp teeth. He snarled and snapped his jaw in Ferris's face. His body shook as he held the monster up, right arm pressed to the male's throat, left throwing punches. Each time his fist landed with a crack against ribs, the bones crunched. The vampire twisted and writhed, but he didn't deter the attack.

"Get out of here, Mouse," Ferris growled.

She let out a strangled, painful sob. *Fuck.* After that fall, she was probably too hurt to run. The vampire clawed at Ferris's chest and his arm buckled from the sharp, tearing pain. Fangs pricked Ferris's neck. He braced for the bite—for the fire it lit inside him—but it didn't come.

The weight of the vampire's body lifted from Ferris and he sprung to his feet. The clear dagger from the shelf protruded from the back of the vampire's head where Mouse had managed to find the strength to stab him. He released a wretched screech, flinging his head from side to side, as black sludge-like blood spilled from the wound.

Ferris swept Mouse off her feet and bolted down the darkened tunnel, his heart slamming in his chest. If they could make it back to the library, maybe they would have a chance of outrunning the motherfucker. Hunger churned within him, his body weak, weaker now that he had to heal from the vampire's bite. Even at full strength, he was still outmatched. The vampire had gone fucking mad and that was what fueled him now. If he had to, he would fight, but he couldn't do that if he was worried about Mouse, and she was clearly not going to leave him to save herself. Unless he could convince her…

"You need to leave me, Mouse," he told her, stopping just outside the room with the relics. The library shelves would never hold against this feral vampire and he needed to give her as much time as possible to escape. The male would likely kill him, though Ferris wouldn't make it easy. Hopefully it would give Mouse enough of a leeway to reach the portal on the edge of Ivory. Then, after he was dead, Wonderland would need to be ready. "Ever has to know what we found and prepare a way to neutralize the threat."

"No." Mouse pushed out of his arms to stand in the tunnel and stumbled into the wall. Her injuries would slow her down but she was brave—she could make it home. "We can do this together."

Ferris looked her up and down. The vampire had ravaged her throat. While it was healing, blood still covered her neck and chest, soaking into her dress. "Luv, please. You need to go. I'll slow him down."

Mouse's eyes widened, her hand going for a dagger but finding it gone from her hip, still lodged in the vampire's head. "He's coming!"

Ferris whirled around, widening his stance, wishing he had a gun on him. It had barely made a difference when Mouse shot the ancient, but maybe if he took multiple shots… *Shit.* The wild look in the vampire's eyes told Ferris that he was too far gone to care about anything but feeding. The vampire ran toward them, hunched, claws out, fangs bared, nearly every bone on display beneath his skin. Mouse's dagger still protruded from his head.

"Fuck!" Ferris shouted. He needed to buy Mouse time to escape. Against all his training as a guard, he turned his back on the enemy, and shoved Mouse through the hole in the wall. She fell backward into the room with the strange relics. "Get out of here."

He couldn't lose her. If he died right now, the fucker would only go after Mouse next—he had to kill him. Ferris whirled around, baring his own fangs at the vampire. Eyes trained on the dagger in the bastard's skull, Ferris sprinted forward using his vampire speed.

If he could get the dagger, he could use it to—

The vampire punched Ferris in the side of the head. Stars burst in his vision and then the momentum of the blow sent him crashing into the wall before tumbling to the ground. His temple took the impact and then… darkness stole his vision. Mouse screamed and he stumbled toward the sound. He shook his head, pressing his eyes shut. The sound of shattering glass and splintering wood echoed through his skull. *Fuck!* Blinking rapidly, the stars finally broke through the blackness. A few more times and he could finally see. Mouse screamed again and he leapt to his feet.

Fucking motherfucker!

Ferris darted through the hole and into the hidden room. Gulping sounds greeted him first. His body froze, the world seeming to crack in half as he locked onto the horrific scene before him.

Mouse, splayed on the floor, surrounded by shattered glass. The vampire straddling her lifeless form. Head bent to her neck. Feasting. His vision faded around the edges, fear and anger blistering through him.

No!

Not Mouse.

Teeth bared, blood boiling in his veins, he dove for the vampire, everything moving in slow motion, and latched onto the dagger in the vampire's skull. Ripping the blade free, Ferris drove it straight down into the back of the fucker's neck, severing the spinal cord.

"Mouse?" He yanked the vampire's lifeless body off her and threw him to the side. "Mouse, are you okay?" Pausing, he waited for her reply, but it never came. "Luv, you need to wake up."

She was silent. Unmoving.

Ferris spared a moment to rip the vampire's head from his body, then to tear his heart out, not willing to risk another attack while he saved Mouse. He barely noticed himself doing it, even as black blood sprayed over his hands. Mouse's throat was torn to shreds, bright red pooling from the wound. Her chest still.

Bone was visible inside her neck. Tendons and muscle exposed. Her glassy eyes stared up at nothing. Ferris fell to his knees beside her. "You'll be okay," he promised her. "I'll save you."

Lifting her to lay her head in his lap, he really noticed just how deep the vampire had torn into her. There were only a few inches of skin still holding her head to her body, but the spine hadn't been severed. It wasn't too late…

It wasn't fucking too late.

He bit into his wrist and pressed his skin to her lips, allowing the blood to drizzle inside her. There was enough in him to save her, even if it drained him dry. All she had to do was drink. But his blood pooled into her mouth and spilled over the corner of her lips.

"Luv?" Tears blurred his vision. "Luv, you have to drink."

Still, her lips didn't move against his skin, not even a tiny twitch.

"Please!" he screamed, the sound reverberating off the walls. "Mouse. Don't do this to me. Don't you dare fucking die!"

His heart thundered painfully in his chest as he pressed his wrist harder against her mouth. The blood leaked down her chin, spilling into the open wound. She was *nearly* decapitated—that didn't count. He'd seen Rav bring back vampires in similar conditions. *Worse.* With their skin peeled back from their skulls, flesh scraped away from limbs until all that remained was bones. All she had to do was fucking drink.

"Please, luv." Hot tears flowed down his cheeks. He bent over her small frame and placed a kiss on her forehead. "Please. I love you. I'll do anything. *Please.*"

This wasn't fucking doing a damn thing. Ferris pulled his wrist away and laid her carefully onto the floor. Rav had used an IV. But Ferris didn't have any needles … hadn't since he'd stopping using drugs. Pressing his ear to her chest, he heard a faint thump of her heart. Too quiet, too irregular. *Fuck!* She wasn't going to make it. He tore across the room, yanking books off the shelves, smashing the glass cases open. Rampaging like the vampire had.

Only one thing mattered.

Mouse.

In his entire miserable life, he'd never been able to hold onto anything good. Not his friends nor his family. Not Ellie. Their baby. Everything he touched turned to fucking shit. It withered and died. But not Mouse. She was immortal. Too full of life for it to be real.

Ferris stood amid his chaos and gasped for breath.

But she was gone. Her eyes … they were just like Ellie's had been that day in the car. They were *dead* eyes. He collapsed beside Mouse, gently wiping the hair from her face, a crackling sob breaking in his chest.

There was no stopping the tears now. No mending the shatter of his heart.

Mouse was dying because he couldn't save her. He became a vampire for that very reason. She had given him his mortal life back the day she'd drank the drugs from his system, let him live on borrowed time. And all he wanted was to give her *forever.*

But he was a damned failure.

"I love you," he whispered, closing his eyes. There was nothing left for him now. Not without her. "I love you. Please, please, please…"

And all he could think about in that moment was how she would die just like Ellie had.

"It's raining." Ellie turned to face him and cradled a large baby bump. "Maybe we shouldn't go today."

Ferris chuckled. "I know you don't like going out in this type of weather, but it's Oliver's birthday party."

Ellie crossed her arms. She wore a blue and white striped jumper, her hair neatly curled. "I have a bad feeling today."

He paused, watching her chew her bottom lip, and pulled her closer. Her baby bump brushed against him. "If you really don't want to go, we don't have to. We can stream a movie or something."

"No, I'm being silly." She stretched up to give him a quick kiss. "We should go for Oliver, but afterward we can have a cozy night on the sofa."

Ferris bent down, speaking to Ellie's stomach. "How does that sound, Luna?"

"She says she likes the idea very much." Ellie giggled.

Ferris held an umbrella over Ellie and rushed her to the car so she wouldn't get soaked before hopping into the front seat. Rain was coming down hard as he drove them to Oliver's, pelting the windscreen, making it nearly impossible to see. He eased off the accelerator, slowing the car.

"We should pull over until it lets up," he said.

Ellie nodded in agreement. "I think there's a place around the curve that—"

The squeal of breaks stopped Ellie mid-sentence. Ferris's grip tightened on the wheel, drawing a sharp breath as he saw the inevitable too late, a car coming straight toward him. The other car slammed into theirs, jerking them sideways, the tires skidding over the side road. His head struck the side window, glass shattering. Then there was only silence, smoke, and the white of the airbag.

"Ellie," Ferris rasped.

No response. The smoke faded a little as he turned to face her and a strangled cry tore from him. Ellie's eyes were glazed with death, blood running down her forehead. More blood pooled between her legs. Their baby…

"*Ellie!*"

Fuck. No. No no no.

"*You promised you'd never leave me!*" *he cried.* "*Ellie! Wake up!*"

Wake up!

Wake up.

Wake.

Up.

"Ferris?" Mouse whispered.

CHAPTER TWENTY

MOUSE

"Ferris?" Mouse murmured, holding back a scream as pain roared through her. She tasted blood in her mouth, *Ferris's*, and panic coursed inside her chest. Every single one of her nerve endings felt as if they were engulfed in flames. Her gaze locked on Ferris—he was above her, holding her, *alive*, his eyes red-rimmed and puffy, but he didn't look hurt. "Where is that bastard at? I'm going to rip him apart," she seethed, choking on a cough that only made the aching throb once more. Mouse didn't know if she could stand, but it wasn't like the days beneath the rubble. She could move her body, but everything was heavy.

"Mouse?" Ferris said with a choked sob. "You're alive."

She remembered the ancient vampire storming into this room, cabinets breaking, glass shattering, him yanking her head to the side as his teeth tore into her flesh. Mouse knew he was furious after she'd stabbed him twice so he hadn't been gentle with her in the least.

"After everything I've been through, do you honestly think I would die so easily?" Mouse tried to smile but could only clench her teeth together as sharp aches radiated up her neck. "I'm sorry I went in there. I just couldn't sleep and didn't want to wake you to explore quickly, but then I came across the ancient."

"It's all right—I killed the fucker," Ferris growled, drawing her to his chest as if she would fade away unless he held her. "I decapitated him and ripped out his heart a few moments ago."

Mouse pushed up with her hands but she was too weak to hold her weight. Ferris's lovely scent caressed her nose and she reeled in the temptation to drink from him as her fangs dropped. But then another heavier, metallic smell made her eyes flutter. It wasn't the decaying scent of the ancient that called to her, but his *blood*.

"I'm famished and don't want to hurt you," she said. "Will you bring me a pouch from my bag?" There was a legend that blood from ancients contained fast healing properties amongst other things, but she didn't want to risk drinking from a dead vampire. Perhaps that was another reason the Red Queen had kept them, to use their blood to bathe in while drinking it until she grew bored with them and put up a wall to hide them. Even though she believed that was the truth, Mouse would never know the precise answer.

Ferris nodded and lowered her to the floor, careful to not jostle her. A rustling echoed as he fished out her canteen and the powdered blood from her bag. She held her breath to avoid inhaling Ferris's alluring scent, running her tongue over the back of a fang while she waited. He shook the mixture and she greedily snapped the canteen from his hand. She gulped it down, the flavor making her moan as it brushed her tongue and drifted to her stomach.

As soon as she finished, Ferris gave her the second canteen. Her body was sewing itself back together, the blood working wonders even though she would've rather had a mortal's in that moment.

"Drink," Mouse rasped, forcing herself to stop but not wanting to.

"I wanted to make sure you didn't need another first."

"This is enough for now."

Ferris nodded and reached for his backpack, not taking his gaze away from her. He wasn't worried about himself, but *her*.

As her appetite sated, Mouse felt more like herself than she ever had in the past two years. Perhaps part of it had been due to the vampire bite the ancient had given her. Only a bit of exhaustion lingered, and she realized how close she'd been to death. If the ancient had only pulled a little harder on her head, shifted her body further in the opposite direction, he would've severed her spinal cord.

After Ferris finished his canteen, her eyes fluttered and she managed to get a few words out. "I need to rest a little. I don't think I can make it home right now."

"I'll find you a better room without a corpse." Ferris collected their bags, then scooped her into his arms, cradling her close to his chest. "You're not leaving this castle until your strength is up. I don't care if I sound like an arsehole or not."

"Mmm, I like when your alpha side slips out." Mouse's voice slurred as she smiled, and she could no longer hold her eyes open, yet she relished the way his muscles flexed against her body while he carried her through the tunnels.

"This will have to do," Ferris said and she became alert once more, finding they were already in a room.

The space was nicer than the other ones she'd seen thus far. Only a few layers of dust covered the area and besides a mirror, nothing else was broken. Other than the bed, a spinning wheel was propped in a corner and across from it rested a dresser and a vanity.

Ferris lay Mouse on the bed and slid off her boots. "Let me help clean you up, then you can rest."

She nodded with a yawn and he helped her remove her clothing until she was bare before him. He took out a cloth from his bag and poured water from the canteen. With delicate motions, he cleaned the blood from her throat. She bit her lip, watching as he continued his tender movements.

"Thank you," Mouse whispered once he was finished. Tiredness washed over her and she couldn't focus on what he said, yet she felt him pull the covers over her while she drifted away again.

Mouse cracked open her eyes and looked around the room, now that she could focus clearly. There wasn't as much dust as when Ferris had brought her into the space. That was strange. Had he cleaned it for her?

Where was he? Mouse caught a glimpse of his brown hair outside the open door, finding him sitting in the hallway.

"Why are you out there?" Mouse called, drawing the blanket tighter around her naked form.

"You're awake." Ferris whirled around and shoved up from the floor. He smiled, but it didn't reach his eyes. "You didn't sleep long, only about an hour. We can spare a few more if you need it."

"I'm fine." Mouse couldn't fall back asleep even if she tried. She was too alert now. "What were you doing in the hallway?"

He ran a hand across his square jaw. "Thinking, but mostly I wanted to stand guard outside your room in case some other fucker decided to show up."

Her chest tightened. "I don't want you to worry about me. I don't mind being saved, but I don't want you to think I have to be protected all the time."

"Luv, I think you're stronger than me." When he smiled this time, it finally met his eyes.

"We'll have to arm wrestle on that sometime." She laughed.

"Are you strong enough to head back to Ivory?"

She was about to nod, but a thought crossed her mind and she mulled it over. While in Red, they'd faced werewolves, the Jabberwocky, an ancient vampire, her fear of libraries, them falling into a cavern, her attacking Ferris. It was as if she'd survived a lifetime of tragedies. Between the road home from Red to Ivory, Mouse didn't know what they would come across next. And frankly, she was sick of it. She wanted to put an end to the never-ending Shakespearian tragedies in her life and become something not so bleak. It didn't have to be perfect, only something where she and Ferris were happy.

"There's something I want to do before we return home," Mouse finally said, fidgeting with the blanket.

"What's that?"

Heart pounding in her chest, she leaned forward, her voice breathy. "Remove your boots and turn around."

Ferris arched a brow and smirked but did as was instructed. Taking a deep swallow, she drew back the blankets, her bare feet touching the cool floor.

With her body still bare, Mouse slowly walked toward him, her gaze never leaving his muscular form. Once she reached his warmth, she brushed her hands against his hips, then trailed her palms up Ferris's defined chest beneath his shirt.

"So, I take it we won't be leaving soon?" he said in a gruff voice.

"We have a few hours to spare, as you said." She grinned, grasping the hem of his shirt, and he helped her lift it over his head.

"Mmm, taking a few hours to ourselves after the shitstorm we just faced sounds fucking amazing."

Mouse traced the lovely tattoo on his back, following each curve of ink, gliding across the gears, making him shiver at her touch. She shifted forward, pressing her breasts to his back, and skimmed her fingers over his abs to the front of his trousers. His breath caught as she unfastened the button and peeled the fabric down his legs.

"Do you want me to touch you?" she asked as she stood, her hands sliding up his thighs to just beneath his navel.

"All the fucking time," he groaned. "But how healed are you?"

"Completely." Mouse grasped his hard length, slowly

pumping him, her finger circling the piercing at the tip that she loved so much. "You can turn around now."

She released him and he spun to face her. He didn't hesitate to hoist her up, eliciting a squeak from her as he backed her into the wall. Her legs circled his hips and his cock pressed against her core. Ferris's lips crashed to hers, the kiss rough, just the way she needed it. She nipped his lower lip before tangling her tongue with his, the taste of him sublime. Gripping his shoulders, she dug her fingernails into his flesh as he slid his delicious length up and down her slickened folds, his piercing adding a wonderful sensation.

"I love you," Mouse murmured in his ear, not ever wanting to hold back those words. She'd said them in the room with the ancient, she said them here, and she would keep saying them because he deserved to hear how she felt. "I love you so much it hurts."

"Fuck, I love you. If you were dying, I'd rip out my heart and place it inside your chest."

"Your words are a hundred times better than Romeo's." Mouse grinned.

"You woke something in me the day you saved me," he rasped, gripping her hips, grinding into her even harder. "It's been building and building and *building* for four years. I fucked Imogen to save you. The whole time I was in bed with her, I didn't think of anyone but you."

Jealousy didn't burn within her that he had to tumble Imogen, only sorrow and rage. But the queen was dead and Maddie had gifted her precisely what she'd deserved. Otherwise, Mouse would've faced her fears now and gone back to the palace to rip out the queen's throat for how she'd treated Ferris.

"Then it looks like we deserve to let that dam break." She threaded her fingers in his hair as she kissed below his jaw. "I want you to make love to me the way lightning strikes, the way thunder roars."

"Then let's make it fucking storm," Ferris growled. His cock slid down her core once more, then he thrust inside her, making her gasp in pleasure.

"Keep going," she moaned. "Don't take it easy on me."

In answer, he thrust again, hard, so bloody hard that when she was about to cry for more, he did it again. Blissfully again and *again*.

He carried her away from the wall and to the bed, bringing her into his lap. "Ride me," he ground out, his dark eyes fastened to hers.

Wildness rose within her, but she hadn't done this before. Yet, as his hands gripped her hips, urging her to move forward, her body naturally gave in to the motions. Slow at first, then her pace picked up, going harder and harder until she was the one fucking him. A pleasureful feeling thrummed at her center as his hand cupped her breast and his mouth captured hers once more.

They continued this delectable dance, and as she grew close, so close to frenzy, she pulled away from his mouth to whisper in his ear. "Take me from behind and we'll come together." Mouse's sexual exploration had been quiet for centuries and she wanted Ferris to wake everything within her. No longer was there fear or worry about someone stealing something from her they shouldn't.

He didn't hesitate, easily rolling them so she was on all fours. She only missed him inside her for a moment before he slid back into her, making them both groan in satisfaction. His hand trailed up her spine as he drove into her over and over, his piercing delightfully rubbing her inner walls, until their bodies were both slick with sweat. And then she felt a tempest brewing inside her, prepared to wipe out all of Wonderland. Her eyes fluttered as lightning struck, the earth splitting open. Thunder roared, rumbling fiercely, then the rain poured within her. Paradise rolled through her entire being, touching all the way to the tips of her fingertips and toes. With each quake that came, she whispered Ferris's name.

"Mouse." Her name fell from his lips in a low growl as he spilled himself inside her.

Ferris slowly kissed his way along her spine, to the back of her neck, his arms holding him up on either side of her. Their chests heaved in sync, his soft skin on hers, then he scooped her up, keeping her back against his chest as he brought them to their sides.

"That was perfect," she breathed. It had been worth it for her to wait centuries to find him.

"Fucking perfect," he murmured. "I love touching you. I love you touching me."

Heat spread through her at his words and she arched into him. "I think we have time for one more round before we head home, don't you think?"

Ferris grazed his hand to her breast, his thumb caressing her nipple as he hardened again. He drifted his fingers down her stomach to between her thighs and, as her heart screamed in anticipation, he buried his length deep inside of her once more.

CHAPTER TWENTY-ONE

FERRIS

"Do you feel okay, luv?" Ferris asked.

Mouse snuggled closer into his side beneath the blankets and wrapped an arm around his waist. Her breasts pressed against him, stirring his lust. But after worshipping her body three times last night, it was safe to say they were both too worn out for another round. Still, he trailed his fingertips up and down her bare back. Having her next to him like this made him feel like he would combust. Like he was free. He couldn't remember the last time he'd felt so … content.

"Mm-hmm," Mouse mumbled around a yawn.

"I hate to say this since it's so cozy in this bed," Ferris said as he kissed her forehead, "but we've both finally gotten the rest we needed, so we should head back to Ivory."

"We should." Mouse sat up slowly and stretched her arms over her head, giving him a view of her full breasts, nipples peaked. "I don't like going back empty-handed though. None of the things we found answer any questions about the

Jabberwocky."

"Me either, but they'll worry if we don't come back soon." All they'd found in Red were fucking monsters. Rogue werewolves, the Jabberwocky, a rabid ancient. A few foreign relics and finger bones, for whatever those were worth. If there were answers, it would take longer than they had to locate them, especially with all the hidden rooms. And that wasn't even counting the rest of Red. The answers could be anywhere in the territory.

"That's certainly true." Mouse gave him a lingering kiss on the mouth, then shoved the blankets from her lower half and climbed out of bed. "Maddie is probably losing her mind by now."

Ferris chuckled and swung his legs off the bed, standing. Mouse's gaze raked him up and down, her lips tugging up at the edges. He smiled, turning around so she could admire his backside. That they were comfortable enough to look at each other naked with nothing unspoken between them put a smile on his face.

Ferris leaned over to get his trousers. Mouse followed suit, gathering her dress and shaking the wrinkles out. He grabbed her panties and held them out to her, dangling them from his fingertip. "Missing something?"

Mouse laughed and snatched them from him. "Are you sure you wouldn't prefer it if I left them off?"

"Of course I fucking would, but then I'd be distracted the whole way back to Ivory." He winked at her and they both finished dressing. Mouse fished out a dagger from her backpack, one from the relics room, and tucked it into her boot. With a quick peek inside their bags, he realized they only had six blood pouches left. That would be plenty enough to get them back home, but their canteens needed to be filled. "We should stop at the lake for more water before we head out."

"You read my mind." Mouse brushed a kiss against his cheek. "Let's go."

Ferris followed her through the palace, throwing glances

down at her to make sure she was all right while keeping an ear out for the Jabberwocky's boisterous screeching. His free hand lifted subconsciously to the ring hanging beneath his shirt. Circling the metal through the fabric, a sense of peace descended over him. Like he was finally ready to let them go. No—maybe that wasn't the right way to explain it. Ellie and their daughter would always be with him, but he was ready to let go of the guilt over the accident. To move on and allow himself to finally fucking *live* again. They would want him to be happy.

"I love you," he whispered to Mouse.

Though he'd said it before, her eyes lit up like she was hearing it for the first time. "I love you too," she murmured.

"Let me make sure the coast is clear," he said when they reached the broken front doors. Stepping out first, Ferris scanned the sky for the Jabberwocky. The horizon was lightening to a soft gray as morning rose, but there was no sign of a threat. "All right, luv. Come on."

Together they went back to the same lake they'd bathed in the day before and he listened again for the return of the Jabberwocky. Only silence greeted him as they reached the water's edge. Clouds reflected on the glassy surface and, as Ferris dipped his hand into the cool liquid, goosebumps prickled his skin. It was colder than last time—or maybe he hadn't noticed because he'd been too focused on Mouse. Still, he cupped the water in his palms and splashed it on his face. He'd give anything for a warm bath or shower after this journey.

Mouse handed him one of the empty canteens and they filled them in companionable silence. When they were finished, she tucked them in the backpack again. "I can't wait to be home," she said, digging through Ferris's bag for the other two canteens. "To feed Des a new leaf, to watch my sister work on a new hat, to hear Ever's viola. I still wish we had better news to bring."

"We'll figure it out," he assured her. "There's always more than one way to fix a problem."

"But if someone could've killed the Jabberwocky, why—" Mouse's body froze, her eyes growing wide before she shot to her feet and pointed across the lake toward the dead gardens. "Do you see that?"

Ferris sucked in a breath and stood, his heart pounding as he saw what she was staring at. Bright green light shimmered in the air. What looked to be an emerald rectangle expanding, glimmering wider, until it formed a doorway. It carried a light, earthy scent, like a field after it rained. And it … it seemed to be a portal. That was impossible though. Portals just existed where they were—they didn't appear out of nowhere like this.

"What the hell is that?" Ferris hissed, grabbing Mouse by the wrist and hauling her over the low stone wall that circled the lake, kneeling behind it. It was best to see their new potential foe before they were seen *by* it. Ferris could assess the probability of winning a fight or if they needed to haul arse out of there. Honestly, as much as he enjoyed taking down a rival, his body was a wreck. He'd healed from all the injuries he'd received over the last few days, but he needed a live mortal to feed on to truly regain his strength.

"Stay low," he whispered to Mouse. They both peered over the top of the wall, waiting to see what would happened next. He held his breath and reached in his bag to retrieve a weapon. Except—*shit*. Their bags were still by the lake. A few yards away. "Do you still have that dagger on you?"

"Yes." Mouse pulled the blade from her boot and handed it to him.

Just as he wrapped his fingers around the handle, a form stepped from the green doorway. A shadow at first, then a fully formed male. Dark silky hair hung down his back and he wore a loose white shirt, shoved up to his elbows like he'd just walked out of a renaissance faire, with a brown satchel slung over one shoulder. Another looming form appeared behind him. Taller. Carrying an axe. He had long silver hair, a blue tunic, and fucking green sparks shooting from his hand. They exchanged a few words, but Ferris was unable to hear from this side of the lake. Whatever they'd said had the dark-haired male rolling his eyes as a swirl of red smoke curled around his arm.

A quick flick of the silver male's hand and the doorway snapped shut with a crack. Whatever the fuck was going on—this was unnatural, even for Wonderland. Ferris stared at the space where the green light had just been, mouth parted. No one could create portals and make them vanish at will. They needed to get back to Ivory to tell Ever and Chess that there might be a more serious problem than the Jabberwocky. He couldn't risk fighting them, not if they were… What the fuck were they? Sorcerers? It sounded insane, but he would've said the same about vampires a little over four years ago.

The pair walked around the lake with slow, cautious steps and examined their surroundings. The silver male shifted his axe as he turned, walking backward for a few paces, while the dark-haired stranger carried no weapon. At least not in his hands. Which made him the more dangerous one, Ferris thought, because he certainly didn't look like a fool. This male would undoubtedly have another way to defend himself.

"What should we do?" Mouse whispered.

Ferris swallowed. "We need to get back to Ivory. *Now*."

"But how? They'll see us if we run."

He had no answer. They were trapped between the palace and the lake. Unless the fuckers turned their backs or wandered away from the lake, they were screwed. It would only take a second for Ferris and Mouse to get away with their speed. If these two would just look the hell away… But they seemed focused on the palace. To get there, they would pass right by Ferris and Mouse.

The two males were in no rush, studying the surface of the lake, the dead trees in the distance, the crumbling walls of the palace, with grim expressions. Their booted feet carried them closer and closer by the second.

Bloody hell! Ferris's mind screamed at him to attack—he and Mouse were strong enough to take down two males—but they were using *magic*. They didn't stand a chance.

"Looks abandoned." The silver male paused and lowered his axe a fraction. From this distance, Ferris could see his pointed ears. Was he a fucking *elf?* Ferris held his breath, letting the reality sink in. The newcomer turned his head, surveying the sky, and exposed the silver metal snaking over his left cheek. "Did you give me the right coordinates?"

"Do I *look* like an amateur?" the other male said. Their accents were strange, light and airy. "Of course I'm right."

"Tik-Tok, I swear to the fucking stars, if you don't stop being an ass, I will leave you here."

The dark-haired male—Tik-Tok—laughed, humor lighting his red irises. His right arm caught the faint moonlight. Ferris squinted at the limb, making out gold, mechanical joints. *What the fuck?* "And tell your daughter that you abandoned me in a world full of blood-thirsty vampires? Nice try, Tin. She'd have your head on a platter."

Tin grumbled as they rounded the edge of the lake, then stopped short. "Someone's here."

Shit, shit, shit. Ferris followed their line of sight to the bags they'd left beside the water. His pulse sped up and he shifted to balance on the balls of his feet. Fighting these two pointy-eared males was a bad fucking plan, but he would do what had to be done, if need be.

Tik-Tok stalked over to the bags and crouched. With his golden arm, he rifled through them. "Water, some clothes..." He pulled out one of their remaining blood pouches and held it up to show his companion. "Whatever the fuck this is."

"They have to be close. There's still water on the outside of the canteens," Tin said. He stood tall as he scanned the area. Ferris yanked Mouse down beside him before they could be found peeking over the wall. They were boxed in, their backs to the lake and too much space to the palace. If they tried, they would be seen.

Tik-Tok sniffed loudly. "Mmhmm."

There was a long pause and Ferris reached out for Mouse's hand. They were both fast, but there was no telling if these males were faster. Still, they would need to risk it. With any luck, they could outpace the magic too. Run straight to the edge of Ivory and leap into the portal that had brought them there. Ever and Chess could send guards to figure this shit out.

But before Ferris could inform Mouse of his plan, Tin said, "Do your thing."

"My *thing*?" Tik-Tok scoffed.

"Yes, your fucking thing, jackass."

"Calm your tits, *Father*."

Tin growled. "I will never understand what my daughter sees in you."

"Aw, you love me. Don't deny it," Tik-Tok purred. "Stand back."

Fuck! Whatever this *thing* was, Ferris had no intention of sticking around to find out. "We have to go," he whispered in Mouse's ear.

She nodded, then let out a cry. "Ferris!"

Stone crept over her body, encasing her legs. Rising up her thighs to her torso. Panic sliced through him. How could he stop this? How could he save her? What the fuck was happening? Ferris tried to shift to better face her but his own legs were hardening, becoming heavy. Swallowed by stone. He glanced at Mouse and his wild fear reflected on her face. His fangs dropped, his lips pulled back into a snarl.

There wasn't time to scream, to beg, fight. One moment, the stone was creeping up their chests, the next it had turned them fully into statues. Ferris strained his muscles, trying to break free, but it was impossible. He was trapped. Made of stone, yet aware of his surroundings. Of the crunch of two pairs of boots on the ground. Of Tik-Tok's *hmm* of intrigue. And the two forms that now loomed over them.

"Interesting," Tik-Tok said. He leaned down in front of Mouse. "I expected them to be bigger."

"Didn't you say they were human once? They're appropriately sized." Tin dropped to his knees in front of Ferris and poked at his exposed fang.

Even made of stone, they were sharp enough to cut flesh. Evidence of which beaded on Tin's index finger. Ferris could still sense the blood, smell the strange, sickly-sweet notes it carried.

"Well, damn," Tin murmured. "Let's avoid getting bit while we're here."

Tik-Tok chuckled. "Lucky for you, axe man, they're easily killed by decapitation."

"Let's not rampage through this world if we can help it. Release only their heads so we can talk to them."

"If I had the ability to turn certain body parts to stone, I would've started with your mouth," Tik-Tok said, raising a brow as if challenging him.

"I dare you to try that shit on me again. Once was enough." Tin's gaze fell to the dagger still clutched in Ferris's hand. "They have fae weaponry."

"Good," Tik-Tok said, studying the blade with a smirk. "We're close then."

CHAPTER TWENTY-TWO

MOUSE

Mouse's flesh was now stone, and she tried to scream, yet nothing would escape her mouth. She couldn't shift her eyes, only focus on what was directly before her. Which looked to be two males who had come straight through a portal from *A Midsummer Night's Dream*. She wouldn't be the least bit surprised if Shakespeare had conjured up his play after seeing them. Their pointed ears, the light way their words flowed from their mouths, their elegant movements. Their *magic*. Magic that had turned her and Ferris into stone statues that could still see, hear, and smell. The unwanted guests had said the dagger was fae weaponry… Were they truly fae like in the stories?

"Now," Tik-Tok cooed, his red irises sparkling with mischief. "Which of these two should we unleash first?"

"Just fucking pick one," Tin seethed, his shoulders broad like Ferris's, his muscles bulging beneath his blue tunic. Silver hair hung down his back in a beautiful thick sheet.

Tik-Tok tapped his chest with his hand, one that appeared as if it was constructed of golden metal. And were those bolts she was seeing? "I'm only trying to protect us so we *both* return to our females in a safe fashion."

Tin's fingers tightened around his axe. This was no itty-bitty little weapon—either side of its sharp blades could easily slice cleanly through her throat. She would brush her fingers across her neck at the moment if she could.

Mouse's heart jolted in her chest as Tik-Tok crouched in front of her, cocking his head, studying her. A sandalwood scent drifted up to her, accompanied by a rush of metallic. His blood smelled of pure heaven, the way Tin's also did. She tried to burst from her stone prison, but not one inch of her budged at all. Only he could free her, if he chose to. Panic set in as she realized this was another prison, *trapping* her…

Tik-Tok moved his finger back and forth between her and Ferris before he finally spoke. "We'll go with the female since she's unarmed." He glanced up at Tin and chuckled. His attention focused on Mouse but, thankfully, he didn't try to touch her stone flesh. "Now, listen, and listen closely. I'm going to release you, but you will not attack either one of us. If you can accomplish that, then we won't have to remove your pretty little head. Do you understand? Tin here never misses with his axe. And if you die, I doubt your friend here will be of much help to us. I'd prefer us not to have to get our hands dirty." His grin spread across his face, lighting up his red irises before he turned to Tin once more. "I do love it when they have a partner that we can use to threaten them with. Do you remember the game I played with our good friend Jack when I first met him?"

"I would've rather come with him," Tin grunted.

"Too bad he doesn't have one of these." Tik-Tok smirked, flashing some type of golden ornament to Tin.

Mouse wanted to hurl herself at his throat, dig her teeth in and rip it to shreds, all while lapping up his otherworldly blood. But his words sank in, and as they did, it made some sense. They wouldn't hurt her … if she didn't hurt them. Even in the palace, Rav and Imogen had never given her that ultimatum. It was only hurt, hurt, *hurt*.

"I'm going to take your silence as a yes." Tik-Tok chuckled, straightening and popping his back as if he had all the time in the world.

"Do you always talk this much when you're threatening people?" Tin growled.

"I find it more effective than swinging a weapon around." Tik-Tok clucked his tongue.

Tin only narrowed his eyes and clenched his strong jaw. The silver scar was twisted like spiderwebs across his cheek, and his blue eyes mirrored pure ice, as though he was used to being feared. But for some reason, she didn't fear him, even though he held an axe.

"Remember what I said," Tik-Tok cooed at Mouse while lifting his hand, his fingers covered in thin silver rings with jewels of various colors.

Her body loosened as the stone gave way to her flesh. She fell forward, her fists catching on the grass while she took deep breaths. Ferris rested beside her, still stone, his fangs protruding, and her heart sank at seeing him this way. "Release him," Mouse rasped, her fangs still lowered, but she didn't leap forward, didn't attack, or even hiss. She had to control herself for Ferris's sake. "Please."

Tik-Tok tapped his canines. "Now, now, first tuck those little fangs of yours away. From the tales I've heard about vampires, I know you can. And as for this handsome fellow—your lover, I assume, since you both reek of each other's scents—that will come in due time. Depending on you, that is." He then reached into the pocket of his trousers and drew out a small black vial. "I need you to drink this so you won't feel the urge to attack us."

Mouse eyed the vial. "What is that?"

"Fae blood. One sip is strong enough to keep your appetite sated for days."

"So, you *are* fae," Mouse murmured. "Like Puck from a *Midsummer Night's Dream*."

"Sorry, can't say that I know a Puck. Unless he's dead." Tik-

Tok's lips curled up at the corners. "But yes, I'm fae, directly from Oz. I'm Tik-Tok, Captain of *The Temptress*, and this grumpy male is Tin, a once-famed assassin." He motioned at the ground. "How about we sit down and you can tell me your name, then how your friend came across the fae dagger he's holding." Tik-Tok lowered himself beside her as if they were to be guests at one of Maddie's tea parties, then handed her the vial. "And drink up."

Mouse stared at the black glass, peering over at Ferris who was most likely yelling at her not to do it—but there was no other choice. Don't drink it and be turned to stone, possibly have her head cut off, or worse—Ferris remain as he was if she refused. She uncapped the vial, letting the sweet aroma caress her nostrils. With prayers that she would live after this, she tossed the contents back. A bright flavor burst along her tongue, delicious, divine, as it slid down her throat. She handed the container back to Tik-Tok, wishing there was more, but the hunger wasn't there—her appetite filled for the time being. Mouse couldn't deny that she liked the way it made her feel, that she didn't have to lose control.

Tin continued to stand, glaring daggers at Tik-Tok but remaining silent. However, his fingers didn't loosen on his axe as his gaze turned to her.

"I'm Mouse," she said softly to Tin. "I do indeed find your axe rather pretty."

"I suppose." Tin's voice came out gruff, his brow arched. Tik-Tok side-eyed him while smiling, appearing amused.

"Ferris and I were here in Red to learn how to deal with a threat in another part of Wonderland, where I'm from."

"Would this threat happen to be a flying vicious beast?" Tik-Tok drawled.

Mouse gasped. "You know about the Jabberwocky?" How would he know? Was this not their first time in Wonderland? "Have you been here before?"

He shook his head. "No. There used to be a portal in the sea, but decades ago, it vanished. I only recently convinced Tin to open one on land for me. His portal magic can be quite handy when he bothers to use it."

She wondered if they ever went to the same mortal world. Never once had she seen a fae before … unless they used glamour like in the stories… "We can venture to the mortal world, but our portals have always been here."

Tik-Tok leaned back on his hands, drawing a knee to his chest, getting comfortable. "Let me tell you a story. I have a sea witch friend who has visions after a good fucking. A crew member of mine has been ravishing her for almost a century and we were told that two lone vampires would be here to assist us. That means *you*."

Mouse frowned, glancing at Ferris, wishing he was there to give his thoughts. "We found nothing on how to kill the Jabberwocky. Its body is like iron and nothing penetrates it."

"Damn, you're vicious. We don't want to *kill* him," Tik-Tok purred. "Centuries ago, a fae male was cursed by a nasty bitch named Locasta. She was one of the witch rulers in Oz, who was rather good at hiding her deceitfulness before she was slaughtered. I don't know Pipt's full backstory, but somehow this male was cursed as a beast and hidden in your world by her."

Mouse inhaled a sharp breath and mulled over what he'd just confessed, how she'd always wondered where the Jabberwocky had come from, why there had always only been one. The beast wasn't from Wonderland at all—it—*he*—was from Oz. A fae male cursed as a beast, one she didn't know anything about, but if she were to guess, perhaps in his true form he was never vicious at all. "So, do you know if he was ever meant to destroy our world? He's part of the reason this territory looks like this, and I believe he's going to end up doing the same to my home."

"I don't believe that was the intention," Tik-Tok started. "A trusted witch knew him and said he was a good male. A bit reckless but good. If he's destroying your world, he likely doesn't mean to or can't control himself anymore."

Mouse knew what it was like to not be in control of oneself. She may not have been under a curse, but when she'd slaughtered those mortals in the donor building, her hunger had felt like she was. "I'll help any way I can, but tell me how to cure him."

Tik-Tok rubbed his hands together. "This is the fun part. It's simple really. My compass will lead us to his location, then we will need to pour the potion the sea witch provided down his throat."

Mouse's lips parted, her eyes widening in horror. "You can't just waltz up to the Jabberwocky and pour something down his throat. He'll eat you whole! Are you mad?"

"Sometimes, perhaps." Tik-Tok's grin grew wide. "But I think I've traveled to other worlds that are more dangerous than this one. If we set a trap, it should be easy enough."

"If it were that easy, it would've been done already," Mouse huffed. The vampires in Red had tried relentlessly until they'd finally abandoned the territory. "You had centuries to claim him and you didn't. He's done so much damage here." Tears pricked her eyes as she looked at Ferris who could've been killed when the Jabberwocky had broken into the palace.

Tin gritted his teeth. "If you tell her the rest, you ass, she would understand more and we'll be finished here."

Tik-Tok flicked his hand in the air. "And you're the one to talk. You've been silent almost this whole damn time." His intense gaze locked on hers once more. "The fae didn't come sooner because no one knew what Locasta had done with him." He paused, flexing his fingers. "This would've been much easier if North was here. She's Tin's daughter, my North Star, but he's the only one who can open land portals. You see, she's with child, our first child, and she's been bedridden. The sea witch needs Pipt to return for her own purpose. If we bring him back to her, she'll give us a concoction to heal North." It was the first break in his cocky expression. He tightened his gold fist, his eyes glassy for a moment.

Mouse blinked, her chest tightening. They were both doing this for love. Tik-Tok's lover and Tin's daughter. She knew that feeling, would do anything for Ferris if circumstances arose. "We'll do everything we can."

"You still didn't answer how you came across a fae dagger," he said, his smirk returning.

"When we were searching the palace, we found a secret room with ancient relics. I suppose they are all from your world."

"Interesting." Tik-Tok rubbed at his chin. "We should have a look in there."

"Fuck that." Tin frowned. "We're here for one purpose."

"It is quite a bloody mess after we encountered an ancient there and most of the things are now broken anyway." She held up a finger. "But before I go any further with helping, you will break the spell on Ferris now."

"That's fair," Tik-Tok said. Just as he lifted his hand and the stone unfurled from Ferris's flesh, a boisterous screech broke out in the distance.

The Jabberwocky.

CHAPTER TWENTY-THREE

FERRIS

The Jabberwocky's cry shook the ground beneath Ferris the very moment his body was no longer stone. He gasped for a breath, finally able to fill his lungs, and leapt up to stand beside Mouse, pulling her close. He'd heard every word the fae had spoken and wasn't sure exactly how they were meant to help these two fuckers. A sea witch? Bullshit.

But he'd think on the conversation as soon as they figured out where the beast was. Not a beast—a cursed fae. Whatever the fuck he was, the Jabberwocky would eat each and every one of them if given the chance. The sky was still free of danger, even though the beast's screech had echoed from a distance.

"Ferris, I presume," Tik-Tok said, then held up a golden compass. The face looked normal enough with the usual north, south, east, and west, but it emitted a soft golden glow. And, instead of pointing north, the needle aimed in the same direction from where the Jabberwocky's sounds had come. "And *that* would be Pipt."

"Yes, that's the Jabberwocky," Mouse confirmed.

"Here, take this." Tik-Tok tossed a black vial at Ferris without looking up from his compass.

Ferris caught it and rolled the glass between his fingers. Even though the fae's blood pumping in their veins had an intoxicating smell, he had no desire to lay a single fang in them. "I'm not going to bite you."

"Nevertheless," Tik-Tok quipped.

Bloody hell. Was he really going to ingest mystery blood just to humor this asshat? But Mouse had drank it, so that meant he would risk it. Only for her. Popping the top off with his thumb, he sniffed it. *Fruity. Tempting...* Ah, fuck it. He tipped the contents into his mouth and swallowed the thick liquid. Savory, alluring, and it sated his hunger completely.

Tin held out his hand to Ferris. "Dagger."

"What?" He wasn't giving up the dagger to this conceited looking fucker—especially not now. The fae claimed to want their help but Ferris wasn't about to lower his guard before he was sure of them. Not after having survived in the Ruby Heart Palace where trust didn't exist. "Fuck you."

"Fuck *you*," Tin retorted. "That's a fae blade and iron hurts like a bitch. I won't risk you using it on one of us."

"Well, now that I know it's extra effective against you..." Ferris tucked it into his belt and offered a smile, his fangs bared. He cast a glance at the axe over Tin's shoulder. "Besides, you already have a weapon."

"Play nice, you two." Tik-Tok pulled his satchel off and held it out to Mouse without looking away from his compass. "What we need is in here."

"And you want me to carry it?" she asked.

"Your paramour can, if you prefer it."

"No, it's fine." Mouse grabbed the leather bag and tilted her head at Ferris in confusion. When Tik-Tok released it, her arms dropped from the unexpected weight.

"It's spelled to carry more than its size and helps lighten the load," Tin explained, though no one questioned it.

"I've got it." Ferris took the bag from Mouse—not because she couldn't carry it but because it was the gentlemanly thing to do—and swung it over his shoulder. *Damn*. It had to weigh almost as much as he did—if this was *lightened*, what the fuck was in there? Lifting the flap, he peered inside to find a ludicrous amount of large, heavy-linked chains. He picked up a section to test its weight and his brows rose. "That's a good fucking spell," he mumbled to himself. Just one of the links had to be around nineteen kilos.

Tin released a sharp breath. "It's beginner magic."

Well, la-de-fucking-da. "So, what's the plan then? Because I hate to break it to you, but chains won't do shite against the Jabberwocky."

Tin's nostrils flared when he looked down at the chain in Ferris's hands. "Those are iron chains, dumbass."

"And they will do jack-shit," Ferris said again.

Tin tilted his head and tapped the metal trailing over his cheek, wincing. Twisting silver lines covered most of his right cheek. If iron hurt fae so much, why would this fae imbed it on his cheek? Unless it wasn't there by choice...

"It will do plenty against a fae," Tin said in a low voice.

"That's where you two come in," Tik-Tok interjected. "Tin and I will distract Pipt. You'll immobilize him with the chains, just long enough for me to turn him to stone." He snapped his fingers. "Then voila. Cured."

"Just like that?" Mouse asked in disbelief.

"I may have skipped a few minor details." He glanced at Tin, his red eyes alight with mischief. "Are we moving out or do you prefer to stand here all day?"

Tin hefted his double-sided axe back onto his shoulder. "The sooner we get this over with, the better."

Ferris couldn't agree more.

Mouse shifted closer to Ferris, eyeing the two fae as they spoke a few lines in a soft, lyrical language full of rolling letters. "Are you okay with this?" she whispered.

Was he? There didn't seem to be much of a choice—Tik-Tok

would easily turn them to stone again if they refused. But what other options did they have? If these two had a shot of ridding Wonderland of the beast, he and Mouse would be fucking insane not to give it a go. And then he thought of something they'd said that made his chest tighten. Helping Tik-Tok's wife and child in the process wasn't something he could deny either. He hadn't been able to save his girlfriend and daughter, but maybe he could help them.

"For now," he replied quietly.

She stuck close to his side as they followed the fae through Red and away from the castle. They passed the wreckage of a city with half crumbled walls, then meandered through a forest of rotting trees, and climbed a small, craggy hill. While Tik-Tok stared at his compass and Tin kept a sharp eye on their surroundings, Ferris watched *them*. They moved with a fluid grace, not completely unlike vampires, though they gave off otherworldly vibes. Different than both Wonderland and the mortal world. Cocky, mysterious bastards.

"Ferris, was it?" Tin asked when they'd been walking for a good while.

"Yeah," he replied warily, side-eyeing the fae. They entered a prairie with patches of brown crunchy grass and a dried-up stream.

"I'm curious." The silver-haired male slowed his steps until he walked beside Ferris instead of Tik-Tok. His axe rested casually on his shoulder. "How does one become … like you?"

Ferris scratched the side of his neck where Imogen had torn into him. It hadn't been a pleasant experience—feeding her, fucking her, drinking her blood. He'd hated every second of it, not knowing if Imogen would uncover his plan with Maddie through his memories. It was the painful ones of Ellie the Queen of Hearts had seen though. But Mouse was worth it. If it had been someone else… If it had been *Mouse* who'd turned him, Ferris was sure it would've been a vastly different experience. "Why? Are you interested?"

"In drinking blood? Fuck no. You're immortal, I hear, yet

your kind can't walk in the sun. It sounds even more pathetic than having iron imbedded on your face." He switched his axe to his other shoulder and stared out over the emptiness that was Red. "I don't understand why anyone would choose to live eternally in a shit place like this."

"All of Wonderland isn't like Red," Mouse drawled, motioning at the bare trees. "Ivory is beautiful and thousands live in Scarlet."

"Not everyone chooses this life," Ferris added. Maddie certainly hadn't. Imogen and Rav had never asked anyone's opinion on the matter. Noah's sister, Alice, flashed through his mind. The journey Noah and Maddie took to save her life after Imogen turned her was nothing short of perilous. "The Queen of Ivory and the King of Scarlet are working together to make sure no one is forced anymore."

Tin's brows furrowed, then smoothed out as he shrugged. "Tik-Tok once turned me to stone."

"Fucking brutal." The sense of suffocating, of being unable to move, but being fully aware of everything was torturous.

"He does it to everyone who might attack. Cowardly, if you ask me," Tin grumbled. "He kidnapped North right in front of me and her mother. There wasn't a damn thing we could've done about it because he'd turned the entire ballroom into statues."

Mouse gasped. "Kidnapped her? I thought—"

"Yes," he said in a hard voice. "They're together now. Going on almost a century at this point, so I've given up trying to get rid of the bastard."

A screech blasted through the air and pebbles shook against the parched ground. Ferris threw a protective arm around Mouse, looking toward the sky, catching sight of the Jabberwocky's silhouette following above them. "He's too close."

"On the contrary." Tik-Tok threw a smirk over his shoulder. "We're not close enough."

"I don't think you fully understand what the Jabberwocky is," Ferris mumbled. They were in the middle of a damn *prairie*.

Nowhere to hide. Nowhere to run.

"Pipt doesn't breathe fire, does he?" Tin asked the vampires. "Or have any long-range attacks?"

"Not that we've seen," Mouse said. "He's a relatively new risk to those outside of Red, but no one has ever reported him breathing fire."

Tik-Tok tucked the compass away in his back pocket. "If I need to turn him into stone to knock him out of the sky, we'll just have to hope no limbs break off when he lands. Celyna never said anything about bringing him back in one piece."

"Who?" Mouse asked.

"The sea witch." Tik-Tok shrugged. Ferris's eyes lifted to the sky just as the Jabberwocky's shadow fell over their group, his wings giving a deafening clap. The shadow moved swiftly, swallowing them and spitting them out just as fast. "Show time."

"Take out the chains," Tik-Tok ordered Ferris. "We'll lure the dreadful creature down. As soon as you've got him tangled, I'll handle the rest."

With that, the fae sprinted ahead, leaving Ferris and Mouse to stare after them. Their feet barely seemed to hit the ground. Red magic sparked off the tips of Tik-Tok's golden fingers and Tin lowered his axe to hold with two hands.

"They're giving us a lot of trust here." Ferris turned his eyes up to the gray sky. A tip of a taloned foot dipped below the clouds, then the giant beast came into view, throwing his head back to release a rumbling roar. *Fuck.* "Either that, or they're using us as the perfect appetizer to distract him."

"The chains," Mouse hissed.

"Shit." Ferris reached into the bag and handed one end to Mouse. She took two steps back, helping pull the links out, until there was a massive coil between them. Finally reaching the other end, he wound it around his fist once for a better grip.

The two fae spoke loud enough to draw the Jabberwocky's attention from where it circled above them. Scuffing their feet on the dry earth, they kept their gaze trained upward. Waiting for him to attack.

But the beast cracked his wings, lifting higher into the thick clouds, and disappeared. He didn't reemerge—not a single sound came from the Jabberwocky as though he was *toying* with them, his prey. *Oh shit.* Ferris held his breath. This couldn't be good.

His gaze scoured overhead for any sign of the Jabberwocky. A shadow, the dip of his tail. But there was no hint of the sneaky fucker. Not before he tore from behind a cloud, teeth bared, wings pressed against his body, diving down from the sky—straight toward him and Mouse. *Bloody hell!* This wasn't the plan. The fae were the bait. Ferris lunged for Mouse, knocking her down and rolling them both out of the way just as the Jabberwocky crashed to where they'd been standing. The ground shook, trees rustling, chain clanking. A roar vibrated the air around them and the fae shouted. Ferris leapt up, dragging Mouse to her feet beside him.

The Jabberwocky's cry turned to a whine. Ferris tightened his grip on the chain and turned to find gray stone slipping over the beast's body. It oozed down the quills, sliding over dark fur, around his abdomen and neck. He stomped his taloned feet, but then the stone was there, too, holding him in place. And, finally, silence, as the last of his snout hardened.

"Damn it," Tin muttered. "How are you going to get him chained up now, fucker?"

"Oh, I'm sorry. Did you want *them* to become a snack?" Tik-Tok adjusted his rolled sleeves, exposing more of his golden arm, and peered around the Jabberwocky to smile at Ferris and Mouse. "You're welcome."

"Cut the shit, pirate. The cure takes time to work. Unless he's flesh and bone, he can't ingest anything and if he's not tied down, he's going to use our bones as toothpicks." Tin let the head of his axe thud to the ground and squeezed his eyes shut.

"It's fine. This might work better than expected. Fangs"—Tik-Tok pointed at Ferris—"wrap him up nice and tight."

Mouse snorted in disbelief, scanning the fae up and down.

"I wonder how much we could sell their blood for if we bottled it," Ferris said. "With the Jabberwocky turned to stone like this, they can't release him so our problem seems to be solved."

"Oh, feisty! I like it." Tik-Tok laughed, seeming to be completely unfazed by the threat. "Unfortunately, if I get too far away, he'll turn back into a beastie. So, get wrapping."

Ferris rolled his eyes. He'd like to wrap the chain around Tik-Tok's throat instead. "Let's just get this over with."

Dragging the chain between them, Ferris approached the stone Jabberwocky. The beast remained crouched like he was still about to attack, lips pulled back slightly, exposing the tips of his sharp teeth. But there was something else in his expression. Shock, fear. His furry brows were slightly lifted in surprise. If this worked, he would be able to go home after all this time.

"Hopefully he still remembers how to speak." Tik-Tok rapped his fingers against his golden arm. "If he's not rational after the cure, you can knock him out."

"May I?" Tin drawled.

"Just don't hit him too hard and kill the poor male." His red gaze landed on Mouse. "Chop, chop, my pink little confection."

A low snarl left Ferris. He would love to attack Tik-Tok just once if it weren't for the unknown magic shit he'd retaliate with—somehow, he doubted Tin would help until the very last moment too. But there were more important things at play, so he wrapped a loop of chain around the Jabberwocky's left leg, ensuring it was nice and tight, before dragging more toward his back one.

Mouse mirrored his movements, throwing the chain to each other over the beast's back and beneath his stomach, until they were out of links. Tangled as he was, it would take forever for him to escape and, given that the chain was made of iron, Ferris was confident they would have enough time to cure the cursed fae.

Or get the fuck out of there if Tik-Tok's concoction failed.

"Now what?" Ferris asked, wiping his sweaty palms on his trousers.

Tin reached into his tunic and produced a gold vial. "We get him to drink this."

Mouse blinked, her lips set in a thin line. "I suppose we'll find out if this final act becomes a tragedy."

There was no way they were going to get close enough to the Jabberwocky's mouth to feed it jack-shit. Not unless they were also determined to lose a hand in the process. But, hey, as long as the Jabberwocky got the cure, it made no difference to him if one of the fae lost a limb. Maybe Tik-Tok wanted a matching set.

Tin turned to the cocky fae and grabbed him by the shirt. "If you fuck this up and I get eaten, remember that you have to face my very expectant, bed-ridden daughter."

"If you get eaten, I won't be facing another fae for a *very* long time, will I?" Tik-Tok brushed him off. "You're my ticket home, so fear not."

Tin let out a string of low curses as he approached the Jabberwocky and popped open the vial. "Stand back," he told Ferris and Mouse. Then he took a deep breath. "Fucking do it."

The magic faded from the Jabberwocky, lightening dark stone to his gray hide. His growl rumbled lower than before, his lips pulling back into a sneer, and his eyes narrowed as he waited for the moment he could move again. Attack. Devour.

But then the iron links touched his hide instead of stone and his jaw fell open on a high-pitched whine. Tin shoved his hand into the beast's mouth, pouring bright purple liquid onto his red tongue, before flinging himself backward just before the Jabberwocky snapped his mouth shut and released a blood-curdling howl.

Mouse grabbed Ferris's wrist and drew him out of the Jabberwocky's range of attack. If this failed, they'd just royally pissed off the most dangerous creature in Wonderland.

"Is it working?" Ferris shouted over the wail.

"Fuck if I know," Tin grunted.

CHAPTER TWENTY-FOUR

MOUSE

The Jabberwocky's body shook, the quills along his head vibrated, then his wild orange gaze found them. Mouse was about to use her vampire speed to drag Ferris and get out of this horrid situation, when a mixture of emotions in the beast's stare gave her pause. Suffering, regret, sadness.

Compassion stirred within Mouse. He was a cursed fae male who hadn't chosen to become this, just as she hadn't chosen for her hunger to become monstrous. They'd both been hurt and altered in different ways and no pain rivaled another—pain was pain.

The Jabberwocky's legs buckled beneath him and he collapsed onto the dirt, releasing a low wail as he tried to push himself up before falling once more. He writhed within the chains, his eyes rolling back in his head. And then his body stilled, his breaths decreasing.

"Bollocks, I think he's dying," she said, racing to his side. He didn't appear strong enough to fly or escape as his body continued to tremble.

"He better not fucking die," Tin growled. "We need him." Even though the fae's face was icy, his gaze held worry, most likely for his daughter.

Mouse pressed her hand to the beast's stomach while it rose and fell from his ragged breaths. Ferris stood beside her, not as inclined to comfort the Jabberwocky, but he didn't ask her to move away.

"Just wait," Tik-Tok cooed.

Wait for what? And then in answer, small whines escaped the Jabberwocky. But that wasn't what he was referring to—the beast's body shook once more, only this time it was more of a convulsion, bright white foam spilling from his mouth.

"It's all right," she whispered in a soothing voice. But she honestly didn't know if it was at all. The dark fur sank beneath his flesh and the skin turned golden, then became lighter until it looked as if his outer layer had been kissed by the sun. Sun she hadn't seen in so long, and frankly, never truly missed. Deep green, almost black strands of hair sprouted from his head, growing longer, his body shrinking, until he was no longer a beast. Mouse stripped away the chains that were too big for him now, then dropped to her knees beside the fae male, his face ethereal and beautiful like Tin's and Tik-Tok's. His ears came to sharp points and his cheekbones were high.

Pipt's orange eyes met hers. "Water," he croaked.

Ferris was already unzipping his pack, fishing out a canteen for him. Pipt's hand trembled as he took it, then guzzled the liquid down.

"I would give you clothing, but I'm fresh out, mate," Ferris said, rifling through his pack again.

"Just give him the shirt you're wearing," Mouse said, staring at the fae's lithe and toned form. "He can cover himself with it."

Ferris lifted his shirt over his head and ripped it down the front for Pipt to wear around his waist like a towel.

"I remember you," Pipt said, pushing himself to sit, not doing anything to cover himself with the shirt while exchanging a glance between Ferris and Mouse. "In the tunnels. I couldn't control myself, even though I'd wanted to." His gaze shifted to Tin and Tik-Tok. "Who are you?" He squinted, seeming to try to recall if perhaps he knew them from Oz.

"Your rescuers, of course," Tik-Tok cooed. "We're from Oz."

Pipt's lip trembled and tears beaded his lashes. "Locasta, she—"

"That bitch is dead," Tin grunted. "Reva and Crow killed her. If you remember them. They sure as fuck remember you and your reckless magic."

"What about Glinda? She was helping me master my magic, but then I made a grave mistake and went to Locasta, not knowing she was truly an evil witch in disguise."

"Sadly, Glinda is gone." Tik-Tok sighed. "You'll discover a lot has changed when we return. And dare I say, for the better."

Pipt peered down at his hand where black vines were tattooed on his ring finger. His eyes cleared, and he pushed himself to stand, wrapping Ferris's shirt around his waist. "My wife!"

"Is still marble," Tin said. "Reva knew you would ask about her and she's safe."

"I did this." He sobbed, his head falling into his hands. "It was an accident with the Liquid of Petrification."

Tik-Tok tapped a golden finger against his chin. "Yes, reckless magic you shouldn't have been toying with. I'll help return her to you, but you must first meet with the sea witch."

"Celyna?"

"So, you *know* her." Tik-Tok smirked.

Pipt ignored him and surveyed Red's bare trees, the dead bushes, the dust in the air. "I didn't mean to do this to your world. I didn't mean to do any of this."

"Wonderland is safe now," Mouse whispered, grasping his hand and giving it a gentle squeeze. "*You're* safe."

"We're wasting time," Tin grumbled. He lifted his free hand and chanted words in that lyrical language of his while drawing a small rectangle in the air with his fingertip. A green outline formed in the same shape, only taller, wider. A portal like the one she'd seen earlier by the lake.

Tik-Tok removed a jeweled ring from his golden finger. "I'll owe you one favor, if you ever need it. Put this on and I'll know you're ready to call it in. It will only work once though, so don't be hasty." He handed her the ring and it glowed a light red, tingling against her fingers. She unzipped the front of her pack and slipped it inside, hoping she would never have to use it.

Tin stepped forward, his axe relaxed at his side, his gaze shifting between Mouse and Ferris. "You did well today."

"I hope your daughter feels better," Mouse murmured.

Tin gave a small nod, lifting his weapon over his shoulder while stepping toward the portal.

Pipt ran a hand across the back of his neck. "It was a curse I never believed I would be free from. Centuries like this. Thank you all for freeing me."

Mouse felt as though she didn't do much, only threw chains across the Jabberwocky to hold him in place, but the four of them had done it together.

The trio of fae then walked through the portal and the green light flickered before vanishing. Mouse pressed her hand into the space where the portal had been and she felt nothing, not a single buzz of magic.

"This was an unexpected ending," she said, dropping her hand back to her side.

"Or a fucking miracle." Ferris sighed, drawing her into his side as she wrapped her arms around him.

"*Now*, we finally go back to Ivory." If this wasn't all a wonderful dream, then that meant the Jabberwocky would no longer terrorize Red, wouldn't attempt to do the same to Ivory. Rav and Imogen were gone. And now the Jabberwocky was gone. Wonderland could become better. The seductive touch of a vampire, their dark habits, and ravenous appetites would still rule the nights, yet no one would have to worry about getting eaten by a vicious beast.

Mouse and Ferris journeyed back through the forest, finding no sign of any rogue werewolves, only bones scattered or in piles across the ground. After a bit, they reached the edge of Ivory, then crossed into the mortal world since it was still nighttime.

"Are we sure we want to use this portal, luv?" Ferris asked. "I think I know what's going to happen when we pass through since we had to leap off the bridge to get to it."

"Why, Ferris, have you never gotten a little wet before?" she drawled, then leapt into the portal with a laugh as he cursed behind her.

"I'm never going through that portal again," Ferris said once Mouse grabbed his hand, helping him up from the Thames.

"The Knave who is always up for anything, even risking his life to break me out from a palace, is afraid of a little water?" she teased.

He traced a finger across her lips, sending a delicious shiver through her. "Tonight, you'll pay for making me go through it twice." A grin spread across his face. "With my tongue between your thighs."

Mouse blinked, heat creeping up her neck and into her cheeks as he turned and walked away from her. "You can't go teasing me like *that*," she shouted, catching up with him.

"Oh, well I just did." He chuckled.

"See you at the palace then." She smiled and took off with her enhanced speed toward the portal in the cemetery. It didn't take them long before they crossed back into Wonderland, the alabaster gothic-like palace resting before them.

Noah stood in his Ivory uniform, guarding the front of the castle. "You're back. It's about damn time," he said, pulling open the door for them. "Ever already put a search party together and they were going to leave in two days."

"Suppose she'll have to cancel that then, yeah?" Ferris asked.

Noah cocked his head. "Cancel?"

"You'll find out soon enough."

Mouse patted Noah's shoulder. "Let's just say we don't have to worry about the beast any longer."

Noah's brows shot up as they stepped inside the palace. Mock lingered on guard near the stairs and his lips parted in surprise. "I knew you two would come back."

"I'm glad you were so confident," Mouse whispered with a smile. "Can you tell us where Ever is?"

"She's in the study." Mock studied her, his lips curling upward. "I like this talking side of you. Don't go back to being quiet around me."

"I'll try." Mouse left Mock to continue guarding and walked beside Ferris to the study, where the deep sounds of Ever's viola spilled into the hallway. Mouse could tell by the faster sounds that the queen was stressed, nervous, and she had more than an inkling of why. Not only because they hadn't returned but because her territory had been at risk.

Ever stood in the middle of the room near a plush white chaise while Chess watched her from behind the desk. He held a stack of papers in his hand, but he wasn't focused on them—all his attention was on Ever. Chess was the first to notice them, rising from his seat. "Well, well, look what the cat dragged in." He gave them both a once over before cocking a brow at Ferris. "Do you own a shirt?"

Ever's hands stilled, the music coming to a screeching halt as she whirled around. "You're here!" She rushed to Mouse, wrapping her into a tight hug as if she thought she'd never return. "Maddie is already packed and prepared to hunt the Jabberwocky with a party of guards."

"No one has to go," Mouse said, stepping back from Ever.

"The Jabberwocky isn't in Red anymore," Ferris added.

"Then where the fuck is it?" Chess arched a brow. "The beastie hasn't played in any of the other territories since it was here last."

"Have you ever heard stories of the fae?" Mouse asked,

running her fingers over the end of her plait.

"I don't think we need a bedtime story." Chess scowled.

Mouse rolled her eyes and continued, "The Jabberwocky isn't what we thought he was. He's from another world known as Oz and was cursed as a beast before being banished here. Two fae came through a self-made portal, then we helped them break the curse. They're all now back in Oz so we're safe."

Ever held up a hand, a frown on her face. She wasn't as relieved as Mouse thought she would be. "Should we be worried about an attack? Two fae came here from another world, who can just return at any time they would like without our knowledge? What if something worse comes?"

Mouse hadn't thought about that, and perhaps that was one of the reasons she wasn't and would never be a queen. "I know it's foolish, but I trust them. They won't come back, only if I ask them to. The portal doesn't remain open as ours does with the mortal world. There's a lot to discuss."

"Do go on then." Chess sat on the edge of Ever's desk, leaning back on his hands. "We have plenty of time."

Ferris clasped Mouse's hand, seeming to know what she needed. "I'll fill them in. Go to Maddie."

Mouse nodded and before she left the room, she heard Chess purr, "It appears the two of you discovered *other* things while in Red."

She bit the inside of her cheek to stop from smiling about the pleasureful things she and Ferris had done together as she ventured back into the sitting room to find Mock. "Do you know where Maddie is?"

"She's in the drawing room," he said.

Even though his eyes weren't puffy like they'd been when she left, she knew he wouldn't ever forget about Didi. He was going on, day by day.

"Thank you, Mock," she whispered, then hurried down the halls to the drawing room.

Maddie's legs hung over the chair arm and Mouse quietly padded in, watching as her sister's fingers thoroughly pushed her threaded needle in and out of a violet and cerulean checkered top hat.

"I've returned," Mouse whispered.

Maddie's hands froze, her head jerking up. "Mouse!" She leapt from the chair and threw her arms around her. "I've been going positively mad here, making hundreds of hats."

"Hundreds?" Mouse laughed. "That seems like a record number."

"You're laughing," Maddie said slowly, studying her as if she had twenty eyes on her face. "Like you used to."

"I should hope that's a good thing."

"It is." Maddie grinned, hugging her again.

"I have an interesting story to tell you." Mouse didn't wait for Maddie to respond before discussing the journey, starting with the rogue werewolves, the queen and her husband, the ancient, the relics, the fae, and their magical portal. A beast who wasn't one at all, but an ethereal male who had matters of his own to sort when he returned home. Like they all had to do.

"Well, that"—Maddie tapped her chin and smiled wider—"is quite the tale. But you're leaving out parts, aren't you?"

Mouse had… She'd left out the parts where she'd almost died, where things had gone too far with the ancient because those parts didn't matter now.

Before she could speak, Maddie waved a hand in the air. "I know what it is. You and Ferris *fucked*."

Mouse gasped. *Oh, bollocks, it isn't what I had thought at all.*

"It's all right. I know it's hard for you to discuss these things, but I'm happy for you." The smile slipped from Maddie's face as she peered at her hands. "However, I do have news to give you about Des."

"She *died*?" Mouse shrieked.

"What? No!" Maddie grasped her by the arm and turned her to where the chess set rested on top of the table. Only, beside the set was something blue, an odd almost oval shape.

And then Mouse's eyebrows shot up as she glanced back at her sister. "It's a cocoon! *How?*" Caterpillars in Wonderland never formed cocoons, never became a butterfly or a moth.

"Species evolving? Maybe she's special? Perhaps her sadness did it. She had remained blue for a while, her yellow coloring gone." Maddie shrugged. "But she's been like this since the day you left."

"This is my fault." Her heart sped up and she blinked away tears.

Maddie wrapped her arm around Mouse, drawing her close. "We'll wait and see what happens when she emerges from it. She'll be fine, I promise."

Mouse didn't know what to think, but she would try to be positive the way Maddie always was. She hugged her sister, then sat in the chair across from Des. "Thank you for watching over her."

"Of course." Maddie took a seat opposite her. "How about you tell Des everything that happened while we play a game of chess? I'm certain she'll be able to hear you." She paused, scanning her over. "Unless you would rather bathe or nap first?"

"No, I'm not tired and I can have a proper bath later. I want to spend time with the two of you for now." Time that she should've been spending with them before instead of moping about.

Maddie inched a white chess piece forward. "Now tell me, what precisely led you and Ferris to fuck in Red?"

"Maddie!" Mouse laughed while moving a black pawn forward. She then turned to Des's cocoon and murmured, "Ignore my sister, she's too nosy for her own good."

CHAPTER TWENTY-FIVE

FERRIS

Ferris paused outside of the drawing room after talking to the royals, listening to Mouse and Maddie laughing together. A smile tugged at the corners of his lips. This was how it used to be with them—how it *should* be. They had laughed together all the time before Mouse was taken by Rav and the Queen of Hearts, spent hours joking. Ferris hadn't always known what it was they'd found funny, but the sound was so contagious that he had nearly always laughed along with them.

Mouse and Maddie needed this time together. Ferris wasn't one to eavesdrop, so he stuffed his hands in his pockets and made his way through the hallways, up the stairs, until he reached the bathroom a few doors down from his bedroom. After turning on the water as hot as he could stand it, he peeled off his clothes. Usually he would take a shower, but he needed to soak the ache from his muscles.

Stepping into the massive granite bath, he released a low groan and sank down into the water with his eyes closed. The warmth was an instant relief to his body after the journey in Red. But, as frustrating as their trip had been before the fae arrived, Ferris would do it all over again if it meant he and Mouse could be together.

Ever and Chess had found the information about fae troubling, not that Ferris could blame them. Magical beings who could create a portal anywhere they wanted could be a problem. What was to stop them from portaling into a throne room and vanishing with a royal? But Tin and Tik-Tok had seemed eager to leave Wonderland. They might be back one day if Mouse ever decided to put on the ring Tik-Tok had given her, but until then he wasn't overly concerned.

Surfacing from the water, he dragged in a breath and found a bar of soap. The lake had done well to wash off the blood and dirt in Red, but by the time he finished scrubbing himself, Ferris felt refreshed. After sparing another moment to wash his hair, he drained the bathtub, dried himself, and wrapped the towel around his waist.

He padded toward Mouse's room, but the door was wide open, the bed perfectly made, the lights off. A small twinge of disappointment pinched his chest. He wanted to see her, to touch her just to reassure himself she was real. That she was safe and here, with him, but he knew she would find him when she was ready.

Returning to his bedroom, he passed by his drum set and ran a finger over his cymbal. It gave a low chime when he flicked it. He smirked and grabbed one of the sticks from where it sat on his snare. "Hello, beauty," he whispered to the instrument, twirling the stick between his fingers. "Did you miss me?"

Soon he would play them again, but there was no music drumming in his mind right now. He set the stick back down and stretched his arms over his head, yawning. Now that they were home, he had no doubt that he could sleep for days. He stood between his bed and the dresser. Ever had told him to go rest, so he likely wouldn't be bothered again tonight. There was no need to get dressed. *Not even for Mouse,* he thought with a grin. He pulled the towel from his hips and walked to the chair, draping it over the back to dry.

The only thing he wore now was his necklace with Ellie's ring. It felt heavy around his neck now, uncomfortably so. He lifted the jewelry from where it laid against his chest and stared at the white gold band. The small solitaire diamond. He'd worn it every day since the coroner returned it to her family, who then returned it to him, to remind him of Ellie and their daughter. To carry them with him as he struggled through life, knowing they were gone.

But he wasn't struggling now. He missed them and would always miss them, but he had finally accepted the hard truth of it. Ellie and Luna lived in his heart and always would. This ring though… Ferris hadn't been carrying their memory around his neck. He had been carrying his guilt.

Biting his lip, Ferris carefully lifted the chain over his head and ran his thumb over the ring's stone. It was time to let go of the bad and remember only the good. To stop wondering *what if* and start living again. Truly living. He opened the top drawer of the dresser and set the chain inside, closing his self-blame away.

Ferris loosened a breath and perched on the edge of the bed, feeling lighter than before. So light, in fact, that he was no longer tired. His hand itched to draw. To bring beauty to life on page. He smiled to himself as he took his sketch pad and pencil from the bedside table.

Flipping past sketches of looming castles on cliffs, glass-like portals, of Ellie, Mouse, and Maddie, Ferris put the tip of the pencil to the page and began drawing.

"Ferris." A soft voice broke into his sleep. "Ferris, wake up."

"Hmm?" He cracked one eye open to see Mouse leaning over him. *Oh, shit.* He hadn't meant to fall asleep. One minute, he was sketching his third image of Mouse, then the next, she was waking him. Sitting up, he blinked the sleepiness from his eyes. "What's wrong?"

"Des somehow formed a cocoon. Maddie wanted to watch over her for one more night so I'm letting her." She gave him a soft smile. "I wanted to climb in next to you, but you're hogging the whole bed."

He rolled off his stomach and onto his side to give her room, not thinking that he was giving her a view of his dick. Pink rose in her cheeks but she didn't hesitate to lay beside him. She propped her head up on her hand. His gaze traveled down from her damp, loose hair to the large black T-shirt she wore. *His* T-shirt. And from the looks of it, nothing else.

"What are you drawing?" she asked, interrupting his lazy perusal.

Ferris glanced at the lines of what would've been Mouse's sleeping face had he finished and closed it. "Nothing."

"Liar." She reached for the book. "You always let me see."

He clutched the spiral spine a little harder, unsure how she would feel about the other two drawings he'd created before falling asleep. "I might have to rethink that policy."

"Oh?" Mouse's brows rose playfully. "And why is that?"

"Subject matter may no longer be suitable for all ages." He flashed a sheepish smile. "I might have drawn a couple things that, in retrospect, I should've asked permission for."

"Well, now I'm twice as curious," Mouse drawled. "Since I'm much older than you, it really shouldn't be a problem." She slowly pulled the sketchbook from his hand and he let her, giving silent permission. Flipping through to the end, she paused at the unfinished page. "What will this one be?"

"You," he said. *Fuck.* He really should've asked her if she minded being the subject of sexually charged drawings before he did them. It wasn't too late to burn the whole damn book… If she was uncomfortable, he would destroy the images and never do anything like it again. "You look peaceful when you sleep, so I was trying to capture that."

She beamed, then turned the page. The smile faded.

"Ferris…"

"I'm sorry."

"What? No." She looked up at him. "Don't be sorry. It's just … is that how you see me?"

Ferris glanced down at the image of Mouse. It was the view he'd had when she was pressed against the wall as he licked her to orgasm. Her arched back, peaked nipples, eyes hooded with pleasure. His cock stirred at the reminder of how sweet she'd tasted on his tongue. "I'm not the best artist in the world so I couldn't capture your perfection. Do you not like it?"

"I just look so… I don't know." She let out a small, disbelieving laugh. "I've always been seen as quiet, reserved, which I can be, but you see more than that. You see all of me."

"So, you don't mind? That I drew you like this?" Ferris asked nervously. He really hoped not—he loved drawing her this way.

"No. As long as you don't show anyone."

He inched closer to her on the bed and used his index finger to tilt her chin up. "No one else will ever see that expression on your face. Not on paper and certainly not in real life."

"Only ever you." She gave him a small smile as she turned the page again to reveal a drawing of her on her knees, fingers wrapped around his pierced cock, mouth parted. She slammed the book shut and slid it back toward him, laughing. "That's quite enough of that. Perhaps I'm not brave enough to see my face in such a sexy way. But do go on and continue drawing whatever you wish of me."

Ferris chuckled and pulled her body flush with his, the warmth of her legs against his made him only want to feel more of her skin. In answer, she slid over his hip, giving him a definitive answer to his earlier wonderings. She did *not* have anything else on under his T-shirt. Her slick heat brushed against his semi-hard cock. Instantly, there was no longer anything *semi* about his hard-on.

"Would you like to fuel my imagination a little more?" Ferris asked, brushing his nose against hers, his hand trailing down to cup her arse.

"Hmm. I'm not sure," she replied, teasing, and rolled her hips once. "Do I get to benefit from *your* imagination too?"

Ferris grinned. "Are you asking if I have a new bedroom trick to share with you?"

"I'm asking if you have *multiple* tricks." She nipped gently at his bottom lip. "Though, if you don't, I'm not opposed to helping you figure out some."

"Oh, luv, I have *many* things I'd like to do with you, but not without talking them out first. And we'll need to take a trip to the sex shop. For now, though—" He rolled her onto her back and knelt between her thighs. The motion made the shirt slide up around her waist, giving him a view of her, wet and eager. His cock throbbed with the need to be inside her. "For now," he said again, his voice gruff. "This will have to do."

"What will?"

Ferris reached behind him and grabbed one of the pillows. "Pick up your hips for me." She bit her bottom lip and lifted them from the mattress. Sliding the pillow beneath her arse, he groaned at the sight of her slick folds. "Is that comfortable for you?"

Mouse relaxed into the pillow and nodded.

"Good." Ferris skimmed his hands down the outside of her bare legs, across her knees, and back up her inner thighs to her wet center. He leaned down and pressed his lips to hers. In response, she dug her fingers into his hair. He took ownership of her mouth, his tongue stroking across hers, as Ferris found her clit with his thumb, rubbing gentle circles.

"Faster," she breathed.

"So bossy," he said with a smirk against her mouth. And he fucking loved it. Loved that she was comfortable enough with him to tell him *exactly* what she wanted. He would give her anything she asked for and more. While his thumb moved faster, Ferris's middle finger slid inside, pumping. She squirmed beneath him, panting, and a pearl of cum beaded on the end of his cock. *Fuck.* He wanted to please her, bring her to oblivion numerous times, but he needed to feel her clench around him.

"Would you like to see the trick now?" he asked. "Or should I use my mouth again first?"

"The trick," Mouse panted.

Thank fuck. Ferris kissed her again and removed his hand to line his cock up with her core. She sucked in a breath when it passed over her folds. Ferris grinned and slid the pierced tip through again, before burying himself deep inside her with one thrust.

"Oh!" Mouse cried.

Ferris stilled inside her. The pillow made for deeper penetration, but was it *too* deep for her? "Do I need to stop?"

"No." She grabbed at his arse, pulling him forward, urging him to move, while widening her legs. "More."

Ferris groaned. Were those words ever sexier than when coming from her mouth? He pulled nearly all the way out, then pressed back in, slow, but firm. Unable to take his eyes off hers. When he'd first seen Mouse, he believed her to be an angel. While she might not be from Heaven, she had still saved him. In more ways than one. He loved her so fucking much and with each roll of his hips, he showed her. Again and a-fucking-gain. Until she dug her nails into his back so deep she drew blood, making Ferris growl in pleasure. His thrusts increased. Faster. Harder. With no real rhythm, only him and her making their own drumming beats.

Mouse tilted her head, exposing her neck. Her mouth brushed against his wrist. "Ferris." She flicked her tongue against his pulse point. "I'm so close."

Oh fuck. His balls tightened, his own release nearing. "Bite me," he rasped, fangs dropping.

Mouse extended her neck a bit more. "Together."

He lowered his head to her throat and ran his tongue up the vein, tasting the salt of her skin, then placed a lingering kiss there. When her fangs grazed his wrist, his thrusts became fast and erratic. "Damn, luv," he murmured, and sank his teeth into her flesh. Pleasure stormed through him, starting at his wrist where her fangs pierced. He drove his cock into her as her blood flowed over his tongue, her flavor driving him toward oblivion. Once. Twice.

"Ferris!" she whisper-shouted, pulling herself from his wrist to arch into him. Her walls fluttered around his cock in orgasm. The sounds she made tipped him over the edge and he roared out her name as he came inside her.

They stayed like that, his gaze locked onto hers as they panted. This moment right here, between him and her, was everything he'd ached for over the last few years. The way she looked at him… He knew it was mirrored on his face. And he wanted that expression on paper, to draw her just like this. *His* Mouse. Even though he didn't want to, Ferris found the strength to roll off her. Placing a kiss on her temple, he whispered, "I'm never going to get enough of you."

"I should hope not." She turned to him and smiled. "You have a lot of paper left in that sketchpad to fill."

Ferris chuckled. "I'll need to buy out the art shop."

"Oh?" She laughed softly, shifting the pillow out from beneath her hips and climbed toward the head of the bed. She snuggled beneath the covers then motioned for Ferris to join her. "I suppose on the way we can stop by the sex shop you mentioned."

Ferris grinned as he slipped under the blankets and wrapped an arm around Mouse's waist. "If you insist."

"I do." She closed her eyes and sighed, content.

"Let's rest," he said. "We deserve it after all that shit in Red."

"I already told Maddie I wasn't getting out of this bed for at least a day." She pressed closer into his embrace and yawned. "I love you."

Love didn't feel like a strong enough word for the emotions burning within him for Mouse. They'd saved each other's lives, sacrificed and suffered. She was his eternity and he would continue to protect her with his life. He drew her close and kissed the top of her head. "And I love you. More than I can say."

EPILOGUE

MOUSE

According to Maddie's estimate, from the time Des had first hidden herself away in a silk cocoon, twenty-two days had passed. Ferris had brought Mouse a book from a mortal library that read how it generally took five to twenty-one days on average for a butterfly or moth to emerge from their protective casing. Yet, some could be tucked away for as long as *three* years.

With Des resting beside her on Ferris's bed, Mouse thumbed through a book with more thorough butterfly and moth details, along with a collection of pictures of different species. She tapped her foot against the mattress to the beats coming from Ferris's drums. Every so often she would glance up to watch the way he bit his lip, how his muscles flexed while hitting a cymbal or a snare, and how the perspiration slowly slid down his chest and taut abs. The song was chaotic and beautiful and she hoped Des heard every glorious sound within her silk. Ever since they first moved into the Ivory Palace, the caterpillar had loved hearing Ferris play, standing on her hind legs as the top half of her body would sway to the music.

Mouse peered beneath her lashes at Ferris once more, recalling all the new activities they'd experienced together. Emotionally and physically. Heart-to-heart chats, making love, him showing her what it was like to be truly sexually liberated. Although Mouse hadn't snuck another peek at the additions Ferris had drawn inside his notebook, she was tempted. Perhaps at some point, she would. The drawings had made her blush, and it was different seeing her face that way, happy and blissful. Something she hadn't been in a long, long time.

Soon, Ever and Chess's castle would be finished, and Mouse was excited for this new chapter, to truly unite Wonderland, start something fresh. It was what the vampires in Ivory and Scarlet both needed.

Mouse's stomach still felt heavy from her earlier meal. She continued to struggle with her hunger at times, but on those days, she would ask Ferris or Maddie to go with her to feed, to make sure she didn't become a ravenous monster. Unless she chose to be, when she would still hunt those who'd hurt others.

Movement beside Mouse's hand caught her attention, and she averted her gaze from Ferris. She blinked as the blue silk casing wiggled. For a moment, she thought it was from the vibration of the drums or her foot tapping. But then Des wiggled again.

Her heart slammed in her chest, and she shouted, "Ferris!"

He halted his movements, the drumsticks clenched in his fists, and looked at the cocoon now resting in her hands. It wiggled a little harder.

"Come on!" Mouse didn't wait for his answer as she left his room, skipping over steps while descending the staircase. She flew past Mock, his eyebrows raised to his hairline when he glanced her way.

"I'm fine," she called to the guard.

Before heading out the door, she looked back, and Ferris was nowhere in sight. She didn't wait as she hurried past the blossoming trees and toward the garden near the sparkling lake.

White zinnias were in full bloom and vines weaved through the backs of the iron benches. Mouse halted in front of one of the benches but didn't take a seat, only continued to cradle Des in her palm.

The sky was dark and a swarm of crimson ravens flew overhead beneath the silvery moon and bright stars. Ferris's footsteps finally crunched across the pebbles of the garden pathway and Mouse whirled around. "Took you long enough," she teased, her gaze pinned to his captivating dark eyes.

"I had to grab something really quick." He shrugged, a smirk crossing his face.

She arched a brow, finding nothing in his hands. "Well, good thing you haven't missed Des's big return to Wonderland."

"I think Des would've waited for me."

Mouse rolled her eyes, then focused back on the blue silk. It shook a few more times, then remained still. They waited with bated breath, whispering encouraging words to Des as she worked to break out. She would stop, then go again, then stop. If it was a stressful endeavor for Mouse, she couldn't imagine what it must be like for Des. The sky slowly lightened in the garden until the morning's gray tones crept in, the stars and moon hiding away for the day. It had been a long while since Des's last movement.

"Maybe it was a false alarm. We should head back inside," Ferris said. "We've been standing out here for almost an hour."

"You can take a break, but I want to wait. I want her to be out in the open, free, when she hatches. Not cooped up in the palace after being in this cocoon for weeks."

"Even if it takes as long as it said in that book of yours?"

"Yes," she deadpanned and pointed at a comfortable spot near the flowers. "I'll sleep right there."

"I believe you would too." Ferris chuckled. "I guess I'll have to grab us camping supplies for *three* years."

"It won't take *that* long!" At least she hoped it wouldn't. In answer, the silk shell twitched, the soft casing on the left side tearing open. "Ferris, look." Mouse beamed, her eyes wide.

"I see it, luv." Ferris's arm slipped around her waist as they watched together.

A blue wing with obsidian edges slipped out, followed by a thin leg. It was one of the most beautiful things she'd ever encountered. Not once had she ever seen an insect come out of a cocoon in the mortal world. And then the rest of Des emerged—one of the most gorgeous butterflies in existence. She might be biased though since it was Des, but it was true. The assortment of blues and blacks shimmered, her antenna a glittering cerulean. Unlike the butterflies she'd seen in the book that came out wet and wrinkled, her friend was dry, her wings prepared to fly if she wished.

"Des," Mouse said softly.

The butterfly stood, her head lifting so her pale blue eyes, no longer black, could meet Mouse's.

"You're the first butterfly in Wonderland," Mouse murmured, tears beading her lashes. "I do hope you're not angry with me for leaving you here while I went to Red, but I couldn't put you in danger. Not after you risked your life by staying with me in the palace and helped me through my whirling emotions."

Des crawled up Mouse's palm and nuzzled her finger as she always did. She batted a wing at Ferris, and he brushed a finger across one. "You're the prettiest butterfly in Wonderland," he said.

"She's the only butterfly in Wonderland." Mouse grinned, then watched Des for a long while, knowing her friend needed a journey of her own. "You've been trapped in places long enough. How about you fly for a while. Experience the outdoors, *the world*." She held her hand toward the sky. "Return whenever you wish."

Des looked back at Mouse, and she gave her an encouraging nod with a smile. Somehow, Mouse knew she was smiling too. Then the butterfly fluttered her wings, lifting into the air, then took off toward the forest.

"I hope she'll be all right," Mouse said, watching her friend drift farther and farther away.

"I'm sure she'll be fine." He took his hand from her waist.

Mouse stared after Des long after she disappeared, hoping to catch another glimpse of her. But all she could see was the rustle of trees from the wind and a content smile crossed her face. Des was free. They both were.

"I wonder if there will be more butterflies in Wonderland now." Ferris didn't answer and she turned around to find him knelt before her. She cocked her head and studied him. "What are you doing down there?"

Ferris smirked, fishing out a silver ring from his pocket. Black and white diamonds embedded in the band glimmered. "I told you I had to grab something before coming out here, didn't I? I've been waiting weeks for this moment and was praying it wouldn't be three fucking years. And, just so you know, I even whispered to Des what I was planning."

Mouse took a deep swallow as she stared down at the loveliest ring she'd ever seen in the fingertips of the loveliest male she'd ever seen.

Ferris took her shaking hand in his, his thumb rubbing gently against her skin. "Will you marry me, luv? Not to entice you to say yes, but I'll even dress up as a Shakespeare character at the wedding." His grin grew wide, lighting all the way up to his dark irises.

"Yes!" she screamed, throwing her arms around him and pushing him to the ground. "Even without the Shakespeare, it would've been yes!"

"You knocked the ring from me." He chuckled, his hands trailing to her waist, his digits pressing in just right.

"We'll find it in a moment." She brushed her lips across his as he drew her even closer. Her tongue parted his lips as she rolled her hips against his.

"What is all the screaming?" Maddie shouted, rushing toward them, the purple feathers atop her black hat bobbing. She came to an abrupt stop farther back by the trees, staring at them. "Oh, are you two…?"

"We're getting married!" Mouse shrieked to her sister, her

voice echoing through the gardens.

Maddie laughed, waving a hand in the air. "Finally, Ferris! Now we'll have the tea party to celebrate."

"We will"—Mouse grabbed a grinning Ferris by the hand—"but first we're finding the ring."

Did you enjoy Vampires in Wonderland?

Authors always appreciate reviews, whether long or short.

Want to enter a sexy fae world? You may want to check out Faeries of Oz, beginning with the short story prequel, Lion.

Langwidere has an obsessive habit—collecting heads. She wears a new one each day, changing them out like she does her ivory dresses. But Langwidere doesn't have the one thing she truly wants: complete power over the territories in Oz. When Lion—the once cowardly fae—shows up at her doorstep, he offers her an opportunity to achieve her desires. Will he use the courage the Wizard gave him to help her succeed, or will he betray her in the process?

ALSO FROM CANDCE ROBINSON

Wicked Souls Duology
Vault of Glass
Bride of Glass

Marked by Magic
The Bone Valley
Merciless Stars

Cruel Curses Trilogy
Clouded By Envy
Veiled By Desire
Shadowed By Despair

Cursed Hearts Duology
Lyrics & Curses
Music & Mirrors

Untamed Darkness Series
Dearest Clementine: Dark and Romantic Monstrous Tales
These Vicious Thorns: Tales of the Lovely Grim
Savage Delights: Two Dark Tales

And Then There Was Silence
Her Cruel Dahlias
Between the Quiet
Hearts Are Like Balloons
Bacon Pie
Avocado Bliss

ALSO FROM AMBER R. DUELL

The Dark Dreamer Trilogy
Dream Keeper
Dark Consort
Night Warden

Forgotten Gods
Fragile Chaos

The Prince's Wing
When Stars Are Bright

Faeries of Oz Series
Lion (Short Story Prequel)
Tin
Crow
Ozma
Tik-Tok

Vampires in Wonderland Series
Rav (Short Story Prequel)
Maddie
Chess
Knave

Once Upon A Wicked Villain Series
Spindle of Sin

Acknowledgments

Thank you, amazing and wonderful readers, for diving into our retelling of Wonderland! We'd like to thank our families and friends for being with us through our high and low points. To Amber H., thank you two for always being ready to help us! And to the awesome people who helped us on this journey—Brandy, Vic, Elle, Jerica, Hayley, Lindsay, and Ann.

I hoped you had a good time with our vampires in Wonderland. They would love for you to join them at their tea party!

About the Authors

Candace Robinson spends her days consumed by words and hoping to one day find her own DeLorean time machine. Her life consists of avoiding migraines, admiring Bonsai trees, watching classic movies, and living with her husband and daughter in Texas—where it can be forty degrees one day and eighty the next.

Amber R. Duell was born and raised in a small town in Central New York. While it will always be home, she's constantly moving with her husband and two sons as a military wife. She does her best writing in the middle of the night, surviving the daylight hours with massive amounts of caffeine. When not reading or writing, she enjoys snowboarding, embroidering, and snuggling with her cats.